I LEFT THE bedchamber and found Harwood focused on Mendi, but the others turned to look at me as I entered the firelit audience chamber.

"What is happening?" Yarrow asked.

I gathered my wits and told them, seeing their faces reflect the shattered dismay I felt. Harwood had ceased probing Mendi, and he asked in disbelief, "Did you say *everyone* will die?"

"Everyone," I said, and I seemed to hear the high mocking sound of Ariel's laughter.

ALSO BY
ISOBELLE CARMODY

◆

THE OBERNEWTYN CHRONICLES

Obernewtyn
The Farseekers
Ashling
The Keeping Place
Wavesong
The Stone Key
The Sending
The Red Queen

◆

THE GATEWAY TRILOGY

Night Gate
Winter Door

◆

LITTLE FUR

The Legend Begins
A Fox Called Sorrow
A Mystery of Wolves
Riddle of Green

ISOBELLE CARMODY

THE DREAMTRAILS

THE OBERNEWTYN CHRONICLES

Includes two complete novels

WAVESONG • THE STONE KEY

BLUEFIRE

Wavesong copyright © 2008 by Isobelle Carmody
The Stone Key copyright © 2008 by Isobelle Carmody
Cover art and map copyright © 2008 by Penguin Group Australia

All rights reserved. Published in the United States by Bluefire, an imprint of Random House Children's Books, a division of Random House, Inc., New York. The works in this collection were originally published together in a slightly modified version by Penguin Books Australia Ltd, Camberwell, in 2008. Published here by arrangement with Penguin Group Australia, a division of Pearson Australia Group Pty Ltd.

Bluefire and the B colophon are registered trademarks of Random House, Inc.

Visit us on the Web! randomhouse.com/teens/strangelands

Educators and librarians, for a variety of teaching tools, visit us at randomhouse.com/teachers

Library of Congress Cataloging-in-Publication Data is available upon request.
ISBN 978-0-307-93219-8 (tr. pbk.) — ISBN 978-0-307-97584-3 (ebook)

Printed in the United States of America
10 9 8 7 6 5 4 3 2 1
First Bluefire Edition 2012

✦ CONTENTS ✦

✦ Character List ✦

Angina: Empath guilden and enhancer; twin brother of Miky

Ariel (aka H'rayka, the Destroyer): sadistic enemy of Obernewtyn; distorted Talent; allied with the Herder Faction and Salamander

Atthis (aka oldOne): Agyllian or Guanette bird; blind futureteller

Avra: leader of the Beastguild; mountain mare; bond-mate to Gahltha

Blyss: Empath guilder

Bram: Sadorian tribal leader

Bruna: Sadorian; daughter of Jakoby

Brydda Llewellyn (aka the Black Dog): rebel leader

Calcasuus: horse; companion of Jakoby

Cassy Duprey: Beforetimer, later known as Kasanda

Ceirwan: Farseeker guilden

Daffyd: former Druid armsman; farseeker; brother to Jow; beloved of Gilaine; unguilded ally of Obernewtyn

Dameon: blind Empath guildmaster

Dardelan: rebel leader of Sutrium

Darius: Twentyfamilies gypsy; beasthealer

Dell: Futuretell guilden

Domick: AWOL Coercer ward; former bondmate of Kella

Dragon: powerful Empath guilder with coercive Talent; projects illusions

Druid (Henry Druid): renegade Herder Faction priest and enemy of the Council; charismatic leader of a secret community that was destroyed in a firestorm; father of Gilaine; presumed dead

Elspeth Gordie (aka Innle, the Seeker): Farseeker guildmistress; powerful farseeker, beastspeaker, and coercer, with limited futuretelling and psychokinetic Talent

Fian: Teknoguild ward

Gahltha (aka Daywatcher): Beast guilden; bondmate to Avra; a formidable black horse sworn to protect Elspeth

Garth: Teknoguildmaster

Gavyn: Beast empath; beasts call him adantar

Gevan: Coercer guildmaster

Gilaine: mute daughter of the Druid; farseeker bound to Lidgebaby; beloved of Daffyd; slave in the Red Queen's land

Gilbert: former armsman of Henry Druid

Grufyyd: bondmate to Katlyn, father of Brydda

Gwynedd: Norselander; rebel leader of Murmroth

Hannah Seraphim: director of the Beforetime Reichler Clinic

Harwood: powerful coercer

Helvar: Norselander and shipmaster of the *Stormdancer*

Iriny: halfbreed gypsy; half sister to Swallow

Jacob Obernewtyn: Beforetimer; wealthy patron of Hannah Seraphim

Jak: teknoguilden; bondmate to Seely

Jakoby: Sadorian tribal leader; mother of Bruna

Javo: Obernewtyn's head cook

Jik: former Herder novice; Empath guilder with farseeking Talent; died in a firestorm

Jow: former follower of the Druid; brother to Daffyd; beastspeaker

Kader: Healer with empathy and farseeking Talent

Kasanda: mystical leader of the Sadorians; left signs for the Seeker to help in her quest

Katlyn: herb lorist living at Obernewtyn; bondmate to Grufyyd, mother of Brydda

Kella: Healer guilden with slight empath Talent; former bondmate of Domick

Lark: Norselander from Herder Isle; son of shipmaster Helvar

Lidgebaby: powerful coercer-empath; an infant bound to the Druid's Misfit followers at birth

Lina: young, troublemaking beastspeaker

Linnet: coercer-knight

Louis Larkin: unTalented highlander; inhabitant of Obernewtyn; honorary Beastspeaking guilder

Malik: traitor to the rebellion, allied with Herders

Maruman (aka Moonwatcher, Yelloweyes): one-eyed cat prone to fits of futuretelling; Elspeth's oldest friend

Maryon: Futuretell guildmistress

Matthew: Farseeker ward with deep probe abilities; slave in the Red Queen's land

Merret: powerful coercer with beastspeaking Talent

Miky: Empath guilden; twin sister of Angina; gifted musician

Miryum: AWOL leader of coercer-knights

Pavo: Teknoguild ward; died of the rotting sickness

Powyrs: rebel sea captain

Rasial: white dog with powerful coercive abilities; second to Avra in Obernewtyn Beastguild

Reuvan: rebel seaman from Aborium; Brydda's right-hand man

Roland: Healer guildmaster

Rushton: Master of Obernewtyn; latent Talent

Salamander: secretive, ruthless leader of the slave trade

Sallah: rebel mare; companion to Brydda

Seely: unTalented caretaker of Gavyn; stranded on west coast

Straaka: Miryum's Sadorian suitor, killed in the rebellion

Swallow: Twentyfamilies D'rekta, or leader

Zarak: Farseeker ward with beastspeaking Talent

WAVESONG

*. . . we travel the path of waves,
which is full of contradictory currents
and mysterious diversions . . .*

*for my brother Ken,
who climbs mountains when you
least expect*

PART I

◆

SONG OF FREEDOM

◆ 1 ◆

IT OUGHT TO have felt momentous, going through the pass and seeing the highlands spread out in the pink-gold morning light, because, for the first time, I was riding down to a Land that was free and where I did not need to hide who or what I was.

Yet it was impossible to feel complacent or even secure, because soon, for the first time, Landfolk would vote for their leaders, who might undo all that the rebels had achieved since overthrowing the Council. And where would that leave Misfits like me? The hatred and prejudice against us, which the Council and Herder Faction had encouraged, had not ended with their reign. The wrong leader could easily fan the flames of resentment and unease into a fire that might yet consume us. But as the rebel leader Dardelan had so often said, there could be no true freedom if people were not able to choose their own leaders.

I let my eyes rove along the neat line of trees that bordered Bergold's orchards on the left side of the road, trying to take comfort in their order. But my eyes were drawn inexorably to the other side of the road, where the ground dropped away steeply and suddenly into the dense, complex wilderness of the White Valley. I could see clear across the green treetops to Tor, Gelfort, and Emeralfel—the mountains that separated highland from lowland—and to the Blacklands that bordered the White Valley. It looked untouched and impenetrable, but I knew how many secrets lay hidden there.

It was the way of things, I thought morosely, and it was better not to forget it.

I lifted my face to the sky and closed my eyes, trying to focus on the sun's warmth and on spring's sweet green smell, but too many worries crowded in—the looming elections, of course, and the forthcoming trial of the rebel Malik, as well as whatever was going on in Saithwold. But most of all, I was troubled by Maryon's insistence that Dragon accompany us to Sutrium. Dragon's presence meant that I must constantly face her fear of me. This was painful, because she had loved me once; however, my invasion of her mind, which had been the only way to save her, had destroyed her trust in me. It had been a shock to discover that, upon waking from her coma, Dragon had forgotten our friendship, forgotten my rescue of her from the Beforetime ruins where she had dwelt as a lonely urchin. I had believed Kella and the other healers when they said Dragon would remember in time, but she had not done so. She viewed me only as one who brought pain, and so great was her fear of me that we had been unable to manage a single conversation since she had awakened. Dragon had been willing to make this journey only because both the healer Kella and the old herbalist Katlyn were going.

In truth, I had proposed the expedition as much to get away from Dragon as to fulfill my promise to return the Twentyfamilies gypsy healer Darius to his people. Then Maryon had announced her support for the expedition, because she foresaw trouble looming on the west coast, and I would be needed to deal with it. Naturally, she had offered no further explanation or details. Almost as an afterthought, she had added that Dragon must go to Sutrium.

I felt a surge of anger and fear at the memory of her fore-telling, for it had been just such a journey to Sutrium that had initiated the events that left Dragon in a dangerous coma. A cooler voice reminded me that sometimes good comes from bad. Without the coma and my journey into Dragon's mind, I would not have discovered that Dragon is the daughter of the Red Land's murdered queen. And though her fear and hatred distressed me, I now knew that something locked in Dragon's memories would ultimately help me complete my secret quest to destroy the Beforetime weaponmachines. Per-haps this journey to Sutrium would provide me with this knowledge.

"Why cannot ElspethInnle just accept? Why always think-ing/gnawing, trying to change the shaping of things?" Maru-man sent the acerbic query to me without shifting his languid position on Kella's lap in the wagon.

"If you are irritated by my thoughts, you could stay out of my mind," I sent back tartly.

The old cat did not condescend to answer, but Kella gave me a sidelong look. She had no farseeking abilities, but her healing empathy meant she could not help but feel the emo-tions flowing between Maruman and me. She turned away at once, not wanting to pry, but her bleak expression told me that her own thoughts were no more happily disposed than mine. Doubtless she was thinking of Domick. He and Kella had been in love, but the coercer's spying before the rebellion had so tormented and divided him against himself that he had finally rejected her and Obernewtyn before disappearing under mysterious circumstances. Kella blamed herself, and I thought it was as much guilt as the desire to heal that was taking her to Sutrium. But I said nothing. Empathy was the one Talent I lacked entirely, and its want made me awkward with emotions and reluctant to trust my own feelings, let alone anyone else's. Besides, what could I say to comfort her, unless it was true that misery loved company.

"One cannot flee from/avoid difficulties of life, Elspeth-Innle, but perhaps it is possible/necessary to outrun them for a time," Gahltha sent. I felt a rush of affection for the horse's passionate nature and laid my hand on his sleek black neck. The flesh quivered with impatience.

"The wagons are not made for speed," I sent regretfully.

"I/Gahltha am! We will gallop away and then return," he responded eagerly.

With a laugh, I told Kella that we would scout ahead. Gahltha neighed to Welt and Belya, who drew the wagon, then cantered to the lead wagon where the young farseeker Zarak sat on the foremost bench with Louis Larkin. Zade and Lo whinnied a welcome to Gahltha as I explained I would ride ahead for a time. Dragon was in the back of the wagon with the plump old herbalist Katlyn and one of the two injured soldierguards we were transporting to Sutrium. The other lay on the floor of the second wagon.

"It is a perfect day fer a ride," Zarak said wistfully.

As though his words were a signal, Gahltha sprang away. If I had not learned from hard experience that he loved to leap into a gallop like this, I would have tumbled backward over his rump. I tangled one hand in his mane and caught the thick black whip of my plait with the other. Joy steamed off his body as heat and a kind of vibration that filled me with exhilaration. How many times had we ridden like this in the high mountains, sharing the rush and the wild freedom of our speed?

My muscles soon protested, reminding me how seldom I had ridden of late. My duties as guildmistress at Obernewtyn left little time for self-indulgence. Fleetingly, the weight of that role pressed on me, but then the sheer physical demands of the ride emptied me of thought. I let myself merge with Gahltha until I was no more than an extension of the powerful black horse racing along the road.

It was a reckless pace, but the way was clear well ahead, and walkers rarely traveled the lonely stretch between the turnoff to Bergold's orchards and the pass into the mountains. Aside from the fact that poisons dangerous to the naked flesh streaked the ground and walls of the pass, the rumor that plague had destroyed Obernewtyn had been enough to discourage the curious. Of course, the rebel leaders now knew that Obernewtyn was intact and home to our Misfit community, and I had no doubt that knowledge of our refuge was spreading into the wider community. Even so, I doubted we would have many casual visitors.

Rounding a slight bend in the road, Gahltha stopped and reared suddenly, almost unseating me. I lurched violently onto his neck and saw that a whole section of the ridge had broken away to crumble down into the White Valley, taking a chunk of the road with it. What remained was narrow and badly eroded on one side, and though it would still serve a walker or a careful rider, the wagons could not possibly pass along it. The landslide must have been recent, since the messenger from Sutrium had not mentioned it when he visited Obernewtyn a mere sevenday ago.

"Damn," I muttered. In drier weather, we might simply have run the wheels along the edge of the roadway, but this soon after the thaw, the ground was soggy and the wagons would sink to their axles. I slipped to the ground and sent Gahltha back to warn the others.

After the black horse had galloped off, I began to cast

7

about for boughs and flat stones, laying a border to increase the width of the road on its inner edge. The passage between Guanette and the mountain pass leading to Obernewtyn had been eroding ever since I had first traveled it years back as a sentenced Misfit. Since we had taken over Obernewtyn, the Teknoguild had spoken many times of the need to repair it, but fearing unwanted attention in the valley, they had done nothing. For this reason, travel into the White Valley had always been limited to small expeditions on foot or horseback. It was only in recent times that discreet ramps for wagons had been created from scree.

It was hot muddy work, but I found myself enjoying the simplicity of the makeshift repairs. I tried to imagine a life that required of me no more than this and then realized that such an existence could seem desirable only to one who did not have to do it all the time. In truth, I enjoyed being mistress of a guild at Obernewtyn, despite all the meetings and negotiations and the sheer amount of talk required. My role would change now, though, for Misfits no longer needed to be rescued.

When the wagons arrived, Louis, Kella, and Zarak alighted at once to sigh and shake their heads, before unhitching the horses. Dragon climbed down, too, casting a look of violent blue-eyed dislike at me. As Maruman leapt down beside her and pressed against her legs, I wondered somewhat bitterly why she felt no antipathy for the old cat, since I had been able to invade her mind only with his help.

Katlyn and Darius remained in the wagons to watch over the soldierguards, but Garth, the Teknoguildmaster, descended and, upon seeing the broken road, began to mutter about this shoring-up technique and that stress.

It took two hours to widen the road enough for the wagons to pass. Katlyn suggested we eat midmeal before continuing, but I did not want to stop until we had reached the White Valley. The habit of caution was strong, and given what the Sutrium messenger had said about robber bands terrorizing remote holdings, I deemed it wiser not to break that habit just yet. Admittedly, the messenger had been referring to the upper lowlands, but it was possible that robbers might roam higher.

When we set off, Dragon sat beside Louis Larkin, with Maruman perched contentedly and rather smugly on her lap. Zarak now rode Zade, for despite being a mare, Lo was large and strong, and she had no difficulty in pulling a wagon alone. Leaving Zarak and Zade to accompany the lead wagon, I dropped behind to speak to Kella, but she had climbed into the back to help Darius tend to the injured soldierguard whose bandages had been dislodged.

My feelings toward the soldierguards were ambivalent. Being in our care all through the wintertime had forced them to see us as different from the monstrous freaks that the Council had labeled us, but these men had killed people and horses I knew and cared for. Rushton, ever focused on the present, had said the most important thing was that they had agreed to tell the new Council of Chieftains exactly what had happened in the White Valley, when Malik had betrayed us. Rushton had also suggested that since I required two wagons, I should use them to return the soldierguards to Sutrium. They were not entirely recovered, but with both Kella and Darius traveling with us, the guards would be well cared for, and by traveling now, they would have time to recover from the journey before the trial.

Garth spoke, interrupting my thoughts to suggest that, given the delay, we should spend the night at the Teknoguild encampment in the White Valley. "You will never reach Rangorn before night now, and Maryon did not urge particular haste, did she?"

"Maryon would never be so hasty as to urge haste," I said dryly. "She said only that I am needed to deal with danger on the west coast."

"I do not see how, since the ships that the rebels were building to reach the west coast have been destroyed. Dardelan's message said there is no chance of landing a force on the west coast for at least another half year."

"Not a force, perhaps," I said, "but I am sure that Dardelan's request for a plast suit means he will try to send a spy across the Suggredoon." We were transporting two fragile plast suits, which the Teknoguild had made during the wintertime; one was for Dardelan and the other was for Swallow, the leader of the Twentyfamilies gypsies, as a gift of thanks. Swallow had requested it as a reward for thwarting Malik's murderous intentions.

Garth regarded me narrowly. "You are thinking of offering yourself as their spy?"

I hesitated, but unlike the other guildmasters, Garth regularly flouted the unspoken convention that leaders of guilds ought to keep themselves out of dangerous situations. "It would explain why Maryon sent me to Sutrium," I finally said.

The Teknoguildmaster grinned. "Very noble of you to ensure the veracity of the Futuretell guildmistress's prophecy." Then he grew serious. "I daresay the others would protest, but it does make sense. After all, you are powerful enough to coerce the guards on the other bank, so you wouldn't be killed upon climbing from the water. You could also farseek Merret or another trapped Misfit to find out what has been going on there."

Garth continued. "I must say I am curious to learn how the Herders managed to sneak a ship into port, burn the rebels' half-constructed ships, and sneak out again, all unnoticed. And what was the use, since the rebels will simply build more ships anyway?"

"We will know better once we meet Brydda," I said.

"Why don't you ask Brydda to ride to Saithwold with you? I doubt anyone would have the courage to hinder the Black Dog, even Chieftain Vos." Garth stumbled a little over the unfamiliar title. Under the old regime, town leaders had been called Councilmen, but the messenger from Sutrium had informed us that the rebel leaders who had replaced the Councilmen were henceforth to be known as *chieftains*. As their leader, Dardelan was to be known as high chieftain.

"Maryon did not foresee trouble in Saithwold, but it is true that Vos has no love of Misfits. And Khuria's letters to Zarak certainly suggest that something is going on there," I said. "It may be worth stopping at a roadside inn to see if we can glean any gossip about Saithwold."

"We can be sure that Vos is unhappy with Dardelan being made high chieftain," Garth said dryly.

"I wonder how Malik took it," I said.

Garth laughed. "I think it is safe to assume that he loathes it. Not only because he coveted the position himself, but also because he knows that Dardelan will allow us to make formal charges against Malik before the elections."

I frowned. "Do you think Malik knows that the soldierguards intend to testify against him?"

Garth gave me a sardonic look. "I think that Dardelan's sense of fair play would ensure it."

I sighed, realizing he was right. The new high chieftain's first decree after being elected ultimate leader of the rebels had been that, after a year, he and all the rebel chieftains would step down from their positions to allow the Landfolk to freely elect future chieftains. Rushton had thought this sensible as well as honorable, but like most of us, he thought Dardelan ought to have kept power for a longer period to ensure stability within the new regime. Others felt that Dardelan ought not to have given such an undertaking at all until the west coast had been secured. But the young rebel was as determined as he was honorable, and the elections were looming.

"Dardelan is not completely naive," I said. "Otherwise he would not insist upon charging Malik before the elections."

Garth grunted. "I think it is only concern for justice that motivates our young high chieftain. I am sure he would say that justice delayed is justice denied. If he was a little more pragmatic, he might have kept the details of his proposed Beast Charter to himself until he had been elected high chieftain. He is well liked, but the idea that no beasts can be owned, that they must be paid for their labor, has alienated most of Dardelan's supporters and enraged his enemies. It might well cost him the election."

"Surely when it comes time to elect their chieftain, people will remember that it was Dardelan who led the rebels in the virtually bloodless coup that rid the Land of the Council and the Herder Faction," I said.

"Isn't it true that Dardelan wants to establish Obernewtyn as a settlement in its own right *before* the elections?" Garth asked. "If that happens, we will vote for our own chieftain."

I nodded. Rushton had been ambivalent about Dardelan's proposal. Having our own chieftain would give Misfits a voice in running the Land, but it would also require the chieftain of Obernewtyn to travel regularly to Sutrium for Council of Chieftains meetings. It was as obvious to Rushton as to the rest of us that he would be our choice as chieftain, and just as obvious that he did not relish the thought. There had been some discussion of the matter in the last guildmerge. Some said that the proposed new settlement would cause un-Talents to resent us even more than they already did. Others worried about transforming what had long been our refuge into a village that anyone could enter. We would have to make a decision before Rushton rode down to Sutrium for the ceremony to formalize the Charter of Laws, which was to take place just before the elections. Dardelan wanted us to lay charges against Malik straight after the ceremony and before the elections.

"Hard to know what is best," Garth grunted, his thoughts no doubt running along similar lines.

I said, "In any case, to respond to your suggestion, we will stay the night in the White Valley."

"Good," Garth said. "There are a few things I would like to show you, for I know you have an interest in the past that our good leader does not share." His expression changed, and before I could extricate myself from the conversation, he added reproachfully, "I must say that is why I was so disappointed when you voted against opening Jacob Obernewtyn's tomb. Surely you want to know more about the Beforetime Misfits who once dwelt at Obernewtyn? Or how Hannah Seraphim is connected to Rushton?"

I suppressed a sigh. Garth was aware of my interest in the Beforetimer who had established Obernewtyn, but he did not know why I was interested in her, and of course I could not tell him. I said, "I am not convinced that opening Jacob Obernewtyn's tomb will add to the sum of our knowledge about the Beforetime or indeed of anything. I see no evidence to suggest there would be diaries or journals kept there."

"If it is no more than the resting place for a body, why create such a solid structure, and why set it on an obscure path where there are no other graves?" Garth reasoned. "Do you know that it was even marked on Beforetime maps we found of Obernewtyn's grounds? And some believe that with Jacob Obernewtyn's body are not only the records we have been searching for, but Hannah Seraphim's body as well."

"In the same grave?" I demanded skeptically.

"The Beforetimers did sometimes bury bondmates together, an' even whole families, though of course nowt at the same time," Zarak broke in, apologetically. "But if they put more than one person in a grave, there should ha' been two names on it and the birth and death dates of each."

Irritation flickered over the Teknoguildmaster's ruddy face. "If Hannah Seraphim died during or soon after the Great White, as we surmise, I doubt there would have been a stone-carver handy to chisel another name into the gravestone. And if Hannah is not in that grave, then where is she?" This last was directed sharply at me.

Before I could frame an answer, Garth looked back at Zarak. "Besides, the Beforetimers did not always date graves. Jacob Obernewtyn's was undated."

"Maybe dates seemed pointless after the Great White," I murmured, but neither of them heard me.

"Maybe Hannah Seraphim was away from Obernewtyn when the Great White came," Zarak said. "She might have been visitin' the Reichler Clinic Reception Center under Tor. There would ha' been a lot of coming and gannin' betwixt the two places."

"Even if I *had* voted to open the grave, Garth, all the other guildleaders still would have refused you, just as on every other occasion you've raised the matter since the grave was found."

Garth scowled. "True enough. If Maryon would just—"

"She is entitled to her opinion and her visions," I said evenly. Inwardly, I cringed at my hypocrisy, for I had often wished the Futuretell guildmistress would keep her thoughts and visions to herself.

Garth was not diverted. "The trouble is that the others are overly swayed by her opinions, because they imagine them to be based on futuretell visions that she chooses not to divulge," he growled. "Without her influence, I am sure I could have convinced the guildmerge to see it my way."

"Maybe she *is* basin' her resistance on things she has foreseen," Zarak suggested.

Fortunately, at this moment, we reached the scree ramp down to the White Valley. Zarak dismounted, pulled aside the woven foliage that obscured it, and scrambled down. The two wagons followed slowly, steadied by Zade and Belya, and checked by ropes belayed around tree trunks, paid out slowly by Gahltha, Lo, and the big piebald, Welt. When the others were all safely down, I drew the foliage screen back in place.

Once on the floor of the valley, I felt less anxious, though I was never able to feel entirely at ease here. Nor was I alone in this. The White Valley was generally regarded as being cursed by numerous tormented Beforetime wraiths. And maybe it was, I thought soberly. I did not know what had stood here in the Beforetime or what had become of it, but the valley attracted trouble like a lodestone attracts steel. The renegade Herder Henry Druid had established a secret encampment here, which had been wiped out by a terrible firestorm. I, too, would have died here, if not for the

15

intervention of the mysterious Agyllian birds who had taught my body to heal itself. And here in the White Valley, Malik had betrayed us.

But cursed or not, the White Valley was undeniably beautiful. The trees were a delicate haze of bright new green around damp charcoal-black trunks and branches, and shoots and buds burst from the rich dark earth on all sides. The ground was soft, so we kept to the stone-studded track laid by the teknoguilders. This soon brought us to an avenue where the branches of trees had been interwoven overhead, creating a green tunnel. I guessed that Garth had commanded this new arrangement to conceal the track, part of which had been visible from the ridge road. If anything, the Teknoguildmaster was more concerned now about Landfolk stumbling onto his guild's research site than before the Council had been overthrown.

Because the wagons were hard to haul over the uneven track, we were all walking now, except Katlyn, Darius, and the two soldierguards. Louis Larkin walked behind them with Dragon, while Garth strode ahead, eager to reach his guild's new settlement at the foot of Tor. His intention was to make a formal claim on the land where it stood, including the cavern leading to the submerged Beforetime city under Tor, which we now knew as Newrome.

"I always think of Jik when I come here," said Zarak, catching up with me. "If I had nowt been farseeking without a guide an' without permission, I would nivver have made contact with him, and we nivver would have brought him out of his cloister in Darthnor. He would nivver have come here to die."

"Do you think he would have fared well among Herders?" I asked. "Something more dreadful may have happened if he had remained in the cloister."

"More dreadful than dying in a firestorm?" Zarak asked in a low voice.

"Jik was terrified of being taken to Herder Isle. He said the priests knew about Misfits and experimented on them. Maybe if he had stayed in the cloister, that would have happened to him."

Zarak was silent for a time, then he said, "Why do ye suppose they took some Misfits an' burned others like they did seditioners?"

"Jik said they were always more interested in children with Misfit powers and that some abilities interested them more than others."

"Maybe they wanted to train them to catch us," Zarak suggested.

"Maybe they used them to help create demon bands," I suggested.

Zarak made no response, and when I glanced at him, he was looking at me. For a moment, I saw myself as he must: a long lean woman with a tight-bound plait and overly serious moss-green eyes. I said gently, "Do not blame yourself for Jik's death, Zar. Many things happened to bring him here, not simply the foolish disobedience of one young farseeker."

"Do ye remember that dog Jik insisted we rescue with him?" Zarak said suddenly, half smiling. "He was th' ugliest creature I ever saw."

"The Herders breed them to look like that," I said. "Darga."

"Yes, that was his name. I had forgotten." Zarak gave me a look of curiosity that I pretended not to notice. It was generally assumed that Darga had perished with Jik in the firestorm, but the Agyllian birds that saved my life claimed he lived. They said he would return when it was time for me to

leave Obernewtyn to undertake the final stage of my quest—
to destroy the deadly weaponmachines left by the Beforetimers.

I had been waiting so many years for that moment that I
sometimes wondered if it would ever come.

Zarak had drawn ahead, no doubt discouraged by my silence, but Kella took his place. I glanced at her, wondering if
she would regret leaving Obernewtyn to run the healing center she had established in the old Sutrium Herder cloister during the rebel uprising. She and Dardelan had developed a
genuine liking and respect for each other during that time, so
it was hardly surprising when he asked her to come and run
the center and establish a teaching facility for healers. But
Kella's acceptance had startled me.

Roland, the Healer guildmaster, had been enthusiastic
about his guilden's new venture, and Rushton, too, praised it
as an excellent way of further impressing ordinary Landfolk
with the usefulness of Misfit abilities. I seemed to be alone in
feeling that Kella's departure marked the end of an era. Of
course, it was time for us to live in the Land openly. Wasn't
that what we had fought and longed for? Yet my heart ached
for the days when Obernewtyn had been our secret refuge,
just as it had been for the Beforetime Misfits.

Kella gave me a quizzical look, no doubt sensing something of my feelings.

"I was just thinking of the Beforetimers," I told her quickly.

To my surprise, she bridled fiercely. "We are not like them.
We would never do to our world what they did to theirs."

Would we not? I wondered morosely. Or was it only that
we did not have the ability to destroy as efficiently as they
had?

✦ 2 ✦

I HEARD A shout and looked up to see the slender, brown-haired teknoguilder Fian burst through the trees with loud halloos that scattered birds from nearby bushes. Garth beckoned to him impatiently and they spoke, then the Teknoguildmaster strode on, and Fian came beaming to greet me.

At Obernewtyn, I was accustomed to being honored and held in awe for my powers and for what I had done, but I was unused to being liked. Yet Fian liked me. In part, he knew me better than most, having taken part in several farseeker rescues that I had led; moreover, the year he had spent in Sador with the Empath guildmaster, Dameon, had given him an independence of thought and attitude that allowed him to see everyone as an equal, despite differences in rank and power. I valued his friendship as well as his cleverness and unfailing good humor. The fact that he had also unwittingly adopted several of Dameon's mannerisms only endeared him to me more, for the Empath guildmaster was my closest friend.

"Is Dameon nowt with ye?" Fian asked, as if he had read the name in my thoughts. He nodded a smile to Dragon, who shrank behind Kella.

"Dameon has decided he would rather ride to Sutrium with Rushton and the coercer-knights next sevenday," I said.

Fian's eyes widened. "Did ye say he would *ride*?"

I nodded. "He has been practicing with Faraf, and he

wants to see how well he can manage. She knows he is blind, of course, and that she must be his eyes." I spoke as if it was a minor detail, but in fact I wondered very much why Dameon had become so determined to ride when he had always seemed satisfied with being driven in wagons. I could not believe it had anything to do with the case against the cousin who, in order to inherit his property, had reported Dameon to the Council as a Misfit. There were many such cases now, as people who had been dispossessed of their property sued for its return.

"What will Dameon do if he gets his farm back?" Fian asked curiously. "I canna believe he wants to run it himself."

"He means to establish it as a cooperative farm run jointly by beasts and unTalented humans. He hopes ordinary Landfolk will see that it is possible to work with beasts to our mutual advantage, even without Misfit translators. It is a brilliant idea. I am only sorry that it will not be established in time for the elections."

"Alad thinks Dardelan ought to present the Charter of Laws and his Beast Charter at the same time."

I shook my head. "If he did, both would be rejected. By keeping the two charters separate, no matter what happens in the elections, Dardelan will have at least established a basic set of good and fair laws for the Land. And people who dislike the idea of rights for beasts might still vote for him, since Dardelan is known for listening to the opinions of many different people and might be talked out of it."

"He'll nowt change his mind," Fian said stoutly.

I smiled. "I don't think so either."

More teknoguilders came toward us now, but my attention was caught by the long, low, curving building I could see in the clearing beyond them. Constructed from wood and stone, it faced the section of the Suggredoon River from whence I had once set off on a raft to escape the renegade Herder Henry Druid. I had a fleeting but vivid memory of the gallant, red-haired druid armsman Gilbert. He had been one of the few to survive the firestorm that had killed his master.

"Ye see how the buildin' masks th' openin' to the subterranean city?" Fian pointed out enthusiastically. "Garth designed it that way, because he said we want to distract strangers from noticin' the cave an' wonderin' where it leads."

I nodded, impressed by how much had been achieved in the few weeks since thaw. But as I came closer, I saw that there was no glass in the windows, and when I looked through one of them, I saw that the floor had yet to be laid.

"It's nowt finished," Fian said unnecessarily. "Guildmaster Garth felt it were more important to get the whole thing up so that from a distance it would look finished. In case any Landfolk come into the White Valley. We are about fencin' the land now to keep anyone from comin' too close. We can complete th' inside of the homestead later." This was said so carelessly that I wondered if the Teknoguild would ever finish it. Their researches were generally so compelling to them that anything not utterly vital was put off. It would not surprise me to find that in a year, when wintertime returned, the Teknoguild homestead still lacked a floor and windows.

Fian led me around the back of the building to the tents and shacks that presently housed the resident and visiting teknoguilders in the White Valley.

At first glance, the camp reminded me of a Sadorian desert camp, which was not surprising since the excellent cloth huts the guild used had been gifts from the Sadorian tribal leader,

Jakoby. But there was also something of a gypsy encampment about the settlement, for there were boxes and bales piled haphazardly and clothes laid out on the grass to dry. Sadorians possessed little, so they did not produce clutter, whereas for both teknoguilders and gypsies, clutter seemed a natural consequence of busy and active lives. Indeed, as with any gathering of teknoguilders, a quiet but intense sense of purpose and concentration pervaded the scene. Here and there, teknoguilders sat cross-legged on the grass, scratching their heads over notes they were making, or perched on barrels or bales reading or poring over some queer Beforetime object brought out of the subterranean city. The day was warm enough that most wore shirtsleeves or light shifts, but there was a fire burning in a stone-lined pit in the midst of the rough semicircle of tents. Judging by the smells coming from pots suspended over it, something good was simmering away. It was long past midmeal, but the teknoguilders never bothered with formal mealtimes except on special occasions.

"Are ye hungry?" Fian asked, seeing my gaze. "We expected ye hours ago, but there is still plenty of soup."

"Starving," I said, my mouth watering. I had skipped first-meal, unable to face Rushton sitting stiffly by me and making polite, meaningless conversation with everyone in the dining hall looking on, knowing something was amiss yet being unable to help. The only time we seemed able to behave normally was during guildmerge, when we were guildmistress and Master of Obernewtyn.

Fian hastened to lay his kerchief over a bale for me to sit on, and Garth looked about vaguely as if he wondered where the table and chairs had been put. But the idea did not gain sufficient focus for him to realize that furniture was something else put off until later. Instead, he found a wide barrel, sat on it, and began examining something one of the tekno-guilders wanted to show him. Katlyn, Kella, and Dragon came slowly to the fireside with Darius. The gypsy's crooked body, awkward movements, and prematurely gray hair always made me think of Darius as old, but when he laughed at something Katlyn said, it struck me that he was only a few years older than Rushton.

We all ate with good appetite, but afterward, instead of someone producing an instrument and suggesting a song, as would happen around other campfires, Garth heaved himself up and said that he needed to go into the mountain to see something too large to be carried out. He invited anyone interested to accompany him, and most of the teknoguilders stood at once, as did Zarak. Darius and Kella said they had better see to the soldierguards, and Katlyn wanted to look for certain herbs that did not grow in the high mountains. The herbalist intended to try growing them in a cave high above Obernewtyn where the teknoguilders had discovered a hot spring. At Katlyn's request, the cave's top opening had been roofed in thin, nearly transparent plast sheets, for she was sure the warm, moist atmosphere would allow all sorts of unlikely plants to grow there. For her, the gathering of seeds was the expedition's main purpose, apart from seeing her son. When the older woman rose, Dragon went with her, giving me a backward glance that told me her desire was less to gather herbs than to avoid me.

Garth looked at me expectantly, but I shook my head, pretending not to see his disappointment. I had been into the subterranean city many times, and my mood was already too melancholy to endure the complicated mixture of wonder and dismay I always felt at seeing it. Louis Larkin made no response to Garth's invitation, for straight after eating, he had stretched out on his back and now snored loudly.

Once the others had gone, I regarded the old man with fond amusement and thought about the day, many decades past, when he had seen two gypsies come to Obernewtyn to offer carvings to Marisa Seraphim, then Mistress of Obernewtyn.

The carvings, containing secret messages from the seer Kasanda, had become part of the front doors to Obernewtyn. I had long since learned their secrets, but I wanted to be able to see and hear the gypsies who had brought them to Obernewtyn in the hope of learning how they had come by the carvings.

Of course, I could not delve into Louis Larkin's memories without seeking his permission first.

Feeling restless, I farsought Maruman, but I could find no trace of the cantankerous old cat. No doubt he had gone to sleep somewhere. It was almost impossible to probe a sleeping mind unless you knew where the sleeper lay or could make physical contact; even then it was sometimes impossible to enter Maruman's mind. Gahltha had once told me this was because the old cat often went *seliga* when he slept. This was one of the few beast words I did not understand clearly. It meant something like "before" and something like "behind."

I decided to walk to the monument created by the Twenty-families gypsies in memory of the Misfits and beasts who had perished in the White Valley because of Malik's betrayal. A lone teknoguilder sat on a log by the fire, engrossed in a book. I did not know her name, but when I touched her arm to tell her my intention, she looked at me in astonishment. I told her where I was going, and she promised to let the others know if they returned before me.

I had not been walking more than fifteen minutes when I sensed that someone was following me. I sent out a mind-probe but found only the minds of numerous burrowers and other little creatures dwelling in the valley. It occurred to me that Dragon might be following me. It would not be the first time she had done so, and she was the only Misfit whose coercive strength would allow her to evade my probe.

I stopped, shaped a probe to her mind, and swept the area again, but it would not locate. Yet my sense of being watched was stronger than ever. I considered turning back but decided against it; if Dragon was following me, she might finally allow me to talk to her. If it was not her, then it must be a large animal with a small brain. This did not frighten me, for all beasts seemed to recognize that I was the Seeker when I beast-spoke them. For animals, the Seeker was not the person who was supposed to find and end the threat of the Beforetime weaponmachines but was a legendary figure destined to lead beasts to freedom from humans. I was fairly sure that the mystic Agyllians had concocted this legend to ensure that beasts would protect me, for the ancient birds set my quest to destroy the weaponmachines above the welfare of any individual creatures, human or beast.

Reaching the track leading to the cul-de-sac where Malik had instructed us to lure the pursuing soldierguards, an eerie sense of the past stole over me, and I forgot about the possibility of being followed. I seemed almost to see the empath twins Angina and Miky; the handsome, ebony-skinned Sadorian warrior Straaka, towering over sturdy Miryum; all arrayed about me, and I glanced up to the tree-lined lip of the cul-de-sac, as I had done during the rebellion, wondering why Malik and his men were taking so long to show themselves and order the soldierguards we had lured there to lay down their weapons. Then the soldierguards had begun to shoot their arrows.

I shivered, thinking how many more might have died that day if the Twentyfamilies gypsies had not intervened. I brought my gaze to rest on the white marker stone that the gypsies had carved. Swallow, who had succeeded his father as D'rekta of the Twentyfamilies, had shown it to me once before, but it seemed less white today. Maybe it was my imagination, for when I came closer, I could see that the stone showed no signs of weathering. I knelt to look at the names carved so beautifully and minutely into it, knowing that the Sadorian mystic Kasanda had taught the Twentyfamilies gypsies their famous stone-carving skills. I had no absolute proof that Kasanda and the original D'rekta were one and the same person, nevertheless, there was no doubt in my mind that Cassy Duprey, the young Beforetime artist of whom I sometimes dreamed, had adopted both titles at different points in her long life.

I continued reading the names of the dead, beast and human, chiseled into the marker. The last name was Straaka's, although he alone of the dead was not buried in the valley. The coercer Miryum, whom he had died to shield, had taken his body and vanished, and we had neither seen nor heard of her since. The coercer-knights she had once led were convinced that Miryum had taken Straaka's body to Sador, for Sadorians believed that their bones must rest alongside those of their ancestors lest their spirits wander. That seemed as likely a possibility as anything else, for Miryum had been out of her mind with grief and guilt.

The coercer was not the only guilty survivor of that day. The empath Miky constantly anguished over her twin brother, Angina, for although he had recovered from his wounds, he would never regain his former strength. Once, I had used spirit eyes to look at the lad's aura, and I had seen clearly how the red slashing mark, which echoed the fading scar at his temple, leeched brightness from the rest of his aura, draining it of vitality. The boy's body had been healed, but his spirit had been savagely wounded, and no one knew how to heal such a thing.

I spoke each name on the marker aloud, remembering the owners of the names with a grief that made my eyes sting.

"Do you pray to Lud to mind their souls?" a voice asked.

I gasped and overbalanced trying to turn and stand at the same time. A tall woman with short silken yellow hair and piercing blue eyes stood a little distance away, hands on hips, watching me.

"You are Bergold's sister, Analivia," I said, recognizing her, for she had once saved me from a whipping.

She nodded to the marker. "I heard that many of your people died here. Those are their names scribed on the marker?"

I nodded and said, without really knowing why, "There are the names of animals as well as humans. How did you . . . ?" I stopped, finding it hard to speak of my Misfit abilities openly, even now.

A mercurial smile played about her mouth. "You wonder how your Misfit powers did not detect me? I have always had a knack of being able to remain hidden." Her smile dimmed. "In the house where I grew up, it was wiser to be invisible."

That did not surprise me. Her father had been the brutal and oppressive Councilman Radost, who had once ruled the Council and Sutrium with an iron hand and heart. Not long before the rebellion, he had sent his sons, Bergold and Moss, up to the highlands to establish new Councilfarms, since one man was permitted to hold only so much land. Analivia had

27

lived with Bergold, the eldest of the three. Since the rebellion, Moss and his father had been sentenced to long terms on Councilfarms, but Bergold, a fair and kindhearted young man, had been permitted to continue running his orchards, as a cooperative venture. The fruit-bottling industry he had established was so successful that they had employed many Darthnor miners who could not work while the road to the smelters and west coast industries remained closed.

"Are you hunting?" I asked politely.

"You might call it hunting, if curiosity can be called a weapon and knowledge prey. I have been watching your people. I have been inside the mountain. The Beforetimers must have loved darkness to build in such a place, but what do your people seek there?"

"Some of us are curious about the Beforetimers and how they lived," I said, realizing that she must have explored the caverns when the teknoguilders were inside them. Given how little awareness the teknoguilders had of anything outside their studies, I was not the least bit surprised, but Garth would be horrified.

"Why are you curious about us?" I asked.

She shrugged. "It interests me that you survived when so many people wanted to kill you. I am interested in survival." She glanced down at the memorial marker. "I suppose you know that Malik is not the sort to give up his hatred because of agreements and treaties. My brother and father were like him. Hatred ran through their veins like fire, devouring all else."

"I heard that they were killed trying to escape from the Councilfarm," I said, uncertain whether to express sympathy, since it was known that Analivia's brother and father had both mistreated her.

But she merely said rather cryptically, "Hatred does not die so easily." She looked around the cul-de-sac. "This is a pretty place to be marked by so much hatred and death."

"Marked?" I wondered if she was referring to the carved monument.

She saw my confusion and said soberly, "I think that terrible happenings mark a place so whoever comes there after feels a kind of echo."

I said slowly, "Do you feel the mark of what happened here?"

She did not answer, seeming suddenly distracted.

"Will you come to the encampment with me?" I asked presently.

She shook her head but said that she would walk some of the way back with me. I half expected her to interrogate me, but instead, as we walked, she told me about her life as a girl. Her father had bonded only for a son to inherit his properties and power. It soon became clear that Bergold, his firstborn son, was nothing like his sire, lacking Radost's ruthless ambition and brute will. So Radost turned his attention to his second son, Moss; they were like two vipers in a nest. Only his desire to increase his properties and extend his area of influence had made Radost send Bergold and Moss to establish Councilfarms in the highlands. He had intended, in time, to weld the properties together as one, under his control, but the rebellion had ended his ambitions.

"I am glad of the uprising," she said. "I prayed for many years that the rebels would have the courage to do it."

"Not all Landfolk welcome the change," I said mildly.

She shrugged. "People fear that if the old ways come back, they will be punished for failing to oppose the usurpers. They have to learn not to be afraid. When the Council ruled, fear clogged the air like mist above a moor. You could not breathe without drawing it in."

Abruptly she stopped, and I saw the wagons. Analivia said goodbye and in the twinkling of an eye, she was gone. I tried to probe her but to no avail. I made my way toward the Teknoguild camp, wondering if the yellow-haired woman had learned to conceal her presence because of her childhood or whether she had a trace of Misfit ability. I was passing the second wagon when I noticed one of the soldierguards sitting up and gazing out. I stopped reluctantly to ask if he needed anything.

"I was just thinking that it had been a peaceful wintertime." He laughed humorlessly. "The truth is, I am uneasy about going back to the city. Everything will be changed, and I don't suppose it will be easy for an ex-soldierguard to find employment."

"I am sure that High Chieftain Dardelan will find a place for you," I said coolly.

"You don't like me, do you?" the soldierguard said. "I do not blame you for it, but you don't realize how it was back then for us. How your kind was made to seem . . ." His voice trailed off, and though I waited politely, he appeared to have forgotten what he meant to say. I bid him good day.

"I am not a forgiving sort of person," I muttered as I walked on.

"That is because you are strong," said a familiar voice.

I started violently and then saw the beasthealer, Darius, sitting before me, under a tree. "I'm sorry," I said.

"Sorry about what?" he inquired gently. "About me, because I am so insignificant that you almost walked past me? About that man back there, who must daily grow in awareness of what he did in this valley? Or are you sorry about yourself for having such a nature? But, no, people who are strong forgive themselves least of all."

Darius smiled gently and with a graceful gesture invited me to sit. I lowered myself to the knobbled knee of a tree, shocked to notice that from a certain angle, Darius bore a strong resemblance to Swallow. It was hardly remarkable; Twentyfamilies gypsies seldom bonded to outsiders. Indeed, bonding among them required the approval of the old women who kept track of genealogies so the match would not be too close. I felt a stab of pity for Darius, to have such a face set above a dreadfully misshapen body. Then I wondered at my thought. Should I wish him a face as distorted as his body?

His gentle smile widened as if he heard my thoughts, and I felt the blood heat my cheeks. Twentyfamilies gypsies could see spirit auras with their normal eyes, and who knew what mine told him?

I rose, offering to send food, but Darius heaved himself awkwardly to his feet, saying he would come with me. Back at the camp, Katlyn and Kella were chopping mushrooms and garlic, and the healer looked up and smiled at our approach. She said that Dragon had found several huge rings of mushrooms, and they had decided to make a proper meal. I asked where Dragon was, and Kella told me that she had taken some grain to the horses. Darius examined the herbs Katlyn had gathered. I wanted to tell Kella about Analivia, but Darius held up a small scarlet flower with a crow of delight.

I left them to gloat over their herbs and sat on an upturned barrel beside Louis Larkin. Awake now, the old man was prodding moodily at the fire in a desultory way. Maruman lay curled asleep in his lap.

"He seems to do nothing but sleep lately," I said.

Louis shrugged. "Carryin' a deal of years is a terrible wearisome business."

I did not doubt it, but in Maruman's case, I did not know if it was just age. Until recently, the cat had been a great wanderer; his adventuring had earned him many scars and cost him an eye. But during the wintertime just past, he had not once gone wandering, choosing instead to sleep. I had been glad, but now I worried that the old cat might have abandoned his physical adventures to travel on the dreamtrails, which could be far more dangerous. In his dream journeying, Maruman did not have old bones and weary flesh, but any wound or hurt taken would be echoed by a real wound that would afflict his spirit, and this would affect him physically.

On impulse, I said, "I have been thinking of those Twentyfamilies gypsies who came to Obernewtyn when you were young."

Louis gave me a knowing look. "So that's th' way of it, then. That Swallow."

I stared at him in bewilderment for a minute, then realized what he was implying. Opening my mouth to give him the sharp edge of my tongue, I had a sudden clear vision of Swallow, leaning forward to kiss me after rescuing me.

I wondered if Swallow even remembered that kiss. So much had happened since. He had become D'rekta of the Twentyfamilies gypsies, with all the responsibilities of leading his people and fulfilling the mysterious ancient promises that lay at the heart of their community. Our realization that these promises connected to my secret quest meant that Swallow knew more about me than any other human. So much so that the Agyllians had made use of him more than once when I had been in danger. The overguardian of the Sadorian Earthtemple had even told me that one of Kasanda blood would accompany me to the desertlands where I would receive Kasanda's final message for the Seeker. I knew that Swallow had spoken of me to the seers among his people, and though he had never told me what they said, these days when we met, he was always very stern and serious. I wondered if I had not preferred the devilish gypsy who looked at me with admiration and kissed me without permission.

Louis was still looking at me expectantly, so I said, "Louis, would you let me enter your memory of the gypsies' visit to Obernewtyn?"

The older man's face creased in a scowl. "Ye'll keep out of me brain, girl, be ye Mistress of all Obernewtyn! Look at what happened to Dragon when ye meddled with her!" His voice had risen and I felt the other three look at me. Louis pushed Maruman unceremoniously to the ground and stalked away stiff-backed.

"Cannot funaga control themselves/emotions?" Maruman sent coldly as he climbed onto my lap. I said nothing, for my throat was tight with unshed tears. Louis's words seemed to highlight a growing feeling of my own inadequacy and dis-placement. Again, I found myself wondering when my quest would claim me.

"It claims you now," Maruman sent. "It has never stopped claiming you. All that you do, ElspethInnle, serves the old Ones and the quest."

✦ 3 ✦

THE FOLLOWING MORNING, we rose in the thin, gray, predawn light, having said goodbye to the teknoguilders the night before. We did not bother lighting a fire, for we would eat at one of the inns in the upper lowlands. Both wagons had already rattled off, and I was preparing to follow the others when Garth came shambling out in his nightshirt, a blanket draped around his massive shoulders.

"I have been thinking about this daughter of Radost. This Analivia . . . ," he began.

"We have spoken more than enough on that subject," I interrupted him firmly, for he had speculated at length about the young woman after I told him of our meeting. "She might be Radost's daughter and Moss's sister, but she is also the sister of Bergold, who mistreats no human or beast. For Lud's sake, it is common knowledge that her father loathed her! She is no danger to Misfits, and she might very well be one of us."

A look of real agony passed over the teknoguilder's wide face. "But if she continues spying . . ."

"Garth, why are you so worried about people finding out about the sunken city?" I demanded, exasperated. "Do you really think they will rush here to see it or try to prevent your guild researching the past? Most likely, normal Landfolk will merely shudder at your interest and name it ghoulish. The Council has gone. We are free people in a free Land."

He stared at me, speechless, and I grew silent, for my words had the weight of a futureteller pronouncement and I felt slightly abashed.

"What you say is true, Elspeth," Garth said at last. "But this freedom is new and precarious. The world can turn back in an instant, and all our care and work would be lost if it should be decided that Beforetime sites are taboo. At the least, it is better to continue as we have begun, in secrecy, until Dardelan is elected. For all we know, Malik has found new favor during the wintertime. Instead of being made to answer our charges, he might be elected high chieftain! Or the Herders on Herder Isle might be building a secret weapon. Or the Council on the west coast might be on the verge of a successful counterattack. I must protect what we have learned."

I nodded wearily and closed my coat's fastenings, reaching down to pick up Maruman. As I draped him about my shoulders, he sank in his claws to make himself secure and comfortable. Garth still looked as if something further might be said or decided, so I nodded and turned away decisively. I glanced back once to see him still standing there, peering after me.

"Funaga . . . ," Maruman began.

"I know emotions annoy you," I beastspoke the old cat tersely, "but, unfortunately, they are as much a part of us as our bones. We can't set them aside to please you, even if we wished it."

Not even to please ourselves, I thought privately.

"They are untidy/disturbing," Maruman responded with a fastidious mental shudder that was rather like having someone sneeze inside your head.

"Well, there is nothing to be done about them."

He fell silent, but his indignation was loud. I bit back a desire to tell him that his own emotional emanations were fairly disturbing, but of course he caught the thought and sent a huff of irritation rippling through my mind. I endured it doggedly, concentrating on finding the best footing, until his stiffness softened and he slept, his breath sawing in and out by my ear.

Only then did I reach up and stroke the battered head with a tenderness and pity I would never have dared express when he was awake. Louis had been right in saying the cat was old, though I hated to think it. Maybe it was true that his sleeping of late was no more than a sign of age. I did not know how old Maruman was, but he had not been a kitten when I first overheard his thoughts at the Kinraide orphanage, and I wondered, as I had done countless times since, where he had been born and how he had come to Kinraide. Most likely, he had survived a farmer's attempt to drown an unwanted litter, but that beginning, however traumatic, would not explain his mind's strange distortions. It was possible, of course, that he had simply been born as he was, just as I had been born Misfit. Perhaps I would ask Atthis about his origin when next she communicated with me. After all, the Agyllian mystic ruthlessly used the old cat's distorted mind as a conduit, because those distortions meant he could not be spied upon.

Such memories summoned the pale face of my nemesis Ariel.

When I had first met him, at Obernewtyn, he had been a beautiful, sadistic boy. When we took over, he had fled and somehow wormed his way into the confidence of both Henry Druid and the Council. Later he had joined the Herders, and rumor said he was now high in their ranks. He had lost none of his beauty in the intervening years; the last time I had seen

Ariel, he had been a tall, slender man with a cascade of silky, nearly white hair surrounding that astonishing face. He hated Obernewtyn and had harmed us, directly and indirectly, whenever possible. But his antipathy to me was more specific and malevolent; in fact, I believed that Ariel was the Destroyer, destined to resurrect the Beforetime weaponmachines if I failed to disarm them. Atthis had never named him the Destroyer, but Ariel had hunted me on the dreamtrails just as Atthis had warned me the Destroyer would. If I had needed any more proof, Maruman called Ariel *H'rayka*, which means "one who brings destruction" in beastspeak.

The last time I had seen Ariel, he had been aboard a Herder ship laden with Landfolk who were to be sold as slaves in distant lands. One of those slaves had been the farseeker Matthew, and the memory of my final moments with him still anguished me, though Maryon had foreseen his survival. From time to time, those of us who had known Matthew experienced fragmentary true dreams that showed him living in a port city in a hot desert land. Gradually, we had come to believe that Matthew was in the Red Queen's land, which many believed to be a myth. Brydda's seaman friend Reuvan had assured us that it was very real but was so unimaginably distant that few had ever traveled there. True dreams of Matthew showed a brutish horde that had enslaved its people occupying the Red Land. Matthew and others taken from the Land also served the slavemasters, working at extending the city or in the mine pits outside the city.

In my dreams, Matthew had become a grown man with broad shoulders, muscled from breaking stone and working in the mines. I had seen him striving to convince the enslaved people to rise up and overthrow their oppressors. To

Matthew's great frustration, they refused because of a prophecy foretelling that the people would overcome the slavemasters only when their queen returned. Their queen, however, had been slain. One day, Matthew had seen a wall frieze depicting the Red Queen and noticed her uncanny resemblance to Dragon. Matthew had realized then that the filthy urchin we had rescued from the Beforetime ruins on the west coast was the Red Queen's lost daughter. Which meant *a* Red Queen *could* return. But the last time Matthew had seen her, Dragon had lain deep in a coma.

In my most recent dream of him, I had seen Matthew trying to persuade people that they had misread the prophecy, that they had to overthrow their oppressors *before* the Red Queen could be restored to them. It had not been hard to guess that Matthew wanted to free the Red Land and bring Dragon to her kingdom in hopes that this would wake her. He did not know that she had awakened and that the shock of remembering her mother's betrayal and murder had erased from her memory everything except her time alone in the ruins. Like Matthew, I dreamed of restoring Dragon to her land, but we could not reach the Red Land without ships capable of making the journey, not to mention maps and charts to show the way.

Over time, I had taken to reviewing the beautiful intricate dream maps the futuretellers compiled from dream journals that each guild kept, looking for dreams about Matthew. From these I learned that the farseeker had ceased trying to convince the people of the Red Land to rise and had begun thinking of returning to the Land. He had the support of other Landfolk who had been taken as slaves, but they were insistent that any plan to steal a ship must be foolproof, because if caught, they would be sentenced to work in a mine within a chasm where a monster dwelt, a fearsome creature called an Entina. I did not know what it was, but Garth speculated that it must be one of the rare creatures spawned on the Blacklands, which had adapted to the tainted earth. Why else would it not venture from its chasm in search of victims?

Several of Matthew's companions had been caught stealing weapons and had been assigned to the deadly mine. Those taken by the beast uttered screams of such intense terror and pain that grown men had fainted hearing them.

I wished, as I had done many times before, that I could communicate with Matthew to tell him he need only bide his time, for as soon as possible, we would come to him with Dragon.

The misty dawn had given way to a soft cool morning when we reached the main road and hauled the wagons back up the scree slope. It was a pleasant ride, and we saw nobody for several hours.

"I had a queer dream last night," Zarak said as we rode along. "I was in the mountains near the hot springs, an' I saw Miryum and Straaka walkin' together. I suppose it was bein' in the White Valley that put them in my mind."

I frowned, remembering that there had been other recordings of dreams about Miryum and the Sadorian tribesman Straaka. It was impossible that they were true dreams, since Straaka had died to protect Miryum, but there must be some reason why people were dreaming of them. When we returned to Obernewtyn, I would ask Maryon.

I was about to say as much when I noticed several wagons coming along a small road that joined the main road just ahead. Given that the wagons were heavily laden with furniture and that there were children and women as well as men on them, I guessed the travelers had come from Darthnor. We had heard reports that some miners had rejected Bergold's offer of work, preferring to pack their families' possessions and leave the region. Despite the rebellion, the miners retained their old loathing of Misfits and blamed us as much as the rebels for the loss of the smelters and metal works in the west that had meant the closure of the mines.

I knew it would be obvious that we were Misfits, given the direction from which we were coming, and my heart began to hammer as we approached the smaller road. I forced myself to nod to the wagoners, and to my relief, we received courteous but unsmiling nods in return. We were far down the road and out of sight before I relaxed, and I smiled ruefully at the memory of the stirring speech I had given Garth in the predawn light about being free people in a free land.

It was late in the day before we passed the blunt black face of Emeralfel, but a purplish haze obscured our view of the whole lowlands spread out beyond. I told myself the day would clear, but as we continued, heavy gray clouds massed overhead. It was foolish and superstitious, but I felt the darkening day to be an ill omen. On impulse, as we approached the hamlet where we had decided to stop for supplies and information, I suggested that Katlyn and Kella continue on in their wagon and wait for us on the road to Rangorn. After they had gone, I tied Gahltha to the wagon and sat on the front bench with Zarak, drawing a simple shawl over my hair.

The hamlet was only one of many nameless clusters of buildings and stalls grown up willy-nilly by the roadside to serve travelers who could not be bothered leaving the main way to replenish their supplies or get a meal in one of the villages or small towns. I had stopped at this one before the uprising, but I had no fear of being recognized. Those who worked in such places were often wanderers themselves, earning a few coins before traveling on. When visiting such villages before the rebellion, I had invariably gone disguised as a gypsy. As we approached the inn that was the hamlet's centerpiece, I noticed several new trading stalls and a number of cottages, and there was now a sign of a horseshoe painted on a board, denoting a blacksmith. Was this growth a sign of prosperity brought about by the changes in the Land? I climbed down and bade Lo pull the wagon around behind the inn, just in case any wagons came along and decided to take a closer look.

Zarak was unhitching the horses when he sent to ask if he ought to make some pretense of hobbling or restraining them. I sent a terse no, suggesting to the horses that they merely graze discreetly among the trees surrounding the hamlet. In the meantime, Zarak ought to fill the feed bins and replenish the water barrel.

The inn was the same rudimentary building I remembered, constructed of timber and stone, its front standing open to the road. I approached the wide serving bench and sat upon one of the stools set before it.

"What will ye, young mistress?" asked the gray-haired woman behind the counter in a friendly but businesslike way.

"I would like apple cider if you have it. I remember it was very good the last time I came this way." I tossed out the information to suggest I was a regular traveler, and I knew that my lowland accent would tell her and anyone else listening that I might not necessarily have begun my journey in the highlands, though my wagon had come from that direction.

"Will ye have it warmed? It's turned chilly."

"I will," I said equably, knowing that warming the cider

41

would take time in which she might be prevailed upon to gossip.

"Where are ye bound?" she asked as she set a pot of cider to heat over a small fire.

"Saithwold," I answered. "My brother is a woodworker and we have a hire there."

"Saithwold?" she repeated. Then she leaned closer and asked skeptically, "Who offered the hire?"

"The ex-Councilman of Saithwold, Noviny." I spoke loudly, turning slightly to see how the other customers reacted to my words. Most were busy with their own conversations and meals, but at a nearby table, an older man with muddy boots, sitting with a young woman, was clearly listening, as were two tough-looking men by the wall. I could not tell from any of their faces what they felt.

"How long ago did he offer yer brother work?" the woman asked, her voice pitched low now.

I shrugged and dropped my own voice, intrigued by her almost furtive manner. "Before last wintertime, Master Noviny sent word that he had work that needed doing on his homestead, but we could not leave the job my brother was engaged upon. Now we go to Saithwold to see if there is still work and also as a courtesy. It is no matter either way, as there is another hire waiting for my brother in Sutrium."

The woman made a noncommittal gesture, her eyes flickering past me as she poured my mug of warmed cider. I sipped at it, wondering aloud where my brother had got to and resisting the temptation to probe the woman in case she was a sensitive. I knew that Zarak was filling the water barrels from a well behind the inn, but I did not summon him. Glancing casually about the room, I saw that the man and the woman who had seemed to be listening to us were now conversing in low voices, but the two hard-looking men by the wall were still watching me.

"If you have them, I would like fresh bread, honey, and butter," I said. "My brother will want something a bit more substantial. Eggs maybe?"

"I can offer cured bacon as well as eggs," the woman said. "Though it will cost yer. It's the last of an old store, and meat will not be so easy to get if this animal charter is made law."

"Do you think that is like to happen?" I asked, having shaken my head to the bacon.

"I cannot see folk gladly doing without their meat," she answered, giving me no hint of her own opinion.

"The hunting of beasts who prey on humans is allowed within the charter, is it not?" I asked, watching her closely. "The way I heard it, a man might have bacon if he is prepared to face down the boar for it."

"Do ye ken this fingerspeech?" a voice behind me asked curtly. I turned to see the man with the mud-crusted boots, whom I had decided was a farmer. Beside him, the young woman sat with eyes demurely cast down.

"I know a little of it," I admitted warily. "A jack showed it to me and my brother."

"Is it true speech?" the man asked truculently. "Is it nowt some play of speaking? A trick?"

"To what end?" I asked. "My brother and I were skeptical, too, but the ability to communicate even a little with beasts has proven very useful. It is handy to be able to ask the horse or dog accompanying a man if he is trustworthy."

From the corner of my eye, I saw the two men at the other table exchange a purposeful glance as they rose, donning coats and throwing some coins down before they strode out.

"Mark my words, it is a trick," the farmer muttered

stubbornly, and turned his back on me.

"You best not speak of fingertalk an' the Beast Charter if you're going to Saithwold," said the woman behind the counter, still in a low voice. Her manner was less guarded now, which seemed to confirm that she had been wary of the two men who had left.

"Is Master Noviny opposed to the Beast Charter, then?" I asked, knowing it was not so.

"Sirrah Noviny isn't chieftain of Saithwold," the woman said crisply as she went to pick up the men's coins.

I sat back, trying to connect what she had implied with what Zarak's father, the beastspeaker Khuria, had written to his son about Saithwold. Before the rebellion, Khuria had gone down to Saithwold to help establish a chain of farseekers between Darthnor and Sutrium, enabling communication among the Misfits. It had quickly become clear that although Noviny was a Councilman, he was also an honest man much admired by those in his region. After the uprising, Khuria had told the old man the truth about himself, and Noviny had invited him to remain in his household. Khuria had been glad to stay, for he found Obernewtyn's bitter winters harder and harder to endure. Judging from Khuria's letters to Zarak after the end of the rebellion, a genuine friendship had grown between the two men. The letters had made it clear that Noviny was almost certain to be reelected chieftain of the region as soon as the people of Saithwold were allowed to make their own choice. Vos, the rebel who currently served as chieftain, knew this and resented it bitterly, but attempts to force local farmers to agree to vote for him had only increased his unpopularity.

Once the pass had been closed with snow, there had been no more letters until thaw. But as soon as the pass had opened

44

and messages arrived, Zarak had shown me the pile of letters from his father, asking grimly if I would read them and tell him what I thought.

They had been arranged from oldest to most recent. The first, sent at the start of wintertime, had reported Vos's growing anger at the Beast Charter and Noviny's willingness to embrace it. There had been several confrontations between Noviny and the new chieftain in which Vos had ranted and Noviny had remained calm and dignified, saying that he was a private farmer and was concerned only with his own affairs. The letter was written with Khuria's characteristic bluntness, but there was a marked change in the tone of the letters that followed. The scribing became strangely formal, and instead of offering incisive evaluations of Saithwold's situation, Khuria offered all manner of irrelevant and even trivial details of daily life. There was no more mention of Vos, nor of beastspeaking and agreements with beasts. The last letter, sent only a sevenday or so before the thaw, seemed maudlin and spoke of infirmity and the wings of time. This missive was so altogether unlike Khuria that either he had not written it, or he was striving to make it seem false.

"He wishes to communicate but he cannot write freely," I had suggested to Zarak.

"That is just what I thought," he had responded worriedly. "On his deathbed, my father would nivver whine like this."

The serving woman set down a platter of fresh-baked bread, interrupting my reverie. As she arranged crocks of honey, jam, and butter, she said softly, "If there is trouble in Saithwold, ye can be sure Chieftain Vos is behind it." She spoke his title with a sneer. "He is determined the people of Saithwold will elect him chieftain again whether they like it or no."

45

"He can't make anyone vote for him," I told her. "Each person's name will be marked off as they make their choice for chieftain. That choice will be scribed in secret, then folded, and put into a box that will remain locked until it reaches Sutrium."

"I ken that as well as the next person who can read a notice, but who do ye think will guard the box of votes and bear them to Sutrium?" the woman snapped. "The armsmen of each chieftain, that's who."

Zarak entered, hailing me jovially and commanding the woman behind the counter to bring him a brace of eggs, a mountain of fried bread, and a slab of sharp yellow cheese. The same again was to be wrapped up for our companion who lay ill in the wagon.

A faint unease passed over the woman's face at the mention of illness, but I knew this was only an unconscious remembering of the plague that had swept the Land some years previous, killing many and scarring more. The woman offered Zarak a cider, which he accepted, and as she set about preparing the rest of his order, I told him aloud that there might be strife in Saithwold over the coming elections and suggested we reconsider going there. At the same time, I farsent a command to Zarak to disagree in an arrogant brotherly way.

"It is naught to do with us," Zarak said airily, carefully emulating lowland speech to match our accents. "We are not to vote for the chieftain of Saithwold." He stretched languorously and said that he would rather eat outside and soak up a bit of sunlight. Ordering me to bring him the eggs when they came, he ambled out, humming to himself. I had to repress a smile at how well he played his part.

The woman shook her head at me, provoked just as I had

46

hoped. "He is a comely lad, your brother, but a dear fool," she said tartly. "Ye'll be lucky if he gets no more than a sound beating when ye try getting past the blockade."

"Blockade?" I thought I must have misheard her.

"There is a blockade set up on the road to Saithwold. It is supposed to keep out brigands, but if you ask me, it is the brigands mannin' it," she said, breaking eggs forcefully into a pan. "They provoke trouble with anyone who wants to go to Saithwold and use that as an excuse to stop them entering the town."

"They stop people going to Saithwold?" I asked with mild skepticism.

"Exactly that," she said sharply. "And the blockade doesn't only keep people out. It keeps in them as wants to leave. You try scribin' a letter to Sirrah Noviny to tell him yer coming to take up his offer, and ye'll get back a polite missive from him saying he has no work for yer brother." The woman glanced about, then leaned closer. "I've a sister who went to live in Saithwold wi' her bondmate years back. We have visited back and forth over the years, but at the beginnin' of this wintertime just past, I sent her an invitation an' got back a missive full of small news. My sister nivver even mentioned my suggestion that she come an' visit. I wrote again an' asked her more bluntly. Again she wrote a lot of queer prattle about recipes an' descriptions of th' weather and all manner of news about people I didn't know, but still no answer. I have scribed two more letters since, and it were th' same both times when she scribed back. There is something amiss; I know it well, but I can't go there to see her because of yon blockade." The woman's eyes suddenly brimmed with tears. "There is so much trouble about. Robbers creeping along the road at night in gangs, burnin' an' destroyin' homes, an' kitchen gardens, an' planted fields of good people. . . . Many's the time I wish fer the Council back. I hated their corruption, but at least I could see my sister."

Her voice had risen and I glanced around, but the other patrons appeared indifferent to our conversation. The woman visibly mastered herself. "My advice to ye and that handsome ninnyhammer of a brother waitin' for his eggs is to ferget about Saithwold. If ye've a promise of work in Sutrium, go there and take it up." Her eyes searched my face; then she said quickly, "But if ye do go to Saithwold, mayhap ye'd consent to . . . to take a missive from me to my sister? She's a rare fine cook and ye'll nowt be sorry. . . ." She stopped in confusion, her eyes again filling with tears, which she dashed away angrily.

I said softly, "Scribe your missive and tell me her name. My brother may look a fool, but he is resourceful. If your sister will scribe a message to you, I will bring it out and give it to a jack I know who comes this way regularly. You have been kind to give a stranger so much information, and I am sorry for your trouble."

The woman nodded and vanished for a time. When she returned, it was with red eyes, a laden plate for Zarak, a package of food wrapped in cloth, and a small folded paper that she surreptitiously pressed into my palm. "I'd like not ter charge ye for your meal, but my master is over at that table," she said apologetically.

I paid her, carried the plate out to Zarak, and sat with him while he ate, telling him what had transpired as he wolfed down the food.

"My father made no mention of any blockade, but perhaps he kenned the letter would nowt be allowed to leave Saithwold if he did. Can Vos really expect to force the people of

48

Saithwold to vote for him? He can nowt keep the town closed away forever, and as soon as anyone can leave, they will complain to the Council of Chieftains in Sutrium."

"Perhaps he hopes that whoever is voted head of the Council of Chieftains will refuse to hear any complaints against him," I said.

"There is something else odd," Zarak went on. "Dardelan mun have heard about the blockade from people turned away. Why hasnae he sent up a force of armsmen to investigate?"

He was right, and I could think of no reason for Dardelan's failure to deal with the blockade unless his grip on power was a good deal more fragile than we had been led to believe. Zarak continued. "As for the election, as soon as we tell Dardelan what Vos intends, he mun send some of his armsmen to make sure the votes are nowt tampered with." Zarak warmed to his idea and began to elaborate on how Dardelan might disguise his true intentions under a festive façade.

Suddenly eager to reach Rangorn, I bade Zarak prepare the wagon to leave. I took the plate inside, and some impulse made me ask the woman if the rebel chieftain Malik ever came by.

This time fear flashed in her eyes, but anger, too. She glanced around before saying, "His men have camps set up all along this coast to keep watch for any Herder ships that try to land, but they spend most of their time at inns buying ale and gaming with the local layabouts. Those two who left earlier drink with them regularly, and there is always trouble when they come." She hesitated and then said, "Anyone foolish enough to speak against Chieftain Malik or in favor of his enemies or rivals in their hearing is like to find their house burned down around their ears. By robbers and brigands, of course," she sneered. Then she added uneasily, "I hope I haven't made a mistake and you aren't one of Malik's spies."

"You can be sure that Malik is the last person I would serve," I said.

✦ 4 ✦

As we set off again, I told Darius what we had learned, suggesting he might not want to come into Saithwold with us. But to my surprise, he insisted.

"There may be danger," Zarak pointed out hesitantly.

The crippled healer smiled peaceably and said, "It was ever dangerous to be a Twentyfamilies gypsy, and there is a thing in Saithwold I wish to see."

At these words, I struggled to keep my composure.

Khuria had once told me of a magnificent statue of a man in Noviny's garden, and his description had made me wonder if it had been carved by Cassy Duprey, when she had been D'rekta to the Twentyfamilies. Swallow had told me enough of the ancient promises that bound the Twentyfamilies to make me aware that their first leader had charged his people with the maintenance and protection of the carvings she had created to communicate with the Seeker. If I was right, the statue in Noviny's garden might very well be a message to me. Darius's interest certainly suggested it.

So far, I had found only one of the signs mentioned in the clues carved on the original Obernewtyn doors: an enormous glass statue with my face in the sunken city under Tor. I had dived to see the statue, convinced that I would find concealed in it one of the keys mentioned on the Obernewtyn doors. But instead of a key, I had found only an inscription and the

51

artist's name: Cassy Duprey. Soon after, water had filled the protective airlock, shattering the statue, and I had been devastated, convinced that I had failed my quest at the first test, because I had not found the key.

But later, the teknoguilder Reul had mentioned that Beforetimers communicated with their computermachines by pressing on scribed letters built into the machines, spelling out sentences. This, he had explained in his dry crisp way, had been called "keying in a command." Seeing my rigid attention, he elaborated, saying that a key word or phrase might also be required before a computermachine would accept a command or offer any information.

This had made me realize that the phrase carved into the glass statue's base—*Through the transparency of now, the future*—might be just such a "key."

That had led me to wonder if the other keys referred to on the Obernewtyn doors might not be physical keys either. Indeed, one bade me "seek the words in the house where my son was born." Whatever those words were, I was sure that they, too, would prove to be a key to the mechanisms of the Beforetime weaponmachines I must find and destroy.

Discovering the glass statue had also made me realize that Cassy Duprey's decision to leave messages and clues for me had been made much sooner than I had supposed—not when she had been living in the Land as D'rekta of the Twenty-families, as I had thought, but *before* the Great White, when she had carved the glass statue.

Of course, it was possible that the glass statue and the words upon it were no more than a significant gift to a new friend and perhaps the seed from which the eventual plan to send messages to the Seeker had grown. But the Agyllian mystics had insisted I return in haste to the highlands to find "the last sign" before it was lost, and finding the glass statue seemed to fit their warning too well for it to mean anything else. Only later had it occurred to me that the Agyllians might have summoned me to the highlands to save Dragon, whose deepening coma threatened the keeping place of another sign referred to on the doors—something locked in her suppressed memories.

I visualized the words to the second and most obscure of the clues as Fian had translated them from gadi:

[That which] will [open/access/reach] the darkest door lies where the [?] [waits/sleeps]. Strange is the keeping place of this dreadful [step/sign/thing], and all who knew it are dead save one who does not know what she knows. Seek her past. Only through her may you go where you have never been and must someday go. Danger. Beware. Dragon.

I was sure that Dragon was "the one who does not know what she knows" and that Cassy or Hannah had foreseen Dragon and all that had brought her to me, impossible though that seemed; however, Fian's translation had so many alternative possibilities and blank spaces and ambiguities that sometimes I was afraid I had misread all the signs. During the early part of the winter, I had even flown the dreamtrails again with Maruman to try to take a clearer rubbing of the doors' carvings, for they had been destroyed in reality, but our first visit had affected the dreamtrails, so we had been unable to find them again. Or that is what Maruman had said, though perhaps he had simply been unable to focus his mind well enough to lead me to them.

We had not long taken the turnoff to Rangorn when Zarak spotted the other wagon waiting by the wayside. We stopped briefly to share what had happened at the inn.

As we rode on, the others began to speculate about Saithwold and Vos. Finally, Katlyn said comfortably, "I expect Brydda will explain everything." The others nodded so readily that I wondered if we were not putting too much faith in the big rebel. He had been a true friend to us and to beasts, as well as to his rebel comrades, but Brydda and Dardelan were no longer trying to overthrow a vicious and oppressive authority. *They* were the authority now, and they must control the Land and protect its people while living up to the ideals they had expounded during the years of oppression.

At length, we passed the rutted, little-used back trail leading to Kinraide. I glanced along it and thought of my early years in the Kinraide orphanage and my brother Jes. How long ago that day in the orphanage seemed when he had embraced me and promised he would come for me at Obernewtyn as soon as he had his Normalcy Certificate. How certain he had been that he was in control of his life. And I, borne away in a carriage bound for Obernewtyn, had felt utterly powerless. One day, when there was time, I would go back to Kinraide and see if I could lay flowers upon my brother's grave.

The road passed the dense, eerie Weirwood, within which lay the deep narrow chasm known as Silent Vale. As a girl, I had been marched here from the Kinraide orphanage with other orphans to gather deposits of poisonous whitestick. We had been given gloves and special bags, for merely brushing against the stuff could cause vomiting, blisters, and the loss of teeth and hair. Of course, in those days, there had been an overabundance of orphans to be disposed of, I remembered bitterly.

On the other side of the road was the stream, which was all that remained of the Upper Suggredoon after it flowed through the mountains and drained through Glenelg Mor. It was forded just before a cold, dark, poisonous river from the Blacklands joined it, transforming it into a wide, fast-moving, and now tainted river known as the Lower Suggredoon. As the wagons lumbered across the ford, I looked downriver and saw the white patches of the Sadorian tents used by the men of the rebel Zamadi, who had been given the task of guarding the banks of the Suggredoon to prevent an invasion of west coast soldierguards.

It was growing dark by the time we headed north on a smaller road to bypass Rangorn and cut across sloping green fields. The path turned to follow the lower edge of the dense forest that ran all the way from Rangorn's perimeter back to the foot of the Aran Craggie range. Here, where the river flowed out after its tumultuous journey through the mountains, Grufyyd had found Domick, Kella, and me washed up on the riverbank following our dramatic escape on a raft from the Druid's encampment.

The road brought us at length to the narrow track leading to the land where Katlyn and Grufyyd had once lived with their son. I wondered how Katlyn felt, knowing that she must soon look upon the charred ruins of her home. As a child, I had dwelt in this region, too, with my brother and parents, but I had no desire to see the ruins of my old home. It could only remind me of the dreadful death my parents had suffered at the hands of the Council.

We reached the clearing where Katlyn and Grufyyd's house had once stood, and I gaped in disbelief, for *there stood the house,* exactly as I remembered it, perfectly whole and utterly unmarked. I turned to find Kella looking no less astonished. At the rear of the wagon, Katlyn sat staring, pale and stunned.

We climbed down silently from horses and wagons, and before anyone could recover enough to speak, the front door of the little homestead opened, and out stepped Brydda Llewellyn, huge as ever, the brown beard and great shaggy mop of his hair shining in the light from his lantern. Hanging it on a hook beside the door, he strode forward, scooped up his gaping mother, and kissed her soundly, asking how she liked his surprise.

"I know you never wanted to come back here after I destroyed the old place to prevent the soldierguards from doing so, but I have a fondness for this hill and this view, so I have been rebuilding the cottage, little by little, since the rebellion. I think there is not a finer house in all the world, and though I know you and Da are happy at Obernewtyn, I thought you might like to spend the wintertimes down here."

Katlyn answered him, but she was laughing and crying at the same time, so not a single word was understandable. He lifted her again and swung her around with a laugh. I noticed Dragon gazing at Brydda, a shy, bemused smile upon her face, but when she caught me looking at her, her face shuttered.

Brydda noticed this, but even as I began some vague explanation, I found myself swept into a bear hug that crushed the breath out of me. I had not expected the embrace or how much it would warm me. These days, no one touched me, not in friendship or in love, I realized and was horrified to discover tears blurring my eyes. *It is your own fault for being so prickly and remote,* I told myself savagely.

Fortunately, Gahltha chose that moment to approach, and Brydda released me to greet him and the other horses warmly in the fingerspeech he had invented. I did not know it well, having no need of it, but my beastspeaking ability allowed me to understand that Brydda was telling Gahltha that Sallah grazed in the fields beyond the forest. She was a large fiery mare who would accept no human as her master; she allowed Brydda to ride her only because she regarded him as a friend and an ally.

Once the horses had left, we told him the news from Obernewtyn in between ferrying items from the wagons into the house for Katlyn. There was not much news, but the big rebel listened with grave courtesy. Once the fetching and carrying was done, Katlyn and Kella shooed out all of us except Dragon so they could prepare a feast fit to celebrate a home's resurrection. We would have to eat it outside as a picnic, Brydda said apologetically, for he had not yet arranged to have furniture sent up, and he began to set out a rough trestle table and upturned log seats, hoping it would not rain.

I asked Zarak and Louis to walk down to Rangorn during the meal preparations to see if they could learn anything more about the blockade in Saithwold. Darius went to tend the soldierguards, then took a short walk to ease his cramped muscles. That left Brydda and me.

"Maryon insisted that we bring Dragon," I said without preamble.

Brydda frowned. "I gather that she has not remembered you?"

I shook my head. "Roland told me that she will. Maybe that is why Maryon sent us on this trip together." I changed the subject and told him about Khuria's letters and what I had heard at the inn. Brydda was not surprised by any of it.

"For the last moon or so, we have had numerous reports from people turned away or beaten up at this blockade," he said. "We have also had complaints from people who received letters like Khuria's. Dardelan sent a messenger to question the blockaders, but Chieftain Vos claimed that he is protecting the people of the Saithwold region from brigands and ruffians. I wanted to ride to Saithwold with a troop of armsmen and shake him until his teeth rattled, but Dardelan would not allow it. He says that we must not be seen as oppressors who can solve problems only with force."

"Surely Dardelan will not sit back and let the people of Saithwold be forced to vote for Vos against their will," I said indignantly.

"He will act only if someone from the region lays a formal charge against Vos before the Council of Chieftains. You see, it is too well known that Vos allies himself with Malik and that Dardelan and Malik are at odds. If Dardelan acts against him of his own volition, people will say that he is not impartial, and he can't risk that, given that he will be one of those to judge your charge against Malik."

"But how is anyone in Saithwold to lay a charge if they are not allowed to leave or scribe a letter without fear of it being destroyed?" I demanded. "And what of Malik? I have heard that he is behind the so-called robber burnings."

"I have heard the same. But, Elspeth, think," Brydda said. "In a very short time, Obernewtyn will lay a serious formal charge against him. I have no doubt that, with the soldier-guards' testimony, the Council of Chieftains will agree that there is a charge to answer. In which case, Malik must remain in Sutrium. That will severely limit his mischief. It will also make anyone think twice about voting for him as a chieftain. And when he is found guilty after the elections, as I have no doubt he will be, he will have to serve a long sentence on a community farm."

"And what about Vos?"

"Straight after the elections, you can be sure that Dardelan will find some pretext to enter Saithwold and deal with him."

"Are you so sure that Dardelan will be elected high chieftain, Brydda? I understand there is some concern about his proposed Beast Charter."

The big man rolled his eyes. "I did suggest he wait until after the elections to reveal the Beast Charter, but you know Dardelan. He said it would be dishonest to hide his intentions. However, he means to make it very clear that the charter will not be formalized until all Landfolk have had the chance to offer their opinions and ask questions. Given how gently he went about publicizing the Charter of Laws, allowing people to argue for changes in it, I doubt anyone will feel he is like to force anything on them."

Brydda's certainty and calmness began to allay my fears. I said, "You might mention this to him. On the way here, Zarak had an idea about how Dardelan might ensure that Vos does not cheat in the election. He suggests that as many chieftains as are willing march into Saithwold on voting day. Dardelan can claim they have come to celebrate the first elections. For that reason, there should be tumblers and musicians and other sorts of entertainers, and if possible, the chieftains should bring their families to lend the day a festive air. Needless to say, the chieftains would bring a substantial honor guard of armsmen. Vos will not dare to complain, nor will he dare to bully anyone or tamper with votes if other chieftains are looking on. Maybe Dardelan could even open the sealed box of votes and count them on the spot so Vos can't later claim they were tampered with."

Brydda's eyes glinted with amusement and admiration. "During the rebellion, I thought that Zarak had the makings of a fine strategist, and now I am sure of it." He sobered. "If you will take my advice, we should go directly to Sutrium tomorrow and leave Saithwold alone for the time being."

I shook my head. "I promised Zarak."

Brydda sighed. "It may not be a bad thing. You can spread the word in Saithwold that Dardelan knows what is happening, so people there won't do anything rash. If you don't object to riding back along the main road, I could ride with you as far as the blockade. I doubt that whoever is manning the barrier will refuse you entry, knowing that I will witness it. But you will have to coerce yourself out again if they are really preventing people from leaving."

"I will do it if we need to, but why must we go to Saithwold by the main road? It would be quicker to go via Kinraide and Berrioc."

"It would," Brydda agreed, "but I need to speak with a rebel who lives just after the Sawlney turnoff before I go back to Sutrium. It would not take long, and we can just go on from there to Saithwold."

I opened my mouth to agree with the change of route when a cold premonition of danger flowed through me. At the same moment, Kella, Katlyn, and Dragon emerged from the house laden with platters of food. Brydda leapt up to help them set the plates on the trestle and to fetch more lanterns. By the time this was done to Katlyn's satisfaction, the premonition had faded.

Louis and Zarak returned red-cheeked from their walk as we were sitting down to eat, and Zarak explained that there had been little talk in Rangorn about the blockade outside Saithwold. The gossip was all of Zamadi's men and the soldierguards stationed on the opposite bank of the Lower Suggredoon.

Listening to his description of the camps, I realized that if both riverbanks were heavily guarded even this high upstream, it would be impossible to enter or emerge from the Suggredoon, even in a plast suit, unless there was a diversion. But it would have to be something very clever, since the Councilmen and soldierguards would expect just such a trick.

As we ate, the moon rose and a chill wind began blowing at our backs. But the fire gave off waves of delicious warmth, and we shifted to sit around it as we finished the meal with slices of plum tart. Only then did I think to ask Brydda about the ship burning. I told him what Garth had said, and he nodded.

"It would be impossible for a ship to come into port, decant enough men to set fire to the ships being built, and then vanish, all without anyone noticing anything; therefore, we know that the raiders did not come by ship."

I stared at him. "You mean someone from the Land destroyed them?"

He nodded grimly.

"But who would do such a thing? And why?" Kella cried.

Brydda shook his head. "As to why, most of the Council of Chieftains believe the ships were destroyed to prevent us from landing a fighting force on the west coast. But since the shipbuilding began again as soon as the debris was cleared, nothing was accomplished but a delay. Dardelan thinks *that* might have been the reason for the burnings."

"A delay?" I echoed. "To what end?"

Brydda shrugged. "Maybe to give the Council more time to prepare their defenses, or maybe to allow time for some other plan to unfold. Maryon's futuretelling about trouble on the west coast all but confirms it, and there is no doubt that our enemies are plotting to regain this part of the Land."

"But who burned the ships?" Kella repeated her earlier question. "The Councilmen and all soldierguards who did not die or escape over the Suggredoon are in prison or working on Councilfarms, and all of the Herders left."

"They are to be called *community farms* now," Brydda explained. "It may be that some Herders or soldierguards did not leave, either by accident or design, and are now bent on working against us so that their masters can return. Or maybe the saboteurs are people who have lost power or property since the rebellion and want things back the way they were."

"The sabotage couldn't have anything to do with Malik, could it?" I asked.

Brydda met my eyes. "It occurred to me, but how would it serve Malik to have the ships burned? More likely he would want them completed sooner, knowing that Dardelan will insist upon taking part in any west coast landing, where he might be killed or injured or simply fail."

The others began talking more generally of the elections, and I told Zarak what Brydda had said about Saithwold. As expected, he was still determined to go there, but he agreed that it was worth the extra time to go back via the Sawlney turnoff if it meant that Brydda would escort us to the blockade.

"Brocade will likely be reelected chieftain of Sawlney," Brydda said, answering a question from Zarak a little later. "He has spent a good bit of time currying favor with powerful farm holders in his region. In truth, his election would not necessarily be bad. Brocade openly opposes the Beast Charter, but he dislikes violence and is moderate in other areas."

"Who do ye predict will be made chieftain of Darthnor?"

Louis asked, no doubt thinking of his friend Enoch, the old coachman who dwelt on a small property in Darthnor with Rushton's defective half brother, Stephen Seraphim.

"Lydi may win, but the locals are divided between him and one of their own, Webben. He is a mine overseer who wants the road to the west reopened. He is constantly making representations to the Council of Chieftains, demanding that they negotiate with the west coast, despite the fact that we have no means of communicating with them, nor the slightest indication that they desire it. Do you know the man?"

"I do," Louis grunted. "He dislikes Misfits but mayhap more out of Darthnor tradition than any real conviction."

"Is there no possibility of Bergold being elected?" I asked.

Brydda shook his head. "He is thought to be too . . . eccentric. In any case, he has not put his name forward."

I said nothing, for it suddenly seemed to me that, for the beasts and Misfits, it did not matter who won each town's election, so long as Dardelan was returned as high chieftain, for his honesty and ideals would influence the rest.

At last, Darius rose slowly with a groan, saying he needed to sleep. Watching him hobble away, I saw that he moved a good deal more stiffly than before. I mentioned it to Kella, who explained that his joints were becoming inflamed from the wagon's jostling. She rose, saying that she would see if he would allow her to drain off some of his pain. After she had gone, Katlyn told us that the healer had twice on this journey performed the service for the gypsy healer, though he had protested each time.

"Maybe he feels a man ought to bear his own pain," Brydda said.

"Or he is afraid of becoming dependent on the relief she offers," I countered.

"It might not be pride or fear of dependency that makes him refuse her help," Katlyn said, regarding both of us with slight exasperation. Before I could ask what she meant, she rose, kissed her son, and bade us all good night. She held out her hand to Dragon, who went with her, yawning like a cat. She neglected to look back at me with especial dislike, and I felt unexpectedly cheered. Perhaps this trip would at least lessen her dislike of me, even if it did not restore her memory. Maybe I had made a mistake in trying to make her remember our friendship and all along ought to have been trying to form a new one.

Brydda rose to get more wood for the fire, and Louis and Zarak packed up the meal and carried away the dishes to wash them in a bucket of water drawn from the well. I stayed where I was, for Maruman had crept into my lap during the meal and had fallen asleep. I did not want to disturb him, because he had been unusually subdued all day, either sleeping or simply gazing at the passing world from Kella's lap or my shoulder, offering few of his usual acerbic asides. And he had not even once glared at the moon, now glowing overhead. I looked up at it, as yellow and ripe as a wheel of cheese, and thought again of the premonition I had experienced earlier that night.

✦ 5 ✦

"I HAVE SOME Sadorian choca," Brydda said, jolting me from my reverie as he dropped an armful of wood beside the fire. "Would you like a mug before you go to bed?"

"Is the sky wide?" I asked dryly.

Brydda threw back his head and laughed. He knew as well as I that the delicious, sweet brown powder was both scarce and violently expensive now that Sadorian ships no longer docked at Sutrium. The Sadorian tribal leaders had ruled that neither of the two precious remaining greatships would make port at the Land until Salamander ceased preying on ships that sailed into Sutrium. Their policy of nonaggression meant that they would not engage Salamander's notorious *Black Ship* in battle unless he attacked Sador, and as far as I knew, he had never even landed there. This meant that choca and other Sadorian luxuries had to be transported by the difficult coastal route or carried by smaller vessels daring or greedy enough to brave the hidden shoals close to shore, where Salamander's larger vessel could not venture.

Brewing the choca carefully, Brydda explained that it had been a gift to him from Bruna, Jakoby's headstrong daughter.

"Has she returned to the Land on horseback, then?" I asked with some surprise.

Brydda shot me an enigmatic look. "She never left. After the destruction of the *Zephyr*, when Jakoby departed by land,

Bruna stayed. She has been an honored guest in Dardelan's house ever since. Bruna's mother sent the choca."

Brydda handed me the fragrant brown liquid and asked if I had brought the plast suit Dardelan requested. I nodded, explaining that it was laid flat in a special compartment within the wagon's base and that, although the plast was impervious to taint over a certain period, the fabric was nonetheless very fragile. I asked openly if Dardelan meant to use it to smuggle a spy across the Suggredoon.

Brydda looked at me like Garth had. "Dardelan had thought of asking you or another coercer to swim across the river and spy for us. We had even begun planning the diversion of all diversions, but then we learned that all soldierguards guarding the other bank wear demon bands."

I stared at him in disbelief. Not long before the rebellion, the Herder priests had created demon bands to prevent Misfits from coercing or farseeking their wearers, but only upperrank priests and a few Councilmen and soldierguard captains had ever worn them. "You can't mean that *everyone* guarding the other bank has a demon band?" I asked, thinking I must have misunderstood.

"All," Brydda repeated flatly. "You can see them when you look with a spyglass, once you know what you are looking for. Obviously, the Herders are producing and supplying them. We only knew it after Reuvan found a Port Oran man washed up on a bit of sandy shore near the mouth of the river. Some drunken soldierguards had thrown him into the sea after he had objected to their manhandling his daughter. He had drunk too much tainted water to be saved, but he told us quite a bit, about the demon bands, for instance, and that the Herders have formed an alliance with the west coast Councilmen. Of course, we guessed as much. He also said that

Salamander is working openly for the Faction, or with it. He runs three smaller ships that patrol our coastline now, as well as the *Black Ship* that regularly sails between Norseland and Herder Isle and across the strait to the west coast. Salamander openly buys any prisoners in the Councilmen's cells, so he must have made some accommodation with them as well."

"Did the man say anything about the rebels?"

"Only that there are no rebels left in Port Oran or any other towns close to the Suggredoon. He did say rebels are rumored to be causing havoc higher up the coast, in Aborium and Murmroth. But things are bad over there. Food is scarce in the cities, because most of their grain and vegetables came from this side of the Suggredoon, as well as ore for their smelters. There are small farm holdings all down the coast as well as in the hills about Murmroth, but their produce is limited by the land's barrenness. The man said most people survive only by fishing, but even that is being affected by the poisons the Council spilled along the remote and unguarded portions of the coastline before our ships were burned."

"It sounds awful," I said, aghast.

"The man cursed us for the disaster our victory brought to the west coast, and then he begged us to invade and save his daughter," Brydda said grimly.

I did not need to ask if the man had already died. It was in his face. "So if even a Misfit cannot slip across the Suggredoon now, why did you ask about the plast suit?"

"Because Dardelan intends it to be worn by a spy who will swim ashore on the west coast just past the river mouth. The area is unguarded, because a rocky shelf extends a long way into the water, just under the surface, making it too shallow even for a ship boat, and no one swims there because the water is tainted."

"Whoever wears the suit will have to be very careful not to tear it on the rocks—and they will have to be a strong swimmer, because the sea around the river mouth is very wild."

"Reuvan all but has fins," Brydda said, smiling.

"Reuvan!"

"He volunteered."

"Why didn't Dardelan's messenger mention any of this?" I asked.

"Dardelan wants it kept quiet, given that the ship burnings mean we have secret enemies. Only he and I and Reuvan know about the man washed ashore, and now you. That is partly why I suggested this meeting: to tell you in person what has been happening and to make sure you brought the plast suit. Reuvan will leave as soon as he has it."

"Once ashore, what will he do?" I asked.

"Conceal the suit and make his way to Port Oran, where he will see if anything of the rebel network remains there. If there is no one, he will move from town to town up the coast. Once he makes contact with the west coast rebels, he will let them know what is happening in the Land. But his main task will be to learn what the Council is planning. Because there is no doubt in Dardelan's mind, or mine, that something is afoot, else why the demon bands? Of course, Reuvan will try to reach your people as well. That is another reason I wanted to speak with you. We need to know how to reach anyone not in communication with the rebels."

"How will Reuvan share what he learns with Dardelan?" I asked. "Will he signal over the river?"

"That would be dangerous, because he would have to get close enough to be seen from our side of the river. The best place for that would be the old ferry landing, where the banks draw closest to one another, but the soldierguards have a barricade there to keep everyone well back. And the remainder of the river is patrolled and makeshift watchtowers have been erected. The plan is that Reuvan will carry the suit back to the coast, put it on, and let the current carry him back to Sutrium. We will be watching for him, of course."

"What if the suit is damaged on his way there or if he is washed out too far? Even ships don't go out into the middle currents."

"And who told you that?" Brydda asked, straight-faced.

I sighed. "Reuvan."

"Just so. If the suit is damaged, he will find some way to signal us," Brydda said. But he looked suddenly weary, and I knew that, for all his apparent confidence, he was worried about the young seaman.

I thought again of the premonition that had assailed me earlier. "I begin to fear that we were too quick in letting people know of our refuge."

Brydda shook his head. "If you had kept your refuge secret, it would have made Landfolk even more mistrustful and suspicious of you. Take heart, for all is not ill in this new time. The Council is gone from this part of the Land, and with them, the soldierguards and Herders and their whole machinery of corruption. Good new laws are about to be established, and soon people will elect their own leaders. Of course, some still fear your kind, but many more do not, having seen clearly your loyalty during the rebellion. Do not be impatient, for the changes have begun and will continue." He lapsed into silence for a moment, then said, "When people first began to speak of the rebellion, I imagined that once the Council was gone, the Land would become a sort of paradise. But of course, it is not that simple. It will be many years before we have real stability, and no doubt there will be almost as many steps back as forward."

"You could just walk away from it all," I pointed out, once more hearing the fatigue in his voice. "No one would ever say you had not done enough."

"I would say it," Brydda said with gentle finality. "Enough is not measured by what you give but by what is needed." He reached out and took my hand in his. "Something is wrong between you and Rushton, isn't it?"

I cursed his knack of knowing what he could not know, but still the words burst out of me, low and raw. "Rushton has changed since he was imprisoned in the cloister in Sutrium. He does not remember what happened, but something is broken in him. I cannot look inside his mind to see if it can be mended, for he will not permit it. He does not want my Talent, and he does not want me. There is nothing to be done."

I looked down at Maruman, who slept on obliviously. I was glad, for my grief would have irked him.

"Elspeth." Brydda said my name gently, and when I looked up, I saw pity in his eyes. "Come. It is time you were asleep." He reached down, scooped Maruman into his arms, and pulled me to my feet. He led me to the bedroll Zarak had spread beneath a wagon, and I lay down, feeling suddenly utterly exhausted. Brydda placed Maruman gently beside me, and the old cat rolled close with a soft snore. He had not even awakened, and I wondered if he slept or traveled the dream-trails.

"Sleep," Brydda commanded gently, and left me. I closed my eyes, and sleep rolled over me like a soft, heavy blanket, obliterating consciousness with a gentle finality.

✦ ✦ ✦

I dived through the cloudy swirl of memories and dreams that clamored at me in the upper levels of my mind, shielding myself until I was deep enough for them to fade into a thick brown silence. I continued to descend until I heard the siren song of the mindstream that runs at the deepest level of all minds and that contains the thoughts and memories of all minds that have ever existed. The urge to join the stream and give up my individual existence was as potent as ever, but I held myself until the pull of the mindstream was in exact balance with the pull to rise to consciousness.

I had come deep to avoid dreaming, but even as I looked down into the shimmering beauty of the mindstream, a bubble of matter detached itself and rose toward me, as shapeless and shining as air rising to the surface of the water.

The bubble engulfed me.

I saw Cassy Duprey sitting in a Beforetime flier. I could not tell if it was the same flying machine I had seen her in before, but she looked different, subtly older. Perhaps it was just the plain dark clothes she wore, instead of the bright colors she usually favored; or maybe it was the fact that her wild mass of dark crinkling hair was restrained in a complex coil against her neck. A very beautiful, haughty-looking older woman with the same choca-toned skin as Cassy sat opposite her. A certain likeness about the facial bones suggested they were related. Could this be her mother? I wondered. She did not act like a mother, for Cassy wept, and the woman made no move to comfort her.

"What did you expect, Cassandra?" she finally asked, her tone irritated. "He was a spy."

"He might not be dead," Cassy said in a voice thick with tears and despair.

"Don't be foolish," the woman responded crisply. "Samu

vanished while spying on officials in the Chinon Empire. If he is not dead, then he will wish he were."

Cassy groaned and leaned over as if she had a stomachache, her forehead pressed to her knees.

"Don't you think it is time to end this orgy of grief?" the woman said, glancing at her watch. "Samu knew the price he would pay if he was caught. He thought it was worth it. If you loved him, you might honor his choice." Her lips twisted into an ugly shape as she said the word *love*, but Cassy, head on her lap, did not see it.

"Must people always pay the worst price for doing what is right in your world, Mother?" she whispered.

The older woman glanced out the window at the sky for a long minute, her expression remote, as if she were thinking about something completely different. Finally, she returned her gaze to her daughter. "I did not say he was doing the right thing, Cassandra. Only that he thought he was. People always think what they are doing is right. Look at your father and his Sentinel project. He and the government think it is right to put the world's fate into the hands of machines. He thinks it is responsible and mature to relinquish control of the weapons we have created. We may all pay for his doing what he thinks is right." There was a queer expression on her face, and the queerness had spread into her voice.

Cassy lifted her head and gave her mother a long, bitter look. "If you think Father is wrong, Mother, why don't you tell him so? Why don't you tell the whole world? You have the power to do that, and it would not even cost your life."

"Wouldn't it, Cassy?" her mother asked: "You think the government would allow me to criticize its pet project? You are such a child."

"What are you talking about?" Cassy demanded.

72

"I am talking about the real world, Cassy, where we all live. Not the world of heroic and foolish boys and girls. I chose to leave your father, because he had become a man I did not like, a man who believed in things I could not believe in. He let the world and his own fears turn him into a puppet. I can't stop what he does any more than I can stop what the government does. The best I can do is stay away from him and his world and keep you away from it. I don't want to hear any more about you going back to that place. I don't want you there again. Not ever."

"But, Mother, he has invited me, and I need . . . I mean, I want to go. It will be the last time."

Cassy's mother gave her a hard, coldly intelligent look. "Why would you want to go there again, when you resisted going there so violently in the first place, despite my having no choice but to send you?"

"I . . . I just . . . I was doing some painting there. Yes, I hated it, but I want to finish the work I began."

Her mother regarded her for a moment and then smiled. "You are lying. But I will make you a bargain. You tell me why you suddenly want to switch to the university at Newrome, and I will allow you to visit your father this one last time. But I want the truth, and I will know if you lie."

Cassy's face changed, and a peculiar expression filled her wide, almond-shaped eyes. "Do you really want to know, Mother? Because if you do, I'll show you."

Her mother frowned. "Cassandra, I have had just about enough of these childish—"

Cassy cut her off. "Remember that big splashy series of advertisements sent out by the Reichler Clinic a while back, Mother? The ones asking for anyone who thought they might have paranormal abilities to come and be tested? Well, I went—"

"But that was a hoax. There was a scandal over falsified research results. Surely you were not foolish enough—"

"Yes, there was a scandal, but it was about the man who was running it—William Reichler. He supposedly wrote a book, only he hadn't come up with the testing methods the clinic used or written the book. It was another scientist, who died. Reichler stole his work and put his own name to it. He was after money, and he got it by conning rich people into making donations, convincing them that everyone had paranormal abilities, which could be awakened with the right techniques, just as the book said. Then he was exposed and there was the scandal. But not everyone he hired was crooked. A lot of the researchers who worked for the Reichler Clinic really believed in what they were doing. So when William Reichler died, they kept the clinic running. . . ."

"The clinic was destroyed," Cassy's mother said. "Reichler burned it to cover his tracks, only he was killed before he could get away."

"William Reichler was killed. And the building that had housed the clinic at Inva was destroyed, but the Reichler Clinic is an organization, not a place. It relocated to Newrome. It is still operating."

Her mother's lips curled in disgust. "And I suppose whoever is running this place persuaded you when you visited Newrome last month that you have paranormal abilities. Cassy, will you never grow up?"

Cassy smiled. It was as cold as her mother's. I felt her mind reach out. She had fashioned a mindprobe so clumsy that it must have hurt her mother badly as it entered her mind and spoke her name. I heard the older woman gasp with pain and clutch at her head.

"Is that proof enough for you, Mother?" Cassy asked

aloud. "Or are your own senses as untrustworthy as you keep telling me mine are?"

Her mother's mouth hung open. Her eyes bulged in disbelief. "You . . . what did you . . . ?"

The memory dissolved, and the mindstream sang its song to me, alluring, infinitely sweet, promising release from pain, sorrow, and desire. I dared not stay there any longer. Wrenching myself upward, I was too weary to armor myself against the strands of thought floating past. One brushed me, and all at once, I was inside the old dream of walking along a dark tunnel, hearing the drip of water into water. Ahead was the dull yellow flash, flash, flash of light, like a signal.

"Stop," said a woman's voice, beautiful and strangely loud. "Do not enter or you will die."

The shock of hearing a voice in a place where I had never before heard one woke me. I opened my eyes and found myself blinking into daylight, the dreams slipping away like dawn mist. I thought of the vision I had experienced of Cassy, weeping at her lover's death, and then of her mind forming a clumsy but powerful probe to invade her mother's mind. Clearly, Hannah Seraphim had taught her to use her Talent. Cassandra, her mother had called her. Not far from Kasanda . . .

"Get up, ElspethInnle," Maruman sent peevishly. "I am hungry."

We were on the road again by midmorning, having bade Katlyn farewell. She was to remain in Rangorn, herb gathering until Grufyyd brought down a wagon in a few days to collect her. When we left, the herbalist was tying what she, Kella, and Dragon had collected into bunches to hang up and dry.

The rest of us parted just over the ford. Kella, Dragon, and Louis Larkin set off in one wagon for Sutrium via Kinraide and Berrioc with both soldierguards. Zarak, Darius, and I took the other wagon and went with Brydda back the way we had come, first to the Sawlney turnoff and thence to Saithwold. I had tried to convince Darius to go with the others, partly because I worried about his inflamed joints and partly to see if he might give his true reason for wanting to go to Saithwold. But he simply smiled serenely and said he would stay with us.

I rode Gahltha to begin with, but once Brydda had made his brief call at the farmstead on the Sawlney turnoff, he suggested I dull Gahltha's coat, tie him to the back of the wagon, and ride inside. "A young woman of your description riding a magnificent black stallion would be as good as a message to Vos that Elspeth Gordie is visiting Saithwold," Brydda said.

I was not sure I was as well known as Brydda seemed to think, but I did as he suggested, drawing my shawl over my head and lifting Maruman into my lap as I joined Zarak on the bench seat. Darius lay in the back. I wished again that I had managed to convince him not to come, but perhaps all Twentyfamilies gypsies regarded it as their sacred duty to check on their D'rekta's carvings whenever they had the chance.

When at last we reached the turnoff, I was surprised that there was no sign of armsmen or blockade on the smaller road, but Brydda said the blockade was not immediately visible from the main road. Sure enough, around the first bend, we came upon it: a solid barrier of planks nailed together and running from dense underbrush on one side of the road to the other. The surly looking fellow slouching before the barricade gave an unmanly squeak of fright as Sallah pranced to a stop. Brydda roared laughing, but before the red-faced man could unleash a tirade of abuse, the big rebel called out a greeting, naming him Tam Otey.

The man squinted shortsightedly at Brydda, and then his face changed. "Brydda Llewellyn, are you riding to Saithwold?" He sounded truculent, but there was alarm in his eyes.

"Will you try to stop me if I am, Tam?" Brydda asked in a mocking voice that made the other man's expression twist with anger.

"Chieftain Vos will not like that you sent no word of your visit."

"I have no wish to visit your precious chieftain, man. There are a lot more than him living in Saithwold province, though maybe he has forgotten it." Brydda's voice had a hard edge, and the other man scowled, but before he could respond, a man standing behind the barrier spoke in a cold, authoritative voice.

"No need to get shirty, Llewellyn. Tam here only asked if you intend to enter Saithwold region."

"Stovey Edensal," Brydda said flatly. "It is strange to see you here minding Vos's front door. Were you not once Malik's man?"

"Answer," the man said in a stony voice. "Do you wish to enter this region?"

"I intended to escort these good people, whom I met upon the road, to Saithwold. The lass is anxious about the rumors of brigands. But seeing how well you have the road guarded, I can leave them and return to Sutrium," Brydda said.

"We have orders to find out what they want before we let them through," Stovey Edensal said stiffly, after a slight hesitation.

Brydda nodded to Zarak. "Tell the man your names and business, lad."

"I am Zar and these are my two friends, Ella and Darius. We mean to visit my father, who works for one of the farm holders in Saithwold region," Zarak said, suppressing his highland accent.

"Is your father expecting you?" the armsman demanded.

"He is not," Zarak answered equably. "I had a missive from him some while back, and he sounded a bit low in spirits. I decided to call on my way to Sutrium to cheer him up."

"There!" Brydda said with cheerful impatience. "Neither the boy nor his companions are robbers, so you may set the barrier aside with a clear conscience."

Stovey looked from the wagon to Brydda and made a gesture with his hand. Three tough-looking armsmen emerged from each side of the bushes where they had been concealed, and my heart began to race, but all six merely set about moving the barrier to let the wagon pass. After Lo and Zade had pulled the wagon through the gap, the barrier was replaced and Zarak turned to shout thanks to Brydda for his kindness.

"You owe me a mug of good ale for my troubles," Brydda bellowed. "Look for me at the Inn of the Red Deer when you arrive on the morrow."

"We might stay a night or two with my father," Zarak called, "but I promise you'll have your ale within a fourday."

"I look forward to it," Brydda roared.

Their prepared speeches completed, I beastspoke the horses to urge them on. My last sight of the blockade was of Brydda astride Sallah, talking down to Tam Otey. He had reckoned that no one would come after us while he was watching, and it seemed he was right.

The moment we were out of sight of the blockade, the

horses broke into a gallop. Maruman complained bitterly at the ride's roughness, but I ignored him. I had never been to Noviny's homestead, but I knew that his property ran along the outer edge of the Saithwold region. The entrance should not be far along the road, and with luck, we could reach it before we were pursued. At last we saw a gateway with Noviny's sigil and name painted on a metal shingle swinging from a post beside it. The gate stood open, but it was so narrow that it took a good deal of maneuvering to get the wagon through. The track beyond it was only a little wider and badly rutted, which surprised me, for Noviny had struck me as a meticulous man.

"Noviny gave my da a cottage not far from the front gate," Zarak said, looking around, but it was Darius who spotted the thatched roof that rose above the trees a little way from the entrance. A clearing at the start of the path leading to the cottage enabled the horses to draw the wagon off the track, where it would not be visible to anyone glancing into the property from the main road. I suggested we unhitch the horses and shove the wagon under a huge spreading tree with weeping branches to hide it from the sight of anyone coming along the track as well.

Zarak had to help Darius down, and when I saw his strained expression, I asked if he would not rather stay in the wagon and rest.

"It will be better for me to walk about a little," he answered, but his rigid smile alarmed me. However, there was nothing to be done immediately, and at least he could lie down in a proper bed in Khuria's cottage. Noviny might even employ a healer. With the horses' help, we shoved the carriage out of sight. I arranged branches to conceal the protruding part of the wagon while Zarak hurried off to see if his father was asleep, as neither of us had been able to farseek him. Darius lowered himself to a log with a stifled groan as I sent a general probe in the direction of Noviny's homestead. It was blocked by areas of buzzing rejection that betokened tainted earth. I remembered that the Saithwold Herders had laid caches of tainted material during the rebellion to confound the ability of Misfits to communicate with one another.

We heard footsteps and turned to see Zarak alone, a worried expression on his face. "He's nowt there, an' it looks as if nobody has lived there for some time." Anxiety strengthened his highland accent.

"He probably just shifted to the main house during the wintertime," I said soothingly. "There's too much tainted stuff about to farseek him, though." I looked at the gypsy. "Can you walk, Darius? We had better leave the wagon where it is, given the state of the track."

Gahltha offered to carry him, but when I conveyed the offer, Darius thanked him and said he would rather walk. We set off, moving slowly and leaving the horses to graze near the wagon so they could warn us if we were pursued. They would follow us up to the homestead later. Maruman lay across my shoulders in offended silence, his claws sunk in painfully deep. I kept trying to farseek the homestead, but areas of tainted resistance continued to block me. I wondered if Noviny realized how much poisoned material was strewn about his land. It ought to be cleaned up before it began to seep in and poison the groundwater. But perhaps Noviny knew about the tainted matter without having any idea how to remove it.

After a time, the sound of dogs barking filled the air. Four great hounds with faces as ugly as Jik's friend Darga came racing down the steep, rutted road, gnashing their teeth menacingly. I beastspoke them and they stopped at once. They came to me, the lead dog whining and baring his neck in such a show of inferiority that Zarak gave me a curious look. Unlike Talented communications between humans, beastspeaking was audible to anyone with the Talent; other beastspeakers had often seen animals behave reverently or heard them address me as Innle, which was the beast word for Seeker. I had found it wiser to offer no explanation, for people were usually too shy or awed to question me. But Zarak was neither.

"Try farseeking your father again," I said quickly.

Distracted successfully, his face took on the distant focused look all farseekers acquire when they send out their minds, but after a moment, he shook his head in defeat. We walked to the top of a long slope, and there stood a graceful, low, stone homestead and a cluster of well-kept outbuildings. The front door burst open, and Khuria stepped out carrying a cudgel and frowning suspiciously. Zarak gave a relieved shout and ran to embrace his father.

Khuria was a taciturn man, but after holding his son tightly for a long moment, he looked at the three of us in open consternation. "I dinna expect ye to come here!" he said.

"The letters you sent Zarak were designed to summon us, were they not?" I said, puzzled by his reaction.

"Aye! But I dinna imagine anyone would manage to get past th' blockade. I thought the letters would bring Zarak there, an' once he'd been turned back, he'd ride to Sutrium and tell Dardelan. I fear I have brought all of ye into deadly danger." His eyes settled on Darius, whom he had never met, and Zarak introduced the beasthealer to his father. The older man greeted the gypsy with warmth; then he sobered abruptly. "I only wish I were nowt meetin' ye under such circumstances."

"Don't worry, Father," Zarak broke in eagerly. "We know what Vos is tryin' to do, and High Chieftain Dardelan knows it as well. We saw Brydda Llewellyn last night in Rangorn. He rode with us to the barricade, the only reason they let us through without a fuss. He told us Dardelan will deal with Vos after the election."

The old beastspeaker ran gnarled hands through his thinning hair. "I wish that we had only Vos's ambitions to contend with. Well, I will say nae more, fer this is Noviny's story to tell. Come inside an' ye will hear it soon enow."

I wanted to insist on some immediate answers, but I noticed that Darius was looking grayer than ever, so I held my tongue. We had barely stepped inside the door of the homestead when he fainted dead away. Zarak managed to catch him, and the young woman coming along the passage toward us commanded we carry him to a small bedchamber. Once Darius was stretched out on a bed, she examined him with a swift efficiency that marked her as a healer. Then she said, "He is very hot. I will prepare something to lower his fever." She drew a sheet over Darius's twisted form and ushered the rest of us through a well-appointed kitchen, where the staff gaped at us, and into a large round room containing a fire pit sunk deep into its center. She introduced herself abstractedly as Noviny's granddaughter, Wenda, and bade us wait while Khuria fetched her grandfather.

"I must go back and tend to your friend," she added, and left.

Somewhat dazed by the speed at which things were happening, I set Maruman down and eased off my muddy boots before lowering myself onto one of the worn embroidered cushions set around the fire pit. Maruman was already kneading one enthusiastically when Zarak joined me.

"What do ye think is the matter with Darius?" he asked.

"I don't know, but I wish I knew why Khuria looked so appalled to see us."

We heard footsteps, and the door opened to reveal Khuria and the older man I remembered as Councilman Noviny. Although the man was straight-backed and had a very direct gaze, his hair had turned snowy white, and there was a frailty about him that I had not noticed during the trials. But he smiled warmly as Khuria brought a carved chair with a very upright back and set it close to the fire. Noviny turned his eyes to the leaping flames for so long that I wondered if he had forgotten us.

Finally, I said gently, "It seems there is more trouble here than Vos wanting to win an election."

Noviny sighed and looked at me. "If Vos were wise or even sensible, he would know perfectly well that Chieftain Dardelan and the other rebels will never allow him to usurp the leadership of Saithwold. But he is vain and foolish, which has made him the perfect pawn for a true villain whose own ambition is darker than anything Vos could imagine."

My heart sank. "What villain?" I asked. But even as I said it, I thought of Brydda saying, *"Stovey Edensal . . . Were you not once Malik's man?"*

✦ 6 ✦

"Before I say anything more, I must ask how you got past the barricade," Noviny said.

I let Zarak explain, and Noviny nodded. "I thought it must have been something like that, since you could not have used your Misfit powers."

"What is going on here?" I asked. "Why was one of Malik's men guarding that barricade?"

Noviny gave me an approving look. "Stovey Edensal, I imagine. And he is manning the barricade, because he is mind sensitive to the Talents exhibited by your people. Unlike the other men there, he will not wear a demon band, for his task is to identify any Misfit attempting to use Talents to enter the region. It is sheer luck that you did not attempt to enter his mind."

"Demon bands!" I said, unable to believe I was hearing about them again so soon after Brydda had mentioned them. On the other hand, Malik and Vos had managed to get their hands on demon bands even before the rebellion. Indeed, a demon band had prevented us from realizing that Malik meant to betray us. No doubt more had been found in the abandoned Saithwold Herder cloister.

"Ye mun have noticed," Khuria now said, "that ye were unable to farseek us here."

"It is no secret that the Herders here and elsewhere in the

Land made a practice of laying tainted matter and studding the tops of the cloister walls with poisoned fragments, knowing it would inhibit Misfit Talents," I said.

"That was done before the rebellion," Khuria said grimly. "But Vos's men continue doin' it. They have poisoned the region's entire perimeter as well as many fences within."

"But to what end?" I asked. "Surely not so that Vos can be reelected chieftain."

"No, although that is certainly what Vos believes," Noviny said. "Let me tell my tale from the beginning. It will be quicker and more orderly."

I stifled a feeling of impatience and nodded.

He continued. "When Vos's men began to call at homesteads in and about Saithwold before wintertime, demanding that folk pledge their votes to him in the coming elections, I thought him a fool. Once Dardelan learned what was happening, the Council of Chieftains would deal with Vos. But Vos's oppressions increased. People's letters left Saithwold only if they were not critical of the chieftain or the situation here. Vos issued a decree forbidding citizens to travel without permission because of the danger of being waylaid by brigands. Then the blockade was set up, supposedly to prevent robbers or unsavory folk from entering our region. Little by little, we realized that no one secured permission to travel and that the blockade was as much to keep us in as others out.

"It was obvious to me that the other rebel leaders would soon realize what Vos was trying to do, but I could not see Dardelan moving against him until after the election. Therefore, I advised neighbors and friends who sought my advice simply to wait. All would be put right in time.

"But having assured everyone that all would be well, I became troubled, for the dogs told Khuria of men creeping

85

about my property. Khuria kept watch, and he saw Vos's men laying tainted caches and overheard them saying it was being done on Malik's advice. That made me very uneasy. Vos is foolish enough to suppose he could get away with forcing himself upon this region as its chieftain, but Malik would know his efforts were doomed to failure. So what was Malik up to?

"Then I heard a rumor that a second blockade had been set up on the other side of Saithwold—that is, on the road leading from the town to the cliffs. The new barricade was meant to prevent robbers creeping into the town from that direction, but I began to wonder if its true purpose might be to prevent anyone venturing near Malik's main coastal camp. Then I decided that this might be the purpose of both barricades."

"Are you trying to say that Malik does or does not want Vos to become chieftain of Saithwold?" I asked, trying to contain my impatience.

"I am saying that Vos's chieftainship and all that he has done to ensure it is irrelevant to Malik except as a distraction," Noviny answered.

There was a soft knock at the door, and Wenda and a servant entered, carrying trays laden with mugs, jugs of ale, bread and cheese, and pie. Noviny remained silent as his granddaughter and a red-faced lad laid a small table. When they had finished, Wenda assured me in her gentle voice that Darius was sleeping.

"Do you know what is wrong with him?" I asked.

She nodded. "His fever is the result of severe joint inflammation. But I am preparing some poultices that will ease him, and he will be more comfortable by tomorrow."

"I trust Wenda," Noviny said when the door closed behind his granddaughter. "But she does not know what I am about to tell you. Nor have I dared to impart it to any of my friends or neighbors or even to trusted retainers."

"Tell us," I said simply.

Noviny nodded. "As a young man, I went on long rambles about the wild parts of Saithwold, and though I am no longer young, I know this region like the back of my own hand. I announced my intention to take a ramble toward a lake I know, not far from the Sawlney border. I set off at a deliberate old man's pace, making sure any number of farmworkers and neighbors noticed me, until I reached a dense copse through which a stream flows. Within the copse, the stream cuts into a deep gorge. It appears utterly inaccessible, but I knew from my boyhood adventures that one could enter it and follow the stream to the other end of the gorge, where it emerges in thick wood not far from the coast.

"I am no longer the agile boy I once was, and it cost some effort to clamber into the gorge, but once inside, it was not hard to follow the stream. Some hours later, I came out of it and was immediately assailed by the scent of the waves. I knew well where I was, but I did not know the exact location of Malik's camp. I very nearly walked into the midst of a group of Malik's armsmen. Indeed, I would have if the wind had not brought a man's voice to me. I froze, and it was just as well, for had I taken another step, I would have tumbled into a deep hollow where Malik's men had made their camp.

"I retreated hastily and made my way carefully around the hollow until I could see into it. I was disappointed to find it was not the main camp but an outpost obviously set up to keep watch over the steps leading down to the beach below. There are three such ways up from the beach, which here is a mere strip of sand so narrow as to be invisible from above unless you are close to the cliff's edge.

"I knew I had not the strength left to find my way to Malik's proper camp, but I reasoned that if I could get close enough to these men, they might speak freely enough of their master's affairs to confirm my suspicions. I walked up the coast until I could no longer see the camp, and I crawled along the edge of the cliff using the sea grass as cover until I was near the camp. I could go no further without crossing the stone steps that go down to the beach, but when I lay still, I could hear the conversation quite well.

"I do not know what made me look down. Maybe I wanted to be sure I was not too close before I settled myself properly to listen, but what I saw gave me so great a shock that I nearly cried out."

"What did ye see?" Zarak whispered.

"A ship," Noviny said grimly. "Anchored so close to the beach that it must have been in danger of running aground. Men were rowing a ship boat toward the beach, and a group of Herders got out when it was dragged up. Malik and some of his armsmen came across the sand to meet them. They must have been waiting at the base of the cliff, out of my sight. Several of the priests heaved wooden crates from the boat and set them on the sand, and then Malik and the priests held a long conversation. It was clear that this was not their first meeting, and eventually Malik's men took up the crates and the Herders hustled some of the people who had come with Malik into the ship boat. I had not noticed before, but now I saw that they were not only men but women and children. And they were roped together."

"Slaves?" Zarak hissed in disbelief.

Noviny nodded. "I believe that the poor wretches were farmers and their families and servants, taken by Malik's men in the guise of brigands before their land and homesteads were burned to make it seem they had been killed. I have no doubt they were given to Salamander. It was dreadful to lie there and know I could not help them. At last the ship boat was rowed away while Malik and his men carried the crates toward the steps. Fortunately, they were heavy, and Malik and his men were concentrating so hard on them that they angled straight across to the camp without even glancing in my direction.

"I dared not move as the afternoon wore on, and after Malik rode off with a couple of his captains, night fell and the armsmen lit a fire and cooked their supper. Still I lay there, hungry, thirsty, cramped. I was too stiff now to crawl backward, and I knew I must wait until it was dark enough to stand without being seen. The wind blew in from the sea, so I could hear little conversation, but I had heard enough talk between Malik and his men during that long afternoon to know that he had made a pact with the Herders to allow and aid a secret invasion."

"An invasion!" I echoed incredulously.

Noviny looked grim. "Finally, it began to rain, which put out the cooking fires and drove the armsmen into their tents, giving me my opportunity. I got up and hobbled away, praying no one would look out and see me.

"It was a difficult trip back here. By the time I arrived home, I was fevered. For days I was ill, and Wenda and the servants feared that I had stumbled into a tainted trap on my ramble. It was fortunate they thought so, for this was the tale that traveled into town, which Vos would have heard and passed on to Malik."

A faint smile crossed his crumpled features. "I daresay our chieftain hoped I would perish and was much disappointed when I did not. I have taken care since to seem permanently weakened by what happened, to assuage his jealousy. In truth, the adventure did take something from me that I have not managed to regain."

He sighed. "Since that time, my sole concern has been how to get word of the invasion to the Council of Chieftains." He shook his head. "I could not leave Saithwold, nor send a message clear enough to be useful. Sevendays passed and then winter was upon us.

"In desperation, I confided in Khuria, thinking he could communicate with one of his beast friends and ask them to carry a message to Obernewtyn. But none of the beasts could safely cross the poisoned perimeter. At last he suggested scribing letters to his son that would not mention our plight at all but would be so uncharacteristic that his boy would seek him out."

Noviny looked at Zarak. "We expected you to be turned back at the blockade. Khuria believed you would then return to Obernewtyn and seek the aid of your master, who would ride out with coercer-knights only to find they were unable to penetrate the region with their abilities. Again they would be turned back at the barricade, but they would have discovered that the armsmen guarding it wore demon bands. This would prompt the Master of Obernewtyn to ride to Sutrium and demand that Dardelan investigate what was happening in Saithwold. It was an unwieldy plan, but we could devise no other."

"The last thing we expected was that you would manage to get through the blockade with a sick man an' the guildmistress of the farseekers, and you would be trapped here, too," Khuria said gruffly.

"We came knowing something was wrong and accepting the risk," I said firmly, and I explained my encounter with the tavern woman. Noviny took the note she had scribed, smoothed it out, and read the name and address upon it. Then he nodded.

"Lacent Ander," he said. "I know her, and her husband, Rale. I will see this note is taken to her, but I fear that you will be unable to make good your promise to bring a letter out for her sister. Like Khuria, I must apologize for having dragged you into danger."

"You are right in guessing that Dardelan will do nothing before the election," I said, "but if he adopts Zarak's suggestions about how to deal with Vos, he and a group of other chieftains and their armsmen and women will arrive in Saithwold without warning on the day of the voting, ostensibly to celebrate. There will be too many to forbid entry, and the minute Dardelan rides in, I will farseek him to let him know what Malik is about."

"I'm afraid that will be too late," Noviny said grimly. "You see, the invasion is to happen before the election. Malik spoke of the timing with great amusement."

I mastered a surge of panic, realizing this was what had lain behind the premonition I had experienced in Rangorn. "All right. Then we have to do something ourselves to stop the invasion. You said there are steps down to a small beach? Are they narrow steps such as outside Arandelft, which will not allow two men to walk abreast?"

Noviny nodded. "Narrower and steeper, but there are three sets of steps along the Saithwold coastline, and I don't know which the invaders will use."

"Then we will keep watch over all of them. Surely every man and woman in the region will help, especially if you ask it."

"Guildmistress, you do not realize how things are in Saithwold province these days," Noviny said. "We live under constant surveillance by Vos's men. Even movement from one farm to another is regarded suspiciously unless it is a regular event. If a person visits another unexpectedly, he is like to be brought before Vos for questioning. And Vos reports everything to Malik, who has camps of his men right along the stretch of coastline from the road to Sador down to the end of Saithwold province, because his men are supposed to be guarding it. Even if we could muster a force without it being discovered, how are farm holders, however brave and strong, to deal with the likes of Malik's men? For that is who they would have to fight before they could even begin to think of defending the beach steps."

I scowled at the fire. "I am a fool. I had forgotten about Malik's part in this."

"He is not a man who can be overlooked," Noviny said wearily. "You can be sure that Stovey Edensal will soon be riding to report that three people in a wagon escorted here by Brydda Llewellyn managed to enter the province."

"One thing I dinna understand," Zarak said. "What sort of invasion can priests mount? They are nowt warriors, after all. Will they command Malik's force, or will they bring soldierguards from the west coast?"

"There was no talk of Councilmen or the west coast in what I heard," Noviny said. "As far as I can understand, this is a Herder invasion. But those sent will certainly be warrior priests."

"Warrior priests . . . ," I echoed, some memory nagging at me.

Noviny nodded. "You say that priests are not warriors, lad, but there have always been priests trained to fight. There was a name they called themselves, but I do not recall it. A number of them inevitably accompanied the higher cadre priests as honor guards when they came to the cloister here.

Having seen them practice, I do not doubt their skill.

"And while it is true that initially these warrior priests were just a small force within the priesthood, even before the rebellion, that was starting to change. The head priest of Saithwold—a Nine and a proud, cold man—often spoke disparagingly of the Faction's soldierguards. More than once he implied that his masters were growing weary of spending their coin on the temporary loyalties of soldierguards. Once, he said that a soldierguard was a cur whereas a warrior priest was intelligent, courageous, and loyal unto death to the Faction's principles and ideals. When I admired their discipline after seeing the warrior priests exercise, the Nine told me that they trained on Norseland under the most stringent conditions," he said.

"Warrior priests . . . ," I muttered again, and then I remembered. Domick had mentioned warrior priests several times in the last garbled messages before his disappearance, and I was sure that he had even mentioned a vast training camp, though he had not said it was on Norseland. I could see that Faction leaders would much prefer fanatical warrior priests, who did not have to be bought, to soldiers for hire, and it made sense that, having fled the Land, they would do all they could to increase their numbers against future need. An army of their own kind would free them from having to rely on or accommodate anyone outside the Faction. And, of course, they would have at their disposal all the young novices and acolytes from the abandoned cloisters in the Land.

"Do you think the west coast Councilmen know anything about this invasion?" I asked.

"I have thought much about this. I think the Herders did not warn the Councilmen this side of the Suggredoon about the rebellion, because they wanted them to be defeated. And

I think they warned the Councilmen on the west coast, not because they favored them but to ensure that we did not take over the whole Land. They were practicing a strategy called *divide and conquer.* They knew they had not strength enough to confront the east and west coast Council and its legion of soldierguards, so they allowed the rebels to defeat them in this part of the Land. The rebellion thus had the effect of producing two lesser powers, each in control of one part of the Land, with the added advantage that each saw the other as the primary enemy. That has left the Herders free to develop a force and play their own secret game."

"But how does Malik fit into this?" Zarak asked.

Noviny shrugged. "I have no doubt he has been offered wealth and the sort of power he yearns for in the Land, after the Faction reclaims it. Remember, he failed to be voted high chieftain, and he is now about to face a trial here for his betrayal of your people."

A chill slipped down my spine at the realization that, in coming to Saithwold, I had put myself within the reach of Malik, who hated me. I was about to ask how many knew that Khuria was a Misfit, when Zarak asked, "But how did the Herders get to Malik in the first place?"

" 'Tis my guess he signaled the ships and offered to betray the rebels, lad," Khuria said. "He was in the perfect position to do it without anyone kenning it. But it might also be that someone here got to him and made him an offer, fer it is well kenned that he loathes Misfits an' Dardelan's championing of ye. Then there is th' Beast Charter."

"Are you sure that the west coast is not involved in the invasion?" I asked, thinking of Maryon's prediction of trouble in the west.

"I do not doubt it," Noviny answered. "The Councilmen

see the Herders as allies, and the Faction would encourage that. Not only can the Herders control Council activities to some extent but they can also make sure no pact or truce is made between the west coast Councilmen and the rebels here. But rest assured that when they are ready, the Faction will dispense with both the Council and the rebels and take control of all the Land themselves."

Zarak leapt to his feet. "I am sorry to interrupt, but, Guildmistress, ye said we would have to wait until the election before anyone would come here. Yet what of the Master of Obernewtyn? Surely the moment he arrives in Sutrium for the ceremony to celebrate the new Charter of Laws, finds ye absent, an' hears what Brydda says, he will ride here with the coercer-knights. And I dinna think they will be turned away, for even if they cannot use their Talents against men wearing demon bands, they are skilled fighters. It will be nothing fer them to overcome those louts guarding the barricade."

In that moment, Zarak reminded me of Matthew, who had been much given to notions of romantic rescues. But I knew that the last thing Rushton would do when he discovered my absence would be to ride to Saithwold. He would accept Dardelan's decision that matters be left as they were until the elections and be relieved that I was not in Sutrium. Grief and desolation clawed at me, but I stifled them and said aloud that we dared not wait and hope to be rescued. Too much was at stake. Then I stopped, realizing that I had no more idea than Noviny how to stop the invasion. After an uncomfortable silence, Noviny sighed and suggested we eat.

I took little food, my appetite gone, but Zarak had heaped his plate high, and between mouthfuls he said, "I can nowt believe Malik has made this bargain after he fought to free the Land."

Noviny said wearily, "I think he fought, as many do, not to rid the Land of oppression but to create a situation in which he could gain power. Instead, he is to be tried for betraying your people. So not only does he stand to gain the power he wants from the Faction, but he will also take revenge on the rest of us."

"It will not come to that," I said through gritted teeth. "We will get a message to Sutrium."

"How?" Zarak asked eagerly.

"I am not sure yet," I admitted. I looked at Noviny and asked, "Is it common knowledge here that Khuria is a beast-speaker?"

Noviny shrugged. "It was clear from the beginning that Vos would torment any Misfit in this region, so we never spoke of it openly; however, there are many who probably harbor suspicions."

"Okay," I said. "Now, who normally shops for your household?"

"Wenda and one of the servant girls take a small cart into town once every sevenday," the older man answered, looking perplexed.

"If you will permit it, then, tomorrow Wenda will take me to town to see what patent medicines are available for my crippled companion. Better to act as if we are innocents who got into the region by chance."

"You will be harassed by Vos's armsmen, if they do not insist on taking you to him. And they will all wear demon bands, so you will not be able to prevent it," Noviny warned.

"I *want* them to take me to him, because I assume that is where Vos's men live as well. If I can reach a single armsman, I can impose a coercive command to remove his band whenever a certain control word is spoken. That means I can get to

96

him later and coerce him to help us spread the word to Dardelan and the others. I will also do my best to stop anyone regarding us as a threat, by playing the innocent fool. Just one thing: Is Malik like to be there?"

Noviny shook his head decisively. "Malik rarely enters the town, and I doubt very much he will be at Vos's property. His plans require him to stay very much in the background at this stage. But you can be sure he will demand a full report from Vos."

"Will Vos not recognize you?" Zarak asked.

"I think the chance is slim, because Vos is the sort of man who does not look at anyone properly, especially not those he believes are his inferiors. But just in case," I added, "I will change my appearance."

I retired early that night, more to think than anything else, for I was wide awake. I kept turning over and rejecting plans, occasionally getting up to gaze out the window at the dark wood behind the homestead and wonder what had become of Maruman. He had stalked off in a rage when I told him that he could not accompany me to town, refusing to listen when I explained that if I carried him on my shoulder, I might as well put up a sign announcing myself as a Misfit. Gahltha had told me not to worry, saying he would go and find the old cat, but neither had returned, and now I worried about both of them.

My mind shifted to Zarak's touching certainty that the Master of Obernewtyn would ride to my rescue. Absurd and impossible as it was, I wished it were so. But Rushton would not come. It was not that he hated me or wished me harm; it was only that he no longer loved me or wanted to be near me.

Why, I wondered bleakly, was it so much more hurtful to

love him hopelessly now than before I had known that he cared for me? I cursed myself and turned over, forcing my mind back to the problem of sending a message from Saith- wold about the invasion. It was deep in the night before I fi- nally slept.

I dreamed I was walking along a wharf toward a knot of peo- ple. There were men and women and boys, all roped together. *Slaves,* I thought, recognizing the wharf, though it was not the one in Sutrium.

What am I doing here? I wondered. Then one of the slaves turned and I recognized his face. It was Matthew, but he was a boy again. It was a memory dream.

"Elspeth!" Matthew farsent urgently. "Ride on past, fer Obernewtyn's sake!"

I beastspoke Gahltha, asking him to slow down and pre-tend lameness, and then I slipped to the cobbles, pretending to examine his hooves. On one level, I knew that I was dream- ing of my last moments with Matthew, but another part of me was in that moment, desperately measuring the distance to Matthew, trying to see the lock on his shackles and calculate how long it would take to unlock it, mount Gahltha with him, and gallop away. The nearest soldierguards were close—one carried a short sword, and two held bows in their hands; all of them were wary and alert. Perhaps I could coerce them into fumbling or even into not seeing me move.

"It's no good," Matthew sent, resolution and despair in his mindvoice. "Ye mun let 'em take me."

"Matthew, they're taking you away on a ship!"

"I ken it," Matthew sent calmly. "An' ye'll let them because we are outnumbered. I'm nowt afraid. . . . I love ye, Elspeth. I'm sorry about Dragon. . . ."

His mental voice faded as he walked over the gangplank, over the water.

"Matthew!" I sent in anguish. The cry, coming from the self who had lived through that awful parting and the self who now dreamed of it, was so strong that it catapulted me out of the memory dream. I had the sensation of falling through darkness, and suddenly I was on a steep stony road following a line of men with picks and other digging implements hoisted over their shoulders. The man directly in front of me turned, and I gasped, for I saw that it was Matthew, but now he was a grown man. I had dreamed of him like this before, but the dream had never felt so real. At the same time, I was very conscious that I was not present in the dream, save as a watcher, for though his eyes seemed to search mine, I knew he could not see me. A man ahead called out to ask him what the matter was.

"It's nowt," he answered, turning away from me. "I thought I heard someone shout my name."

A hand grapsed my shoulder, shaking me gently.

"Matthew?" I mumbled.

"Guildmistress, I am sorry to disturb ye." It was Zarak, looking pale and excited. He whispered, "I have an idea I mun tell ye."

I sat up and shook my head, my mind still full of the dream, which had begun as a memory and then turned into something else when I cried out Matthew's name.

"What time is it?" I rasped, gathering my wits.

"Just before dawn." The farseeker leaned forward in his eagerness. "I have been thinking that Malik's betrayal could be made to serve us. If we let the Herders land an' disembark their force, rather than trying to stop them, we could commandeer their ships. Just think of it! With a ship, we could gan to the west coast immediately, rather than waiting months and months for the new ships to be finished!"

I blinked at him, trying to take in his suggestion.

"There is no way the west coast Councilmen could be prepared for an attack so soon," he continued. "And if they are not involved in plans for this invasion, they might not even ken it is happening. Seeing Herder ships approach, they will assume they came from Herder Isle. We could land in their midst before they realized it."

My mind raced ahead, seeing further possibilities. If we took possession of the Herder ships and captured the west coast, I could then petition Dardelan to send a ship to the Red Queen's land, restore Dragon to her kingdom, and free her people, free Matthew, and find whatever it was that Cassy had left there for me.

"It is a good thought," I said. "The only problem is that we would have to allow ourselves to be invaded to get the ships. We would need a force ready and waiting to capture the invaders, which means getting word out to the other chieftains."

"We *have* to find a way," Zarak said.

"If we are fortunate, I will learn something today that will help us. Now go away and let me get dressed. I will see you in the kitchen."

After he had departed, I sluiced myself with cold water, dried, and dressed, wrinkling my nose at the stale smell of my shirt. Despite the hour, everyone was up and eating first-meal when I entered the kitchen.

We spoke of Vos and his ambitions, and of Darius's health. Then I announced that I wanted to go and see what kind of patent medicines the town had. Wenda nodded, saying that her grandfather had mentioned my desire to go into town and that she would take me. Then she asked apologetically if I would like to borrow a skirt and shirt of hers. I accepted with alacrity, knowing that her demure style would make me look quite different if I dressed my hair to suit. Besides, her offer told me I probably smelled worse than I realized. We could stop at the wagon on our way back from town so I could collect a change of clothes.

After firstmeal, Wenda brought an armful of dresses, shirts, and jackets to my room, and eventually I emerged wearing a narrow gray skirt, a yellow shirt, and pale green jacket, my long hair braided and pinned into a bun at my neck. Before we departed, I visited Darius, who was eating from a tray and looking a good deal less frail than upon our arrival. I waved away his apologies for his collapse and briefly related what Noviny had told us. He agreed we must get word of the invasion to Sutrium at all costs, though to my disappointment, he had no more idea than I how this might be done.

Despite my impatience, it was midafternoon before Wenda and I were traveling along the main road to the township in a little, open two-seater cart pulled by Gahltha. He had refused to let me go to the town alone. Touched by his devotion, Wenda had suggested that he pull the cart.

It was a gray day with low dark clouds, and feeling a spit of moisture, I glanced at the sky apprehensively, aware that rain would render me unable to coerce anyone without physical contact. Wenda was a peaceful companion, for she spoke little, but instead of making plans, I began to worry about Malik. Noviny had assured me that the rebel chieftain seldom entered the town, but in my experience, those things you most passionately wish not to occur have a way of happening.

As we approached the town, I could see stores lining either side of what was effectively one long, empty street. In other times, the wares from those stores had spilled onto these same verandas on long trestle tables, and other sellers had sold food and drink to a cheerful throng of people from tables in front of the verandas. Now, both street and veranda were so empty that the town looked deserted. But there were people about. I noticed one man standing against a wall and another leaning over a balcony, armsmen wearing Vos's colors. We passed yet another one fletching arrows and whetting the edge of his short sword. Another lounged on a step smoking, a cudgel laid across his knees. All of them watched us pass without smiling, and my skin rose into gooseflesh, for each time I tried to probe one, I encountered the buzzing resistance that told me they wore demon bands.

Although I could see smoke dribbling from more than one chimney, there was no sign of life in the houses built between the stores, save the occasional movement behind a curtain. At last we reached the cluster of stores and businesses at a crossroads that was the heart of the town. Wenda eased back on the reins, and Gahltha drew up obediently to the hitching post. She climbed down gracefully from the carriage and gathered up her shawl and basket. I followed, feeling awkward in the skirt's unfamiliar narrowness. I wished that I was wearing my own comfortable clothes, but it was just as well to present a picture of feminine helplessness for the watching armsmen to report back to their masters. Certainly, no description they would give could evoke in anyone's mind the name of Elspeth Gordie.

We had just entered the store when it began to rain. My

heart sank, but then I realized it did not make any difference, for I could not probe any of the armsmen. The store was the good solid sort at the center of any small town. Shelves all about the walls were piled with various goods, but there were also many empty shelves. No doubt it was difficult to amass stock when everything coming in and out of the region had to be brought by people approved by Vos. Several tables in the shop's center were heaped with bolts of cloth, ribbons, and ropes; bottles of buttons and other fittings; cards of needles; and several shining sets of scissors. Presumably, this pretty display had been set up to divert attention from the half-empty shelves.

"Good day, Mistress Arilla," Wenda said to the woman behind the counter.

"Good day, Wenda," the woman responded crisply. "I am afraid our supplies have not come in from Sutrium yet."

"I only want flour and salt, Arilla, though my friend here wishes to see your patent medicines." Her tone was reserved, and I had the sense that both of them were playing a part. Then I realized that the woman's restraint arose from my presence.

"What is your ailment, lady?" she asked.

"I am not ill," I said, adopting a fussy and overly cultured lowland accent. "It is my friend who has need of medicines. He is crippled and his joints have become badly inflamed on our journey. It is very tiresome, for we had meant to go on almost at once to Sutrium." I sighed. "It is quite likely we will have to remain in Saithwold for a sevenday or more, unless you have some elixir that can help."

The woman flicked a glance at Wenda, no doubt wondering why she did not offer her own herbal lore. This spurred me to add, "Wenda has offered various herbs, but I am not a great believer in herbal lore, if you will forgive me for saying so, my dear," I prattled. Wenda's face showed no emotion, so the woman indicated a case of brown bottles. Labels about the neck of each bottle had the benefits of its contents scribed on them, and I went over and pretended to read them.

"What will you have, Mistress Wenda?" asked the shop woman again in a cool, flat voice.

"Just a small measure of salt and some flour, if you please, Mistress Arilla," Wenda said.

"We have only rough-ground flour, I am afraid. Will that do?"

"It will have to do," Wenda sighed. She addressed me then. "Have you found anything that might ease your friend's sickness?"

"I am not sure if these medicines will do," I said in a querulous voice.

"What he needs most is rest," Wenda said, pretending impatience. "I can mix a tisane that will do him more good than those patent medicines."

I gave her a bothered look and joined her at the counter. The storewoman put the flour down by the smaller parcel of salt, and Wenda paid her out of a thin purse. We crossed to the door and opened it to find that it was now pouring. I pulled up my coat collar and walked out onto the veranda, only to have an armsman step into my path. He was a big powerful-looking man with thinning brown hair gone to pepper and salt and shrewd blue eyes in a face that I might have liked, had he not worn Vos's colors.

"Ye mun be one of them the Black Dog escorted to the barricade yesterday," he said. "Are ye aware that ye neglected to mention whose property ye were visiting?"

"Why should I have mentioned it?" I snapped before remembering I was supposed to be frivolous and silly.

The man frowned, but I thought there was amusement in his eyes. "Th' men at the barricade were supposed to ask ye. But nivver mind that now. I see by yer companion where ye're stayin'." He gave a mocking bow, rain spilling from the brim of his hat. "I am Kevrik, armsman to Chieftain Vos who governs this settlement, charged with learning the names of the newcomers to Saithwold."

"I am Ella," I lied haughtily. "And now if you will be so good as to stand aside, we wish to leave."

The armsman stepped aside, and Wenda came out onto the veranda beside me, closing the door behind her. She gave the armsman a brief cool look before going to the carriage and thrusting her basket into the sheltered space beneath the seat. Then she climbed up and swiftly unraveled a sheet of waxed cotton over her head to serve as a makeshift cover. She beckoned to me, but the man caught my arm. "I assume they also neglected to mention at the barricade that it is the custom for all who enter Saithwold province to pay their respects to its chieftain?" He spoke loudly to be heard over the rain.

"If the manners of those louts at the blockade are anything to judge by, I can understand why your chieftain must order himself up guests," I said tartly. Before he could respond, I added, "But custom you said. Did you mean that a visit to your chieftain is a courtesy or a law?"

"Dinna ye think a courtesy ought to be observed as strictly as if it were a law?" Kevrik asked mildly.

"Courtesies are best preserved in free air, I think," I snapped. "However, you may tell your chieftain that I will wait upon him tomorrow or the next day. There can be no rush, since we are delayed by my friend's illness."

I tried to pull my arm free of his grip, but he kept a firm

hold of me, saying, "Ye mun wait upon Chieftain Vos now, my lady."

"I cannot force Wenda to journey with me in this rain, and I need to take some medicine back to my friend," I protested.

The highlander nodded. "Then it is simple. Wenda will return to Noviny's homestead with the medicine for yer companion, an' I will take you to pay your respects to the chieftain."

I scowled, looking down to hide my elation at the thought of being taken exactly where I wanted to go. Ironically, Wenda insisted that if I must face Vos, she would accompany me. The rain having abated, I coerced her into agreeing to leave without me, and then I had Gahltha to contend with for he refused to obey Wenda when she tried to leave. I laid my hand on his warm wet neck under the pretext of calming him, hoping I could buy myself enough time to convince Gahltha not to make a scene.

"I warned you this would happen," I sent him.

"You said you would be taken to see this chieftain. You did not say you would go alone," he sent.

"I must go with this man willingly, or he will force me," I sent.

"I will not allow him to harm you," Gahltha sent wrathfully, shifting angrily so that the small cart creaked and tilted.

"Be still, my dear," I bade him. "It is not only him. There are many other armsmen in these streets, with knives and arrows and clubs. If you fight, you and the girl will be hurt, and still they will take me. Let me go with him now, and I promise that I will soon return."

I could feel his anger fade into resignation. He said dryly, "Maruman/yelloweyes will be furious, for he made me promise not to leave you."

"I fear that is true," I sent, suddenly conscious that the armsman had returned and was watching me. I pretended to adjust the bridle. "Now, let me go and I will come as soon as I can."

Kevrik hurried me along the muddy street to a covered wagon and gestured for me to climb up to the seat. Then he climbed up beside me. "I've nivver seen that horse before. It's yours, en't it?"

I hesitated, and, irritatingly, he took this as an admission. "I thought so. Yer one of them beastspeakers, aren't ye? Like the old Misfit that serves Noviny." His eyes widened. "That's who th' boy who came with ye is kin to! An' I suppose he is a beastspeaker, too."

My heart sank at the realization that Noviny had been wrong in thinking that Khuria's Talent might be a secret. The only consolation was that Kevrik had only just connected me to Khuria, so neither Vos nor Malik would know yet that Zarak and I were Misfits. That meant I had a little time to maneuver. Being identified as a beastspeaker would make Vos less likely to realize who I really was.

"Two of use are beastspeakers. Our crippled friend is not a Misfit," I said at last. "And none of us owns the horse. He is my friend, and I had to beastspeak him because he was refusing to leave me with you."

"He dinna want to leave ye," Kevrik marveled, shaking his head in wonder. He took up the reins purposefully. I squinted at his horse's neck and, to my astonishment, saw the glimmer of a demon band. Kevrik made the sort of chucking noise used by men who have no other means of reaching the mind of a horse, and the copper horse set off at a sedate canter.

✦ 7 ✦

"This horse is wearing a demon band," I said, suddenly glad there was no need to pretend I was not a beastspeaker. We had left the town behind, and a wall of thick forest ran along either side of us, broken by the occasional gate leading to a road that must wind its way to a farmstead.

Kevrik shot me a look. "I suppose ye tried to communicate with her."

I struggled against outrage and lost. "It is barbaric that you put a demon band on a beast without asking if it agrees to accept the danger."

"Danger? What are ye blatherin' about, lass?" the armsman asked.

I stared at him, wondering if he and all the other armsmen wearing demon bands did not know that tainted matter gave the devices their power and that it would eventually penetrate the metal tubing and poison the wearer's bones and blood. Then it occurred to me that Garth had only warned us about the dangers of the demon bands in guildmerge just before wintertime; how would those here have learned of it?

I drew in a sharp breath, suddenly realizing that the heavy crates Noviny had seen the Herders deliver to Malik had probably been filled with demon bands.

"Tell me what ye meant by sayin' demon bands are dangerous," Kevrik prompted.

"They cause wasting sickness," I said, careful not to reveal that I knew he and the other armsmen wore demon bands, for how should a beastspeaker know that?

"That's a lie," Kevrik said sharply, his hand going unwittingly to his collar. "You see for yourself that the mare is not sick."

I shrugged. "Demon bands are no more than metal tubes encasing matter taken from the Blacklands. The taint will not hurt immediately, just as it does not kill a man immediately to walk on tainted Blacklands. The sickness comes later when the bones crumble and the flesh wastes from them. The demon bands take longer, because the taint is much weaker and has to seep through the metal casing."

I glanced away into the dense wood at the roadside, and said, "But surely your chieftain has told you of the danger?" I pretended not to notice the armsman's blank face and added, "Unless . . . Can it be that Chieftain Vos does not know the demon bands contain tainted matter?"

Still the armsman said nothing, and I went on as if musing to myself. "I guess he found a supply of them in the abandoned cloister and thought to use them to prevent Misfits from manipulating his mind. But surely the Herders did not leave demon bands for horses?"

From the corner of my eye, I saw Kevrik's brow crease, and I wondered where he and the other men imagined the horses' demon bands had come from. And what had Malik told Vos to explain the appearance of demon bands big enough for horses? Kevrik shifted uncomfortably on the seat beside me, and I guessed with satisfaction that he itched to wrench the demon band from his neck, but he had probably been ordered to wear it at all times.

The road we had been traveling along was the same one

that turned from the main road to Sutrium, but now we came to a place where the road forked. One way led to the coast and the other turned down toward Sutrium. Kevrik took the latter, and I said, "Wenda mentioned that there is a second blockade this side of the town. I suppose it is on the other road?" Kevrik said nothing, so I went on as if he had answered. "Why do you need a barricade this side of town? How many brigands will dare to come along the coast with Malik's watch camps set up all along it to make sure the Herder ships don't come in to land?"

I watched the armsman closely from the corner of my eye, because although I could not reach his mind to read it, I still had eyes to see a start or a look of guilt that would tell me Kevrik knew about Malik's bargain. But he only said distractedly, "The brigands are insidious, and it is just as like that they would take a secretive route."

He might believe that, I thought, or maybe he knew that Malik's men were the brigands and had decided to hold his tongue. Or perhaps he simply thought the second barricade was making sure that none of the region's inhabitants could leave to report Vos to the Council of Chieftains. But could he really be so foolish as to imagine that Vos would get away with oppressing the people he was supposed to represent and lead?

My mind turned to Vos. If he had been any other rebel leader, I might have tried telling him the truth about Malik's treachery and the pending invasion, but Vos would undoubtedly go straight to Malik to report what he had been told.

"How . . . how long does it take for a demon band to cause harm . . . to a horse," Kevrik asked, somewhat jerkily, and I realized he had hardly been listening to anything I had said since I had mentioned the taint inside the demon bands.

I had to work to keep triumph from my voice when I answered. "I am not sure, but given that a horse is flesh and blood, as we are, it would take the same time as for a man. That is several months. Of course, that would depend on whether it had been worn constantly or not. A horse cannot take the band off at will, as a man can." I did not quite succeed in hiding a renewed jab of anger.

Kevrik said, "Vala is my horse and I care for her, no matter that you beastspeakers think yer the only ones to have any love fer beasts."

"We love them as friends and fellow beings. You love this mare as a possession," I said coldly. Before he could say anything, I added, "But if you love her in any way, you will remove the band as often as possible."

There was a long silence, and then he said, "Is it true some of you Misfits can enter a person's mind even if they are nowt near?"

"Some Misfits can. It is called *farseeking*, but usually farseekers only communicate with other Misfits who have that ability. To farseek someone with no Talent is more difficult," I added. In fact, it required both farseeking and coercive abilities to manage it, but I did not say so, because the perception among many unTalents was that a Misfit could have only one ability, and it was always better to be underestimated by enemies. "But why do you care?" I asked. "We Misfits have given our word to the Council of Chieftains not to use our powers on any person, save those who are enemies and wish harm to us."

The wagon slowed as we drew near a wide gate with ornate carved posts, and I knew we had reached Vos's homestead when the mare turned into it so willingly.

"What if ye suspected harm was intended but could nowt

be sure? Would a Misfit wait to see or penetrate a man's mind to find out if he was an enemy?" Kevrik asked once the wagon was through the gate.

"In such a circumstance, that Talent would be as a weapon. You might take out that knife in your sheath, if you thought a robber was stalking you. But you would not use it on him until you were certain he was a villain."

He nodded and said nothing more until we came in sight of another gate. This one led to a cobbled courtyard surrounded by fenced enclosures and various barns and outbuildings. Set back from these, in the midst of a smooth lawn, was a large rambling farmhouse with wide stone steps leading to a veranda and an ornate front door between two fluted stone columns. Kevrik stopped the carriage on the cobbles, then bade me wait while he announced my arrival to his master. It was again raining, but lightly, as he ran to the house, so I climbed down from the carriage and went to the mare. Despite being in contact, the band would not let me reach her mind, and I gazed into her long face and gentle eyes, wondering if she could tell I was the Seeker or whether that knowledge would only come to her when our minds touched. I murmured soft nonsense to her, and she put her ears forward in a friendly alert fashion that suggested Kevrik had probably spoken the truth when he said he cared for her.

I examined her face and neck and listened to her heart, but there was no sign of the wasting sickness. The hair on her coat was not even rubbed under the demon band, which suggested that she had not worn it long. The catch was a simple hook, and only the fact that the mare was yet unhurt kept me from it—that and the certainty that Kevrik would remove the horse's band and his own as soon as he could.

The front door opened, and a group of armsmen spilled

from the homestead into the rainswept yard.

"What were you doing to the horse, Misfit?" demanded one of the armsmen brusquely.

"I wanted to see if she showed any sign of wasting sickness," I said truthfully. This was greeted with blank silence, which told me that although Kevrik had obviously reported that I was a beastspeaker, he had not mentioned what I had said about the demon bands. I said, "It is caused by demon bands if they are worn too long."

The anger in one or two faces gave way to apprehensive expressions, but most burst into rough laughter or jeered in disbelief. "Do not think to trick us into taking our bands off, Misfit," said one man in a mocking voice. "We are not the fools you take us for."

I widened my eyes innocently. "You are wearing them, too?" Before any of them could speak, I asked, "Where is your chieftain? I have come to pay my respects to him." I turned and marched across the yard to the door and through it. The armsmen, clearly sent to force me hence, crowded hurriedly after me, muttering and treading on one another's toes.

The front door led unexpectedly straight into an enormous front parlor. Here, rather absurdly, Vos sat upon an ornate chair on a raised dais. He wore a demon band that had been polished and set with jewels, his collar laid back so that it could be clearly seen. I wondered waspishly how he would feel when he realized what a pretty death it was. His narrow-jawed face made him look more ratlike than ever, despite his fine red-dyed robes and oiled hair. He observed me with such exaggerated disdain that I knew he hardly saw me at all for admiring his own posturing.

"What is your business in this region, Misfit?" he demanded in his thin bullying voice.

I made an exaggerated bow that anyone less arrogant would have perceived as a mockery, and said, "Good day, Chieftain Vos. My name is Ella. I am a Misfit but I prefer you to call me beastspeaker." Vos reddened with anger, but before he could think what to say, I went on smoothly. "As to what I am doing here, that is nothing more than an accident." I gave a light laugh. "You see, I was traveling to Sutrium when my friend Zarak expressed a desire to see his father, the beast-speaker Khuria who serves Sirrah Noviny. Saithwold was not much out of our way, but I feared encountering brigands. We were arguing the matter when the rebel Brydda Llewellyn heard us and offered to escort us to Saithwold. As it turned out, there was no need for him to bring us all the way because of the blockade you have set up near the main road. We meant to remain in Saithwold only a night, but, unfortunately, one of our party is now ill. Sirrah Noviny's granddaughter has some skill in healing and seems to think it will take at least a sevenday and maybe two before he will be able to travel. It is a pity, but what can be done?"

Vos scowled and a bold idea flashed into my mind. "I had not thought to come here today, but now that I am here, I wonder if there is any possibility of my sending a missive to Brydda Llewellyn with your next messenger to Sutrium. We were to meet him in a twoday or so, and I would let him know that we cannot now come to Sutrium so soon."

Vos gave me a cold smile. "I am sure that Sirrah Noviny had much to say to you and your friends about matters here that you are eager to report to the Black Dog."

I shrugged. "I do not know what you mean. In truth, I have had little chance to talk with Sirrah Noviny, for we ar-rived only yesterday, and my friend's sickness has preoccu-pied all of us since then. Khuria and his master do complain somewhat about the barricade, to be sure, but I cannot see why when it is for their own protection. They ought to be glad of it, but in my experience, men do hate to be locked up as much as cats, even when it is for their own good. All the same, it seems to me they exaggerate its effect on their lives, for Zarak's father said people cannot pass the blockade. But that is nonsense, for how else should Zarak and Darius and I have come to Saithwold?"

"What did he say to that?" Vos asked.

"More of the same. But it is the nature of old men to grumble, and I daresay they did not mean me to take it seriously." I looked around as if distracted and said vaguely, "Well, I will see for myself how Saithwold is in these next sevendays, will I not?"

"You will see what I permit," Vos snapped.

I pretended to have mistaken the threat in his words for an offer.

"You are most kind, Chieftain!" I gushed. "It would be very agreeable if you would allow your armsman to take me about in his wagon. Ours is unwieldy and Noviny has only a small uncovered cart, and there has been so much rain!"

Vos was clearly confounded by my inability to realize that I was under threat, and I reminded myself to be careful not to overdo it. All that I said would be reported to Malik, who was far from a fool. It was enough that I had sown seeds of trouble concerning the demon bands. As the chieftain sat glowering at me, I gathered my wits and sent a probe roaming through the house, but I could not find a single mind to enter.

Vos suddenly twisted his features into a gruesome parody of a smile. He had realized that it would be to his advantage to let me write an innocuous letter to Brydda, for he now announced that a rider bound for Sutrium would come first thing in the morning to collect my missive. My heart leapt in triumph, but I arranged my face in a mild expression of gratitude and bobbed a curtsy. "I thank you, Chieftain Vos. You are a man of courtesy, though I had heard it said you have no love for Misfits. I hope the armsman who brought me here can convey me back to Sirrah Noviny's homestead, for my friends will be anxious."

Vos nodded curtly toward Kevrik, who stood amidst other armsmen to one side of the dais, his expression preoccupied.

Outside, I discovered that the rain had again stopped. As I climbed into the wagon, I cast out another general farseeking probe. Once again, I could not locate a single unbanded mind. Either the armsmen and servants wore bands constantly, or they had donned them upon my arrival. I turned my thoughts to the letter I would scribe to Brydda. On the surface, it would praise Vos's courtesy, and for good measure, I would scribe disparagingly of Noviny's overreaction to the barricade, pointing out our own ease of entry as proof that he was wrong. But as soon as Brydda saw the pricks I would make in the page, he would recognize the language Dameon used to scribe messages, and soon after that, they would know about the invasion. I could hardly wait to get back to Noviny's farm.

Kevrik suddenly asked, "Did ye speak true about the demon bands?"

"I did," I answered. I thought he would ask other questions, having broken the silence, but he lapsed back into frowning reverie. By the time we reached the town, it was beginning to rain again. My initial feeling of triumph faded into fear that Malik would guess that I meant to use the missive to send a hidden message. I told myself it did not matter if he assumed this, since he could not possibly know that we knew about the invasion. He would envisage any secret communication as being solely about Vos's activities, which could only serve him.

Just so long as he did not guess who I truly was.

By the time the carriage approached Noviny's gateway, it was raining harder than ever, and thunder rumbled ominously in the distance. It was only dusk, but the stormy sky made it seem much later. To my surprise, instead of urging the mare through the gate, Kevrik pulled the wagon to a halt, explaining that the track was too narrow and ill kept for it. "I am afraid ye mun walk up to yon household," he said with unexpected courtesy, and to my surprise he handed me a blanket, bidding me drape it over my head for some meager shelter from the rain.

Turning to trudge up the muddy track to Noviny's homestead, I wondered why a man as courteous as Kevrik seemed to be would choose to serve Vos. By my judgment, the armsman was not a natural bully, nor did he appear to be a man who hungered for power over others. Perhaps there had been no other way of making a living save to bear arms, and he had offered himself to Vos with no knowledge of what the man was like.

I was shivering with cold, for the clothes Wenda had given me had been soaked through more than once that day. Doubly regretting the rain because it prevented me summoning Gahltha to fetch me, I stumbled suddenly and fell to my knees, muddying and ripping the sodden skirt. I felt like cursing Noviny for the state of the track, but he had explained that it was kept narrow and uneven to inhibit Vos's armsmen from coming in wagons.

It occurred to me that I must be near Khuria's cottage and

the concealed wagon. Indeed, I had intended to stop there but had forgotten. By the time I groped my way to the wagon, unlaced the canvas, and slipped inside, the storm was directly overhead, and rain was hammering down. I tied the canvas shut, deciding I might just as well wait out the storm. It was dank and chilly inside, but I lit a lantern and a small fire in the cooking brazier. Teeth chattering, I drew water from a barrel and set it to warm for soup. Then I peeled off my sodden borrowed finery and toweled myself briskly, thinking I would have to replace the skirt when I had the chance. I felt more myself dressed in my own comfortable trousers and shirt as I crumbled herbs and dried mushrooms into the soup. While it cooked, I tried squeezing some of the moisture from my boots, then set them as near to the brazier as I could, for I had no other footwear save a pair of thin sandals.

As the wagon slowly filled with warmth and the wholesome fragrance of the soup, I was glad I had not gone straight up to the homestead bubbling with triumph, for I realized now that I could not simply rely on a missive with a secret warning to stop the invasion. There was too much danger of that plan going awry. And now that I had ceased to fret at it, a different idea for dealing with the invasion had begun to form in my mind. I pondered it, wondering if I dared put it into practice, for it would be very dangerous. I had no doubt that were I to present it at guildmerge, it would be rejected as far too risky. But I was not at Obernewtyn with strong allies about me. I was trapped in a hostile province with dangerous enemies on all sides.

I drank the soup, alternately refining the plan and wishing there was some way to let the others know I was safe, but it was too wet and wild outside. The wagon gradually grew so warm that I began to drift to sleep, but I woke at once when the rain stopped. I tried farseeking the house, but the tainted patches of earth still blocked my probe. I was about to reach for my boots when it occurred to me to try farseeking Gahltha, since he might be grazing nearby. To my delight, the probe found him at once. He was not far away, but the contact was tenuous. Relief that I was safe filled his mind, but fearing that our connection would be broken, I wasted no time in asking him to go to the house to let Zarak and the others know where I was.

"I/Gahltha will come and carry you there," he offered, but I refused, saying I was warm and dry and might as well wait where I was until daylight. Reluctantly, Gahltha obeyed, warning me that I had better be prepared to face Maruman's wrath. The probe began to dissolve. I sent a swift farewell, extinguished the little fire in the brazier, and lay down. Able to relax at last, I fell immediately into a deep sleep.

I dreamed of Matthew standing on a red rocky bluff gazing hungrily out over a dawn-bronzed sea. As on the previous occasion, I was aware that I was simply a disembodied watcher in the vision dream, which again had a remarkable clarity. I did not need to hear Matthew's thoughts to guess he was thinking of the Land, for there was an unmistakable yearning in his face. Then he turned, and I saw a long puckered scar down one lean brown cheek that I had not noticed before. Matthew smiled as Gilaine came to join him, and once again I was glad they had found one another; the mute empath-farseeker had met him when he and I had been taken captive by her father, the fanatical renegade Herder Henry Druid. I did not know how they had encountered one another in the Red Land, but it was no great surprise, since Misfits were naturally drawn to each other.

For a time, they merely gazed companionably out to sea, until Matthew sighed and said, "Ye ought not to be seen talking to me, just in case there is trouble over this." He touched the puckered scar.

Gilaine did not speak. Indeed, she could not, for she was mute, but when Matthew sighed and shook his head, I realized that they were farseeking.

"I am careful," Matthew now said. " 'Tis just that I nivver expected to be attacked by another slave. I kenned the people here dinna want to fight the slavers, because the Red Queen is supposed to come an' set the whole thing in motion, accordin' to their prophecy. But I always thought they refused me because they believed it would be impossible to win without her. I dinna realize they'd think of me as a threat fer trying to make them act before the prophecy had come true. Pity Naro did nowt realize I have abandoned my plan of rousin' the people against their oppressors." He shook his head to whatever Gilaine said. "I canna tell them about Dragon, because they will nowt ken that she is truly the daughter of their queen without seein' her. An' even if they did believe me, how should I tell them about her bein' in a coma?"

Another pregnant silence, and Matthew frowned. "I wish I *could* believe she has woken, Gil. But that's too much like the happy ending in an empath storysong. When I were a lad in th' Land, I saw life as a grand story full of heroes an' villains an' sleepin' princesses that mun be wakened with a kiss. I nivver guessed it might be a sad story that ends in misunderstandin' an' tragedy." A silence. "I have nivver lost heart. I just ken that mebbe I have been wrong tryin' to force a battle. Mebbe the prophecy is true, an' Dragon mun come here before this Land can be free. I mun gan back to th' Land. I am sure I can convince Elspeth an' th' others to let me bring

Dragon here, once they understand that it may be th' only thing that will wake her."

Gilaine laid a hand on his arm, and he flushed, then paled. "I dinna expect her to love me. I scorned her affection when she was a lass, so how could she love me now? An' she will be a queen. It'll be enow fer me if she can be restored to her people an' will let me serve her." There was a caressing quality to his voice that made me think of the blaze of wonder I had seen on his face when Dragon had tried courageously to save two children from a Herder just before she had fallen into her coma. He had been enchanted by her heroism, but something in his voice and face now suggested that boyish infatuation had ripened into something deeper and more real.

They were staring out to sea again, and Matthew said in a different voice, "I dream of them sometimes—Elspeth, Dameon, an' Rushton. Th' others. They all seem older. . . ."

Gilaine looked eagerly at him, and he smiled at her. "Well, of course ye do, for if anything could reach across all that distance, it must be the love between Daffyd an' you." His smile faded and again he looked out to sea. "I just wish I kenned what is happening in th' Land. The slavemasters talk of it but mostly in their own language to one another, as ye ken. The slaves from th' Land talk, but it's hard to glean much more than that the rebels have driven out both Council and Faction on one side of the Suggredoon, while the Council and Herders have the west coast, an' from what you saw of Daffyd . . ." He broke off as a man whose face was vaguely familiar joined them. It was not until he spoke that I recognized Jow, Daffyd's elder brother. Both brothers had once served Henry Druid, before realizing they were Misfits.

"You'd do well to keep your mouth shut hereafter, lad," Jow said. "It'll be the Entina pit for you if you're caught fighting." Gilaine must have made some protest, for the man touched her cheek gently. "Speaking of it won't make it happen, child."

"He is right anyway," Matthew said grimly. "It is only lucky that no one saw Naro attack me, so I could claim I had fallen. The masters were suspicious, of course, but as an overseer, I get more work out of a crew than any other, so it would be a terrible waste to feed me to th' Entina."

Jow laughed. "You conceited young whelp. But it's true you have a gift for moving men about a job that would be hard for the masters to replace. Still, you'd best lie low for a while."

I woke with the complete certainty that I had not merely truedreamed of Matthew; I had seen him and the others *in the present*. The only way to have done so over such distance was on the dreamtrails, which meant I must have drifted onto them in my sleep. I had too little knowledge of the mysterious and dangerous dreamtrails to know how this could have happened, but to feel sure I was right, I had only to think of my previous dream of Matthew, in which he had seemed to hear me call out his name. The thought that I had made contact with Matthew in the Red Land was thrilling and revolutionary, but it went with another thought I had sometimes had: that true dreams were merely dreams experienced while the mind drifted close to the dreamtrails. I decided to endure the discomfort she always made me feel and discuss it with Maryon when we were back at Obernewtyn. If I was right, perhaps I could ask Maruman to guide me to Matthew on the dreamtrails.

But what had woken me? By the darkness, it was still night, though perhaps not far from dawn. I got up, shivering with cold, and peered through a small gap in the laced canvas. The chink of sky visible through the overhanging branches was the dense starless indigo of predawn, and the air was so damp that it must have rained again while I slept. I decided to walk back at once, rather than waiting for Gahltha to arrive. I would be able to tell the others of the letter I would scribe for Vos and outline my plan over firstmeal. I began marshaling the arguments I would need as I groped for my boots. I was about to pull them on when I heard a branch snap loudly.

I froze and sent out a probe. It would not locate, but when it brushed several areas of buzzing resistance, the hair on my neck prickled, for that could only mean men with demon bands. I was able to distinguish four separate areas of resistance close by and two farther away in the direction of Khuria's cottage.

Another branch snapped, and then I heard a man hiss softly that the wagon must be close. I felt sick. Their knowledge of the wagon's whereabouts meant they had been up to Noviny's homestead to question the others. Worse, the stealthy approach meant that they knew I was inside it, for Zarak would never willingly give me away.

Hearing another footfall very close, I reached down and carefully unfastened the disguised hatch in the wagon floor that was the lid of the compartment where Swallow's plast suit lay. Lifting it open slowly to prevent the hinges creaking, I climbed carefully into the cavity. Hauling my boots and wet clothes in with me, I lay down flat and lowered the hatch. Once it was in place, I felt for the pin that would allow me to secure it from beneath.

I relaxed my muscles, trying to calm my breathing so that I could hear, for the coffin-like compartment had been built solidly to ensure that it would not give out a telltale hollow sound if it was knocked. Minutes passed until I heard a hiss of triumph and a furtive rustle as the canvas was thrust aside. The wagon rocked as first one, then a second and a third man climbed in, their boots loud on the wooden boards over my head. I heard one curse, and through a crack to one side of the compartment's lid, I saw a light flare.

"Empty," snarled a voice. "The boy lied."

"I dinna think so," said a man in a rough highland accent. "She has been here, all right. And from the smell of it, she cooked."

"Where is she, then?"

"She got away. Vos won't like it," said another man.

"Malik will like it even less," responded the highlander. He bellowed an order for a thorough search of the area surrounding the wagon. There was the sound of a locker opening overhead, then rummaging and banging and our belongings shattering. Finally, someone hammered at the floor. I trembled as the point of a knife showed between the boards, but Grufyyd had done his work well, and the knife would penetrate no deeper because of crisscrossed metal strands laid in a grid under the wood. After a moment, the knife was withdrawn.

As the search continued, I learned from their talk that a troop of armsmen had ridden to Noviny's homestead during the night, and Khuria had been tortured to make Zarak say where I was. It was horrible to think that this had been happening while I slept. But why had Vos sent his men after me? Or were they Malik's men, dispatched when he heard about the meeting with Vos? And where were the others now? They might still be in the homestead, but it seemed more likely they would have been taken to Vos's property where, as chieftain, he would have cells.

But what about Maruman and the horses? Gahltha must have been taken prisoner, or he would have come to warn me, so I tried to beastspeak Maruman. The probe would not locate. I told myself it was inhibited by the tainted ground between us, but at the same time I had a dreadful vision of the armsmen slaughtering all the beasts to ensure that none could help me.

The wagon rocked, and I realized that the armsmen were climbing out of it. I pressed my ear to the wood to listen. The other searchers had returned with news that there were no tracks or any other sign of me. The rain had been too heavy.

One of the armsmen said they must take the wagon back to Vos's and suggested using their own horses to draw it. Another pointed out that it would be impossible since the wagon had no proper harness.

"Let's burn it, then," said another.

Hearing this, I turned onto my belly and closed my fingers around the pin that held the bottom of the hidden compartment in place. Grufyyd had created the second opening in case a person concealed there needed to slip away. But finally the highlander, who appeared to be the group leader, said that the wagon had better be taken back to Vos's in case Malik wanted to look it over.

There was much groaning as they dragged it out from under the tree and pushed it onto the track, where they tried to hitch two horses to it. By the time the wagon set off at the uncomfortable jerky pace that comes of mismatched horses, my senses told me that dawn had come and gone. I tried to beastspeak the horses, but both wore demon bands whose strength was such that it produced a queer discomforting numbness in my mind.

✦ ✦ ✦

"What is this?"

Hearing Malik's cold unmistakable voice made my scalp crawl.

"This is th' wagon that th' mutants used, Chieftain," answered the highlander who had elected to ride along with the carriage after commanding the others to continue searching for me. As he explained where they had found the wagon, it became clear that Malik had neither sent the men nor instructed Vos to do so. It was also clear that Malik knew I had vanished but did not know who I was.

"I should have been informed before anyone made a move against Noviny and these mutants," Malik said, his voice sharp with displeasure.

"Chieftain Vos commanded that the servants were to be sent home, an' Noviny an' his granddaughter be taken prisoner, along with the mutants an' the horses. One of the mutants turned out to be a gypsy, but the armsmen took him as well, just in case. All other beasts were killed, as well as two maidservants an' a man who refused to leave."

I bit back a cry, thinking of the servants I had seen and the dogs that had greeted me upon our arrival. And Maruman!

"You said the mutants were questioned?" Malik prompted.

"They were nowt questioned until they were brought back to Vos's homestead. That is when we realized th' female mutant, who had presented herself to Chieftain Vos, was not among them. At first the mutants tried to tell us that one of the women killed was the missing woman, but after we tickled the mutant lad's da, he told us she had sent a horse to tell him that she was waiting out the storm in the wagon."

"Probably the other mutants used their freakish powers to warn her as they were being taken away."

"They couldn't have, Chieftain," the highlander said. "The armsmen put demon bands on the lot of them at Noviny's place. But mebbe the female mutant saw them pass. . . ."

Malik grunted. "What did the mutant boy say they were doing here?"

"Only what th' female told Chieftain Vos yesterday: that they were headed for Sutrium an' had merely stopped here on th' way fer the lad to see his da. But it's clear they came because of something the old man scribed in a letter. Chieftain Vos had th' captives thrown into the cells an' gave orders for us to find the woman. That is when I sent a rider to ye, Chieftain."

There was a silence; then Malik said, "Very well. Take the wagon to Vos and make sure the prisoners are not questioned again. I will deal with them myself when I come. Tell him to concentrate his men and his efforts on finding that female mutant. With luck, she has stumbled into one of the perimeter traps and is dead. If so, I want to see her body."

I heard the sound of horses galloping away, then the slushy clop of hooves and the jingle of harness as the wagon lumbered on. I laid my face on a fold of the plast suit, insisting to myself that Maruman had not been slain and wondering if I really had the courage to put my plan into action.

✦ 8 ✦

I MUST HAVE fallen asleep for I woke to the sound of horses' hooves clattering over cobbles and realized that we had reached Vos's holding. I tried to picture the layout of the yard I had seen the day before. When the wagon turned left and came to a halt, I reckoned we had stopped in front of the barn that stood nearest the grass surrounding the main house in a sea of green. As the horses were freed from their makeshift bindings, I sent out a probe for Gahltha and then tried to reach Lo and Zade, to no avail. A large area of buzzing rejection came from what I guessed to be the direction of the corral. Perhaps Gahltha and the others were in the midst of the banded horses, and the collective disruption of their demon bands prevented me from reaching them. I farsought Zarak and Khuria with no more success, before remembering the highlander had spoken of their being demon banded.

After the two horses that had drawn the carriage were led away, I rolled on my back and was reaching for the pin that held the overhead hatch when I heard the voice of the armsmen who had brought the wagon in with the highlander.

"I do not see why we should be worried about making sure Chieftain Vos does what Malik commands," he said in a low, truculent voice. "He is not our chieftain."

Another voice told him authoritatively not to be a fool. "Do you think Chieftain Malik camps in Saithwold province these long winter months because he is concerned about protecting our coastline? He could just as well leave that to his men. I believe he intends to offer his name to the Council of Chieftains as candidate for Saithwold."

"But Chieftain Vos—"

"Will do nothing because he will be under charges for setting up the blockade and trying to force the people here to vote for him. Why else would Malik encourage him to do such things? But the main point is that Chieftain Malik is like to take on those of us who have proven useful to him."

"All right, but how are we supposed to make sure Vos obeys Malik's command not to question the prisoners again?"

The other man answered in a sneering voice, "Vos can be steered as easily as a sheep. Didn't you hear the highlander say in Vos's hearing that it is Malik's practice to keep prisoners in isolation and solitude to weaken their wills? If he follows his usual pattern, Chieftain Vos will simply appropriate the idea as his own."

The banging sound of a door came from the direction of the main house, ending the conversation. I heard the sound of many boots approaching and then Vos's voice, sneering at the wagon's smallness and its "grotesque and freakish ornamentation." To my horror, one of the armsmen again suggested burning the wagon, adding that the prisoners be made to watch. But Vos said loftily that he had decided the prisoners would stay where they were for the time being. A bit of isolation would stew their terror and make them more amenable when they were again questioned.

Vos derided the wagon for a little longer, then ordered it to be dragged out of his sight. There was a good deal of pushing and shoving before I heard the muffled sound of receding boots, and I prayed that the wagon had been pushed into the shed. It would be much easier to sneak out under cover.

After listening for a long time to be sure there was no one close by, I turned onto my belly, pushed aside the plast suit as carefully as I could, and pulled the pin at the bottom of the concealed section to release the lower hatch. I hung my head out, startled to find myself looking down at thick green grass. The wagon was not in the barn after all but on the grass beside it. With a sinking heart, I visualized all the windows in the long side of the homestead that would face me as I crept out.

I opened the hatch farther, hung my head right down, and looked around, but it was not until I gathered my courage and climbed out that I discovered that the wagon had been pushed under a weeping tree growing beside the shed. Better still, the barn door was flung open so wide that it blocked part of the wagon from view. I closed the hatch and crept along the side of the barn into the dense trees surrounding the homestead, giving thanks for the barn door's protection. All I had to do was stay hidden until dark, then slip inside to find the others. I refused to let myself dwell on how I would rescue them when all of the armsmen wore demon bands. I told myself that I should first find the horses. They might be able to tell me where the prisoners had been taken, and Gahltha would know what had happened to Maruman.

I moved through the trees behind the barn and around to where I had seen the corral, only to discover a large empty yard I would need to cross before I could reach it. I could not see any armsmen about, nor could I check for smaller buzzing areas of disturbance because it had begun to rain again.

My heart leapt into my mouth when, among the horses, I spotted a coal-black head I would have known anywhere. *Gahtha*. I beastspoke him and was close enough that I ought to have reached him even in the light rain, but he did not respond. The buzzing repulsion and the glint of metal about his neck gave it away. He had been banded! Gahltha could not reach me any more than I could him, yet his sense of smell was acute. He lifted his head and wheeled suddenly, causing an eddy in the slow swirl of horses. Then he was at the edge of the yard, his nose quivering.

I crouched and slipped through the fence posts into the empty yard. I ran across it, bent low, for I had spotted a group of armsmen sitting on the front porch of the homestead, talking and cleaning their weapons. Assuring myself that they could not possibly see me with all the moving horses between us, I had almost reached Gahltha when, to my astonishment, he laid back his ears and bared his teeth at me!

I stopped incredulously. What was the matter? I moved toward him, but this time he reared up slightly and gave a low, urgent whinny, stopping me again. I recognized the whinny he had given as a warning and looked around, but I could see no one. Baffled, I took another step. Gahltha snorted and shook his head.

"Gahltha?" I whispered, and reached out to him. But this time he snapped at my fingers and backed away, making the horses nearest him shift and prance. Was he in pain? The possibility that he had been harmed filled my mind with such a red blaze of anger that I struggled to compose myself. I was signaling laboriously for him to come when I heard a soft voice behind me.

"So, I was right."

I spun, heart hammering, to find the armsman Kevrik standing by a door I had not noticed in the side of the nearest outbuilding. With the delicacy of a true dagger handler, he held a short throwing dagger, point first. This was what Gahltha had been trying so hard to convey.

"I ken well how to use this, lass, in case yer thinkin' of makin' a run for it," Kevrik said in the same soft voice.

"How did you know I would come here?" I demanded, instinctively keeping my voice low.

"I was nowt sure, but having seen ye with yon black horse yesterday, I dinna think ye'd leave without him." I must have glanced at his throat, for he touched the demon band. "I believe ye about these being dangerous, but I can't have ye making me cut my own throat now, can I?" I must have reacted because his smile widened. "Unlike many of my comrades, I ken that Misfits can have more than one Talent. Nowt that anyone is like to listen to me, since I returned ye as I was bidden and am now suspected of letting myself be ensorcelled by ye. Capturing ye would be th' only way to restore my reputation."

"Why didn't you stake out the cell where my human friends are held?" I asked. "Are they so inaccessible that I would have no chance of reaching them, or don't you think we Misfits care about human friends?"

His teeth flashed white. "There are many armsmen in the house, and a guard is posted to stand outside the cell holding yer friends, which is in the basement. That, I suppose, is th' information ye were trying to trick out of me." My anger must have shown, for his grin faded and he tossed the knife purposefully up and caught it by the handle without ever taking his eyes from me. "I have to admire ye, lass, still plottin' to turn this moment to yer advantage when ye ought to be in despair. I'd nivver expected Misfits to show such courage and determination, nor to be loyal or clever. The stories told to us would have ye as vicious and cowardly near-beasts."

I opened my mouth and then closed it, suddenly struck by the fact that he had not made any attempt to call for help. Perhaps he intended to take me straight to Malik, since he was in disfavor with Vos. "Maybe you should be as clever," I said fiercely. "Of all people, Malik does not deserve anyone's loyalty."

Kevrik lifted his eyebrows, once again throwing the knife and catching it. I took a small step toward him anyway, growing reckless in my urgency. "You say you believe me about the demon bands? I will tell you something else that you ought to believe. Malik is a traitor—and not just to Misfits. Even now, he betrays you and Vos and all the rebels."

The amusement in the armsman's eyes was gone. "What are ye blatherin' about?" he demanded.

"Haven't you wondered why he supports Vos's pointless plots, which any fool can tell will not gain more than the most temporary chieftainship of Saithwold? Perhaps you imagine, as some others here do, that Malik supports Vos's folly the better to usurp his claim on Saithwold. If that is what you think, you are wrong. Malik desires vastly more than being chieftain of Saithwold. He is using Vos and Saithwold and all of you as a distraction to stop anyone from learning what he is really doing, until it is too late."

"Too late for what?"

"To stop him," I said, heartened by the fact that the armsman had not defended Malik. I took a deep breath. "Malik has made a pact with the Herders. Noviny saw him meeting with them down on the beach. He agreed to let a force of Herder warriors land, and he has used Vos's activities as a way of isolating Saithwold so none of the other chieftains will get wind of it. The tainted traps laid all about the province's perimeter and the demon bands that you and the horses wear are simply to make sure no Misfit scries in this region and learns what Malik is up to. If not for them, I could

133

have farsought someone to warn Dardelan and the Council of Chieftains about the invasion. As it is, I am trapped here, my friends are prisoners, and soon hundreds of Herder warriors will invade. I do not know what has been promised Malik for his treachery, but you can be sure that all who aided the rebellion will be slain or given to Salamander as slaves to be sold over the seas."

"How did Noviny just happen to witness a secret meeting between Malik and the Herders?" Kevrik asked.

"Noviny suspected him of being behind the burnings up the coast, so he went looking for proof. Since learning of the invasion plan, he has done nothing but try to get word to Dardelan. That is why he had Khuria scribe those letters to Zarak. He thought the lad would be turned away and would make enough of a fuss that Dardelan would have to send in some armsmen. He never imagined that Brydda would ease us through the blockade."

For a long moment, Kevrik looked at me, knife poised; then he lowered it. "Most of us have believed that Malik meant to take over Saithwold. Some felt it would be a better billet to serve him, while others, me among them, dinna much like the idea of being Malik's man but saw little else for it. Yet if all ye say is true . . ." He paused for a moment. "It is said that Malik betrayed many of yer people to their deaths."

"No one has better cause than me to know it, for I was one of those who survived his treachery," I said fiercely. "He knows me and hates me specifically, though not by the name I gave Vos, for he strove against me in the Battlegames in Sador. We Misfits lost the Battlegames and, therefore, the chance to join the rebellion as equal allies, but Malik's ruthless tactics caused him to forfeit the respect of his fellows. That is why he is not high chieftain. He blames Misfits for that, and if you take me to him, have no doubt that you will win his favor." I stopped, breathless, praying that I had not misjudged the armsman's essential nature.

The highlander gave me a long look, then in one smooth movement, reached up, undid the demon band, and removed it. "The favor of a treacherous leader is a precarious thing," he said. "Me mam used to tell me dreadful tales of monstrous Misfits who would come and eat me if I dinna heed her. I am no longer that wee lad, an' meetin' ye yesterday has troubled me, lass; I tell ye straight. Ye admitted to being a Misfit, but I dinna find ye evil-natured or freakish. Indeed, yer bonny and braw and clever, and in coming here, ye have proven yerself a true friend. I think we can be allies, unless ye now use yer powers to make me slit my own throat and prove me wrong."

I drew a deep shaky breath and managed a soft laugh, hardly able to believe that I had managed to convince him. "I will not slit your throat nor even read your mind, for with these words, you have made us allies, and because of them, I will tell you the plan I have to thwart Malik. Indeed, with your help, it just might have a chance of succeeding."

"What can I do?" he asked simply.

My gratitude was so great that I had to blink away a hot rush of tears. Only then did I realize how deeply I had feared being unable to save the others. I mastered myself and said, "First, we must get my friends out of their cell."

"I fear that is impossible," Kevrik said regretfully. "I could gan to the cell easy enow. It is the first in a long corridor of basement cells an' can be reached by descending a flight of steps. I might manage to trick the guard outside their door into letting me take the prisoners by telling him Vos has changed his mind an' wants to question them again, but the key to the cell hangs around the chieftain's neck, an' all men ken it. There's no way to get it from him, save knockin' him on the head. An' since he has ten armsmen with him at any moment, I dinna think we will manage that very easily."

I pondered his words. "Could you persuade the guard watching the cells to remove his demon band for a moment?"

"Probably," Kevrik said. "But that would nowt solve th' problem of opening the door."

"What about the other guards? Could you persuade them to remove their collars?"

He shrugged, frowning. "I could say th' catches on some demon bands are faulty an' Vos wants me to check them. But if suddenly everyone lacks demon bands, it would soon be noticed an' the alarm given," Kevrik said.

"The bands only have to be off for a few moments. I can put a command into the mind of each armsman that will endure for some time even after the band is restored," I said.

Kevrik blinked. "What command?"

I told him, then asked, "Is the door of the cell made of bars, or is it solid?"

"Solid," Kevrik said apologetically, not realizing that this was what I had hoped. He went on, "But what of th' lock."

"I can open the lock."

Kevrik's eyes shifted, and he said hastily that I had better uncollar my friend. I turned to see Gahltha glaring down at me, his nostrils flared wide with indignation. With an exclamation of remorse, I turned and unclasped the demon band, wincing at the mental tirade that the black horse immediately poured into my mind. I stopped him by telling him my plan.

"No! There is too much risk to you/ElspethInnle," Gahltha sent at once.

"This is the only way to stop Malik, and if we succeed, Dardelan and the rebels will be able to defeat the Herders and then go and free the west coast, so that I can pursue my quest. And if my plan fails, all will be lost anyway, for the Herders will reclaim the Land and Misfits will be put to the flame or made slaves."

"What of your quest if you are hurt or killed, Elspeth-Innle?"

I sighed. "I don't know, Gahltha. So many times in my life, I have put my quest first, but often, even when I did not think it, I discovered that I was serving it. Perhaps Maruman is right in saying that all I do serves my quest." I swallowed a hard lump of fear in my throat. "Tell me . . . what happened to him? I heard that the animals were killed save for the horses."

"Not Maruman," Gahltha sent. "He warned me they were coming, but they were upon us before I could beastspeak Zarak or Khuria. The dogs and a goat were slain, and five milk cows with their calves. None of them saw Maruman, but he was watching. The last message he sent was that he would find you and warn you of what had happened."

I felt a rush of relief. "He must still be out there somewhere," I said aloud.

"Lass, it is too dangerous to stay here like this," Kevrik said urgently, glancing across at the homestead.

I nodded and looked into Gahltha's eyes. "Do you think the horses here will be able to find their way to Malik's camp without riders?"

"I will lead them where you have said, ElspethInnle," Gahltha sent. "But your plan could fail."

"If it does, then you must do your best to reach Brydda or someone from Obernewtyn who can warn the others about the invasion. You will have to jump the barricade."

He looked at me.

He did not say that the armsmen guarding it would not

hesitate to use their weapons on him. He did not say the chance of his getting by alive was so slender as to be almost nonexistent. I lay my face against his silky black neck and felt his pulse against my cheek. "Tell Zade and Lo and the other horses that I can't uncollar them yet, because an armsman might notice. But if we succeed, they will be free of the foul things forever."

Kevrik wanted to wait until full dark to move, but I was filled with a sense of urgency almost as strong as a premonition. Fortunately, miserable weather kept the armsmen inside, except for those who had some duty. Kevrik came and went, gradually describing the layout of the house and making the few preparations we needed, as I worked out what to do. I told him that we would use the rear entrance to the house, which was toward the back of the long wall facing the barn. I would go along the tree line until I was opposite the entrance, and when it was safe, he would signal so I could cross the grass to enter. The greatest danger would come when I was out in the open, for anyone glancing from a window would see me. Kevrik advised me to push my hair beneath the collar of the armsman's cloak he had brought, saying I would be taken for an armsman if I acted like one.

When I was in place in the trees, with a good view of the rear door, I saw armsmen stacking firewood against the wall beside it. Kevrik went to speak to them and then went back in the direction of the barn, only to emerge fifteen minutes later in the trees beside me, panting.

"Dinna worry. They will go in when they have finished, because it is nearly time for nightmeal, an' most men who have no duty will gan to the dining hall, which is toward the front of the house."

"Tell me about the demon bands for the horses," I said as we settled to wait. "I am certain the Herders created them and gave them to Malik, but why?"

"I dinna ken why, but a sevenday back, Malik rode up and gave Vos a crate of them. He said that since Noviny harbored a beastspeaker, we mun protect ourselves from the possibility that our horses might be manipulated to give messages or even to harm us. A lot of us wondered where Malik had got the bands, but none of us dared question him. One of the men asked Vos, an' he called the man a fool. He said, of course, that they had been found in the cloister. But we searched that cloister—" He broke off and nodded to the door. The men stacking wood had gone in. I ran my eyes along the side of the building and saw that several windows that had shown light were now dark.

Kevrik went back through the trees toward the barn. A few minutes later, I saw him cross the cobbled yard to the front of the homestead and disappear inside. My heart raced with apprehension until he reappeared at the back door. He glanced about once, then beckoned. I took a deep breath, rose, and stepped out purposefully. I had retrieved my boots from the wagon, but at the back door I hastily pulled them off so I could move silently in my socks.

I followed Kevrik as he moved deeper into the house. The passages were empty, but I stayed a little way behind him, knowing that at any minute someone might step out. The rooms we passed were both unoccupied and unfurnished, but this was no surprise, for Kevrik had told me that the house had been built to accommodate the number of servants and armsmen Vos imagined he would eventually amass.

Suddenly Kevrik splayed his fingers downward in the warning signal we had agreed upon. I flattened myself against the wall and froze. I had wanted Kevrik to leave off his collar so I could reach his mind, but he said that would look suspicious if noticed, as was bound to happen when he raised the subject of demon bands.

Kevrik looked at me. "Are ye sure?" he mouthed.

I nodded, then listened anxiously as he turned a bend in the passage ahead and spoke a greeting. We had agreed that he would greet each man he met by name so I would know how many there were. One, then. I crept closer to the corner and heard Kevrik explain that Vos had ordered him to check all demon band catches, for some had proven faulty. When I heard the snick of the fastening mechanism, I shaped a delicate coercive probe and carefully entered the armsman's mind. It took only a moment to fashion a simple block that would prevent his noticing me as I passed or noticing the others when we returned. I waited impatiently as Kevrik examined the demon band at length, obviously imagining I needed more time. At last he told the other armsman his band seemed fine, and I heard the snick of its being fastened on again.

I padded around the corner. The armsman stood looking at the wall, as I had commanded, and he did not turn as I ghosted past him, leaving an astounded-looking Kevrik in my wake.

"I canna believe it worked," Kevrik whispered when he caught up with me. A faint unease in his expression told me he was wondering if I could tamper with his mind as easily. Then he flushed, and I guessed he was wondering if I was reading his mind now. I made no comment, because although his fears were scribed clear upon his face for anyone to read, if I tried to allay them, he would regard my awareness as proof that I had invaded his mind.

"How long does it last?" he asked when we had gone

around another bend in the passage.

"About half an hour, as long as nothing happens that opposes the suggestions I have put into his mind."

"Like an alarm being given?"

"That still might not cause the block to crumble, but if we were in the process of creeping past at the moment an alarm went . . ."

"I see." Kevrik sucked in a breath of air and blew it out. "I suppose—" He stopped because we heard voices and footsteps around the next bend in the passage. Kevrik strode quickly ahead, and I heard him greet two men and explain in an authoritative voice that Chieftain Vos wanted all demon band clasps examined as some had proven faulty. There was a little silence, and then I heard the men remove their bands. One of them made a bawdy comment about Kevrik's skill with his hands, and as Kevrik responded in kind, I slipped into the minds of first one and then the other. When I glided around the corner past where they stood with Kevrik, momentarily blank-eyed, they turned to the wall.

He joined me a few moments later, his face pale. "I am nowt sure I can take too much of this, lass. I keep expecting someone to see ye an' shout an alarm."

Despite his anxiety, we managed to negotiate the passages without difficulty, leaving three more armsmen coerced behind us. The worst moment was when we encountered a group of five men. When Kevrik spoke their names, I began to sweat. It was not the number of men that troubled me, but the fact that five were enough to produce an amorphous group mind that had also to be coerced. Knowing the notorious instability of group minds, I instructed each man to hand his demon band to Kevrik and then to forget that he had done so. Having the armsmen unbanded meant that I could check on their blocks and refresh them if they began to crumble. There was the risk that the absence of the bands might be noticed, but I had no choice. I kept control of their minds and made them all turn to the wall as I passed so that no matter what happened, they would not remember my face. When Kevrik joined me a few moments later, he held out the bands with a questioning look. When I explained, he thrust them atop a high shelf we passed.

At last we reached the steps leading to the basement cells. Kevrik descended and I followed, grimacing when the stone became slimy underfoot. But I was less concerned about my socks than the knowledge that there was only one way in and out of the cells; if an alarm was given now, we would be trapped. My blood churned with a mixture of nervousness and excitement that I welcomed, knowing it would sharpen my responses.

Kevrik touched his finger to his lips as he reached the bottom of the steps, and I stopped and listened. I heard him greet the armsman guarding the cells and was relieved that there was only a single man. Kevrik offered his tale, but the armsman refused to remove his demon band.

"Not with them freaks so close!" he expostulated. "Maybe this is just what they've been waiting for."

"Dinna be a fool," Kevrik said jovially. But the guard insisted he would wait until Chieftain Vos himself came to give the order. There was a bit more arguing, followed by a great thump and silence.

"Ella!" Kevrik hissed. I went down and saw a tall armsman crumpled on the ground at Kevrik's feet.

"He would nowt be reasonable, so I had to knock him on the head and take off his band," Kevrik said, his accent thickened by agitation. "Can ye make it so that he won't remember what happened when he wakes?"

"I will have to wake him to coerce him, which will require physical contact." I wrinkled my nose as I laid my hand on the armsman's thick and none-too-clean forearm. I inserted a coercive probe into his sleeping mind and made him wake. When his eyes flew open, Kevrik started back with a gasp of alarm, but the guard only lay glassy-eyed and placid, his gaze fixed on the pitted rock wall of the basement passage as I had coerced him. I was able to make it stronger than the others because I was touching him. Finally, I restored his demon band. When I rose and stepped back behind Kevrik, the armsman yawned, rose to his feet with a guilty expression, and then walked away from us to the far end of the row of cells, rubbing his jaw absently.

I turned my attention to the cell door, which was just as solid as the armsman had said. I did not bother trying to farseek Zarak or Khuria or the others, knowing that they all wore demon bands. I put my fingers on the lock, closed my eyes, and focused hard to transform mental energy into a physical force. I felt out the shapes inside the lock carefully, struggling to understand how they worked. It was more complex than I had expected, and Kevrik shifted impatiently beside me.

"A person's thoughts weigh nothing," I gasped at him. "To move matter with your mind is the hardest thing. Opening this lock is like trying to move a wagon with a spoon."

At last, I heard the tumblers click and sagged back in relief, trembling with fatigue. I had closed my eyes for a moment, which was when Kevrik turned the lever and opened the door. Before I could stop him, he had stepped into the cell, and my heart sank as I heard a sickly thud.

✦ 9 ✦

Zarak stood over Kevrik's unconscious form triumphantly, but when he looked up and saw me in the doorway, his face sagged in disbelief.

"I am glad you took to heart farseeker rescue instructions to keep yourself ready to escape at any moment, no matter how hopeless the situation," I told Zarak, trying for irony. "Unfortunately, poor Kevrik will have a terrible headache that he does not deserve."

"He is one of Vos's armsmen," Zarak protested.

"He was," I said, taking in Khuria, Noviny, and a pale but determined-looking Wenda sitting together in one corner. Darius was awake, too, but he lay with his head in Wenda's lap. They all looked alert, though Khuria had a bloodied face.

Zarak looked down at Kevrik in dismay. "I am sorry, Guildmistress. . . ."

I shook my head impatiently. "Never mind that now. Take the others up the steps and make your way toward the back of the house and out the back door. The guards ought not to take any notice of you, because I have coerced near a dozen of them. But be ready to strike if anyone reacts, for it might be someone I did not meet coming in. You will have to do it physically, because they will be wearing demon bands, and we do not now have Kevrik to convince them to remove the bands. Take his dagger and his cloak. That ought to give any-

144

one you encounter pause enough for you to deal with them. But make no noise, else we will have the whole house down on us. Once outside, go straight across to the trees and make your way to the barn. You will find our wagon this side of it, pushed under a tree. Lo and Zade are waiting behind the barn. Hitch them up to the carriage, get in, and wait for me."

They all stayed where they were, gaping, and I felt like stamping my foot to wake them. At last Zarak went to help his father and then Noviny to their feet. I bit my lip, seeing how badly the old beastspeaker limped, knowing he had been tortured so Zarak could allow me more time to escape. But he gave me a crooked grin that told me his spirit was as strong as ever. Noviny had not been as badly hurt, but he looked years older as he bent to help Wenda with Darius. The gypsy showed no marks of violence, but his face was bloodless under his dark skin.

"Can you manage?" I asked, knowing that if they could not, we were all doomed.

"We must," Noviny said, and Darius managed to nod. As they passed by me, I saw that the gypsy's face shone with sweat, and his breath sawed harshly in and out. But there was nothing I could do for him.

"What about you, Guildmistress?" Zarak asked.

"I must wake Kevrik and relock the cell door so it seems you are still inside. Go and help the others. I don't know how long the blocks on the armsmen will last. One of them was on a group mind."

Zarak looked alarmed, spun on his heel, and went. I dropped to my knees beside Kevrik's limp form and laid a hand on his cheek. Unconscious, he looked younger. I reached a coercive probe into his mind to bring him to consciousness and then thought better of it.

✦ ✦ ✦

Several minutes later, I hurried past armsman after armsman, each of whom obligingly looked the other way. Kevrik had been right in saying there was much less movement during mealtimes, and in any case, most activity and attention in the homestead was focused toward the front of the building and the entrance to the property. I got outside without mishap and arrived at the wagon just as Zarak was helping Darius into it. I was about to summon the strength to unlock Zarak's demon band when Gahltha farsent me urgently. I ran lightly along the back of the outbuildings and through the empty yard after a hasty scan to be sure there were no armsmen near. Gahltha was waiting at the side of the corral, and he gave a soft whinny of greeting before telling me that three funaga had ridden in while I was gone, leaving their mounts tied to the other side of the corral. The horses were demon banded, but he had learned that they had come from Malik's camp.

"I have told them who you are and what you want the horses here to do, and they are ready to help," he said. "They have offered to throw their riders and trample them, if you wish it." Gahltha's eyes were fierce, as if the idea pleased him. I climbed into the corral and moved through the horses to the side closest to the homestead. I could easily reach the three tethered outside, and I undid the demon band of the first I reached, a big dappled-gray beast with intelligent eyes. Fortunately, none of the horse bands had locks, for Malik and his ilk only ever feared that beastspeakers would coerce the minds of their mounts. It never occurred to them that beastspeakers were not animal coercers and that horses might collude to attack of their own free will. Freed of the demon band, the gray horse greeted me as Innle and told me that his name was Dovyn. I asked him to explain to his comrades that I

146

would not undo their bands because one missing could be an accident, but not three. Then I explained what I needed them to do when they returned to Malik's camp.

Gahltha was questioning Dovyn's companions about the number of men and horses in the camp. I could not hear their answers because of their demon bands, so I left him to it and returned to the wagon in time to see three men wearing Malik's colors striding across the yard. I prayed that Dovyn's missing band would go unnoticed. The three riders mounted up and would have galloped away at once had Vos not come hurrying from the homestead to command them to stop. They obeyed, but none of the three dismounted. I was afraid that Vos might notice Dovyn's bare neck, but the horse kept his head down so his mane fell forward. Vos began to speak, his voice querulous and indignant, as he bade the armsmen tell their chieftain that he was sorely needed. One of Malik's men answered coldly that his chieftain had heard that message already. Malik's answer was what they had come to deliver, namely that Chieftain Vos must concentrate his efforts on finding the Misfit his men had managed to lose.

To my horror, Vos pointed frantically toward the barn and asked if they wanted to see the wagon where the Misfit had hidden. Fortunately, the barn door partly blocked the view of the wagon from the yard, and it was now dark, so no one noticed that there were horses tethered to it. Dovyn's rider said his master had already seen it and that it was not a wagon he wanted but the missing woman. Then the three wheeled their horses and rode off. Vos stared after them for a scowling moment before storming back into the house.

Afraid that he might be headed for the cells to interrogate the others about me, I called Zarak. He came to the open canvas, and I reached through and laid a hand on the demon-band lock. Gritting my teeth, I focused my mind, but the band's taint was so strong that it would not let me concentrate energy into force. Frightened that the empty cell would be discovered even before they had escaped, I reached deep down into myself where my black killing power lay coiled in the depths. The last time I had awakened it, I had nearly lost control, but this time I drew on it without waking it. I heard the lock in the demon band click.

My mind felt numb from contact with the taint, and my head spun from the effort of opening a second lock so soon after the first, but I was elated to discover that it was possible to harness that black and terrifying power within my mind without being overmastered by it.

Zarak wrenched the band off his neck with a look of profound revulsion, and seeing that he meant to hurl it from the wagon, I bade him keep it. Wenda came forward expectantly, lifting her hair from her throat.

I shook my head regretfully. "I have no more strength now. I am sorry," I croaked. Swiftly, I wove a coercive net to take in the fatigue clouding my brain, and farsought Zarak. "I am going to create a diversion to draw Vos's household to the back of the homestead so you can escape. Get Darius as comfortable as you can, because Lo and Zade will gallop as soon as they are out of sight of the homestead."

"But where will we gan?" Zarak responded. "Th' main road is barricaded, an' there will be armsmen all over th' roads lookin' fer you."

"Most of them have been sent to Noviny's property or to the barricade. And you will not be going that way."

"The coast road is barricaded as well. . . ."

"You will not be going that way either." I sent him the mental picture I had given Lo, when we had let her out of the

148

corral, of a track leading off the main road just before it forked. Kevrik had suggested it.

"The abandoned cloister?" Zarak sent in disbelief. "But there is only one road in an' out."

"The armsmen will be looking for Misfit fugitives who want to escape Saithwold. They are not going to look in an empty cloister on a dead-end road," I sent with a tartness that made the young farseeker wince. "If you encounter anyone on your way there, Lo or Zade must beastspeak their horses to throw them. You won't be able to do it because of the demon bands. Bind them and take them with you. Put them in one of the old cloister cells. Ask the horses to follow you."

"What about you?" Zarak asked.

"I have other matters to attend to," I said in stern guild-mistress tones to discourage him from asking any more questions. Then I bade him and the others farewell and leapt down from the wagon.

I made my way back along the tree line until I had reached the same place where I had hidden earlier, opposite the rear door. Forming a coercive probe, I sought the minds of the five armsmen I had left unbanded. To my delight, four of them were together playing cards in a room near the end of the homestead. Their minds told me that they were on duty, guarding Vos's armory. I smiled.

A moment later, one of the men leapt up crying out that he smelled smoke. The others "smelled" smoke, too, and one managed to "see" flames without any coercion at all. To my surprise, instead of trying to rescue the weapons in the armory, the four men fled down the hall and outside, bellowing in terror. Puzzled, I dipped into one of their minds again to find that piled in one corner were eight small wooden kegs filled with a black powder, which the armsmen believed

149

would explode and destroy the house.

It seemed highly unlikely, but in moments there was a wild clangor of bells, and people began spilling out of the building from all directions, giving credence to the armsmen's belief that the whole house was in danger of being destroyed. I waited until they had all run down toward the rear of the homestead and then farsent Lo and Zarak. I found one of the men without bands and made him "see" a host of armed strangers creeping through the woods toward the back of the house, and a senior armsman ordered the others to investigate while he tried to find out where the fire was. He ran back into the homestead, and I knew I did not have much time.

I farsought Zarak again and was delighted to find that the wagon had already left the cobbled yard and was swiftly nearing the entrance to the property. By my reckoning, it was not more than half an hour to the road leading to the cloister, and with luck, they might make it all the way there without being seen.

"We will deal with anyone we meet," Zarak sent determinedly.

I withdrew from him only to find that the search for the fire and intruders was beginning to flag. Doubts were flowering, and any minute it would dawn on someone that they had been tricked. I reached into the minds of the unbanded men and managed three more sightings of people creeping about the house, prolonging the search for another half hour. Then someone discovered that one of the armsmen guarding the armory had no demon band. In a short time, all five unbanded armsmen were found and brought before their chieftain.

"The Misfit is here and trying to release her companions," Vos screamed at his men. "Find her!"

I ran back through the trees to the barn and across the

cobbled yard toward the corral. I heard a shout and ran faster, but my wet socks slipped on the damp cobbles, and I went down hard. I was surrounded in seconds, and it was all I could manage, as I lay there, winded and dazed, to command Gahltha to do nothing, for I knew he could see me from the corral. If he tried anything, he would be killed. All the armsmen glaring down at me held knives or bows with arrows already nocked. I lay very still.

"Get up," snarled a senior armsman as he arrived with a lantern and took in the scene before him.

"I'm not sure I can. I think I have sprained my leg," I gasped.

Another armsman reached down, obviously intent on dragging me to my feet, but the senior armsman told him sharply not to be a fool. Was I not the Misfit witch who had forced their comrades into removing their demon bands and serving me? Who knew what I would do to someone who touched me?

The armsman snatched his hand back and gave me a look of frightened loathing.

"I will need a . . . stick if you want me to stand," I said, levering myself awkwardly into a sitting position as more armsmen emerged from the house.

Before any of them could decide whether there would be any risk in giving me a stick, Vos came hurrying along the side of the homestead with more of his men. I noticed Kevrik among them, a purple swelling over the eye where Zarak had struck him. But from the smug triumph on Vos's face, he had no idea yet that his prisoners were gone. I tried to reach Kevrik's mind, but the demon band he now wore made it impossible. He looked down at me coldly.

"So," Vos sneered, his eyes glittering with triumph in the

lantern light. "You thought you could use your filthy powers to rescue your friends, but see how you have failed. Here is the man you used to help you trick others into removing their bands." He was pointing to Kevrik.

"Let me kill th' witchling who made me betray ye, Chieftain," he begged hoarsely.

Vos laughed. "You shall have her, but first, Chieftain Malik will wish to question her."

"Then let us ride now and take her to him!" Kevrik snarled.

A look composed equally of arrogance and unease crossed the chieftain's narrow features. "It is dark now, and Chieftain Malik commanded that none should come to his camp without first sending a message."

"Sirrah, surely that could not mean you?" Kevrik demanded. "Are ye not the equal of Chieftain Malik, since ye are both chieftains, an' ye are within yer own region? Let us take the freak to him, for will he nowt be eager to ken that she is taken prisoner? Let Chieftain Malik witness how yer men captured the Misfit when his own armsmen failed."

"You speak well, Kevrik," Vos approved, his cheeks flushed. He turned to the other armsmen. "I have decided that we will ride immediately to the camp of Chieftain Malik and deliver this creature to him."

Several of the other armsmen, one of them the highlander whose voice I recognized from the wagon, sought to dissuade Vos, but the more they talked of Malik's commands, the more stubborn Vos became.

"Am I Malik's armsman to be commanded hither or thither? Besides, I wish to see Malik, and since he cannot be bothered to come here, then I will go to him, and in triumph, bringing him what he most desires."

Still some of his captains argued until Vos flew into a rage and ordered them to make ready to ride.

Malik was the same solidly muscled, gray-eyed, gray-haired man he had been the last time I saw him, but he wore his arrogance with a vicious new edge that must have been honed by the secret bargain he had made with the Herders. He listened impassively to Vos's description of my capture—by his telling, a brilliant coup in which Vos himself was a central figure. Without the congratulations and accolades from Malik that Vos clearly expected, the story at last foundered to an uncertain end.

"Did I not inform you that I wished you to send word that you had caught the Misfit? Did I not command that a messenger be sent if you intended to come here?" Malik inquired coldly. The light from lanterns hung about the encampment gave his face a sinister ruddy glow.

Vos's bluster about being Malik's equal shriveled, and he said, "You did, however . . . ah . . . it is a dangerous Misfit that my men caught. Not just a beastspeaker but a powerful coercer."

Malik all but curled his lip in derision. "Your men caught her after they first let her escape and after you acted against my express orders to do nothing about Noviny or his visitors until I gave you leave." Vos tried to speak, but Malik ignored him. "But I am sure Chieftain Dardelan will be most understanding when you expalin to him why you took Noviny and his granddaughter and their guests prisoner and interrogated them."

Vos paled. "But . . . if the freaks had used their powers to escape, they would have reported me to the Council of Chieftains."

Malik gave a bark of laughter. "Do you really imagine that the Council of Chieftains will be forever ignorant of what you have been doing here?"

"You said I would have your full support if it came out," Vos stammered.

"So you would have, had you not decided to take prisoners against my orders. And now you march into my camp, though I warned you against it."

"I am sorry, Chieftain Malik," Vos gabbled, unraveling with fear. "I hope that you will not take this . . . eagerness of mine amiss. I will take this creature and return with my men to my homestead."

"The mutant might as well remain here," Malik said. He turned to look at me. He had glanced at me indifferently when we arrived, and I thought that he had not recognized me under the mud and dirt. But now, seeing the look of gloating hatred in his metal-gray eyes, I knew I had been wrong. He knew exactly who I was.

A cold shiver of terror ran down my spine. I forced myself to seek the mind of the horse Dovyn, whom I had unbanded, but the probe would not locate. His missing band had probably been discovered and replaced.

"Why are you here in Saithwold?" Malik demanded.

My mouth was so dry with fear that I had to work my tongue to produce moisture enough to speak. "We had letters from the beastspeaker Khuria, who serves Master Noviny. The missives did not sound like him, so we—"

Almost casually, Malik drew back his hand and struck me in the mouth. It was an openhanded blow with the back of his knuckles but hard enough to make me stagger sideways.

He asked in an almost bored voice, "What did you know of matters in Saithwold before you came here?"

"Nothing until a woman at an inn mentioned the blockade. She said that Chieftain Vos was trying to force people in Saithwold to elect him."

Vos let out a strangled cry of dismay, but Malik silenced him with a cutting gesture.

"And the Black Dog?"

"Brydda said the high chieftain knew what Vos was trying to do but that Dardelan didn't want to act against him until after the elections. He did not want us to come here, but when I said that Zarak was determined to see his father, he offered to help us get past the barricade."

Malik sneered. "You would have me believe that despite knowing there was trouble in Saithwold, Brydda Llewellyn, a known friend to freaks, escorted here the guildmistress of Obernewtyn and doxy to its master, and left her without protection?"

I heard Vos gasp at hearing my title, but Malik ignored him.

"Brydda didn't think there would be any real danger," I said. "The worst we imagined was having to wait in Saithwold until after the elections, and in the meantime I would be able to stop anyone from doing anything rash, by telling them that Dardelan meant to deal with Vos."

Malik struck me again, this time with a closed fist that glanced off the side of my head and knocked me to the ground.

"Get up," he said coldly.

I struggled to my knees with difficulty, because my wrists were bound. The blow had set off a great explosion of pain in one ear, and I fought a blackness that fluttered about the edges of my vision, wondering what Malik wanted from me. I was answering his questions truthfully, and he could have no idea that we knew of his bargain with the Herders.

"Get up," Malik said once more.

Trembling, I obeyed. When he stepped toward me, I instinctively lifted my bound hands to protect my face, but he sank his closed fist into my stomach. I doubled over, gagging at the force of the blow, and fell to my knees. When I managed to heave in a breath, he ordered me up yet again. I obeyed as slowly as I dared, tensing for another blow. Instead of hitting me, Malik asked what Noviny had told me. When I opened my mouth to answer, he punched me again in the stomach.

I fell badly this time because of my bound hands, banging my head on a rock, and when Malik told me to get up, my limbs would not obey. I stayed curled on the muddy ground, praying that he would not kick my head or face. When he did not move or speak, I looked up to find him staring down at me, his features utterly empty. The moon had risen and seemed to ride on his shoulder. No wonder Maruman hated the moon, I thought dazedly. It was on Malik's side.

Malik turned to Vos, who looked frightened out of his wits. "Do the other prisoners know that you have caught this one?"

"No," Vos said in a thin voice. "They have not been questioned since the first interrogation, just as you ordered."

"Good. Go back to your homestead. Remove Noviny and his granddaughter to their homestead and have them kept there under guard. Do not speak of this Misfit's capture to them. Offer no explanation and make sure your men are equally silent. The other two Misfit freaks and the crippled gypsy are to be questioned again. Edel," he addressed one of his own men, "accompany Chieftain Vos and conduct the interrogation. Begin with the cripple and torture him until he dies, regardless of what he does or does not confess. Make sure the other two witness it, then begin on the boy. That will loosen the old man's lips if they are keeping anything back. Find out why they came, what they have learned here, and what they intended to do. I will expect a report by tomorrow."

Edel nodded, but Vos stammered a protest. "The . . . the Council of Chieftains will want to know what happened to the Misfits, Malik. And if this woman is truly the bondmate of the Master of Obernewtyn . . ."

"This is a freak, not a woman," Malik snarled. "I will deal with her as all mutants ought to be dealt with. It is nothing to do with you. As far as anyone else will know, you saw her but once when she came to pay her respects to you, and then you had her taken back to Noviny's property."

"But if she talks—"

"You need have no fear of that."

Vos swallowed the meaning of this as if it were a stone. "But the other Misfits . . . Noviny and his granddaughter will say that they and the cripple remained my captives when they were returned to their home."

"If you are ever accused of anything, you will let it be known that Edel performed the interrogation of the Misfits at my command." Malik's tone was so indifferent that it sounded like boredom.

"But the Council of Chieftains will—"

"I will deal with the Council," Malik said with cold finality. "Now go."

Vos hesitated, perhaps expecting something more formal to pass between them, but Malik made no face-saving speech. Finally, with as much dignity as he could muster, Vos commanded his men to mount up and ride back to his property. They obeyed silently, watched by Malik's men.

Malik was now speaking quietly to one of his men, and I closed my eyes for a moment, battling fear. My tongue found the jagged edge of a chipped tooth, and my lip stung where it had been split. I could also feel the drain of energy as my body tried to repair itself. There was no way to stop the process, for it was not activated by my will, and opening the locks had depleted me, though that fatigue was still coercively netted. I did not dare push the pain I now felt into the same net, because pain trapped in this way doubled and tripled in a very short time.

I was so intent upon my thoughts that I failed to notice Malik's armsman circling behind me. When Malik abruptly ordered me to get up, I obeyed, relieved to find that my limbs would obey. But even as I stood, swaying slightly, I felt the cold metal of a demon band snap around my neck.

◆ 10 ◆

To MY HORROR, I discovered that my powers were trapped inside my mind like a bear caught in a cage. I told myself that this was merely normality, but the thought that this dreadful isolation and passivity of mind could be called normal sickened me. No wonder unTalents loathed us. At the heart of their hated must be bitter envy.

I might have been better able to stifle my horror and fear had I not known that, in banding me, Malik unwittingly left me unable to play my part in the plan I had set in motion. I fought a suffocating wave of panic and tried to focus a probe to work the lock, but the taint emanating from the band was too strong. Desperately I tried to reach the black power at the bottom of my mind, but pain and the healing of my body drained me of the energy I needed to rouse it.

"Ye ken Vos will nowt keep his mouth shut," grunted the man who had fastened the demon band about my neck as he poured a mugful of some dark liquid and handed it to Malik. The chieftain drank it off, then shrugged.

"I have given him makework enough to occupy him for the time being, but the fool's role is almost at an end."

"What about her?" The armsman nodded in my direction.

"The freak is irrelevant," Malik said dismissively.

"Obernewtyn's master might nowt agree if the woman is truly his doxy. He might come riding in looking for her with some of those coercer-knights of his, regardless of what Dardelan wants. It would be inconvenient if their arrival coincides with other matters."

He is talking about the invasion, I thought.

A smile curved Malik's thin lips. "I doubt Rushton Seraphim will be in any haste to get his woman back. After the priests had their fun with him, I am amazed that he could stomach her presence these long months. He might look like a man, but all that makes a man is gone. He is no more than a shell."

Bile rose in my throat, and tears stung my eyes, for what Malik said was true. Had Rushton not said as much to me himself? For Malik to know so much, the Herders with whom he had struck his bargain must have boasted of what they had done when they had Rushton imprisoned in the Sutrium cloister. I ground my teeth in fury, and some of the quaking terror left me.

"If all is so well, Chieftain, why do ye have a troubled look about ye?" ventured the armsman.

A flicker of impatience in the cold face of his master faded into a brooding puzzlement. "It is true," Malik said slowly. "I am troubled. Something nags at my mind." To my dismay, he turned to look at me. "How did that fool Vos manage to capture her, of all mutants? That is what nags at me."

My heart hammered because Malik knew me as only a former opponent can. Perhaps he was remembering the last occasion on which we had faced one another, when victory had turned to ashes in his mouth. I tensed as he took a step toward me, but he stopped, hearing the sound of horses' hooves drumming. Malik and his men turned to face the road, no doubt imagining that Vos and his troop were riding back. But when the horses came in sight, they were riderless, though many wore saddles and even dangerously dangling reins. Malik and his men stared, perplexed and astonished.

Malik was the first to regain his wits. "Shoot! Shoot them, you fools, for they are coming to save the freak." His men tried to obey, but it was too late. The stampeding horses were upon the camp. Men screamed in terror and pain as they fell under flashing hooves. A few men shot arrows or threw a spear or knife, but not a single horse fell. I realized with elation that the men did not know how to fight horses, for their training had always focused on their human riders. Without warning, more horses leapt from the bushes. They were unsaddled and unbridled, which told me they were the horses that had been left in the corral back at Vos's property. Gahltha had released them as I had requested. Then I saw him, black and powerful in the moonlight, rearing and stamping down hard, his nostrils flaring.

Huts were trampled, lanterns smashed, and brief flames extinguished as the horses rampaged through the camp. Men who had not been trampled fled from the devastation, only to find their own horses, led by Dovyn, herding them back. An armsman who tried to attack the horses was crushed so savagely that others threw down their weapons at once. I had run to one side of the camp the moment the horses appeared. Now I saw Gahltha turning his head this way and that, clearly wondering why I was not beastspeaking him.

I drew breath to call his name, but a hand closed over my mouth, and I was lifted from my feet. My captor turned and ran with me into the trees bordering the camp. I could not fight because of my bound hands, and I could not summon help with my mind because of the demon band, so I tried to bite the hand pressed over my mouth in order to scream. I was suddenly hurled to the ground so hard that I was winded. It was dark away from the campfire and lanterns, but a shaft of light, reaching through the trees, briefly illuminated Malik's face, contorted with urgency as he used his kerchief to gag me. I could still hear the horses and men screaming and shouting when Malik threw me over his shoudler. Then he began to run, dodging trees and crashing over bushes and fallen branches. Gradually, the sounds of the camp faded into the monotonous thud of his boots and the snap of foliage breaking or swishing as it sprang back after we had passed. Malik was breathing hard but regularly, revealing his strength and stamina. My heart sank at the realization that he might go on in this steady way for half an hour. By then we would be far from the camp. Worse, I was sure that none of the horses had seen him take me.

Malik ran without stopping or slowing for what seemed an eternity. When he did finally stop, he was panting, but he clearly still possessed strength. He drank some water from a bottle on his belt, seemed to listen for a time, and then he set off in a slightly different direction, this time walking. I could hear nothing but the creak and rustle of trees and wondered where he was taking me. Not to the coast, as I had expected, to signal his Herder friends. As far as I could tell, we had traveled parallel to the road back to Saithwold town.

A sickening hour of hanging half upside down passed before Malik stopped and hurled me to the ground. Sheer luck kept me from hitting one of the snaking tree roots protruding from the leaf litter, but instinct made me lie very still as if I had been knocked unconscious. I could tell by Malik's breathing that he was weary now; if he felt safe enough to sleep, I might have a chance to escape, for my legs were not bound.

I heard Malik moving and sensed that he was looking into my face. I kept my breathing slow and even, knowing he would not be able to see clearly in the dappled tree shadow. There was a long silence, but I continued to feign unconsciousness. I was just beginning to think I must have been mistaken in thinking he had been looking at me when I felt a knife's cold edge against my face, and the gag fell away.

I gasped and opened my eyes to find Malik's moonlit face so close that I instinctively recoiled. He pressed the knife against my neck and gave me a cruel, knowing smile that exposed my hope of escaping as the foolishness it was. His eyes told me that I would never escape him. Not alive. I felt a shudder of terror as I suddenly understood that Malik had brought me with him not as a hostage, but to finish what he had begun in the camp. Madness glimmered in his eyes along with a pleasurable anticipation that told me he meant to take his time in killing me, exacting as much pain as he could. He wanted me to grovel in terror before him.

He sat back on his heels as if the fear in my eyes had assured him that I understood his intentions. He took the knife from my throat and ran his thumb across the edge of his blade in a caressing gesture, never taking his eyes off me. His nostrils quivered as if he hungered for even the odor of my fear.

"You are a monster and a coward," I said, looking directly into his eyes.

He laughed with real enjoyment. "You think I am that idiot Vos, to be taken in by feigned sleep or provoked to hasty action by an obvious attempt to anger me? No. I mean to take my time killing you, and nothing you do will hasten your dying. I have in mind to deprive you of all your senses first. Hearing, speech, smell, touch." He pressed his knife in turn to my ear, my lips, my nose, my bound hands as he spoke the name of each sense, and then he lifted the tip of his blade and rested it under my eye. "But first, your sight."

"You are wasting time in which you might escape." I tried to sound cold instead of frightened, but, oh, I was frightened. I had never been more afraid.

He said very calmly, "What makes you think I need to escape?" He grinned at the consternation I could not conceal, for his words seemed to imply that there was something I did not know. Was he referring to the invasion, or was there something else? His look of terrifying concentration quenched my attempts to think. He lifted his knife and kissed the flat of it in a deadly salute.

I closed my eyes and let terror roil through me and flow away. I turned my mind from what was to happen and pictured Maruman and Gahltha, Dameon, Dragon, Matthew. And Rushton. The memory of those I loved could not be cut out of me, I told myself fiercely. Even when I died, my vision of them would live on in the mindstream. I wished that I could harness my mind's power and give myself to the mindstream, depriving Malik of the satisfaction of hurting me, but the demon band would not allow it.

I summoned up a mental image of Rushton as he had been when we had parted last. I saw his coldness with compassion rather than disappointment and sorrow. I felt boundless gratitude that he had come into my life to show me how deeply I could love, and it was a little burst of light in that dark moment to realize that being able to love was life's real gift. Without those people and creatures who had made me love them, I would be a lesser being. Even the pain of loving was a gift that had deepened me.

I felt the knife point scratch along my cheek just under my eye like the single claw of a kitten—a testing, teasing touch. I kept my eyes closed and thought of my quest. There was an unexpected peace in surrendering to the knowledge that I could not fulfill it. I had been willing to give up everything, including my life, but now it was time to die. I would try to keep silent when he hurt me. I could do no more.

I heard a thump and resisted the temptation to open my eyes, certain that was what Malik was waiting for. He meant my last sight to be of him. Instead, I pictured Maruman. I saw his battered body and his single bright eye, and I waited.

Then I heard the breathing of two people, though I held my own. One was heavy and regular and the other, fast and uneven. I opened my eyes to see Kevrik leaning over an unconscious Malik. He looked up at me and grinned. "I hit him hard enow to brain a bull, but he's still breathing."

"Oh, Kevrik," I gasped. "I have never been so glad to see anyone!"

"Doubtless," the armsman said wryly. He gently pulled me upright and grabbed Malik's knife to cut the ropes about my wrists. I shook my head and asked him to untie them. "We will need the rope for him," I croaked, nodding at the unconscious Malik.

Kevrik laid aside the knife and set about loosening the ropes, talking as he worked. "I've been following ye since he took ye from the camp. I thought he would nivver stop. Then when he did, I heard what he said, an' I was afeard he'd stab ye afore I could get near enow to hit him with the rock. It was cursed ill luck that I dinna have my dagger." He frowned over a stubborn knot. "I have nivver seen anyone look at any creature wi' as much black hate as Malik looked at ye before he struck ye. An' when it took me longer than I expected to fall far enough behind Vos an' th' others so I could turn back to th' camp, I near went mad. I was sickened by what he had done to ye, but more sickened by the fact that others did nowt to stop him. Men I have laughed and drunk ale with and regarded as strong and courageous, all standin' by and watching a man beat a bound maid." He grimaced as if he had bitten into something foul.

"When I finally came within sight of Malik's camp an' saw ye'd nowt been kilt, I was so relieved that I dinna wonder why ye were nowt talking to me inside my head as ye said ye'd do in that dream ye put in my mind when I was unconscious outside the cells. When I did notice an' wonder, I thought maybe ye'd been stunned. I was still ditherin' like a ninnyhammer when the horses Vos an' his men had ridden came gallopin' hell fer leather along the road. It was only because I'd been looking at ye that I saw Malik grab ye. If I'd blinked, I would ha'e missed it. I just plunged after ye."

The ropes loosened and fell away, and the armsman began to massage my wrists gently. I winced at the pain, but that pain was life, and incredulous joy swept through me. I had expected to die. I had prepared myself for it, and yet here I was, still alive. My quest had not relinquished me after all. Kevrik unhooked a water bladder from his belt, and I took it from him gratefully and drank. Then he took a long draft and restored it to his belt.

"What now?" he asked.

The welling delight I had felt a moment before faded as I thought of Gahltha and the horses. "I need to return to Malik's camp. I was so sure I would be there to tell the horses what to do that I told them nothing save that they should stampede the camp and disarm as many men as they could. But even if they succeeded in that, how can horses keep humans prisoner?"

"It's a long walk back," Kevrik said. "The best or worst will have happened by now."

I felt sick at the knowledge that he was right. "Do you

think we are closer to the road or the old cloister?" I asked.

"The road," Kevrik said decisively. "But it's still a good long walk. More if ye mean to bring him."

"I'm afraid we've no choice," I said. I plucked at the demon band about my throat. "I wish I could get this off, because then I could farseek Zarak to come and help us." Malik stirred and groaned. "Better tie him up well before he wakes. Then we'll make a litter and drag him between us."

"I can carry him some of the way," Kevrik said as he tied the chieftain's hands.

I fashioned bandage sandals for myself from strips of Malik's shirt. Then I helped Kevrik get the rebel across his shoulders, grateful the armsman was almost as big as the chieftain. Even so, Kevrik staggered slightly under his burden before standing upright. We walked almost a half hour before Kevrik's knees began to buckle. While he rested, I used the time to replenish the tattered bandage sandals. Then we constructed a rough litter. I did not look forward to pulling it, for my stomach hurt, and a fierce jabbing pain in my chest suggested that Malik had cracked one of my lower ribs. But worst was the weariness as my body fought to repair the damage and cope with the netted fatigue I had released. When we rested again after another bout of walking and dragging the litter, I had to fight the overpowering urge to just lie down and sleep.

When we headed off again, the moon had set and the forest darkened, making it harder to see our way. It was growing cold, too. This, as much as a desire to reach the road and find out what had been happening, kept us moving. As always when I was in physical discomfort, I found myself longing for absurd luxuries instead of simple necessities: a freshly made bed or a long soak in one of the hot springs in a mountain valley. I imagined eating a fresh-baked roll with butter melting into it as I sat in the battered chair that stood on my little turret-room balcony, Maruman lying on my lap.

Thinking of Maruman frightened me, because Gahltha had said the old cat intended to seek me out, but he had not done so. Hours had passed between the time the others had been taken from Noviny's place and when the armsmen had returned for me—easily time enough for Maruman to have found his way to me. I feared less that he had been injured than that what happened had sent him into one of his fey wandering states.

I wondered if the blue-black night sky would ever lighten. It was impossible to believe that it had only been the previous evening when I had sat in the wagon on Noviny's property, listening to the rain and brewing soup.

"How long until the sun rises?" I asked.

"Three hours maybe," Kevrik panted, squinting up at the sky. The next time we stopped, I borrowed Malik's knife and nearly cut my throat trying to pick the demon band's lock so we could summon aid. Kevrik tried, too, but after only a minute he shook his head and said he had not the nerve for it. I must be patient and he would get a key for the band.

Malik muttered something in a slurred voice, and Kevrik and I exchanged an alarmed look. He was definitely waking. The highlander fetched a stone and gave the chieftain a solid knock on the head. By the time we went on again, the sky was lightening to a deep indigo. To pass the time and to take my mind off the horses, I asked Kevrik what happened after he had awoken outside the cell in Vos's homestead.

The guard had awakened him, he said. The man remembered being hit by Kevrik, who had pretended to recall nothing and "noticed" that neither was now wearing a demon band. Kevrik remembered all that had happened between us, of course, but he also had a "memory" in which I told him how he had been knocked out and how I had decided to use this accident to make sure Vos did not regard him with suspicion. Kevrik then told the cell guard that the alarm bells they could hear must signal the capture of the Misfit who had tampered with their minds. Ironically, that had been the simple truth, and Kevrik had arrived just in time to do as I had asked: suggest to Vos that I be taken at once to Malik's camp.

"You took a great risk, yet still I do not understand what you meant to achieve."

"How else could I have made sure that I would be in the camp when the horses stampeded? I knew that we needed to overcome Malik and his men and take them prisoner as swiftly as possible so that someone could be sent to Sutrium to warn the Council of Chieftains about the invasion. Of course, I did not bargain on Malik grabbing me, but I daresay he did not bargain on you. How many of your men will stand with us if they know the truth about Malik's plan?"

"A good many of them," Kevrik answered. "Once they are convinced it is not a trick. I would suggest letting Noviny speak to them. He is known as an honorable man."

We walked very slowly now, for we were both weary, and my bandage sandals were wearing thin once more. Kevrik began to talk again, perhaps to distract himself from fatigue. He said that he had tried to saddle Gahltha to ride to Malik's camp, thinking the black horse would want to go along. But Gahltha had backed away so determinedly that the armsman realized he had some other instruction.

"He was to release the other horses from the corral and deal with the armsmen who would try to stop them," I said.

He nodded. "I realized as much when th' black horse an'

th' rest came past the tree where I was hidin'. I could tell they kenned I was there an' on their side because your black horse came an' butted his head against me." He laughed softly at the memory. "Then th' other horses came gallopin' along the road an' stampeded through the camp. Your black horse leapt out and the rest followed. No wonder Malik an' his men stood there like dolts through it."

We both fell silent, lacking the breath for anything but dragging. Then, at long last, just as the rising sun stained the sky with a pink and lemon glow, we saw the road.

Not until we had almost reached it did I notice the dead armsman lying in the middle of the road. From the queer horrible angle of his neck, he looked as if he had broken it when thrown from his horse. Sickened, I wondered how many men had died as a result of my commands.

We propped Malik against a sturdy tree, and Kevrik dragged the armsman's body off the road, for it seemed disrespectful to leave it lying there. I was shocked to see him riffle through the man's pockets, but then he held up a small gray key with a shout of triumph, and a moment later the demon band was unlocked.

I resisted the urge to hurl the loathsome thing into the trees and instead set it on the ground, knowing that sooner or later, someone was going to have to clean up the tainted material around Saithwold. Then I gave over thinking in the sheer joy of being able to send my mind spinning out. Having briefly experienced normality, I thought it such a wretched limited state that I wondered how Malik could value it so.

First I sought out Gahltha. He was still at Malik's camp, and his welcome and relief were no less than mine at finding him safe. To my amazement, he said the horses were in control of Malik's camp. The uninjured armsmen were penned up against the cliff edge, guarded by horses. Gahltha had sent Dovyn and a few horses back to Vos's property, for the gray horse had a plan to ensure the humans there did not leave. They were too far away for him to beastspeak, Gahltha explained, but he was confident that Dovyn would manage, despite the fact that the men had weapons and a house to take refuge in. Indeed, he seemed surprised at how worried I had been. It occurred to me with some shame that, in imagining they would need a human captain, I had underestimated the horses almost as much as Malik had.

Predictably, Gahltha wanted to come and get me at once, but I insisted that I was safe and bade him stay to keep a close watch over his human prisoners. "We can't risk any of them signaling the Herders; they might call off the invasion."

"Is that not what you want?"

"It was, but now it seems we ought to let them land so we can take their ships, as Zarak suggested."

During the laborious walk through the trees, I had done some thinking about Zarak's idea of permitting the invasion so we could commandeer the ships. It would be a brilliant coup, allowing us not only a swift and unexpected way to reach the west coast, but also the means of bringing Dragon to the Red Land. To simply turn back the invaders would be a lesser victory, and the Faction warriors would be stronger when they invaded next. My only fear now, other than someone signaling the Herders, was that Malik might have planned to give some final signal to let the Faction know it was safe to land. The only way of learning would be to probe Malik. This would also allow us to learn the exact timing of the invasion. The thought of delving into Malik's mind filled me with revulsion even as Kevrik removed the unconscious man's demon band.

Withdrawing from Gahltha, I tried to farseek Zarak, but I realized he and the others must have set up camp close to the cloister's tainted walls, for the probe would not locate. I sent my mind back to Gahltha, asking him to send a horse to let Zarak and the others know what had happened and to suggest they bring the wagon in the direction of Noviny's property, where they would find Kevrik and me waiting by the roadside.

I farsought Dovyn, who sent that many of the thrown riders had walked back to the homestead by the time he and the other horses had returned. Dovyn said the humans believed that the horses had been forced to throw their riders. Instead of regarding them as enemies, they had begun herding them into the corral. Dovyn had expected this, and he had urged his equine warriors to allow themselves to be corralled, for Gahltha had shown them how to unlatch the gate and escape whenever they wished.

Nothing had happened for some time, and then several funaga-li came to saddle horses and ride off. The horses had thrown them as soon as they were out of sight of the homestead and returned at once, to the evident dismay of the humans, again allowing themselves to be caught. As Dovyn had surmised, the funaga-li were incapable of understanding that the horses acted under their own volition, and all of them had retreated into the house, clearly believing they were under siege by a human army. Soon the doors and windows of the homestead were bristling with armsmen who shot arrows out into the darkness all night long, though no one had approached. I could guess that Vos imagined an army of vicious Misfits surrounding his property and killing every rider he sent out.

Stifling laughter, I asked what had happened to the

thrown humans, and Dovyn explained that dogs had been enlisted to keep watch over them. The two species did not normally cooperate in this way, but neither did they normally make war on funaga. The gray horse added that dogs were perfect guards, because their acute sense of smell allowed them to scent the intention of a captive funaga-li to attack or attempt escape. I guessed their human prisoners were far more unnerved at being attacked and guarded by a pack of dogs and horses than they would have been by a group of humans.

There had been no arrows fired since dawn, Dovyn sent, for the funaga-li had been able to see that there were no enemies creeping closer. Vos must be sadly puzzled about what was going on. He would have discovered by now that his prisoners had vanished, and he could have no idea how that had happened.

Dovyn also told me that the men at the blockade had fled at the sight of riderless horses galloping back from Malik's camp.

I felt a touch on my arm and bade Dovyn farewell. When I opened my eyes, Kevrik nodded at Malik.

He looked unconscious, but if he was awake, I wanted to know it. I shaped a probe and had barely entered the black tumult of his mind when I was engulfed by a ghastly vision of torture, where I was the victim and Malik stood over me with bloodied hands. His eyes flew open.

"Get out of my mind," Malik hissed through gritted teeth.

I withdrew, shaken to discover that he was mind-sensitive. It explained much, though not all. I wondered what he would say if I told him of Garth's belief that this sensitivity was itself a minor Talent, which made him a Misfit, too.

"Check his ropes," I told Kevrik calmly, holding Malik's

burning gaze. Then I said coldly and purposefully, "I have no wish to enter the cesspit of cruelty and violence that you call a mind, Malik, but I will do so if you speak another word that angers or offends me, or if you try to escape. I will enter it and wipe it clean. Do not doubt that I can do it."

Malik seemed to teeter on the point of exploding; then abruptly all the tension melted out of him and his face grew calm. Watching this transformation, unease snaked through me, and I remembered his avowal that he had no need to plan an escape. To find out if he was referring to something other than the invasion, I would have to probe him. I decided it could wait until I reached Vos's homestead.

"You and your kind—" Malik began.

"Are here to stay," I concluded savagely. "Now keep your mouth shut, for I meant my threat." I turned my back on him. I was trembling slightly, but not out of fear. Malik's relentless hatred had disturbed the black killing power deep inside me. I felt it stir, like someone sleeping, almost waking, and then settling back. It frightened me. The last time I had fully awakened that power, it had proven to have a dark will of its own, and I had a ghastly vision of myself coercing Malik to cut his throat or set himself on fire.

To distract myself, I tried farseeking Zarak again, and this time my probe located immediately. "Where are you?" I asked.

"We are coming to get ye just as Gahltha told me ye wanted. We have just turned onto th' main road," Zarak sent. "I suppose ye could nowt reach us before, because we were camped inside the cloister walls. It was empty as ye thought, though it looks as if something had been planned there, fer there is a great pile of earth an' rock just inside the walls, an' all manner of tools. To tell ye th' truth, I regretted settin' up inside, fer the cloister is a strange creepy place full of ghostly

174

bumps and echoes. We were in the midst of breakin' camp to move outside th' walls fer tonight when Gahltha's messenger galloped up. Is it true ye were Malik's captive?"

I winced. "I will explain everything later," I sent briskly. "Right now, Malik is my prisoner, and Malik's men and Vos and his men are sieged by the horses. They have done brilliantly, but they need some human hands to deal with their prisoners. Ask Noviny to start thinking about who we can ask for help."

"I'd like to know how the horses managed to get away from Vos and his men," Zarak said, and then laughed. "I know! Ye'll explain everything later. There is one other thing, Guildmistress," Zarak said, and the tone of his voice was suddenly subdued. "You should know that Darius is worse."

A chill ran through me. Yet how should we have achieved so much without any casualties? Did not life always demand its sacrifice? I sent to Zarak to ask Wenda about the most experienced healer in the region, determined to send for that person as soon as possible, but then I felt Kevrik's hand on my arm again. I opened my eyes to see him looking with consternation toward Saithwold town. I followed his gaze and almost groaned aloud to see men on horses galloping toward us. They could only be armsmen who had been stationed at the main barricade or who were searching for me, and I cursed myself for lacking the wit to stay off the road and out of sight. Too late now to untie Malik and hide with him, for if we could see the riders, they could certainly see us.

"There is no need for you to be caught," I told Kevrik. "Go into the trees and hide. Wait for my friends in the wagon."

"I will stand with ye," Kevrik said stoutly. "They will be Vos's men, so maybe I can convince them of the treachery Malik planned."

From the corner of my eye, I saw Malik give the armsman a look of burning fury. But I had no time to think of him. I stepped into the road and shaped a beastspeaking call, praying that one of the approaching horses was unbanded. To my surprise, my probe slid into the lead horse's mind as smoothly as a hot knife into butter. Then I realized why. I knew her.

"Esred!" I sent, hardly able to believe my own senses. The horse responded with delight, but as she returned my greeting, incredulous relief splintered into a confusion of longing and despair, for riding upon her back was the Master of Obernewtyn.

Rushton.

PART II

◆

SONG OF THE WAVES

✦ 11 ✦

RUSHTON CLIMBED DOWN from Esred and went to help Dameon off Faraf. The long-legged Empath guildmaster ought to have looked absurd on the small pony, but Dameon had a way of conferring dignity on anything he did. Rushton hung back to allow Dameon to sense his way to me. I ought to have been glad, as my feelings for the Empath guildmaster were a good deal less complicated than those roused by Rushton. But what I longed to do with a passion that shocked me was to rush over and fling myself into Rushton's arms. Ironically, that was a thing I had never allowed myself to do, even in the days when it might have been welcomed.

Dameon embraced me, and I gave myself to the kindness and affection that flowed from the empath as naturally as warmth from the sun. Fortunately, affection for me had not caused him to abandon the emotional barrier he erected habitually to protect him from the overwhelming force of other people's emotions, because the fierce tangle of emotions I was experiencing would have felled him.

"So, you are a rider now," I said. "How does it feel?"

"Painful, but only in one place," Dameon said dryly in his cultured lowland voice. He held me a little away from him now, and his milky eyes seemed to examine my face. "What have you been up to?"

"I will tell you in a moment," I temporized. "First tell me

179

how in Lud's name all of you come to be here."

"Maryon," Dameon said simply.

Of course. "Would that the Futuretell guildmistress had seen that we were riding into danger in Saithwold *before* we left Obernewtyn," I said tartly.

"She visioned it the day after you left," Dameon said. "Of course, the knights would have ridden out at once to stop you, but Maryon—"

"The Futuretell guildmistress said you must not be stopped." Rushton finished his sentence.

My skin prickled at the sound of his velvety voice, with its grainy hint of highland accent. Girding myself, I looked into his handsome, craggy face, into dark green eyes that had once caressed me as tenderly as his hands had done. Something inside me ached and twisted, but I was careful to offer only my cool guildmistress's expression, knowing he wanted no more than that from me, as I asked calmly, "Why?"

"What happened to your face?" Rushton asked in a strange, flat voice.

I lifted my hand to my cut lip self-consciously, realizing I probably looked dreadful. And what did Rushton feel seeing me like that? Certainly there was no hint of emotion in his expression. "This is nothing," I told him lightly. "I would have been dead if not for Kevrik. He is, or I should say, was, one of Vos's men." I looked at the armsman. "This is the Master of Obernewtyn, Rushton Seraphim."

Several expressions chased themselves across the highlander's face, but he stowed Malik's knife and said solemnly, "Sirrah, I am pleased to meet ye. I have always been taught to regard Misfits as dangerous human-shaped beasts or worse. I am shamed now by my former ignorance. I have nivver seen such courage and determination as this young woman has shown, an' if all Misfits are like her, then 'tis an honor indeed to meet their master, be ye beast or human or some part of both."

"There is none to match the guildmistress of the farseekers," Rushton said, but there was no warmth in his voice.

"You asked what Maryon foresaw to stop us coming after you immediately, Guildmistress," Rushton said. "She said that despite the danger you would face, you would avert a catastrophe. I assume that the prediction had somewhat to do with your prisoner." He glanced at Malik, who gave him a stony look, then added, "Maryon was almost certain you would triumph without our help."

"Almost certain," I echoed, and was startled by how bitter I sounded.

Of course, I understood. If I had been stopped from entering Saithwold, no one would know about the invasion. Or if they had come soon after I had entered Saithwold, Malik would have warned the Herders to postpone their invasion, and it would only have been his word against Noviny's if he were accused. Instead, I had come to Saithwold, and with Kevrik's help and the horses' courage and cleverness, I had triumphed over Malik. Maryon had been right, yet I could not help but remember that dreadful moment when Malik had held his knife to my eye.

"What has been happening here?" Rushton asked with a touch of impatience.

I told them almost everything, from Brydda's assistance in getting us through the barricade to my rescue by Kevrik, and I watched Malik pale when I told of the invasion. By the time I had finished my story, his expression was stony again, giving away nothing.

I concluded by telling them Zarak's idea about taking the

invaders' ships. "But before we can plan anything, we will need to coerce the details of the invasion out of Malik."

"I will take him to Sutrium this night, so one of the knights can coerce all he knows from him, before the Council of Chieftains," Rushton said. "We must ensure that no one can accuse us of putting words in his mouth."

"Where are Zarak and the others now?" Dameon asked.

"They were hiding in the old cloister, but they ought to be along any time," I said. "We were going to Vos's property—"

"We will ride ahead to secure it," Rushton said decidedly and bade Asra and Hilder ride to Malik's camp to help Gahltha and the other horses herd their prisoners to Vos's property.

Dameon chuckled as the knights rode off. "This seems to have been as much a victory of beasts as of humans."

"Clearly, Maryon was right in saying you had no need of us," Rushton said coolly. There was something in his tone that I did not like, but before I could fasten on it, he turned to Kevrik. "Will you ride with us, armsman? You can speak with your fellow armsmen and explain what Malik has been about." When the armsman nodded, Rushton suggested that Dameon wait with me for the wagon so Kevrik could ride Faraf.

"I will bear the funaga-li as well as you," Esred sent to Rushton, stamping her hoof and farseeking to me and those who could hear her. "But tell him that if he so much as tickles my belly with his heels, I will give him a brand that will mark him forever." I took some pleasure in relaying the threat, but Malik said not a word as he was mounted up on the mare, his hands still tied behind his back.

Kevrik mounted Faraf gingerly, but she bore his weight stoically, commenting to me that she did not suppose they would gallop. Abruptly, as Kally and Linnet remounted, Rushton asked if it was Malik who had beaten me. I had carefully glossed over how I had got into Malik's hands, but even as I opened my mouth to suggest we exchange stories later, Kevrik began eagerly describing how I had been captured by Vos's men and taken to Malik. My heart sank as Rushton led the armsman deftly to relay what had happened at Malik's camp—in particular, the beating interspersed with questions.

"You watched and . . . did nothing?" Linnet asked him scornfully.

"If she had nowt made me promise to do nothing to interfere in what happened in Malik's camp, I could nivver have stayed still," Kevrik told her, flushing slightly. "But th' worst of it was when Malik grabbed her and ran, in the midst of the stampede. It was sheer luck that I saw her taken." He described the headlong run through the trees, and when he repeated Malik's threats just before he had rescued me, there was a profound silence.

"Thank you for saving the life of the guildmistress, for it is clear that she would not have survived her adventure without you," Rushton said. He turned to me and asked in a low, glacial voice, "Am I correct in assuming that you deliberately allowed yourself to be handed over to Malik? Does it matter at all to you that you contravened the agreement of all guild-leaders not to put themselves into danger?"

Anger rose in me, as clean and hard as a blade. "It is strange that you should object to my putting myself in danger, given that you and Maryon were prepared to allow me to ride here knowing there was danger waiting for me. At least I chose it with Malik, but neither you nor Maryon gave me the choice. Why did you not come after me and simply tell me what she had seen? Do you think I would have balked at coming here if you had told me that facing danger would enable me to avert a catastrophe? Have I given you such cause to doubt my courage? Was I not conveying Dragon to Sutrium, even though she hates me, because Maryon said I must? And what of *that* foreseeing?"

Rushton had grown very pale. "I asked that of Maryon, and she said that one foreseeing did not negate another, even when they appeared to conflict. You were to take Dragon when you left for Sutrium, and so she has gone to Sutrium. Nothing was said of you arriving with her, Maryon says. And her foreseeing concerning Saithwold was that no one must go after you, else you would not do what you were meant to do. You speak as if I chose this."

Dameon reached out to lay a quelling hand on Rushton's arm. "This is a difficult time, and it is not yet over," he said gently.

Rushton gave a jerky nod and said in an expressionless voice that he was sorry if I thought he had done wrong in obeying Maryon. He bowed to us both, turned on his heel, and mounted Esred behind Malik, saying that he would see us at Vos's homestead. In a moment, he and the others continued along the road.

Watching them ride away, I found myself thinking of the night before I had left Obernewtyn. Rushton had come to my chamber with the letter for Dardelan, which contained Obernewtyn's formal charges against Malik. Taking the missive, I had summoned the courage to ask why he had been avoiding me for most of the wintertime. Rushton had answered in a weary voice, "Do you not understand, Elspeth, you who are so bright? Is it not obvious? There is nothing left in me to feel emotions with."

The quaking in me grew, and I began to tremble so hard

that my teeth chattered. I was furious with my weakness, but I could not stop. Dameon gave an inarticulate exclamation and put his arms around me, drawing me close.

"You are in shock, dear one," he said compassionately, leading me to the side of the road. "Let us sit down to wait for the wagon."

As soon as we were seated, he began to emanate a low, soothing flow of emotions. He told me of a walk he had taken through Obernewtyn's orchards with Alad to visit the teknoguilders in their caves. He had sensed that they were being followed by the strange, silent boy Gavyn, whom beasts called *adantar*. Dameon had called his name, and I imagined the boy stepping out and coming to the blind empath, accompanied by the dog Rasial, who had become leader of the Beastguild at Obernewtyn in the absence of the mare Avra.

"He so rarely speaks, and yet I felt his desire to communicate very strongly," Dameon said softly. "I asked if he wanted to tell me something, and he said that Seely was coming to see him."

"*Seely!*" I echoed.

Before the rebellion, the unTalented Seely had fled with her young Misfit charge all the way to the mountains from the west coast for fear of what the Council would do to the boy at the behest of his stepmother, Lady Slawyna, who guessed her stepson was a Misfit and wanted his Councilman father's property to pass to her own son.

I had found the pair and brought them to Obernewtyn, but during the rebellion, Seely had returned to the west coast with the teknoguilder Jak to help set up a refuge in the Beforetime ruins. Like all of the Misfits I had sent there to aid the rebel groups, she had been trapped there when the Suggredoon had been closed. Gavyn had never seemed to miss her, though he had once or twice mentioned dreaming of her. But how could she visit him unless the west coast was won from Council and Faction? Was this a sign that we would capture the invasion ships and use them to reach the west coast?

Forcing myself to calm down, I asked Dameon if, since my departure from Obernewtyn, there had been any new dreams of the Misfits I had sent to the west coast recorded in the dream journals. He said that he had inquired after the strange encounter with Gavyn, and there had been only one recorded dream. In it, the young empath Blyss and the coercer Merret had been waiting outside a city for a messenger from the rebel Gwynedd.

"The city must be Murmroth," I said, but Dameon shook his head, saying the dreamer had scribed that the city was right on the coast. Murmroth was the only coastal town not situated right on the coast.

"If messages are being exchanged between us and the rebels, it may be that Tardis is less opposed to us than she was," I said.

"I think hers was an inherited hatred rather than the fierce and fanatical hatred her father apparently had for Misfits, and it may be that circumstances have so altered in the west that old prejudices have melted away. But it might also be that something has happened to Tardis, because from what was said in the dream, it sounds as if Gwynedd is the leader of the Murmroth rebels now.

"And, no," Dameon went on, anticipating my next question with a smile, "there have been no dreams of Matthew, save for one brief dream I experienced only last night." The empath went on to describe the dream, in which Matthew and another man had been speaking of a ship anchored offshore from the Red Land, which rumor said was delivering a new shipment of slaves. Matthew had been insisting that the ship was the very same that had brought him to the Red Land, in which case it was likely to go back the way it had come once it had emptied its holds. The remainder of the discussion had been about the possibility of boarding the ship and stowing away, which both men had acknowledged as difficult and deadly. Then there had been some incomprehensible talk of something called The Spit, which Dameon said seemed to have put Matthew off the idea of stowing away.

"A true dream?" I asked, knowing it was always harder for Dameon to tell, for his dreams were scent and smell and sometimes taste dreams.

"It felt real, but it was too brief to be sure," the Empath guildmaster said.

Suddenly Dameon stiffened. "I hear a wagon."

I scrambled to my feet and saw the wagon in the distance. I farsought Zarak with relief and found that he already knew about the arrival of Rushton and the others, for Asra and Hilder had stopped to speak with them. But when Lo brought the wagon to a halt, Zarak looked shocked.

"What happened to your face?"

"It looks worse than it is," I said lightly, taking his hand and climbing into the back of the wagon. Darius lay bolstered on all sides by blankets and took up most of the floor space.

"We will send for a healer as soon as we can," I said as Zarak helped steer Dameon to the seat opposite his father, where there was room for his long legs. As the wagon lurched forward again, Khuria introduced Dameon to Noviny and his granddaughter. Dameon held out a hand, and Wenda put her own awkwardly into it. The empath released her hand and asked if she was a healer. She looked startled, nodded, and then flushed, realizing he could not see her.

Noviny asked me what had happened at Malik's camp, for Gahltha's equine messenger had not been much of a tale-teller. I obliged, describing the stampede and concentrating on the courage and brilliance of the horses. When I concluded, Noviny gave a great sigh and said it was a relief that he no longer had to worry himself sick trying to think how to notify the Council of Chieftains about the invasion.

I noticed the glimmer of metal at Darius's throat, and remembering the key Kevrik used to free me from my demon band, I drew it from my pocket and crouched down beside Darius to insert it into the lock. His waxen skin felt clammy and cold against my fingers as I unclipped the band and pulled it gently out from around his neck. Handing the key to Zarak to remove the other demon bands, I pulled the blanket higher around the gypsy's neck.

"Poor man," Wenda said as Zarak removed her band. "His limbs were already inflamed and giving him pain, and then he was so roughly handled by the armsmen. They did not care that he was hurt." She added, "I was able to find some good healing herbs near the cloister to bring the swelling down and ease his fever. But then he fell into this still, cold sleep. I do not know how to treat him, for I do not understand what ails him, unless it is shock. That can sometimes come after an event and have strange and deadly effects, especially on someone who is already ill."

"If it is shock, I can help him," Dameon said, and he asked Wenda to guide his hands to the cripple's chest. This done, he closed his eyes and concentrated. Then he drew back and shook his head. "He is not in shock," the empath said with authority. "There is something causing him so much hurt that he withdraws from life rather than endure it."

Dameon now turned his blind eyes to me. "I cannot cure what ails him, Elspeth, but I can help him rest more serenely until we reach the healing center in Sutrium."

I bade him do what he could, and we all watched in silence as the Empath guildmaster closed his eyes again. There was no sign of his empathising and no great change in Darius, except that, to me, his expression seemed to grow more peaceful. When Dameon opened his eyes again, he looked weary but serene as ever, and Wenda let out a breath she had unconsciously been holding.

"It must be confusing," she said, smiling shyly at Dameon, "to feel what another feels. How can you tell it is not your own feeling?"

Dameon gave a soft laugh. "There are times when it is *very* confusing to be an empath," he agreed.

By the time we came within sight of the gate to Vos's property, we were cramped and hot, but despite my eagerness to get out of the wagon, I bade the horses wait until I farsought Dovyn. He told me that Rushton and the funaga had arrived and had subdued the funaga-li, and he bade me enter without fear.

Presently, Zade and Lo were unhitched from the wagon and released to join the other horses grazing peaceably on the homestead's green lawn. The rest of us stretched our limbs gratefully, save Wenda who said she would remain in the wagon with Darius until he could be carried to a bed. Sover, standing by, heard her and promised to arrange it at once. He was that rarity, a coercer with secondary abilities as an empath.

He went into the house and returned with Rushton and several frightened-looking servants. As Zarak, Sover, and

Harwood gently lifted the injured gypsy, Rushton greeted Noviny, who introduced his granddaughter, naming her a healer and explaining that she had been caring for Darius. Rushton bowed to the girl, thanking her so warmly for her care of the crippled gypsy that she blushed prettily. To my shame, I felt an ugly stab of jealousy at this proof that only I left the Master of Obernewtyn cold.

You are a fool, I told myself savagely, and felt Dameon flinch. Contrite, I reined in my emotions and forced myself to calmly ask Rushton what had happened upon their arrival. As he turned to answer me, I saw his reluctance, and it made me realize something that I had not known or maybe had not wanted to acknowledge. It was not that Rushton felt nothing for me. It was the opposite. It was as if he constantly struggled to control a powerful aversion to me. This thought gave me such pain that I nearly gasped, and I was glad for Dameon's sake that he had moved away.

As if from a great distance, I heard Rushton explain that it had been a simple matter to take control, since Vos gave himself up as soon as he saw them ride in with Malik as their prisoner. The rebel leader had been horrified to learn Malik's true intentions and insisted that he had known nothing of this dastardly plot, that everything from the barricades to the attempt to have himself made chieftain had been Malik's idea. He had been tricked and bullied. Rushton said this speech had made Malik turn a look of such blazing fury on the rebel chieftain that Vos had nearly passed out. Vos was now confined to his room, as were those of his men whom Kevrik said could be trusted. The rest were in the cells.

As we all went inside the house, Rushton told Noviny that he and some of the knights would be taking Malik to Sutrium as soon as they had eaten.

"Perhaps you would like to come. I believe it would be far more effective for you to tell the Council of Chieftains what you saw that day from the cliff rather than our reporting it secondhand," Rushton said.

I did not hear Noviny's answer, because Linnet was telling me that she had prepared a room and a bath for me.

I sank blissfully to my neck in a bathing barrel filled with fragrant hot water. The air was full of steam and made me feel as if I had drifted into a dream, but I made myself wash my cuts and my hair until it floated about me like strands of black silk.

There was a soft knock at the door.

A swift probe revealed that it was Dameon and not Rushton, as my treacherous heart had hoped. "Come in," I called, and after a slight hesitation, he entered, gasping a little at the clouds of steam that enveloped him, and then his face turned toward me unerringly.

"I have been sent to fetch you for the meal," he said, standing in the doorway.

"I am just trying to summon the energy to get out," I said.

Dameon smiled, but there was an awkwardness in his expression. For a moment, it came to me that he was troubled at my being in a bathing barrel, but then I chided myself for being absurd. Even if I had stood naked before the empath, he would not be able to see me. Something else must be bothering him. Ashamed that I had been so full of my own troubles and doings that I had not even thought to ask Dameon how he had been faring, I said, "Stay a little and talk to me, if you can bear the steam. There is a bench along the wall on your left where you can sit."

He made his way to the seat so clumsily that I was

startled. Dameon's usual grace made it hard to believe that he did not see. Then I almost laughed as I realized he was in pain! I remembered all too well the awfulness of my early riding days, and I asked, as delicately as I could, how he felt. He took my meaning at once and laughed, seeming suddenly to relax.

"Wenda has given me some salve that I am told will help." His smile faded. "In truth, I am more bothered by imagining you at Malik's mercy than by my own small discomforts. Do you think he meant to kill you?"

"I think when he beat me in front of Vos, he was making a point to him and his men. But the more he hit me, the more he wanted to hit me."

"I cannot bear to be near him," Dameon confessed. "His hatred is like some putrid fountain whose noise and stench I cannot ignore."

I sighed. "I wonder how the other rebels will react to all that has happened here. Especially those who have supported Malik."

"Rushton wants to question him in front of the other chieftains to make sure we cannot be accused of falsifying anything. But it is my feeling that his former allies will discover they always suspected him of being a traitor," Dameon said with rare cynicism. "Ironically, his treachery is more likely to bring peace and stability to the Land than anything anyone else has done, because no matter what the individual chieftains believe or how their desires conflict, none of them wants the Councilmen or the Herder Faction back. Their outrage at Malik's betrayal will force the chieftains to stand united for the first time since the rebellion was won, and they will have to work together to meet this threat, rather than concentrating on their own regions. Rushton hopes that Dardelan will use the threat of invasion as a reason to postpone the elections a moon or so, and that will please the rebels, too. Indeed, it may be put off longer still if Dardelan decides to do as Zarak has suggested and take the ships, for he is certain to want to use them immediately to surprise those on the west coast."

As he spoke, I climbed out of the barrel and began to towel myself. Dameon tilted his head, his sensitive hearing allowing him to track my movements as I padded over to the clothes Linnet had left me.

"Tell me how Maryon's futuretelling came about," I said, taking a towel to my hair again now that I was dressed.

Dameon nodded. "I was in a meeting with Rushton and the coercer-knights when one of the younger futuretellers came running in to say her mistress wanted us urgently. When we arrived at the Futuretell guildhall, Maryon was still drifting in and out of a trance. She told us much that seemed to have no meaning, but what was most important and unambiguous was that danger awaited you in Saithwold. The coercer-knights set up a great baying that you must be rescued. But Maryon bade them be silent, for she needed to think. Then she was quiet again for a long time. At last she said that no one must go after you, because a path awaited you in Saithwold that was yours alone to tread. There was some puzzlement at this, because Zarak at least would be with you, unless something was to happen to them. Rushton asked, but Maryon said she did not see anyone in your party coming to permanent harm. You were the only one in danger, and the probability of your surviving was high.

"Rushton asked what was so dangerous to you in particular, but Maryon just said there was danger there that would eventually threaten everyone in the Land and that your going to Saithwold would avert a catastrophe. Then she mentioned something about ships, which made no sense until you told us of the invasion and Zarak's idea about capturing the ships."

"So Rushton agreed to let things unfold as they would?" I asked coolly.

Dameon laughed. "He told Maryon in that icy, cutting tone he sometimes has, which is worse than being shouted at, that she ought not to tell us someone was in danger if we were to do nothing about it. Maryon only said rather loftily that we would need to ride to your aid but not yet. She would let us know when it was the right time. And so she did, though it seems that you had managed everything by the time we arrived. Unless our part is to finish what you have begun by taking Malik to Sutrium."

"You saved me from having to coerce Malik," I said fervently. "For that I am more than grateful."

Dameon stood and said gently that he had better go back to the others or they might think he had lost his way. At the door, he turned back to tell me that Gahltha and the prisoners—scathed and unscathed—from Malik's camp had arrived and had been dealt with.

After he had gone, I crossed to the mirror that hung by the door to comb and plait my hair. Wiping the moisture from the glass's surface, I grimaced at the sight of my battered face. Before the bath, many of the bruises and grazes had looked like dirt. But now that I was clean, I saw that the whole of one cheek and my temple were a mass of black and blue swelling around a long angry-looking gash. My lip was also swollen and split in two places, and I had a spectacular black eye.

I sighed and told myself I was lucky no one could see the bruises on my body.

⋆ 12 ⋆

THE PASSAGE WAS cold after the bathing room's steamy warmth, and I shivered as I padded along it toward the front of the homestead. I farsent Gahltha briefly and learned that he was in the midst of speaking with the other horses, so I withdrew, promising to come and see him later.

I did not know where the kitchen was, but I followed my nose to the big front room where Vos had interviewed me to find the carved chair had vanished and the pompous dais had become a trestle laden with platters. There was no formal seating, and everyone was merely filling plates of food and going to sit about a fire in the enormous hearth. I was startled to see a number of strangers filling their plates. Near me an old woman with a ruddy face spoke intently to a stocky younger man wearing farm clothes and an air of authority, and closer to the fire, two older men and a young woman were talking with Noviny.

There was a brief hiatus as I entered and everyone saw my face. In that momentary silence, I had the strange sensation that they all saw me as I truly was: an outsider who had only seemed to belong.

"Hurry up, Guildmistress," Zarak called, "or the savages will fall on this food I've managed to save for ye." There was a burst of laughter from the coercers about him, and the feeling of remoteness faded as I made my way to the fire.

Dameon smiled at me, seeming as ever to sense exactly where I was, and patted the seat beside him. Only then did I notice Maruman sitting on his lap, glaring balefully at me.

"Maruman!" I cried softly. But when I reached for him, the old cat hissed and turned his head away. I tried to enter his mind, but it was closed to me.

Dameon winced, giving me some indication of the level of Maruman's ire, and said, "Rushton sent Harwood and Yarrow to get him, and they only just returned. I am afraid Maruman did not much enjoy the ride."

I was grateful to Rushton for his thoughtfulness, though I had no doubt he had done it as much for Maruman as for me, for he had always been fond of the old cat. And I ought not to be surprised that Maruman was angry, since Gahltha had warned me that he had regarded my failure to return to the farmstead as a personal affront. An affronted Maruman was a formidable prospect, and I sat down and regarded him with longing. I took the plate Zarak handed me, asking, "Who are the strangers?"

"A couple are Vos's men that your Kevrik says can be trusted, and the others are locals Noviny sent for after Rushton asked him to summon a few of the leading members of this community capable of making serious decisions about Saithwold now that Vos and his followers have been ousted."

"But surely Noviny will—" I began.

"He would take over. Indeed, these locals asked it of him the moment he told them what had been happening. But Noviny has agreed to ride to Sutrium tonight with Rushton," Dameon said.

"If it were only a matter of governin' Saithwold, it could wait until he returns," Zarak put it. "They're takin' Vos with them as well," he added, scowling. "As a *witness*."

"A witness!" I echoed wrathfully. "He meant to cheat in the elections, he allowed your father to be tortured, and he unlawfully imprisoned Noviny and the others of his own free will! And he was going to let one of Malik's men kill Darius and torture you!"

Dameon laid a restraining hand on my arm, nodding pointedly at Maruman sleeping in his lap. But he only said, "A contrite and helpful Vos will be of far more use than a resentful prisoner, since he will not be disagreeing with everything that is said and defending himself. Indeed, he has already voluntarily handed chieftainship of Saithwold to Noviny, saying it has been a burden that he is glad to set down, if you can believe it."

"I can believe he said it," I replied, determined that once the invasion had been dealt with, I would lay charges against Vos to the Council of Chieftains.

Rushton raised his voice to announce that he and Noviny and some of the others would ride to Sutrium with Malik within the hour. "Other than that, I want to remind you of the urgent need to make sure that word of what has happened does not leak out of this province. For that reason, neither barricade will be removed at this time. Some of Vos's men, recommended to us by Kevrik, will man it so nothing here will appear to have changed. A coercer will be at each barrier at all times, dressed as an armsman and ready to probe those wanting to enter the region, in case they serve Malik. Those wearing demon bands are to be taken prisoner and coerced after their bands are removed to see if they are aligned with Malik. Malik's camp will be reconstructed and peopled by coercers clad in his colors. Anyone who comes to the camp for any reason is to be taken prisoner."

He glanced at the little group of townsmen. "Life here

should appear unchanged to those outside this room, until we can find out what Malik knows and High Chieftain Dardelan summons a force to deal with the invaders. By my reckoning, that will take no more than a threeday."

He added that after the invasion had been dealt with, those armsmen who had served Malik would be taken to Sutrium to be judged, but for the time being they would remain in cells beneath the homestead.

Then he turned again to the townsfolk. "We are relying upon you locals to monitor your neighbors and make sure you do all you can to prevent any rumor starting about changes here," he told them sternly. "I know that some of you are concerned about being dishonest to friends and even family, but console yourself that this is for a short period and that it is only to protect them and the Land. Soon you will vote for a new leader, and both peace and freedom will return to Saithwold province."

"It will return when Noviny is chieftain," said a woman whom I suddenly recognized as the one who had served Wenda and me in the shop. Those about her laughed and said aye, and Rushton smiled, too, dropping his stern expression for a moment. Then he continued seriously. "I have no doubt who you will choose to lead you when you are free, but for now, remember that it is Noviny who chose *you* to serve Saithwold through the dangerous days that lie ahead. I leave here the head of the coercer-knights, Linnet, to advise you and to aid you, as well as to perform the duties I have mentioned. If you have any trouble or fear during this time, send a messenger to seek out Linnet, and she or another knight will come to your assistance. If you see her and the other knights about with Vos's men or even Malik's men, have no fear. They will be coercing them.

"Finally," Rushton continued, his eyes moving to the fire where I sat between Zarak and Dameon, "Elspeth, guild-mistress of the farseekers, who has been instrumental in defeating Malik and freeing Saithwold and is a powerful coercer, and Dameon, who is guildmaster of the empaths at Obernewtyn, will remain to act as joint chieftains until Noviny returns. Know that it was Noviny's suggestion and one of which I heartily approve. They will coordinate the activities of the coercer-knights, and for the time being, it is to them you must look when you need guidance."

I clenched my teeth, outraged that Rushton had not bothered to consult me before deciding that I would remain in Saithwold rather than go on to Sutrium. As if he felt my indignation, Rushton's eyes, green and unreadable, met mine briefly. Then he turned to speak to one of Vos's armsmen. The noise level rose again, but instead of engaging in the conversations about me, I picked at the food on my plate, my appetite gone.

Maruman turned to glower at me and leapt down from Dameon's lap to stalk over to a partially opened window. I half rose to go after him, but Dameon caught my arm to stay me, saying gently, "Let him go, Elspeth. You are too emotional to deal with him right now."

Knowing he was right, I sat back down. Rushton was coming toward the fire with Noviny and Linnet. The older man was describing the Herder warriors' training exercises, which he had witnessed, and gradually the heat in my anger faded as I listened, for he might have been describing coercer training, with its emphasis on breathing and balance as well as on strength. Noviny added that the warrior priests' favored weapons were a short metal-shod pole and a handheld sickle-shaped blade.

Noviny went on to say that although the warrior priests wore robes and had their heads shaven, there were distinct differences between them and ordinary priests, even in their attire. The tunics of the warrior priests were a much darker gray than the traditional pale gray worn by Herders and were split on one side so they could reach their weapons, which they carried in holsters attached to belts.

Hearing this, Linnet suggested they must see themselves more as warriors than priests.

"I am not sure that is true," Noviny said. "When I heard the warrior priests speak and move about, it seemed that they see their weapons and their ability to fight as a kind of prayer that they dedicate to Lud. For them, fighting is praying."

Again prompted by Rushton, he speculated about the increase in numbers of the warrior priests just before the rebellion and about how many more there would be if the priests had trained as warriors the hundreds of acolytes and novices who had fled with the rest to Herder Isle. The figures he mentioned took my breath away.

Rushton thought for a moment. "Given what you have said, Noviny, I think a coercer would be a match for a warrior priest in an equal battle, and though they may exceed the number of coercers we can muster, the cliff paths are all too narrow for more than one person to ascend at a time. Even so, we would need to capture the warrior priests immediately and silently so as not to warn those coming behind. We cannot allow them to form a massed force."

I was still infuriated with Rushton's decision to keep me in Saithwold, but I could not undermine his authority before the others, so I said in a voice harsh enough to show my anger, "The warrior priests are certain to wear demon bands, so the coercers' Talents will be useless."

Before Rushton could respond, one of the locals called out to say he hoped *they* would not be expected to fight, for what had farm folk to do with battles.

Rushton turned to look at the man, but when he spoke, he spoke to all those gathered. "There is a battle to come, make no mistake about it, and it will be fought in this region. The coercers from Obernewtyn will fight, but understand that this is not a battle between Misfits and Herders. Nor are the rebel conquerors defending a land they have stolen from others. We are all—Misfits, rebels, and ordinary Landfolk—free men and women who must fight to remain so. This will be *our* battle for *our* Land.

"As for the details of our defense, that is not something that can be decided here." His eyes flickered my way without ever meeting my gaze. "That will happen in Sutrium once we have learned the precise details of the invasion from Malik."

Noviny went to speak with the man who had spoken, and Rushton turned back to me. "I am sorry I did not have the chance to warn you about what I would say, but I assumed you would wish to remain until Darius can be taken safely to his people. That will be at least a sevenday according to the healer who now tends him," he said in a low voice.

His explanation ought to have mollified me, but his cool formality stripped the words of comfort. I was still trying to think how to respond when Zarak said, "I have been thinkin' on how we can gan to the invaders' ships without havin' to fight our way to them. Noviny was tellin' me about these deep caves at the foot of the cliffs, just along from the stone steps, where he saw th' Herders meet with Malik. . . ."

"I have said already that we will not know where along the coast the invasion force will land until Malik has been interrogated," Rushton cut in sternly.

Zarak flushed and looked mortified, but Rushton reached out to grasp his shoulder. "You have a fine mind, lad, and I think if your guildmistress will permit it, you might ride along with us to Sutrium tonight, for we will need such skills in the days ahead." Rushton released him, saying in a louder voice, "It is time for us to leave for Sutrium. Make your preparations."

A babble of talk erupted, but rather than becoming engaged in it, Rushton turned on his heel and strode across the room toward the door.

Zarak looked at me pleadingly, and despite my own emotional turmoil, I could not help but smile. Even if I had wanted to refuse him, I could not have done so anyway with Khuria standing behind his son, beaming with pride. I nodded, and Zarak hugged his father and raced to get his things.

As the room gradually emptied, those locals who had attended the meeting came to bid Dameon and me a rather stiff farewell, but after the empath spoke a few words to them, they were smiling, and I knew he had bathed them in waves of calmness and trust. I wondered, as I had often done before, at the morality of this, for was it not another form of coercion, even if it was benevolent?

". . . Garth was completely astonished," Dameon was saying.

"Astonished about what?" I asked, realizing he had been speaking.

He smiled wryly. "I was saying that Rushton summoned Garth back to Obernewtyn the same day you left the White Valley and ordered him to open Jacob Obernewtyn's grave. As you can imagine, the Teknoguildmaster wasted no time. You know how obsessed he is about Hannah Seraphim. Strangely, there were no bones in the grave, nor any sign that a body had even been there. Instead, there was a suit, which Garth says is the Beforetime version of our plast suits, and a notebook with the pages sealed in plast. The writing in the notebook begins as a letter to Hannah Seraphim, though later parts seemed more like a journal, from what I heard."

"*Jacob's* journal?" I guessed, my interest quickening.

Dameon nodded. "He scribes that he is weary of his loneliness and has decided to leave Obernewtyn. He says that he will take with him the key Hannah left behind. Since she never returned, it will never lie with them in the grave they had prepared to hold their bodies."

"Never returned from where?" I asked, baffled.

"He did not say where, but the letter appears to have been written over a period when he was making elaborate preparations to leave. Some of what he scribes makes me sure he intended to go into the Blacklands beyond the mountains above Obernewtyn."

"Poor man mun have been mad," Khuria said.

"If he is speaking of the Blacklands, then the letter was scribed after the Great White," I said. "But what does he mean about being alone? Even if Hannah was not there, there would have been others."

"The letter tells that the others had decided to take refuge from the missiles and something called a *fallout* in what used to be the building that housed the teknoguilders of their time. And you know what happened to it, of course. The upper levels were destroyed and the lower levels crushed, not by weapons but by immense movements in the earth, which were the result of the Great White.

"Jacob scribes that Hannah had warned them that Obernewtyn would be the safest place for them during the holocaust, but when it all began, everyone was frightened that she might have made a mistake. After all, she had never foreseen her own absence. So they voted to go into the lower chambers of the Teknoguild laboratories. Jacob scribed that he would have been with them, but he was in the house trying to reach Hannah on a computermachine. From what he says, he spoke to her, and that was when she promised him that she would return, for she had foreseen that their bones would lie together at the end with the key."

"What is this key he speaks of?" Khuria asked curiously.

Dameon shrugged. "Jacob said only that it had been given to Hannah in trust and that she was supposed to hold it safe for someone else, though I do not know how she could have done that if they were supposed to take it to their grave."

"I wonder where Hannah went," I said.

"It mun have been as my lad has always thought," Khuria offered. "Hannah were in Newrome under Tor when the Great White came, an' she died there."

"But Jacob scribed that he spoke to her, so maybe she escaped the flooding of the city under Tor but had no way of getting through the mountain pass to Obernewtyn," Dameon said. "Remember, the pass would have been a good deal more poisonous right after the Great White."

"Jacob had a plast suit, though. Why dinna he use it and gan to *her*?" Khuria wondered.

Dameon frowned. "He must have had two suits, because he scribed that he was going to wear one and leave one for Hannah in the tomb so she could follow him. But I don't know how he thought she would manage that, since he did not leave any information about where he meant to go."

Khuria said grimly, "I have seen a glimpse of what lies beyond the high mountains, and I tell ye that no one could gan there an' live, even if they wore a plast suit. It is a vast unending desolation that stretches to th' horizon. Jacob'd nowt last more than a sevenday there without food, an' less without water, and if he took off his suit to eat or drink, he'd die eventually of wastin' sickness."

"He would not last long," I said. "The air above tainted earth would also have been poisoned back then, Garth says. He would be dead within hours."

"No," Dameon said. "Jacob scribed that he was taking an air purifier and food and water in special containers that he could use without taking the suit off. He also had some sort of device to eliminate waste."

"Even so, he was alone, and how much food and water could he have carried?" I said.

"Poor man," Khuria murmured. "He mun have been driven mad waitin' in vain all those years for the woman he loved."

"We don't really know if there was anything between Hannah and Jacob, despite what Garth thinks," I pointed out, somewhat startled by the old man's romanticism.

"They mun have loved one another, else why choose to share a grave?" Khuria asked.

"You could not read his words and doubt that he loved her," Dameon said slowly. "Yet maybe *she* did not love him."

"Why did Rushton command the grave be opened?" I asked.

"Maryon said it must be so," Dameon said. "She did not say why."

The others began speculating about why the Futuretell guildmistress would want an old grave opened. I said nothing, for it seemed to me quite likely that Maryon had been manipulated by the Agyllian birds guiding my quest, to ensure that I knew the key that ought to have been in the grave

205

was not where it was meant to be. But if that were true, what was I supposed to do about it? The only thing I was sure of was that the key Jacob had taken with him must be the one referred to in the carving on the Obernewtyn doors.

". . . that key which must be [used/found] [before all else] is [with/given/sent to] she who first dreamed of the searcher— the hope beyond the darkness to come. . . ."

Which meant I had been wrong to think that the words on the glass statue under Tor, created by Cassy Duprey and given to Hannah, were the key referred to by this line. It must be as I had first thought: that the key had been sent to Hannah concealed in or with the glass sculpture. Hannah must have promised Cassy that the key would go with her to her grave, neither of them foreseeing that the Great White could separate Hannah irrevocably from the key or that Jacob would go into the Blacklands, taking it with him.

But I refused to fall into despair—at least not until I had read Jacob's journal, for there might be a clue in it that only I would understand. Or maybe the clue waiting for me in the Earthtemple in Sador was the result of a later futuretelling by Kasanda, which would direct me to the missing key. Perhaps it was good that Rushton had not asked me to come to Sutrium, for it left me free to return directly to Obernewtyn. After all, Dameon could surely manage Saithwold in my absence.

A question occurred to me. "How did Garth react to Maryon's command to open the grave?"

Dameon laughed. "As you can imagine, given her previous opposition to his requests, he was torn between wanting to embrace her and wanting to strangle her."

A gust of cold wind blew around us, stirring the flames in the fire, and I turned with the others to see that the outer door had opened. Zarak stood there, wearing boots and greatcoat, his cheeks pink with exertion and excitement. "Rushton said to tell you we are about to leave," he said.

The wind had the smell of the sea in it, as well as the scent of storms to come. Apt, I thought. The sky was blanketed in cloud that allowed neither moonlight nor star shine to show through. But several of the coercers carried lanterns whose flames danced and fluttered even behind their glass shields.

I breathed in the sweet wild air, realizing that thinking of my quest had cooled the anger I felt toward Rushton. I looked at Malik. His face might have been carved of rock for all the emotion it showed. This thought reminded me that I had yet to see the statue that stood in Noviny's garden. At least the delay in our departure would give me time to find out if it was another sign from Kasanda to the Seeker.

I saw Kevrik preparing to mount up, and realizing that Rushton must have asked him to go to Sutrium as well, I went to bid him farewell. I was interested to see his clumsy attempt at fingerspeech. He flushed and smiled when the horse made no response. "I have already learned a few words in beast-speech, an' young Zarak has promised to teach me more as we ride. He says he owes me a lesson fer th' headache he gave me in the cell."

"I have not thanked you properly for saving my life," I said seriously.

His expression sobered. " 'Tis I who should be thanking ye for allowing me the chance to become a free man. I dinna mean that I am nowt in a cell either. I mean free of foolish prejudices that are as bad as bars. Some of th' men who served Vos feel the same way after meeting Linnet an' the knights, and your Rushton is an impressive sort of man, by anyone's standard."

I gritted my teeth at hearing Rushton referred to as mine, but before I could correct Kevrik, Rushton was calling everyone to mount up. Kevrik obeyed with alacrity as Rushton came over to me. "I wish you a safer journey than thus far, Guildmistress," he said formally.

"Give my good wishes to Dardelan and Reuvan," I managed to say composedly, but as he mounted Esred, I thought again of what had passed between us the night I had ridden out from Obernewtyn.

"You must tell me what is wrong," I had pleaded. "Why do you not touch me or smile at me or look at me?"

He had sighed, and when he did look at me, I had seen only a deadly weariness. If I could have stopped him answering then, I would have. For I suddenly knew, as if I were a futureteller, that if he spoke, his words would destroy something precious. But it was too late.

"Do you not understand, Elspeth, you who are so bright? Is it not obvious? There is nothing left in me to feel emotions with," Rushton said slowly. He glanced toward the turret window, which overlooked the wall encircling Obernewtyn and the jagged mountains surrounding us, their tips blanketed in snow. Then he looked back at me. "We loved, you and I. That is a truth. But not all love lasts forever, and that is also a truth. I do not love you any longer. Since I woke from my . . . time in the cloister, I have felt nothing. It is as if all capacity for feeling has been burned from me. I remember love, but I do not feel it any more than one who has had a limb amputated. At some moments, there is something . . . and I have waited to see if it would grow into true feeling, but it has not, and I know now that I am nothing more than a limbless person who experiences an itch in a leg that is no longer there."

"Rushton, if you would only let me help you remember what happened in the cloister, perhaps your ability to feel would return," I said.

"I do not wish to remember," Rushton answered flatly. "I am sorry, for I know that what I say must give you pain, and yet you need to know the truth so that you can be healed of . . . of what you feel for me." He looked out the window again, his green eyes remote.

The pain of his words cut so deep. But I could see that even the pity he expressed was nothing more than a mimicking of that emotion. He could not truly feel pity any more than he could feel love. Yet he seemed to have lost none of his devotion to Obernewtyn. Or was that just another simulation? How cruel pain made me in that moment. How I wanted to scratch at that calm face to see if he felt even that.

"I . . . see," I managed to say, the words jerking from my mouth. "I am glad you have explained it to me. I had not thought of love as a wound that might need healing. Well, it must be possible, for you have managed it without even a scar. Maybe it is not so difficult as I might have imagined."

The metallic taste of blood woke me to the present, and I realized that I had bitten my lip. Everyone had mounted now, and they were riding out the gate. Malik was at the back between two coercer-knights, and he turned to look back. I expected to see loathing in his eyes, but instead he gave me a look of vicious triumph.

A shiver of premonition came to me as I remembered Malik saying in the woods that he had no need to escape. I had felt sure he meant the invasion, but he knew now that we were aware of the bargain he had struck with the Herders, so why that look of triumph? I shaped a probe to call them back so we could coerce Malik at once and learn what lay behind that look. But the thought of facing Rushton again stopped me sending it. Whatever secret Malik nursed would be wrested from him by a coercer in Sutrium on the morrow.

I stood for a long time after the sound of the horses' hooves faded, only half conscious that the wind had grown stronger. No one spoke to me as they drifted back inside, and I guessed they imagined that I pined for Rushton. No doubt they thought that we had quarreled. Would that it were so simple, for quarrels could be mended. I had felt myself devastated by what Rushton had said that last night at Obernewtyn, but I understood only now that I had not accepted his words. When Rushton had ridden up on Esred earlier that day, I had looked for signs of his love, feeling certain that such love as we had shared could not simply be extinguished like a fire.

But now hope was truly dead.

Whatever the Herders had done to Rushton had changed him irrevocably. Hearing of what Malik had done to me, he had behaved as if an injustice had been done that he would see was put right. Remembering Malik's sly hateful words about Rushton being hollowed out, I wondered if what lay behind his triumphant look of malice was his awareness that Rushton could not love me. After all, he witnessed the coolness between us as Rushton bade me farewell.

I had meant to look for Maruman to mend the rift between us, but my heart and mind were full of turmoil and grief. I stumbled along the side of the house to the back door and went directly to the bedroom I had been shown earlier. Opening a window in case Maruman recovered from his dudgeon and came seeking me in the night, I farsent Gahltha to say good night, only to find that the old cat was with him. Relieved that he was safe, I withdrew and lay on my bed, fully clothed. I fell at once into a dream.

I dreamed vividly of the day my parents had died. I saw the soldierguards burst through the door of our home as my mother prepared nightmeal. One soldierguard grasped my mother about the waist, and Jes flew at him. The soldierguard swatted him away as if he were an insect, and Jes hit the wall with a loud crack and fell down, lying half stunned against it. I ran to my mother and tried to climb into her arms, but another soldierguard tore me away from her and hurled me over to where Jes was beginning to stir. My mother was dragged outside, and then two soldierguards pushed us after her. I heard her calling out to neighbors and friends to help us. But though people's faces appeared at windows, no one tried to stop the soldierguards or the Herders directing them.

We were brought to the central square of Rangorn, where moon fairs and sevenday markets were held. Here a small crowd stood gathered about a man tied to a pole in the midst of a woodpile. I realized as we came nearer that the man was my father. He spoke my mother's name with grief, and she cried out his name and then our names. Anguish crossed my father's features as he saw us, and he cursed the Herders standing by, pale and gray-robed, their heads bald and gleaming in the sunlight. My mother only begged the priests to take us away so we would not see the burning.

The older of the priests answered her in a dry, fussy voice, saying that we were the children of seditioners and must see where our parents' treachery had led so we would not follow in their footsteps. Then one of the soldierguards held us while another daubed our cheeks and foreheads with the stinging dye used to mark the children of seditioners.

"Don't let them do this," my father cried out suddenly in his strong rich voice. "There are more of you standing here than these foul priests and the few brutish soldierguards that serve them. Rise up and bind them and let us begin the rebellion here and now, which this Land needs to cleanse itself."

I looked at the Herders and saw unease cross the face of the younger one, but the older priest only gave a prim, cruel smile and leaned forward to light the kindling with his torch. I saw no more, because Jes pulled me to face him and held me tightly so that I could not see the burning. But I heard it and smelled it.

I felt my brother's trembling, suffocating embrace, and days later, my upper arms still bore the hand-shaped bruises of Jes's grip. I heard my father groan and curse the Herders and the Faction, and I heard my mother plead over and over with her friends and neighbors to care for us before her voice rose to a scream. When the screams and groans stopped and a terrible smell filled the air, I looked up at Jes and saw tracks of fire running down his cheeks, where tears reflected flame.

I wept then, too—the desolate weeping of a child deprived forever of her life and family.

✦ 13 ✦

I WOKE BEFORE dawn, hollowed out by the vividly detailed memory dream.

I was too wide awake to go back to sleep, for it was near morning. Resisting the temptation to farseek Maruman, I decided to find out what sort of mood the old cat was in without actually beastspeaking him. I lit a lantern, washed my face, and dressed before pulling on my boots and brushing my hair. As I left the room, a few intrepid birds were already giving out notes, tuning themselves for the dawn chorus. Rather than going straight outside, I decided to go find some food. Aside from being hungry myself, food was always a good way to coax Maruman out of a temper. If I could find some fish, the battle would be half won.

It took me a little time to find the kitchen, but it was not deserted, as I had expected at such an early hour. A young boy was seated on a bench before the stove, poking at the fire. He leapt to his feet when he saw me and began to stammer an explanation. His father had sent him to rake up the embers and stoke a fire for firstmeal.

"Good," I said. "I need someone to give me directions to the larder. Do you suppose your father would object if we had a bite to eat before he comes?"

The boy said, "There is some bread we could toast, Da told me not to touch any food . . ."

"I will make you a bargain," I said, hiding a smile. "If you will toast some bread, I will spread jam upon it. And let us light a lamp."

In just a few minutes, we were seated companionably before the fire, eating thick, half-burnt slices of bread smeared with a delicious tart blackberry jam. Gazing into the fire and listening to the boy tell me that his little sister had picked the berries for the jam, I thought of Jes and how tightly he had held me to stop my seeing our parents' awful death. He had done his best for me. The strangeness that had come over him before I had been charged Misfit had been no more his choice than the repression of those memories had been mine. Our minds devised these responses to help us survive. And maybe Dameon was right about Rushton's love being buried beneath what had been done to him by the Herders.

Hope stirred in me, small and frail, but hope nonetheless.

The sound of a door opening interrupted my thoughts, and I turned to see Linnet enter. She said in a grave, urgent voice, "You'd better come, Guildmistress."

I handed my plate to the boy and followed the coercer, my heart beating fast with apprehension. "What is the matter?"

"I'm not sure. One of Malik's armsman offered us information in return for his release. He said the only reason he had continued serving Malik, once he had made his pact with the Faction, was because he would have been killed if he had seemed to waver in his loyalty. He has a woman up in Sawlney who is carrying his child, and he wants to go to her. I told him that we would get all the information we needed from his master, but he said that it would not come soon enough to save us from the invasion. I asked what he meant."

"Why didn't you tell him that the quickest way to prove he was telling the truth would be to let you probe him?"

"I did, and he agreed to it. But I made the mistake of put-

214

ting him back in his cell while we cleared another to conduct the interrogation. Another armsman attacked him, and he is so near to dying now that anyone entering his mind would be at risk of being taken with him."

We had reached the steps leading to the cells, and I ran down them, past the waiting coercers. A big armsman lay on the floor in a pool of blood. I recognized him from Malik's camp. I knelt next to him, noticing that his breathing had an ominous whistling sound.

"Can you hear me?" I asked. His eyes found my face, and I saw that he was able to understand me. I leaned close to his ear and said, "Tell us what you know, and we will find your woman and see that she and the child are cared for."

The man's eyes widened, and I saw the effort it cost him to move his lips. "Klah . . . los . . . ," he gasped. Rosy blood bubbled from his nostrils.

"It must be the name of his woman," Linnet said.

But I was looking down into the armsman's face and saw his eyes move rapidly left and then right. No.

"Try again," I urged him.

"Clos . . . ," he spluttered.

"Close?" I guessed. Again his eyes flicked left and right. A cloudiness in them indicated that we had very little time.

"Please," I said. "Let your child be told that his father fought to keep the Land free."

This time the tendons in his neck stood out as he spoke. "Clois . . . Kloh . . ." He sank back, his lips sheened with blood.

"Dead," I said softly, and reached forward to close his staring eyes.

"Could he have been trying to say *cloister*?" Linnet guessed.

215

"It may be. You had better coerce the man who attacked him. I think we can say this is serious enough to warrant it."

"I doubt it will do any good. The dead man claimed to be the only one who knew what he was offering to tell us. Indeed, he said Malik would have killed him for what he knew. The other armsman attacked him purely because he meant to collaborate with us."

I looked down at the dead man and remembered Malik's triumphant look as he rode off. "He said that any information obtained from Malik would come too late to save us from the Herder invasion?" Linnet nodded. "That makes no sense, for Malik will have been coerced by tomorrow or the day after, and Dardelan will send a force here immediately to prepare for the invasion."

"It was before wintertime that Noviny overheard Malik, and the timing of the invasion might well have been changed since then," Linnet pointed out.

She was right. "Then if the armsman spoke truly, the invasion would have to take place tomorrow or even today!" I thought again of Malik's look of triumph. "We must organize our own defense immediately."

"But what are we to defend? There are three places where an invasion force could come ashore in Saithwold," Linnet said.

"We must put watchers at each set of steps and instruct them to send word the moment they spot ships approaching," I replied. "That will give us time to move a force to meet them. In the meantime, we need to gather a fighting force."

"We must send word to Rushton and Dardelan," Linnet said.

"So we will, but we need something more than a few choked words from a dying man. I will ride to the cloister and look around."

Linnet nodded decisively. "I will send out some knights to watch for ships at each accesspoint."

"You might also send someone to investigate those caves Noviny mentioned to Zarak as well," I said. "See what sort of force we could conceal in them."

Linnet gave me a searching look. "You still intend trying to take the ships?"

"I think we must try," I said. "With luck, Dardelan and the others will arrive in time to help."

Linnet strode out of the cell, and I heard her instruct a co-ercer to summon Khuria and all the knights to the kitchen. I glanced down at the dead man one more time before going after her.

As we ascended the steps, Linnet said she would ask Khuria to gather the men and women nominated by Noviny to help guide Saithwold in his absence. "We will need their help to assemble a force big enough to deal with any warrior priests we take as prisoners," she explained. "But we knights must be at the top of the steps to receive these warrior priests."

"Given the sort of numbers we will have, it might be wiser to try trickery at the top of the steps, rather than force," I said. "Why not coerce a group of Malik's men to meet the invaders and lead them into a trap away from the cliffs?"

"The invaders are going to expect to see Malik," Linnet pointed out.

"Then prepare for that. Have the coerced men claim to be taking the invaders to Malik. If we are right in guessing that the cloister is a secret armory, the Herders can be told Malik awaits them there."

"Maybe one of Malik's men will know," Linnet suggested. "I will coerce the leaders among them as soon as I set the others to their tasks. It is a pity your friend Kevrik left."

"Talk to those of Vos's armsmen that Kevrik said were decent people. One of them is bound to know which men Malik might have confided in," I said, but I had no great hope he would have confided in anyone.

By the time we reached the kitchen, some of the coercers were beginning to assemble, but I did not linger, for I was eager to find out if we had been right in our guesses about the cloister. Farseeking Gahltha to meet me in front of the house, I fetched my greatcoat and went outside to find he was already waiting. I grasped his mane, threw myself onto his back, and in minutes we were galloping hard along the road. It then occurred to me that the slaves Noviny had seen might have been held in the cloister to be handed over to the Herders. Remembering the pitiable state of the prisoners we had found locked in Sutrium's cloister cells after the invasion, I farsent Linnet to ask her to send Wenda and the carriage after me, just in case there were any poor wretches in the cells.

The sun was near to rising behind the trees as we approached the rutted track to the cloister, and I could see the pale, stone wall that enclosed it quite clearly. It stood as high as the tallest trees in the mist-wreathed forest that hemmed it on three sides, and had a secretive air.

I slipped down from Gahltha's back, hot from the exertion of the gallop, and approached the enormous metal gate sagging off its hinges. I could feel the numbing buzz of the tainted walls, and my heartbeat quickened. Why freshen the taint in the walls, if not to keep something concealed from Misfit Talents?

I was about to go through the gate when I noticed Gahltha hanging back. Guessing that the taint was troubling him, I stroked his soft nose and told him to wait outside since he could not come into the cloister buildings with me anyway. He agreed with relief, and I went through the gateway alone. But I stopped again inside, assailed by a premonition of danger. As usual, it was so vague as to be useless, save as a reminder that I would not be able to reach Gahltha's mind until I came back through the gate. Then I chided myself for being a fool, for of course I could call out to him.

I took a deep breath and looked around. Cobbles ran from the gate to the front of the cloister, but on either side of the cloister building were green swathes of grass. On the south lawn apple trees grew in neat lines parallel to the side of the building. The sun had not yet risen high enough to cast any direct light on them, and it struck me that I had foolishly failed to bring a lantern or candles and a tinderbox. Since it was too dark to enter the building, I decided to look at the tools and piles of earth Zarak had mentioned until Wenda arrived, for there would be lanterns or candles in her wagon.

I walked through the trees toward the back of the cloister, passing under long glassless windows set into the cloister wall at intervals. These gave me the discomforting feeling of being watched, and my unease grew until suddenly I realized what was causing it. Despite the sun having risen, I could hear neither bird nor insect. The profound silence inside the cloister wall reminded me of the deadly Silent Vale.

Reaching the back of the cloister, I saw more fruit trees growing here, and behind them, against the wall, rose several high mounds of earth and the tools that Zarak had mentioned, resting against a small stone shed. Going closer, I saw that the mounds had a hard crust, which meant they had been exposed to the weather for some time. They were the same dark choca hue as the earth showing through the wet grass;

but there was enough earth to fill a great pit and no sign of a digging site.

The most likely place to bury something dangerous would be in the cells, which traditionally had earthen floors. If I was right about farm holders being held here before they were given to the Herders, Malik could have used them to dig in secret, for once locked in, they would have required no guards. The armsman killed might have stumbled onto knowledge of what was happening by overhearing a prisoner, for armsmen would have been required to escort them to the coast. Perhaps under the floor of every cell I would find that a crate of weapons had been buried, or barrels of the explosive black powder that had so frightened Vos and his men. If so, the number of crates might indicate the size of the invading force.

The rear door of the cloister was a great oaken slab that was firmly closed and would not budge, so I returned to the front of the cloister, where the door, like the gate, had been wrenched off its hinges and lay splintered and graying on the cobbles. The sun was now high enough that it cast a dull brightness inside the stone-flagged entrance hall, which was covered in a dense litter of leaves and dust. Three doors led out of the hall, and a set of steps went up to the left. Two of the doors led to passages that ran toward the back of the building, and one led to a room on the right, partly visible through a half-opened door.

Half an hour later, I had walked through numerous chambers, around the kitchen, and along all the subterranean passages, but none of the rooms or cells was occupied. Nor had I found any evidence of digging in the cells, the passages, or their walls. As I stepped out into the sunlight, I thought of the tools left leaning against the stone shed.

In minutes, I was standing in front of the shed, holding the heavy metal lock that fastened the door. It was hard to form a probe dense and delicate enough to manipulate the lock workings this close to the tainted wall, but at last I heard the telltale click.

I opened the door and stared, even though I had been expecting something of the sort. There was no floor in the shed, save for a rim of earth around the walls. The rest was a great gaping hole and a ramp of earth descending into darkness. A tunnel!

There was a row of lanterns and a tinderbox on the earth ledge, and I selected one, checked the oil reservoir, and lit the wick, before venturing into darkness. I pictured a chamber at the end of it, full of crates of weapons and barrels of black powder, but ten minutes later, I was still walking, the sloping earth ramp and earthen walls having given way to a natural passage through the region's soft rock that must have once been a subterranean watercourse. Aware that such a passage could go on for miles, I wondered if this was an escape tunnel of the sort the Faction had often built to allow secret movement in and out of cloisters. Judging from the packed-earth floor, much of what had been dug out of the tunnel had been used to fill the bottom of the rift and create a flat base.

Another fifteen minutes and I was regretting that I had not told Gahltha what I intended to do. But having come so far, I could not bring myself to turn back.

Another fifteen minutes passed, or so I judged it, and the tunnel still led downward. I could no longer believe this was merely an escape tunnel, for it would have surfaced long before now. I wondered if Wenda had arrived at the cloister yet. If so, she would come looking for me, but it would take time to find the tunnel entrance. When she did, I hoped that she would wait for me with Gahltha or even return to the homestead to tell Linnet and the others about the tunnel. Very soon I would have to turn back, whether or not I wished it, for the lantern's oil reservoir was nearly empty. If only I had thought to take two lanterns. But who could have guessed at the tunnel's length?

Suddenly, the flame in the lantern was snuffed out, and I was plunged into darkness.

I knew I ought to turn back, but the draft of air that had blown out the flame suggested I might not be far from a shaft leading to the surface. If there were steps, I could get out that way and farseek both Linnet and Gahltha.

I set the lantern to the side and went on cautiously, hands outstretched to keep from running into anything. Then, in the stillness, I heard a voice. I held my breath and listened hard, but I had not been mistaken. Someone was talking, and if there was a speaker, there must be at least one person listening. Was it possible there were Herders here already?

I hesitated but could not resist going on, for I wanted to hear what was being said and get some idea of how many Herders there were. If I was truly fortunate, they would not be banded, and I could learn everything we needed to know from them. I walked very carefully now, anxious that I might alert the speakers to my approach. Even so, I stumbled several times, because the ramped earth that had leveled the tunnel higher up had given way to undulating stone.

Finally, I stopped to remove my boots and tuck them under my arm, knowing that I could move more stealthily without them. I was very aware, too, that the speakers might suddenly decide to come along the tunnel. In that case, I would have no choice but to fly back to the cloister like a fox with hounds on its tail.

The flow of air grew stronger, and there was a tantalizingly familiar scent in it. The air smelled of the sea!

My mind raced, for though by my reckoning I had been moving constantly in the direction of the coast, I did not think I could have reached the cliffs. Then a thought struck me. At several places along this part of the coast, narrow inlets opened up and the sea flowed in. What if this tunnel opened into one of them? It was an intriguing idea, but even if a ship-master could maneuver his vessel along such a narrow channel at high tide and manage to disgorge Herder warriors in a tunnel opening, how would the ship turn to leave?

I was so intent on my thoughts that I tripped and fell sideways, stifling a cry and throwing out my hands, but there was nothing to catch ahold of. I landed with a sickening crunch.

✦ 14 ✦

I OPENED MY eyes to pitchy blackness. Both hands were pressed against my body, and when I tried to move, pain lanced through my head. At first I thought I had been captured and tied up, but there were no bindings about my wrists or body. I could not move because there was stone all about me. Swallowing hard, I told myself I must have fallen sideways into a crevice running off from the tunnel, and now I was wedged there. I felt about with my fingers and toes and butted my head gently forward, trying to get an idea of the space into which I had fallen, but to my dismay, the movement caused me to slip farther down into the crack.

Suppressing panic, I lay completely still, willing myself to calmness. I felt extraordinarily weary, which meant that my body had been draining my energy to repair whatever damage I had done in the fall.

Ruthlessly, I quashed fear and imagination and commanded myself to think, for only I could get myself out of the predicament into which I had literally fallen. Using my fingertips and toes, I began very slowly and carefully to ease myself back up the crack. Only because I had fallen sideways into the cleft instead of headfirst did I notice the play of light against the stone as I inched myself upward. I froze and saw that the light was growing stronger, which could only mean that someone was coming along the tunnel with a lantern.

I kept my eyes fixed on the crack, for if it was Wenda, I would have only one chance to call out softly and stop her from blundering into whatever lay at the end of the tunnel. Then I became aware of the thud of feet; not just the feet of one person, but of many people marching in time. Surely that could mean only one thing: *The invasion was under way!*

At least I am not a captive, I told myself, fighting a wave of despair. Once the marchers had passed, I would have to go in the opposite direction to warn the others. But what of Wenda?

The light grew brighter, and now I could feel the vibration of the marchers' boots through the stone. Soon they were passing the opening: an endless line of grim-faced, shaven-headed Herders in dark gray robes moving up the tunnel toward the cloister. Save for the color of their attire, they looked no different from any other Herders, except they were more powerful-looking, and I seemed to feel their relentless purpose. These must be the warrior priests Noviny had described. No wonder Malik had looked at me in triumph. He had known that the invasion force was on the verge of arriving.

I willed the column to end so I could renew my efforts to escape the crack, praying that Wenda would hear the thud of the Herders' feet if she was coming along the tunnel.

By the time the last warrior had passed, my whole body ached with tension, but I did not move until the light had faded completely, and even then I lay for a time listening.

Finally, I gathered my courage and strength and began moving myself carefully back up the crevice. Once I managed to get one arm free, it was easier, though I muttered a curse at the realization that I must have dropped my boots into the crack when I fell.

Back in the tunnel I took a deep breath, considered a

moment, and then set off in the same direction as before, for I reasoned that I would sooner or later reach the tunnel's end. The only trouble was that the tunnel was still angling down.

After a time, I heard someone speak again and froze. He sounded quite near, and a faint light showed ahead. These things and the draft suggested I was right about the tunnel ending in steps or a shaft that led to the surface. Elated to think I might be able to escape the tunnel in time to warn the others, for the marchers could not possible have reached the cloister yet, I hastened my steps.

Suddenly, the tunnel curved into a large cavern. I stopped dead, unable to see into the cavern properly because of the angle at which the tunnel entered it. There were chinks of fire or lantern light high up, and I decided to climb the inner wall that separated the end of the tunnel from the cavern to see what was there.

The cavern was enormous, with the same undulating stone floor and walls as the tunnel, and the light came from a small fire built in a pit. From the blackened patches in other places, it looked as if there had been many fires lit. This and the number of bedrolls strewn about made it clear that the invaders had been here for some time. The warrior priests I had seen must have come ashore and hidden here.

The sole occupants now, however, were two inner-circle Herder priests, each sitting on either side of the fire. One was elderly and wore the golden armband of an inner-cadre priest. This made him the likely commander, so why had he remained here when the warrior priests had marched up to the cloister? Unfortunately, both priests were banded, as the marchers had been, so I could not probe them.

A gust of sea-scented air blew through the small hole in the stone wall I clung to, and I could actually hear the muted boom of waves, and I thought again that the tunnel must lead to one of the inlets.

The lesser of the priests began to speak. "Salamander said he wants as little killing or maiming as possible because it is a waste."

"What Salamander wants is irrelevant," said the senior priest coldly. "The One feels that a high number of deaths is desirable, both as a lesson and to cut down the corrupted population, which has accepted the dominion of freaks and Luddamned mutants. Once the Land is stabilized, we will breed a people without such undesirable tendencies as courage, inquisitiveness, and aggression. Far better to have a population born to obedience. The idea is to have a population that knows nothing but slavery and reveres its masters as superior beings that rule by Lud's will."

The two were silent awhile; then the younger spoke again. "What is the relationship between Salamander and Ariel? I have always wondered."

"It is my understanding that they met over the sale of the rabble left after the firestorm that destroyed Henry Druid's secret settlement. During that exchange, Ariel suggested to Salamander that he might serve himself in serving us."

"Salamander must be wealthy beyond the dreams of ordinary men, and yet he is ever greedy for more slaves to sell. And his greed is matched by the greed of those who rule the Red Land for slaves to work their mines."

"Only after he began to serve the Faction did Salamander acquire real power and wealth. The One says that this is a sign he is doing as Lud requires."

"Even so, it seems strange to me that, despite the new ships he has purchased, he continues to master the *Black Ship*," said the younger priest.

The older man shrugged. "The *Black Ship* is unique, both in its ability to attack other ships at sea and its capacity to carry men. It is because he agreed to take part in this invasion that we were able to bring as many Hedra as we have. His *Black Ship* alone took double the number of the other two ships."

Crouched precariously upon the high stone ledge, I frowned. Surely far more men than I had seen marching along the tunnel would have fit on three ships, especially if one of them was Salamander's *Black Ship*. But if that was so, then where were they?

"... his price was the rebels and their supporters alive and saleable," the younger priest was pointing out. "Which is why he desires as few deaths as possible."

"He will have slaves aplenty after this day's work, regardless of how many are killed in the invasion," the older priest said indifferently.

The pair was silent for a time, and the younger priest said, "I am told that those who rule the Red Land are heathens who do not believe in Lud. I have wondered sometimes whether it can please Lud that we enable Salamander to send them so many slaves."

"The purifying flame will sear the Red Land someday. Lud will suffer no unbelievers. But Ariel has been to the Red Land, and he assures the One that his influence is strong there. When the time is right and Lud wills it, Ariel will open the way for the Faction."

"What do you suppose motivates him? Ariel, I mean," the younger priest asked, now adding wood to the fire. "There are times when his words make me doubt his faith."

"That had troubled me on occasion, as it has others among our brethren. But though he is high-handed and arrogant, Ariel has served us well. He, after all, proposed allowing the rebels to overtake the Council in this part of the Land in order to lessen the power of the Councilmen. And he suggested that this Malik would be willing to open a way for our invasion. Even these were his ideas and his invention," added the priest, tapping at the demon band about his neck with a grimace. "I wish he would find some way to protect us from the taint, but at least we need wear them only on land."

"Is it true that he also suggested building a force of our own warriors who would be pure in mind and body? Who would fight not for glory or gain, but for Lud?"

"Yes, the creation of the Hedra was his idea, and it so pleased the One that he agreed to let Ariel build his own dwelling on Norseland. It is a pity he won such decisive favor with the One."

The younger priest frowned. "I do not understand."

"Well, Ariel has great influence with the One, and there are times when we have been glad of it. But there are also times when Ariel makes speeches to the One about Lud and retribution and the Herders being chosen to rule the world, which render the One . . . very excitable. And when the One is excitable, there is almost always blood. Sometimes the bloodletting is less than convenient. More than once, good informants have been rent limb from limb because the One required them to be purified immediately."

"I heard that the One wanted every single man, woman, and child in the Land slain," said the younger priest, lowering his voice as if the words shocked even him.

"The One is very pure. How should he not be when he is so dear to Lud and knows his grief at the waywardness of his children? But on this occasion, Lud, in his infinite wisdom, prompted Ariel to offer words to the One that stayed his hand."

"Are you saying that Ariel influenced the One?" asked the younger priest, sounding shocked.

"Of course not," snapped the older. "Naturally, being the chosen first of Lud, the One is incapable of being influenced by lesser beings. Say rather that Ariel is the instrument of Lud, and for this reason, you must take care never to speak against him. Even some of the questions you have asked me might be cause enough for the One to become . . . excitable. Remember what happened to the last priest who questioned Ariel's motives? They say he died screaming, driven mad by Lud for his blasphemy."

"All who displease Lud die screaming and raving," the younger priest said piously.

"It is one thing for slaves and novices to be put to death," the older man said querulously, "and quite another for inner-circle priests to suffer the same rough end. The priest who died was as I am, an inner-circle Nine, for Lud's sake! And his death meant a host of others had to be put to death, because they had sworn loyalty to him. It was an unnecessary violence. . . ."

"It is rumored that the One offered to make Ariel a Nine, and he refused. He told the One that Lud desired him to serve the Faction as an outsider, until such time as the Herders had dominion over the world."

The older priest said nothing, and the younger priest glanced at him, then leaned forward to gaze moodily into the fire. I sat back on my heels. The exchange between the priests was fascinating, but I could not sit up here forever like a roosting pigeon when anything might be transpiring above us.

I readied myself to climb back down, but a movement caught my eye. It had come from the shadowed end of the cavern, and I gaped to see a man emerge from the darkness. He was tall and lean and swatched in a hooded black cloak that made it impossible to tell if he was a warrior priest or an ordinary priest. But when he reached the two by the fire, he pushed the hood back. I saw that, instead of being shaven, his head was entirely covered in a loose black cloth similar to that worn by the nomadic Sadorians when they travel across the blazing white heart of their desert land, only he also wore black bandages about his face, concealing all but fierce yellow eyes.

Salamander.

If I had not been holding my breath, I would surely have gasped aloud, so great was my surprise, for seldom did anyone see the infamous slaver so close, let alone so far from the sea and his *Black Ship*. I wondered what he hid so carefully under all those layers of black, since a simple mask would have disguised his identity well enough. It took only a moment to confirm that he wore a demon band.

"Where is Malik?" Salamander asked. His voice was deep and smooth, but the words were distinct despite being slightly muffled by the cloth over his face.

"He has not come. I think we must assume that something has gone wrong," the older priest said.

"It matters not," said Salamander. "If he has been exposed, Ariel has made sure the rebels will get nothing out of him. When one of the freaks attempts to read Malik's mind, it will collapse, taking the intruder's mind with it."

"And if they torture him physically?" the younger priest inquired.

"He will not be tortured," said the other priest with a sneering laugh. "The boy chieftain does not approve of torturing prisoners."

"Then we proceed with the next stage of the invasion?" Salamander asked.

"Yes," the older priest said. "The Hedra will soon be in place in the cloister."

"We must leave at once," Salamander said decisively.

The priests gathered up their cloaks and slung cloth bags over their shoulders while Salamander took up a resin torch, lit it, and then kicked the fire apart. When the priests announced themselves ready, he turned without hesitation and began to walk back the way he had come.

They disappeared into the shadows at the far end of the cavern, taking the lantern light with them, and I realized that I had been right. There was a way to the surface from this end of the tunnel! Fortunately, there was a faint glow from the embers of the fire, and I climbed down from my ledge and hurried after the three men, picking my way around bedrolls and other obstacles.

Thinking of what I had overheard, I realized that if Rushton and the others had *not* ridden into Saithwold when they had, I would have coerced Malik and died. Was that why Maryon had sent the others after me? Instead, another coercer would die trying to probe him. Surely that would make Dardelan realize something was wrong and send a force of fighters to Saithwold.

I had reached the shadows now and saw another tunnel leading off the chamber. It was dark and had a dank smell that made me gag, but there was light ahead. I went toward it carefully, because I did not want to stumble into Salamander and the priests. Gradually, the drumming of the waves grew louder and the briny reek of the sea stronger.

At the end of the tunnel, I peeped out. What I saw took my breath away.

Before me was a cavern many times larger than the one where the priests had sat, but instead of being floored in stone, there was a vast pool of water that reflected a great opening in the side of the cavern. Daylight flowed through it, and I could see the sea washing against the stony spikes that edged the opening. But I could not see the sky, only a long, sun-streaked stretch of cliff wall, which told me that I was looking into one of the narrows. But the truly astonishing thing—the *impossible* thing—was that three greatships were floating on the cavern lake, one of them as large as the giant Sadorian spicewood vessels. Its black hull told me it was the infamous *Black Ship* mastered by Salamander.

He and the two priests had reached the edge of the lake, where a ship boat had been pulled onto the steeply sloping stone shore. As I watched the three men climb into it, my head rang with the strangeness of what I was seeing, for how had the ships got into the cavern? Obviously the sea would flow into the cavern at high tide, but a ship could not possibly pass through the stone spikes.

But then I saw that this was not quite true. There was one section where there were no stone spikes, but it was barely the width of the *Black Ship*.

The ship boat had almost reached the *Black Ship*, and I was struck again by its similarity to Sadorian ships. But there were many additional constructions on the *Black Ship*'s deck, not to mention the great ugly bulb of wood and metal spikes protruding from the prow, which must be used as a battering ram.

So absorbed was I in my examination of the ship, I did not immediately notice how many people stood on its deck, and when I did, I looked at the other ships and saw that it was the same. At least as many gray-clad warriors stood upon the three ships as I had seen marching up the tunnel. Doubtless the rest were to be set down on the beach where Malik had received the crates from the Herders, or divided among all three beach accesses to the Land in Saithwold province. The Faction had left nothing to chance.

I tried to think what to do. Obviously, the only way to reach the surface was to climb back up the tunnel, but if I did that, I would walk straight into the hands of the Herder warriors in the cloister.

My eyes fell upon the ship boat, now tethered to the *Black Ship*, and I saw with mounting excitement that the other two greatships also towed ship boats. Those aboard the *Black Ship* were now weighing anchor, and as I watched, long oars came out and the ship began to turn its misshapen prow toward the gap in the stone spikes.

I licked my lips and looked at the two remaining ships. The nearest was not so far away, and its ship boat tugged and bobbed on the waves in my direction. It was not dark, of course, but I doubted anyone would be looking back into the cavern. All attention would be fixed on the *Black Ship*, which edged toward the gap in the spikes.

I thought of the inner-cadre priest in the other cavern, fingering his demon band and saying he was glad they had only to wear the devices when they were on land. If he spoke true, and I could board a ship, then I could take it over by coercing first its shipmaster and ultimately everyone aboard. I could learn all the invasion plans and even use the ship and those aboard to help me stop the other ships from escaping.

Heart pounding, I worked my way around the side of the cavern, keeping low. Then I crawled down to the water's edge behind a rib of stone and put my hand into water that was so icy I shuddered. But I dared not dither, because I would be seen more easily out of the water than in. Gasping at the cold, I entered the sea and struck out for the ship boat. I was delighted to find that the tide flowing toward the cavern's opening was carrying me straight toward the ship. But it was so strong and swift that delight turned to horror as I found myself being swept inexorably *past* the ship boat.

The tide was ferocious. I could not stop myself.

I was dimly aware that the *Black Ship* had left the cavern and that the second ship had turned to approach the gap. It hit me that if I made it past the stone spikes into the narrow, my only chance of survival would be to board one of the ship boats. I glanced back to see the second ship moving rapidly into place. I gave up struggling against the pull of the waves and arrowed forward, steering myself between the stone fangs. For one terrifying moment, I seemed about to smash into a looming pillar, but I shot past it into the inlet's violent waters, which immediately dragged me under.

I kicked hard to reach the surface and managed to suck in a breath of air, but then I was dragged under again. By the time I fought my way back to the surface, I saw the second ship leaving the cavern. Dragged under again, this time I swam hard toward the middle of the inlet. I surfaced in calmer waters, but two ships had already gone down the inlet toward the open sea.

I had just readied myself for the last ship when a wave crashed over me again, pulling me under the water. It was like being eaten by a whirlwind. I tumbled and turned, and water forced its way up my nose and down my throat. My chest began to hurt with the need to breathe. I remembered the shipmaster Powyrs telling me that the sea was unforgiving to those who tried to fight it and forced myself to go limp.

Incredibly, as if it had only been waiting for me to

surrender, the sea spat me to the surface. I had time to gasp a breath of air and to see a few streaked purplish clouds in the blue slice of sky before a green shadow reared up and struck me down again. I went under three more times before I managed to reach less savage waters, but my relief was short-lived, for the third ship was emerging from the sea cavern. Even as I watched, I could see that the ship was not approaching the gap at the right angle to pass through. The shipmaster had miscalculated, and I heard a terrible grinding sound as the ship hull was ground against the side of one of the stone spikes. After a long moment, the tide turned the ship enough that it passed through the gap and turned to sail after the others!

Exhausted, I let the tide carry me down the narrow in the ships' wake. Despair filled me, for no matter how I conserved my strength, I could not swim all the way out of the narrow and around to one of the beach accesses.

"Oh, Maruman," I whispered, knowing I would never see the old cat again.

I noticed a large stone pinnacle jutting up from the water in the shadows near the stone wall of the narrow. Without hesitation, I struck out for it, knowing that if I could just get a decent foothold, I could wait there until the tide turned and then swim back to the sea cavern.

Driven by the outgoing tide, I hit the stone pinnacle hard enough to stun myself, but instinct made me cling to the rough, porous rock until my senses returned. I climbed above the waterline. Immediately, the wind cut into my chilled skin like icy blades. I tried hard to ignore the voice telling me that I would freeze to death if I stayed until the tide turned, because what was the alternative?

For a time, I thought of everything I could have done differently. The thought of the Herder warriors waiting in the cloister filled me with fear for my friends, but my mind also jumped to the food they might have left behind and the warm fire I could have kindled from the embers of their cook fires. I shook my head and told myself not to sit there like a fool daydreaming about food and fires as I slowly froze to death. If there was one stone spike, there would surely be others, or maybe some rocks at the base of the cliffs where I could rest. Somehow I had to make it to one of the beaches. I did not know which of the narrows I was in, but I did not believe I was far from the beach where Noviny had seen Malik and the Herders. Once out of the narrow, I would only have to swim around to it.

I lowered one numbed foot into the water, seeking for a grip on the stone so I could lower myself easily. Then I gasped, jerking my foot up instantly, *for something had pressed momentarily but firmly against the sole of my foot!*

I peered into the shadowed waves, trying to see what had touched me. I had just about convinced myself that I had merely touched a part of the stone pinnacle, when to my horror, I saw a long dark shape rise to the surface of the water. My mind leapt immediately to the many-toothed fish that Reuvan had once described, saying that he had seen it attack and tear to pieces a seaman who had fallen overboard. *Shark*, he had named it, and I clenched my teeth to stop whimpering with fear. Reuvan had said that the savage creatures were drawn by blood, and I had a dozen grazes all bleeding into the sea, sending out a deadly summons.

Was there any possibility of reaching the creature's mind? I wondered. I did not know of any beastspeaker who had ever managed to communicate with a fish. Water inhibited the ability to communicate mentally for some reason we did not understand. To even try to reach a fish's mind, physical contact would be necessary.

I peered down, wishing I could see through the shadows and the shifting reflection of cliff and sky. Finally, in desperation, I lowered my foot and slapped it on the surface of the water because Reuvan had said that vibrations also attracted sharks.

It must have been waiting just deep enough that I could not see it, for the enormous fish erupted from the water right under my foot, pushing up so hard that it dislodged me from the stone spike. As I fell, I opened my mouth, but I did not utter the scream shaping itself in my throat. For in that moment of contact, a bell-like voice sounded in my mind, offering help.

✦ 15 ✦

I MIGHT HAVE drowned if the fish had not nudged me back to the pinnacle, for fright had drained the last of my reserves. As I clung to the rock, I no longer feared that I would be eaten, for even that brief contact had shown me a female mind with no trace of the rapacious hunger or mindless aggression that Reuvan had said characterized sharks. Indeed, as I watched her circle, I saw that she was not a shark at all, but a warm-blooded ship fish of the kind that were said to have occasionally rescued drowning seamen.

She butted my leg and again I heard her bell-like voice in my mind. "This one is Vlar-rei. Name of Ari-roth."

The words were like music. I was so enchanted that it took me a moment to realize that she had responded to a thought, even though we were not in physical contact. That meant that while I needed to be in touch to hear her mindvoice, she could "hear" my thoughts without contact.

"I am ElspethInnle," I thought.

"Morred-a," she sent, brushing against my leg.

I realized she had translated my name into her language. Then I thought of the name she had applied to herself. *Vlar-rei.* It was not her own name but the name of her kind, and I knew that I had heard it before. Yet how could that be when I had never spoken with a ship fish?

Then it came to me. Locked inside Dragon's coma dream,

I had seen her mother, the Red Queen, leap from the slave ship that had stolen her and her little daughter from their homeland. She had summoned whales to destroy the ship and her tormentors. Then she had summoned a ship fish to bring Dragon to shore. She had told me that ship fish called themselves *Vlar-rei* and that in human speech this meant "children of the waves." I shivered with wonder because that this really was their name proved what I had guessed from Dragon's coma dream: her mother—the Red Queen—had been a powerful beastspeaker with a rare ability to commune with sea beasts.

A sleek gray head emerged from the water in front of me, and the ship fish turned slightly to fix one round, gray eye on me. Lifting her smooth snout, she uttered a long, complex, musical call. Somehow I knew that the trilling call was a language that did not echo her spoken words but elaborated and explained them—except I had no means of understanding it.

"This one answers the call," she sent, swimming close to make contact so I could "hear" her.

"The call?" I thought.

Her smooth body touched my leg again, and I heard her beautiful voice. "What is needful?"

"Can you help me to reach land?" I was so cold now that it was becoming hard to think clearly.

Ari-roth responded with a coiling trill of notes. Then she brushed me again and said merely, "Morred-a must make a mindpicture of the place she wishes to go."

Gingerly, I passed an arm around her smooth leathery flank and let go of the pinnacle. She took my weight, and I had the queer sensation of her mind swimming through mine. Like Maruman, she ignored my shield as if it did not exist.

I formed a mental image of the beach Noviny had described, hoping it would be enough. The ship fish merely gave another fluting call and bade me take hold of her more securely by the side and back fin, but to avoid her blowhole, for it was sensitive. I adjusted my position as she had instructed, and she moved smoothly away from the rock and along the channel.

Without my noticing it, the sun had set, and this time when I looked up, I saw stars caught between the black jaws of the cliffs. *Can so much time have passed since I rode to the cloister?* I wondered. Gradually, as we passed along the dark narrow, I realized that I was no longer cold.

"This one feeds Morred-a," Ari-roth sang imperturbably.

"Feeding me what?" I echoed, uncomprehending.

A bright picture swelled to fill my mind. It showed my body, as if seen through spirit eyes. It was no more than a dim shadow amidst a fluctuating halo of colored light, but the light was dim and the colors faded. Even the vivid slash of red corresponding to the damage done to my spirit by the life I had once taken was pale and faded. A ship fish shape emanating blue light appeared in the vision, and a tendril of light reached out from the ship fish to me. Gradually, my aura grew brighter and the colors stronger.

"This one feeds ohrana to Morred-a," Ari-roth sent as the vision faded.

"You have my gratitude," I told her, realizing that *ohrana* must be the ship fish word for "spirit energy." I wondered, too, how many ship fish had rescued seamen and helped them in this way without their ever realizing it.

"No," Ari-roth sang, answering my private thought as if it had been directed to her. "This gifting given only by Vlar-rei to Vlar-rei. But Mornir-ma asked that help be given to

Morred-a when she called." She lifted her head and gave a rising trill.

"Mornir-ma?" I echoed, confused. Did she mean Dragon, for the beasts called her Mornir?

"Mornir-ma sings to friends who swim long ago, of Morred-a who will swim in the waves to come. Very beautiful is the song/singing. Those who listened sang she song, too, that the waves would remember it. Now all who hear waves, hear the plea-song of Mornir-ma for Morred-a."

I drew a long shaky breath, wondering if I could be understanding her correctly, for she seemed to be saying that she had fed me from her aura, because someone had asked it long ago on my behalf. Mornir-ma. Dragon's mother?

It was fantastic to imagine, but Cassy might have future-told my need to the first Red Queen, who, like her descendant Dragon's mother, may have possessed the Talent to commune with sea beasts. But even if the first Red Queen had sung to sea creatures to ask help for a woman she had never met, how could Ari-roth have known I needed help now? She had spoken of a call, but I had not called anyone.

"Morred-a called," the ship fish responded calmly.

"What did I call?" I asked, utterly bewildered.

"Mornir-ma sang in the long ago, that Morred-a would call. *Mar-ruhman*. Ari-roth heard and followed the ripples back to Morred-a."

Mar-ruhman, I thought incredulously. *Maruman?* Then I remembered. I had called his name in sorrow and longing when I had thought I would drown. Cassy had foreseen me do so on the verge of drowning. A great chain of legend had been forged through time, to make sure that I would be saved.

"What did Mornir-ma sing of me?" I asked. I was trembling but not from cold.

"That Morred-a would say the sacred word *Mar-ruhman* to the waves when she was in dire need, and all aid must be rendered unto her, even the gift of ohrana, for by her deeds would the song of the waves go on, and without her, the song would be sung no more."

I felt astonished by what she told me, yet my life was caught in a web of prophecies, so how should I be surprised that sea creatures subscribed to the land-beast legend, which made me their Savior? But as always when I encountered the faith of others in those prophecies, I felt a dreamy powerlessness, which the dark water all about me seemed to emphasize. I tried to take in the knowledge that by calling Maruman's name, I had summoned the aid of the ship fish because of a song sung by a woman I had never met but whose daughter I had befriended and whose memory held a secret that I needed in order to complete my quest. My mind reeled at the complexity, and I could not even begin to understand how my cry had reached Ari-roth.

Oblivious or perhaps indifferent to my confusion, the ship fish swam in my mind and the waves so swiftly, yet serenely, that it seemed no time at all before we were passing out of the narrow inlet. For a long time, we swam straight out to sea, for Ari-roth explained that there were shoals all about the mouth of the narrow, where the currents were treacherous even for ship fish.

The open sea was far calmer then it had been inside the restricted inlet, and seeing the vast starry sky stretched over an inky sea where stars floated, I became calmer, too. Ari-roth turned and began to follow the Land's high shadowy coastline. As we cleaved through the water, I was enchanted to see patches of phosphorescence shimmering on the water's smooth surface. The despair and hopelessness I felt earlier evaporated. I was not cold or hungry or tired, and all my aches and pains had faded.

It was the effect of being fed Ari-roth's ohrana, but it seemed that, however long I lived, at the end of my life, this time of fluid serenity would be one I could summon to remind me of the beauty of living. I found tears upon my cheeks.

"Morred-a makes an offering to the waves." Ari-roth spoke the words in my mind with approval.

The moon now rose, a rich yellow-gold, shining like a burnished coin shaved at one edge. I thought of Maruman and imagined how he would glare at it. As it rose higher, its yellow richness fading to silver, I brought my wandering attention to bear on the land. We were passing along the coast of Saithwold province, but I could not see any of the three beaches or the steps cut into the cliff. As if sensing my desire, Ari-roth angled toward land. But the moon had climbed high before we passed the jutting brow of the cliff that hid two narrow beaches. Two ships were anchored close to shore at the first beach, but neither of them was the *Black Ship*. Salamander must have taken the warrior priests aboard his vessel to the third beach, closer to Sutrium, perhaps even directly to Sutrium. I decided to ask Ari-roth to set me ashore on the second beach. I could mount the steps and farseek Gahltha to come and find me. But first I needed to see if the warrior priests aboard the ship had gone ashore, as I suspected.

I asked Ari-roth to bring me closer to the ships, and though I doubted anyone would be looking out to sea, I adjusted my position and sank lower in the water so that my head barely rose above Ari-roth's shining fin. Soon I could make out steps cut into the cliff and several darker patches at the base of it, farther along the beach, which might be the caves Noviny had mentioned.

Turning to the deck of the nearest ship, I saw so little movement that either the entire force was belowdecks, or they had gone ashore. My instincts told me the latter, for the ships had surely arrived well before the moon had risen, and any commander would have taken advantage of the darkness.

I knew that the wisest course would be to ask Ari-roth to set me ashore on the second beach, but I had spotted the ship boat bobbing against the hull of the nearest ship. If I could get aboard, and it remained against the hull of the greatship, I might manage to farseek someone and learn what was happening ashore. It occurred to me that I could do what I had meant to do in the sea cavern: take over the minds of those aboard the ship.

"Does Morred-a wish to go ashore?" Ari-roth asked serenely.

"No," I told her, "just as far as the small vessel, but I must not be seen by those aboard." To be sure she understood, I pictured the ship boat.

Ari-roth sang soothingly that the funaga saw only what they expected to see, but just in case, the sea would conceal our approach. Then she bade me hold my breath. Seeing her intention, I sucked in a lungful of air and tried not to be afraid as she dove under the water. Our speed was so great that I felt as if I had put my head under a waterfall. My ears began to ache as the weight of water above us grew, and I prayed that Ari-roth would realize my lung capacity was not as great as hers. Ari-roth heard and bade me calm myself, lest the song of my fear summon azahk. The image she offered told me she spoke of sharks. I would have felt frightened at their mention, but my need for air was too urgent. To my relief, Ari-roth turned back toward the surface, and we sped upward even more quickly than we had descended. Before I had the chance to gasp in a breath and register the looming bulk of the greatship and the smaller shape of a ship boat, I heard a voice say distinctly, "Did you hear that?"

Without hesitation, Ari-roth twitched me from her back and leapt into the air, rising from the shadow cast by the ship into the moonlight. For a moment, she was gloriously limned in silver, then she dived back into the waves, only to leap up again. Someone cried out in delight, and a man shouted to someone else to come and see. A stern voice commanded them all to shut their mouths lest they wake every fool who slept on the Land. The men fell silent, but still Ari-roth leapt and cavorted so magnificently that I knew their eyes would track her.

I caught hold of the edge of the little ship boat and was elated, if surprised, to discover that it had been lashed to the metal rungs of a ladder leading up the side of the ship. I soon realized why. A number of boards had been roughly hammered on to patch a splintered gash in the hull. This must be the ship whose shipmaster had miscalculated the gap when leaving the sea cavern. The ship boat had obviously been lowered and lashed to the ladder to offer a stable platform from which repairs could be carried out.

I shivered and realized that I was growing cold without Ari-roth's aura to keep me warm. Hunger and thirst were returning, too, along with the pain of my cuts and bruises and a deadly weariness. Ari-roth had leapt out of sight now, but the stifled cries of admiration and splashes told me she had gone around to the other side of the greatship to give me the best chance of boarding unseen. Unfortunately, I was much weaker than I had thought, and it took several attempts to lever myself up onto the edge of the ship boat. To my dismay, my grip slipped, and I slithered forward to land in the bottom of the boat with a distinct thud. Immediately, I reached for a crumpled canvas lying at one end of the boat and pulled it over myself, wrinkling my nose at the stench of fish. I was not a moment too soon, for almost immediately, I heard the sound of boots and a voice directly above.

". . . heard something?" a man's voice asked.

"One of the boards might have sprung free." The answer came in a voice that sounded far too young for a shipman. Both speakers had the soft-edged accents of Norselanders.

I heard someone else approaching, and the older Norselander said with stiff politeness, "The sighting of a ship fish augurs well, Master Herder."

"Superstitious nonsense, Shipmaster," snapped another man in a sharp, disapproving voice. "There is only the righteous will of Lud for good or ill, and as we are his chosen and serve him, we have no need of omens to know that we will be victorious."

I caught my breath, for surely it was the voice of the old priest I had heard in the cavern. But I had seen him and the other Herder board the *Black Ship,* so Salamander must have come here to let the Herder transfer to this ship. Perhaps he had also set down his force here. I sent out a probe, focusing on the Herder, knowing that if I could reach and control his mind, I would be able to use his authority to prevent the remaining ships from leaving. To my intense disappointment, I encountered the unmistakable buzzing rejection of a demon band. The older Norselander was speaking now, and I tried his mind. It was barred as well, which could only mean that everyone aboard was demon-banded because of their closeness to the Land. On impulse, I tried their younger companion and was astounded to find he was unbanded!

His name was Lark, and as I had guessed from his voice, he was little more than a boy. But not just any boy. He was the son of the Norse shipmaster who commanded the vessel! Delving into his mind, I found that he did not wear a demon band, because he had stowed away to be with his father, so no band had been provided for him.

I turned my attention to the conversation between the two older men, reflected in the mind of the boy, and heard the priest bid the shipmaster come with him to look at a map. The older man gave the boy a quelling look, which the boy took in well enough for me to momentarily see the shipmaster. He was a tall, handsome Norselander with long, fair, side plaits; direct, very blue eyes; and a weary, troubled air.

Left alone, the boy turned to look down at the ship boat where I lay hidden. To my relief, he was not worried about an intruder so much as the hasty repair coming undone, for the Herders had refused to allow them to stop and repair the hull properly. If only they would let his father do his job! All would have been well if the priests aboard their ship had not insisted on deciding when the ship would leave the sea cavern, for the resulting damage was a good deal more worrying than the priests seemed to realize. *Perhaps they thought their precious Lud would keep a holed boat afloat because of the righteousness of its passengers,* Lark thought sourly.

Underneath the boy's concern about the damaged ship, I found a deeper fear arising from the knowledge that only his father's refusal to allow it had stopped him from being hurled overboard when the Hedra captain had discovered him hiding in the hold. The boy's mind told me that both the Norselanders and the Herder priests called the warrior priests of their order *Hedra,* and I remembered that the priests in the cavern had used the same term. The boy thought of how his father had defied the old Herder priest, saying bluntly that if the boy was killed, he would not master the vessel, and none of the other seamen had the skill for it. The Hedra captain, Kaga, had then proposed that Lark's tongue be cut out as a punishment, but again his father had refused to permit it.

I dropped beneath the boy's conscious thoughts and began to scour his mind for memories of his movements about the ship to familiarize myself with its layout. In doing so, I learned that twelve shipmen and eight priests were on board, and six of these were high-ranking Hedra, with Hedra Kaga most senior. All of the Hedra but Kaga and the other five had gone ashore with the Hedra from the *Orizon* and the *Black Ship* before the latter had returned to Herder Isle to report to the inner cadre on the progress of the invasion.

Lark's fear of the cold, brutal Hedra Kaga was very strong, but he was far more afraid of the inner-circle priests, especially the inner-cadre Nine. Delving deeper into his fears, I discovered that the boy was terrified that the Nine would punish his beloved father for daring to oppose his will. According to Lark, inner-cadre members were proud and vengeful; if his father was arrested and taken into the Herder Compound on Herder Isle, it was unlikely that he would ever return.

I shivered at the potency of the boy's fears, and again I had to force myself to remember my own needs. I was lucky to have found him, and he would have access to his father, who was the shipmaster. Not that I had any illusion about who was master here. The Nine was the ultimate authority, but he and the other priests must rely upon the sea skills of the shipmaster, who would have some power until they returned to Herder Isle.

I had always assumed that the Norselanders willingly

served the Hedra, but from what I saw in the boy's mind, they were an occupied people forced to serve and obey the Faction. This news would greatly interest the Council of Chieftains, but I had much to do before I could share what I had learned.

The first step was obvious. I needed the boy to convince his father to remove his demon band, and then I would coerce the shipmaster to secretly order his men to remove *their* bands. Once I had coerced them, they could overcome Kaga, and as soon as they removed his band, I could use him to deal with the other five Hedra aboard. Then I would have the ship signal the *Orizon* and have the Nine command the ship to remain anchored. No seaman would be a match for a trained warrior, I reminded myself, so I must be careful not to incite any open confrontation. Now that I understood that the Norselanders were little more than slaves, I could not in good conscience put them in danger to further my own plans.

Lark moved toward the foredeck, deciding he would go below into the hold to check the repair and see if the leak was worse. Delicately, I changed his mind and directed his attention to Ari-roth. He noted that she was still leaping spectacularly from the waves, glittering with phosphorescence, but she was moving steadily away. Lark observed that the leaping ship fish would make a fine image to render as an offering to the goddesses to ease his passage into the longsleep. I was startled at his use of the term that beasts used for death, and my curiosity again led me further into his mind. At a deeper, half-repressed level that connected with memory, he was thinking that ship fish were supposed to be the willing servants of the three goddesses of forbidden Norse myths, which his mother whispered to him at night. The myths were banned by the Faction. Once he had asked his mother why they must be kept secret, and she had answered that until the Norse Isles were free, the stories must remain secret, for anyone repeating them would be burned.

Lark's mind told me that his father and mother had been born on Norseland, and I delved deeper, seeking to understand how his parents had come to dwell upon Herder Isle. I was very surprised to learn that Herder Isle was actually an island divided in two by a channel, where once there had been an isthmus. A vast, walled Herder Compound occupied most of the larger island, which lay closer to the Land, while the Norselanders dwelt in villages on the lesser island, arrayed about the edge of a great swampy expanse of land surrounding a single low hill at the center of the island. The smaller island was called Fallo after a Norse city that had once stood on that side of the isthmus. This bridge of land, called the Girdle of the Goddess, had been destroyed by the Faction, along with the cities of Fallo and Hevon. Hevon had stood on the larger island, facing the bay and the Land, and had been surpassing fair. I tried to find out how the Faction had destroyed two cities and an isthmus, but the boy did not know. Indeed, much of his knowledge came from tales his mother told him and, occasionally, by what he had overheard from his father's shipfolk.

Lark, his parents, and all the shipfolk lived in the village nearest the channel. His mother and father had been brought from Norseland to dwell upon Herder Isle so they would be better placed to serve their masters as shipfolk and shipwrights. The *Orizon* was one of several smaller greatships built at the Herders' behest, Lark's mind told me with faint disparagement. Many of these had foundered at sea, Lark believed, because they had not been dedicated to the goddesses who protected the Norseland shipfolk. But the *Stormdancer,* which was the ship his father mastered, had been built by one of his own ancestors and had been sailed in the days of freedom, before the Faction came. Now the Herders owned all the ships, and the Norselanders served them as they required, for anyone who defied them was taken to the Herder Compound for questioning, where they faced death by burning, or worse.

I wanted to know what "worse" entailed, but this part of Lark's mind was darker and more sensitive, because it connected to his fears of what might happen to his father upon their return to Herder Isle, so I dared not venture there.

I turned instead to Lark's childhood. He had no memory of Norseland, for his mother had given birth to him on Fallo, but he had many glowing visions, fashioned in his imagination through his mother's stories of the island. These were peopled with noble men and women akin in strength and courage to the Norse kings who had made the high rocky island their ancestral home, who farmed and tilled and wrested a living from the barren island, yet who never forgot to keep their blades sharp. His favorite fantasy was that those upon Norseland were planning an uprising and would someday come to free Fallo and Herder Isle from the Faction. But I saw from his memories that the Norselanders who served aboard ships traveling regularly to Norseland spoke of only a few scattered villages of farmers and two sizeable towns, the entire population of these being less than the number of Hedra in the training camp there.

Brydda, too, had spoken of the training camp for warrior priests on Norseland. I remembered that, according to the priests in the cavern, Ariel had a residence on Norseland, too.

The boy looked up at the moon. I saw it clearly in his mind's eye, a shining sphere across whose face now unraveled skeins of purplish cloud. I sent him to the other side of the ship to survey the Land, and the sight of the high dark cliffs evoked in him uneasy apprehensions about Landfolk whom the Herders described as little better than savages, preyed upon by dreadful fanged mutants.

I could not resist constructing and implanting a question as to why the Faction would invade the Land if it was full of savages and bestial mutants. The boy's mind immediately seized on the question but could come up with no answer. This troubled him, and he decided he would ask his father. Then he began to think about the training exercises the warrior priests had practiced on the decks. He wondered if those techniques would aid them against the mutant hordes. Seeing the exercises in his memory, I noticed they truly were very like coercer training exercises. Gevan had devised these with the help of Beforetime books unearthed by the Teknoguild, so perhaps the warrior priests were also using Oldtime books, despite their being forbidden by the Faction.

The boy's mind registered the shipmaster's summons, and he hurried to meet him, love for his father filling his mind. The shipmaster's cabin was not the best chamber aboard, as was traditional, for that had been taken by the Herders. Through Lark's mind, I saw his father close the cabin door firmly after them and turn up the wick on a lantern. The boy sat on the edge of the bed, anxiously waiting to see what his father would tell him. I prompted him to ask the question I had placed in his mind, interested to discover that it had already formed strong connecting threads to other doubts and questions. If I had not encouraged the boy to ask why the Herders were invading a land inhabited by monsters, it was clear that Lark would soon enough have come up with it for himself.

The boy watched several expressions chase one another across his father's face: astonishment, anger, concern, and, finally, wariness. But last of all, he smiled, and Lark knew this meant that his father would tell him something true, something dangerous.

"Perhaps the Landfolk are not the bloodthirsty monsters the priests preach about but are only folk who do not wish to be ruled by the Faction," the shipmaster said quietly. "But you must never speak of that possibility with anyone but me or your mother."

Lark nodded seriously, pride swelling in his mind at the trust his father placed in him. Then, prompted by me but not yet controlled, he asked, "Why do you wear a demon band if you think the people of this Land are not mutants with dreadful nullish powers?"

His father frowned. "Because it is what the priests command."

"Can I look at it?" I made the boy ask, holding out his hand.

His father hesitated, then sighed, and the boy watched him unfasten it. "Just for a moment, then." As the lock opened, I abandoned the boy for his father's mind.

His name was Helvar, and his mind showed that he was, incredibly, all that his son believed him to be: noble, strong-minded, compassionate, and generous. He was also troubled by Lark's sudden interest in the demon band and his questions about the Land's inhabitants, and he was aware that his answers, repeated, would see them both burned. He had answered Lark truthfully, because he knew the boy would appreciate his trust. He believed the questions his son had asked were a manifestation of the lad's fear of the Nine. Helvar knew very well that Lark was afraid the Herders would punish him for protecting his son, and he feared that, too. But his fear was not that he would vanish into the Herder Compound, for his skills as a shipmaster and shipwright were too valuable to be wasted. Besides, the priests' punishments were always cruel and subtle. They would be far more likely to do what both Helvar and his wife feared, which was to claim the boy as a novice.

Ever since Lark had been born, this possibility had haunted Helvar, for most Norse boys were taken from their families to become Herder novices. Helvar had done what he could to protect his son; he had taught the boy all he knew, hoping that, by the time he was old enough to be considered as a novice, he would have too many valuable ship skills to waste. And it might have been so, save that by stowing away, the boy had drawn himself dangerously to their masters' attention.

I threw up a thin coercive shield, realizing I was becoming dangerously absorbed in the compelling thoughts of a man I could not help but like and admire. My control loosened, and Helvar immediately reached out to pick up the demon band, remembering that it was death to be caught without it and wondering at his carelessness in failing to put it back on immediately.

I coerced him to set it aside again and cast about to find a thought I could use before making him ask Lark to fetch their nightmeals on a tray from the galley. As the boy closed the door behind him, his father reached again for the band, and again I had to turn his mind away. Helvar knew that the bands were dangerous, and he had told his son the truth when he had said he wore it only because he must. I made him button his shirt to the neck so the demon band's absence would not be noticed if someone entered the cabin.

Leaving his conscious thoughts, I delved deeper into the shipmaster's mind, searching out his knowledge of Herder plans for the Land. Unfortunately, he knew no more than the boy's mind had already yielded, the Norselanders being little more than a source of bonded labor and novices for the Faction. Helvar's memories showed me that he and the other shipmaster had been informed only two days before the journey that the *Stormdancer* and the *Orizon*, led by the *Black Ship*, were to carry a Hedra invasion force that would reclaim the Land from the mutants who had driven out the Faction and enslaved the Landfolk.

The shipmaster of the *Orizon* had asked where the force would land and had been told there was no need for him to know. He need only follow the slavemaster Salamander and obey the Herders' commands.

Helvar had been as amazed as the rest when Salamander had led them up the narrow inlet, with its towering stone walls, and through the impossibly tight space between the stone teeth that lined the vast sea cavern. He loathed the slavemaster but acknowledged that he guided a ship as if touched by the goddesses. For all his skill and experience, Helvar would not like to have led two ships into such a rough and narrow passage, and he had wondered if they were all sailing to their doom, for the way was too narrow and rough to turn a ship.

Half the Hedra on the three ships had disembarked immediately and vanished through an opening in the cavern. The ships had remained anchored through several tides, until Salamander had fetched the two inner-cadre priests, whereupon he had bade them sail back down the inlet.

Anger flowed briefly though the shipmaster's mind at the memory of the arrogant Hedra captain who insisted on judging the timing and angle of their departure from the sea cavern. His error of judgment had resulted in substantial damage to the ship, and I felt Helvar's anger turn to apprehension at the thought of the roughly patched hull. He was aware, as Lark had not been, that the damage would make crossing the strait a perilous enterprise. But Helvar told himself that once the Land was taken, the Nine would surely agree to the ship being properly repaired. Priests might preach about the meaninglessness of flesh compared to spirit, but they were as devoted to protecting their own skins as any man. Not the fanatical Hedra, of course, who believed that their spirits were so pure that Lud guided and blessed their every action.

Anxiety about the ship gave way to renewed anxiety about Lark and the realization that Kaga often eyed the boy with grim purpose. Helvar regretted that the captain had not gone ashore with the rest of the force because then at least the brute might have been slain. Though who would be brave or foolish enough to attack Kaga, whose bulk and strength alone would intimidate anyone, without their even seeing his deadly ability with a knife and pole?

There was a tap at the door, and Helvar rose to open it for his laden son. I waited impatiently while they ate, constantly fending off Helvar's desire to put on the demon band in case one of the priests entered. Love for his son now slightly distorted the older man's mind. He told himself that he ought to prepare the boy for the possibility of being taken as a novice, yet he could not bear the thought himself, so how should he comfort his son? And what if he was chosen to be turned into a null? He had shown no nullish abilities, but they sometimes came on when a lad's voice changed. It would kill Gutred if the boy was taken by that demon-spawn Ariel. She must already be frantic at her son's disappearance. Lark swore he had left a note with his friend Alek, explaining his intention to stow away on the *Stormdancer*. The note would say nothing of an invasion, because Lark had not known of it. But Gutred knew because Helvar had whispered the truth to her in the night. She would be mad with fear for them both.

At last the meal was done, and I immediately coerced Helvar to have Lark return the tray to the galley. Then I moved deeper into the shipmaster's mind, seeking to learn more about nulls. His conjectures had given me the horrible suspicion that nullish powers were Misfit powers.

I had to proceed more carefully, because the information I sought was contained within the area of Helvar's mind made sensitive by fear for his son. I learned that the boys who would become nulls were chosen from among the new intake of Herder novices. Ariel inspected them as soon as they entered the Herder Compound, and he tested them with a machine. Helvar had never seen the machine, but he had heard the Herders speak of it as something that fitted over a boy's skull and caused intense pain, which somehow caused them to reveal any nullish powers they possessed, even those unbeknownst to the lad being tested. Salamander then transported those whose nullish powers had been revealed to Ariel's residence on Norseland, to be purified to receive messages from Lud.

Helvar did not know what *purification* meant, save that those who survived it, and many did not, returned to Herder Isle many sevendays later, transformed into shambling idiots whose babble and wild nightmares were interpreted by Ariel as visions sent by Lud. Helvar wanted to dismiss their transformation as a cruel and insane charade, save that the nulls were known to predict the truth.

I gritted my teeth, sure that the visions seen by the nulls

were coerced into their minds by Ariel to conceal the fact that they arose from his own Misfit powers.

When I had climbed into the ship boat, I had intended to take over the mind of the shipmaster so he would summon and unband his crew. But having entered into his mind and learned the sort of man he was and that the Norselanders were being forced to serve the Faction, I found myself deeply reluctant to use him as a puppet. Helvar was a good, courageous man with no evil in him, and in other circumstances, I had no doubt that I would be glad to regard him as an ally and even a friend.

I made my decision.

"Do you wish to save your son?" I farsent, using coercion to reach his untalented mind.

✦ 16 ✦

I felt astonishment shudder through the shipmaster's mind. But Helvar was a strong man with a cool head, and he mastered himself to ask aloud, "Who speaks?"

"For your own safety, Shipmaster, do not speak aloud. Think what words you wish to say, and I will hear them, for I am one of those your masters name *monster* and *mutant*. They name me so not because I am deformed physically, but because I can speak to your mind. When I was no more than Lark's age, the Herders occupied the Land, as they did yours, generations ago. They dragged my mother and father to the fire and burned them in front of me. My parents were guilty of nothing more than opposing the Council's oppressive rule."

There was pity in Helvar's mind, but he thought a hesitant question. "You are able to reach my mind because I removed the demon band?"

"It was I who made your son ask you to remove it. I was able to reach his mind because he does not wear a band."

"Then it is true that you have the ability to control minds?"

"I could have simply made you help me. Indeed, it was what I meant to do, until I saw from your mind that you and your people are not in league with the Herders, nor do you serve them willingly. So instead I ask your help. Indeed, I think we can help one another. Your son is in danger, and I have seen what you fear for him. Knowing the Herders, I think your fear is reasonable. You believe that you have no alternative other than to accept the situation, but I will show you a way to save Lark and yourself and maybe even to bring about the peace and freedom that your wife desires."

"I cannot stop the invasion," Helvar said.

I could only admire the firm calmness of his response, for I could feel that his senses were reeling at how effortlessly I had plucked from his mind knowledge of him and his family. "I do not ask you to stop the invasion," I said. "The people of the Land, who are people like me as well as ordinary folk like you, know of the Herders' plan to invade, and they have made their own preparations."

"I hope they have many warriors, for the Hedra have made themselves the weapons of Lud, and their sole purpose is to kill anyone who opposes the Faction," Helvar said.

His words chilled me, but I did not let doubt enter my mindvoice as I replied, "I believe that the Hedra will be defeated and driven back to their ships. But it is my hope that their ships will not receive them."

"You want the ships," Helvar guessed.

The swiftness of his mind did not surprise me. I sent, "The Herders burned our ships when they fled the Land a year ago, and recently, they had their agents burn replacement ships we had begun to build. It will be many months before new ships are ready, but with these two ships, we could carry a force to the west coast immediately and free the people there. Once this is done, we will unite to deal with the priests upon Herder Isle and Norseland."

"I understand what you are saying, but what if you are wrong about your friends triumphing? You have never seen the Hedra fight. . . ."

"And you have never seen my people fight," I sent. "But I swear to you that if matters go ill for my friends, and the Hedra do win this battle, I will coerce the Herders aboard this ship not to recall that you helped me overpower them. They will think only that they were bewitched by mutants who crept aboard. I can even make them remember both you and Lark defending the Nine, and you and your shipfolk driving off the horde of invading monsters so heroically that any plan to punish Lark for stowing away will be forgotten. Then I will swim ashore."

"You could do this?"

"I could, but only if the Nine and the other priests are not wearing demon bands."

"But once they restore them . . ."

"The coercion will hold even after the bands are put back on. I promise. If you agree to help me, summon your seafolk one at a time and have them remove their demon bands so that I can be assured they are trustworthy."

"My crew will not betray me," he said, and his mind projected an image of his first shipman, a tall, scar-faced man called Oma, with dark hair rather than the usual Norse blond, who was his best friend. "Indeed, it may be *you* who has to prove that you have the power to undo what you begin, for the sake of their families."

"I will convince them," I promised. "But I must first be sure for myself that they can be trusted. We have been betrayed more than once by those who pretended to be allies."

"Very well. Then what?"

"You and your men must overcome one of the Hedra. Preferably the Nine."

"Impossible. The captain of the Hedra, Kaga, watches him constantly, and there are not enough of us to overcome him,"

Helvar answered. Then he frowned. "But I can ensure that a potion is put into his nightmeal."

"If he is dead, I cannot use him to command the other Hedra to unband."

"I speak only of a sleep potion. We have plenty aboard, because many of the Hedra suffer wave-sickness. Without Kaga to deal with, I think we could overcome his immediate underling, Ruge. But it might be simpler to drug all the Herders aboard, for then there will be no need to guard them."

"We will require at least one of them with sufficient rank to deal with the other shipmaster and any Herder aboard his ship. My suggestion is to drug Kaga, if he is as formidable as you say, and overcome the Nine to remove his demon band, for once that is gone, I can use him to control the rest."

"That can be done," Helvar said. "Where are you?"

"It is best that you do not know until we have control of the ship," I told him. This produced a surge of suspicion, as I had anticipated.

"If I refuse to help you, will you not simply use your powers to force me, despite what you have said about our not being your enemies?" Helvar asked.

"I would not force any man or woman or child to obey me, nor enter their mind and thoughts without their leave, save in direst emergency. Would you judge it so, sirrah, when your land is invaded by fanatics who will kill anyone who resists them and enslave the rest? The answer is yes, I will force you to help me, although there are many of you and I might fail, for I am alone. But before you judge me evil, remember it is not I who threatens your son. Our enemies are your enemies."

Abruptly, the connection between us dissolved as rain began to patter down on the canvas. My heart sank. Within minutes, I heard the sound of boots ringing on metal and a thud as someone jumped into the boat. The canvas covering me was wrenched away, and I found myself looking into the face of a Norselander with his unmistakable blond side plaits. He carried a lantern, and his expression in its light was so completely astonished that I wondered if I had been mistaken in thinking that Helvar had sent him to find me. I could not probe him, of course, because a demon band glinted at his throat.

He gestured brusquely for me to get up, and I obeyed, stifling a groan as my stiff, battered body protested. The Norselander immediately removed his voluminous rain cloak and draped it around my shoulders, mimicking that I should draw up the hood. I obeyed, hope burgeoning at his civility. He climbed up the ladder first, and I went after him, clenching my teeth and coercing my fingers to hold on, for I was still exhausted from my long immersion. Just as I reached the top, the hood slipped forward, blinding me. When I tried to push it back, I slipped, but before I could fall, a strong hand grasped me by the wrist. I muttered thanks and looked into the deeply scarred face of the powerfully built, dark-haired Oma, whom I had seen in Helvar's mind.

"Thank you, Oma," I said.

He looked shocked, but only muttered something to the blond Norselander, which sent him hurrying away down the deck, then he jerked his head for me to follow him. The rain that I had cursed now served us, for it had driven the Herders inside. Oma led me to a stairwell. I followed him down spiraling metal steps into a dark passage, reminding myself that Helvar trusted him like a brother. Oma had not bothered to get a lantern, but he was clearly very familiar with the ship, for he continued on swiftly, though I could see nothing. Then he stopped so suddenly that I cannoned into him, and I heard a door opening. Oma guided me through it and closed it. Only then did he light a lantern.

We were now in a tiny compact cabin with a porthole above a narrow bed fixed lengthways to the inner hull wall and a single long locker at one end. Sitting on the bed was Lark, a gaunt-faced lad a little younger than Zarak, with very long, very pale hair, partly braided as Oma's was.

I pushed the sodden hood back, and the boy gasped. "You are a woman!"

Only then did I understand the surprise of the man who had come to find me. It had not occurred to me to mention to Helvar that I was a woman, and Oma had obviously been sent to find a man. Lark was frowning. "Who did that to your face?"

"The man who betrayed the Land to the Herders," I said.

"You are not afraid?" Oma asked in his rough and yet oddly pleasant voice. He hung the lantern neatly on a hook.

"I am not, for Shipmaster Helvar will not turn me over to the Herders."

"You have the means to prevent him betraying you?" Oma asked coldly.

"I meant only that betrayal is not in his nature," I said.

The bleakness faded from the other man's ravaged face. He said, "Shipmaster Helvar asked me to bring you here. It is safer than his cabin, where the Herders might enter at any moment. This is my cabin, and it is far from the priests' sleeping chambers." He gave me an openly appraising look. I did not know what he saw, other than a lean woman with strings of drenched black hair, sodden clothes, and black and purple bruises. His eyes fell to the floor where a puddle of water was forming about my feet, and he frowned and bade me remove the cloak.

I struggled to obey, but the cloth was heavy and clung. With a murmur of exasperation, Oma reached out, peeled it off me, and hung it on one of the hooks set into the door. His fastidiousness reminded me of Reuvan, but perhaps it was more that there was so little room, even upon a greatship, that any clutter or mess could not be tolerated. In its weariness, my mind meandered like a lost sheep, and I tried to think what I should say that might convince Helvar to agree to help me. I swayed, and Lark leapt to his feet. Catching my arm, he steadied me as Oma laid a towel on the bed so I could sit.

Oma said, "Val—that is the man who found you—will have let Helvar know that you are here, and he will come to speak with you when he is able. In the meantime, Lark, see if you can't go and beg some food from the cook."

"Can I have some water?" I croaked, speaking aloud for the first time.

Lark hurried away and Oma poured water from a silver jug into a beaten metal cup. "How did you get aboard?" Oma asked as I drained the cup.

"I . . . swam," I said, too tired to explain what would not be believed.

"Helvar says your people are waiting for the Hedra."

"We knew of the invasion, but there were some aspects of it we did not expect. I got caught up in one of them, so I don't know how things are going."

"The Hedra all wear demon bands." He touched his own.

"We expected it," I said. I met his gaze and found it watchful. "What I did not expect to find was a man like Helvar Shipmaster serving the Faction."

Oma gave a snorting laugh. "Hel's greatest enemy is his nobility of mind. It has always got him into trouble."

"You believe he should not help me," I guessed.

He shrugged. "If the Herders have successfully invaded the Land, and they learn that we helped you, we will be doomed along with our bondmates and children and family. The fact that we were dead would not prevent their slaughtering our children down to the last babe."

I nodded. "I know that there is risk in your helping me. But I assure you I can do as I told Helvar and erase from the Herders' minds anything that will cause you harm, if things go ill for my people."

He frowned. "You disconcert me, woman. I expected to hear you argue that yours is the right cause and we ought to help out of the goodness of our hearts."

Before I could answer, there was a loud clanging of bells and the sound of raised voices from above. Oma stiffened at the sound of boots running back and forth on deck and in the passages on the underdeck. Suddenly the door opened and Lark burst in. "The Hedra are retreating! Your people have driven them back!"

He sounded elated, but Oma's face was somber. Like me, he realized the consequences of what Lark was saying. The Hedra were retreating before I had begun to coerce the priests aboard, and now there would be no time to do so. I had lost the chance to win us the ships!

Lark's delight faded as he saw our faces and understood, too. "I am sorry," he told me. He looked at Oma and said, "Kaga has ordered our shipfolk to go and get them. All the ship boats are going out now."

"I must get off the ship," I said. "I will swim to shore."

"I am sorry," Oma said. "There is no possibility of your leaving the ship unseen now. All the priests, including Kaga, will be on deck, and we will have to go up as well. You must stay here and be silent."

"Here is what the cook gave me," Lark said, thrusting a bread roll and a mug of milk into my hands. Oma snuffed the lantern, and they both left, closing the door firmly behind them. I groped for the shelf I had seen set into the wall by the bed and then got up to unfasten the porthole. Rain flew into my face, driven before a rising wind, and I could hear distant shouts, but I could see nothing because the porthole faced away from the Land.

I sank to my knees and buried my head in my hands. *Fool!* I cursed myself. If only I had not come aboard the ship. How conceited I had been to believe I could single-handedly stop the Herder ships from leaving.

Hours seemed to pass as the Hedra were gradually ferried aboard, and I sat helpless, listening to their boots hammering on deck, wondering if they had merely been driven down the steps or if there had been fighting on the beach. I could not imagine what had happened ashore, and a thousand possibilities crowded through my mind as I vacillated between joy at the fact that we had forced a retreat and despair at the realization that I had trapped myself. Then I heard the unmistakable sound of an anchor being hauled in, and a chilly terror flowed through me at the thought that I was being taken to Herder Isle.

I knelt up at the porthole again and watched as the ship turned, until I saw the long wet cliffs of the Land as they hove into view, silver-sheened wherever the moonlight had found a rent in the clouds. I saw specks of orange light moving rapidly down the cliff where the steps would be and knew that must be people descending, carrying lanterns; Landfolk, for the ships were moving away from the Land on the tide. Watching the lights cluster along the beach, I wondered with a wrench if Rushton carried one of them. Certainly he would have ridden in with Dardelan and the rebel force, for they must have arrived, otherwise, how else would the Hedra have been defeated? Then it struck me that even if Rushton was standing on the shore, neither he nor anyone else could have any idea that *I* was aboard one of the fleeing Herder ships.

I watched helplessly until I lost sight of land, and then I sank back on my heels, appalled at the mess in which I found myself. I was trembling, and I told myself sternly that it was because I was cold. Glad to have some activity to distract me momentarily, I climbed off the bed, peeled off my sodden outer clothes, and hung them and the towel under the cloak on the back of the door. Last of all, I dragged one of the blankets from the bed and wrapped it around me, grateful for the prickly warmth. I sat back on the bed and sternly told myself not to panic. Helvar and his crew would hide me, for if I was found aboard, they would be suspected of helping me. I was going to Herder Isle, but not as a prisoner.

Not *quite,* said a voice drily in the back of my mind.

I ignored it, telling myself that the Norselanders could smuggle me into their village on Fallo, and I would simply hide there until Dardelan and the others built their ships and came to deal with the Faction. I had no doubt they would come, though I dared not guess how long it might take, for lacking the ships we had hoped to capture, they would have to build them first. In the meantime, everyone I loved would think I was dead or taken captive. Unless Maryon foresaw what had happened to me.

I gritted my teeth in anger at the thought that the futureteller might have foreseen it already and chosen to remain silent. Then I chided myself that she would only have done so if she truly believed that it was necessary. But what good could possibly come of my being carried against my will to Herder Isle? And how long could I hope to remain hidden on Fallo before the Faction learned of it? A village was not like a city where a lone person could live unnoticed. And if I was discovered, it would not just be the seamen aboard the *Stormdancer* who would die, but all those in the village.

I ought to have been too frightened to sleep, but I was weary to the bone, and as I sat there growing warmer, my eyelids began to close. I fought sleep for a little while; then I lay down, simply too tired and wretched to worry about someone finding me.

I dreamed the old dream of walking through a dark tunnel filled with the slow drip of water into water. The dream seemed colorless and remote, as if it were the memory of a dream. I slipped from it into another dream in which I was flying. It was vivid and thrilling. *I'm free,* I thought. Then, without any sense of the dream changing or any feeling of disruption, I was somewhere dark, and Matthew turned to me, smiling reassurance.

"I need to gan close enow to hear," he whispered.

"What do ye think ye'll learn?" asked another voice.

"Listen, these slavemasters of ours came here; they murdered th' queen an' enslaved her people. No one kens where they came from or why," Matthew said. "An' now this ship has come with its strange white-faced lord, who wants to negotiate the purchase of a great many slaves. Thousands! That is what I heard one of the masters say yesterday. He said someone suggested breedin' us to meet the demand. But the white-faced lord said that breeding slaves would take too long. Th' masters mun provide full-grown slaves in a year. The white-faced lord says he will return with ships enow to carry them and with payment. Why do they want so many slaves all at once?"

"An' ye think ye'll find answers to yer questions pokin' in th' heads of a few ragtag seamen?" The speaker sounded older than Matthew, and weary. But I could not make myself see him. The vision was fixed on Matthew.

"Seamen ken more than anyone else about other lands," Matthew said. "I want to find out where this white-faced lord comes from."

"What difference does it make? It's all th' same to us."

Matthew shook his head impatiently and leaned forward to peer around the corner of the building in whose moon shadow they stood.

I opened my eyes to see Lark's face illuminated in a spill of sunlight from the porthole, and the events of the night flooded back into my mind with devastating clarity.

"What is happening?" I asked, pushing the dream of Matthew to the back of my mind.

"It's morning. Let's speak inside my mind as you did with my father," Lark whispered. "It will be safer than talking aloud."

I nodded and evoked a picture of us in his mind.

He flinched.

"This will make it easier for you to speak to me with your thoughts," I farsent the explanation to him.

"Is it true as Oma said that you made me get my father to take off his demon band?" Lark asked, his image laboriously articulating the words loudly and slowly.

"Yes," I told him, resisting the impatient desire to simply sift the information I needed from his mind. "What has been happening?"

"Kaga is furious. He demanded to know why the Hedra who went ashore here retreated without even engaging in battle. The captain who had led the force up from the sea caverns said he had commanded the retreat, because almost all of his Hedra had been killed or taken prisoner by a host of mutants and beasts as well as ordinary men and women whose minds were controlled by the mutants, he said no human force could oppose them, however brave. Kaga killed him. He wanted to lead another attack, but the Nine has forbidden it. We are going back to Herder Isle."

I had known where we must be bound, yet it was still a blow to hear the words. "How many Hedra are aboard the *Stormdancer*?"

"Over half. It is a pity more were not killed, for both ships are overloaded, since they must bear all those who came here on the *Black Ship*, and the *Stormdancer* is taking on a lot of water. We are lagging behind the *Orizon*, because we dare not go any faster."

"What will happen when we reach Herder Isle?"

"We will anchor in Hevon Bay, which is very close to the entrance to the Herder Compound. Usually, the ships are anchored out from the shore in deeper water, but my father will ground the *Stormdancer* so we can repair her damaged hull. My father thinks that the Hedra and the priests aboard the *Orizon* will have gone inside the compound by the time we drop anchor, but the crew of the *Black Ship* are not Norselanders. They always remain on board, save for Salamander, who will go inside for a time. My father says you must remain hidden on board until it is safe to move. We will cross to the channel in Fallo in small ship boats as soon as we land. I am to go with Oma because my father may have to go into the compound to make a report."

272

I did not need to be an empath to read the boy's fear for his father. "Lark, I am sure that the Herders will be too concerned about the failure of the invasion to worry about your stowing away. What happens after Helvar makes his report?"

"If they allow it, he will come home, too, in our ship boat."

"Perhaps I can come to Fallo with him?"

"You must wait until the next day," Lark said. "The Hedra always set a watch on the ships, but they change them every few hours. Oma says you must slip into the water when the watch goes ashore and remain in the shadow of the ship until the new watch comes aboard. They will inspect the ship as the old watch marches back to the compound, and that is when you will be able to swim to the boulders at the end of the beach. Wait until the third watch to move, for the Hedra will be less alert. Oma says to hide in the rocks and wait until my father and the others return to clean the ships and begin repairs on the *Stormdancer*. We will tether our ship boats by the rocks, and while we are working, you can get aboard and hide under the canvas that will be there. The boat is called *Gutred,* after my mother. At the end of the day, we will bring you home with us."

My heart sank at the thought of hiding in the rocks for a night and day. "Can't I just swim across to the village? The channel cannot be very wide."

"Nor is it. But there is a watch-hut atop each corner of the wall surrounding the Herder Compound; one overlooks the channel. You would be seen if you tried to swim across," the boy answered. "I must go back out now. I will try to come again later in the day." He rose to his feet, but I forestalled him to ask how long it would be before we reached Herder Isle. "It is not long past dawn now, but because of the currents and the shoals, we will not arrive at Hevon Bay before tomorrow night."

After Lark had gone, I got up and stood indecisively in the darkened cabin. I would have paced except that I feared making any noise. Eventually, I ate the stale roll Lark had brought, drank the milk, and then lay on the bed. But there were shouts and thuds and footsteps in the hall outside the cabin, and I leapt up a dozen times in fright before I decided to make a seat for myself in the locker. I left the door open and stretched out my legs, knowing that I need only pull them in and close the locker door if anyone entered.

For a time, I cheered myself by imagining the shock the warrior priests must have got at finding themselves opposed by beasts as well as humans in Saithwold. I wondered what would be made of my disappearance. Linnet, Khuria, Gahltha, and Wenda all knew where I had gone, and eventually the tunnel in the cloister would be discovered and followed to the sea cavern where the debris left by the priests would tell its own tale. Then what? They would assume I had been caught. I doubted anyone would judge me fool enough to willingly board one of the ships, though that was exactly what I had intended to do.

Weary of thinking, I drew the locker door closed and made myself as comfortable as I could. Sleep claimed me then, and I was glad. After a good night's sleep, I would be physically ready to face what the morrow brought, if not mentally.

A thunderous crash brought me out of the locker, my heart hammering. It sounded as if a great cliff of ice had fallen on the ship, but there had been no impact. I scrambled up onto the bed, opened the porthole, and peered out. It was night still, and I could see the lanterns that marked two ships in the distance. One was likely the *Orizon*, though it was impossible to tell at that distance in the darkness. It looked as if the larger ship was approaching it. There was another great clap of sound, and I saw something bright red fly in a swift high arc from the larger ship to the smaller. Then there was a violent explosion, and a flower of orange and white bloomed against the velvet-dark night as the smaller ship burst into flame. I cried out in shock and then, realizing in horror what I had done, pressed my hand to my mouth, but no one came to investigate my cry. Probably everyone had rushed up on deck, hearing the first crash, and so there had been no one to hear a woman scream on a ship of only men.

I looked out the porthole again and saw that there was now a wedge of drowning flame and a single ship visible. I had no doubt it was the *Black Ship,* for no other ship had such deadly power. But why would the *Black Ship* strike its ally?

I remembered suddenly that I could reach Lark's mind. I sent out a probe that located swiftly, but rather than communicating with him, I merely listened to the information his senses were bringing to his mind. Incredibly, it seemed that the *Black Ship* had fired on the *Orizon,* and from the furor among the Hedra, no one had any idea why. Then Lark registered with frightened excitement that the *Black Ship* was signaling them. I waited within Lark's mind, sharing his anxiety as the shipman reading the flags spelled out the message: *The other ship was sunk because it had been boarded by mutants.*

My ears roared, but I forced myself to remain within Lark's mind in case there was more.

"How could Salamander know there were mutants aboard?" he heard one of the warrior priests ask another.

"He has one of Ariel's nulls aboard," the other answered impatiently.

"But everyone knows their visions can only be interpreted by Ariel," another spoke.

My blood turned to ice in my veins at the thought that Ariel had been aboard the *Black Ship* all this time. And how long before he knew that I was aboard the *Stormdancer*?

Lark did not come until dawn lightened the sky, staining the clouds rose-gold. He brought a tray heaped with food and a privy pot that he handed over with a blush, explaining that his father had pretended to be angry and had sent him to Oma's cabin. Most of the crew were on deck, and the Hedra were practicing their martial arts, so it was unlikely anyone would come along the passage, but, he warned, we must be careful to keep our voices very low.

I nodded and asked where Oma had been sleeping. He answered that the big shipmate had slept on the deck like others of the crew. Fortunately, this was a common practice, so no one thought it odd.

Lark began to tell me what had happened to the *Orizon*, but I told him that I had seen its destruction. I told him what I had overheard and asked if it was true that Ariel was aboard. To my intense relief, the boy shook his head. He said, "Salamander always keeps at least two of Ariel's nulls aboard his ship, and it is said he can read their visions almost as well as Ariel himself. The flagman told me that the *Black Ship* had been on its way back to Herder Isle so the Herder could make a report to the Three when Ariel's nulls began screaming that mutants had taken over the *Orizon*. I have known those shipmen all my life, and now they are dead. But I think you must grieve, too, for your people were also aboard."

I nodded, my mind still groping to take in the news that nulls were capable of seeing the future even when Ariel was not with them. Which had to mean that they were real futuretellers! Then I thought of those who had perished aboard the *Orizon* and felt like weeping. "I do not know which of my friends were aboard or how they managed it. But Ariel has been responsible for too many deaths of people I loved," I said, feeling the weight of my grief.

"Ariel is responsible for many deaths on Herder Isle, too," Lark said. "But you need not fear that you will be exposed by the null as your friends were, for the flagman sent that both nulls died confirming the vision. Nulls are fragile and rarely last more than a few visions."

"It is strange that the nulls did not see the failure of the invasion," I said.

Lark shrugged. "They do not see many things, but what they do see is almost always true."

I did not want to think about which of my friends might have died, so I forced myself to change the subject. "Tell me what you know about Ariel's residence on Norseland."

He answered that he knew little, save that the residence stood on a rocky knoll at the high island's less populous end. The closest settlement to it was Cloistertown, which had grown up around what had once been a Herder cloister. It had been abandoned, and now all the priests on Norseland dwelt in the island's only other cloister. This was walled, Lark added, and its watch-huts overlooked Main Cove where all ships anchored to unload those who would climb the narrow road up to the top of the island. Covetown had grown up around the top of the trail from the Main Cove and was the largest settlement on the island.

"I heard there was a training camp on Norseland," I prompted.

He nodded. "That is on a plateau that rises up from the flatland behind Covetown and the cloister."

"How did the Herders take control of the Norselands in

the first place?" I asked curiously.

"Partly by treachery," Lark said. He went on to explain that some generations past, when the Norse king was making his annual journey from Norseland to Herder Isle for the sevenday summer festival, a great storm had blown up. After the storm, a broken ship carrying thirty-nine Herders was found cast up on the beach at Hevon Bay. They were brought to Hevon City to be cared for, and when the king asked where they had come from, they said only that their homeland was no more. Pitying the stranded priests, the old king had offered them land on which to build homes. He also gave them permission to woo and bond with the Norse women that they might settle more truly. But these men wanted no women, and it was not homes they built upon the rocky land behind Hevon City but a small compound where they lived communally and worshiped their punitive Lud.

Next summer festival, when the king came to Herder Isle, the priests bade him forsake the three goddesses worshipped by the Norselanders. The old king laughed and said the priests might worship a male god if they chose, but he preferred the softness of the three goddesses. Being a generous and good-humored man, he granted the priests' request for more land to extend their cloister, for they had persuaded a shipwright to rebuild their ship and had begun to make trips across the strait, bringing back young boys they claimed were converts to the Faction.

No one thought to question the boys, who had been immediately taken inside the compound for the cleansing period of isolation and silence the priests claimed was needed to prepare them for the Faction. Indeed, the king was often heard to comment that life in the Land across the strait must be harsher than it had been when Norselanders had gone there to trade, for why else would any lad agree to join this loveless order?

"Eventually," Lark continued, "by dint of wheedling and begging and demanding, the Faction took over an entire section of Herder Isle. The Norselanders gave little protest because the area included a patch of deadly Blacklands. But there were some rumblings of discontent when the Faction began to build a high wall around the land they had been given. The Herders claimed this was merely to protect the compound and its farmlands from bitter sea winds."

I guessed that this must have happened about the time the Council had formed an alliance with the Faction, bestowing upon them land to build their cloisters in each province. No doubt they had recognized that an alliance with a terrifying religious order could only strengthen their hold upon the Land. I had not realized that the Herders had first established themselves upon the Norselands, but I had no doubt that the boys who had supposedly wanted to become novices were given no choice. "But you still have not said how they took control," I prompted.

Lark nodded and went on to explain that the old king had been interested in the order's apparent vigorous growth and the stern discipline it imposed on its converts. They worked very hard and did not speak, and their silent dedication seemed to him admirable. He thought his own son an overindulged weakling, too much under the sway of his mother, grandmother, and aunts, so when the One of the Faction offered to educate the boy in the austere ways of the cloister, he agreed. By the time the king died, his son was a devout believer in the Herders' Lud.

Lark went to get some water from a wooden barrel behind a wall panel and to listen awhile at the door. Then he came back to sit on the bed and continued his tale. "By the time the old king died," he went on, "there were many more priests, and the Faction all but ruled the Norselands through the old king's son. He came to be known as the Last King, for when he died, the Herders claimed that he had abdicated in their favor. There was no proof of it, and there was an uprising to oppose it. That was when the cities of Hevon and Fallo were destroyed and Herder Isle divided."

"But how . . . ?"

"The Faction used Beforetime weapons. My father believes they brought them when they came to Herder Isle, though then it was all named Fallo Isle. In any case, once they had taken over, they sailed to Norseland. Instead of fighting, they released several people who had witnessed the destruction of the cities on Fallo and the Girdle of the Goddess. The Pers—they are our leaders—refused to surrender, for how could the invaders manage to get their dread weapons up onto the land?

"Again the Herders struck, using some terrible weapon that flew like a bird, and the great city of Kingshome and the cliff upon which it stood, broke away and plummeted into the cove. Not one person survived. What else could those who remained on the island do but lay down their arms? The Herders have ruled the Norselands ever since. To begin with, they ruled from Norseland, but after the compound was complete, that became the center of power," Lark concluded solemnly.

A picture rose in his mind of great black metal gates, set in an impossibly high stone wall, opening slowly to reveal a big black square surrounded by stone buildings similar to cloisters, save that they were formed of black rock instead of the gray of the Land. The compound buildings had the same high narrow windows and sloping roofs as Land cloisters, but they were roofed in some dark stiff thatch instead of being tiled, as was the custom in the Land. Herders passed back and forth in gray robes, and there were smaller figures in white or black robes. All moved like objects underwater, as if driven not by their own will but by a slow inexorable current. The vision was very dark and loomed oddly and unnaturally, which told me that the memory was distorted by Lark's emotions. Even so, it was clear that it was not just a large cloister behind the wall but a city. A city of Herders.

I slept on and off through the long slow day that followed. The moon had risen before I was roused by the sound of the horn, which Lark had told me would signal our approach to Hevon Bay. I could see nothing from the porthole in Oma's cabin but open sea; however, I was able to catch glimpses of the island in Lark's mind. At my request, he made a careful point of visualizing whatever he thought might interest me. In this way I saw that unlike the Land, there were no high dark cliffs to be surmounted. Like the west coast, the moonlit island was very flat, yet it was impossible to see the channel that now divided the island, or the villages on Fallo, or even the hill that was said to rise from its swampy heart, for an immense stone wall rose up all along the island's coastline, so high that it obscured everything behind it. It had been built so close to the edge of the island that it looked like a wall rising straight from the sea. Indeed, when the tide rose high or was storm driven, it must crash against the base of the wall. From Lark's description, I knew that the wall surrounded all the land that had once been Hevon City and that it ran right along the channel that separated it from Fallo Island. The only bit left unwalled was a wide flat spit of land that curved around the beach that formed Hevon Bay. As we passed along the wall, which surely could not be as high as Lark's mind showed it, I noted the watch-house overlooking Hevon Bay and remembered that Lark had spoken of another surmounting the corner of the wall facing the channel. No wonder he had said I could not swim it without being seen.

"Why build a wall?" I asked when Lark came down a little later.

"No one knows, but it is said that they were matching a bit of Beforetime wall at the end of the island near the patch of Blacklands," Lark said. We heard a shout, and the boy stiffened and listened a moment before saying, "We are about to anchor. I had better go up on deck. Remember, stay hidden until the third watch is sounded, and find a place in the rocks to hide as close as possible to where the ship boats will be tethered. You will see the places where pegs have been driven into the stones," he told me earnestly. Then he muttered a curse and added, "I am a fool. I forgot to tell you that the *Black Ship* is not here."

"Not here? But it was coming here to report to the Herders."

"It was here not two hours past, the flagman on the walls signaled. But now it has gone to Norseland. The route passes on the other side of Fallo, which is why we did not see it leaving. You will be pleased to know that Ariel has gone with him."

I was more than pleased; I was relieved. After Lark had gone, I climbed into the locker and locked the door. I could undo it from inside the cupboard, but we had agreed that it would be safer for me to be locked in since each new watch would make a cursory inspection of the ship when they came aboard. I was trying to find a comfortable position that I could maintain for some hours, when the ship lurched hard and gave a loud creak. It was coming about, I guessed, and then I heard the rattle of a chain as the anchor was lowered. The noise of disembarking that followed seemed to go on forever, but I distracted myself from the cramped locker by watching it in flashes in Lark's mind. In the end, I left him because his fear for his father now filled his thoughts and had begun to rouse my own fears. When I tried to reach Lark a little later, I could not contact him, which meant that the Norseland crew had gone ashore, and the boots I could hear now all belonged to Hedra.

It was hot and stuffy in the locker, but I resisted the temptation to unlock the door and get out. Better to be uncomfortable and alive, I told myself. Suddenly, I heard footsteps coming down from the deck. From the sound of the boots, several people were coming along the passage toward the cabin where I was hidden.

". . . that is what he told us . . . ," a man said.

I heard the next cabin door open and then close. Then Oma's door opened, and I held my breath.

"This is it," said a man's voice.

Footsteps and then the locker door rattled. "It's locked," said another man's voice.

"Break it open," said the first speaker. "She must be there."

◆ 17 ◆

THERE WAS A great crash, and wood splintered under the force of a hard heel. I had a brief glimpse of a group of Herder priests, bald, robed, and demon-banded, peering at me, and then the sundered remnants of the locker door were torn aside and a rough hand reached in to haul me out by the hair. A Hedra captain stared into my face with eyes that burned with a fanatical icy fire above a thin nose and a lipless slash of a mouth.

"A woman!" he said in disgust.

"Not a woman, Bedig," said the slow quavering voice of an old man.

The Hedra dragged me around to face a tiny wizened priest with coal-black eyes set in a face collapsed into a nest of wrinkles. The thick gold band about his upper arm denoted him a Three and one of the most powerful men in the Faction, save for the mysterious One. Ignoring the younger priest's half-incoherent bleating, he drew closer to me and peered into my face.

"A female mutant," he said with a soft, hissing emphasis that brought gooseflesh to my arms.

Another younger priest appeared at the cabin door, panting, "Master, the Norseland shipfolk have already gone across to Fallo, including their master. He was dismissed by the Nine."

The Three turned to look at the younger priest. "I bade you inform me the moment the *Stormdancer* anchored."

"Master, the null said the ship was damaged and that it would be near morning before—"

"It is a fool who relies upon the visioning of a single null. Did you confirm the vision, Daska?"

The other seemed to shudder under the old man's glaring disapproval. "Master, there was only the one null left," he whispered. "They die so easily. . . ."

"I know that, you fool. Why do you think I bade you organize a watch?"

"I spoke to the watch—"

"I told you to organize a separate and specific watch for the ships."

"The *Orizon* . . . ," Daska began.

"Ariel told us what happened to the *Orizon* at the same time he informed us of the null's prediction that another mutant was hidden aboard the *Stormdancer*. But none of that is your concern. Why did you not do as I commanded?"

The other priest cringed. "Master, forgive me. . . ."

The Three turned to the Hedra holding me. "Bedig, see that Daska is whipped and then confined to a tidal cell for a fourday," he said indifferently. "Let the crabs teach him obedience."

"Master," the Hedra captain intoned.

"Also, I want this ship's master and his crew brought back for questioning immediately."

"Their families, Master?" Bedig asked.

The Herder considered it, then shook his head. "Not yet. Let the Norsemen hope that they can prevent us from punishing their families by offering us information. Then when we bring the families in, the pain of learning that they have been taken will be much greater because it will contain true despair." He spoke blandly as if he was telling someone how to arrange a vase of flowers or lay a table. "Now let us get this mutant into the compound and see what we can learn about why it boarded this ship, rather than the *Orizon*."

"Master, is not the interrogation of the mutant to wait until Ariel returns from Norseland with his interrogation machine and the special null?" asked Bedig.

"Ariel left instructions that the creature not be damaged, for the interrogation will be vigorous and requires a subject in good condition. However, despite his undeniable usefulness, Ariel is not one of the inner cadre. Now band the mutant," snapped the Three.

The demon band was heavier than the one Malik's armsman had put on me and the taint so strong that it made me feel sick. But it turned my stomach less than the knowledge that Ariel had known I was aboard the *Stormdancer*. Bile rose in my throat, and I leaned forward and vomited.

The Three uttered a disgusted sound and went out, leaving Bedig to drag me after him. Strangely, after that first overwhelming moment of sick terror, I felt no fear as they marched me through the ship and up onto the deck. It was as if I had vomited it out. It was dark enough that lanterns had been lit, for the tide of black clouds I had seen from Oma's cabin now covered the face of the moon, and even as I was hurried down the ladder and into the ship boat, I heard the rumble of thunder, and it began to rain.

I ought to have felt guilt, knowing that the shipfolk would be taken into the compound because of me, but my emotions seemed to be locked in a distant room. Once the boat had run aground, Bedig pulled me out and marched me up the shore. A flash of lightning revealed a monstrous wall, which was easily as high as Lark's mind had shown, and giant metal gates opened to receive us like a great black maw. As I was ushered through them, there was a long, low growl of thunder, and it came to me that I would never leave this fearsome place alive. As if to underline this truth, the gates swung closed behind me with a dull clang that rang in the air with deadly finality.

It was so dark now that I could see no more than patches of the wall's great hewn stones where lanterns hung. Lightning flashed, and I saw that we had entered the wide yard surrounded on three sides by the black buildings I had glimpsed in Lark's mind. The façade of buildings was broken here and there by narrow streets. From one of these, a number of bald, white-robed novices came hastening with lanterns. No doubt the gate watch had seen us approach and had summoned them. One carried a fresh cloak for the Three, and the old man allowed himself to be ministered to without acknowledging the novice. For his part, the boy replacing his wet cloak was so self-effacing that I had the feeling he strove to be invisible. Thunder rumbled again as another novice held out the basket he carried, and the Three and the other priests removed their demon bands and placed them in it. Then Bedig barked a command, and the other Hedra departed, the terrified-looking Daska in their midst. The novices left, too, save one with a lantern, and at an impatient signal from Bedig, he set off and we followed, the Hedra once again grasping my arm.

I tried to control my mind's skittering by mentally building a map as we passed along one narrow street after another. I had invented the technique and taught it to farseekers as a way of controlling and calming the mind as well as gaining useful information. Its effectiveness was weakened by my knowing that I was unlikely to have the chance to use that knowledge.

As we passed along yet another black, rain-swept street, lightning flared on the long blank face of the buildings on either side of us, and it struck me that I had not seen a single door in any of the buildings, which meant that all the buildings must be connected. Indeed, there were even elevated stone walkways passing overhead from one side of the street to the other, linking the buildings. This was not a city filled with Herders working and living individual lives; it was a nest such as ants or bees construct, with the whole community living for one single idea and purpose.

At last we came to a deep-set black door atop a short flight of steps. There were Hedra standing before it, but seeing the Three, they pressed their hands to their throats as if in salute and stepped smartly aside. The novice with the lantern ran up the steps to open the door, and as we followed the Three inside, I thought, *I will never leave this place alive.*

This time, strangely, the cold weight of the thought calmed me.

Two boys clad in hooded black robes awaited us in the shadowy foyer, each bearing a lantern that swung from a stick. There was no sign of the white-clad novice, and I realized that he had probably departed when we entered the building. I had no idea what the black attire signified, but if the novices had seemed to wish themselves invisible, these boys were invisible, for neither Bedig nor the Three even looked at them. I could not make out their expressions, for they kept their heads tilted forward.

The Three had taken two steps across the foyer when a young Herder priest, accompanied by yet another black-clad lantern bearer, emerged from the door farthest to the left and bowed to the Three. His armband revealed him to be an inner-cadre Nine, which surprised me, for Farseeker research had shown that seniority ruled all matters in the Faction, yet he was no more than Rushton's age. He commiserated with the Three about the rain, and there seemed something in his voice less obsequious than there ought to have been, given that he was speaking to a Three. Perhaps the Three thought so, too, because the old man made an impatient silencing gesture and asked sharply what he wanted.

The young Herder bowed and said, "Master Mendi, the One bids you come to him at once. He wishes to see the mutant whose presence upon the *Stormdancer* was foreseen by Ariel's null."

The Three frowned. "The One cannot wish to trouble himself with this creature, Falc."

"I do not presume to know what the master wishes. I tell you only what he told me to say, Master Mendi." The delicate malice in his words was unmistakable.

The Three hesitated a moment, then snapped, "I will come as the One commands, of course. I am only concerned for his comfort and health."

"The comfort and health of the One have been much disturbed by the failure of the invasion," the young priest said, going back through the door by which he had entered.

"That has disturbed all of us," Mendi responded coldly, keeping pace with him and ignoring the hooded lantern-bearer who had slipped ahead to light the dark passage. "It is only a pity that Ariel's nulls did not foresee it or the loss of the *Orizon* in time to avert it," the Three added.

"Perhaps you will convey your displeasure with Ariel's nulls to the One, Master Mendi," Falc said with an arch smile. "Or maybe you would prefer to wait until Ariel returns so you can make your complaints directly to him."

Mendi's lips tightened. "Shall we make haste? I am sure the One will not be pleased that I was slow to answer his summons, because you felt the need to air your thoughts on the way."

Falc stopped before a door and curtly bade us enter. We obeyed and found ourselves in a very narrow passage of rough stone with a roof high enough to defeat the weak light shed by the lanterns. The passage ran straight for so long that its end was lost in shadow. We had been walking along it for some time before I realized that its stone floor sloped slightly upward. Despite the absence of doors or windows, the air was fresh, which suggested vents leading directly to the outside. I wondered why anyone would bother building a roof and walls over such a long walk.

We must have gone on for ten minutes before I saw a light ahead coming from an open doorway. Two Hedra bearing metal-capped staffs stood before it, but they moved aside when Falc commanded it. The younger priest hurried through, leaving the rest of us to follow, and I glanced back to see the black-clad lantern bearers withdraw. The chamber we entered was long and narrow and was empty except for a large carved chair drawn up to a fireplace in which flames crackled brightly. It was not wood burning in the fireplace but some queer red-brown rock that gave out great heat but almost no smoke. The floor was carpeted from wall to wall in thick overlapping animal pelts, and one wall was entirely curtained in heavy gray cloth, making the room stiflingly hot.

Falc went through a door on the fire's other side, and I heard the low, deferential hum of his voice, then he reentered, followed by two more black-robed boys. One carried a small enamel table and a goblet of water, and the other had two soft gray cushions, which he arranged carefully on the carved chair, then he crossed the room to draw the curtain. It must have been heavy, for he struggled with its weight. The curtain parted to reveal an enormous window with a wide, spectacular view of the dark, rain-swept sea, lit momentarily by a flash of lightning. I forgot about the mystery of the black-clad boys, for how should a building have such a view inside a monstrously walled city?

Then I understood. I thought of the long narrow tunnel we had followed and realized the passage and this chamber must be embedded *within* the wall surrounding the compound!

Bedig's grip tightened painfully on my arm, and he sank into a low bow along with everyone else in the room, dragging me with him, as an enormously fat old man wearing a gold-edged robe and a thin golden circlet about his brow was helped into the chamber by a solicitous Falc and two slender, black-robed boys. Because I was on my knees, I caught sight of the thin face of the nearest black-robed boy, who could be no older than Dragon, and for a fleeting second, his shadowed gray eyes looked into mine. He turned away, and I was left to study the huge, querulous-looking bald man being settled into his chair. It was hard to believe that this old man with his obese helplessness was the supreme priest of the Herder Faction: the terrifying One in whose name my parents and hundreds of others had died.

More than anything else, he reminded me of a great fat baby, for although his body was corpulent, the hands protruding from the gold-edged sleeves of his robe and the feet in their soft woven slippers were tiny, and his mouth was a very small, wet red bow. Only his eyes betrayed his age and power: small and as black as obsidian, they glittered with malevolent purpose.

Belatedly, I realized that fierce gaze was now fixed on me.

"The creature dares to look at me. Put out its eyes," the One said in a queerly feminine voice.

"Of course they must be put out, Master," said another voice, and I turned with everyone else in the room to see another Three enter the chamber. Unlike Mendi, this was a man in his prime, with a barrel chest and well-muscled arms. If not for his gold band, I would have taken him for a Hedra. The robust newcomer crossed the room, dropped to his knee before the One's carved chair, and lifted the tiny plump fingers to his forehead.

I glanced at Mendi, who regarded this obeisance sourly. The newcomer lifted his head and said in his smooth, creamy voice, "You should not trouble yourself to command what is as obvious as the sun rising, Master. For how should a mutant be permitted to gaze upon the glorious face of the first-chosen of Lud and then look upon anything hereafter? Its eyes and its life will be extinguished as soon as it has been questioned."

The One glared at the newcomer. "Where have you been, Grisyl?"

"It has pained me to take so long to answer your summons, Master," the Three answered, rising gracefully to his feet. His eyes flickered toward me. "I presume this is the mutant revealed to us through Ariel's null and by Lud's grace?" His voice might shame honey with its warm, sliding sweetness.

"Ariel," crooned the One, his expression an odd mixture of frustration and irritated indulgence. "Yes, our faithful and clever Ariel; what did he recommend before he left, Falc?"

"To leave unharmed the mutant we would find hidden in the shipman's locker until he returns. He will bring special devices to force it to speak the truth and a special null with the power to prevent its foul powers hindering us during its interrogation, and such an interrogation will require a strong, healthy body," Falc answered eagerly.

"So Ariel said to me also," Grisyl agreed smoothly. "Of course, once the mutant has been drained of information, it will die, and that death must be slow and painful, for such a mockery of Lud's highest creation cannot go unpunished."

The One made a sound like the greedy mewling of a baby spying its mother's uncovered breast.

Mendi spoke then, his voice dry and harsh after Grisyl's mellifluous tones. "It is puzzling that Ariel's nulls did not foresee the failure of the invasion."

The One turned his black gaze onto the Three, but before he could speak; Grisyl said, "Ariel has told us many times that the nulls are unstable tools."

"Where is the Nine who commanded the invasion force?" Grisyl asked Mendi. "He was one of yours, was he not?"

Mendi gave him an impassive look. "I have ordered a period of penance and fasting, after which I will question him."

"Where is Zuria?" the One demanded.

"He is interrogating Kaga and the other Hedra who survived the abortive invasion," Grisyl said. "Naturally, he is especially anxious to learn why it failed." There was a lick of malice in his words.

Mendi opened his mouth and then closed it, as if thinking better of whatever he would have said. From what had been said, I guessed Zuria had been most strongly in favor of the invasion. But given the structure of the Faction, the invasion would never have been undertaken without the One's approval. Not that anyone would remind him of that now.

I thought of Ariel and wondered about his intentions. He had told the Herders that he would return to interrogate me, and I had no doubt that he would do so, but I doubted he would want to question me in front of the Herders about the signs and keys Kasanda had left for me. Most likely, he would contrive to get me alone. A terrible weariness assailed me at the knowledge that I would have nothing but my own will to shield me from his questions, for I had little faith in that. Long ago at Obernewtyn, Ariel, Alexi, and Madam Vega had tried to torture information from me using a machine. It had not been courage that had kept me from speaking, but a tenuous physical contact with Rushton that had allowed him to absorb part of the pain.

But there would be no rescue this time. Ariel would force me to tell him all I knew of Kasanda's instructions and the signs that would have led me to the Beforetime weapon-machines. My only comfort was that I did not know all I needed to know, nor had I all I needed to have in order to complete my quest. Perhaps Ariel intended to use me to find the remaining clues. The only way to prevent that would be to wipe my own mind clean. *Memory-death,* we called it.

I clenched my fists and felt my nails dig into my palms. Why hadn't a premonition stopped me from climbing aboard the ship boat? Why hadn't Atthis warned me not to do it? I groaned softly, realizing that even if the bird had tried to warn me, she would have been unable to reach me, for Maruman was her conduit, and he and I had been separated almost the whole time I had been in Saithwold.

Maruman, I thought, and grief stabbed at me with the knowledge that I would never again hold him or feel his dear heavy presence in my mind.

"Of course, Master," Mendi was saying. "I am only pointing out that it might have been useful to discuss what happened before Ariel hastened off. But I suppose the delay will not be so great if he returns immediately."

"Ariel must go first from Norseland to the west coast to accomplish Lud's will," said the One, giving Mendi a glare of malevolence that made the older Three step back. "You have never served Lud as well as he, Mendi, for while you seek a scapegoat for the failed invasion, Ariel is already thinking of another way to strike a blow for Lud." A fit of coughing shook the old man's enormous body. He looked at me, and his expression suddenly registered exaggerated disgust. "Who dared to bring a woman into my presence?" The words were almost a shriek.

"She is a woman only in appearance, Lord," Grisyl said swiftly, and began to stroke the One's hand as if he were a fractious child.

"Get her out of my sight." His face filled with sudden rage. "All of you get out of my sight." Grisyl offered a goblet, but the old man smashed it from his hands. "Get out, I say. Get out! Falc! Summon my shadows!" The last glimpse I had was of several black-robed boys converging silently on the One while Falc wrung his hands.

"Do not imagine that your manipulations go unnoticed, Grisyl," Mendi said as we again traversed the long wall corridor. The two Threes walked ahead, illuminated by the lanterns, and I came behind with the cold-faced Bedig, his fingers locked about my arm.

"What do you mean?" Grisyl asked coolly.

Mendi gave a sneering laugh. "You seek to ingratiate

yourself with the One. But as you see, Lud has his own means of shielding our beloved One from those who wish to pursue their own desires."

Grisyl gave him an ironic look. "Of course, Lud knows the selflessness of his two faithful servants, Zuria and Mendi."

The older Herder made a scornful sound. "I do not say that we have no ambitions of our own. But this is not the time to be divided. You seek to ally yourself with Ariel, because he is favored by the One, but Ariel is as unreliable as his precious nulls."

"I will not be held accountable for this disastrous invasion, Mendi," Grisyl said with sudden anger. "I was not with him when Ariel broke the news, thank Lud, but Zuria was, and he said the One ordered the shadow serving him to be flayed alive, because a drop of fement spilled on his robe."

"Better a hundred shadows than one of us," Mendi said dryly. "The One will calm down when we can offer him an explanation for the invasion's failure, or at least a scapegoat. I suspect we were betrayed by Malik. I said all along that it was ludicrous to trust an ex-rebel. Personally, I am more interested in learning how the mutants on the *Orizon* took control when all aboard should have been wearing demon bands until the anchor was raised. Unfortunately, we have no one from the *Orizon* to interrogate, since Salamander sank the ship and all aboard. We have only his word and the testimony of a null, now dead, that the *Orizon* was boarded at all."

"What could it serve Salamander to sink one of our greatships?" Grisyl asked. "Zuria is furious about it, of course."

Mendi grunted. "What about Ariel being sent to the west coast after going to Norseland? What is he to do there?"

Grisyl shrugged. "Lud's will, apparently. But perhaps the One simply confuses Ariel's present journey to Norseland with the longer journey he has been planning to make to the Red Land."

"I had the feeling from the One's words that Ariel is to undertake some specific task on the west coast," Mendi persisted. "Did he not specifically say that Ariel will strike a blow in Lud's name?"

"Something like that," Grisyl agreed, frowning. "And now that you mention it, I *have* heard that Ariel has been working on something special. Something to do with two nulls he has kept locked in his chamber. He has taken them with him, you know."

Mendi said, "My concern is less what Ariel has gone to do than that he chose to go or was sent without our being consulted. I dislike this policy of secrecy that excludes us but includes one who is not of the Faction."

"You speak as if Ariel desires it to be so, but you know as well as I that our master has grown more and more . . . *particular* in these last few years," Grisyl said. The two men exchanged a look as if Grisyl meant another word that Mendi knew.

"All I am saying is that Ariel should not undertake some important activity about which we have not been informed," Mendi said.

"I agree, but I doubt either of us is likely to express our indignation to the One," Grisyl said dryly. "Or have you forgotten the last Herder foolish enough to criticize Ariel to our master? Whatever Ariel will do in the west, the One has approved it, and therefore it has Lud's blessing."

Mendi scowled. "That is so. But tell me, why did the null aboard the *Black Ship* warn Salamander about the boarding of the *Orizon* yet fail to reveal the mutant aboard the *Stormdancer*?"

"Perhaps the null did reveal it and Salamander failed to understand," Grisyl said indifferently. "In any case, it is fortunate, since Ariel says that this one ranks high among the mutants and is a friend of the Black Dog and the boy chieftain. I will be most interested to hear what she can tell us."

"I, also, yet it is strange that someone so important would board a Herder vessel alone," Mendi continued. "It makes me uneasy, and I do not like that we are bidden not to interrogate her until Ariel returns. Especially if he has not merely gone to Norseland as I was led to believe. It could be a sevenday before he returns."

Grisyl nodded. "Longer, depending on what he is to do there. And you know how much more *particular* the One becomes when he is frustrated or impatient." He turned and gave me a cold, appraising look. "No doubt this mutant had some specific part to play in whatever scheme the mutants aboard the *Orizon* had in mind, for Ariel said she is extremely powerful and warned that she must not on any account be unbanded. Apparently, the null spoke her name, and Ariel knew it. He said she is the woman of the Master of Obernewtyn."

Mendi's brows rose high. "That *is* interesting. I suppose Ariel learned of the woman when the Master of Obernewtyn was our guest. But remind me, did not Ariel have some grand scheme for him?"

"Ariel has many schemes," Grisyl said dismissively. "In any case, whatever it was clearly failed. Rushton Seraphim is returned to the mutants and leads them as if nothing ever happened. Indeed, given the results of the invasion, it would seem he is more effective than ever as a leader, even if he is broken as a man. It may have been a great mistake to leave him behind in the cloister." He stopped abruptly and gave me a speculative look. "I wonder . . ."

"What?" Mendi asked impatiently.

"Well, it just occurred to me that this woman may know Ariel. After all, he did originally come from Obernewtyn, before the mutants took control."

"What of it?"

Grisyl frowned. "Perhaps this talk of special implements is merely a way to control how much the mutant tells us. I always thought there were too many gaps in his tales of what occurred in those days."

Both men glanced back at me speculatively, and Mendi said slowly, "You know as well as I do that someone will have to pay for the failed invasion. And a dozen shadows, a few Hedra, and even a Nine will not satisfy the One. But I see no reason why we should be blamed for a plan that was not of our choosing. Zuria proposed it, and Ariel supported him. Instead of trying to ally yourself with Ariel, you might see this as a perfect opportunity to drive a wedge between him and the One. None of our desires will be harmed if Ariel has less power."

"Zuria may not agree. . . ."

Mendi laughed scornfully. "Oh, I think Zuria's infatuation with Ariel will be well and truly extinct since the *Orizon* sank. Some of his best people were aboard. Besides, I doubt he will object to seeing this failure laid squarely at Ariel's door, for otherwise he must bear the brunt of the One's anger." A pause, then, "My intention is not to dispose of Ariel or harm him in any lasting way. He has been useful to us over the years, and he will no doubt continue to be so, especially when it comes to dealing with the heathens from the Red Land. I merely feel that it would be wiser to curtail his power."

"What are you suggesting?" Grisyl asked. We had now reached the entrance hall, and he turned to face the older

Three. The two men acted as if Bedig, the hovering black-clad shadows, and I were trees growing about them.

"I think that we might question this woman ourselves," Mendi answered. "As a Nine, I believe you showed a rare talent for interrogation that left no marks."

"What of Zuria?" Grisyl asked. "Should he not be present?"

"Let us leave him to his interrogations for the time being." The two men exchanged guarded smiles of complicity.

"You would have us believe that Ariel is a mutant?"

I gasped for breath. "He was at Obernewtyn. Why . . . why else would he have been there?"

"He was the son of Alexi, who was in the employ of Stephen Seraphim," Grisyl snapped. I must have looked as stunned as I felt, for no one had ever whispered that Alexi was Ariel's father—unless it was all a fabrication.

"He is a Misfit," I said. "He sees into the future."

"His *nulls* see into the future," snapped Mendi.

"How would he locate Misfits among your novices if he was not one himself?" I asked.

"Do you dare to mock us by claiming that he is like you?" snapped Grisyl. "Why would a mutant work against its own kind? I will cut the mouth from your face if you lie to me again."

"But not yet," Mendi drawled, sounding bored and irritated.

"I must cut her to make her speak. If I hold her under the water any longer, she will drown," Grisyl snapped.

"Perhaps you have not the skill needed for this task after all," Mendi said.

"I have the skill but am hampered by your prohibitions."

"Ariel's prohibitions," Mendi corrected.

I was lying in a puddle of water I had vomited up, marveling bitterly at the irony that I had told them the truth about Ariel, yet for all their suspicions and doubts about him, they did not believe me. They were now arguing about whether to go on asking about Ariel or to try finding out how I had come aboard the *Stormdancer*. They were convinced that I had been in alliance with the mutants aboard the sunken *Orizon*, but they could not see why a group of mutants would come to Herder Isle at all, when there were thousands of Hedra to oppose them even if they managed the impossible and breached the wall and the black gates.

I felt a renewed ache of sorrow for the coercers who had drowned when the *Orizon* was sunk. My thoughts shifted to Ariel, and I wondered what plans he could have had that would involve allowing us to find Rushton.

I stifled the urge to cough, knowing it would draw the deadly attention of the Threes. *If only I could faint*, I thought. They would not be able to do anything to me until I woke. But for all Mendi's sneering, Grisyl was a skilled torturer. Darkness had fluttered at the edge of my vision many times since we had entered the cell, yet Grisyl had never once allowed me to lose consciousness. And he had known when I had tried to pretend. Time and time again, I swallowed the foul water into which I was dipped, but the moment I could hold my breath no more and sucked it into my lungs, I would be hauled out, thrown on the floor, and the water pushed out of me by Bedig.

And all this was a prelude to what Ariel would do when he returned. Fear slipped through me like a cold blade, but I thought of the scribed words of a Beforetimer that Pavo had once quoted to me: *A brave person dies but once; a coward many times.* I thought of Lark and wondered wearily whether he and his father and the crew of the *Stormdancer* were even now in the compound being interrogated, too. *Save them,* I prayed to the three goddesses worshipped by the Norselanders.

"Try again," Mendi said, dragging my head up by the hair. "Make her tell you how she got aboard the ship."

"Why don't you try?" snarled Grisyl.

"Defeated already?" Mendi asked scornfully. "You have no stamina. I will show you how to have her begging to speak the truth. Bedig, remove her clothes."

Before the Hedra captain could obey, boots approached the cell door. Mendi dropped me to the floor as the door swung open with a rusty whine. I forced my eyes open, wanting to see who entered, but the barrel into which I had been repeatedly dipped blocked my view.

"Zuria," Mendi said warily.

"You are to come at once, both of you. The One summons us," announced a cold, haughty voice.

"We have spoken to our master already, Zuria. You will have to make your report yourself," Mendi said slyly.

Zuria replied sharply, "It was the One who sent for all of us to attend him. Shall I go and tell him you two are otherwise occupied?"

"We will come, naturally," Grisyl said.

"Of course we will, but I do not understand this summons when we were with the One not two hours past," Mendi grumbled. "Are we to bring the mutant with us?"

"Mutant?" Zuria asked.

"The mutant found hiding aboard the *Stormdancer*. The one Ariel's null foresaw," Mendi said irritably, pointing down at me.

Footsteps came toward me. Someone knelt beside me, and

I clenched my teeth to steel myself against the pain of being lifted by my hair. But instead I was turned gently onto my back and the sodden curtain of my hair lifted away from my face.

If I had possessed any breath for it, I would have cried out in astonishment, because staring down at me, clad in a split Herder robe, his head shaven, was the Misfit coercer Harwood.

✦ 18 ✦

"GUILDMISTRESS!" HARWOOD CRIED, shock draining his face of color.

"Har, what are you . . . ?" The face that appeared above his shoulder was that of another coercer, Veril. He, too, wore a Hedra robe and was shaved bald. Seeing me, concern became incredulity. "Guildmistress!" he gasped. "But how . . . ?"

"Quiet," Harwood told him urgently, keeping his voice low. His eyes sought mine. "Guildmistress, can you speak? Are you badly injured?"

I managed to shake my head and relief flashed in his eyes, but it was nothing to what I felt—astonishment so great that it was as if a hot river surged through me, warming my over-wrought flesh and numb spirit. Harwood bent closer to examine the demon band and then shook his head. "It needs a key." He turned his head and looked at someone out of my sight. After a moment, he sighed in frustration. "None of these bastard Threes or the Hedra have one! Help me get her up, Veril."

They lifted me to my feet, but I was so dizzy and nauseated that it took me some seconds to notice that Zuria, Mendi, Grisyl, and Bedig were standing docilely in a row against the wall, staring at the floor. My knees buckled and I retched, but I had already voided the contents of my stomach. Harwood helped me to a stool against the wall, looking worried.

"How . . . how did you both get here?" I rasped.

"Aboard the *Stormdancer*. Eleven of us came as part of the so-called retreating Hedra force. But you?"

"I was aboard the *Stormdancer*, too. . . . I didn't sense you."

"We wore demon bands. We had to or we would have been recognized as impostors, and there was no time to have false ones made. But how did *you* get aboard the *Stormdancer*?"

"Later," I said. "What happened in the Land?"

Harwood shrugged. "I don't know a lot of it. After you left for the cloister, Linnet sent the eleven of us down to the sea caves with supplies and instructions to wait for the invading ships. She told us to board if we had the chance. We shaved our heads and planned to steal robes from Malik's men and coerce them to ease us on board. We had plenty of demon bands that we had taken from Vos's armsmen. But Linnet and Reuvan came to tell us that the Land was swarming with Hedra who had been hiding within the old cloister.

"Reuvan said that Aben died trying to probe Malik when they reached Sutrium. Dardelan had immediately begun assembling a force to ride back to Saithwold. Reuvan had been sent to warn us and rode into the middle of the fighting." The coercer took a steadying breath and said, "Linnet said the knights, Vos's armsmen, and all the fighters Noviny had been able to muster were concentrating on keeping the invaders away from the beach, because they had learned from a captured Hedra that three ships were to drop hundreds of Hedra on the beach where we were hiding. Reuvan said that Dardelan had specifically charged him with making sure that the ships didn't leave."

"Why were they keeping the invaders away from the beach?" I interrupted.

"Because Linnet had coerced a Hedra captain and his men into believing they had been defeated. The plan was to send them rushing to meet the arriving Hedra with such dreadful tales of massacre and mayhem as would turn them back, convinced that the force from the sea cavern were all dead except these few. The retreat would give us cover to board the ships. As soon as they had retreated, one of the coerced men was supposed to break down and admit that he had been forced to say what he had said, and then he would tell them that the battle was still raging. The Nine would immediately command the Hedra ashore again, and that would leave the way clear for us to take control of the ships. And hopefully by the time the Hedra did get ashore again, Dardelan and his people would have arrived to reinforce Linnet's band of fighters."

"So what happened?" I asked.

He shrugged. "Everything went according to plan to begin with. The Hedra went ashore, and after a time, they began to retreat. Then things started going wrong. We had intended to get aboard the *Orizon*. We talked it over and decided to focus on one ship rather than spread ourselves over three, and the *Orizon* was anchored closest to the caves. But when the retreat started, the *Orizon* got under way much faster than we expected, so by the time we had caught our eleven men, stripped them, and donned their clothes, we had no choice but to board the *Stormdancer*."

"You know that the *Orizon* . . ."

He nodded soberly. "We saw it from the deck of the *Stormdancer*. I guess Ariel's null envisioned us talking about the *Orizon* in the caves and missed the last-minute change of plan."

"Maybe," I said. "So what happened when you got aboard?"

Harwood sighed. "None of us had reckoned on the ship's actually leaving, because the coerced captain was supposed to break down and admit he had been made to lie, whereupon everyone would rush ashore again. Unfortunately, Kaga was so furious about the retreat that he killed the captain who had ordered it, so no one could reveal that the Hedra were not truly defeated. We dared not call attention to ourselves by suggesting the dead captain might have been coerced, so before we knew it, we were on our way to Herder Isle. We were not too worried, because Linnet had told us the bands were always taken off once the ships lifted anchor. We figured that once that happened, we would take control and coerce the shipmaster of the *Stormdancer* to put in at Sutrium. But the Nine was so frantic about the Hedra captain's description of our force that he commanded everyone to keep their bands on. We might still have managed to get control, but then the *Black Ship* turned back and sank the *Orizon,* and we knew that if the *Stormdancer* did turn toward Sutrium, Salamander would destroy it. So we had no choice but to let the ship come here. Before we knew it, we were marching with the rest of the Hedra through the black gates. I have to tell you that when they closed behind us, I thought we were all doomed." He shook his head. "Then up comes a boy in black with a basket, and we all take off our demon bands! By the time Kaga had marched us to our barracks, we had control of him and a good many of the other Hedra.

"Our initial plan was to escape from the compound, but when Zuria marched in demanding to know what had been happening, I realized that we could take him with us to ease our way, for who would dare to oppose a Three? Taking him with us would also give us a unique chance to learn more about the Herder Faction and its long-term plans. I was just beginning to coerce him when a message came from the One summoning all the Threes. Veril suggested we take all of them with us as prisoners. In one stroke, we would deprive the Faction of its head and have the means to learn everything about its inner workings! It was a brilliant idea, so I coerced Zuria to take Veril and me with him to find the other Threes. That is when we found you!"

I looked at the Threes, still standing in a row, their faces bland. "You have coerced them all now?"

"And the Hedra captain, Bedig, but Zuria is the only one deeply enough coerced that I can send him out to act alone. How do you feel now? Could you walk?"

I nodded absently. "Harwood, you said you thought it would be a good idea to take all three of the Threes with you. But take them where?"

"Why, to the *Stormdancer*, of course," Veril said eagerly. "Once we get out of here, we will have Zuria dismiss the men guarding it, hoist the anchor, and be gone before anyone realizes. The beauty of it is that no one can follow us, because all other ships are anchored in Main Cove in Norseland."

"You can't sail the *Stormdancer* back across the strait," I said. "The hull is damaged. Surely you heard the shipfolk speak of it when you were on board? That is why the *Stormdancer* was lagging behind the *Orizon*. The shipmaster has grounded her so she can be repaired, but I do not know when that will happen, because Mendi ordered the entire crew to be brought in for interrogation."

Harwood and Veril exchanged a look of consternation. "I'd better let the others know," Harwood muttered. "We will have to hide on the other part of the island. I heard one of the Hedra speak of it as a wilderness."

"Wait," I said, realizing that he was about to send out a

probe. I told him what I had learned from Lark and his father about Fallo. "From what I could see in Lark's mind, the swamp is full of quicksand and sinkholes, as well as poisonous plants and swift, deadly vipers. No one lives there for good reason, and we would not survive it without a Norselander to aid us. But how can we ask for their help when I am already responsible for bringing disaster to the shipfolk from the *Stormdancer*? Even if they were willing to fight, they have no arms and would be outnumbered by Hedra. There is only one thing we can do. We have to take over the compound."

Both men stared at me as if I had lost my wits. "You can't be serious, Guildmistress," Harwood said. "This place is the size of a city, and there must be thousands of Herders living here. We can't coerce or kill them all."

"We don't have to control all of them, just the ones who control the rest," I said. "The way the Faction is set up, those with real power are few. We have three of them right here in this room—and an invitation to see their master. We can use them, and the One, and their power and knowledge to get the ship repaired and to keep anyone from realizing we are here. When we are ready to leave, we will take the Threes with us as you suggested, plus all the Hedra captains that can be fitted in the brig cells in the hold, as well as the crew, the shipmaster, and their families, so that they will suffer no retribution."

Harwood had begun to nod. "We will need a safe location to operate from within the compound."

"And we need to find out if the shipfolk are here yet. Where are the others coercers?" I asked.

"In the barracks with Kaga," Harwood said. "We could go there. . . ."

I shook my head. "We need a place where fewer people

will come but where the Threes can logically be seen coming and going." Inspiration struck and I smiled. I was amused to see that this caused Veril to adopt the same apprehensive look Ceirwan sometimes had when I proposed a difficult rescue plan.

"Guildmistress—" the coercer began, but I cut him off.

"The One's chambers lie within the wall surrounding this compound. You can only reach them through a very long passage that runs inside the walls. The One is very old and obese and uses his assistant, Falc, to summon anyone he wants to talk with. If we go there now and coerce the One and Falc, and we have the Threes, we will virtually control the entire compound, so long as no one guesses they are not acting under their own volition. We can send Falc straightaway to demand that the shipfolk be brought to the One."

"You did not tell us how you got aboard. Or how the Herders discovered you," Veril said.

"For now I will tell you only that my getting aboard was an accident. I was discovered because Ariel foresaw it and told the One before he left for Norseland with Salamander. He forbade anyone to interrogate me until he came back to do it himself. He has some machine he would use upon me, which he keeps in his residence on Norseland."

Harwood interrupted. "We will have to leave Herder Isle before Ariel returns from Norseland on the *Black Ship*, else the *Stormdancer* will suffer the same fate as the unlucky *Orizon*."

"We have a little time," I said. "The *Black Ship* has only just left, and Ariel has an errand to perform on the west coast before returning to Herder Isle to deal with me."

"What errand?" Harwood asked.

I shrugged. "The Threes don't know, but we can find out from the One, for it was he who sent Ariel. All I know is that it has something to do with a couple of special nulls. Have you heard aught of nulls?"

Both men nodded, grim-faced. Veril said, "We guess that they are weak futuretellers whose minds Ariel has damaged to make them passive and biddable."

Harwood frowned. "Have you considered that one of these nulls may discern our activities here and that Salamander might return immediately, cut us off in the strait, and sink us as he did the *Orizon*? Or that he will come here with a ship full of demon-banded Hedra? Even if we stay here and coerce the gate guards to lock them out, Salamander could simply bring the *Black Ship* close to shore and use the same weapon he used on the *Orizon* to break open the wall."

I nodded soberly, remembering what Lark had said about the destruction of cities using Beforetime weapons. But I only said, "You may be right, but I don't see what we can do other than trying to get the ship repaired as soon as possible." I explained how to reach the wall passage that led to the One's chamber and bade Harwood ask the other coercers to meet us there. It was unwieldy having to explain in words instead of being able to farsend directions, but I had no alternative until I could remove the demon band. Harwood suggested that one of the knights remain in the barracks with Kaga and the other coerced Hedra so we could summon an obedient force if something went wrong. While he contacted the others, I bade Veril find out if the shipfolk from the *Stormdancer* were in any of the cells. He hurried off, taking Bedig with him to use as a source of knowledge.

Harwood asked, "Are there any guards with the One?"

I nodded. "A couple of Hedra guard the door and, as I told you, the younger priest who serves the One, Falc, but he is no fighter. In any case, all are unbanded, so you can easily

311

coerce them. Oh, there are also several boys dressed in hooded black robes. I don't know how they fit in, but they will have to be coerced, too."

"Maybe not," Harwood said unexpectedly. "From what I can make out, they are mute slaves. The priests call them *shadows,* and they seem to have no more will than a shadow. I don't think we will have any trouble with them. It is the Herder warriors—the Hedra—that we need to be careful about. So far as I can see, they are vigilant and stern watchdogs who don't hesitate to speak against a Herder priest of any level if they believe he is infringing Herder lore."

"Maybe you can gradually put their captains under sleepseals in their rooms," I suggested.

"There are too many to put sleepseals on, because they would all need to be watered, fed, and kept clean," Harwood said. "I would rather deeply coerce them and use them. But that will take time, too."

"We can't do anything until we knew more about how this place works," I said. "We must coerce the One, and then Mendi and Grisyl must be deeply coerced so we don't have to keep a constant watch on them, and during that process, we will gain the knowledge we need. Then we will begin to coerce the inner-cadre Nines and the highest ranked Hedra."

Veril returned with Bedig to report that the Norselanders were not in any of the interrogation cells, but he added that there were several other places within the compound where they might have been taken.

"You'd best investigate," Harwood said. "Take one of the Threes to smooth the way. Take Zuria, since he is deeply coerced. The guildmistress and I go to meet the others in the passage to the One's chamber. Follow us if you do not find the shipfolk, and send a probe if you do. If you cannot reach us, send Bedig." He paused, obviously offering Veril the directions I had given him. Veril nodded.

"See if you can find keys to unlock this demon band as well," I said.

"And some shoes," Harwood said, pointing to my bare feet.

Veril looked at Zuria, who suddenly barked an order for the young man to follow him. The Three stalked out followed by Veril, who winked at us over his shoulder.

Ironically, while we had been in the cell, I had felt safe. Saved. But as Harwood took my arm and we followed Mendi through the labyrinthine interrogation buildings, I thought of the hundreds and hundreds of fanatical Herders within the compound, and my hasty plans began to feel childishly, dangerously foolish. Yet what else could we do? We were on an island controlled utterly by the Faction, with no immediate means of escape and the possibility that Ariel and Salamander would eventually arrive with a shipload of Hedra.

We came through a door into bright daylight, and I stopped in astonishment, hardly able to believe that the whole stormy night had passed while I was in the cell. Unlike the night before, when the rain-swept streets had been all but deserted, now many acolytes, novices, and ranking priests passed back and forth, most accompanied by several of the black-clad shadows.

We set off toward the front of the compound, and I found myself leaning heavily on Harwood, for the hours of watery torment had taken their toll. I was almost trembling with relief when at last we reached the entrance hall where Falc had appeared to command Mendi to bring me to the One. As before, two of the shadows appeared with lanterns. I would have liked to dismiss them, but I knew the long passage was dark enough that we would need light, and it would look odd if we took the lanterns ourselves.

Soon we were following a lantern-bearing shadow along the passage inside the wall, the second shadow following close behind. After some moments, Harwood murmured very softly, "Am I imagining it or does the floor of this passage slant up?"

I was uneasy about speaking aloud, but I was still demon-banded. So I said softly, "The One's chamber is probably halfway up the wall. He has no need to be easily accessible. Indeed, he has probably found it effective to be mysterious and elusive. And he can use the Threes to do anything beyond his rooms."

"It is a wonder the Threes don't overthrow him," Harwood replied. I saw the hooded head of one of the shadows tilt slightly and guessed he had heard the coercer's voice. I nodded pointedly at him, but Harwood shrugged and said softly, "Don't worry about the boy. If he looks like giving us any trouble, I will coerce him, but until then I might as well conserve my energy. When we stop to wait for the others, I want to coerce Mendi and Zuria more deeply so that I need not probe them continually."

Despite my anxiety about the shadows overhearing us, I answered his earlier comment. "The One is not just the head of their order. The priests believe he is the Chosen of Lud and beloved for that reason."

"Feared more than loved, I would say," Harwood said. "But tell me how you got aboard the *Stormdancer*."

Keeping my voice low, I told him what had happened.

"A ship fish," the coercer marveled at the end of my tale. "I had no idea they could be beastspoken."

"How should we know it?" I asked. "We Misfits have

never had that much access to the ocean, and we avoid water because it inhibits our Talents."

"I have always thought it odd that water produces such a strong barrier," Harwood mused. "It has less substance than the earth, after all." He frowned. "There is light ahead." Again I saw the shadow's head lift slightly. He might be mute, but he was certainly not deaf.

"It is coming from the One's audience room," I said softly. "We had better stop here and dim the lanterns or the sentries outside it will see their light."

Harwood made Mendi bid the shadows halt and lower the wick of their lanterns. As they obeyed, I caught a fleeting glimpse of a shadow's face, and though it was unknown, it struck me that there was something odd about it. Before I could discern what it was, Mendi commanded both shadows to sit. I sat down, too, and massaged my cold feet, noting that the shadows sat with their heads lowered. Harwood was now staring fixedly into Mendi's face.

After a time I glanced in the other direction and noticed a light approaching. I stood hastily and touched Harwood's shoulder to get his attention.

"It's all right," he said after a moment of concentration. "It is Sover and the others. Give me another ten minutes, and I will have finished here." He turned back to Mendi.

It was not Sover but Yarrow whom I saw first. He grinned in delight, mugging his incredulity, and then I was surrounded by Hilder, Colwyn, Sover, Geratty, and Ode, all of whom had come to my guild at one time or another to learn to hone and control their coercive probes so they could use them to farseek. Each greeted me with a dozen questions, and then I saw Reuvan, who had hung back slightly.

"It is good to see you," I said. The seaman laughed and

embraced me with some of Brydda's painful force.

"It is astonishing to see you here," he countered, releasing me.

I remembered the shadows then and turned to look at them to see how they regarded our greetings. Two had accompanied the coercers, and now there were four, all standing, for the other two had risen. Rather than gazing steadfastly at the ground, they looked at me. All had thin, pale, delicate faces and unfathomable expressions.

"I forgot," Yarrow said suddenly, drawing my attention back to him. "Veril said you might find a use for one of these." He withdrew a small gray key from his pocket with a triumphant flourish, and in a moment, the demon band lay on the passage floor. I prayed I would never feel one of the foul things about my throat again.

"I have done as much as I can do now," Harwood announced, looking weary as he turned away from Mendi. He cast his eye over us and asked, "Where are the others?"

"I left Asra with Kaga in the barracks, and I sent Tomrick to the watch-hut atop the walls to keep an eye on Hevon Bay and report on any approaching ships," Yarrow said. "Veril said to tell you he cannot farseek you, but he has gone to the black gates to find out if the *Stormdancer*'s shipfolk were brought into the compound."

"The stone in this wall must be too thick or tainted," Harwood muttered.

When we reached the Hedra standing before the door to the One's audience chamber, Mendi barked at them to stand aside. Instead of obeying, one of them said sternly that no one was permitted to enter the One's apartment unless summoned, and no one had been summoned. Then the eyes of both Hedra glazed, and they turned and went into the firelit audience room. We followed, and I had a brief glimpse of a startled Falc leaping up from the One's carved chair before the expression was wiped from his face and he moved to join Mendi, Zuria, the two Hedra guards, and the shadows, all of whom had gone to stand against the wall.

"According to this Falc, the One is asleep through there," Harwood said after a moment, nodding toward the door through which Falc had gone the previous day. "There are also six shadows in there."

We looked at the four who had accompanied us, and they looked back, but their faces revealed nothing. Harwood gently bade them sit down, and they obeyed at once. Then he turned back to me and said in a low voice, "I think the ones inside are like to be as docile as these four, but you'd best be careful just the same."

I nodded and bade Ode, Sover, and Colwyn to come with me. We entered a large dressing chamber hung with gray robes, their gold edging glittering in the light of the lantern held up by a slender shadow who had risen at our entrance. Immediately, he dropped his gaze to the floor.

I wasted no time on him and passed into the next chamber. This was a small but lavishly appointed bathing room, complete with a gold-tiled bath sunk into the floor. There were two shadows here, and both rose to their feet, one holding a lantern, but these also kept their heads meekly bowed and made no attempt to hinder us.

At last we came to the One's bedchamber. The One lay snoring softly on an enormous carved bed piled with white quilts and silken pillows. Three more black-robed shadows sat on the floor in front of a curtained wall, but I ignored them. The overlapping fleeces on the floor swallowed the sound of my footsteps as I approached the bed, but as if he felt my movement in the air, the One opened his eyes and stared up at me in dim confusion.

"You are not Falc. Where is Falc?" he said in a high, quavering voice. Then he came properly awake, and his expression was one of affronted disgust and malice. "You are a woman! How dare you! Who allowed this? Falc!"

"He cannot come at this moment," I said softly, and reached out to probe his mind. The old man gave a thin scream, clutched at his head, and cringed back against the pillows. I withdrew in astonishment and said to the others, "A block has been constructed to cause him excruciating pain if there is any intrusion. If I press deeper, his mind will collapse. Indeed, it seems the block is intrusive enough that it has already eroded his sanity."

"But who could have done this to him?" Sover asked in a low voice. "Such a block would require great coercive skill."

"Ariel," I said bitterly. "This certainly explains how he got the Herders to take him in and why the One favors him so strongly. Go and get Falc." Sover went out and returned with the priest and Harwood. I directed Falc to approach his master, who lay whimpering and clutching his head.

"What is it, Master?" Falc asked in a crooning voice. "Did you have another nightmare?"

"Night . . . nightmare?" the One echoed, peering up at the Nine as if through a mist. "Yes. It was a terrible nightmare! I saw that female mutant that Mendi brought in. The one Ariel wants to question. She was leaning over my bed seeking to possess my mind. I want her killed. Bring her here and do it before me."

"It was only a nightmare, Master," Falc assured him. "The mutant is even now in a cell, awaiting the return of our good Ariel from Norseland."

"Norseland?" The One sounded confused and distressed. "But he will not come from Norseland. He must go to the west coast first." He gave a groan. "Why must he go there? I told him that I need him here. But he said it was Lud's will. . . . My head aches so."

"Master, *you* sent him to the west coast, because he has a vital mission to perform," I made Falc say in his smooth, oily voice. "Don't you remember?"

"Of course I remember, fool," snapped the One. "I ordered him to take the null and unleash the wrath of Lud on the Ludless." He groaned. "My head aches. Where is Ariel? He is the only one who can take away the pain. Lud bestowed upon him the power to heal me."

"I am sure that he will return quickly," Falc soothed.

"Of course he will return swiftly, dolt, else he would be doomed," snarled the One.

"What does he mean?" Harwood farsent urgently.

I shrugged and prompted Falc to speak again. "Master, Ariel will not die. No one would dare to harm him. Lud would protect him from—"

"Shut up!" screamed the One. "No one will harm Ariel. He knows well enough not to linger after he sets the null ashore, lest he perish with all the rest on the west coast." The priest ground his teeth together and rocked in agony, clutching his head.

"The null must have some sort of weapon, and we need to find out what it is," Harwood said softly. "Can't you ease him?"

I shook my head. "Aside from the block, Ariel has constructed a pain mechanism that will worsen each day until he releases it," I said softly. "I can't get into his mind to stop it without breaking open the block. If Ariel does not return within a day or two, the old man's mind will crumble under the pain."

"But Ariel will only just have reached Norseland," Colwyn said. "And a journey from there to here via the west coast will take at least a fiveday."

" 'Perish with all on the west coast.' " Ode echoed the One's earlier words bleakly, and I remembered that Ode's sister was among those assigned to the west coast during the rebellion and trapped there still.

"Nothing but a Beforetime weapon could kill everyone on the west coast," Sover said.

"The Herders used Beforetime weapons to gain control of the Norselands," I said. "Whatever they used was capable of destroying cities. Maybe the null is supposed to go from city to city destroying each."

"That was my thinking, too," Harwood admitted. "I will see if I can dig up any scraps of information from the two Threes about a store of Beforetime weapons. Meanwhile, Sover, perhaps you can ease the One somewhat."

As he departed with Zuria in tow, I looked at Sover, who said, "I have a secondary empathic ability. I can empathise acceptance and serenity in the One so you can question him further." He bent over the Herder, who squinted up at him through streaming eyes. "Who are you! How dare you come in here? I don't want you. I need Ariel!"

"Ariel is serving Lud on the west coast," Sover said soothingly from the other side of the bed. "But he knew you would suffer in his absence, Master. He sent me."

"You are a healer?" the One quavered, his eyes flickering fearfully to Sover.

"I am not gifted, as Ariel is, but I can help you, Master," the coercer said gently. "If you will permit me to touch your head?"

"No! No!" The One cringed back; then he screamed, a horrible thin sound that made the hair on my neck rise. "Yes . . . ," he gasped. "Help me."

Sover placed a gentle hand on the old man's brow, and as the One sank back with an exhausted exhalation, the coercer's face contorted with empathised pain. His expression gradually became one of intense concentration.

"It is working," Colwyn murmured. I forced myself to relax as we waited. Then Sover turned to nod.

"Master," Falc said. I had made him sound too eager and modified his tone before continuing. "Master, I fear that our good Ariel places himself in danger. Surely Lud cannot have intended that."

The One stirred and mumbled, "No man can presume to know Lud's intention."

I decided to risk a direct question. "Can the gain of this dangerous mission be worth the risk?"

The One stirred irritably under his quilts. "I have told you, fool. There is no danger as long as Ariel does not linger after leaving the null ashore. The sickness will not become infectious for some days."

Sover gave me a horrified look, and the One groaned. Immediately, the coercer returned his attention to the older man.

"A plague," Ode hissed into my ear. "It can be nowt else. It were always rumored that the Herders were responsible for the first plague."

I nodded. "But one in three were affected, and only a third of those became seriously ill. Fewer still died."

"Then it is a different plague," Colwyn said. "One that kills three in three if all are to die."

"Why?" Ode asked. "What possible use can it be to th' Faction to kill everyone on the west coast?" His voice had risen in his agitation, and the One heard him but appeared not to realize that someone other than Falc had spoken.

"Lud's will is not to be questioned," he answered dreamily in his strange girlish voice. "He used pestilence in the Beforetime to signal his divine wrath, and he showed Ariel where the plague seeds were hid upon Norseland. All who look upon the desolation that will result from this plague shall know the power of Lud's wrath. And the west coast will be purified so it can be populated with the pure of heart who worship Lud and obey his servants."

"This doesn't make sense," Colwyn hissed. "Why invade one part of the Land if you intend to unleash the ultimate lesson on the rest?"

I could not think past the horror of a sickness deadly enough to kill everyone on the west coast. *Everyone.* "He must be stopped!" I said. "Ask him where the null is to be taken on the west coast."

Sover obeyed, but the One spoke only of a city where sickness would spread like wildfire.

"He means one of the cities," Ode said.

"Even if we could sail the *Stormdancer* within the hour, it would take days to visit and search every city on the west coast," Colwyn said. "And we have no idea what this null even looks like!"

"We need not search every city. We need only put into every port and ask if the *Black Ship* has been there. And Ariel can only just have got to Norseland. He has yet to travel to the west coast before he can think of coming back here. That will give us a couple days' grace. Send someone to find out if Veril has news of the shipfolk yet." I stopped, horrified to realize that I was on the verge of tears, for aside from the thousands of innocent people who would die if Ariel succeeded, among them would be Merret, Jak, Dell, and Ode's sister Desda, all of whom I had sent to the west coast. Mastering my emotions, I turned to Sover. "Keep trying to find out where the null will be taken."

Sover nodded, his expression blank with dismay.

I left the bedchamber and found Harwood focused on Mendi, but Yarrow, Geratty, and the others turned to look at me as I entered the firelit audience chamber, followed by Colwyn.

"What is happening?" Yarrow asked.

I gathered my wits and told them, seeing their faces reflect the shattered dismay I felt. Harwood had ceased probing Mendi, and he asked in disbelief, "Did you say *everyone* will die?"

"Everyone," I said, and I seemed to hear the high mocking sound of Ariel's laughter.

PART III

$$\blacklozenge$$

SONG OF THE WEST

◆ 19 ◆

"Someone must go to Fallo to speak with the shipfolk," I said when Veril arrived to say that the shipfolk had not been brought into the compound, even though a number of Hedra had been sent to summon them. None of us could imagine why they had not yet returned, unless the Norselanders had fled rather than be brought in. The more I thought about it, the more likely this seemed, for what had the Norselanders to lose by fighting?

"I will go," Yarrow volunteered.

"It will take an hour to reach the gate from here." I fumed. "We need somewhere more central as a base."

Harwood touched my arm, and I turned to see that one of the shadows had risen. The boy beckoned and went on silent feet to the dressing room. I followed, intrigued. He went through into the bathing chamber and crossed to the wall behind the bath. Then, to my amazement, he slid open a panel to reveal a dark stairwell. As I went to the opening, he stepped onto the first step and pointed down. Seeing the thin wrists, delicate hands, and slender neck, I realized suddenly what I ought to have seen sooner: the shadow was a *girl*. She began to descend the steps, indicating that I should follow.

"Be careful," Colwyn called down after me uneasily. Stopping, I glanced back and saw that he and the other coercers had followed us into the bathing room, along with the other shadows, and now I saw clearly that all were starveling girls. I turned to the shadow who had led me to the stairs. "You know that I am a Misfit, don't you?" I asked her aloud. "That which the Herders call a cursed mutant."

She nodded, and I was surprised to see no fear in her eyes. Perhaps she had not understood me clearly. I said, "I am called mutant by the Herders, because I have the power to speak inside another person's thoughts and to hear their thoughts as well. If you will permit me, I can enter your mind and speak with your thoughts."

The girl seemed to consider this carefully and nodded, coming back up the steps.

"My name is Elspeth Gordie," I sent, and some impulse made me coerce an image of us both in her mind. She gasped in astonishment as my image smiled reassuringly at her image.

"What is your name?" I asked.

"I . . . I can't . . . oh, I am *speaking*!" Her image lifted its hands to its mouth, and she wept.

"Your name?" I prompted gently when she had recovered herself. Shyly, enunciating very carefully, she told me.

"Cinda," I repeated aloud.

An incredulous smile broke over her pale little face, and she pressed her hands to her cheeks and nodded. From the corner of my eye, I saw the other shadows clutch at one another in evident excitement. Concentrating, I forespoke her image for some time, then she led me down the stairs, where, as she had explained to me, a discreet door opened into an obscure corner of a vast laundry built up against the wall surrounding the compound. Through a door and windows on the opposite side of the laundry chamber, I could see into a walled yard with washing lines strung from one side of the wall to the other. Cinda explained that a gate in this lesser wall led directly to the main body of the compound. From here, it was only a short walk to the black gates.

When we returned to the others, I explained what she had told me, adding that if it were true, we could remain in the One's quarters. Then I charged Yarrow and Veril to go to Fallo, find the Norseland crew of the *Stormdancer*, and bring back Lark's father at all speed. They took Grisyl and were to collect Asra and the coerced Hedra from the barracks on the way, in case they needed a fighting force. After they had gone, using the bathing-room steps, I sent Hilder to the watch-hut atop the wall that overlooked the channel, bidding him let me know the moment he saw a ship boat coming back across. I also told him to let Tomrick in the other watch-hut know what had been happening.

Harwood then ordered Geratty, Colwyn, Reuvan, and Ode to sleep, for we had all been up for many hours and must begin sleeping in shifts if we were to have our wits about us. Sover he bade sleep in the One's chamber in case the One woke and might be questioned further.

"I daresay it is tasteless of me, but I am too hungry to sleep," grumbled Geratty.

"We all need to eat," Harwood agreed, and he asked Cinda, who hovered close by, how the One got his meals. She looked at me, and I entered her mind to learn there was a kitchen that served all in this sector of the compound. Ode went with Cinda and four other shadows to coerce a proper meal out of the kitchen workers. They soon returned with pease pudding, bread, and some queer sour vegetables, and we ate hungrily. We had just finished when Hilder brought news from Veril. Two of those sent out by Mendi to fetch the Norselanders had returned to the compound.

"Veril coerced them," Hilder said. "We were right about the Norselanders guessing what the Hedra intended. The village where they lived was deserted when they arrived. The villagers have taken refuge in the swamp, and the Hedra have been searching for them, to no avail."

"Have Veril and the others left?" I asked.

"They have, but I can reach them from the watch-hut before they cross the channel," Hilder said.

"Do it," I said at once. "Tell them that they probably cannot reach the Norselanders because according to the shipmaster's boy, the swamp is full of tainted patches. Tell Veril to go to one of the other villages. Have them ask for the Per and tell him everything. He may even know how to find Helvar."

Hilder nodded and departed at once. As I turned to speak to Harwood, Cinda came to me shyly with a battered pair of shoes such as shadows wore. I accepted them gratefully, and as I sat to pull them on, I noticed the other shadows watching with sorrowful expressions. I set aside my apprehensions for a moment to enter Cinda's mind and ask why they were so sad; they need not fear they would be left behind when we sailed away to the Land.

"They do not fear being left," Cinda's image explained. "Many of us were taken from the west coast, and although none of us had any hope of returning to our families, we grieve at the thought of their being harmed."

Full of pity for them as I was, it suddenly occurred to me that the ubiquitous shadows might have heard something said that would help us find the null more swiftly. With this in mind, I bade them come and sit with me by the fire. As they obeyed, Sover entered to say that the One had awakened briefly, but in his opinion, the old man did not know where the null was to be left ashore.

"I think the whole idea of a plagued null was Ariel's notion," he added. "The One said that he found plague seeds in some Beforetime storage place, and from what I can make out, he presented to the One the idea of sending a null infected with plague as if it had come to him from Lud. The fact that it would involve a lot of death seems to have made it especially pleasing to the One."

"With Ariel, there might be no intention, save the desire to use what he has created," I said grimly.

Sover ran his fingers through his thick, red-brown hair. "I have soothed the One to sleep again. He needs to rest if we are to get anything more from him." He looked curiously at the cluster of shadows seated by the fire.

"We were just about to talk," I said, and Harwood bade Sover return to the One's chamber and rest while he had the chance. I turned to Cinda and asked her to tell me her companions' names. I was aware of Harwood entering my mind discreetly to listen, but I ignored him and repeated aloud the name of each woman once Cinda's image had conveyed it. As she heard her name spoken aloud, each shadow reacted strongly.

"Most of us do not ever hear our names spoken aloud," Cinda explained.

I asked aloud if any of them knew what Ariel was doing on the west coast. At the mention of his name, several of the girls started in alarm, and one looked sick.

"It was Ariel who chose us and supervised the . . . the cutting. . . ." Cinda gestured to her mouth. "Also, he . . . he uses us as he wishes, and he is very . . . cruel." Then she told me that they knew nothing of Ariel's conversation with the One, for he always made them leave.

Another shadow made several slight gestures with her

hand, and Cinda raised her own hand and made several evocative gestures in return. I realized that the women had invented their own language of signals, just as Brydda had done to enable unTalents to communicate with beasts.

Harwood asked aloud how Cinda had come to Herder Isle, for she was not a Norselander. Cinda and the other shadows gave him a wary look. To her eyes, I realized, he was another Hedra with his split robe and shaven head. I explained to her and the others aloud that Harwood and all of us, save for Reuvan, were mutants in Hedra guise. Harwood added that his Talent was coercion: the use of deep-probe abilities to control the minds of others. Cinda glanced in sudden comprehension at the blank-faced Threes, the Herder Falc, and the two Hedra guards seated in a row against the wall, blank faced and docile, and Harwood admitted that he had manipulated their minds. He added that the shadows need not fear he would use his abilities on them, for Misfits did not tamper with the minds of allies. He smiled as he said this, and although he had a kind face, none of the shadows responded to his smile.

Cinda returned her serious gaze to my face and tapped her head. I took this as a request to raise an image in her mind and obliged, but I told her that the image was not really necessary. As long as I was within her mind, she need only imagine speaking, and I would hear her words. Her image nodded, and she began to tell her story.

She had been taken from the west coast by the Herders, along with her brother, who had been destined to become a novice. He had killed himself before he could be made an acolyte, and she had only learned of it some time after because Ariel had selected her to serve the One, and she had been in the healing hall while her severed tongue healed.

Harwood interrupted to ask if all shadows had their tongues severed, and she shook her head. It had been Ariel's idea that girls be used as body servants for the One, she explained, for although the old man hated clumsiness and roughness, he hated women even more. Ariel had suggested that his body servants ought to be slender girls whose hair was shorn and whose tongues were cut so he need not consider them females. They would serve until they began to develop breasts and were starved to put puberty off as long as possible, for the One disliked change, too. Once the chosen shadows became too old or shapely, they were put to work as invisible drudges in the compound's kitchens and washhouses with the other women, many of whom could speak but did not for fear of having their *own* tongues cut out.

"Are all shadows women?" Colwyn asked, for he, too, had been monitoring the tale.

"There are male shadows, but they work in the mine or at the demon-band works. Their tongues are not cut," her image explained. There was pity in her face, which astonished me, because how could one whose existence sounded so awful find it in herself to feel pity for another?

One of the other shadows, whose name had been given as Lure, made some gestures, and Cinda told me she had said that the Lud of the Herders must have died, else how could we have come to destroy the Faction?

Pity rose in me again, and I said aloud, "We did not come here to do battle. There are too few of us to fight. We must leave as soon as the ship we came on can be repaired. We must stop Ariel from bringing plague to the west coast. But know that in the Land, we have been preparing ourselves for a battle against the Faction, and the day is near when we will come here to fight them."

333

The shadows exchanged looks, and then Lure made some emphatic gestures to Cinda, who nodded and said, "Lure says that you have begun the battle here already, and you must remain to finish it. She said that we will fight with you. All of the shadows will, from child to eldest. We will fight with teeth and nails if you have no weapons for us."

"We are too few," Harwood said aloud gently.

"You are few, but there are hundreds of us," Cinda's image told me in a low, fierce mindvoice. "It is as Lure said. If you will command us, we will serve. We will kill the Herders."

I stared into her stormy eyes, amazed that such savage purpose could issue from such a waiflike figure. And when I looked at the others, their eyes held the same grim fire.

"If you rise up, many of you will be killed, especially if the Herders still have Beforetime weapons," I told her gently.

"They *would* die, if they rose up without any plan," Harwood broke in. "But with a plan, if there truly are hundreds of shadows willing to oppose their masters, it may be that we really can take control here."

I gaped at the coercer in astonishment, for I had always seen him as rather cautious. "You know that when I spoke of taking control, I meant only that we should do so to get the ship repaired," I said.

"I know it. But, Guildmistress, by pure chance we have managed to slip inside the very skin of the Faction, and we have the One and the Threes in our power. Would there ever again come a moment so ripe for the taking, even if we sailed up with ten ships to Hevon Bay? We came here, as you did, by accident, but these shadows have made me wonder if it was not mere chance that brought us here, but purposeful fate."

Cinda and the other shadows gazed at the coercer-knight as if mesmerized.

Cinda touched his arm, and because I was still within her mind, I felt him enter her mind and heard her say, "Lead us and we will fight until the last of us drops!"

"Wait!" I said. "I understand what you are saying, but we have to go after Ariel and stop the plague, or there will be more deaths on the west coast than any of us could imagine in our most terrible dreams."

Harwood rose and came to pull me to my feet. "Elspeth," he said fiercely, "we can do *both*. Once the ship is repaired, you will travel with some of the others to find the null, and I and whoever else remain will lead these shadows."

I farsent to him, "Harwood, only think! These are starveling girls and women with no fighting skills, and the shadow men are like to be the same. If they rise against the Faction, many will die."

"We are dead already," Cinda's image said, for both of our minds were still within hers, and she had heard me. "If we fight, we will fight to live."

Harwood said aloud, "Guildmistress, people died in the Land, too, during the rebellion, to achieve freedom. And we need not wage an open battle here. Look how these shadows move around within the Herder Compound, hearing everything, seeing everything, unnoticed. They cook food and serve drinks that might be drugged. They can go anywhere without anyone wondering why. They deliver messages that can be falsified or altered. Their very meekness and fragility would stop anyone seeing them as a threat. With their help and knowledge and our Talents, we could cut the heart from this place before the Herders know they are in danger."

His words made me think of what my father had cried out before the Herders burned him. If we were to strike a blow against the Herders here, we would be striking at the heart of the foul organization that had killed my parents and my brother. "The Norselanders might fight, too," I said at last, and Cinda and the other shadows nodded excitedly.

Slowly, I nodded. "All right. We will try. But nothing must hinder us from making the *Stormdancer* seaworthy."

Cinda turned to gesticulate urgently at the others, and Harwood sent to me, "I agree. Our first priority must be to stop Ariel, but until the shipfolk return, let us begin to make a map of this place."

His words gave me another idea. Aloud, I said, "Ariel has chambers here. Coerce the Threes to find out where they are, and I will search them for clues about which city is the destination of the plague null."

Cinda reached out to touch my wrist, and when I turned my attention to her mind, she said, "I will take you to my friend. He may know more of Ariel's doings."

Twenty minutes later, I was following the slender girl down the steps from the bathing room again, Falc's hood drawn forward to conceal my hair.

Cinda opened the door to the laundry, and I froze, seeing that it was no longer empty. The coppers were now full, and there were shadows flitting about, their thin dark-clad forms half obscured by dense steam clouds. I hesitated, but Cinda assured me that no shadow would trouble me. Sure enough, the black-clad women paid so little heed to us as we passed that we might just as well have been invisible. But then Cinda stopped and gave me a reassuring look before she clapped her hands loudly. All the shadows turned to look at us, their faces bland. Cinda lifted her fingers and flicked them for a long time. Gradually, the blankness in the women's faces gave way to wariness and then to amazement, hope, disbelief. Some of the women lifted their hands, but Cinda shook her head, fingers still fluttering, and in a moment, all the women had returned to their work, leaving me to feel I might have imagined the brief transformation I had witnessed.

"I told them to rejoice, for we are about to rise up against our masters," Cinda said, leading me out of the overheated washing chamber into the yard, where the numerous lines I had seen earlier now sagged under the weight of wet sheets, towels, and hundreds of white, gray, and black robes. "I told them that you and your friends are powerful mutant spies who have already overpowered the One and the Threes and that you will lead us in the fight to come." She saw my unguarded reaction and read it accurately, saying, "Do not fear that any of us will give you away. All who work in this laundry once served the One and so cannot speak, and the priests know nothing of our handspeaking."

"I do not believe you would betray us even if you could speak," I said, shamed by my momentary doubts.

We reached the gate Cinda had mentioned earlier, and it brought us to a narrow lane that passed along the rear of two long rows of buildings. As we hastened along it, Cinda explained that this way was safer because such back lanes were used only by shadows, novices, and the occasional acolyte. They were called shadow paths because the Hedra rarely used them.

"Are there other paths in the compound?" I asked, and she nodded. We came to a small area outside a door where a Herder novice of about fifteen chopped kindling. Before I could think what to do, he turned and saw us. Cinda stepped forward, moving her fingers rapidly. The youth flicked an incredulous glance at me, but Cinda caught his arm and continued speaking with her hands. I realized this must be the friend she would have me meet, but I had not imagined he would be a novice. He was as tall and strongly built as she was thin and small, but when they turned to me, they wore the same look of yearning. The youth said in an uneven voice, "Is it true what Cinda says? You are the mutant who hid aboard the *Stormdancer*? I heard that you had been taken to the cells."

"I am a Misfit," I corrected him. "And I was rescued by friends who are also Misfits."

"Cinda says you can speak inside her head and hear her thoughts."

"I can listen to what she wants to tell me," I said. "I can show you, if you like."

He shook his head hastily, and Cinda flicked her fingers at the novice and laughed quietly. He scowled at her, red-cheeked. "I am not afraid!" Her expression became contrite, and she moved her fingers until he seemed mollified.

"Cinda asks me to tell you how I ended up here," he said. He glanced warily both ways along the lane and then said, "I never wanted to be a Herder. Hardly any of us do, but those who fail the training are sold as slaves or become mine shadows. Those considered difficult are sent to the demon-band works, and after a few moons there, all of your hair and teeth fall out, and your bones start crumbling inside your skin. So I do my studies and I am obedient. But I am not a Herder, and I never will be," he added almost savagely. "Is it true that you and your friends mean to overthrow the Faction?"

"All that she told you is true," I said. "But there are few of us, and it will take time to establish real control, even with the help of the shadows. We must proceed with care, for the moment your brothers realize we are in their midst, they will put on their demon bands and we will be helpless."

"If you control the Threes and the One, you are far from helpless," said the youth. He glanced at Cinda, then back to me. "She said you need information about Ariel, but you need not trouble yourself about the Pale Man, for he has gone to Norseland. It is said that he will go to the west coast before he returns."

His last words gave me pause, but realizing Cinda had told him nothing of the plague null, I did so, explaining that I needed to know where he might have taken the null. "Faugh!" the lad spat. "It does not surprise me that the Pale Man should come up with such a foul plan. All novices fear him, because when first we come, he tests us to see if we would suit being made into nulls. He smiles when we scream, as if our suffering pleasures him. I know nothing of this matter of the west coast, but I can question the other novices at midmeal. It is unlikely anyone knows more, for the Pale Man's chambers are in a sector on the other side of the compound where few of us have call to go."

"How many sectors are there?" I asked.

"Twenty-one," he answered. "The only reason novices leave their sectors is because a Herder bids them go, and you must go only where you are told and then return directly. Sometimes my master sends me to the ink house or paper press, but occasionally I accompany him to the library, which is right across the compound."

"Is movement controlled?" I asked.

He nodded gravely. "Any unaccompanied novice or

acolyte outside his sector must produce his master's token to show he has been sent on an errand, and the token is marked with chalk to tell where he is meant to go. If he is in the wrong place, a whipping or time in the tide cells would be the least he would suffer." He glanced again both ways along the lane.

I nodded and thanked him. "If you can find out anything that might help us understand more about Ariel's plans on the west coast, even an overheard phrase or gossip, it may mean the difference between saving the west coast and not," I said. "But you must not let anyone guess why you are asking."

"I will be careful," he said. "But you should know that I am not the only novice who would be glad to be free of this robe and this place. There are three I know who would gladly fight if it comes to that. There are more in other sectors, but it is better for us not to know one another in case one is questioned. Yet if there is real hope of getting free of the Faction, then maybe it is time for us to know one another. Where do I find you if I learn something?" he asked.

"Seek out Cinda, and she will bring you to us," I said after the slightest hesitation. It struck me that I did not know his name. I asked him, but before he could respond, the door behind him opened, and an older Herder stepped out. "Novice, why are you taking . . . ?" He stopped, his eyes widening at the sight of Cinda and me. Before he could even begin to formulate a suspicion, I entered his mind and made him come outside and close the door behind him. I felt Cinda and the young novice watching me as I coerced the priest. The novice gaped openly when his master turned, blank-faced, and went back inside, closing the door quietly behind him.

"Right now he thinks he has just told you to hurry up. He won't remember seeing us at all, but later this afternoon he is going to become terribly sleepy and lie down until nightmeal.

Before he sleeps, he will give you a token with his mark. You need only speak Cinda's name into his ear and say whatever you wish him to scribe, and he will do it. Now go back in, and be careful," I warned him.

The novice squared his shoulders, and his eyes flashed. "You asked my name, lady? It is Elkar, and you may count on me."

When we returned to the One's chamber, I was disappointed to find that there was still no word of Helvar, but the compound map was beginning to take shape, complete with shadow paths, sectors, and even details about buildings. Harwood was fascinated to hear about Elkar and as eager as I to see what the lad might unearth. He invited me to look at the map, and I knelt down to study it.

I ran my eyes along the shadow path I had taken with Cinda. From what I could tell, the building Elkar had come from was marked "Scrips." I guessed it must have something to do with scribing since he had mentioned an ink house and a paper press. I searched until I found the library he had mentioned. As he had said, it was on the other side of the compound. Harwood was now explaining that although most sectors were virtually self-sufficient, each had at least one activity that served the entire compound.

"These communal activities seem to be the key to moving safely around the compound," Harwood said. "For instance, here is the food store for the entire compound. Shadows and novices from here make deliveries to kitchens all over the compound, including to the Hedra and the inner-cadre walled garden."

Cinda touched my arm and said that we ought to poison the food meant for the Hedra sector, for we could kill all of

341

them at one stroke. I exchanged a startled look with Harwood, who told her gently that we intended to take control with as little killing as possible.

"Why?" she asked, looking confounded. "Better to kill as many priests as possible, so they can never harm anyone again."

I hid my shock and said mildly that poisoning them would have all sorts of repercussions we could not possibly cope with, such as hundreds of dead bodies that would need disposing of before they rotted. I had thought to bring home to her the grisly reality of her suggestion, but she merely shrugged and said the bodies could be piled up in the exercise yards and burned.

Harwood began asking Cinda about the routines within the compound, but I was puzzled. If Cinda and the other shadows were so willing to see their masters die, why had they not rebelled already?

I turned my attention back to the map, noting the repetition of sleeping halls, meal chambers, and cloister in each sector. I also spotted an unmarked area at the compound's end, farthest from the gate. Before I could ask what it was, Cinda rose and touched my arm, explaining that she and one of the others must go to fetch the One's nightmeal, for it was always made ready at this time.

"Ye gods," Harwood muttered after she had gone. "I thought when she said the shadows would be willing to fight tooth and nail it was romantic rhetoric, but if the rest think as Cinda does . . ."

"They can't, or they would have rebelled before now," I said. I drew his attention back to the map and asked if he knew yet of Ariel's chambers.

He pointed to a small section alongside the library, explaining that they were contained within the wall surrounding the library. Then he tapped another largish section. "That is what interests me. It is the healing center, and it serves the whole compound, according to the shadows who go there to collect medications for the One. I have not scribed it yet, but the whole sector is one immense labyrinthine building with three levels above the ground and two below. Instead of having meal halls kept separate from the healing facility, the acolytes, novices, and shadows live in chambers on one of the subterranean levels while the ranked priests live on the topmost level. I suppose this is because healers have to be available constantly. They are trained within the building and rarely leave it save to go to daily prayer meetings in a nearby sector, because the healing center lacks a cloister."

I touched the place on the map where the Hedra sector ran up against the healing center. "Do priests from the healing center attend the Hedra cloister?"

"No, but the healing center is one level higher than any other building in the compound and two levels higher than most. And it overlooks the Hedra training grounds. One watcher up there—"

"But we already have Hilder and Tomrick on the outer wall."

"They are too far away, and they would have to divide their attention," Harwood said. "If we put even one watcher on top of the healing center, they could watch the whole central area of the compound, including the Hedra sector, and could serve as a conduit for farsought information."

I nodded. "Then do it."

"I was also thinking that the healing building would make the perfect command center," added Harwood. I have just sent Sover there with some of the shadows, supposedly to get

343

something to ease the One. Sover will remain there and begin coercing healers at once. I have sent Colwyn over to take a look at this sector." He pointed to a small area that ran up against the outer wall of the compound behind the Hedra sector. "This is the compound armory. It is walled, and the only way to enter it is from the Hedra training ground. Apparently, it is guarded constantly, but we need to get control of it, given that it may contain the Beforetime weapon you mentioned."

I shuddered; then something struck me. "If you sent Sover to the healing center, who is watching over the One?"

Harwood said dismissively, "Some of the shadows. Geratty is sleeping in the dressing room, and they will wake him if the One stirs." He pointed to the large area I had noticed at the end of the compound, naming it tainted ground.

"Tainted ground?" I echoed.

"Strictly speaking, it sounds as if it is more a patch of blacklands centered on a tainted pool," Harwood said. "The whole area is walled and encompasses the mine where the male shadows work. There are sleeping quarters and an eating hall for the shadows who work there. They never come out, apparently. Lure told me that some of her sisters take in food once a day. I think we need control of it, because aside from the armory, it is the only other place where the priests will be able to get demon bands."

"What of the bands taken from us at the gate?"

"They are returned to the armory," Harwood said.

I pointed to Ariel's chambers again and asked Harwood what he had learned of them.

"Not much," Harwood said, frowning at the map. "The shadows do not go there, any more than novices or acolytes. Apparently, Ariel uses nulls to attend him. I probed Mendi and Grisyl to see what they knew and found they have never been in Ariel's chambers. Moreover, they were remarkably incurious about what goes on there, despite their doubts about Ariel. That lack of curiosity made me dig into Mendi's mind until I found the coercive structures Ariel had set up to ensure that no one interferes with him. It is the same with Grisyl."

"I wonder what is of such importance there that Ariel would keep everyone away," I said.

"Maybe plague seeds," said Harwood. "I would like to do a little more nosing around before you try searching there."

"All right," I said reluctantly. "I will wait until the ship-folk begin work on the *Stormdancer*. But no longer, for there may be information there that will help us find the null quickly."

Cinda returned, accompanied by a beaming Ode who carried a great black cauldron of stew and a basket of bread and boasted of having coerced every person in the sector seven kitchen. Harwood bade Cinda give the One's tray to Falc and sent him to see if he could wake his master to eat. Then he woke Reuvan and Geratty, and we all ate sitting cross-legged on the floor, the shadows among us, as Harwood outlined his plan to take over the healing center and capture the armory. We had barely begun when Elkar appeared at the dressing-room door.

"I did not realize you would be here," he said. "You said to seek out Cinda if I had something to tell."

"You know of the secret stairs to the One's chamber?" I asked.

He glanced at Cinda. "I usually wait for Cinda or one of the shadows on the stairs, but I heard your voice." He was looking about at the others with open curiosity, and I explained who he was and let them offer their own names. Then I said, "Have you learned anything about Ariel?"

"One of the novices in the dining hall told me of another novice who had talked of seeing the Pale Man and his special nulls, but he could not recall who it was. He has promised to try to remember."

"The Pale Man?" Harwood echoed.

"Ariel," I said, and nodded for Elkar to continue.

"Mainly I came to tell you that the other novices are willing to help." He gave a sudden laugh. "Willing! Say rather they are demanding to help. You cannot imagine how the idea of freedom fired them. Even I could not have predicted the strength of their reaction. In truth, none of us *guessed* there was anything to escape to, for it seemed that the Herders were the masters of the world. But then the invasion failed and you came."

I bit back the urge to remind the novice that I had asked him to disclose nothing to anyone yet and said, "Harwood, you should meet with these partisan novices as soon as may be." I added privately that he had better coerce them to make sure there were none among them like to betray us.

But Elkar said eagerly, "That is why I came. There is a prayer meeting tonight that will be attended by all the novices from this sector and by a Herder who will rant at us about serving Lud with a pure heart. I was thinking you could make him stop and then talk in his stead."

"You would have us address all the novices?" I asked in disbelief. "Surely not all of them are ready to rise against the Faction!"

"Of course not," Elkar said. "But you can force the others to obey."

"This is getting out of hand," Harwood sent to me forcefully enough to let me know he blamed me. Then he asked Elkar to describe a prayer meeting. As the novice obliged, Cinda made some signals to the other shadows, which Elkar noticed and translated as a suggestion that all the dissenters had better be killed. The other shadows nodded with such ferocious expressions that I found myself wondering if, after all, they *did* think as Cinda did. Then Elkar said calmly that it might be the best idea.

I farsent uneasily to Harwood that we had best be careful we did not light a taper of rage that would set the whole compound ablaze. The coercer nodded slightly and bade me leave it to him. Then he told Elkar he hoped that the novice had done or said nothing to make his masters guess something was afoot. Elkar laughed, saying that his own master was so excited over a new kind of ink that had been delivered that he would not have noticed if the novice was walking about naked. Then he frowned and added that the Herder who had brought the ink had told his master that Salamander had sunk the *Orizon* not because mutants had boarded it, as had been reported that morning, but because the Hedra aboard had contracted a deadly plague in the Land.

"A plague?" I echoed aloud, unable to see how such a rumor could have arisen unless something had leaked about the null that Ariel was taking to the west coast. I turned to Harwood, but his eyes had the distant look that meant one of the others was farseeking him. After a long moment, he said, "That was Tomrick. He says he walked around the top of the wall until he calculated he was above us, and as he had hoped, he was able to farseek me. He is going to stay in that position now so the others can farseek any news to him to be relayed to us. But he says there is a mist rolling in, and from what he has seen, it won't be long before it comes into the compound. Apparently, Hilder says it is already creeping along the channel."

I stood up decisively. "I am going to Fallo. I need to know what is happening with the shipfolk."

"I will come with you," Reuvan said. "I have slept enough and feel useless here."

Elkar broke in to ask if he and Cinda could come with me. I was about to refuse when Harwood farsent that I ought to let them accompany me to the gates since we would make a reasonable entourage; I could wear Falc's robe again and go as a ranked Herder, accompanied by a lantern-bearing shadow, a novice, and a Hedra escort, for of course Reuvan was bald and clad in a Hedra robe like the coercers.

I told the novice that he and Cinda could come as far as the black gates but that it would look suspicious if they came farther, since Cinda had told me that neither novices nor shadows ever left the compound. And besides that, Elkar ought to be at the prayer meeting. He looked disappointed but acquiesced willingly enough. We were soon descending the hidden stairs and passing through the once more deserted laundry. It was dusk, and the laundry yard was veiled in mist, but Elkar shrugged, saying that the mist would grow much thicker before it abated. I asked if he would not be missed, and he answered that his master would merely assume that Elkar was still in the dining hall.

"Do the Herders keep such casual control of you?" I asked, surprised.

He shrugged. "They keep a tight hold on new novices, but with novices my age, it depends on the master. Mine is old and less strict than many," he added.

Two priests appeared before us in the mist, followed by a lantern-bearing shadow. The Herders nodded to me without breaking off their conversation, but I noticed the shadow flick her fingers at Cinda.

"She asked if it was true that mutants had secretly invaded the compound." Cinda told me what had been signaled.

As we walked, the mist thickened as Elkar had predicted, and I noticed how empty the streets and lanes now were. Was it a curfew or the mist? I wondered.

Soon a group of Hedra came marching along the street toward us. I prayed they would march past without bothering us. But the leader stopped and commanded us to do the same. I obeyed and was relieved to find that there was no barrier as I entered his mind. A relentless fanaticism snaked through his thoughts like a river of poison, sickening me, but there was no time to be squeamish. I took complete and rough control of him, but before I could make him dismiss us, one of the other Hedra asked me suspiciously, "Where are you going, Master?"

"Our master is ill and wishes a potion from the healers," I said in as low a voice as I could manage.

"Who is your captain?" asked the same Hedra of Reuvan.

I jabbed coercively at the Hedra in my control. He gave a loud bray of pain and clutched at his stomach, and the other Hedra looked at him in astonishment.

"It seems my master is not the only one who is ill," I said with pretended alarm. An inspired thought came to me, and I added, "I pray it is not the plague that was aboard the *Orizon*."

A look of deep unease passed between the Hedra, and I made the priest clutching his stomach give another good long bellow of pain, then offered to take him to the healing center, since we were bound there.

"You had better go, too, Gelt," said the Hedra who had questioned Reuvan to one of the others.

I saw from the expression on the other warrior priest's face that he would protest, and I coerced him to nod obediently, then I went back to the mind of the groaning Hedra and jabbed at him again, causing him to utter another groan and double over. The Hedra Gelt stepped forward to take his arm.

"Help them," I ordered Elkar, who had been watching with openmouthed astonishment. He obeyed as the other Hedra marched away.

"It's all right," I assured all of them when we were alone but for the two Hedra, both now silent and blank-faced. "I am controlling them."

"You did that to him?" Elkar whispered, looking at the Hedra who had been shouting and groaning.

"He is not truly ill," I assured him. "I just found a deep memory of a terrible stomachache he once had and grafted it into his conscious mind. Then I gave his muscles a jab to set him off. But let's go on. We can't stay out in the open like this."

"What are we going to do with them?" Reuvan asked softly.

"We will take them into the healing center, just as I said, in case their comrades come back to see what became of this one. This is it, isn't it?" I asked, nodding to the building beside us.

Elkar agreed, adding that the entrance was on the other side, facing sector three. Soon we were approaching the entrance. Mercifully, it was not guarded. I would have liked to leave the others to wait outside, but the door opened before we could reach it, and several low-ranking outer-cadre priests came hurrying out, so immersed in conversation that they did not even see us.

We entered a windowless hall lit by lanterns hanging from

hooks set into the walls. Two outer-cadre Nines standing outside a door a little distance along the passage broke off their conversation to look toward us inquiringly, so I made the Hedra begin bellowing and groaning again.

"What is wrong with him?" asked one of them.

"I do not know," I said, keeping my voice and my head low, for I feared they would see that I was a woman. "I was on an errand for my master when we came upon a group of Hedra. He was in their midst, and I was ordered to bring him here."

Fortunately, the healer was more concerned with the bellowing Hedra than with me, but his companion eyed me suspiciously. Before I could shape a coercive probe to deal with him, an older Herder wearing the gold armband of an inner-cadre priest arrived and demanded to know what was going on. He had the harried air of a real healer, and though his face was much lined, it lacked the coldness I had seen in most Herder faces. Perhaps it was hard to be cold and remote when trying to heal sickness.

I gave the groaning Hedra's mind a hard tweak, and when the Herder bent to examine him, I said anxiously that I would have to go because my own master would wonder where I was. One final jab and the Hedra collapsed. As the three healers tended to him, I withdrew, ushering the others ahead of me. Not until we were outside did I realize the Hedra Gelt had followed us, because I had forgotten to command him to stay.

"He will have to come with us," I decided, and we turned back toward the compound gates. I farsought Sover as we walked, explaining briefly what had happened, and he promised to take care of it.

"What will the healers do when they realize that there is

351

nothing wrong with that Hedra?" Elkar asked softly.

Before I could respond, Geratty's voice scythed into my mind with a force that would have dropped me to my knees had Reuvan not caught me.

"Geratty! What is it?" I demanded, clutching at my head.

"Elspeth, the One . . . Ye gods, it is the shadows. They've killed him!"

Suddenly, bells began ringing loudly.

✦ 20 ✦

I FROZE, BUT Elkar assured me that the bells rang only to announce the beginning of the evening acolyte prayer meetings. "The novice prayers will be in an hour, and then will come the bell for the rest of the outer-cadre priests. . . ." He glanced at my face, and his own grew tense. "What is it, lady?"

"Wait," I said, and stopped. I had to farseek Geratty to find out what on earth he had meant by saying the One had been killed. And by *shadows*! But I could not locate the coercer. I realized he would have had to come outside to reach me, and no doubt he had now gone back inside.

Opening my eyes, I announced that we had to go back to the One's chamber immediately. We retraced our steps along the path. When we drew near the laundry, Elkar announced that perhaps he ought to make an appearance in his master's chamber. He would come after us as soon as possible.

"What's wrong?" Reuvan asked me softly when he had gone.

I told him what Geratty had sent.

He grimaced. "Why?"

"Geratty didn't say, and now I can't reach him," I said worriedly.

Cinda touched my hand. "It does not matter if the One is dead, lady. You can make any Hedra or priests believe he is alive. And you still have the Threes."

I did not know what to say to her, for she seemed to have no sense of the wrongness of murder. She was considering only the consequences of the death, yet this was the death of the most powerful man in all the Faction—at the hands of shadows like her. How could she not be shocked?

Minutes later, we were mounting the stairs leading up from the laundry. A shattered-looking Geratty was waiting for me.

"What on earth has happened?" I demanded.

"Harwood woke me to say he and Ode were gannin' out to deal with some problem with shadows and a Herder priest. He took Grisyl. He said the shadows were feeding the One because he had been asleep earlier when they tried. I was just gannin' a bite to eat myself when I heard a cry. I went to th' One's chamber. The two of them were . . . bending over him. Emaciated lasses more like children than women; they looked so innocent, but their hands were covered in blood." He shuddered. "They had the knives from the meals they had brought. Poor blunt things, but . . . Guildmistress, they . . . they had blinded him and were trying to cut out his tongue!" He looked at me. "They seemed . . . surprised that I was so upset. Apparently, the One woke an' saw one of them without their headdress. He started screamin' for the Hedra to chop their hands off and put out their eyes . . . ye gods." He faltered to a halt, suddenly seeing Cinda gazing at him in bewilderment.

"Is he dead?" Reuvan asked quietly.

The coercer drew a deep breath and shook his head. "I thought he was at first, but no. He lives yet, but he's in a bad way. I tried to reach Harwood or Sover, but my probe wouldn't locate. So I sent one of th' shadows to the healing center. Not one of the two who . . . ."

"Where are the shadows who did it?" I asked.

"In the other room. I . . . I sent them in there while I was cleaning him up." He looked into my eyes. "Guildmistress, I've seen killing before, but nowt like this. Those pretty mild-faced girls with their bloody hands . . ."

The sound of boots coming up the steps behind us brought us to our feet. To my amazement, it was Yarrow, accompanied by Asra and a rather bedraggled Zuria.

"You found the shipfolk!" I said.

"No. We found the Per of Gelan; that is the village on Fallo where your shipmaster dwelt," Yarrow said. "Or at least, the Hedra Mendi sent out had found him and were torturing him when we arrived. He had fled with the rest of the villagers after one of them saw the Hedra take a prisoner off the ship. Apparently, your Helvar realized it was you and guessed that it was only a matter of time before the Hedra came for him, his shipfolk, and their families, so he warned the Per, who ordered the evacuation of the village. They did not want to bring strife to the other villages, so they fled into the swamp. But the Per is old, and when he could not continue, they hid him. Unfortunately, the Hedra found him, and they were so engrossed in their foul labor that we had only to creep up on them and knock them on the heads."

He went on to explain that their rescue of the Per had been fortuitous, because it convinced the old man that they were no friends of the Faction. He had told them that his village had been abandoned, because Helvar had given aid to a young mutant from the Land. "I let him rattle on, because I wanted to see whether he or maybe this Helvar had any resentment toward you over what happened. They don't, by the way."

"Where did the Per think you came from?" I asked.

He grinned. "He was so relieved to have his head on his shoulders that it took him a good bit of time to wonder that. When he did get to it, I said we were friends of yours who had come aboard the ship disguised as Hedra. I explained you hadn't known we were aboard any more than we had known you were aboard."

"I'm glad they're not full of ire," I said, for I could not truly have blamed the Norseland shipfolk for resenting me.

Yarrow went on to say that although the Per did not know where the shipfolk and their families were hiding, he had only to tie a swatch of cloth to the topmost branch of a certain tree to communicate with them. A red swatch warned that the person flying the flag was summoning them under duress. A yellow flag, on the other hand, denoted that it was safe to return.

"He said he was glad we had come along to save him the mortification of flying the red flag," Asra added.

"So you hung out the yellow cloth?" I asked.

"A blue one," Yarrow said. "That means that it is safe and to come in haste. But the Per said that how much time it took Helvar and the others to respond would depend upon where in the swamps they had taken refuge. He promised that as soon as they came out, he would send them across with tools to repair the *Stormdancer*."

"Did you tell the Per what is happening here?"

"I told him that we had rescued you and that we had control of the gate guards and the wall watch, so the Norselanders need not fear an attack. I showed him how we could make Zuria dance a jig and a Hedra stand on his head, which was enough to convince him I was not exaggerating. I also told him we had control of the other two inner-cadre Threes and the One . . . What is it?" He was looking at Geratty, who had flinched at his words.

My elation faded. I said tiredly, "Reuvan will explain what has been happening here. In the meantime, Geratty, you had better go down to the laundry and wait for the healer."

"The shadow said he would come along the wall passage, so I will wait there," the older coercer said. He went through to the firelit audience room, and I followed him. It was easy to see which of the shadows had attacked the One, for they sat huddled against the wall near a blank-faced Mendi, watching us with huge, lost eyes. I went over to them. I saw with revulsion the blood on their hands and asked Cinda to fetch warm water so they could wash. I knelt down before them, seeing that both were little more than Dragon's age when I had found her in the Befortime ruins. If not for the blood on their hands, I would have found it impossible to believe that they had done what Geratty had described. I reached into the mind of one, meaning to reassure her that she would not be punished, and I recoiled from a vivid, bloody vision of myself torturing her. I realized with horror that even though they knew we were allies, they imagined I would resort to torture to seek information or punish them.

The words I had intended to say died on my lips, for I saw that I could say nothing about what they had done that would make any sense to them. They had spoken to the One in the language he and his foul brethren had taught them— the language of cruelty and pain—and it was the only language they knew.

"Come over to the fire. No one will hurt you or punish you," I told them.

They obeyed, and as Cinda came with water and began to

wash their hands, I tried to think of something that would allow us to bridge this moment. Nothing came to mind, and when Cinda sat back on her heels, I asked her rather desperately to tell me Elkar's story, adding the inward request that she tell the story with her fingers as well as her mind. She looked puzzled, but she obeyed, and as I had hoped, the blank devastation ebbed in the eyes of the two younger shadows as her tale unfolded.

Elkar had been born on Herder Isle, Cinda explained. Like so many other Norse boys, he was taken from his family to become a novice. He had resisted the training until he and the other novices had been taken to see the mine and demonband works, and he had understood that this would be their fate if they did not succeed in becoming novices. Elkar had given up his rebellious refusal to cooperate and had tried to forget his family and believe the words of Lud, as expressed by his masters. He had worked hard, and when it was found that he had an aptitude for scribing, he was sent to the Herder scribes. Eventually, he had been assigned to his present master who, although devout, was one of the few Herders with a passion for something other than worshipping Lud. Although friendship was impossible, Elkar had come to respect his master's ability to read and scribe.

The boy had proven so quick and willing to learn that almost before he had realized what he was doing, the old man was teaching him to read and scribe. This was forbidden, but his master had known that Elkar would work more swiftly and efficiently if he could read and scribe, and his own eyesight was beginning to fail. Elkar was careful never to reveal his abilities, realizing that he would be killed if anyone learned that he knew how to read. In time, his master trusted him so well that he had given over the scribing of older scrips to Elkar.

"Why rescribe older scrips?" I interrupted.

"The reason given was that they were old and falling to bits," Cinda explained. "But more often it was because a bit of the scrip had become unacceptable and needed to be altered. This was supposed to be done by Elkar's master and merely copied by the scrip novices."

That scrips said to have come to the One in visions sent by Lud were altered and sometimes even reversed made it impossible for Elkar to believe in the Herders' Lud. But he was older now and wise enough in the ways of the Faction to make sure he never revealed his disbelief.

Cinda ceased her story as Geratty reentered and passed through the chamber with a blank-faced Herder priest carrying a healer's bag. Instead of referring to the interruption, I asked her how she and Elkar had become friends. She smiled shyly and said that he had noticed the shadows' finger movements. Elkar had studied the movements of the shadows, and one day, when Cinda had been serving food to him, he had made the signal that he believed was a greeting between shadows. She had started so violently that she had spilled hot soup on him, but the novice had said nothing. Frightened and confused, she had managed to stay away from the meal hall for some time, and when she had to go there, she had been careful to avoid him. Yet she had not been able to forget the movement of his fingers, which had expressed the word *friend*. Then one day as she was taking a tray to the One, Elkar had been outside the scrip cutting kindling. He had approached Cinda, again using the finger signal for "friend," then told her aloud that he wanted her to teach him the signal language.

"I was afraid at first," Cinda said. "I knew that many of us would be killed if our masters knew how well we could communicate. Yet I feared to refuse him. I decided I would pretend to be very dull-witted and show him only the simplest language so he would believe we used it to communicate only what was necessary for our work. I hoped he would grow bored, but he was so clever and quick. He would make this or that signal and ask what it meant. My sisters told me that we must poison him, but I did not know whom he had told about me, and I wanted to know before I killed him. As time passed, I understood that Elkar had told no one what he had guessed. I asked why he wanted to know how to speak to a shadow, and he answered that he was curious and that he envied our freedom of speech."

The words Cinda used in her upper mind were less eloquent than the picture in her undermind, which was loud and radiant. Cinda had at first feared the white-clad novice, but she had soon learned that his regard was not unfriendly. Indeed, to her astonishment, it had dawned on her that it was the opposite: He was lonely and wished them to be friends. She resisted until, one day, he said that he would repay her for her lessons by teaching her to scribe and to read. Knowing that he could be killed for being able to read, she had taken it as an offering of friendship. But by now, her own feelings for him ran deeper than that, though she never dared let Elkar see how she felt.

Then came the day that she had scribed her name for the first time with a thrill of pure terror, and Elkar had read it aloud. She had looked up at him in wonder and sorrow, for she had not heard her name spoken aloud since her brother had been dragged from her arms, screaming it. She wept, and Elkar had taken her in his arms and kissed her tears away.

This gentle tenderness had shown Cinda that his feelings ran as deep as hers.

When Cinda's image spoke again, it was to say that Elkar's feelings for her made him sympathetic to the plight of all shadows, whose lives he realized were much harder than any novice's. He had become determined to find a way to help the shadows, but save for being as kind and considerate as he dared, he could not think how.

Then one day, Cinda asked if he could scribe a note that would transfer a young shadow from one sector to another, where the girl's sister labored. Since shadows were used as messengers, it was no difficulty for one to deliver the note Elkar had scribed, and soon the sisters were reunited. With this note, Elkar had proven himself to all the shadows, and thereafter he had become their secret champion.

More requests followed, and Elkar came to recruit others among the novices and acolytes, and even one ranked priest, who felt as he did. The little secret group passed among themselves messages of hope, warnings, and occasionally books Elkar had stolen from the library. Some were from the Beforetime and told of a world that was nothing like the Beforetime of the Faction's preachings, which passionately interested all of them. But their main task was to ease the lot of the shadows. And the shadows found ways of helping them, too. A novice being punished would be starved, but the shadows would bring him food; a note sent to command the punishment of a novice would be brought to Elkar, who would rescribe it and simply send the boy to another sector. Cinda assured me that there was little danger, because no priest could ever imagine anyone disobeying him, so he did not check that his orders had been carried out.

I wondered why Ariel had not foreseen what was going

on, unless, like the Herders, he simply never focused his attention on the shadows.

Yarrow was hovering, and when I rose, apologizing to Cinda for interrupting her story, he drew me into the dressing room where Geratty waited. The older man told me that the healing Herder had given the One medicines to soothe his pain but that his mind, already teetering under the weight of Ariel's block, was broken altogether now. Certainly it would be some time before they could even attempt to enter it.

I nearly shuddered at the thought.

"Has Harwood been in contact yet?" I asked them.

Geratty shook his head. "Asra has been outside trying, but neither he nor Tomrick has heard a peep from him since he summoned Hilder down from the wall, and now they can't reach him either. They will keep trying."

Yarrow said suddenly, "You know, I don't think Ariel ever meant to come back here."

I stared at him. "We know he is going to the west coast before he returns to Herder Isle," I said.

"No, I mean I don't believe he meant to come back here at all."

"What makes you think that?" I asked.

"Because he must have known that he would not return from the west coast in time to save the old man's mind, and yet he set no safeguards against its being destroyed. Why on earth let him die or go mad when he had been so useful? Unless Ariel had no further use for him."

"Maybe he plans to let one of the Threes take his place. After all, the One's mind is disintegrating."

"True enough, but it is more than that," Yarrow said. "Ariel has always contrived never to be there when something he is involved in falls apart. And now, when we are making a good start at bringing this place down, Ariel is else-where. Maybe he foresaw that Herder Isle would fall."

"If he did, then why didn't he take steps to stop it?" I asked.

"Maybe he foresaw that it can't be stopped," Yarrow suggested.

"He has access to an army of Hedra on Norseland," I said. "He could have had Salamander blast the wall down."

"He *could* if he wanted to protect the Faction, but why would he? He has just been using them to further his own interests, hasn't he? The way he used Henry Druid and the Councilmen. He has never hesitated to betray people in the past."

"You are saying you think he has left this place for good? Left it to us?"

"That is what it seems like to me."

"Where would he go after he has poisoned the west coast?" I asked. Even as I spoke, my mind flew to the Red Land.

But Yarrow said, "He has a stronghold on Norseland. It seems to me that he will return there after he has left the null on the west coast. I was speaking to the Per about Norseland, and it sounds as if it is virtually unassailable, being all high cliffs, save for Main Cove, where there is a single narrow road leading up to Covetown, overlooked by the cloister. Not far from there the Hedra have their own permanent encampment, inhabited by an army in waiting. I do not doubt that Ariel can coerce its captains into accepting his authority, but maybe he would not need them to defend himself. I was also poking around in Zuria's mind on our way back here, and it seems that Ariel found other weapons from the Beforetime when he found the plague seeds, and the Threes believe he keeps them in his residence."

My blood ran cold at the thought of Ariel in possession of Beforetime weapons.

"But if Ariel knew he would not return to Herder Isle, why leave instructions that the guildmistress be left unhurt until he came to interrogate her?" Geratty asked.

Yarrow frowned. "Hmm. I had forgotten that." He fell silent, mulling it over, but I knew why Ariel would have ordered me not to be harmed. He needed the Seeker alive. He may even have foreseen that I was the Misfit aboard the *Stormdancer* and acted to make sure I would not be tortured before the coercer-knights took control of the compound. That he had not stayed to take me captive himself meant he knew that I had not yet gathered all I needed to find and disable the weaponmachines that had caused the Great White. Perhaps Yarrow was exactly right, and Ariel would return to Norseland once he had done with the west coast, to wait until he futuretold that I was ready for the final stage of my quest. Then what? Did he plan to capture me then or simply follow me to the weaponmachines so he could snatch victory from my hands?

What did not fit was that at least one of the remaining clues was on the west coast, and though Ariel need not know it, he must know it might be possible. Yet he was willing to spread a deadly plague. Did he know that my body's capacity to heal itself could survive even exposure to a deadly sickness, or had he reasoned that once the last plague victim died on the west coast, the plague itself would die?

Suddenly Yarrow stiffened, and seeing his absorbed expression, I waited impatiently for his eyes to clear, my heart sinking at the grim expression on his face.

"That was Tomrick. He says that Harwood farsent him," he said at last. "Colwyn and Hilder are trapped with the

Hedra. Harwood wants all of us to come now, and we are to bring Zuria and Mendi."

Less than half an hour passed before Geratty, Reuvan, Yarrow, and I approached the dye works where Harwood had bidden us meet him, having left Asra to watch over the shadows, the Hedra guards, Falc, and the One. Cinda and two other shadows had accompanied us, bearing lanterns for pretense more than need.

Harwood looked pale and grim as he ushered us through the door of the dye works and closed it behind us. A row of Herders tied up along the wall glared at us, watched by a composed Ode and a little cluster of frightened-looking shadows hovering in the back of the large room. Cinda went to greet them as Harwood explained that he had taken over the place, because we would draw attention if we were all standing out in the open.

"You did not coerce them?" I nodded to the bound priests.

"I did not want to waste my energy, for we may need it," Harwood said.

"How were Colwyn and Hilder caught?" I asked.

Harwood shook his head. "I did not say they were caught. They are *trapped*. About two hours ago, one of the shadows came to us to say that a group of shadows had locked a Herder in a cellar. He had been beating one of them, and instead of standing back and watching as they would normally, the shadows attacked him. Fortunately, they had the sense to send to us for help. Ode and I came to sort it out. I coerced the Hedra to believe he had fallen down some stairs and sent Ode to take him and Grisyl to Sover while I calmed the shadows. I was growing concerned about Colwyn, because I had not been able to reach him since I had sent him to investigate the

365

armory. So when Hilder farsought me to say he might as well come down from the watch-hut because the mist made it impossible to see anything, I sent him to look for Colwyn. As I discovered later, Hilder found him still awaiting an opportunity to sneak across the Hedra yards to the armory. I had not been able to reach his mind, because he was too close to the tainted wall." Harwood sighed and said that before the two coercers could retreat, one of the Hedra captains spotted them and commanded them to take their places in the ranks for the evening exercises. They had no choice but to obey, for every Hedra in sight was streaming down to the exercise yard.

"I knew none of this yet, of course, because now I could not reach Hilder either," Harwood continued. Worried, he had gone close enough to the armory to discover that the wall was tainted, but there was no sign of either coercer. "Finally, I spotted Hilder going through an exercise movement with a vast troop of Hedra. I tried to reach his mind, but it was locked to me. It was the same with Colwyn."

"The Hedra must have been wearing demon bands," Yarrow said. "If there were enough—"

"No," Harwood interrupted. "In exercising together with such precision, concentrating their whole minds upon the synchronized movements of the rest, the Hedra create a group mind that is impenetrable save to one who would mesh with it. Colwyn and Hilder would have had no choice but to mesh."

Yarrow and Geratty looked horrified.

Harwood said heavily, "That is why I summoned all of you here. I want to get control of the armory tonight, and it might take all of us to break the group mind."

"But surely Colwyn and Hilder will be free as soon as the exercise ends?" Yarrow said.

"That is what I believe. If not, I will send Zuria in. I did not send for the rest of you to rescue them. I want to go ahead and penetrate the armory, but if something goes wrong, it may be that the Hedra will form a group mind when they fight. If that is so, I will need your help to break it."

"What is your plan?" Yarrow asked.

"We will wait until this exercise ends, in the hope that Hilder and Colwyn will be released. I should be able to reach them then, and I will send them to the armory to tell whoever is in charge that Zuria and Mendi are on their way to make an inspection at the One's behest. Soon after, we will march in with the Threes, and during our so-called inspection, we will coerce every Hedra we encounter until we have control. If at any point the Hedra form a group mind, we merge to crack it open."

"Who controls the Hedra group mind?" Yarrow asked.

"I have been thinking about that," Harwood said. "In an ordinary unconscious group mind, the group itself has a natural leader, but in the case of the Hedra, there is no central mind. That is what makes it impossible to probe. I think the group mind is actually centered on some sort of shared illusion of the Herder Lud, and the group does what it believes this Lud desires. Our one advantage is that the Hedra form this group mind unconsciously, so they are unaware of the advantage it gives them over us."

"What if you can't crack it?" Reuvan asked.

"Then we had better discover that sooner rather than later," Harwood said grimly.

I drew a deep breath and bade Geratty explain what had happened to the One. Harwood grimaced as Geratty told his story, and once it was concluded, he remarked almost sadly, "I thought we could take over this place as stealthily as beetles burrowing into wood and with as little bloodshed as when we took the Land from the Council. But it is the Herders we are dealing with, and the Faction traffics in death and brutality so readily that it is no wonder even the shadows have learned it." He glanced at a time candle he had set on the table. "According to the shadows, each set of exercises goes on for two hours, which means we have less than an hour to wait."

Harwood turned his attention to Yarrow, asking what had been happening on Fallo. The coercer explained all that he had told me and concluded, "Veril will farseek Tomrick as soon as he gets across the channel with the Norselanders, but given what the Per said, I doubt that will happen much before morning. Maybe it's just as well given what we are about to do."

Harwood nodded.

The others began to discuss the need to find somewhere to put prisoners, for we could not be forever rearranging the priests' memories, and unless deeply coerced, they had to be coerced again frequently. I left this to the others and wrapped myself in my cloak to sleep while I had the chance.

It seemed but a moment before Harwood was shaking me gently awake.

"I just spoke to Sover. He says the rumor you began is spreading like wildfire. Several Hedra have come to the healing center to ask if there is plague in the compound. Hard to believe a rumor could spread so swiftly from such a small event. It seems that the failure of any of the Threes to return to their cottages these last two nights is being seen as proof that something is wrong. I have told Sover he might as well put Grisyl into a bed and let it be known that he is ill, for it occurs to me that the rumor of sickness could serve us very well."

"The rumor of sickness was already established," I said. "Remember, Elkar told us he had heard talk that the Hedra aboard the *Orizon* had caught plague in the Land and that this was the real reason Salamander had sunk the ship."

Harwood opened his mouth to speak and then stiffened. A moment later he nodded and looked relieved, saying aloud, "That was Colwyn. He and Hilder are both fine, but they are being marched to a meal with the other Hedra. They will have to wait until after the meal to go to the armory." He fell silent again, and as I waited for him to finish communicating with Colwyn, I farsent Tomrick and bade him check how the One was. After farsending Asra, Tomrick reported that the One was still alive and that several shadows had come looking for Cinda, as had Elkar. "Asra said the lad insisted on knowing where Cinda was, so I told him you were in the dye works. He is like to be there any minute."

I withdrew and told Harwood what I had learned. He nodded, but I could see that he was preoccupied. When I asked what troubled him, he said that he thought we should use the enforced wait to search Ariel's chambers, given that they were so near the dye works. We quickly decided that he and I would go alone. Yarrow was left in charge and, in case anything went wrong, was bidden to take the armory as planned.

"Do you expect anything to go wrong?" I asked as we left the dye house.

Before he could answer, a figure emerged from the thick misty darkness, but it was only Elkar. Once he heard what we intended, he insisted that he lead the way, for Ariel's chambers were *through* the labyrinthine library. He also insisted that Harwood wear the cloak of an ordinary priest, for Hedra never went to the library. Once the dye-works master had been divested of his cloak, we set off again.

The lanes and streets we passed along were thick with mist and very dark, but Elkar now carried the lantern I had been carrying, having pointed out that no Herder priest of rank would do such a thing. Glancing at the stark black stone buildings on either side of us, I marveled aloud that anyone would deliberately create such a dreary place to live. The mist was so thick, muffling even the noise of our steps, that I had no fear of speaking aloud. "Do these priests think their Lud dislikes beauty as well as women?"

Elkar gave me a quizzical look and answered softly, "My master would say that a woman's beauty is an illusion."

"Is the beauty of a tree also an illusion, then?"

"I do not think that Lud objects to trees," Elkar said. "It is only that trees will not grow here, nor any flower or plant or lichen."

"But what of the walled garden if the land is so barren?" I asked.

"It is barren, save for the earth behind that wall," Elkar insisted. "It was many years before I was born, but the One commanded a garden to be created to honor Lud, so earth was brought from Norseland to allow things to grow."

I gaped at him, unable to imagine how much earth would need to have been shipped to Herder Isle from Norseland to allow *trees* to grow.

"Here," said Elkar, gesturing to an open gateway in a wall. Beyond was a cobbled yard swathed in mist. "The library is on the other side of that yard," whispered the novice. "There are no guards outside."

We went through the gate with some trepidation, but as Elkar had said, there were no guards at the entrance to the large library building. But after we had entered the doors, two young Hedra stepped forward. Elkar nodded to them familiarly, introducing Harwood and myself as his master's new assistants, and they moved aside to let us enter. In a moment, we had passed out of their sight. Almost at once we came to shelves full of books separated by narrow aisles. Interspersed between them were tables where priests sat poring over tomes and making crabbed notes, lanterns pulled close to their elbows. I tried to look studious, though Elkar had promised they would pay no heed to us, as long as we did nothing to draw their attention.

We passed through two more chambers and then came through a door to a small courtyard. From the smell of it, there were privies here, but Elkar indicated a door set into a wall on the opposite side of the yard, saying this was the entrance to Ariel's chambers.

The door was locked and a taint emanated from it, strong enough to make it hard to focus my mind as I laid my hands over the lock and closed my eyes. The mechanism was so astonishingly complex that it could only have come from the Beforetime. I took a deep breath and concentrated all of my will on it. Then I stepped back, the cold chill of premonition touching my heart. My mind had shown me that anyone opening the lock without a key would set off a small explosive device. It was so small that I doubted it would have force enough to break the door down, yet the premonition of danger had been so strong that nothing would bring me to try disarming the lock.

"What is it?" Harwood asked.

My mouth was so dry that I had trouble speaking. "No one must touch this door," I said. "There is . . . some terrible danger here."

"You had a premonition?" Harwood guessed.

I nodded, and shivered. "No one must enter this chamber."

"Very well. Let us return to the others, then."

We had been gone scarcely a half hour, but by the time we got back to the dye works, Yarrow and the coercers had gone, taking Zuria and Mendi and leaving Cinda and the shadows to watch over the trussed and rather red-faced Herders. She explained that Yarrow had tried to reach us, and when he had failed, he had elected to go on with the plan, for Hilder and Colwyn had got away sooner than expected and had gone at once to the armory.

I bade the shadows loosen the Herders' gags slightly so the priests could breathe but to have a rock handy in case they tried anything. I spoke more as a warning to the Herders than as a direction to the shadows, until it occurred to me the women were all too likely to batter the priests' heads in, given what had happened to the One. I bade Elkar wait with them.

Outside, it was now raining, which dismayed me, because it would be impossible to farseek the others. It would also prevent Veril from farseeking Tomrick. He would have to come into the compound, and of course he would go first to the One's chamber. I regretted that I had not sent Elkar back there to wait, but it was too late to do so now. Harwood cursed the ill timing of the rain, but I said that although it was inconvenient, at least rain would ensure that no one would be outside, save those commanded to be there, so we likely would have an easier job ahead of us.

We spotted the end of the narrow path that ran between the walls surrounding the library yard and the inner-cadre garden; beyond lay the Hedra buildings. Someone reached out from a darkened doorway and caught my hand. I stifled a cry, for it was Yarrow, and pressed into the doorway behind him were Reuvan, Ode, Geratty, and Zuria, their faces slicked with rain.

"What is happening?" Harwood asked, wasting no time. He spoke aloud because the taint from the armory wall was strong enough to make farseeking impossible, even if it had not been raining.

"Hilder and Colwyn presented themselves at the armory gate and were taken to the Hedra master," Yarrow said.

"Did you say Hedra master?" I repeated.

He nodded. "It seems that he is one of seven Hedra generals who run the Hedra force, and from Zuria's memories, he is the most powerful, for he reports each new moon directly to the One. That means he will likely take this inspection by Zuria as interference at best and an insult at worst. We will need to be very careful how we proceed, especially if even a lesser number of Hedra can form this group mind outside of an exercise."

Harwood said, "It is a great pity we cannot reach Hilder or Colwyn to find out how they have been received by this general."

"Colwyn did send a mental picture of the yard," Yarrow said, and both Harwood and I reached out to make physical contact so we could take it from his mind. I saw a dark rain-swept yard paved in black cobbles and a single blocklike building set against the outer wall of the compound. Before its two huge metal doors stood ten armed Hedra.

"It seems small for an armory," Harwood muttered.

"A lot of protection for seemingly little," I said.

"Therefore, there must be more than there seems," Harwood added.

"There might be levels underground," Reuvan suggested.

"Let's find out," Harwood said.

"Who goes there?" demanded the Hedra at the armory gate, his bald head gleaming wetly in the light of the lantern he carried.

Zuria stepped forward as he had been coerced to do and asked sharply if the two Hedra sent ahead had not arrived to announce him. "If they have not delivered my message, I will have them confined in the tidal cells," he snapped.

The other Hedra made the throat-tapping gesture that we now understood denoted obedience and said that two Hedra had arrived a short time ago and had been taken to the Hedra master.

"And are two Threes to wait in the rain while two Hedra are questioned?" Zuria snarled.

"I am sorry, Master," said the first Hedra. "If you will accompany me, I will bring you to the Hedra master."

We followed him along the path, which ran to the right of the gates and along the inside of the armory wall to a barracks built against it. I bit my lip, aware that being so near the tainted wall would prevent us from coercing anyone, including Zuria or Mendi. I moved close enough to make contact with Harwood and pointed this out. He said calmly that he had anticipated it and had already given both Threes their instructions. Moreover, he would stay close enough to both to be able to make contact.

I nodded and, falling behind again, glanced across the wet cobbles at the lantern-lit face of the armory with its phalanx of guards. It looked bigger than it had in Yarrow's memory vision, but even so, it was smaller than I would have expected, given the number of Hedra warriors. Reuvan might be right about levels underground, but how many could there be in such a flat island?

The two Hedra on duty at the barracks door snapped to attention as we approached and stepped aside. The guard pushed open the door, and we followed him into a long, low room that was bare save for a battered-looking desk. Behind it sat a muscular man whose stiff bearing and frigid gray gaze reminded me chillingly of Malik. I had no doubt he was the Hedra master, for he emanated authority and his eyes were calculatingly intelligent.

The Hedra master's eyes turned to Zuria and Mendi. "Masters Zuria and Mendi, as foretold," he said. He did not rise, and this calculated discourtesy seemed to confirm Yarrow's feeling that there was bad blood between the Hedra master and the Threes.

"As you have been informed, we have been sent by the One to inspect the armory, Master Hedra," Zuria said in his hard, clear voice. "Will you accompany us?"

The Hedra remained seated. Indeed, he sat back as if to make himself more comfortable and asked why the One had sent them to inspect the armory at such short notice.

"The One has experienced a vision that troubled him," Zuria said haughtily.

"What was the nature of this vision?" the Hedra asked.

"The One did not confide that to us, nor did we think it meet to question him about it," Mendi said reprovingly. "Shall we proceed? The One is impatient for an immediate report."

"Very well," the Hedra master said smoothly, at last rising to his feet. "When you return, I will accompany you in order to offer any additional information our illustrious One may need about the armory." It was not a question, and rather than waiting for a response, he led us into the rainy night.

"Where are the two men sent to inform you of our imminent arrival?" Zuria asked as we crossed the yard.

"The men you sent lacked proper discipline," the Hedra master said. "They need reminding of the standard expected of them. You may take Volent and Davil here in their place."

"I do not like the sound of that," Yarrow farsent, having maneuverd himself close enough to touch my arm.

"Nor I," I sent. "See if you can make contact with any of the Hedra as we go out, to learn where Colwyn and Hilder are."

Within moments, we stood before the great metal doors, and the Hedra master commanded them to be opened. They were heavy enough that it took all ten men standing guard to open them—five to lift the great metal-shod bar and the rest to open one of the heavy doors.

We entered the cavernous darkness beyond and stood a moment in a slice of dim light that flowed through the open door. But even as the door was heaved closed, the Hedra master snapped his fingers, and the Hedra Davil opened the flaps on his lantern. The glow that flowed out seemed to move slowly, as if the darkness resisted or had some heavier form than ordinary air. Gradually, I saw that we were in a big square room rimmed with doors; here and there, instead of a door, a narrow set of steps rose sideways to a second tier and then to a third tier of doors that ran just under the ceiling. They were all low doors and the tiers narrow, but it was an ingenious design that made much of little.

"What do you wish to see?" the Hedra master asked. There was a thread of mockery in his tone.

"Everything," Zuria said.

✦ ✦ ✦

The first several doors led to long narrow cells lined with shelves piled high with the metal-shod poles favored by the warrior priests. The next contained short swords and another daggers. There were enough for five hundred men but not more. Of course, double that many had been taken for the invasion. There were also metal shields, though I had seldom seen those used. The Hedra master said in the same amused tone that the poles were conveniently placed on the lowest tier, because they were used constantly in training exercises. Zuria observed that the swords and daggers had a shine that made them look fresh-honed, and the Herder master said they were indeed, for each man was responsible for the weapon he used, and all were inspected before their return to the armory. Anyone whose weapon was not spotless and well sharpened was like to find himself in the tidal cells.

"We believe that all activities are a preparation for Lud's holy war to come; therefore, every activity must be undertaken with discipline and resolution." His voice had taken on a lecturing tone as he led us to another door and snapped his fingers for another of the Hedra with us to open it.

This one and the rest along the left wall contained demon bands, but there were a good many empty shelves here.

"The store is much depleted," Zuria observed.

The Hedra master gave him a narrow look, which reminded me that I could probe him now that we were out of the rain and shielded from the wall's taint. I shaped a probe, but before I could assay it, Yarrow plowed into my mind to stop me, for both the Hedra master and Davil were mind-sensitives. Unless great care was taken, they would know if anyone probed them and would command the other Hedra to capture or kill us. Relieved to have been stopped in time, I thanked Yarrow for the warning and bade him, Geratty, and

Asra coerce two apiece of the Hedra who were escorting us. I would do the same to another two so we would have them on our side when we returned.

The Hedra master gestured at the doors along the rear of the room and Davil and the other men opened them to reveal hundreds of barrels like those I had seen in the minds of Vos's armsmen in Saithwold. It was no surprise when the Hedra master announced that they were filled with black powder. What did surprise me was the Hedra master's casual mention that after Salamander's next trip to the Red Queen's land, they would have even more barrels and a supply of fist-sized compacted powder balls that, when dipped in liquid white-stick, would explode on impact. Davil added enthusiastically that the balls could be fired by catapult or slingshot or even hurled by hand.

The chambers all along the right side of the room contained amphoras of something the Hedra master called *honey fire*. The mind of the Hedra I had entered told me that it was a liquid that stuck like honey to skin and would burn the flesh like acid. I was sickened to catch a fleeting memory vision of the honey fire being tested on two hapless Norselanders.

"It is only a pity this is too volatile to be shipped by sea," said the Hedra master. "Next time we must ensure that we have the makings of it sent to the Land to be concocted."

On the next level, we were shown a room full of small black metal objects that were made to fit comfortably in the hand and which had a protruding metal tube. I had no idea what the devices were, but they had a Beforetime look. The Hedra master lifted one and explained that they had been a recent gift to the armory from Ariel. Realizing we were not expected to know what the devices did, I prompted Zuria to ask. The Hedra master readily explained that each device possessed the capacity to spit out small darts of metal at great and killing speed. I was not much impressed by them, for what harm could a dart small enough to pass through the tiny hole in the tube of the device do? Especially given that, from what was said, Ariel had not been able to explain how the devices could be made to work. But Davil put in with an enthusiasm almost equal to his master's that even now scholars in the library were researching Beforetime texts to learn the device's secret. It was hoped that these, too, would be ready for the next invasion.

"Where were they found?" Zuria asked, this time at Harwood's behest.

"You will have to ask Master Ariel when he returns," the Hedra master answered, moving to the next cell.

"We have to take control now," I sent urgently to Harwood. "We may never get another chance like this."

"I know it," Harwood sent determinedly. "Get ready. I will deal with the Hedra master; Yarrow, you, and Geratty must overpower Davil. Reuvan, you and Ode will hang back and use the coerced Hedra to give help as it is needed." He stepped backward and turned smoothly, lifting his elbow and driving it into the Hedra master's gut—or he would have driven it in if the blow had connected. Instead, the Hedra master stepped back as if he had read Harwood's intention in his mind, lifting his hands to ward off the attack. But Harwood had made his move so that the Hedra was very close to the edge, and he overbalanced and fell. Yarrow and several of the Hedra had leapt on Davil and were bearing him to the ground under their weight as Geratty drew out a dagger. Another Hedra was sprinting toward the door, and I realized that none of us had coerced him. I flung out a probe after him but was horrified to find he had been chewing spiceweed, so his mind was impenetrable.

"Reuvan! Ode!" I called. "Stop him! The door!"

They whirled and raced after the fleeing Hedra, who turned and drew twin swords, his eyes glittering in the guttering light of a lantern that had been dropped and smashed. Its oil was now spreading, and where it spread ran fire. Reuvan and the Hedra began to fight, and Ode stood by, ready to strike if they gave him the chance. They were right against the door, and I prayed it was too thick to allow anyone outside to hear the battle inside or to allow them to catch the smell of burning, for the flames were now licking up the open wooden door to one of the sword cells. Beams ran along the top of all the cell doors, and if these battles were not quickly concluded, we were like to have the place burning about us. A chill ran through me at the thought of those barrels of black powder, and who knew how the vile honey fire would act in heat.

Harwood and the Hedra master were fighting savagely, bare-handed. As I watched, the coercer executed a perfect turn, which ended in a savage gut-level kick that ought to have dropped the Hedra master. But again he swayed back from the strike, agile as a snake, and suddenly he stepped forward and struck a blow that took Harwood full in the face and sent him staggering sideways, blood gushing from his nose. In the hiatus, the Hedra master cast a devouring look around the armory, seeing Davil held by his own men while Yarrow bent over him, Geratty and the Hedra by the door, circling one another, and the other Hedra standing about, their faces blank. His face darkened with enraged comprehension and loathing.

"Mutants!" he bellowed.

Afraid that he would be heard through the door despite its thickness and the rain, I hurled a probe at his mind, only to find that, as sometimes happened with sensitive unTalents, his mind also possessed a natural shield.

"You see, filth," he snarled, turning to look at me. "Not all Hedra are weak and impure enough to allow your maggot minds to devour their will." Without warning, he turned and ran into one of the cells, slamming the door so hard after him that the outer bar fell into place.

"He locked himself in," Harwood said incredulously, mopping blood from his face.

"Your nose is broken," I said.

"Just bloodied," he answered impatiently. I was moving to the door, but the coercer caught my arm. "Let him stay there while we coerce the others. Reuvan and Ode, smother that fire."

It took us twenty minutes to issue instructions about what would happen when we left the armory; the air was acrid with the stench of the smothered fire. I was more than relieved to see it quenched, though the flames had gone nowhere near the black powder barrels.

Yarrow learned that Colwyn and Hilder were in a shallow punishment cell under the barracks where we had met with the Hedra master, and I suggested we coerce Davil to go with him to release them when he left the armory. The Hedra master would come with us. His men had already heard him speak of accompanying Zuria to see the One.

"The only problem is that his mind is both sensitive and has a natural block, so we cannot make him behave normally," I said.

Harwood scowled, still wiping blood from his nose. "Then

we will coerce these men into believing that a weapon he was demonstrating misfired and knocked him out. That will explain my nose. We will render him unconscious, and he will be taken to the healing center."

"What about just sayin' he took a fit an' collapsed?" Geratty suggested. "We can have one of his own men say he caught you in the face with a flailin' fist, and another one can say that their master was just yesterday speakin' to another Hedra who was taken to th' healing center suffering some sort of an attack."

"It would explain the smashed lantern and the fire," Reuvan said.

"It is a brilliant idea," I agreed, remembering how the notion of sickness had rattled the Hedra who had stopped me alongside the healing center.

"Very well," Harwood said. "Yarrow, you will take the coerced Hedra and their master to the healing center. Command some of the Hedra guarding the door to help you. Take him to Sover and explain what has happened. We need him to spread the rumor that the Hedra master is suffering from plague and must be isolated. Coerce the men who carry him to return to their barracks with reports of a fevered delirium and . . . Well, ask Sover what other symptoms he might show if he had some sort of plague."

"The guildmistress and I will leave, ostensibly to report to the One with Zuria and Geratty. We will have Davil demand to come with us in his master's stead. Before he goes, he will command one of the other Hedra to take you, Geratty, to Colwyn and Hilder. Ode, you remain here. I will send in the Hedra who wait outside to close up the cells. Coerce as many as you can and deepen the coercion when possible. Prepare one to send as a messenger if there is any trouble you cannot handle. Station yourself outside the door and let no one enter. Say it is the One's command. I will send relief when I can. Yarrow, when you have done with the healing center, come to the One's chamber. I want to plan how we will take the sector where the demon bands are made, for this night has shown me that, although it is my desire to proceed carefully, events might force our hand, and the Hedra must not have the chance to don demon bands. Any questions before we face the wolf in his den?" Harwood concluded.

There were none, and we set about opening the door to the chamber where the Hedra master was hiding. The falling bar had bent one of the hooks, so it was hard to raise, but once it was done, Harwood grasped the handle and flung open the cell door. To our astonishment, the cell was empty.

"HE HAS CONCEALED himself, the snake," Yarrow cried, but Geratty was already entering the chamber with another lantern. The cell was deep, and the shelves were piled with demon bands. I called out to Geratty to be careful, though in truth the natural block on the Hedra master's mind would make him as difficult to locate as if he had been demon-banded.

"He's nowt here," Geratty said.

"There must be a bolt-hole," Ode said.

"Or a tunnel out," Reuvan added. "Seems to me the Faction make tunnels wherever they go."

My heart began to hammer. "If you are right, the minute he gets out, he will alert the other Hedra to our presence, and they will go straight for the demon-band works."

"Here!" Geratty shouted suddenly, and we crowded in behind him to see the tunnel opening concealed in a fold in the wall. I looked into it and sent a probe after the Hedra master, but even if the stone had not blocked my way, I would have had little hope of touching his mind.

Geratty went into it. I swiftly probed the Threes, only to discover that they knew nothing of this tunnel. Geratty returned and said to Reuvan, "Seaman, ye've th' right of it. 'Tis a tunnel running inside the outer wall like that leadin' to the One's chamber, an' it may be just as lengthy."

"He must not warn the rest," I said. "Yarrow, you and Geratty go after him. He has a start on you, and we must not lengthen it."

They nodded, and Yarrow snatched up a fallen sword and hastened after Geratty, who had already gone into the tunnel.

I watched until their light vanished, and then I turned to Harwood. "We have to secure this place so the Hedra cannot get at the weapons, in case he does manage to set off an alarm."

"We are too few to secure it, given that we cannot reach past the armory wall to farseek help," Harwood said grimly. "We must destroy this place and as many weapons as we can. I had hoped to take this compound slowly and carefully, but it seems that events have decided the matter for themselves."

"All right," I said. As always in moments of high danger, my mind seemed to grow clearer and to work more swiftly. "We will use the black powder. If it is true that fire will run along it, we can lay a trail of it throughout this place, going into every weapon chamber at the front of the building. It will go to a pile of barrels set up near the front wall of the armory. That ought to be enough to prevent anyone being able to get into it. The powder trail must meander far enough that, once lit, it will be many minutes before it reaches its target. I suggest that once the trail is laid, you go back out into the yard with everyone save Zuria, Grisyl, and me. Have Davil explain that their master sent you all out so that he could show the Threes some new secret weapon. If anyone notices that Geratty, Hilder, and I are missing, then you can say that we were needed.

"Harwood, let us say that you irritated the Hedra master, and he struck you. Have Davil confirm it and command you to go to the healing center. Then he can send Ode to find

385

Colwyn and Hilder straightaway. They might be safe enough in a cellar chamber, but best if we can get them out of here, too. Reuvan must be dismissed and sent to his barracks, and he can slip away when he is outside the armory yard."

"What of you and the Threes?" Reuvan asked.

"I will remain to light the trail of black powder and take them with me into the tunnel. When the explosion happens, if Yarrow and Geratty manage to stop the Hedra master in time, we can spread the word that he, the Threes, and three Hedra were killed when he was showing them his new weapon."

There was no discussion, for there was no time. At any minute, one of the Hedra might enter with a message for his master. We piled three barrels of the black powder behind the door. Reuvan punched a hole in another with a dagger and rolled it hither and thither, leaving a thin trail that looked like black yarn. None of us knew how swiftly the flame would move or how much of an explosion would result. The others shut the cell doors save the one leading to the secret tunnel, for we did not want to risk a spark setting off the other barrels or the honey fire.

The moment we had finished, Harwood departed with Reuvan, Ode, and the coerced Hedra. I sent Grisyl and Zuria into the tunnel with a lantern, snatched up a short sword left on the ground and a second lantern, and followed them. I turned back and took a deep breath before hurling the lantern at the end of the black-powder trail. It flared and hissed like an angry viper, and then a thread of flame sped away.

I turned and bade the Threes run, and I ran after them. On and on we ran, and still there was no explosion. I began to worry that something had gone wrong. Perhaps there had been a small break in the trail of black powder that we had not noticed. Or maybe the Hedra had decided to enter before the thread of flame had reached the barrels and had managed to avert the armory's destruction.

All at once there was a deafening thump, and moments later, a wave of heat rushed after us. But we had come far enough that it did not singe us. We had barely slowed to a panting trot when there was another explosion. The ground shook so violently that all three of us were thrown to our knees, and the tunnel was filled with choking, blinding dust. Zuria's lantern was smashed and the flame snuffed out by the dust, so we groped along the tunnel in darkness. I wondered what had caused the second explosion. Then there came a third, which was the worst of all, and it made the heavy stone wall above us creak and shudder so alarmingly that I was terrified it would come down on us.

Knowing that the few barrels of black powder could not possibly have caused three separate explosions, I realized that the flames must have penetrated the thick cell doors, igniting the other barrels or maybe the honey fire. I could only pray that the others had got away in time. The delay had been long enough that I was sure Harwood and Reuvan had escaped, but what of Colwyn and Hilder, and Ode who had gone to find them?

I mastered my apprehension and farsought Geratty and Yarrow, but the passage curved to match the uneven edge of the island, putting too much stone between us. Or maybe they had already reached the end of the tunnel. I wondered uneasily where it came out, given that it was a secret known only to the Hedra master and his brothers. One thought that gave me pause was that it might end in Ariel's chamber, but by my calculation, we had long since passed that point. Indeed, it seemed we had walked the full length of the compound, but distances were always distorted when traveled in the dark and in panic.

The tunnel began slanting down very steeply, and soon it became steps. Then I saw the orange glow of firelight ahead. I coerced the Threes to wait and crept toward the door at the bottom of the steps.

What I saw when I looked out was like a nightmare. There was a vast cave of black stone with many openings going off in different directions. The tunnel had brought me inside the mine in the walled area at the end of the compound. The whole place was lit by a multitude of small greenish fires flickering on the surface of glimmering black puddles of liquid caught in depressions and cracks. I shuddered, for such witchfire burned on lakes and pools in the Blacklands. It seemed the mine suffered seepage from the black pool.

Then I saw the Hedra master not far away, talking to a group of Hedra. My heart plummeted at the sight of Geratty and Yarrow lying at his feet. At that distance, I could not tell if they were unconscious or dead, and when I tried probing one of the Hedra, the vibrating rejection told me he wore a demon band. It did not take long to learn that all wore demon bands. There must be a store kept in the mines or somewhere nearby. That meant the Hedra master had been outside already. But why come back here? Unless he intended to lead them along the wall tunnel to the armory, but no doubt he had heard the explosions. Indeed, there could be no one in the entire compound who had not heard.

I wished I could hear his plans, but the Hedra master suddenly turned to head up one of the winding tracks on the mine's far side. All the Hedra followed, and the last two heaved up Yarrow and slung him between them. This must mean he lived, but Geratty they left lying there, and tears blurred my eyes at the knowledge that he was dead.

You sent him to his death, a cold voice told me.

I gritted my teeth and forced back guilt, knowing that I must get out into the open air to farseek Harwood and let him know that the Hedra master was at large in the compound with a group of demon-banded Hedra. I must also warn Asra of what had happened, for it was likely that the Hedra master would go to the One's chamber. My only hope was that Cinda had been right in thinking that none, save the shadows, Falc, and the Threes, knew of the stair leading from the laundry to the One's chambers, for that would mean they would have to take the long wall passage.

The instant the Hedra vanished, I burst out of the tunnel and ran to Geratty. He was not dead, but his face was a mask of blood, and there was a terrible wound in his chest. His eyes opened when I touched his face.

". . . uildmistress," he gurgled, and blood bubbled crimson at his lips.

"I will get help," I said.

"No . . . use," he rasped. "Bastard ran me through . . . Help . . . Yarrow." His eyes widened, and I realized he was looking at something behind and above me!

I rolled to one side and rose, lifting the point of my short sword and blinking tears from my eyes. But the man facing me was no Hedra, despite him being bald. He was unarmed. Indeed, he was near unclothed, such was the state of the rags hanging from his filthy, emaciated limbs. His eyes were a startling blue in his pallid, withered face, and there was astonishment in them.

"You can talk," he rasped. "I have not heard the voice of a woman in twenty years."

I forced myself to relax, though my heart was still

thudding wildly, for he must be one of the mine shadows Cinda had spoken about. No wonder there had been pity in her eyes.

"I must see to my friend," I told him somewhat breathlessly, but when I knelt again beside Geratty, I saw that the life had gone from his eyes. Swallowing sorrow, I reached out to gently close his lids.

"He is dead. He is lucky," creaked the shadow almost reverently. He muttered something else, but I scarcely heard him, for now I saw that other mine shadows were emerging from dozens of crevices and openings in the mine's walls, creeping and hobbling over the rough floor, edging round the fiery pools, their faces gaunt and filthy. All were bald and most had weeping sores over their bodies, crusted with black filth. Their collective stench as they gathered about me turned my stomach, but I suppressed revulsion and fear. I could see that they had neither the strength nor the will to harm me.

The first man who had come reached out to touch my hair, but when I turned to scowl at him, he cringed back so pitifully that my brief anger faded.

"My friends and I are enemies of the priests," I told them. "We have invaded the compound, and we are trying to take control here. If we succeed, you will be free to leave this place and go where you will."

I saw only incomprehension in their faces and knew I was wasting precious time. I pushed through them, but even as I looked for the path taken by the Hedra, I realized there were numerous twisting paths leading to many openings in the mine's sloping side, and I had no way of knowing which one was a tunnel that would lead outside. I turned back to the growing crowd of skeletal men gazing up at me.

"Please, show me the way out," I urged them.

This seemed to penetrate their fogged minds, but they only goggled and muttered at one another.

"They won't," said the clear piping voice of a child. I looked down and all but gaped to see a small boy of about five gazing up at me from beside the blue-eyed man. He was very thin and bald like the shadow men, but his eyes were bright with intelligence.

"Why won't they help me?" I asked him gently.

"They are afraid of going out lest they be chosen for the black pool," said the boy.

The men crooned and rocked and tried to draw the boy into their midst, but I knelt and looked into his eyes. "How does a child come to be here?"

"My mother was a shadow. My father brought me here when she died bearing me. He is an acolyte. The shadows say he wept. They have looked after me and hidden me from the Hedra since I was a baby. When I am old enough, I am to become a novice so I can change things, but I do not want to be a priest."

"You must," croaked one of the shadows. "There is only that or this."

"I would rather stay here with you and Colyn, Terka."

"You will die if you stay here," said the shadow he had spoken to. "The mine is poisoned by the black pool. . . ."

"Look," I interrupted. "I am sorry, but those Hedra who left are going to kill my friends, and I need to get out of the mine to warn them. Come with me!"

The shadows recoiled.

"I will show you the way out," offered the boy solemnly.

The shadows moaned and fretted, hissing and rustling, and the boy turned to assure them that he would soon return, but they shook their heads and wrung their hands, and I saw that Terka was weeping. I realized that their concern for the boy had roused their wits, though his will was clearly more robust than theirs.

"I will make sure he comes to no harm for helping me," I promised them, grimly aware that I might not be able to keep my vow beyond the next half hour. I asked if they would sit vigil over my companion. Then I pointed to the opening to the wall tunnel and asked if they would bind up the two men they would find waiting there. This request seemed to cause the mine shadows some consternation, but I could waste no more time, and I urged the boy to lead me out.

He set off up one of the paths and I followed. The boy climbed more slowly than I liked, but for all his eagerness to help, he was not strong or in good health. My heart twisted with pity at the thought of his life, but I resisted the urge to question him further, because it would slow him.

At last we approached an opening. As we entered, fresh air brushed my cheeks. The boy felt it, too, and would have spoken, but I shook my head and mimed that we must be silent. But the boy whispered with certainty that warrior priests never stayed long within the wall surrounding the mine and the black pool. They came only to administer punishments or to usher in the female shadows, who brought food and carried away brown rock from the mine, or to collect crates of demon bands. Then they departed, locking the gate behind them and leaving a guard outside. The boy added that the Hedra had been in the middle of choosing those to be punished when the Hedra master had burst from the forbidden tunnel.

"What happens to those who are punished?" I asked, wondering what could be punishment to the poor wretches condemned to work the tainted mine. More than half of my attention strained toward the end of the tunnel, in case the boy was wrong about the Hedra leaving the sector.

"They are sent into the black pool to get stuff for the demon bands we make here," the boy said. "No one who does that lives long."

I shivered.

At last we reached the opening. It was night and there were no lanterns. To my dismay, I saw that it was still raining, which meant I could farseek no one. I crouched down in the tunnel opening, squinting through the slanting rain, but it was too dark to see more than a stretch of broken ground dotted with muddy pools of water.

The boy pointed to the right and said the wall of the compound ran there, and along it was a room for the shadows to eat in and a long hall of beds. Then he pointed to the darkness in front of us, saying that the black pool was that way, and on the other side of it were the demon-band works. Last of all, he pointed to the left, explaining that the inner wall that surrounded the sector lay there, and if I felt my way along it, I would find the door to the rest of the compound.

"But it is locked," he said, adding that even if it were not, there was always a guard stationed outside. Still alert for any movement, I asked the boy his name.

"Terka and Colyn call me Mouse," he answered. "What is your name?"

"I am Elspeth," I said. "Tell me, when do the shadows bring food?" I prayed he would not say morning.

"I hope they bring it soon, for I am hungry," he answered wistfully. All at once, he seemed to grow uneasy. "I do not usually come outside until after the food has been brought, in case I am seen."

"You had better go back to the shadows, then, for they will

be worried about you," I told him gently. "But I promise that all I told them was true. My friends and I are enemies of the Hedra, and if we can overcome them, all of you will be free."

The boy looked searchingly into my face. Then he said, "Will my father come for me?"

Before I could answer, another explosion rocked the ground, and a shower of small stones rained down on us. As I lifted my hands to shelter my head, Mouse leapt up and fled back down the mine. I did not try to stop him, knowing that, for now, he would be safer with his shadow protectors.

I made my way to the inner wall and felt along it, seeking the door. Just as I reached it, another explosion rocked the ground under my feet. My senses told me the explosions were coming from the direction of the armory, but I was terrified that it had not been destroyed and the Hedra were using the weapons there against Harwood and the others.

I heard the sound of voices raised in alarm. People were moving along the path on the other side of the wall. If only the rain would stop, I might have coerced their help. As it was, I pressed myself against the wall and listened to find out what was happening, but the noise of the rain defeated me. When the voices had gone, I examined the door. It was a great heavy slab of wood encased in metal and locked as the boy had warned. I laid my hands over the lock and concentrated hard to form a probe strong and delicate enough to manipulate the lock despite the rain. It was a simple enough mechanism but heavy, which meant it was likely to make a noise. I hesitated, picturing the Hedra outside, standing with his back to the door, his hand resting on the hilt of his sword. His attention would be focused on the explosions, and the rain noise was loud enough that he was unlikely to hear the tumblers turn in the lock, but the moment I opened the door, he would turn, and I had no doubt that he would be armed and demon-banded.

I licked my lips, telling myself that it would be sensible to wait until food was brought and deal with the guard when he was distracted. Except that while I waited, the Hedra master would be getting nearer the One's chamber, where Asra and the shadows waited, unaware of their danger.

I laid my hands over the lock. Moving the tumblers took a great deal of effort, and despite my care, there was a clicking sound. I flattened myself to the wall on the blind side of the door, in case the Hedra had heard it, but there was no mutter of puzzlement, and the door in the wall remained shut.

I drew my short sword, forcing myself to be calm. I did not often fight physically, but Gevan himself had taught me to do so, pronouncing me swift and strong. I reminded myself that, for all my dislike of it, I could fight. I took a deep breath and held it for a long moment to steady myself. Very slowly, I opened the door in the wall.

There was no one outside.

My mouth went dry with fear at the thought of the guard pressed to the wall, waiting for me with his sword drawn. It took all my courage to step out, only to find that the lane was truly empty. I took a long, shuddering breath, realizing that the Hedra master had probably taken the Hedra guard with him.

I set off at a splashing run along the path, visualizing the map as I wound my way back to the laundry in sector seven and blinking rain from my eyes. I heard another small explosion and then a great rumbling and cracking sound just as I reached the laundry yard. Suddenly Elkar stepped out in front of me, holding up a lantern he was half sheltering under a rain cloak. His face and neck were streaked with blood and his eyes were wild.

"We thought you were dead, lady!" he said in a shocked voice.

"What is happening?" I demanded.

"The armory blew up, along with most of the buildings in the Hedra sector and then the whole library. Cinda and I were still in the dye works when it started but decided to come and see what was happening. Then the ground heaved, and the roof of the dye works fell in. The Herders we had tied up and the shadows inside were crushed under the rubble, as well as the Hedra."

"Ye gods," I said, horrified. "But where is Cinda?"

"She was hit by some falling stone. I wanted to bring her to the One's chamber, for I knew there was a healer tending the One, but then we saw the Hedra go in, so I had to take her away. I came back to see if I could find out what was happening."

My heart sank. "You saw the Hedra? They went this way?"

He nodded. I was aware of movement in the rainy darkness behind Elkar, just outside the range of his lantern. I lifted my sword.

"It is only some shadows," Elkar said. "But what happened?"

"There is no time to explain properly," I told him. "We set off the explosions, because the Hedra master escaped, and we dared not leave the way open to the armory. I came to warn Asra and the shadows that the Hedra master is like to come to the One's chamber." I thought for a moment and made up my mind. "I'll go up and see if I can hear what is happening. Send the shadows away and wait for me." I left him without waiting for an answer and crept across the laundry yard to weave through the sodden robes hanging on the lines. Inside the laundry, there were only empty boilers, and I realized the Hedra master would have seen no need to leave anyone to keep watch. After all, who would they expect to be following them? He might think the rest of us had been killed in the explosions. I cracked the door open to make sure there was no guard within the stairwell, and then I ghosted up and laid my hand on the door to the bathing room. It gave way with a slight creak that set my pulse racing, but the bathing chamber lay in darkness. I opened the door wider and saw light slanting through from the dressing room.

". . . forget the Threes." It was the voice of the Hedra master. "They are in the power of the mutants, as are some of our own men," he went on in his cold hard voice. "We cannot rely upon anyone until they have been demon-banded. That is why we must have more bands."

"But the armory has been destroyed, you said, and we took all they had in the demon-band works."

"Yes, but there are three crates of demon bands in sector three waiting to be taken to the west coast. I sent Gorlot and Neel to get a crate each as we were coming here. Once we have them, we will distribute them through the compound. Any Hedra who even hesitates to put one on is to be run through. . . ."

"If only we had the fire-throwers," said another voice.

"The mutants must have come across on the *Stormdancer*, so there cannot be many of them," the Hedra master said. "They will pay for the damage they have done here. I will peel the flesh from their bones as they live and then cook it and feed it to them for what they have done to the One. A pity the shadows who aided them had no tongues to talk. See if you can rouse the mutant. I wish to question him to see if he has any idea where his herd has gone to ground."

I clenched my teeth, realizing he might mean Yarrow or Asra. I tried to reach either of their minds, but to no avail. Either they had both been demon-banded, or they were unconscious. I closed the door carefully and went down the stairs. Elkar was waiting in the laundry, and I stifled an angry reminder that I had bidden him to wait outside and told him what I had overheard. "I want you to go in all haste to the healing center. If Harwood lives, he will be there. If not, then speak to Sover. Tell him all that has happened and bid him gather those who can fight and come here to aid me. The Hedra master must not leave this place and alert the rest of the Hedra. Bid Sover also send a force of coerced Hedra to blockade the tunnel in the wall, in case he and his men flee that way. But he must hurry. Tell him also that the Hedra captain has sent two men to sector three, where there is a small supply of demon bands. I will remain here and keep watch, but if they leave, there will be nothing I can do save follow them. Can you remember all that?"

He nodded. "But I can get help—"

"There is no time for talk," I snapped. "Go now and do as I have told you."

He turned and hurried away, and I went back up the stairs.

Asra screamed.

I clenched my jaw so hard that my teeth ached, but I could do nothing to help him. If I ran in wielding my sword, I would be killed or taken prisoner. I was about to enter the coercer's mind to see if he had noted any weakness I could exploit among the Hedra, when I heard a movement behind me. I turned, half expecting to see Elkar, but it was one of the shadows.

"What are you doing?" I whispered, going into the stairwell and closing the door behind me. "Don't you know that the Hedra might come down at any moment and you will be killed?"

"They cannot kill all of us," she said quietly. Then she looked behind her, and I saw more shadows crowding into the stairwell. I gestured urgently for them to go back to the laundry and followed them to make sure they went.

Once in the laundry, I was astonished by how many shadows stood pressed between the boilers, and by the look of it, more were arriving every moment. "Who sent you?" I demanded.

"We are done with being sent," said the shadow who had come up the stairs. "When we heard the explosions, we knew it was time to fight."

I stared at them helplessly, for though there were at least a hundred of them, they were all thin and undernourished; not one of them carried a weapon. I opened my mouth to tell them not to be fools when it hit me with the force of a blow that I was the fool, an arrogant fool. Here were grown women who had been brutally enslaved from childhood. Now they had the chance to fight for their freedom, and they wished to do so. Who was I to forbid it?

I drew a deep breath. "All right. If you would fight, then listen to me." I told them what had happened at the armory and about the Hedra master, and I told them of Sover in the healing center, and of the crippled ship that must be repaired and sent to the west coast. Some of them knew some of it, but I kept my explanation terse, my neck prickling the whole time with the feeling that the Hedra master was descending the stairs. Last of all, I spoke of the shadows I thought had been murdered by the Hedra and of Geratty and Yarrow, who were their prisoners. Finally, I told them what I had asked Elkar to do.

"And what are we to do?" asked the woman from the stairs. She had gray eyes and a determined look and tone.

"The Hedra master is waiting for some crates of demon bands, which will not come if Elkar has done what I asked. But sooner or later, he will grow impatient of waiting and come down here. There are thirty of them at least, and you know they are deadly and remorseless fighters. Therefore, if you would stand with me, you must find weapons. Go now as quickly as you can, and bring any other shadows who would fight for their freedom. Tell all who come to bring such weapons as they can find. Axes, stones, kitchen knives, pieces of wood, brooms, and pokers. If there are enough, it might turn the Hedra back the other way. They will not know it is closed to them, and with luck, before they return, there will be others to aid us."

I thought there might be questions, but the shadows were accustomed to obedience. With a shudder of movement, all the black-clad girls and women turned and melted away into the rainy dark of the yard with as little noise as leaves blown before the wind. The woman from the stairs remained, and I asked her name.

"I am Ursa, and we are sisters henceforth," she answered.

"I am Elspeth Gordie," I told her. "And it seems we are to play the waiting game together." But then I froze, for *I could hear the sound of boots on the steps.*

"What would you have me do?" asked Ursa. Fear shone in her eyes, but she did not run.

"We ought to hide, but if we do, they will escape. We must try to delay them, but this will be a deadly game."

I turned and backed away from the door until I stood beside Ursa, then I drew the sword I had sheathed. A moment later, the door to the secret stair flew open, and the Hedra master and his men came out. They did not see us at once, for it was dark and we carried no lanterns, unlike the Hedra. But when one spotted us, the silence spread swiftly until all stopped and stared. I was horrified to see that there were closer to forty than thirty. All were demon-banded, and there might as well have been a thousand for all the chance we stood against them.

Yet I spoke in a voice that rang with false confidence. "Give up your weapons, Hedra, for your corrupt Faction breathes its last breath. My people have control of your companions and your masters, and the shadows and many of your novices stand with us willingly. Now is the time to surrender this compound while you can." The insanity of two women demanding surrender clearly unnerved some of the Hedra, and I could almost hear some thinking that no one would make such a threat unless she could back it up.

"Foul mutant!" said the Hedra master. "Cursed of Lud."

"Curse your Lud and his bloodlust," I said savagely. "I am a Misfit, and I do not heed your god. And I wonder if he heeds you. For where was your Lud when we destroyed the armory? Did your Lud protect the One and the Threes from us? Now, your answer. Surrender at once and you will not die, though you will be judged and punished for all the evil you have done in the name of your Lud. Refuse, and you will fall."

"You will die in great pain and very slowly, mutant," said the Hedra master.

"If your Lud is so powerful, why does he need you?" I demanded, letting mockery tinge my words. "Why does he not strike me down himself?" I looked up. "Come, Lud of the Faction, strike me down for my insolence."

Some of the Hedra looked up, and others glared at me and muttered uneasily.

"He does not answer," I said mockingly. "Could it be that he does not exist? Or maybe he exists but is bored with your bloody prayers."

Several of the Hedra snarled curses and drew their swords. But the Hedra master turned his cold gaze on me. "You will die quite soon, mutant, and Lud will hurl you into the fiery pit of hell for your heresy. Before he does, you may dare to ask him why he chose the Hedra to do his will." He glanced at the big Hedra beside him. "Take them, Aleppo, but do not kill the mutant. I would teach her a long, complex song of pain to sing to Lud."

"What of the shadow?" asked the Hedra.

"Kill it," the Hedra master said indifferently.

"Run," I farsent to Ursa, but instead of obeying, she took up a boiler prod and stepped very deliberately in front of me. Oh, it was so gallant and foolish a gesture that it brought tears to my eyes. The Hedra master and his men gaped at the shadow in disbelief.

"Look well at her, brave strong warriors of Lud," I snarled. "Look at the face of courage, for you have never seen it when you look into the mirror."

One of the Hedra laughed, but his laughter dwindled and his face fell. He and the others were now staring beyond us. Wary of a trick, I flashed a look over my shoulder, only to see that the laundry and the yard beyond were filling with shadows. But they were not the shadows that I expected to see. They were the male shadows from the mine, and as they drew close, the light from the lanterns some of them carried revealed how pitifully thin and filthy their limbs were and made their hideous sores glisten horribly. They must have come through the door in the wall that I had not bothered to close. But how had they come here?

"Lady Elspeth, get out of the way!" Elkar called. The urgency in his voice made me obey, and I pulled Ursa back with me, but I lifted my sword in case any of the Hedra tried to seize us.

"Fools!" spat the Hedra master. "You are many, but you will fall before our swords like sheaves of wheat!"

"It is the Faction that will fall," rang out a new voice.

To my astonishment, the speaker was a tall, frail-looking Herder priest of middle years standing in the midst of the shadows. Elkar stood beside him, and between them was the little shadow boy, Mouse.

"Herder Sabatien, you are possessed by the mutants!" roared the Hedra master.

"No," said Sabatien in a measured voice. "I am no longer a priest. I am a Norselander again, and I am possessed by courage for the first time in my life. I stand with these men by choice, and I command you to lay down your weapons in surrender."

"You will die with this filth, traitor," hissed the Hedra master, and he took a step in the direction of the priest. But one of the shadows hurled something. I reared back, as did the Hedra, but instead of an explosion, there was a wet splat as it fell to the floor. Hedra and shadow alike stared, bemused, at the blackened rag lying on the ground, dribbling moisture.

"Mud will not save you," jeered one of the Hedra at last.

"No, but it will kill you if you do not surrender," rasped the man who had thrown it. I saw that it was Mouse's friend Terka, and now he held up his hand, revealing another sodden rag. The other shadows did the same, and I suddenly understood. I moved farther back, pulling Ursa with me. The

403

movement caught the Hedra master's gray gaze. His eyes widened as he, too, understood.

"The cloths have all been dipped into the black pool!" Elkar shouted. "If you do not lay down your weapons at once, the shadows will throw the rags at you instead of the floor. You may then kill them, but look well as you do, for soon you will bear their same ghastly sores and disfigurements."

There was a long silence as the faces of the Hedra sagged with fear and indecision. They would have rushed us in a second if we had threatened them with swords, but faced with disfigurement, crippled limbs, and bleeding sores, they quailed. Perhaps it was merely that the ravaged shadows were the threat made real. One sword clattered to the ground, and though I could not see whose it was, it was the signal for more to fall until the Hedra master snarled at his men to hold.

"Do not be fools! They will kill us if we lay down our weapons," he bellowed.

"No," I said, stepping forward and keeping my voice calm. "That is the way of the Hedra. It is not our way. I told you. You will be judged and punished for what you have done, and in time, you will be given the chance to atone for the horrors you have committed. There may even come a day when you will bless this moment, for the life you have lived within these walls is bleak and loveless, though you cannot see it. Now choose. Throw aside your weapons and kneel if you would surrender."

Another silence, and then another sword fell and another. I felt a great welling of relief, but when the Hedra Aleppo dropped his sword, the Hedra master turned and clove open his chest in a swift flowing movement. Even as the Hedra toppled forward, life gushing darkly from him, his master spun and leapt back into the stairwell, barking orders for his men to follow. Many obeyed, perhaps as much from instinct as loyalty, and more might have followed, except another of the sodden rags was thrown. It flew high and landed against the side of the door, splattering the face of the Hedra about to pass through it. He gave a high-pitched, horrified scream and reeled back, throwing down his sword and clutching at his eyes.

That was the end of it. The rest threw down their swords and knelt.

The shadows surged forward to gather up the swords, and when I turned to Ursa to thank her for defending me, she threw her arms around me, weeping and laughing. I hugged her back and found myself weeping, too, wondering what had happened to cool, untouchable Elspeth Gordie.

"I wish I had been there," Harwood said later when I went to see him in his bed in the healing center. He had been injured badly in the second of the armory explosions, which had killed most of the Hedra. Fortunately, Reuvan had been behind the wall, which had shielded him, so he was untouched. He had managed to staunch Harwood's wounds and bring him to the healing center.

"I am only glad you are not dead!" I told him.

"I might as well be for all the use I am, lying here like a fool," Harwood fretted. "We have a long way to go before this place is secured. Sover said there are still Hedra who have some idea of what is happening, and they have demon bands."

"They are the pair sent by the Hedra master to get crates of demon bands. Unfortunately, they were not taken prisoner, and they have demon bands enough to hand out to at least a hundred men. But you can't do any fighting when you can't even sit up without feeling faint," I said. "Sover told me you had lost a lot of blood."

"I would worry less if your Hedra master would surrender," Harwood responded. "If only he did not have Yarrow and Asra as hostages."

"If wishes were fishes," I said more sharply than I had meant to, because I worried about the coercers, too, despite Sabatien's certainty that it was only a matter of time before everyone surrendered.

Harwood gave me a faint smile. "Gevan would be gratified to know that you have taken his pet sayings to heart."

"Gevan will be gratified if you would cease demanding to get up and relax and heal. Tomrick and Ode have coerced a veritable army of Hedra now, and Ode is ordering them hither and thither, warning the Herders of the plague-crazed Hedra who is setting off explosions within the compound and bidding them lock themselves up tight until he is caught. Tomrick, meanwhile, has coerced and chivvied the inner-cadre priests into agreeing to hide in the cells of the correction house where you found me, if you can believe that. And we have all the other Hedra generals well coerced. They are busy either hunting down their own men or cleaning up the rubble from the explosion under the supervision of a handful of novices and shadows."

Harwood sighed and lay back against his pillows, visibly relaxing. "I must say, I can't believe Elkar did not mention that one of his friends was a renegade Herder."

Elkar had told Sabatien about us, of course, and the Herder had counseled patience and watchfulness, feeling we were too few to truly take over the compound. He had instructed the novices to aid us as much as possible without endangering themselves, but neither Sabatien nor the novices had realized how strongly the shadows would react to the vision of freedom.

Sover entered with a Herder healer, and I shifted out of the way as Harwood's bandage was changed. Sover had told me that Reuvan had found Hilder carrying an unconscious and badly hurt Colwyn from a mess of rubble. Hilder had been in the midst of describing the collapse of the underground cell in which they had been confined for interrogation when another explosion sent a piece of stonework flying, killing him instantly.

Shocked at the suddenness of Hilder's death, Reuvan had shouldered Colwyn and carried him back to the healing center, where he now lay, still unconscious. Reuvan had gone out again to bring in Hilder's body and then again to look for me, Geratty, and Yarrow. I had met him on the way to the healing center after the defeat of the Herders in the laundry.

Looking back, I realized it had been madness to set fire to the armory, for we might have guessed one explosion would set off the rest of the black powder. It was only luck that we had not set off some truly dreadful Beforetime weapon, such as those with which the Herders had destroyed the city of Hevon.

Harwood was convinced that the many subsequent explosions were the result of the black-powder fire reaching hidden weapon caches within the wall tunnel I had taken to the mine. A small explosion in the wall tunnel near the library had set off the much larger explosion that destroyed the library and Ariel's chambers, and given my earlier premonition, neither of us had any doubt that Ariel's chambers lay at the heart of the explosion. Harwood thought that a cache of black powder or something more potent had been set to explode as soon as the chamber's door was forced; he had pointed out grimly that it was proof enough that Yarrow had been right in guessing Ariel had never intended to return to Herder Isle.

The earlier explosions had weakened the wall surrounding the compound, so when the library went up, a great wedge of the wall broke away and fell into the channel, forming a stone ford that had effectively reconnected the islands. When he had brought Cinda to the healing center, Elkar had told me that this fulfilled a legend that claimed the Norselanders would be free when the Girdle of the Goddess had been restored.

"I meant to ask, is the One dead?" Harwood inquired after Sover and the healer had gone.

"Sabatien thinks he is," I said. "He says that as far as he can make out, the One died after the Hedra master killed the healer tending him. But we will not know for sure until the Hedra master surrenders. Sabatien told him if he kills Asra or Yarrow, he and all of his men will be killed, but if he surrenders them, he and his men will be taken prisoner."

Harwood ran a hand through his hair. "What of those poor wretches from the mine?"

"The female shadows are moving those not too badly injured into the inner-cadre cottages in the walled garden. It is a good deal closer than the healing center. The rest are gradually being brought here on stretchers. Indeed, between the mine shadows and those hurt by the explosions, there is not an empty bed in the place."

We were silent a moment, and then Harwood said, "What news of the shipmaster?"

"Veril came in half an hour past to say that Helvar and the Norselanders had come across from Fallo. It seems they actually witnessed the fall of the compound's outer wall."

"That must have been a splendid sight," Harwood said. "What of the *Stormdancer*? How long will the repairs take?"

"Veril left the shipfolk as soon as they had crossed the channel," I said. "I sent Reuvan to assure the shipfolk that we have control here."

"So we do," Harwood said soberly. "Still, Geratty and Ode are dead, and Yarrow and Asra prisoners." He looked at me. "You ought to go down to the ship and talk to the ship-master yourself."

"I mean to," I said. "I just wanted to see how you were first."

"What happened to Zuria and Grisyl?" Harwood asked as I rose.

"They were killed in the wall passage when it collapsed," I said.

Cinda followed me out into the passage, and I was about to bid her go and lie down when I noticed the fragile-looking Sabatien talking with Sover. Mouse was sound asleep on the older man's shoulder. I approached and asked for news of the Hedra master, but there was none.

Sover took the sleeping child from Sabatien, who said, "I will return soon. I just wanted to bring the boy to have his sores tended." He kissed the child's head tenderly and added, "His friend Terka is here. Put the child with him."

Sover carried the boy away, and I asked Sabatien, "He is your son?" He nodded. "He told me his father was an acolyte."

The older man sighed. "I was when he was born. You know, I have spent a lifetime creeping up the ranks of the Faction, hoping I would one day manage to change it, but you and your friends come here like a storm and scour the place out in mere days. I can hardly believe you have managed it, but I am more grateful than there are words to tell."

"It is not finished, and it was not only us," I said. "We could not have done it without Elkar and the other novices, and the shadows." I smiled at Cinda.

Sabatien's thin face grew sad. "The shadows," he murmured. "Some can never regain all that the Faction has taken from them, and yet who would have guessed there would be such ferocious courage in them? Yet was not my beloved Matty brave and strong? How she would have rejoiced to see her sisters rise up as they did." He sighed again and said he must go and try again to convince the Hedra master to surrender sooner rather than later.

"You think he will surrender?" I asked.

"What else? He knows it is only a matter of time before we send his own men against him. That we have not done so already is only because of his hostages, and your Asra is badly hurt."

"I wish to come with you," Cinda told me when I had taken my leave of Sabatien and Sover. I was going down to see to the *Stormdancer* and was about to suggest she wait until daylight, but then it struck me that this would be the first time she had been out of the compound in years. How should I tell her that she had better wait until the sun shone?

It was close to dawn, but still pitch black and raining hard as we stepped out of the healing center. Cinda volunteered to run back and get lanterns, but then we heard boots on the cobbles. My heart sped up as I turned, but it was only Elkar and several novices bearing lanterns and leading a hobbling line of mine shadows.

Seeing me, Elkar sent off the other novices. He spied

Cinda. For a moment, he froze. Then he laughed aloud, took two steps toward her, and enclosed the startled shadow in an exuberant embrace. Cinda's face above his shoulder was suffused by delight as she hugged him back. It was all at once borne home to me how very much had been accomplished.

"Where are you going?" Elkar half shouted to be heard over the rain. She lifted her hands and her fingers flicked. Releasing the shadow but keeping his arm about her shoulders, he looked at me, and I said resignedly that he had better come with us since he had a lantern.

It was raining harder than ever by the time we reached the black gates, but there was no difficulty passing through, for the Hedra guards had been thoroughly coerced by now. The gates swung open, and as we passed out through them, it was hard for me to believe that only a few days had passed since I had been marched inside, and harder still to believe that we had accomplished so much, so quickly. But our victory was already eclipsed by my knowledge that, even now, the *Black Ship* might be sailing toward the west coast.

The Futuretell guildmistress, Maryon, had told me that I must travel to Sutrium to prevent trouble on the west coast, and I had wondered, leaving Obernewtyn, what she could mean. Now I understood that I must find Ariel's plague null in time to prevent the west coast's destruction. I did not know how we were to find a single null, but I told myself that Maryon would not have sent me if there was no possibility of succeeding. I knew too well that even though the chance might be terribly small, still it must be taken. Time was of the essence now, and though the repair of the ship lay in the Norselanders' hands, its course would be of my choosing. I felt that Ariel would take the null to Morganna, Aborium, or Murmroth, because they were the largest and most populous of the west coast settlements. But we dared not neglect the smaller towns, because it would take twice as long to backtrack.

I fell twice in the dark and turned to ask Elkar to walk ahead with the lantern. At the sound of footsteps, I swung round and saw Reuvan coming toward me with a lantern. Beyond him, farther along the shore, I saw a dim shifting cluster of lights near the hull of the *Stormdancer*.

"Are you all right?" Reuvan said, clasping my arm.

"I am," I said. "Do the shipfolk know yet how long it will take to complete the repairs?" I asked.

"They are still assessing the damage." Reuvan's gaze slipped past me, and I glanced back to see Elkar smiling at Cinda over the glowing lantern, which she now held. But even as I watched, her smile faded as her gaze shifted beyond him to the dark, heaving waves now illuminated by the lantern light. She walked down the sand until a wave ran over her sandaled feet; then she stopped and gazed out. As we walked back to where Elkar stood watching her, I noticed that the rain was beginning to abate.

"She was six when she was brought to Herder Isle with her brother, and she remembers nothing of the journey but sickness and fear," Elkar murmured. "It is different for me. I was ten when the Herders came to the village on Fallo and took me. They said it was an honor, but I knew I would never see my mother or father again. I can hardly believe that we are free. I pray it is not a dream."

"If it is, then we are all dreaming it," Reuvan said gently, laying his hand on the boy's shoulder. "Come. Let us find out what Shipmaster Helvar has to say about the *Stormdancer*, for the tide is almost out."

Elkar went to take Cinda's hand and draw her away from

412

the sea, and as we moved on, she lifted her fingers and moved them gracefully. He said, "She says it is hard to believe that so few could bring down the Herder Faction."

"We would never have managed it if we had been attacking the compound from the outside," Reuvan said. "The Faction sets itself up to appear impregnable. That is a defense in itself, for if something appears impossible to break, then no one even tries. But that same appearance of invulnerability is a weakness if those maintaining it believe it, too. The Herders believed their compound was so fearsome that no one would dare enter it save those who had no choice, so they did not defend themselves within its embrace. In a way, taking over the compound has been like taking over the Land in the rebellion. The Councilmen had run things for so long, they could not imagine truly being challenged, yet most of the Council's power rested on our accepting that it could not be challenged."

"When you speak of it in that way, it seems that power is like some strange agreement between the oppressed and the oppressor," Elkar said.

Cinda lifted her hand, and as it flickered, Elkar translated. "She says that power is not a real thing, like a ship, but an idea. And only by accepting the idea do we make it real. She says that freedom is the same sort of thing—an idea that is nothing, until people believe in it enough to make it real."

I turned to look at the slight girl with faint wonder, aware that Reuvan was doing the same. Then I heard my name called and turned to see Lark running along the beach toward me, his face near split in two by his smile. "We saw the compound wall fall! I can hardly believe that you did it!"

I laughed. "I did not do it alone, and we have not completely won the day. But I don't think you need to fear being

413

turned into a novice any longer. Now let me introduce you to my friends and fellow fighters. You have met Reuvan, I think, but here is Elkar, who has been a novice and is no longer, and Cinda who was once a shadow."

Lark looked with open curiosity at the older youth and then at Cinda beside him, her black hood slipped from her head to reveal the dark fuzz of hair above her thin, sweet face. Then his eyes returned to Elkar, and he asked, "You are a Norselander?"

"I am," Elkar answered with pride. They began to talk, and I left them to it and continued along the beach toward the cluster of lanterns. I recognized Oma among the men standing in a huddle talking, and when he caught sight of me, the scarred seaman strode over, grinning, and swiftly clasped my hand.

"I did not imagine we would see you again," he said, suddenly solemn.

"I did not imagine it either," I admitted. "I am glad we were both wrong."

Oma hailed Helvar, who was coming up the beach with a preoccupied look, and the shipmaster came to join us, smiling his welcome and laying a warm hand on my shoulder. "When I first heard your voice inside my head, I little thought how much of a change you would bring to us," he said. "We owe you much, for it seems as if you and your companions have freed us from the Faction's long tyranny."

"I am afraid there is still a good bit to do, for there are Hedra to be captured, and the Hedra master and some few of his men are barricaded inside the One's chambers with two of our people as hostages. But I think he will surrender in the end. I only hope it will be soon enough for my friends. But now comes a hard task, for you and your people must decide what to do with the Hedra and Herders. Indeed, the sooner you can send some of your Pers up to the compound to take charge, the better. I suppose Reuvan spoke to you of Sabatien?"

The Norselander nodded.

"You must meet him and those novices who worked against their masters in secret so that together you may decide what will come next for Herder Isle."

"I would not usurp your place for the world, lady."

I laughed. "I am no more than a friend, Helvar. Indeed, with your help, I will soon depart."

He took my meaning at once and glanced toward the ghostly bulk of the *Stormdancer*. "Veril has told us of your need of our *Stormdancer* to seek this plague-bearing null, which the *Black Ship* will transport to the Westland. Of course, it will be at your disposal as soon as it is repaired."

"Do you know yet how long it will take?"

He sighed heavily, and my heart sank at his expression. "If the damage were no more than when we sailed into Hevon Bay, we could have patched the ship more easily. But we were not able to haul the ship onto the beach, so the damaged portion of the hull has been gnawed at by the currents, and the sea has filled its hold."

"How long?" I repeated.

"A sevenday at the least," Helvar said. "I am sorry."

◆ 22 ◆

THE RAIN CEASED, and the shipfolk began to make preparations to haul the *Stormdancer* higher up the beach once the tide rose, but I was shattered by the realization that nothing I could do would help the thousands on the west coast that would perish of plague. There was no question that Ariel would have left his null ashore to spread plague long before a sevenday passed. Despair extinguished all the joy I had felt upon overthrowing the Faction.

Leaving the others, I walked along the beach toward the mounded boulders where Lark had once bidden me hide. I sat on a smaller stone rising from the wet sand, trying to accept that it was no fault of mine or Maryon's that something had occurred to disrupt the future she had seen, in which I had the chance to stop the spread of the plague. Perhaps it was no more than the accidental damaging of the hull that had ended that possibility, and there was nothing I could have done to avert that.

So why did I feel as if I had failed?

I buried my head in my hands, unable to bear the thought of what was to come, and yet unable *not* to think of it either. There would be death on a scale unequaled since the Beforetimers had lived, for the last plague had killed only some of those who had contracted it. It had caused hundreds of deaths, and many more had been left scarred or permanently weakened, but the One had said this plague would be caught by everyone who came in contact with it, and all who caught it would die. *All*. And among the thousands of innocent people I did not know who would die were the few I did, those whose presence on the west coast was my doing: Merret, Blyss, Seely, Ode's sister, and all the others from Obernewtyn whom I had sent to the west coast. All of them would die because of me.

"It is not your fault," Reuvan said softly, kneeling beside the rock where I sat. He pressed a mug of something hot into my hands and wrapped a warm cloak around my shoulders, bidding me come back to the compound, for nothing could be done until the tide was right. Helvar wanted to meet Sabatien and speak of the future. "Come back with us."

"I cannot feast and plan, knowing what is coming to the west coast," I said blackly.

"Drink something at least," Reuvan insisted, pushing the mug gently toward my mouth. I sipped a mouthful of the hot, spiced fement, because the effort of refusing was too great, but my teeth chattered against the rim. The fiery brew warmed the chill in my bones and gut, but it did not touch the ice that had formed about my heart. I could think of no words to say, so I drank until the mug was empty and handed it back to the seaman. I saw pity in his eyes and wondered why he would pity me. It was not I who faced death.

As if he had heard the thought, he said, "It is hardest when you can do nothing."

"Go with them," I said. "I need to be alone now, but I will return after a while."

"Very well," he sighed, and departed.

I sat for a long time staring blankly out to sea. My head was spinning slightly because of the fement, but I was only dimly aware of the others leaving. I was glad none of them came to talk to me, for I had no desire for conversation. It was not until my chin hit my chest that I woke up enough to realize I had fallen into a near stupor sitting there. I told myself that I ought to return to the compound and sleep rather than indulging in an orgy of pointless grief and guilt. But the effort of rising was beyond me.

If there had been a bed laid out beside me, I would have fallen gratefully into it. As it was, I was sitting upon a rock on a pale beach running down to a gray ruffled sea, with no idea how I was going to get myself anywhere. A delicate rosy light bloomed along the horizon, limning the crippled *Stormdancer*. A seam of dazzling silver opened along the horizon to allow the day to be born, and as the sun rose at last, streams of pale gold light pierced the thinning clouds to give a shimmering edge to the waves rolling in, and the mist wove a gauzy rainbow.

And quite suddenly, *I knew what I must do.*

I got to my feet, shrugging off both the cloak Reuvan had laid about my shoulders and the Herder robe I had worn, and I walked the few steps to the sea's edge. I slipped off my shoes and stepped into the waves. The water was very cold, but I went deeper until I felt it seeping through my clothes to touch my warm skin with icy fingers. I had to brace myself against the strong incoming tide to prevent being pushed back toward the shore. When at last my mouth was level with the water, I shouted aloud and inside my mind.

"Maruman!" I called as I had done before.

Nothing happened, and as I stood there waiting, all the

fatigue I had shed seeped back into me, bringing with it leaden despair.

"Fool," I muttered.

A movement at the edge of my vision made me turn, and I was startled to see Cinda racing down the beach toward me, her black hood flung back, her eyes wide with alarm. She waved her arms wildly, and knowing she could not call out to me, I waded wearily back to shore.

"What is the matter?" I asked, and entered her mind so she could answer me.

"I kept thinking of you, alone here," she told me. "When my brother died, I blamed myself for surviving, but what could I have done to stop his death?" She looked out across the strait. "You must not blame yourself for what you cannot change." Her voice was kind but stern.

"I sent many of my friends to the west coast, and now they will die because they did what I asked. How should I not blame myself?"

The shadow did not answer, but after a long minute, she said, "I saw you go into the water. You went so purposefully that I . . . I thought . . ." She stopped, her face darkening in a blush.

"You thought I meant to drown myself?" I asked gently.

"There were times over the years when I wished I would die. After they cut out my tongue and when I learned of my brother's death. But if I died, I never would have met Elkar." She glanced toward the compound.

"He loves you," I said aloud.

She smiled.

"I was not trying to die. I sought to call a ship fish to me," I told her aloud. Because I had not withdrawn my probe, my emotions and thoughts were laid bare, and Cinda gasped at what she saw fleetingly in my mind.

"You can speak with the minds of ship fish?" she marveled.

"One saved me once, but I must have been mad to imagine I could call it to me here."

Cinda nodded, but all at once, her eyes widened, and she pointed back over my shoulder to the sea.

I turned to see a fin cleaving through the waves, and hope flowed through me like hot fement. Without hesitation, I ran back into the water. The fin vanished, and I stopped, confused. Then a silvery shining head emerged from the water in front of me. Trembling, I stretched out my hand, but the ship fish neither approached nor retreated. It waited, its liquid eyes fixed on me. I was but a finger length away when it surged forward, pressing its head to my palm. It was not Ariroth.

"This one is Vlar-rei. Name of Ari-noor, podsister to Ariroth. Come now and this one will bear she where she must go, Morred-a," the ship fish belled.

I turned back to where Cinda stood shivering at the water's edge and shouted, "She will bear me across the strait. It is the only chance we have of saving the west coast, and there is no time to waste. Tell the others. Bid them repair the *Stormdancer* and sail to Sutrium. Dardelan and the rebels must be warned not to cross the Suggredoon until the next full moon, just in case I cannot stop the plague. Whatever happens will be over then."

Cinda wrung her hands and shook her head helplessly, but I threw my hand over the ship fish, taking care to avoid her blowhole. As she turned and began to swim strongly straight out to sea, I looked back and caught a glimpse of Cinda lifting a hand slowly. By the time I managed to get a better grip and lift my own hand, the girl was no more than a shadow on the sand.

Soon the cold I had experienced upon entering the water faded, along with my mind-numbing exhaustion. This told me that Ari-noor was feeding me spirit energy as her pod-sister had done.

"Morred-a is smaller than this one expected," she sang. Her tone and manner were more formal than Ari-roth's, but I had the same soothing sense of her gliding presence in my mind.

"Ari-roth spoke of me to you?" I asked.

"The waves know the name of Morred-a. It will be a long journey for she," Ari-noor sang enigmatically with several gloomy subnotes. "Longer than the journey with Ari-roth and longer than the journey made by the calf of Mornir-ma. Morred-a must not take shortsleep lest longsleep come. Must not let ohrana flow into dreamwaves. Morred-a must never, ever, let go of Ari-noor."

I tightened my grip and thought about what she had said.

By the "calf of Mornir-ma," she must mean Dragon, confirming once and for all that the red-haired waif had been brought to the Land by sea creatures after she and her mother had been stolen from the Red Land. And so *Mornir-ma* must be a title given by the Vlar-rei to the Red Queens, or maybe to beastspeakers who could commune with them. But what had she meant by warning me against letting my ohrana flow into the dreamwaves? *Ohrana* was the name Ari-roth had used to describe her aura or spirit form, so dreamwaves might be the spirit form cast by the sea; after all, mountains, fire, and all manner of inanimate things cast spirit forms. If I was right, the ship fish had warned me not to let my spirit merge with the spirit of the waves. But that made no sense, for I would have to *assume* my spirit form even to see or be aware of the dreamwaves. Unless dreamwaves were more closely connected to the real sea than the dreamtrails were connected to real places on land.

A different thought occurred to me. If the dreamwaves were connected to the dreamtrails, it might be that Atthis was using the ship fish, just as she used land beasts, to protect and aid me. Yet it was hard to imagine a bird, even one as ancient and powerful as the Elder of the eldar, manipulating these strange fish.

A wave slapped me hard in the face, almost dislodging me, and I tightened my grip. Ari-noor had warned me sternly not to let go of her. I would certainly be left behind swiftly if I did so, for we were cleaving through the water at a far greater speed than Ari-roth had traveled. In truth, I did not see how the ship fish could maintain such a pace. But even if she slowed, I was sure that I would reach the west coast before Ariel's null had time to spread the plague. I had asked Ari-noor to take me to Murmroth landing, because it was closest to Herder Isle. I would have to travel by foot to the city, if the *Black Ship* had docked there. If not, I would acquire a horse and immediately ride toward Aborium. As soon as I was close enough, I would farseek the Beforetime ruins where Jak and Dell had intended to set up a refuge. Then I would have all the help I needed in locating the null.

Something in the waves ahead caught my eye, and I squinted until I was able to make out a fin cutting through the water toward us. At first I thought it another ship fish, but then a chill ran down my spine, for this was the squat black fin of a shark!

"Yes," Ari-noor sent calmly. "Many azahk are here. They

will not harm she while our ohrana are connected. But if Morred-a lost hold of this one, even for a moment, the azahk would catch she in its teeth."

I tightened my grip convulsively. It was fortunate that I did, for suddenly we went from high swells to a great heaving and pulling and churning of white water that told me we had entered the strait's tempestuous central current. I knew that ships preferred to take a gradual diagonal bearing across the strait, partly to avoid the stress of the contrary currents on their ship and partly to avoid a series of long, wickedly sharp, mostly submerged shoals called *The Teeth*. I had supposed that Ari-noor would cut directly across the strait, weaving through the shoals as effortlessly as she had done through the waves, but to my disappointment, she turned into the current. Our passage became immediately smoother, and if anything, our speed increased, yet this new course would take longer, for by the time we left the central current, we would be well down the coast. The ship fish would have to turn and swim back up the coast to deliver me to Murmroth.

In addition, the shark was following us.

Gritting my teeth, I told myself resolutely that the shark was the least of my worries, for Ari-noor was feeding me her energy, and as long as I held her, it would not attack. But my arms and back were already aching, and I had not even been in the water as long as I had when Ari-roth took me from the narrow inlet to the beach at Saithwold.

As the hours wore on, it was not the buffeting of the waves nor physical weariness that troubled me so much as the constant ominous presence of the sharks, for now there were three fins. Sometimes they circled us, as if to mock our slower progress; at other times, one would come near enough that I would see its blunt, pitted snout and blank, black eyes.

"Azahk ohrana is hungry," Ari-noor observed, but her mindvoice was serene. I took this as an indication that I was in no danger, though I could not help wondering how a hungry spirit could be fed by eating flesh.

"What ohrana desires, flesh does echo," Ari-noor sent imperturbably.

As if to underline her warning, a shark fin rose from the water so close to me that I could have stretched out my hand to touch it. I told myself that I was safe, but I also drew in my legs. After a long, anxious period, the fin turned and vanished beneath the waves' churning surface. In relief, I relaxed, and my grip loosened slightly. Ari-noor immediately belled a warning, so I locked my muscles, ignoring their aching protest.

Time passed, and I tried to converse with Ari-noor to distract myself from the thirst and monotony of the journey, but my attempts to engage her won only reluctant and monosyllabic responses. Despite looking similar to her podsister, she was more reserved than Ari-roth and held herself aloof in my mind.

There was no sight of the land on any side now, and I began to fancy the light had changed subtly. Surely it was afternoon. I prayed so, for although I had no more to do than hold tight to the ship fish and be carried to my destination, there was something in the relentless movement of the waves and my being saturated to the bone that made me feel as if the water was sloughing away layers of my spirit. I imagined dreamily that when the last shred of it was gone, I would let go of the ship fish and drift helplessly into the blue void until the waiting sharks bit into my sodden flesh and spongy bones.

"Do not sleep!" Ari-noor sent with surprising sharpness.

I jerked awake, horrified to realize that I had begun to drowse—doubly horrified, for close by, a fin cut through the water like a dark knife. The shark circled away and vanished, as before, and I wondered with an internal shiver if it had come closer because it had sensed that I was falling asleep. Despite the fright I had given myself, my eyes still felt heavy and my mind sluggish. I cursed my stupidity for sitting awake on the beach the previous night instead of sleeping. Yet how could I have known what awaited me?

I told myself that it mattered not if ignorance as much as courage had brought me into the strait, so long as I reached the west coast.

All I had to do was stay awake.

There was a low rumble of thunder, and I looked up, noting the dark, congested clouds overhead, and wondered what sort of storm was brewing. Aside from the danger of being struck by lightning, I welcomed the possibility of a storm, for surely there would be rain, and the thirst of hours before had become a torment. The temptation to drink a mouthful of seawater was so compelling that I was frightened I might succumb.

"Do not drink," Ari-noor warned.

Desperately, I cast about for something to occupy my thoughts. Strangely, I found myself remembering the day I had ridden away from Obernewtyn. In retrospect, there had been a brightness to that day, although I had been in no mood to appreciate it. I had been so full of grief over my estrangement from Rushton and worry about Khuria's letters and Malik's trial that I had not properly appreciated the feel of Gahltha's warm faithful flesh moving under me and Maruman's softness about my neck and curving into my mind.

Then it occurred to me that I was guilty of doing exactly the same thing again. Only a few days past, I had believed that I would never see Maruman or Gahltha or Rushton again, for I had thought myself doomed to a horrible death at the hands of the Herders. Yet now that I knew that I *would* see them again, instead of rejoicing, I was full of self-pity. I felt a surge of disgust for myself and deliberately turned my thoughts to wondering if they had any idea of what had been happening to me. Atthis might have let Maruman know where I was, and the old cat would have let the others know through the beastspeakers. Or maybe not. Maruman was contrary and uninformative at the best of times, and he had been angry with me even before I abandoned him in Saithwold.

Maryon might also have dreamed of me and sent a messenger to Sutrium to let the others know what had happened. But how much could she have seen? Had she known that I would find myself trapped aboard a Herder ship and taken to Herder Isle? I wondered what I would have done if Maryon had brought me into her high chamber in Obernewtyn's Futuretell wing to tell me all that would happen to me after I left the mountains. Would I have gone to Saithwold, knowing that Malik awaited me, even if I had known that his attempt to kill me would fail? And what of the tunnel under the cloister? Would I have taken that, knowing it would lead me to Herder Isle and into the hands of the Herders? And what lay at the end of this journey across the strait, which I had begun so impulsively?

"She mind swims in circles," Ari-noor sent soothingly. "Will the waves change because someone swims through them? What has happened has happened, and what will happen will happen."

✦ ✦ ✦

Night fell subtly, for the storm that threatened all afternoon had not broken despite the sullen mutter of thunder. The clouds that had masked the sun now hid dusk and then the rising of moon and stars. Night gradually darkened from steel gray to black, and I scanned the sea in the distance, seeking the dull blurs of orange light that would denote land, though in my heart I knew it was too soon. By my reckoning, we were still moving along the strait and had yet to angle toward the shore and enter the coastal currents.

I turned my mind to what Elkar had told me when we had first arrived at the healing center after the confrontation with the Hedra master. He had managed to track down the novice who had seen Ariel's special nulls when he had been sent to deliver a message to the One's favorite. Ariel had just locked the door of his chambers, and he had two nulls with him. According to the novice, one had been very small—a midget, he had supposed—until it looked at him, and he had seen that it was a child. It had been impossible to tell if it was a boy or a girl, because its head had been shaven like all nulls' heads, and its face had been horribly scarred. I doubted Ariel would give a child the responsibility of spreading his plague, because a child would be vulnerable and might come to harm before it had done his bidding. But the other null had been described as a grown man, sickly pale as one long imprisoned in a cell without fresh air or sunlight. I was certain he was the null I must seek. But when I learned where the null had gone ashore, I would concentrate my search not on him but on Ariel. Of course, he might not have accompanied the null ashore, but if it were safe to do so, he would be unable to resist the vicious pleasure of walking through a crowd and gloating over what awaited them. All I needed to do was to ask around until I found someone who had seen a fair, astonishingly handsome young man accompanied by a very pale, dark-haired man.

"Just as long as he is not in a cloister," I muttered.

A wave cuffed me hard, knocking the breath out of me. "Anything else?" I gasped wrathfully at the heavens. Another wave broke against me, and by the time I had finished coughing and choking out swallowed seawater, I had ceased thinking of Ariel and the null. The wind had been growing steadily, and it now howled overhead, whipping the waves into high peaks that broke over me until I feared I would drown clinging to the back of the ship fish. Ari-noor seemed unaffected, yet I was buffeted mercilessly by the sea, and every breath was a struggle. When I remembered my surrender to the waves in the narrow inlet, I relaxed, and at once I became aware that a song throbbed in the air, made up of the sea's roar and hiss and the wind's howling. The strange, wild music had a rhythm, and Ari-noor's movements synchronized with it and were part of it. I thought of Powyrs, the shipmaster of *The Cutter*, telling me that the sea was too strong and vast to be fought. One must surrender to it. I thought I had surrendered to it in the narrow inlet, but I had only given up struggling against it. In order to hear the song of the waves, I began to understand that I had to give up singing my own song of fear first. Powyrs had called it *surrender*, but in truth he meant that one needed to cease one's own competing song. Only then could I listen to the song of the waves and become part of it as the ship fish did.

The sensation of being in tune with the vast, mysterious ocean was profoundly soothing, and the wild waves and the roar of the storm overhead and the dreadful thirst I felt were no less a part of it than Ari-noor. I thought of the mindstream that lay at the bottom of all minds, connecting us to one another and to the past and the future. Perhaps the sea and the creatures in it were closer than creatures of the land and air to that final merging of all life that was the end of individuality, which we humans called *death.*

I shivered, noting dimly that I was growing cold. Ari-noor had long since ceased to feed me from her ohrana. Indeed, she no longer scolded me or reminded me to keep hold or stay awake, and I could feel her fatigue. I had the feeling that if I let go of her, she would swim lightly on, hardly noticing that she had lost me. The thought no longer frightened me. Death, too, was part of the song of the waves. A serene fatalism possessed me.

I drifted, and while I did not sleep, sleep was no longer separate from waking. Both states flowed through me, and my spirit become loose and free in my body, as if I need only lean over for it to pour out into the waves. Liquid into liquid. I felt no urge to pour myself into the sea but no fear of it either, and in that utterly passive state, I heard something. It was not music, yet it was; and it was not exactly sound, yet my spirit floating in my flesh heard it. It flowed through the water, wave after wave of exquisite sound. Swells and eddies and currents of sound that, incredibly, moved through me as if I were part of the sea, as if my flesh did not separate us. This was the wavesong that Ari-noor and Ari-roth had spoken of, I realized in wonderment. This was what sea beasts heard and what had carried the song of my need across time and space.

I floated for a long time, listening and feeling the wavesong before I understood that there was meaning in it. Not one single meaning but a thousand meanings flowing side by side. Not meaning that could be understood as words are, but meaning as music carries meaning. Even a musician without empathy can evoke anger or sorrow or fear with music, and this was like that, only a thousand times more complex. Eddies and rills and coils of meaning merged and flowed and seemed to change and develop, as if meaning communicated with meaning.

As I lost myself in the wavesong, I began to feel a warning or a foreboding of something immense and dark and utterly strange. I struggled to understand what it could be, but its meaning was too fluid. There was death in it.

Frightened, I asked Ari-noor what it was.

She made no response. I called again and realized that I could not feel her in my mind. Unease flowed through me, thickening the fluid softness of my spirit, and as I became aware of my body—how cold and stiff it was—the wavesong faded.

Again I tried to farseek Ari-noor, and to my dismay, I discovered that she was *no longer with me*!

Panicking, I tread water and turned, seeking the sleek gray form of the ship fish, but if she was near I could not see her, for a thick, soft, blinding mist swirled above the waves. I called out her name again, mentally and aloud, but there was no response. Either she had been too weary to register my departure, or she had felt that my letting go severed the commitment she had made to bring me across the strait. Or perhaps in allowing the wavesong to enter me, she felt I had no more need of her.

Abruptly, I stopped splashing and shouting, aware that I was alone in the rain-swept sea and that sharks were probably scything through the waves, drawn by the discordant song of fear I had been emanating.

Something banged against my feet, and I would have screamed in fright if I had had any strength. A wave crashed over me, thrusting me downward with such force that it felt as if I had hit something solid. I thrashed my arms, desperate to reach the surface, and grazed my elbow. I imagined sharks seething in the water, snapping at my flailing limbs. I managed one breath of air before another wave pummeled me, this time sending me tumbling head over heels. Dizzy and confused, I was no longer sure which way was up or down. Again my elbow and then my knee struck something hard, and I realized I must have been washed into a shoal! I could be battered to pieces on the rocks just below the surface. Another wave lifted me and threw me down. My head struck something, and I dropped into blackness. I sank like a stone to the depths of my mind. The descent was so swift that I knew I would not be able to prevent myself from entering the mindstream. Instead of feeling fear or desperation, my will dissolved and I ceased trying to slow my descent.

But I came to a sudden violent stop above the mindstream. Stunned at how abruptly my fall had ended, it took me a moment to understand that some other will had stopped me. Only one will was powerful enough for such a thing.

"Atthis."

"Even *I* could not stop your fall alone," sent the Agyllian. "It took all of the eldar, and even we would have failed without your friends."

"My friends?" I echoed.

"The cat and the horse who are your protectors," Atthis said. "The dog Rasial and the funaga Gavryn, Swallow, and Maryon. They have agreed to let us draw on them."

My mind reeled at the names. "But . . . how?"

"I entered their dreams and summoned their aid. When they opened themselves to me, I drew on their spirits to strengthen our merge, just as the ship fish fed you their ohrana," Atthis answered.

431

"Then my friends know what has been happening to me?"

"No," Atthis answered. "They know only that Elspeth-Innle was in great danger of death and must be saved. I asked their aid, and they gave it. Now you must exert your own will and rise, for it drains all of us to hold you."

I tried to do as she bid me, but my mind was sodden and responded sluggishly. "I can't," I sent.

"You are hurt badly," Atthis said. "We have taught your body to heal itself, and it will begin to do so when you withdraw from the mindstream. This close, your body cannot heal. Draw back, and we will send help."

I strove again to focus my mind and rise. This time, I managed to withdraw from the mindstream a little, but I felt the strange, wrenching regret of leaving behind that inevitable final merging with all that had been and would be. I tried to throw off my regret by thinking of Maruman and Gahltha, strange Gavryn and the others, who had somehow allowed themselves to be used to save me. And I thought of Cinda and the little boy Mouse, who had endured such horrors, and their will and courage to go on living. Most of all, though, I thought of the west coast, that I alone had the chance to save. If I died, thousands would die of plague.

"If you perish, a world will die," Atthis sent. "All beasts and funaga and plants. All."

"If I live, I will save them?" I asked.

"You will try, and you may succeed," the Agyllian elder answered. "Now rise, for even augmented, our merge weakens."

I tried again to rise, but the mindstream sang to me, its song as great and alluring as the wavesong, and I was weak. There was only one way to save myself. I delved into myself and tapped the dark killing force that slumbered deep in my mind. I was careful not to rouse it, but its dark hot strength flowed through me, and I heard Atthis gasp as I began to rise swiftly. As I felt Atthis slip away from me, I faltered in my will to rise. A bubble of matter rose lazily and inexorably from the mindstream to engulf me.

". . . I am Cassy," said Cassy. She was smiling at a middle-aged woman.

"I am Hannah Seraphim," the older woman said in a warm, soft voice.

I stared at her in wonder, for this was the first time I had ever seen Hannah Seraphim, leader of the Beforetime Misfits and the first woman to dream of me and my quest. She was shorter and smaller and more ordinary-looking than I had imagined her, but her mouth was full and smiling, and her eyes were extraordinary. They were brown. Not the opaque brown of stone and earth, but the clear transparent brown of a forest stream, a warm, dappled brown with moving glints of green and gold in their depths. Beautiful eyes, watchful and intelligent.

"I only got in this morning," Cassy was saying. "I . . . I couldn't wait until tomorrow."

Hannah answered in her deep slow voice. "I'm glad you are here and gladder still that you've wasted no time in visiting us." Hannah held out a small strong hand to Cassy, and after a slight hesitation, the tall younger woman laid her own in it and smiled nervously.

"Welcome to the Reichler Clinic, Cassandra," Hannah said formally. "I am afraid this is a very grand building of which we have only a small part. Our patron, although he would laugh to hear himself described so, would happily give us the whole building, and indeed he has the means for it." She smiled a private, rather lovely smile. "But what we have here

433

is sufficient and safer." There was a slight grimness to her mouth now, and her eyes were stern.

"Please, call me Cassy," said the younger woman as they began to climb a flight of steps. She looked around, prompting me to do the same, and at once I recognized their surroundings. They were in the entrance foyer of the building that contained the Reichler Clinic Reception Center, in the city of Newrome, under Tor. But I could hardly reconcile the dim, water-stained foyer within the crushed building in a submerged and ruined city into which I had dived, with this shining hall of marble and glass. Through the windows, I saw huge trees and shrubs growing where now there grew a dark submarine forest of waving fronds sunk in an endless emerald twilight.

Hannah and Cassy had reached the top of the steps, to the foyer's main section, and I noticed the absence of the enormous glass statue of a woman surrounded by beasts. It was missing because it had yet to be created. Cassy gazed around, her eyes narrowing speculatively, and I wondered if this was the moment when the seed of the idea for that statue had been planted. "It seems so impossible and so wonderful to be here," she said. "All those years ago when I was tested in one of your mobile units, I was so desolate to be told that I had no paranormal abilities."

Hannah sighed in vexation, and after one swift assessing glance around, she said in a soft voice, "Those mobile units! Who knows how many like you were turned away because the equipment was useless. At the time, I thought William was just technically incompetent because, after all, he had written *Powers of the Mind*. Of course, he had not written the book at all, but it was not until later that I discovered it."

"When will I meet the others?" Cassy asked shyly.

Hannah looked at her and, after another glance around, said very softly, "Cassy, listen to me carefully, because I won't be able to speak like this once we enter the elevator. There are listening devices in it and also in our reception center. The other paranormal students are not here, because despite its name, this is not the Reichler Clinic. The government and the general public believe it is, because that is what we want them to believe. Our real work with paranormals is undertaken elsewhere so we can be sure there will be no repeat of what happened at the first Reichler Clinic facility. I have been unable to speak of this in our e-mails. I have often warned you to say little in our communications, citing competing factions and cyber pirates as the reason. The truth is that we must protect ourselves from the government."

"But where . . . ?"

"The true Reichler Clinic is not so far away, but we will not go there today. Now you are going to meet those who come here to maintain our facade. Some are paranormals and others are not. You and I are about to enact a performance for the spy eyes and listening devices planted throughout our rooms."

"But why bring me here if we cannot speak freely?" Cassy said in confusion. They were approaching a bank of gleaming metal doors, and Hannah laid her hand lightly on Cassy's shoulder as she reached out to press her palm against a glowing square on the wall beside the doors. Cassy's eyes showed a fleeting look of astonishment, but she managed to turn a cry of surprise into a sneeze. Sensing what was happening, I entered her mind.

". . . how we will communicate," Hannah was farsending. "But it was necessary for you to come here because of our communications so far. You are, after all, the daughter of the director of the institute at which kidnapped paranormals are being secretly held, and you have been communicating with and have come to visit the Reichler Clinic from whose destroyed compound they were taken. No matter what you sent me, I have been lukewarm in my enthusiasm. No doubt it frustrated you that I have many times suggested that you are likely to test normal, despite the fact that your e-mails made it clear that you were definitely paranormal."

"My e-mails." Cassy gasped aloud.

"Exactly," Hannah farsent. "But don't worry. After you communicated with us the first time, we knew there would be official consternation. We set up programs to alter all of your communications before they were logged, and we hacked into your computer to erase all traces of the original messages. What the officials monitoring our incoming e-mails read were the rather fatuous and romantic ideals of a girl who believes herself to be special. Not an uncommon feeling among young women, and one that might be expected of a neglected young woman who is the product of a broken relationship between two busy, rather cold parents with careers, who are less than attentive to their only daughter. Forgive me if this pains you."

"It . . . it is only the truth," Cassy said.

"I am sorry, but the truth is always the best shield for a greater truth. The e-mails I sent you were responses to those false e-mails. Of course, you were careful because the captive paranormals would have warned you to be careful. Nevertheless, we removed even your veiled references to the kidnapped paranormals and your communications with them, because although much time has passed, we do not want the government to guess that we know they destroyed the original Reichler Clinic."

"It was not the paranormals who warned me to be careful, and it was not because of them that I contacted you . . . ," Cassy began, her mindvoice clearer as she forgot her self-consciousness in her urgent desire to communicate. "I did not know how to explain without sounding mad, but it was the flamebird—"

"I have some inkling of what you will tell me. But the elevator is coming now, and we must concentrate on our performance for this meeting. The output of the spy eyes and listening devices will be very closely scrutinized because of who you are, and we must give the government nothing upon which to hang their suspicions. You will take various tests that will reveal very slight latent paranormal ability—that you are basically normal. You, of course, will be terribly disappointed. And tomorrow you will console yourself by hiking in the mountains near the entrance to Newrome with a handsome young student of Newrome University who will come this evening to your hotel bar and offer to buy you a drink. But we will speak more of that later. Remember, guard your expression and play your part convincingly, lest you put all of us in danger."

"Your voice is so . . . so clear," Cassy sent.

"In part because I am touching you," Hannah sent. She released Cassy and stepped forward to press at the panel with apparent impatience. Then her mindvoice came again, but with less strength and clarity. "The closer you are, the easier it is. But rest assured, although my mindvoice may seem strong and clear, with very little training, you will surpass us all."

"How can you be so sure?" Cassy asked.

"I have seen it," Hannah said aloud, but softly. Her face was suddenly ineffably sad, and her sadness lapped at me.

I became aware that I was floating. Somewhere in me was a terrible thirst, but before it could surface, I saw that there was a red-haired woman floating in the water beside me. The water about her was red with blood, and I recognized her from Dragon's comatose dream as the betrayed queen of the Red Land—she whom sea creatures called *Mornir-ma.* In the coma dream, the dying Red Queen had summoned whales to smash the slave ship that had carried her and her little daughter from their land. Then she had called a ship fish to bear Dragon to the nearest land, the west coast. There was no sign of Dragon, though, and as the woman's blood flowered into the sea about her, I understood that the ohrana of the sea was drinking her spirit.

"Is this the dreamsea?" I asked.

The red-haired woman opened her eyes and looked at me. Then she answered in the bell tones of Ari-noor. "The sea is without end. It ebbs and flows between. It is the place where all things meet and change. It is infinite."

I am dreaming, I thought. I began to rise again toward consciousness, but I had too little strength to maintain a shield against the drifting tendrils of dream stuff.

Suddenly I was kneeling in rustling brown and yellow leaves, cupping my hands under a rill of water that bubbled from a cleft in an outcrop of stone. The water was so cold that my palms grew numb as I scooped some to my mouth.

"Do not drink," commanded a somber voice in my mind.

I spat out the salty water and turned to see the white dog Rasial, who had once been called Smoke. Her white coat glowed in a dappling of light falling through bare branches interlaced overhead, but even as I watched, the sunlight dimmed, mist rose and coiled about the trees, and Rasial changed. Her coat darkened and roughened until she became dear shaggy Sharna, who had died so many years before, saving my life from Ariel's maddened wolves at Obernewtyn. Almost before I registered his identity, Sharna's fur and muzzle shortened, his color deepened, and his ears sharpened until I recognized Jik's companion, the Herder-bred Darga, whose coming was to mark the beginning of the final phase of my quest as the Seeker.

"Where are you?" I asked, but he only blinked his dark eyes at me.

"Elspeth?"

I turned to find Matthew standing in the thickening mist. His gaze swept over me, partly in wonder and partly in disbelief. "This dinna feel like any dream," he muttered.

My heart leapt as I understood that he was right. This was not a dream I was experiencing. "I think it is real," I sent. "I am farseeking you."

Matthew looked elated, stunned, then confused. "But how can your mind reach me when I am so far away an' over the sea?"

"I am dreaming, but I think I have drifted onto the dream-trails. Matthew, listen to me. I, and others at Obernewtyn, have true-dreamed of you, as you have of us. I know where you are and what you are trying to do. I know that Dragon is the Red Queen's missing daughter, and we will bring her to you as soon as it is possible."

"Dragon is in a coma," Matthew said sorrowfully.

"No! She has wakened, though as yet she has no memory of her life before or after the ruins. She has no memory of me or . . . or you."

"Perhaps that is best," he said, and there was pain in his eyes before he vanished.

"Elspeth?"

I turned again in hope, but it was not Matthew this time. It was Rushton, smiling at me from the center of a hot spring veiled in thick white steam. Snow lay deep on the ground, and my boots crunched through it as I walked to the rim of the pool. *This is a memory dream,* I realized. I could have wrenched myself out of it, but how my heart yearned for him as he floated back in the water and bade me join him. For this was a memory of the last time we had been alone together before Rushton had been taken captive by the Herders. I had ridden from a meeting at the Teknoguild caves to meet him at the spring in the foothills of the highest mountains, and we had swum together. I allowed myself to merge with my dream self to more fully experience the memory. Stripping off my clothes, I entered the water, and Rushton's arms closed possessively about me. But when he kissed me, I did as I had always done when we were so close, drawing back from final surrender, shutting up the core of myself, for how could I surrender my body without surrendering my mind? To lay that bare would mean opening up all that I was, to reveal the quest that lay at the heart of me like a black pearl that none must ever see.

There was hurt in his eyes at my withdrawal, but no reproach. And I saw in the memory, as I had not seen in the moment, that Rushton encompassed my resistance with a grace that I had never noticed, because I had been too busy protecting my secrets. He released me and drew away from me so the misty steam veiled him. Then there was only the mist, caressing my cheeks.

"Rushton!" I croaked.

Tears blurred my eyes, and I knew with sudden, utter clarity that I had been a fool to refuse him then and all the other

440

times. Was not the song of love like the song of the sea? One must surrender to it to understand it. What would it have mattered if I held my deepest mind apart and allowed him to make love to me? I could have taken comfort from his body, giving him the comfort of mine. What did it matter if that black pearl was kept in a hidden chamber? And the cruel final thought came to me that if I *had* loved him, the memory of that loving might have given him the strength to endure when the Herder priests delved so cruelly inside him.

I wept, and as the water about me grew cold, I drifted from memory of dream to reality.

I was lying on my side with rain falling on my face.

Rain!

Thirst roared to life, and I rolled onto my back and opened my mouth to drink.

Upon quenching my thirst, I realized that I was not in the water. I was lying on the sand some way above the waterline, my clothes stiff with dried salt, though the rain was now softening them. I gave a choking laugh as I understood that *this* was what the wavesong had been trying to tell me: land was ahead, a great dark bulk where no sea creature could venture. A vast and deadly mystery for one who could not walk on dry land and live.

I must be on the west coast! I had made it! I looked around, and through the veils of falling rain, I saw, the hazy dark outline of a city. It was not more than an hour's walk away, but I could not tell which city it was, certainly not Murmroth. I wanted to walk there at once. I needed to find out if the *Black Ship* had been there.

But when I tried to move, I was devastated to discover that I was so weak, I could not even sit up. Lying there, I remembered Atthis telling me that I must rise so my body could heal itself. I had been badly injured, she had said, which was why I felt so monstrously weak. My body had drained itself of strength to heal me.

Gritting my teeth, I gathered all of my will and sat up. My head swam with the effort, and I knew that I would not be walking anywhere, at least for a few days. Fortunately, it was not cold, and the rain had enabled me to drink. I was not hungry, but I soon would be, and I would need food to regain my strength.

And gain my strength I would. I thought fiercely. For I had a plague to stop. And when I had done that, I would return to Obernewtyn and I would find Rushton and I would say to him everything I had been too cowardly to say. I would lay myself bare to him in all ways, and perhaps that would be enough to heal the breach between us.

"I am coming, my love," I thought, and hurled the thought forward with all the will that remained in me.

THE
STONE KEY

for Mallory,
who found me on a table
and read me on a plane,
and for Daywatcher Whitney
and Moonwatcher Nick,
who were my guides on this
unexpected and unexpectedly
enchanting quest

PART I

✦

STONEHILL

✦ 1 ✦

I OPENED MY eyes to find a young gull perched on my chest, peering at me with a speculative black eye. When I moved, it gave a startled squawk and flapped away. It stopped atop a rock and watched me.

"Give up, for I am too big for you to swallow, little brother," I croaked, and struggled to sit up. The night's storm might have been a dream, for there was not a cloud in the dazzling blue sky that arched overhead. The sun was hot enough to have dried the exposed part of my hair and clothes. I had drunk as much of the brief flurry of rain as I could, but I was thirsty.

Indeed I had woken thirsty for the last few days, and it was doubtless thirst that had woken me.

Or maybe the gull had pricked me with its claws. I looked around and found it was still watching me like a small baleful sentinel. But then my gaze went past it, for beyond it in the distance, only half visible through a dense golden haze of sunlit sea spray lay the city that had occupied most of my thoughts since I had awakened the first time on the sand. While I had rested in order to give my body time to heal, I had come to feel certain that the city was Morganna, but it was impossible to be sure at this distance. I could see that it was walled, but I could not tell if it was a complete wall or merely overlapping sections of wall.

I had asked the ship fish Ari-noor to bring me to Murmroth, at the other end of the west coast from Morganna, but the currents and shoals in the strait were such that any ship wanting to travel to Murmroth had to begin its journey on the coast just past the mouth of the Suggredoon, so it could very well be that I had lost hold of the ship fish not far from Morganna.

The thought of ships had preoccupied my mind the last few days: somewhere on the sea sailed the *Black Ship* with its deadly cargo of plague that the Herder leader intended to unleash upon the west coast. I had come to the west coast with the sole desire of finding the plague carrier before his sickness became contagious, but I had no idea where he would be left ashore. In a city, certainly, and in my estimation a large city, but which one I had been unable to discover.

With luck, it would be Morganna, but it might as easily be Aborium or even Murmroth. For this reason, my plan had been to call at every city and ask if the *Black Ship* had recently put in anchor there. But I had not reckoned on losing contact with the ship fish that had borne me across the treacherous strait or on smashing my head on a rock in a shoal and nearly drowning. Indeed it was only the aid of the mystic Agyllian birds, who had come to me on the dreamtrails, that had enabled me to reach the west coast alive. The Elder of the Agyllians had warned me that I must rest so the curative capacity the birds had taught my body could heal me swiftly. And I had obeyed.

Other than my apprehension about finding the plague carrier in time, it had been far from unpleasant to sit on the sloping white sand and gaze out to sea. Spending such long periods of time in the water with the two ship fish and hearing the wavesong, or feeling it, for it seemed as much to be felt as to be heard, had given me a deeper appreciation of it. The wavesong had flooded me with appreciation for those I loved, for those who had come to my aid.

The thought of love brought to my mind an image of Rushton, but it was too painful to let my thoughts dwell on the Master of Obernewtyn, given our estrangement. I thought instead of my two protectors, Gahltha and Maruman. I missed them terribly, though I knew they were aware that I was safe because Atthis had sought assistance from their spirits in order to save me.

I turned my head to look out to sea. Despite the day's clarity, I could not see even a shadowy outline of Herder Isle. Two Islands, I reminded myself, for although the Herders had long ago destroyed the isthmus once connecting the two islands, the link had been renewed when the high wall surrounding the Faction Compound had fallen into the channel, creating a stone path from one to the other.

The dangerous, terrifying period I had spent inside the Herder Compound, first at the mercy of the Herder priests and then through the fall of the Faction on Herder Isle, seemed as if it had happened ages ago, rather than only a few days earlier. There had been much still to be done to secure victory when I had left for the west coast. I wondered for the hundredth time what was happening there and whether the Norselanders, the shadows, and the renegade novices had managed at last to overcome the ruthless captain of the Hedra force and his remaining warriors. I wondered if the *Stormdancer* had been repaired yet. I had meant to travel across the strait in the ship, but it had been damaged when the Herders tried to invade the Land, and the shipmaster, Helgar, had told me it would take at least a sevenday to make the ship seaworthy. I had felt such despair hearing his words, knowing it would be too late then to cross the strait and find the plague carrier in time to stop him from infecting anyone.

Only later that night had I thought of calling to the ship fish, Ari-noor, who had rescued me already. She had not come, but her pod-sister, Ari-roth, did.

Against all odds, I had reached the west coast. I reckoned that since the *Black Ship* had to travel from Norseland, having first provisioned itself and made whatever repairs it needed after its last trip, before weaving through various shoals and currents to reach the west coast, the *Black Ship* was only just now likely to be setting its plague carrier ashore. And it would take some days for the plague to become effective. So I had a few days in which to act.

The thought that the ship might even now be anchoring on the west coast made me uneasy. I was glad that I had left instructions for the *Stormdancer* to travel straight to Sutrium so the rebels could be alerted as to what had happened on Herder Isle and to warn them that no one must cross the Suggredoon, in case I failed.

I had ensured that the plague would be contained if I failed. But it sickened me to think of how many would die on the west coast.

"All," had said the One, the supreme leader of the Herder Faction. "All will die."

The memory of these words was enough to thwart my attempt to relax. I sat up and massaged the stiffness from my muscles while looking out over the shimmering waves. I thought of the true dream I had experienced when I had almost died, of Cassy Duprey and Hannah Seraphim's first meeting.

It had been fascinating to see Rushton's Beforetime ancestor Hannah Seraphim, for my Beforetime visions of the past had always centered on Cassy Duprey, a Beforetime sculptress whose father had been director of the Govamen program working on the computermachines that had caused the Great White holocaust that had destroyed their age. I had known that Cassy and Hannah Seraphim had met, but I had not previously seen them together.

I pictured Hannah's pleasant face with its striking brown eyes and expressive smile and felt suddenly that Jacob Obernewtyn *had* loved her, and this was at least partly why he built Obernewtyn and funded her research into the Beforetime Misfits' Talents, called paranormal abilities by the Beforetimers. I had hoped to dream of Hannah again as I lay hour after hour, drowsing rather than waking or sleeping, but past dreams were not something I could control.

I had mulled over the dream endlessly, though.

The meeting between Hannah and Cassy had obviously taken place before the young woman had invaded her mother's mind to prove that she possessed paranormal abilities. The vision held no trace of the grief I had witnessed in Cassy, and I guessed from this that Cassy's Tiban lover had not yet died when she had met Hannah.

The gull's caw startled me from my reverie, and I looked up to see it flap into the air, just escaping the sharp claws of the plains cat that had been stalking it. I sent a greeting to the cat, and she came gliding over.

"Red meat would strengthen ElspethInnle," said the tiny black cat with its enormous tufted ears and wild eyes. "Better than ubu." She dropped next to me several of the prickly cactus fruits that she and her mate had been bringing me since I first beastspoke them for help. She sat down to clean herself.

"My thanks, Mitya," I told her, feeling my heart seize with

longing for Maruman, who had cleaned his ears in exactly the same fastidious way.

The plains cat ceased her ablutions to watch me as I rose carefully to my feet, her nose twitching daintily. I walked back and forth, testing my strength. For two days I had been practicing standing and walking, but this was the first time since I had awakened on the beach that I felt neither pain nor dizziness, and the double vision I had suffered since waking had finally abated. My heart quickened at the realization that I was finally well enough to begin my quest. Despite my fears about the plague, I thought eagerly of reaching the city that had been so tantalizingly out of reach, because it meant food and water. My stomach rumbled loudly.

"ElspethInnle should eat some bloody meat," said Mitya again.

I said nothing, for I had already made vain attempts to explain to the single-minded little plains cat that I did not eat the flesh of anything that lived, for I could live well enough on fruits and vegetables and grains. She and her mate had not believed me, and they had brought me several tiny dead furry plains mice. I had finally convinced them to eat their kill. They had departed with it and returned an hour later with some of the prickly ubu. The cactus fruits had ensured my survival, but they had little taste and scant nourishment; even as I ate those Mitya had brought with her, I thought longingly of a hot bowl of vegetable stew with fresh baked bread and a bowl of rich honeyed milk. It made me salivate like a starved dog.

"I will go to the city now," I beastspoke the plains cat when I had finished my brief meal.

"Many are funaga-li that dwell there," said Mitya disdainfully.

"Nevertheless, I must go there to find my friend," I told

her. "Where is Guldi? I wanted to thank both of you for helping me."

"Guldi prepares a den, for soon I will have kits," Mitya sent. She gave me a look of glimmering pride, and I told her they were certain to be as beautiful and clever as their parents.

"Of course," she said complacently.

I cast one last glance around me, needlessly, for I carried nothing at all with me; then I bid the little cat farewell again.

I set off toward the city, glad that I was able to walk along the sand, for I was barefoot, having left my shoes from Cinda on the shore at Hevon Bay on Herder Isle. It angered me that I had not had sense enough to tie them to my waist before I entered the water. Aside from needing them to walk, there was a real danger that, barefoot and utterly bedraggled as I was, I would be judged a beggar and refused entry to the city. Of course, I could coerce my way out of any trouble, but given that I was still weak from my ordeal, it would be better to do nothing that would require exertion beyond walking. Certainly not before I managed to find some food.

It would be best to slip into the city along the shoreline, thereby avoiding the guarded entrances, but it would depend upon where the tide was when I arrived.

Driftwood lay scattered along the beach, and I began to gather it, reasoning that if I had to go through a gate, I could claim to be bringing wood into the city to sell. Once inside the walls, I would simply leave the wood somewhere and coerce shoes and some respectable clothes from a storekeeper. I needed to smarten my appearance if I did not want anyone to question my possession of a horse when I tried to leave. I would have to steal the horse, of course.

But first I would find food and water, and then I would go

to the waterfront and find out whether the *Black Ship* had anchored there recently.

By the time I was close enough to see that the town was fully walled, I had a good-sized armful of wood. This was fortunate, since the tide was high enough to make it impossible to enter at the shore. The walk had fatigued me, but it had not left me shaking and sickly as even a short walk had done two days past. My body seemed to have finished healing itself, and I was sure that once I had some proper food and water, I would be completely renewed.

Coming along the shore meant that I was approaching the city from the side and would enter through one of the lesser side gates. I had assumed that it would be scrutinized less closely than the city's main entrance gate, for important people and most travelers would come along the main coast road and so enter the city by its imposing main entrance. The only people who used a city's side gates were its poorer denizens—fisherfolk and foragers of various kinds. This was all to the good, for my bedraggled appearance would cause less comment in such company.

As I made my way slowly along the stony ground beside the wall, I found myself so thirsty that there was little else on my mind save reaching a well. I had endured thirst constantly since awakening on the west coast, but somehow it had become harder to bear the nearer I came to the city. Nevertheless, before I reached the gate, I forced myself to stop in the shade cast by the wall and set down my pile of wood. I rubbed my sticky face vigorously to remove the salt, combed my fingers through my hair, and plaited it as best I could. I then wove some strands of the spiked grass to bind the wood together. A real wood carrier would also have a woven shoulder pad, but I did not want to waste any more time.

Taking a deep breath, I shouldered the wood and joined those waiting to be admitted to the city. I was immediately relieved to notice that the bent crone at the front of the queue carried wood, too. I entered her mind to confirm that the city was indeed Morganna, but unfortunately she knew nothing of which ships had anchored here. Nor did the two boys behind her, leading horses. Both were grooms for the same stablemaster, and it occurred to me that I could easily pass for one of them if I pushed my hair under a cap, hunched down, and left the city the same way. Behind the grooms, a big man sat on a cart drawn by a bullock. The cart was piled high with ubu and a brown nut, which his mind told me he had gathered some distance from the city. Directly in front of me were several poor-looking travelers with thin packs, ragged clothes, and pinched faces. A swift probe revealed they were from the tiny farms where people eked out a living along the narrow belt of less barren land that fringed the Blacklands. Their last crop had failed after a mysterious blight had attacked the farms following one of the winds that occasionally blew in from the Blacklands. They meant to seek work and amass enough coin to buy seed and return with provisions before the next planting season. They had come to this gate to avoid the entry tax required at the main gate.

When I came close enough to see the soldierguards inside the gateway, I farsought the bigger of the two but was dismayed to encounter the unmistakable buzzing rejection of a demon band. I cursed my stupidity in failing to realize that the soldierguards would be demon-banded. Hadn't Brydda told me that all soldierguards this side of the Suggredoon wore the bands?

It was too late to leave the line without drawing attention, and I had to enter the town anyway. I would need to coerce a diversion if there was any trouble. To my intense relief, the guards barely looked at me before waving me through.

There were several wheeled stalls and carts set up on either side of the wide street running back from the gate. The man with the bullock and cart had stopped and was haggling with a stallholder over the price of the spiked fruit. A number of men with creels were selling fish to another stallholder, and I realized that the stalls must absorb a good deal of the produce that entered the city.

I edged through the small crowd examining the fish and produce, managing to anger several people by prodding them with the sticks I had collected. Cringing and apologizing, I wondered how any real wood-gatherer ever managed to move along a crowded street without poking someone in the eye.

Desperate to leave the press of people, I turned into the first street running off the wider gate road, only to find the way ahead blocked by three surly young men playing a game of stick and stone. Rather than coercing them to turn their brutish attention away from me altogether, I took the less exhausting step of channeling their aggressive energy into sneers and threats. I had not felt any real danger, yet I was thankful to come to a square where women and men sat on porches sewing or peeling vegetables with children threading about their legs.

I crossed the square diagonally and entered a lane that headed toward the sea. It occurred to me that selling the wood would not only earn me some coin, but it would also allow me to engage in a conversation that might enable me to ask more general questions, such as whether anyone had seen the *Black Ship* of late. Of course, I could delve into people's minds for what I needed, but asking aloud would be quicker and less wearying.

First I needed to find some water, for my thirst was acute. I asked a young woman about a public well, but she spat at my feet and muttered a curse to drive off beggars.

It took another half hour to locate a large public fountain in the center of a busy square surrounded by stalls and barrows. By now my head ached so badly from thirst that I felt ill. Throwing down my bundle, I took up the wooden dipper chained to the fountain, held it under a gush of water, and drank deeply. I dippered and drank two more before forcing myself to stop. I was still thirsty, but I would vomit if I simply drank my fill. I waited a moment and then drank two more dippers. Only then did I notice disapproving glares from the men and women seated about the rim of the fountain. A brief probe told me that I looked too near a beggar to be drinking from any but the beggars' wells in the poorer parts of the city. Ironically, the troublesome bundle of wood prevented those watching me from demanding to see a beggar's coin. This, I had learned, was the coin that proved one was *not* a beggar. In that sense, I thought sourly, the coin was misnamed. Anyone failing to produce a beggar's coin could be reported to the soldierguards, whereupon the poor soul would be beaten and thrown out of the city. I heaved the wood onto my shoulder again, resolving to acquire a beggar's coin promptly.

Leaving the tiled area about the well, I crossed a grassy circle to a small cluster of braziers. Blue smudges of smoke gave me hope that I could exchange the wood for coin, but the first seller I asked offered a bowl of shellfish stew in exchange for the wood. My stomach rumbled, urging me to accept, but I dared not risk being without wood or coin. Shaking my head, I said I needed a coin, and the man shrugged and gave me a copper. Relieved to be free of my troublesome bundle, I went straight to a shoemaker's stall and coerced him into seeing a silver coin rather than a copper, which enabled me to buy a rough pair of sandals and a threadbare but decent cloak from the next stall. I could have made both stallholders see coins where there were none, or made them give me what I needed, but this was safer and required less energy. In truth, I was weak with hunger.

I had two coppers from the cloak seller, and I used one, again transformed coercively into silver, to buy a comb, cheap woolen trousers, and a shirt. I coerced another trader to let me use his changing tent and discarded my rough, salt-stained clothes in favor of the new garments, regretting that I could not bathe first. Once dressed, I used another coerced copper to buy a water bladder, a small knife, and a chunk of fresh onion bread. The latter smelled so delicious that I ate it standing by the baker's stall. He was a sociable man, and it did not take me long to learn that the *Black Ship* had not called at Morganna in recent days. Indeed, the baker wondered why, saying that it was more than six sevendays since Salamander had come to clean out the Councilcourt cells and take his slaves to Norseland. I also learned that he knew nothing of the attempted invasion of the Land, which suggested that the Council truly had been kept in the dark about it.

I asked if the *Black Ship* might have called at Port Oran and was delighted to hear that big ships never went there because of too many hidden shoals. This meant that I need not back-track toward the Suggredoon before going farther up the coast.

Bidding the baker a casual farewell, I decided to try to find a horse and ride out of the city as soon as possible. The next settlement along the coast was Halfmoon Bay, a city only slightly larger than Port Oran. I was almost certain that the *Black Ship* would choose a larger town in which to release its deadly plague, but it would not do to bypass it and find later that I had been wrong. I remembered that Halfmoon Bay had a sectioned wall, which meant that I could simply ride in one side, check the piers to make sure the *Black Ship* had not been there, and then ride out the other side. If I could leave Morganna within the next hour, I could conceivably reach Halfmoon Bay by nightfall.

I walked, farseeking anyone I passed until I found my way to a public stable. Unfortunately, too many customers and workers provided no opportunity for theft. Rather than wasting time locating another public stable, I decided to try taking a horse from the holding yard of an inn. I had passed several already and had noticed that the smaller ones did not trouble much with attendants. As I searched for a small inn, I sent out a general probe in the hope of encountering any of the Misfits I had sent to the west coast to work with the rebels there. I was not surprised when it did not locate.

At last I spotted several horses in an inn's holding yard. I was initially disappointed to see two grooms talking to each other, but they were so deep in conversation that I decided to sidle up to the yard's outer fence and beastspeak the strongest-looking horse among them, a lovely, long-legged mare with a sand-colored coat. As I had hoped, she recognized me as the Seeker as soon as I beastspoke her, saying that it would be an honor to aid ElspethInnle. I was pleased to learn that her owner was a feckless young mistress who would likely remain drinking at the inn until dusk, though it was now barely noon. Indeed, the horse, whose name was Rawen, assured me that her mistress would be so drunk that she would have difficulty understanding that her horse had been stolen, let alone making anyone understand her. The theft of her horse would be reported eventually, of course, but there would be enough of a delay that we need not worry about being stopped.

Asking the mare to wait, I coerced the yard's sole occupant, a serving girl, to fetch me some bread, cheese, and apples from the kitchen and a simple saddlebag from the tack room. When she returned, I bade her keep watch as I stripped off my new clothes, sluiced myself and my hair with icy water, and used the cloak to dry myself before dressing again. It was a rudimentary bath, but I felt wonderfully clean and refreshed as I carried the food and newly filled water bladder back to the holding yard.

Once there, I saw that one of the grooms had departed. I coerced the other to fetch Rawen's tack and fill a saddlebag with oats and hay. When he returned, I had him saddle up the mare, and I thrust the food and my few possessions into the saddlebag, buckled it up, and mounted. I was unaccustomed to a saddle, but I could not ride bareback without drawing unwanted attention.

I bade the lad lead Rawen from the yard and dismissed him after erasing all memory of our dealings and inserting in its place the memory of having seen an older man with blond hair and a furtive manner hanging about the yard.

To my relief, Rawen knew the way to the main gate, which she said was much closer than the side gate. In a short time, we were approaching the city's busy main entrance. I asked Rawen to stop and dismounted, pretending to adjust her saddle as I studied the best way out. A swift probe told me that the six soldierguards on duty here wore demon bands. Five were concentrating on the long line of incoming travelers while the sixth dealt with people leaving the city. He gave only a cursory glance to each, and, reassured, I was about to mount Rawen again when a man leading two horses reached the gate. The soldierguard held out his hand, and the man produced what were clearly the horses' papers. I was dismayed, and sensing it, Rawen asked what the matter was. I explained as best I could, but she assured me that no one ever asked for anything on the rare occasions when her mistress had taken her out of the city to exercise. This sounded so odd that I asked if I could enter her mind to watch a memory of her last departure from the city. She agreed, and it took only a moment to discover that her mistress was the daughter of one of the city's more important traders.

I was appalled, but it was too late now to return the mare to her stable, and if I simply released her, she might come to harm. Then I would still have to find another horse, with papers, thereby losing all chance of reaching Halfmoon Bay by nightfall. I might even find myself locked inside the city. All things considered, there was nothing to do but go on boldly.

Once again, my fears proved groundless, for when it was our turn to go through the gate, the soldierguard looked at Rawen rather than me and advised gruffly that I had better be quick if I wanted to exercise my mistress's horse and return before the gates closed. Under other circumstances, I would have been alarmed that the soldierguard had recognized the mare, but this enabled us to leave without papers. The moment the horse was reported missing, though, the soldierguard would remember me, so I needed to put as much distance as possible between us and the city.

Once away from the gate, Rawen willingly broke into a canter. It was wonderful to ride again, and I was pleased to find that Rawen enjoyed the gallop as much as I did. Mindful of the need to find the null swiftly, I bade her gallop as long as she could comfortably do so, and as we progressed, I conveyed my recent adventures.

We alternated between a canter and a walk, but I had miscalculated the distance to Halfmoon Bay, and it was dusk before we saw the city in the distance. There was little point in entering after dark, so I told Rawen that we would camp near the city. She asked if I might ride her along the sand beside the water, for she liked the sound and scent of the waves. I agreed, and when we reached the sand, I bade her stop, and I dismounted and walked beside the mare. It was pleasant, and by the time we were close enough to the city to make camp, it was quite dark. But even as I removed Rawen's tack, the moon rose and transformed the sea into a sheet of undulating silver that I stopped to admire. The horse rolled in the sand with voluptuous delight, and then she galloped into the waves, rearing and splashing like a child at play.

After she emerged and shook herself vigorously, she devoured the oats and hay I set out for her while I ate cheese and bread. We both drank sparingly from the water bladder. I had no means of starting a fire, and as it grew cold, I began to worry about Rawen, for she had told me that she had never spent a night in the open. Removing my cloak, I would have thrown it over her, but she suggested that she lie and then I could sit beside her, and the cloak could cover us both.

Lying against her warm belly, I gazed out at the sea, which unrolled its waves like silken rugs threaded with silver. My thoughts turned inevitably to Gahltha, for I had often sat in this way with him, sharing warmth and friendship. Where was he now? I wondered. Back at Obernewtyn or in Sutrium? And what of Maruman?

"You are bound to these beasts?" Rawen asked curiously, for she had seen their images in my thoughts.

"We are friends," I sent. "But what of you/your friends?"

"An equine owned by funaga does not have friends," she told me mildly. I asked about her life and learned that she had been bought unbroken as a filly by an owner who had trained her with care and gentleness. After he died she had been bought as a gift for her present mistress. Despite being feckless, it seemed the girl had not been unkind to her horse, for she regarded Rawen as a possession that enhanced her own beauty and value.

I asked how the mare thought her mistress would react to her loss. Rawen said that it did not matter how her young mistress reacted, for her owner was the girl's father, and he would be furious. This disquieted me, for a furious and self-important trader might complain loudly enough that soldierguards would be sent to hunt the thief. Of course, they would search initially for a fair-haired, furtive-looking man, but it would not take long for the soldierguard at Morganna's main gate to give an accurate description of me. And persistent questioning of those who had entered the city might reveal that I had departed in the direction of Halfmoon Bay.

The only way to prevent their finding me would be to enter Halfmoon Bay without the mare. I explained my concern and asked Rawen if she felt able to make her way alone to the other side of the city. I told her that I did not expect to be inside the city for more than a few hours, and when I left, I would summon her. Rawen agreed to the plan, and I decided that we must leave her saddle and bridle. If she was spotted saddled and riderless, she would be pursued as a runaway. It was a pity I could not take the saddle with me to sell, but aside from being too heavy to carry, it was distinctive, and its description might be circulating with that of the mare. I would bury the saddle in the sand, I decided, but the bridle was small enough that I could take it with me into Halfmoon Bay and sell it. With the coin it fetched, I could buy a plainer bridle with which to lead Rawen, more food, a horse blanket, and a tinderbox.

I yawned and was about to close my eyes when I realized that I could send a general farseeking probe into at least part of the city because of the gaps in the wall. I sent out a coercive probe searching for recognizable mind signatures, just as I had done in Morganna. To my complete amazement, I immediately brushed against a mind I knew! I was so startled that I lost contact too soon to identify whose mind it had been, and try as I might, I could not locate it again. But I had not the slightest doubt that I had touched the mind of an Obernewtyn Misfit. Whoever it was must have either been on the verge of sleep or had moved behind a section of wall. The moment I entered the city, I would farseek again. The thought of being able to speak with a Misfit filled me with excitement, and it was some time before I could calm myself enough to sleep.

The night grew steadily colder, and I worried again about Rawen, but hearing my thoughts, the mare sent equably that she was content. Turning to look at her long face, silvered by moonlight, I saw her prick her ears at the sound of the waves breaking on the shore, and then she turned her head and sniffed the air blowing across the open plain. I was close enough to sense that her mind was truly untroubled, and I marveled yet again at the ability of beasts simply to be. Rawen was not wondering what would happen next or regretting the pampered life she had led in Morganna. She was simply *being*.

Envying her serenity, I knew that it was not in me to emulate it. I turned my eyes to the waves and found myself thinking of the null. Lark and Elkar had both told me that Ariel chose his nulls from among the intake of novice boys, so I had to suppose that he had deliberately chosen an older null specifically for this task. It made sense, but why a null at all? Why not simply someone who could be infected by the plague? Or had Ariel wanted someone with no personal desires or intentions to interfere with whatever he had been bidden to do?

There were no answers, and at last Rawen's warmth and the song of the waves lulled me to sleep. I woke not long after dawn, feeling deeply refreshed. Turning out the last of the oats, I left Rawen to her meager firstmeal while I set about digging a hole deep enough to accommodate the saddle. Once it was buried, I tied the ornate bridle under my shirt and ate an apple with pleasure, giving the other to the mare.

She crunched it up, then nuzzled me and bade me be careful before she cantered away along the beach. I watched her until the sunlit haze of sea spray swallowed her up, and then I rolled the empty saddlebag tightly, wrapped my cloak around it, and set off toward Halfmoon Bay.

◆ 2 ◆

"WHERE HAVE YOU come from?" the soldierguard asked the older man.

He was first in the short queue of people waiting to enter Halfmoon Bay at the gap gate nearest the water. Like the three before him, he had come from a grubber farm in the badlands, whose crops had mutated after a series of storms that had blown in from the Blacklands. I knew from conversations with Seely, who had lived most of her life on the west coast, that although the strip of land that ran along the Blacklands was slightly more fertile than most of the west coast, there was a high incidence of mutated crops and livestock. Anything abnormal was supposed to be destroyed, though in practice, life on these farms was harsh enough that many mutations were passed off as normal. When it could not be concealed, the grubbers had no choice but to burn their crop or livestock and abandon their farms to travel to the nearest city. Some never went back, but most tried to earn coin enough for new seed stock and untainted livestock before returning.

I had thought to be a grubber in search of work, but now I feared my tale would sound too similar, so I invented a sick grandfather in need of medicine. My story thus refined, I turned my attention to what I could see of Halfmoon Bay through the section gate, which was little more than a guarded opening between two sections of wall. Instead of the well-stocked stalls and the bustle of trade inside the gate at Morganna, the open area beyond the gap was narrow and dirty, and the buildings appeared to be on the verge of tumbling down. A group of ragged-looking men playing a card game on the back of a cart stopped occasionally to cast furtive glances toward the gate, and a swift probe told me that they were keeping watch for a traveler wealthy enough to follow and rob in the maze of narrow streets leading away from the gate. I was glad my clothes were simple and that I carried only an empty saddlebag and cloak. Even so, I wished that I had gone into the city a different way, for clearly this gate led to one of the city's poorer areas.

The older man was admitted, and as the soldierguard turned his attention to the two men before me, a group of soldierguards strolled up and lounged against the wall. I could not probe any of them because of their demon bands, but I needed no Talent to realize they must be drunk, for their eyes were glazed, and they laughed often and foolishly at nothing. I half expected the soldierguard on duty to reprimand them, but he merely cast them a frowning look before returning to his questions.

The two men claimed to be tailors from Port Oran come to buy special cloth from a weaver. The soldierguard admitted them and shifted his gaze to me. I offered him my story demurely, suddenly very aware of Rawen's bridle tied around my waist.

"*Medicine*, she calls it," crowed one of the drunken soldierguards. "That's a good one, Pyper."

"What skills do you offer?" asked the soldierguard, ignoring him. It was a question he had asked the others, and I had an answer prepared.

"I am hoping to cook in a tavern or maybe tend horses in

a public stable, for I am good with beasts," I said.

The soldierguard nodded, and just as it seemed he would bid me enter, the other soldierguard said, "She don't speak like any grubber I ever heard, Pyper."

I was dismayed to realize that he was right. I had not thought to affect the slow, almost singsong speech of the grubbers who had gone before me.

"My mother was city born," I said quickly.

"Did she come from Halfmoon Bay?" asked the soldierguard named Pyper.

"What is her name? Perhaps I knew her," called one of the drunken soldierguards with a leer.

I ought to have been afraid, but suddenly I was angry. I was seeking to save the lives of these men as well as the lives of my friends, and I had no time for their foolish hectoring and sly hints. I gave my mother's true name and said that she had come from Morganna. As I spoke, I reached out to beastspeak a thin, swaybacked horse standing placidly by the cart where the men were gaming. I identified myself as ElspethInnle and asked if she would rear up and create a diversion so I could slip into the city. She said that she would be beaten unless there was a good reason for her alarm, so I beastspoke a dog drowsing in a doorway. He agreed at once to help, and he even offered with a sparkle of mischief to froth at the mouth so the funaga would think he was rabid. Without waiting for me to agree, he sprang up and catapulted across the street, barking wildly.

The soldierguards swung around in surprise to see a snarling dog worrying an apparently terrified horse, and while everyone was thus distracted, I slipped through the gate and down the nearest lane. It was empty, and I sped along it and turned into another intersecting lane. There were people

470

here, so I slowed to a walk, listening for the sound of pursuit.

Continuing on, I noticed that the houses were less dilapidated than those about the gate, but they still had an unkempt, neglected look. Crossing a square, I spied a public well and stopped to drink. Only then, as I refilled my water bladder, did I remember my midnight encounter with the other Misfit mind. Incredulous that I could have forgotten, I sat on a stone bench beside the well, closed my eyes, and sent out a probe. I searched for some time, concentrating hard, but to no avail. My spirits plummeted, since the probe had most likely failed to locate because the person it sought had left the city.

I shook my head and told myself that the sooner I could get out of the city the better, for it had an unlucky feel about it. Setting off again, I found myself in a street where an open gutter ran down the middle, streaming with privy water and all manner of refuse; it was all I could do not to vomit. The stench was vile, yet people passed along the street or stood by it talking to neighbors, and children screamed or fought or played next to it, all of them apparently oblivious to the noxious mess running by their feet.

I left the street with relief, only to find myself in another just the same, save that the people here all wore rags, and several gave me looks of sullen resentment that made the hair on my neck prickle. I was dressed so plainly that I had given no thought to being robbed, but now it occurred to me that the poverty here was advanced enough to make me a worthy mark. As if summoned up by the thought, a big dull-faced man and a squint-eyed woman stepped out to block my path. Before I could even begin to shape a coercive probe, the dog I had farsought at the city's entrance came charging past me to snarl meaningfully at the pair.

"'Er's got a doggie," the big oaf said, beaming down.

"Shut yer neck, yer gollerin' sheep," hissed the woman, and dragged the big man back into the doorway from which they had emerged.

"Thank you, but I could have managed," I beastspoke the dog when we had passed out of sight of the pair.

"Of course you could, ElspethInnle, but it is an honor to aid you," he sent so amiably that some of my tension abated. I asked if he would lead me to the sea, and as we went on together, he shared, in the highest of good humor, what had happened at the gate. One of the soldierguards had tried to club him, but he had given the funaga-li a bite for his trouble, and instead of being whipped, the horse had been praised by her master for defending herself so bravely against the vicious mad dog. Best of all, he said that as far as he could smell, it was assumed that I had fled in terror, and no one had seemed to care if I had run in or out of the gate.

"Won't your human be angry?" I asked, for a description would be circulated of a rabid dog.

"I call no funaga master," he answered with cheerful contempt.

"A wild dog who lives in a city?"

"I am free, not wild," he said, adding that a city offered good pickings for a smart, free beast. Then he told me that his name was Fever.

"Fever?" I repeated aloud. He barked assent so pertly that I laughed and shook my head. Then I sobered and sent, "I am surprised to hear that there are good pickings here, for this funaga settlement seems poor to me."

"Pickings are not good for your kind," the dog agreed. "But there is plenty of good rubbish for a dog to eat, and water and lots of fat rats as well."

I shuddered, realizing that of course a dog's notion of a

good place to live would differ greatly from that of a human. We came to another street running with filth, and, sickened, I asked Fever if we might go some other way.

"This is the quickest and the safest way to the waves," he assured me, untroubled by the squalor.

I struggled on, batting flies away from my mouth and eyes with my free hand and wondering that this city had not sprouted its own plague. Thinking of plagues made me remember the frail teknoguilder Pavo, who had once told me that the Beforetimers had used sickness as a weapon. He had said that they harvested the seeds of sickness and preserved them, just as one would with fruit or maybe seed and grain, so that they could be planted long after and still germinate. Pavo would never have imagined that Ariel would unearth some of these dire seeds and try to unleash an ancient plague in the Land.

I wondered where the Beforetimers had discovered seeds of sickness in the first place. It was hard to imagine plague in the Beforetimes of my past dreams, where everything seemed so smooth and clean and shining. But maybe there had been places like Halfmoon Bay in the Beforetime, where the squalor and poverty had produced a crop of sickness for the taking. It was a strangely horrible thought.

A breath of fresh air blew into my face, redolent with the sweet, clean smell of the sea. Moments later, we came out onto a boardwalk. The dog turned to follow it, and I noticed a scattering of small fishing vessels anchored in the water ahead, but no greatship. On the shore, a large sea market thronged with traders and buyers despite the early hour, and Fever sent that he had a funaga friend who worked on the far side of the market. He offered me a mental picture of a big, powerful-looking man with springy black hair, a direct searching gaze, and a ready smile.

I was startled to hear Fever describe a human as a friend, for it was seldom that unTalents cared for beasts that they did not regard as their possessions. Perhaps this man could tell me whether the *Black Ship* had recently called at Halfmoon Bay. If I failed to learn what I needed to know before I reached the other side of the market, I decided I would find and speak to Fever's friend. I would buy provisions and a tinderbox, and with luck, I might even manage to sell Rawen's bridle, all as I sought information.

Pushing my way into the crowd, I was struck by the festive attire and jewels worn by many market-goers. Half of them looked as if they were going to a ball, which was strange, because under normal circumstances, the wealthy did not shop for themselves; they sent servants to do it for them. Yet here they were, shopping in a sea market and showing every sign of enjoying it.

"What is going on in this city?" I muttered under my breath.

Fever must have smelled my confusion, for he said, "It is not always like this."

Before I could ask what he meant, he spotted another dog that bristled and offered an immediate challenge. "My friend is on the other side of the market where the trees are," the dog sent, and abandoned me unashamedly to take up the other dog's challenge.

I edged and elbowed my way laboriously toward the end of the market, where two trees grew close together. I tried probing a couple of passersby to find out if the *Black Ship* had put in recently, but none were thinking about the ship. I did learn in my probing attempt that the city was preparing for its moon fair.

I was in the process of exchanging some more transformed copper coins to buy a tinderbox, a pack to carry it in, some food, and fodder for Rawen when I spotted Fever's friend. He looked exactly as Fever had shown him to me, save that his cheeks were smeared with soot. He was sitting at a stall set up between two trees, wearing a leather blacksmith's apron and stoking a small brazier. Not until I was right in front of the stall did I notice that he had one leg thrust out stiffly, showing a wooden knob instead of a foot.

"Do you want something mended?" he asked in a pleasant, rasping voice.

"Will you buy a driftwood bundle if I gather it?" I asked, saying the first thing that came into my mind, since I could hardly say that Fever had sent me.

"Driftwood is not the right sort of wood for my fire, lass," he told me. "It burns too swift and bright. Metalworking wants a fire that will burn very hot and show little flame. There is an art in the making of fire for metalwork."

"Where do you get wood for such a fire?" I asked.

The man gave me a speculative look that made the hair stand up on the back of my neck. "You are not from the west coast," he said softly.

"I was born in Rangorn," I said, letting myself sound slightly defiant. I could imagine people might not be too willing to admit they had come from the other part of the Land, but there must be many on the west coast who had not been born there.

"Don't be afraid," he told me. "I am not one of those who thinks every person born the wrong side of the Suggredoon ought to be reported to the Council as a spy. But for your own sake, I would not tell anyone else here where you hail from. You ought to get some bootblack or hoof polish and rub it over your skin to darken it a bit. It is your pallor that gave you away as much as your accent."

"Thank you," I said. I hesitated and then forced myself to smile a little. "To tell the truth, I am more afraid of Herders than soldierguards."

"There are stories enough about Herder doings to freeze the blood of any maid or man," the metalworker said soberly.

"I came here to buy medicine for my grandfather," I said. "I have a bridle to sell, but it is a family treasure, and I fear that I will be charged as a thief if I go to the wrong buyer."

"A wise apprehension," the man said gravely. "I can recommend a good buyer, but he will not do if the bridle is stolen."

I felt my cheeks redden, and he continued expressionlessly. "There is also a man in a closed tent farther along the boardwalk. He will cheat you but less than other such men, and he is discreet."

I entered his mind to see that he took me for a woman who had fled an abusive bondmate or possibly a brother or father, because he had noticed faint bruises on my face and arms. He thought the stolen bridle belonged to whoever had hurt me and that I had courage to have stolen it and fled. Far from despising me for the theft, he was trying to think of a way to help me without frightening me. He had thought of his sister, who sent him off each morning with a cheerful smile and "Have a pleasant day, Rolf." He grimaced at the thought of someone mistreating her. As always when I had steeled myself to face darkness and hatred, the unexpected sweetness of compassion undid me. I withdrew from his mind, determined not to enter again, for he was no foe.

He said, very casually, "As you might have noticed, I am crippled. If you will take a coin and buy me a bannock or two for my firstmeal from that stall yonder, there will be enough remaining for you to buy one for yourself. You can leave whatever it is that you are carrying so I know you will re-turn." I did not have to read his mind to know that he had added this last sentence because he felt I would fear his in-tentions if he seemed too generous. I laid down the cloak and saddlebag and took his coin, wondering what this man's spirit would look like, were I to see it through spirit eyes.

I made for the stand he had pointed out where the smells made my mouth water, though the woman behind it had a sour expression. I ordered the bannocks and watched her take them hot from the little oven on wheels beside her. She wrapped them and named a steep price. I told her the man at the metalworking stall had given me the coin and that I would have to go back and tell him it was too little. I was backing away when I noticed a wry smile twisting her thin lips. She glanced toward the metalworker and shook her head.

"Aro sent you, then. And I suppose you're to keep one of my bannocks for yourself, for fetching them for a crippled man, even though I always take them over to him?" Dry amusement tinged her voice.

"I . . . He is very kind," I stammered, more taken aback by her transformation than her words. I also found myself con-fused by her calling the man Aro. His sister had called him Rolf.

"He is that, the dear fool. There is not a stallholder in this wretched place for whom Aro has not done some kindness. Indeed, if gratitude were coin, he would be a rich man. Well, have the bannocks, then, and give me the coin." Her voice had gone back to being cool, but there was now humor in her eyes.

"You are kind, too, I think," I said on impulse. She had not the metalworker's natural generosity of spirit, but his sweet-ness had seeped into her.

"Get along," she scoffed.

Strangely heartened, I returned to the metalworker, who bade me sit awhile if I liked. As he ate his bannock with dirty hands and evident relish, I thanked him between bites, and then I told him the same tale I had told the soldierguards at the gate. I asked casually if he had noticed the *Black Ship* pass by recently.

"It anchored nightfall the day before yesterday," Rolf said.

I stared at him, frozen midbite. I choked down the mouthful and stammered, "Y-you mean Salamander the slaver brought his ship here?"

He gave me a warning look. "In Halfmoon Bay, we call him the Raider. Both him and his ship. But you need not fear his collectors, for this time he did not empty out the cells, and he stayed only long enough to deliver Councilman Kana's spiceweed. It seems he had not the time to empty out the cells, but he did hand out coin enough to pay for all who are in them, else the soldierguards might not have let him go."

"He pays the *soldierguards* for the prisoners he takes?" I asked.

"Let us say he pays bonuses to show he is pleased with the number of prisoners available when he comes to fill his hold. The bonuses have made him a favorite with the soldierguards."

Trying not to sound too anxious, though my heart hammered so loudly I thought he must hear it, I asked if he had seen the *Black Ship* anchor with his own eyes.

"I was finishing off a late job," he said. He stopped abruptly and glanced about. Then he said, "Listen, I have an idea. You need coin for medicine, and there is a better way to earn it than gathering driftwood. A laundry down the way belongs to a friend of mine named Metta. She might have

478

something for you if one of her regular women is off sick. Or maybe she will get you delivering. She has a couple boys, but they are shiftless. Tell her the metalworker from the market sent you. Even if she has no work, she will know where else you might try. And she will also know a good herbalist who can prepare something more useful to your grandfather than patent medicines, and at a reasonable cost. You might as well find out how much you have to earn."

Despite my need to know more about the *Black Ship*, I was struck by his generosity. Rather than probe him, I asked, "Why would you help me? You do not know me at all save that you judge me a thief."

"I do not judge you at all, lass," he said gently. "The world is full of people all too ready to perform that service for everyone and everything they meet. Maybe this leg makes me feel the suffering of others and wish to alleviate it, if I can. Or maybe it is that I see no evil in your face; therefore, if I can, and if you will allow it, I would help you."

I stood up and reclaimed the cloak-wrapped saddlebag before looking into the metalworker's face. "It is strange and wonderful to hear you speak so in this city, which *my* instinct tells me is full of cruelty and misery," I said softly. "I thank you sincerely for your kindness, and I regret that I have lied to you. In truth, I am not seeking medicine or coin. I need information."

His expression shuttered, and I held up a hand. "I am not a Council spy. I just want to know if you saw a young man come off the *Black Ship*. He is about my age with long blond hair and a very handsome, striking face. He would not have worn Herder attire, and he was not shipfolk."

"Who are you?" the metalworker asked.

"No one of any importance," I said. "But I came here for

something more important than you can possibly imagine, not only for me and my friends, but for all who dwell on this coast. Please, the fair man. Did you see him?"

After a long searching look, Aro nodded slowly. "Happens I did see a blond man come from one of the ship boats. I did not mark his face, but my friend who sold you the bannocks said that he looked handsome. Una had packed up and was waiting for me, for we generally walk home together. She saw them first."

"Them?" I interrupted, unable to hide my growing excitement.

"The fair man and the Herder," the metalworker said.

"A *Herder*!" I echoed. I understood that disguising his plague carrier as a Herder would be a stroke of brilliance on Ariel's part. No one would dare harm or harass a priest, and he would be able to go anywhere he liked without being questioned. Unfortunately, it also probably meant that he was in the local cloister.

"Where is the Halfmoon Bay cloister?" I asked.

"Some distance outside the city wall, near the main road," the metalworker said. "But I doubt the Herder I saw could have walked so far."

"Why? Was he injured or . . . ill?"

The metalworker shook his head. "Neither, by my eyes. But there was something wrong with him. There was a look in his eyes of . . . I can only call it confusion. He would walk a few steps and then stop, almost as if he had forgotten what he was doing. In each case, his companion led him on until he walked of his own accord again."

"Do you have any idea where they went, if not to the cloister?" I was almost stammering with excitement.

He shook his head. "I am sorry."

"I must find out where he is." I stopped abruptly, for something the metalworker had said struck me. He had spoken of *seeing* the Herder's expression. That meant he had seen the null's face!

It was too good a chance to waste. I formed a probe and entered his mind again. This time I did not confine myself to the upper levels of thought, which run just under speech and merely echo it. I fine-honed my probe and plunged deeper, through the strange mists and half-dreams and phantasms of the subconscious layer of his mind, down into the great body of memory and dream. To enter that level in another person's mind was dangerous, because the compulsion of other people's dreams and memories was even more powerful than one's own. Fortunately, I had long mastered the means of shielding myself from the pull of such dreams and memories. I sought a particular memory, and as I had hoped, our conversation had stirred it to the surface, so it was very bright and easy to find.

I entered the memory, being careful to retain a thin, coercive shield. I saw the market where I stood, but now it was night and most of the stalls were closed or closing, save an ale shop on the other side of the square and a man hawking fried bits of fish to the other stallholders. The enticing odor was making the metalworker think a bit of fish would please his sister with whom he lived. He imagined her delighted expression—"Rolf! My favorite!"—when he arrived home. The bannock seller was packing up as she waited for her last rolls to bake, and Rolf was finishing a special order for a seaman who had paid handsomely for the work to be completed before he went home. The fellow would come soon, and he wanted to be ready.

Una approached Rolf's stand with a swagger and threw a

package on the bench, saying brusquely that he might just as well have them since she had overbaked for the morrow. He thanked her, taking her offering for the generosity that it was.

"You should not work so late, Aro," she scolded.

"I promised," Rolf told her, continuing to work. "Wait a little, and I will walk you home."

She shook her head in irritation. "I am not afraid to walk alone. But someday your determination to keep your word will see you dead."

"Unfortunately, keeping your word is the point of giving it," Rolf said, with a smile to soften the sting.

"Well, let us hope your fine and hasty seaman keeps his word and pays you well for this late work," Una retorted tartly.

Rolf decided not to tell her that he had already been paid. Una liked pretending to be tough and cynical, and he liked playing the naive fool for her.

He finished the last buckle and was polishing it when Una bade him look, in a low voice that caught his attention. She was gazing out to sea where a ship boat was rowing in from the *Raider*. Rolf felt the same disquiet he always did at the sight of the *Black Ship*, for he could not help but think about its wretched cargo. Still, a ship boat rowing ashore from the *Raider* this early was odd. Usually no one came from the ship before midnight, for the slaves were brought out of the cells early in the morning to avoid marching through a crowded market. Not that anyone was like to protest, even if babies and older women were being taken, but the Raider's ways were always secretive. The man himself never set foot ashore save to look over the penned slaves, and once he had approved, he immediately reboarded his ship boat and returned to the *Raider*, leaving his men to complete the transaction.

As he and Una watched, a burlyman caught the tether ropes thrown up from the ship boat, and in a moment, two men climbed onto the nearest jetty. One of the new arrivals wore Herder robes, which was nothing unusual. The *Raider* and its smaller sister ships often brought Herders or carried them away while collecting shipments of slaves or bringing spiceweed for Councilman Kana. But this Herder was not alone, and the man with him, with his long fair hair and fine white cloak, was no Herder. As the pair made their way along the pier, Rolf noticed that the fair-haired man was half-supporting the Herder, who limped and kept halting. Rolf began to industriously polish his buckles, and Una pretended to be utterly absorbed in the activity when the two neared Rolf's stall. It was unwise to take too obvious an interest in the Raider's affairs. But right opposite the stand, the Herder tripped. His hood slipped back, and his face was momentarily illuminated in the brazier fire's ruddy glow.

For an instant, Rolf had looked into the Herder's dark blue eyes, and it was as if someone had punched him hard in the gut. The Herder's eyes had been utterly devoid of intelligence or thought, yet his expression had been one of unimaginable horror. It was, Rolf thought, as if he had seen something so indescribably awful that reason had fled, leaving only the frozen shell of horror etched into his face. He had seen such expressions before on those unfortunates taken from the cloister to Herder Isle, but he had never seen a Herder look like this.

Inside his memory, I was reeling with my own shock, for the gaunt and haunted face of the Herder *was that of the Misfit coercer Domick.*

483

✦ 3 ✦

"WHAT IS IT, lass?" Rolf asked, looking concerned.

I blinked into the sunlit day, feeling as if I had staggered from a dark tunnel. I tried to make some answer, but the discovery that *Domick*, the coercer who had vanished under mysterious circumstances the previous year at the same time the Herders had taken Rushton prisoner, was the person Ariel had infected with a deadly plague—the person I had come to the west coast to find—was beyond any imagining. I understood now that it must have been Domick's mind I had touched the previous night, and I thought with anguish of the coercer, whom I had known for as long as I had known Rushton. Brydda had always claimed it odd that both men vanished at the same time, and I realized now that they had been taken together. One of the Threes had said that Ariel had had plans for Rushton, but he must have been mistaken. It had been Domick around whom his plans had been formed, unless he had originally thought to use Rushton as his plague null. Perhaps that explained the state of Rushton's mind when we found him. Ariel might have tried to use him and failed, so he had taken Domick to Norseland, leaving Rushton in the Sutrium cloister cells, where we had found him.

"Lass, are you well?" Rolf asked, beginning to rise awkwardly from his stool.

I nodded, realizing I must have been standing there for

long moments, pale and gaping. I shook my head with a sobbing laugh. "I must seem mad to you. But it is only that I have . . . I have had a shock."

"Sit down again and catch your breath. You look ill, truly," Rolf said in concern.

"I am not ill," I said, and then gave a wild bleak laugh at the knowledge that soon everyone on the west coast, including this man, would be ill if I could not find Domick.

And what to do when I did find him? I wondered. But that question was too dark to contemplate.

"You must not sit here laughing and weeping," Rolf said sternly. "You will call too much attention to yourself, and someone will trot away to tell the soldierguards there is a wild creature at the market that wants locking up. The cells may be full, but the Councilmen won't want any trouble on the eve of the festival."

That I might bring suspicion on him, after his kindness, enabled me to master my emotions. "I do not want to endanger you, Rolf," I said hoarsely.

He frowned. "How is it that you know my name?"

"The . . . the bannock seller spoke it," I began, but he shook his head.

"Una calls me Aro, which is short for Arolfic Smithson. Only my sister calls me Rolf." His voice was steady, and his eyes looked into mine.

I drew a long breath, forcing myself to be calm. "How I know your name is part of a much greater and more complex story, and I have not time enough to tell it to you. Yet I hope you believe that I would tell it if I could, for I trust you. Why I trust you is also part of that larger story. Let me say only that you offered help, and I accept it. I need to find the Herder who came ashore with the fair man, as swiftly as can be, and get him out of the city. It is more important than you can possibly imagine."

Rolf held my gaze for a long moment, knitting his brows slightly. Then he said, "The Herder is known to you?"

"He . . . was once a friend." I choked out the words. "He is only disguised as a Herder but is not really one. But the Herders have done something to him that could bring deadly harm to all who live here on the west coast. I have come to prevent that."

He nodded slowly. "You are a rebel, then. I guessed as much. Well, I may be a fool, but as you say, I offered help, and help I will give. I don't know where those two went, save that they went north from the market, but that is not the way to the cloister. I have a friend who can help you locate them. Go to Metta at the laundry and tell her I said to introduce you to Erit. Say my name to him—Aro, not Rolf—and tell him I want him to help you. Tell him what you have told me." He gave me clear directions to the laundry, but when I moved to depart immediately, he caught my wrist in a gentle but powerful grip and added that if I needed further help or a refuge, Erit would show me where he lived with his sister by the fifth gate.

"I can promise you a safe, clean bed and a good meal, and then after, I will help you and your friend leave the city."

"I thank you," I said, unable to tell him that Domick was infected with the plague and was, therefore, the last person he would ever want as a guest.

I hurried in the direction he had indicated, weaving and elbowing my way through the increasing press of laughing, chattering people. I reached the street Rolf had described, to find it deserted, and I could not resist stopping to send out a probe shaped specifically to Domick's mind. I did not expect

486

it to locate, so I was not disappointed when I failed.

The laundry was thick with steam and bustling with activity. Amid the smells of soap and boiling washing, I approached a young girl up to her elbows in suds and asked for Rolf's friend Metta. She pointed to a merry-faced woman stirring a steaming boiler of white clothes. She was middle-aged, with enormous splendid breasts, a mass of treacle-brown curls, and the mischievous, flirtatious eyes of a much younger woman. Seeing me approach, she asked courteously what my need was. I spoke the words Rolf had bidden me say, and her smile faded, but into concern rather than animosity.

"I hope Aro knows what he is doing," she sighed, wiping the suds from her hands and arms and drying them. Undoing her apron, she bade a young girl to stir the bleach until she returned. Then she led me out the back door into a crooked lane hung with washing. A little way along it, she stopped and pointed to a narrow passage between two buildings, saying I would find Erit there.

I peered into the weed-clogged opening, which seemed no more than a gap between buildings, wondering if she was joking. But when I glanced back, she only nodded encouragement at me, so there was nothing but to push into the opening. Aside from the first part, the narrow passage had been cleared. It led me to a large angular space at the back of several buildings mounded high with weed-embroidered rubble, but beyond the rubble was a small clearing where a rough lean-to had been cobbled together. Some small, very dirty boys were squatting near the entrance playing a dice game. I hesitated, then went over to them to ask if they knew a man called Erit.

"Who wants to know?" asked the smallest of the boys truculently, a filthy urchin with a gap between his front teeth that made him whistle comically as he spoke.

"Ro . . . Aro sent me to speak with him. I am to collect a favor."

"Aro, eh?" said the whistling boy, looking owlishly around at his ragged companions. Then he looked back at me, his expression suddenly serious. "All right, I'm Erit. You can talk in front of them. What do you need?"

I stared at him, touching his mind to confirm that he was indeed Erit. Then, suppressing my misgivings, I told him that I needed to find a man in Herder robes who had been brought ashore from the *Raider* two nights past by a handsome, fair-haired young man. I described what Rolf had seen.

"Sounds as if the Herder was sick," Erit said. "No doubt his friend took him to the healing house."

"He wouldn't have taken him to the healing house," said one of the other urchins. "Herders have their own healers in the cloister."

"True," Erit said. "On the other hand, something tells me the man she wants is no true Herder, else she would have named him so rather than saying he wore Herder robes." He was looking at me as he spoke, a question in his eyes.

"He is not a Herder," I agreed, my confidence in the urchin rising at this evidence of his sharp wits. "His name is Domick, and he is . . . a friend."

Erit nodded in a slightly absentminded way. "All right. Bally, you go nose about the city healing house. Gof, you and Grim go out to the main gate and see if this pair went out toward the cloister. Might as well make sure they are not in the obvious places first."

I interrupted his instructions to say that I was almost certain that the fair man would have left the city, having taken Domick somewhere safe but innocuous. Erit asked for a description of Domick, and I gave it as best I could from what I had seen in Rolf's mind, adding, "Do not approach him. The Herders may have tampered with his mind, and there is no telling what he will do. Just locate him and come and tell me where he is."

Erit nodded and turned back to his companions to give further directions as to where they might search. At last he gave a decisive nod, and all the boys departed purposefully save for their diminutive leader. Erit turned back to me, an assessing look on his face. "If this man is in Halfmoon Bay, we will find him, but this better not set the Raider upon us or Aro."

"It will not," I promised.

"If Aro trusts you, well and good," Erit finally said. "What will you do once you find your friend?"

I swallowed sorrow. "I must get him out of Halfmoon Bay as soon as possible. I have a horse waiting outside the city, which reminds me I will need some water and fodder for her."

He nodded. "Time enough for that later. Wait here now. There's food and water in the hut. Help yourself."

He was gone in a flash, and after a brief surge of frustration at having to wait while others acted, I relaxed, guessing that my presence would only have hindered the urchins if I had insisted on accompanying them. I ate some of the apples and bread, and I tried again to farseek Domick. When I failed, I paced for a time before spreading out my cloak. It was most sensible to rest in readiness for whatever the night would demand.

Later that day, Erit explained that the famous and ancient masked moon fair lasted three days instead of the customary single day. It had been held in Halfmoon Bay for more than a hundred years and still drew visitors from all along the coast. The fair's fame was not just that it lasted three days and involved an elaborate game of masks, but the Councilman of Halfmoon Bay always presented a real solid gold crown to the wearer of the finest mask, who would become the fair's king or queen.

Erit also told me that although the merriment was now focused on the wealthy area and the better markets, when the fair proper began at midday the next day, the town's entire population would be involved, for anyone seen unmasked thereafter during the fair must serve his or her finder as a slave for a day or forfeit a gold coin. Erit added wickedly that the fair was a great occasion for pickpocketing and gulling fools.

I was unable to smile. His explanation told me exactly why Ariel had brought Domick to Halfmoon Bay. He had known of the masked moon fair, known that people would come from all over the west coast. He had chosen this city and this occasion as the swiftest means of spreading the plague. Domick would probably become infectious on the morrow or the day after, and because the people he infected would not become contagious for some days, they would have time to return to their own cities. Once the deaths began, it would be too late to close any city, for there would be plague carriers in all of them.

In order to allow a margin for safety, I had to get Domick out of the town before midday the next day.

Erit and his friends had not found it difficult to track the coercer. Within an hour of leaving me, the leader of the little band of urchins had returned to say that a strikingly handsome blond man and a sickly-looking Herder had gone to a

Faction house at the edge of a prosperous district not five streets from the sea market. Erit's informant was a maid who worked in a private house opposite the Faction house; the same girl had seen Ariel leave, alone, several hours later.

Erit explained to me that the house was used primarily by priests awaiting a ship to Herder Isle and was operated and guarded by Hedra, those warrior priests whose numbers had grown so alarmingly in recent times. It was strange to think that although we had defeated the Hedra on Herder Island, I must face them here again. Ironically, they were in as much danger as the poorest beggar, for the plague Domick carried would take all who dwelled in the west, no mother their allegiance.

Erit began to describe the interior of the Faction house, saying that there were several sleeping chambers on the ground floor, as well as subterranean cells for prisoners destined for Herder Isle, but I was sure Ariel would not have allowed Domick to be locked up as a prisoner. He needed to be free to roam if he was to spread the plague, and Ariel would have wanted to ensure it without exciting too much curiosity in the Hedra guardians, given that they were also to die. Most likely, Ariel would have suggested that Domick had a specific mission to perform at the behest of the One, which required him to move about freely.

Erit took me to a lane that ended in the street of the Faction house. He pointed out a soldierguard barracks at the end of the street. Its entrance faced away from the Faction house street, but the soldierguards who marched up and down the street in guard duty came every few minutes to the corner, and they glanced at the Faction house regularly enough to see anyone approaching or leaving it. They would also hear any commotion and come to investigate.

"The best thing is to wait till your friend comes out and then speak to him," Erit suggested quietly.

"He may not come out alone, and I need to see him as soon as possible," I said. I tried to farseek the coercer, but not unexpectedly, the walls were tainted. A message-taker entered the street. As we watched, he went to the Faction house and rapped on the door. A Hedra answered and, after looking at some paper proffered by the message-taker, ushered the man inside. When he came out a few minutes later and marched away, I probed him. Unfortunately, he had only stood in the foyer, so I was unable to get any sense of where Domick might be.

"Are you thinking of sending him a message to draw him out?" Erit asked, misunderstanding my interest in the message-taker.

"I do not know if Domick will be capable of responding to a message," I told him. "The message ought to go to the person in charge of the Faction house. And who would it be from?"

"The fair-haired man who brought him here?" Erit suggested. Then he asked if Domick would come willingly with me, once outside the Faction house. I had to admit that I did not know.

"Are you saying that you will have to capture, bind, and gag him?"

"I fear it will come to that," I admitted.

A group of people emerged, laughing and chattering, from one of the fine houses between the accommodation and the barracks at the end of the street. Erit watched silently until they had gone out of sight, then he said that his gang would keep watch on the Faction house to learn its routines and gather information about its denizens and about Domick. "It will be best if you return to the hut to wait," he concluded.

I shook my head, saying I would help keep watch, but Erit said it was not a good idea, for although the moon fair would not begin officially until midday the next day, there was a long tradition of boisterous prefair celebrations that would continue deep into the night. During this time, almost every soldierguard in the city would be patrolling the streets. Erit shot me a glance as he added that one of his boys had heard a rumor of a young woman fitting my description who had stolen a valuable horse in Morganna and had been seen riding toward Halfmoon Bay.

"By evening, every soldierguard in the city will be looking for the thief, for a reward has been offered," Erit said. "It would be a great pity if you were taken for her."

"True," I conceded. "All right, what if I leave the city for the day and return after dark? I need to tend to my horse anyway. If you can get me some suitable clothes, I could pretend to be a boy."

Erit approved the plan, suggesting that, since I had some hours to spare, I might ride Rawen to Stonehill, where there was good grazing and a well besides. I had never heard of Stonehill, but Erit said it was a one-hour ride along the coast, and I could not miss it. Since I was leaving the city, he also suggested that I remain outside until the tide was low enough for me to enter by the sea gate, for it had no permanent guard. It would also be well after midnight, so there would be little danger of encountering fair revelers.

I fretted at this, for it left mere hours before the start of the fair, but Erit pointed out that the safest time to rescue my friend would be early the following morning when the fair revelers, and most of the soldierguards, would be snoring abed. In the meantime, he would speak to Aro and see if he could suggest any plan to wrest Domick from the Herders' clutches without bringing them down on our heads.

Thus it was that I left the city attired as a lad with a small bag of food for myself and directions to Rolf's house, just in case Erit was unable to meet me at the sea gate as we had arranged. I left by a section gap opposite the one I had entered, passing a great chattering crowd of people lined up and waiting to enter the city. By their clothes and fine horses, most were festival-goers, like those I had seen at the sea market. The rest were the usual sort of sellers, wheeling their carts or shouldering great bundles of goods, all waiting to sell their wares in Halfmoon Bay.

As Erit had promised, the soldierguards were intent on incoming visitors and traders, so my exit from the city among a group of lads set on collecting shellfish to hawk was swift and smooth.

I trailed after them to the water's edge, noting many other poorly dressed people fishing or picking through the sand. I noted, too, that the tide was washing so high against the wall's end section that it was hard to imagine it would later withdraw enough to open up the space between the wall and the waves, known as a sea gate.

I set off slowly along the water's edge, shying the occasional pebble into the waves as if I were a lad. The heavy boots that Erit had given me to match my boy's attire were several sizes too big and already rubbing my heels.

"Was there anyone ever with worse luck when it comes to shoes?" I muttered, exasperated that I had forgotten the sandals I had bought in Morganna. Then I thought with a pang of the beautiful handmade and dyed slippers that Maryon had gifted me, sitting at the foot of my bed in my turret room in Obernewtyn, and indulged myself in a moment of passionate longing for that small, well-loved room and its com-

494

forts. Then I thought of Rushton and knew that Obernewtyn could never again be the beloved refuge it had once been for me. However should I tell him that he had been on Herder Isle at Ariel's mercy? No wonder he did not wish to remember what had happened to him.

This dark thought distracted me for a time, but my heels hurt dreadfully. Finally, I glanced back to be sure that I was too far for anyone to see me clearly and removed the offending boots. Their unpleasant odor made me wonder exactly where Erit had got them. Tying the laces, I rose, slung the boots across my shoulder, and walked into the waves to cool my feet.

Standing in the cold shallow froth, I turned inland to watch some young stable hands exercising their charges with an enthusiasm that might have alarmed the horse's owners. Clearly I could not summon Rawen until they had retreated inside the city walls, for a lone and unbridled horse would certainly be pursued, and these lads might have heard the rumor of a horse thief from Morganna. I sent out a probe to locate the mare and found her some distance inland on the other side of the main road. I asked her to meet me after the sun set, explaining that I was walking along the coast away from the city toward a place with both grazing and water. I apologized for having no other directions, but Rawen said if there was fresh water, she would scent it when she was closer.

Bidding her be careful not to be seen, for her mistress had offered a reward for her return, I withdrew and set a swifter pace, wondering if Stonehill would be high enough to gain any farseeking advantage. For some reason that even Garth could not yet explain, it was easier to farseek farther when higher than the person whose mind you wished to reach. The greater the height, the farther the reach. Of course, Stonehill was probably not high at all, for what heights had west coasters to compare it with? The so-called mountains upon whose feet Murmroth stood were really only the tail end of a string of peaks running away from a great range of Blackland mountains. Still, it was worth trying to farseek the Misfits at the Beforetime ruins, for now that I knew the null was Domick, I was more anxious than ever to have Jak's advice on how Domick might be treated.

It was close to dusk before I saw what I first took to be a mass of smoke some way down the beach but which soon revealed itself as a great tower of rocks. Realizing this must be Stonehill, it was not until I was closer that I could see that it was not a mound of stones but a single massive tor, which reminded me of the stone pinnacles where the Agyllians dwelt in the highest mountains. Garth had once said that such pillars were actually the insides of ancient mountains and that these rocks had burst up from the fires at the heart of the world and cooled to such hardness that they had remained when the earth surrounding them had worn away. This hill of stone was higher than the wall about the Herder Compound on Herder Isle and looked to have the surface area of Obernewtyn's farms, but how would one scale such a sheer monolith?

The sun set just as I reached the foot of the immense tor, and I stopped to farseek Rawen. She told me apologetically that she had been delayed trying to cross the road unseen but that she was even now galloping toward me. I sent her a mind picture of Stonehill, and it was not an hour before I heard the sound of hooves coming up behind me. Rawen pranced to a halt, her mind anticipating the heady and unaccustomed pleasures of the fresh grass she had scented atop the tor. There was a hectic excitement in her mind that had been absent when I had first entered it, and it occurred to me that her easy acceptance of captivity and the saddle, and her readiness to do the bidding of others, might have ended now that she had tasted freedom. Nevertheless, she insisted I mount her for the ride up to Stonehill, saying that she had scented a way up but that it was very steep at the outset.

The place she brought us to was so sharp an incline that I doubted any horse would be capable of scaling it. Rawen assured me so confidently that she could do it that I mounted up, telling myself that Erit would not have suggested I come to Stonehill unless it was possible to climb it.

Rawen cantered back some distance from the hill, explaining that she needed a run-up to gain speed enough for the first part of the climb. My heart leapt into my mouth as she turned and galloped full pelt at the dark bulk of the hill, for although she radiated confidence, at that speed, bones would be broken—hers and mine—if we fell. But Rawen did not falter, despite the steep incline. She leapt like a mountain goat from jutting stone to jutting stone, her sure-footedness surpassing anything I had ever seen. After a short terrifying period in which I did little more than close my eyes and cling to the mare's back, the way flattened slightly, and Rawen's speed decreased. I opened my eyes and saw that we had reached a narrow switchback ledge that soon widened to a trail. I did not dare look down, but gradually I relaxed and began to feel the beauty of the sea-scented night.

At length, Rawen stopped, saying she needed to rest. Dismounting carefully, I looked up and noticed that the hill flattened out only a little higher up. Refusing Rawen's offer to carry me again, I bade her go on at her own pace. I would climb up directly and meet her at the top. She obeyed and was soon lost to view.

At first the way was steep and difficult, and I wondered if I had made a mistake in not staying with Rawen, but in a short while, the slope flattened. When I stopped to catch my breath, I decided to try farseeking the Beforetime ruins. Some impulse made me shape a probe to Merret's mind as I sent it in the direction of the ruins. To my surprise, it veered away toward the coast and located. I was immediately conscious of Merret's amazed disbelief.

"Elspeth?!" The strength of the coercer's clumsy but powerful farseeking probe made me clutch my head in pain.

"Ouch! Of course it is me," I sent sharply.

"Sorry!" she sent just as loudly, then I felt her make an effort to restrain her mind—never easy for coercers. "Sorry," she said again. "I was just so . . . But where are you?"

"I am on the west coast," I sent. "I came by sea, and I am just outside Halfmoon Bay on the Aborium side. I was trying to throw my mind to you in the ruins and the probe veered sideways."

"I am on my way to Aborium," Merret sent, her mindvoice again growing strident with excitement. "But what do you mean you came by sea? How many of you are here? How many ships?"

"There are no ships," I told her. "You know, of course, that the rebellion was won on the other side of the river?"

"We know a good deal more than that because of Dell's foretellings, though not all is clear. Is it true that Rushton was found in the Sutrium cloister cell and is once again Master of Obernewtyn?"

"It is, but let me give you some memories. It will be quicker than trying to explain; then we will talk."

Merret made her mind passive, and I evoked a series of memories that covered the main events since I had left

498

Obernewtyn. I concluded with a vision of the One's revelations about Ariel's plague null.

Merret's anger swelled so strongly that it almost dislodged me. "I am sorry, Elspeth," she sent. "But why would even Ariel do such a foul thing?"

"I do not know," I said. "But that is not the worst of it." I showed her the memory I had taken from Rolf's mind, of Domick passing through the sea market with Ariel.

Merret's mind boiled with emotions, but she swiftly mastered herself to say, "So it is Domick who carries this plague, and he is in Halfmoon Bay. . . . Ye gods! The masked moon fair! Half the coast is headed there!"

"I am sure Ariel realized that," I told her bleakly. "But don't worry; I do not think that Domick is contagious yet. Ariel would not have wanted to risk the sickness incapacitating his carrier before the moon fair begins. I think he probably infected him in Halfmoon Bay. The girl who saw them enter the Faction house together said he was there for several hours."

"Then we are all doomed anyway," Merret sent.

"No," I said. "If you gather the others and go to the Beforetime ruins and remain there, you will be safe even if the plague does break out, so long as you allow no one to join you. It will be less than a moon before it will be over, because eventually a plague that kills everyone will kill all carriers. If you act quickly, you will have time enough to warn the rebels. But you need to tell them that unless they can convince or force the Councilmen to close their cities immediately, they had better ride out with supplies and set up desert camps away from everyone until it is over."

"You are going to stay to find Domick?" Merret guessed.

"I know where he is," I sent. "The man whose mind I

showed you is helping me. He has a friend who has located Domick in a Faction house not far from the piers. I do not know whether he is a prisoner or a guest, but they promised to help me reach him. They say it will be best to act in the very early morning, for half the population will be abed, sleeping off tonight's indulgences."

"The city is a cesspit, because Councilman Kana is greedy and unscrupulous and will stoop to anything to line his pockets," said Merret in distaste.

"It does not matter," I said. "It is my intention that by midday tomorrow, with their help, I will be well away from Halfmoon Bay with Domick."

"This Erit is a child," Merret protested, for she had seen him in my mind.

"And what were we when we took over Obernewtyn?" I snapped. "Erit has already proven himself by finding out where Domick is staying."

"He and this metalworker know everything?"

"So far they know almost nothing. They think I am a rebel trying to rescue another rebel who has some sort of weapon. But tonight I will tell them that I am a Misfit, and I will tell them about the plague that Domick carries."

"You trust them." A statement rather than a question.

"Without their help, I would still be seeking Domick, for his mind is closed to me."

"Even so, I will ride to Halfmoon Bay. I can be there by tomorrow morning," Merret sent decisively.

"No," I said. "I need you to warn the others and the rebels."

"I can do both," Merret replied. "I am riding to Aborium to meet Gwynedd and some of the newer rebel leaders. All the original rebel leaders were killed in the Night of Blood, såve Serba, Tardis, and Yavok. Then Yavok was murdered, Tardis died not a month after, and Gwynedd became the leader of what remains of the rebel network."

I did not bother to explain that I knew about Gwynedd saying only, "It is extremely fortunate that you are about to meet Gwynedd."

"Not truly," Merret responded. "We have been meeting once every sevenday this last twomonth."

"Then we are fortunate that this is the day. Tell Gwynedd that Dardelan would have come to their aid sooner, but all the ships were burned during the rebellion, and when the rebels built more, they, too, were destroyed, probably by Malik's men."

"I do not think Gwynedd will be much surprised by Malik's new treachery. No more am I. But though he will be interested to hear of what has been happening on Herder Isle, I think he and the other rebels will be more concerned about what you intend to do with Domick once you have him."

"I will ride with him out onto the plain on the other side of the main road where there is no danger of anyone running into me by chance. Then I will make camp and care for him."

"But, Elspeth, if you are with him when the plague becomes contagious . . ." Merret began.

"Someone must be. Why should it not be me?" I said tersely. I knew that I could not avoid the heroic light that would be cast on my actions, but I was probably the only one who would survive the plague because of what the Agyllions had taught my body. I went on, "Tell Jak everything and see what he advises as treatment for Domick. If there are medicines that will ease his pain or heal him, you can leave them some distance from the camp, and I will walk out to get them."

"Elspeth, this is absurd. You cannot do this alone. As soon as I speak to Gwynedd and the others, I will come to Half-moon Bay to help you. Blyss is already in Aborium, and she can ride back and speak with Jak."

I wanted to refuse, but in truth, I might need help. "Come, then, but remain outside the city. I will farseek you if necessary," I said, growing mentally exhausted now. It was always a battering business to sustain a farsought conversation with a coercer. And sharing memories was tiring with anyone.

"Where are you now?" Merret asked as I was about to withdraw from her mind. I told her, and she said, "How strange that you should find your way to Stonehill, given that it was not where I told you it was."

"I don't understand," I said, unable to remember her ever mentioning Stonehill to me.

"I thought it was on the other side of Aborium," Merret said.

"We can speak of this later," I said, for I was becoming fuddled. I bade her ride safe and withdrew from her mind.

I rested for a time and, drowsing, found myself remembering a vision I had once had of Domick lying slumped in what I had thought was a Council cell, his hair long and matted, his body covered in sores and filth. I had no doubt now that the vision had been of Domick on Herder Isle or Norseland, and I wondered what Ariel had been doing to him all this time, given that he could not have been infecting him with plague.

At last thirst forced me to climb again, and it was not long before I reached the top of Stonehill. A gentle slope rose before me, covered in long grass that swished pleasantly in a slight wind. It was very dark, for the moon had risen behind a tattered veil of cloud and was only fitfully revealed, but I walked steadily, eager to reach a place where I could see the ocean. The wind grew stronger, and I was so intent on leaning into it that I was almost on them before I noticed the outline of buildings near the top of the slope. Drawing closer, I saw that they were ruins. I entered the nearest dwelling. There was no roof at all, and whatever had once been laid down as a floor had gone, too. But the grass growing there was soft, and I was delighted to see a pile of the brown rock that was used for fires on Herder Isle. All I needed were some twigs and dried grasses to start a fire, and I could cook the potatoes Erit had given me.

Once outside, I remembered that I wanted to see the ocean and continued up the slope until I reached the top. The hill flattened out and ran to a cliff edge where the stone looked as if a knife had sheared it off. The moon was shining through the clouds onto the sea, and I stood for a long time looking at it and thinking of Ari-roth and Ari-noor and of Dragon and her mother and of Harwood and the others upon Herder Isle. But the wind that flowed from the sea was chilly, and soon I turned to head back to the ruins. I had one clear glimpse of them and the land about them before the moon vanished again, but I had seen enough to discern that the ruins were not merely a few buildings but a proper small settlement. I wondered why Erit had not mentioned it when he suggested I ride to the top of Stonehill. If there had once been a settlement here, there must be some easier way up the hill than the perilous path I had taken with Rawen.

In looking for some twigs to start a fire, I noticed a hollow to one side of the ruins that had once been walled. Within it grew the remains of a substantial orchard. Queerly shaped stumps were all that remained of the trees, all thickly distorted trunks with little branches. Dead, I guessed, the branches long ago broken off for firewood.

I headed toward the nearest gap in the wall, wondering why Halfmoon Bay had not been built about this hill. It would have provided a magnificent lookout and given the city true distinction.

Then the clouds shifted, and moonlight bathed the thick stumps in a light that transformed them into stone.

◆ 4 ◆

I GASPED, FOR even at that distance and in the moonlight, I recognized in the stone forms the work of Kasanda, who had once been D'rekta of the Twentyfamilies gypsies. That meant that the ruined buildings must be the first and only home of those gypsies before they had struck their safe passage agreement with the councilmen and become nomadic. If I was right, this was also the site of the school for stone workers that Swallow once told me about. Now I understood why Merret had made her cryptic comment about Stonehill. Hearing of my interest in statues, she had once told me that she had heard of a stone garden where sculptors were trained, built upon a sea cliff on the other side of Aborium. She had got the location wrong, but I recalled her saying that she wanted to visit the stone garden. I wondered why I could not remember her telling me about it. Then I realized that had been the last farsought conversation I had had with Merret before the Suggredoon closed.

I stopped dead, my heart beginning to race, for I was remembering the fourth line of clues that Kasanda had carved into the panels that had become the doors to Obernewtyn.

"Who [would/must] enter the [sentinel/guard/watcher] will seek the words in the house where my son was born."

Sentinel was the name of the Beforetime project that had been set up to develop a worldwide retaliatory system of weaponmachines that would deal indiscriminately with any aggression between countries. But something had gone wrong, and these weaponmachines had brought about the Great White holocaust that had destroyed the Beforetime and poisoned most of the world. These were the weapon-machines I was to find and render helpless. And if the clue meant what it seemed clearly to say, words in these ruins would help me gain access to the Beforetime complex with-out harm.

As if in a dream, I turned back toward the ruined build-ings. Whatever message I found here must have been carved during Cassy's time in the Land, yet the clues on Obernew-tyn's door panels had to have been carved after Cassy had journeyed to Sador, for how else could she have learned the gadi in which they had been scibed? But if she had made the panels after she went to Sador, how had they fallen into the hands of the gypsies Louis Larkin had seen bringing them to Obernewtyn? Was it possible that Cassy, now Kasanda of Sador, had sent them back to the gypsies who had remained in the Land, and if that were so, why hadn't Swallow men-tioned that the revered Sadorian seer had once been D'rekta of the Twentyfamilies gypsies? Or had he known but not mentioned it to me?

Setting aside the puzzle, I looked about and tried to en-visage how the ruins had looked when they were whole and occupied. A number of smaller dwellings had been built in a semicircle, facing a larger building of which little remained. The larger building had most likely been communal: an eat-ing place or maybe a sculpture hall. I methodically went through all the smaller buildings, checking what remained of the walls and patches of flagged floor, seeking the words Cassy had left for me.

I found none, though I did discover a well with a stone cauldron beside it between two of the huts. I drew up a bucket of icy water and drank thirstily, wondering again why a settlement with water and fertile ground in a desert land had been left abandoned after the Twentyfamilies gypsies had left. Pouring some water for Rawen into the stone cauldron, I continued searching the remaining smaller buildings and then inside and outside the walls of the larger building, but I found no carved words.

I went back to where I had left my bag, took out the potatoes and the battered tinderbox Erit had given me, and set to making a fire. When the brown rock glowed hotly, I pressed the potatoes into the embers, took a stick of lighted wood, and revisited the walls of the ruins to see if I had missed any small carved words, but still I found nothing.

The moon was shining brightly now, and the sight of the thirty or so statues glowing in the pallid light made the hair on my neck stir, for it came to me that the Cassy of my past dreams, whom I had seen commune with flamebirds and mourn her lover and fight with her parents, had once stood in this very place as a grown woman. She would not just have been a woman, but a mother. An even stranger thought occurred to me. She had known my face as she stood here, for had she not carved it from glass in the Beforetime? And perhaps she had thought of me as she stood here with her little son in her arms. Or maybe she had thought of her friend the Red Queen, and the queen's brother, who had fathered the child. It struck me forcibly then, for the first time, that Cassy's bond with the queen's brother meant that her son was a distant cousin to Dragon! Was *that* why Cassy had dreamed of my meeting with Dragon *even before* she left the Red Queen's land? She must have, for why else would she have left something there for me that Dragon alone could reveal?

I thought of what I had seen in Dragon's Comatose mind. Her dying mother had bidden her remember the grave markers of the first Red Queen and her brother. The dream had been a vision dream, full of symbolic images, but I had no doubt that this part had been true. Dragon's mother had spoken of the grave markers of her ancestors, who had known Cassy.

I summoned from memory the sixth line from the Obernewtyn doors.

That which will [open/access/reach] the darkest door lies where the [?] [waits/sleeps]. Strange is the keeping place of this dreadful [step/sign/thing], and all who knew it are dead save one who does not know what she knows. Seek her past. Only through her may you go where you have never been and must someday go. Danger. Beware. Dragon.

Despite being sure that the "one who did not know what she knows" was Dragon, there was still much in the clue that mystified me. But all at once it occurred to me that what Kasanda had left for me in the Red Queen's land might not be a thing but words, and if that was true, then the obvious place for the words would be on the grave marker of the Red Queen's brother. Indeed, what would be more natural than for Cassy to have sculpted a stone for the grave of her dead lover? But would she truly have been capable of using his grave to leave me a message? Perhaps it had been his sister who had suggested the stones, for Cassy must have spoken to her of the Seeker and the need for her ancestor to know that

I would someday come to the Red Land to find the sign left for me.

I shivered and realized I had been standing as still as the statues before me. Thrusting my numb fingers under my arms, I went to look more closely at them. The nearest was a cloaked man and was less refined than the wall friezes Cassy had created in her latter days as Kasanda in the Sadorian Earthtemple but was more subtle than the glass form she had made for the Reichler Clinic foyer in the Beforetime. I bent to look at the base for any words carved there, but there was nothing but a faint C.

I went to another statue and then to others, stopping to study the faces as much as the stonework that shaped them, wondering if they had been people whom Cassy had known. From what Swallow had said, the workshop and school she had established here had been very successful in the early days, and in addition to the many ordinary young Landfolk who had come to learn Cassy's technique, many more had come to have their forms sculpted. Some of the stone figures were clearly Twentyfamilies gypsies, judging from their attire and facial characteristics. One, the statue of an older gypsy woman, had an expression of great pride but also a hint of stern sorrow.

Some of the pieces were not Cassy's, though it was clear she had taught the maker. And although these were fine, none surpassed the mastery of their teacher. Several of the better pieces were inscribed with an *E,* and I wondered who "E" had been.

In one corner, I came upon several groupings of children that seemed sentimental. These were not Cassy's work, and I guessed they had been done by her novices or acolytes, but in their midst was a statue that Cassy had obviously done, of a boy about Erit's age, posed in sitting position, hands clasped loosely about his knees. This boy lacked the tough, good-natured brashness that animated Erit's engaging face. He looked more vulnerable and reminded me somewhat of the Norse boy, Lark, whom I had met on the way to Herder Isle. I stood for a long time, marveling that Cassy had been able to capture the nature of a boy's yearning so well and so tenderly. It came to me that this might be Cassy's son, who had taken over the Twentyfamilies when she had left the land.

How had he felt, I wondered, when his mother had vanished? Swallow had told me once that, although many of the tribe had believed their D'rekta had been stolen away from the Land against her will, her son had always insisted that she had known she would be taken and had allowed it. If she had known what would come, she must have told her son, who went on to make the pact with the Council that had brought the Twentyfamilies to their nomadic existence. This enabled the gypsies to watch over and protect the messages and signs for me that she had strewn about the Land. Maybe Cassy's son had even distributed some of them.

Had he lost that gentle yearning once he became responsible for the Twentyfamilies, I wondered, and what had he yearned for as a youth anyway?

I left the statue and went farther down the field than I had gone before. There was more novice work here, but there was still the occasional form that could only have been wrought by Cassy. I came to the statue of a girl about my own age, standing and gazing into the middle distance, frowning slightly. She had lifted one hand as if to shade her eyes from the sun's glare, and like the statue of the boy, the face had been modeled with great care. Some moments passed before

I realized that it seemed familiar. The person it resembled most was Hannah, whom I had just seen for the first time in a vision when I come to the west coast. It was curious that Cassy had chiseled Hannah as a girl, given they had not met until Hannah was middle-aged. Had she dreamed of her mentor as a younger woman? It might be so, for the likeness was not exact. The brows were wrong, and the mouth was more full then those of the older Hannah, the chin softer. Whatever it might lack in accuracy, the statue was an exquisitely rendered work that showed its maker's affection for the subject. Both the young woman and the boy had been posed gazing outward, but where the boy's expression had been poetic and full of yearning, the statue of the girl was characterized by determination and strength. It was as if she, unlike the boy, was looking for something very important and very specific. Certainly this was not the face of a dreamer.

I heard a sound and turned my head, expecting to see Rawen, but instead I saw a woman coming toward me, her face hidden in shadow. Stumbling backward in fright, I caught myself from falling by grasping the hand of the stone girl whose face I had been studying. The woman did not speak, and for one wild moment, I thought she was a ghost. Then I saw her face and my shock subsided, for I recognized the strong, willful face of Swallow's half sister, Iriny, whom I had once saved from burning, though she had cursed me for it.

"You!" I gasped.

"I," she agreed caustically, her odd two-colored eyes gleaming. "I gather that is your fire back there? Your potatoes."

"I . . . Yes. And there are apples and bread," I stammered, made foolish by astonishment. She quirked a brow, saying that if this was an invitation to nightmeal, she accepted, but we had better go back and rescue the potatoes, for they smelled well and truly done to her. Not until we reached the ruin and were out of the wind did I pull myself together enough to ask, "Iriny, however did you get here?"

"The plast suit," she said simply, kneeling and rolling the potatoes out of the fire with a stick. She knocked one toward me and set aside another to cool for herself. "The Master of Obernewtyn brought it the night he returned Darius to us. That was when we learned of the Herders' attempt to invade the Land with the help of the traitor Malik."

"How is Darius?" I interrupted, stupidly trying to open my potato when it was still too hot. "He was so ill when I saw him last."

She reached into the bag Erit had given me and withdrew the dark loaf, tearing a piece and wolfing it down before she answered. "He was sick when I left, though your healer Kella was treating him." She shrugged and ripped off another piece of bread before handing me the loaf.

I tore off a piece and ate it, asking, "You used the plast suit to cross the Suggredoon? Why?"

I was thinking of Atthis, who had told me that she used Swallow, among others, to save me when I had been near death trying to cross the strait. It would not be the first time the D'rekta of the gypsies had saved my life at the behest of the seer.

Iriny said, "Swallow dreamed that one of us needed to come here. He said it was a matter of the ancient promises. He wanted to come himself, but the elders would not permit the D'rekta to put himself at such risk when he has yet to father a child to take his place." She gave a sour grin. "I volunteered to come, and the elders agreed. We needed a diversion to draw the attention of the watchers, so we used the rafts we had prepared for the day that we might cross the river again. Not to cross the river, for anyone trying that would be an easy target, rather, we stuffed clothes with straw and set them afire as we pushed them out into the water. It was night, and they made a wondrous bright diversion that let me slip unnoticed into the river wearing the suit.

"As soon as the soldierguards on this bank spotted the rafts, there was an uproar. I waited in some rocks until some of the soldierguards on the bank opposite me moved downriver slightly to see what was amiss, then I swam across. I am a good swimmer, and because the suit has a tube that enabled me to breathe while underwater, I did not have to expose myself."

She pulled out a knife and skewered her potato, deftly cutting it open and scooping out its steaming contents.

She went on. "The soldierguards soon realized the burning rafts were a diversion, but they were looking for an unlit raft carrying a spy, never imagining a person would immerse herself in the tainted water. In all the commotion, it was a simple matter to reach the barrier the soldierguards have set up to keep people from the old ferry crossing and slip over it, because of course it was designed to keep people out, rather than in.

"Once I had crossed the open space between the barrier and entered a rough sort of village, I knew no one would catch me. All I had to do was get rid of the suit, so I skirted the village and went some distance onto the open plain to bury it. Then I made my way back into the settlement and mingled with the folk there."

She leaned forward and flicked out two more potatoes from the embers. While they cooled, she went to get some water, saying that she had found herbs with which she could brew a hot drink.

Left alone by the fire, I ate one of the apples from the bag and thought of the first time I had seen the halfbreed gypsy. She had been tied to a pole, yet she had dared taunt the Herder torturing her. I had intervened on impulse, spurred on by her courage, yet the act of saving her had brought me to Swallow. Almost every meeting with the D'rekta had been somehow connected to my role as the seeker, and in a sense, Swallow knew more about that part of me than any other human. And Iriny had come here at Swallow's insistence . . .

I stopped midbite and cursed myself for a fool, for surely he had sent Iriny here because Atthis had revealed to me that I would need someone to tell me exactly where the D'rekta's son had been born so I could find the sign Cassy had left here for me!

Iriny returned but before I could speak, she said, "I should tell you. Before I left, my brother told me that you are the one referred to in the ancient promises. That he told me violates the ancient promises, and it troubled me. But I guess now that he knew you would be here, and he sent me to give you aid. If my brother is right and you are truly the one to whom the ancient promises refer, it must be that the end days are here when all promises will be fulfilled. Therefore, I will serve you in whatever capacity you require."

I drew a deep breath and said, "As it happens, I do need help. I must find words that were carved where your first D'rekta's son was born. I think that one of the statues in the stone garden must have once stood in the house of your D'rekta, for I have searched the ruins and can find nothing on the walls . . ."

She was shaking her head. "Evander was not born here."

I gaped at her. "Isn't this the first and only settlement your people had in the Land?"

"It is, but the D'rekta's son was born in a rough hut constructed at the front of a cave in the base of Stonehill. It was built when my ancestors first came ashore, to shelter the D'rekta who was very near to her birthing time. They did not build atop Stonehill until later, after they had constructed the road. Not until the boy neared manhood did the D'rekta make a carving in the cave."

"Take me there," I said, half rising, but again she shook her head.

"A rockfall destroyed it just before my ancestors brought Evander here to die. When he learned of the avalanche, he commanded that the cave be dug out. But too much stone had fallen, and in the end, he carved the words from the cave into a stone and invoked the ancient promises when he bade the Twentyfamilies set the stone into his death cairn and tend it as if it were one of his mother's sacred carvings. He spoke at length to his son in private, to pass on what needed to be told, and thereafter, he died."

"Where is the cairn?" I asked with excitement, hardly able to believe that in the midst of all that had happened, when my quest was far from my thoughts, I had stumbled on another sign from Kasanda.

Iriny had risen, and now she took up a stick from the fire and went out into the night. I followed her past the walled stone garden. The night had gone still, as if the world held its breath in anticipation of what I was about to see. The cairn rose up out of the grass, formed from many rocks shaped and fitted together so perfectly that they needed no mortar to bind them. Iriny went around to the side of the cairn that faced the sea. The glow from embers at the stick's end allowed me to read the two groups of words carved into one of the stones. The first said that these words had first been carved in the cave where Evander had been born, and under them, in a more ornate script, was carved

I come unto thee, Sentinel. Judge my hand and let me pass, for all I have done was in your name.

"Do you know what the words mean?" I asked Iriny as we made our way back to the ruins.

"I do not know nor do I think the Twentyfamilies who made the cairn knew. Once I heard a seer say that the words in the cave referred to some infamous event that had happened in the past, but they did not say what it was, for the ancient promises instruct us never to speak of the days before our people came to the Red Queen's land. My brother may understand the meaning of the words, though, for each D'rekta has passed on his secrets to his successor through the generations."

As Iriny added brown rock to the fire, I asked what sickness Evander had died from.

"It was not sickness but an accident," she answered. "Our people had come from the highlands down to Sutrium to make the yearly tithe at the Councilcourt. There was a storm, and just as our wagons entered the city, a great shaft of lightning struck a building, setting its roof ablaze. Evander's horse was young, and it reared. Though he was a good rider, he fell, and it was a bad fall. At first it seemed that he would recover, but some weakness crept into his broken body, and he began to waste away. When the healers had done all they could, it is said he smiled and announced that he was glad, for he might now return at last to the only place where he had been truly happy, for that was where he would be buried. And he bade them bring him here."

"What if he had been killed immediately when he fell?" I asked curiously. "He would not have passed on his knowledge to his son."

She shook her head. "One of the seers would have warned him. It happened once with another D'rekta. A seer visioned that he would die suddenly, so he told his son what was needful. A sevenday later, he died during a firestorm."

"What if a D'rekta has no son?"

"Then his brother or sister or his daughter becomes D'rekta, and if there were none of these, the seers would have warned of that, and he would have adopted a son or daughter by the blood rites and passed on his knowledge. If the child was a babe, the knowledge would be passed to a guardian D'rekta. That, too, happened once. The seers named an old woman as the babe's guardian D'rekta."

I marveled at the determined fidelity of the gypsies to their vows as Iriny wiped her knife on the grass and put it away. I wiped my sooty fingers and thought of Evander calling Stonehill the only place where he had been truly happy. "I suppose Evander must have loved his mother very much, and that is why he wanted to come here at the end."

Iriny shrugged. "I think it would be an uncomfortable thing to have a mother so full of destiny and so preoccupied by a future that she and no one else could see. My father . . ." She stopped, licking her fingers. "Well, those who must love their duty have little left for other things, and the first D'rekta had a very great and terrible duty."

Her words made me wonder if Evander had meant that he had been happy on Stonehill because his boyhood had been free of that heavy duty he had been forced to assume as a young man. It was sad that his life had seemed an exile from his golden youth.

"Did you notice the carving of a girl shading her eyes?" asked the gypsy. I nodded. "She is not a Twentyfamilies gypsy, but she came to the Land with my ancestors from the Red Queen's land as a toddler. It is said that the D'rekta loved her like a daughter and that Evander loved her, too, though apparently not as a brother loves a sister. She went away to the mountains after his mother was taken by slavers. Some say she went because Evander desired her and she felt toward him only sisterly love. Still others say she went to the mountains to seek her own mother. Whatever the truth of it, Evander sought her out whenever the Twentyfamilies' wanderings brought them near the place she settled in the highlands, but in the end he bonded and bore a child to a Twentyfamilies pureblood as he was duty-bound to do."

There was sadness in her face, and I knew she thought of her own halfbreed mother, set aside by Swallow's pureblood father for a Twentyfamilies girl when he was forced to become D'rekta after his brother died childless. Suddenly, Iriny rose to her feet, as lithe as a snake at the sound of hooves.

"It will be Rawen," I told her, and we went to greet the mare, who was drinking thirstily from the stone cauldron I had filled. I shaped a probe to tell her who Iriny was, but as I did so, I noticed that Iriny was making rudimentary beast-speaking signals to the mare.

"She does not know beastspeech," I said aloud, conveying the meaning of my words to Rawen. "We met in Morganna, and I suppose no beast has ever been there who knew it."

I was surprised when Rawen lifted her dripping muzzle and disagreed, commenting that some creatures in Morganna had spoken of a special sort of signaling some humans used to communicate with beasts, but she had thought it a myth. Then she asked if I still wanted to go back to Halfmoon Bay. That made me realize that I had not yet told Iriny about Ariel and Domick.

I told her as succinctly as I could of the overthrow of the Faction on Herder Isle and of Ariel's journey to the west coast to deliver someone whom he had deliberately infected with a deadly plague. Painfully, I explained my discovery that it was Domick, whom she had met. Iriny's frown deepened as my tale unfolded, but she did not interrupt. I concluded that I was going back to Halfmoon Bay to take Domick from the city before his sickness became infectious. "In case I fail, you should go to a safehold we Misfits have here until the plague runs its course, for all who contract it will die."

"I will remain with you and give what aid I can," Iriny said in a voice that brooked no argument.

I replied, "You understand that Domick might be contagious now."

"I will come with you," she reiterated simply.

Seeing that she would not be swayed, I suggested we descend. We did so using the road the Twentyfamilies had built, which was somewhat less precipitous than the path I had taken earlier.

"Evidently, they had some special device from the Beforetime that enabled them to cut through rock as if it were butter," Iriny said, explaining the impossible smoothness of the road spiraling down. She glanced at me and asked why the Herders wanted to kill all who lived on the west coast. "Are not their own people here as well?"

"I think the priests regard their order as more important than any individual priest, or even any cloister. But it was the One who rules the Faction who desired this terrible thing, and he was a madman. Mind you, it was Ariel who shaped the notion in his mind." I looked at her to see if she understood who I meant, and she nodded. "As to why he would want to kill so many people, I cannot say. But he is defective, so perhaps it is foolish to try to come up with a rational reason for his actions."

"There is still reason in madness, though it be flawed," Iriny pointed out.

I shrugged. "In one of his fits, the One said something about the destruction of all life here being a wonderful example of Lud's power and wrath."

"But it would be the Herders' might that would be shown, *their* power."

"The One did not see it so, and if the other priests had known what he planned, I think many of them would have approved and called it Lud's judgment," I murmured. "Or maybe I should say that it would serve the Herders to see it so. The Herders preach that Lud made people in his image, though we are flawed and so must strive for perfection. But I think the Herders made Lud in their own image, to serve as scapegoat and excuse."

"How can people make Lud?" Iriny asked.

"I do not know, but look at the Lud of the Gadfians who regarded women as less than beasts and beasts as nothing. The men of that race believed that Lud made women for no other purpose than to beget and nurture more men who would worship Lud. As the men believed, so their Lud was said to believe, and if he disagreed, he never told anyone so."

"Did their Lud not desire the worship of women?"

I shrugged. "According to the Gadfians, Lud desired only fear and obedience from women, not love or worship. That is why the women and a few men left and formed a new exiled race in Sador. They rejected their ancestors' Land and Lud. And how should a Lud be left behind like a land from which one has sailed, unless he was no more than the invention of the men of that land?"

Iriny looked thoughtful. "Even if this Lud had some hand in the making of humankind, as the Herders preach, might not he have planted us like a gardener plants a seed, tending it for a time and then leaving it to grow as it will?"

"That is an interesting idea," I said. "But if there were such a Lud, I wonder what it would make of the intolerant Lud of the Gadfians or the punitive Lud of the Herders."

"It would not think of them at all," Iriny said.

Once at the base of Stonehill, Rawen, insisted she could carry both if us as long as we did not ask her to gallop, and we rode slowly to Halfmoon Bay. It was nearly four in the morning when I bade the mare stop and let us down. A quarter league from the city, I could hear the muted sounds of laughter and music as we dismounted, which suggested that many were still celebrating the coming masked moon fair in advance. Rawen cantered briskly away along the sand, promising not to stray too far so that she could come swiftly when I summoned her. Then we walked the rest of the way along the shore on foot. I had no fear that we might be seen, because the moon had set now and it was very dark.

The sea gate was not completely open when we reached it, for waves still nibbled at the base of the wall, but I decided not to wait. When I turned to say as much to Iriny, I saw that she was already unlacing her sandals. I took off my own boots, wincing at the blisters on my heels, and followed her as she waded through the water around the end of the wall and into the city.

"What now?" Iriny asked after we had replaced our shoes.

"We will go to Rolf's house. Erit must have been delayed," I said. I had told her in more detail, as Rawen plodded along, all that had occurred in Halfmoon Bay before I had come to Stonehill.

The sound of boots marching in unison on the cobbles made us exchange one swift glance and then dive under the boardwalk that ran along the seaward edge of the city. When the tide was in, the waves would run right up under it, but now it was dry enough, though the sand was too wet to sit on, so we crouched down to wait.

I held my breath, listening as the boots came closer. Iriny lifted four fingers to indicate four walkers, and I rolled my eyes. Then there was the sound of wood thudding. The boots came to a halt almost directly over our heads, and I sent out a probe. That I could not reach the minds of any of the walkers told me they were soldierguards wearing demon bands. They began to speak of the morrow, one congratulating the other for having managed to be off duty on the first day of the masked moon fair. The other grumbled that women were much more inclined to smile at a man in uniform. Better if he had the last day of the fair off, having had the chance to flaunt himself first in his uniform. The other laughed, sneering at him for needing such trappings.

Iriny grimaced at their crude boasting, but I thought it better to listen to the utterances of fools than to have them looking about attentively. Once they had marched away, we decided to wait before coming out.

"This city has a bad feel to me," Iriny muttered. I asked if it had always been so, and she said that she had never been here before, which surprised me. She shrugged, saying, "I have been to Stonehill several times since my brother permitted halfbreeds to join the Twentyfamilies, but I never came into Halfmoon Bay. Swallow did, of course, and others of the tribe, for there was always a good market for our more complex and costly work here, but I do not enjoy cities."

Again we heard footsteps, but these were light and quick, and when I sent out a probe, I found Erit wondering where I was. Iriny and I emerged to find him standing a little distance away scratching his head. I called his name softly, and he swung round. His eyes widened at the sight of Iriny.

"You are a gypsy," he said when we approached, the bluish radiance of predawn slicking his ratty little dirt-streaked face.

"I am, and what sort of burrowing animal are you?" Iriny asked, sounding amused.

The boy bridled and stuck out his chin. "I am Erit and I'm not afraid of you."

"Good," Iriny said. "I am not afraid of you either. But I hope this house we are going to has something more than bread and potatoes, for I am fearfully hungry."

"There is no time to waste in gorging ourselves," I said, knowing it was mere hours now till midday and the start of the masked moon fair.

"We can do nothing until the sun has risen and the city begins to stir," Erit said.

"Aro has a plan, then?" I asked eagerly.

He nodded but said he would let Aro explain it. "Is she coming with us?" Erit asked, looking at Iriny. "I suppose you found her visiting their ghosts?"

"Ghosts?" I said, puzzled. "You mean the statues atop Stonehill?"

"The stone garden is said to be haunted by the ghouls of dead gypsies," he said.

That explained why no one else lived atop the hill, I thought. "Why did you tell me to go up there, if there are ghouls?" I asked as Erit turned and beckoned for us to follow.

He looked over his shoulder at me. "It is said the ghouls only drink the blood of those who are treacherous and evil-hearted."

I blinked, startled to realize that I had been tested.

✦ 5 ✦

IT WAS NOT far to Rolf's house, which stood at the end of a row of small dwellings. No light showed at the windows, but the moment Erit knocked, the door was opened by a woman so like Rolf that she could only be his sister. She was older by perhaps a decade, and her hair was gray-streaked where his was dark, but her smile had the same warmth as she bade us enter the main room before we introduced ourselves. Rolf was waiting there, sitting at a scrubbed wooden table, his face and hands clean and his hair combed. He urged us to sit, too, for he could not easily stand. We obeyed, and I introduced Iriny.

"I am Arolfic and this is my sister, Mona. Erit you have met, though probably he had not manners enough to offer his name to you, or ask yours," Rolf said in his rumbling voice.

"She is a gypsy," Erit said.

"I do have eyes enough to see it, boy," Rolf said. He looked at me. "I once heard that rebels across the Suggredoon have had some dealings with the Twentyfamilies."

"It is true. But Rolf, before we go on, I must tell you the truth about myself and the danger my friend Domick poses to you and the west coast. My name is Elspeth Gordie, and I am a Misfit."

He shrugged. "I know that Misfits worked with the rebels. Indeed, I once heard the rebel leader Serba speak out passionately against those who regard them as lesser beings because they are different."

"Domick, whom we hope to rescue, is a Misfit, too. But some time ago, he was captured by the Herders. We did not know this until recently when I learned he had been delivered to Ariel, who is not a priest but serves them and is high in their councils. That is the blond man you saw bringing Domick from the *Black Ship*. When you spoke of seeing the man with him yesterday, I used my Talents to look at your memory. That was when I saw that the man with Ariel was Domick. That was why I was so shocked. Until that moment, I did not know the person I followed was a friend."

"But if you did not know, then why were you following him?" Rolf asked.

"Because I learned that the blond man, Ariel, had brought a man here from Herder Isle whom he meant to infect with a deadly plague that would spread to all who came into contact with him, once it became contagious. I know the west coast has endured plague before, but this will be worse, for all who contract it will die. I came to find the man Ariel had brought here, because I wanted to stop the plague."

Rolf's face had gone pale, and I saw that his sister had pressed a hand to her mouth in dismay.

"You said *once it became contagious*," Erit said.

I nodded, once again appreciating his quickness. "There is a delay of several days between when a person is infected and the moment he can infect others. Domick is infected, but there will be a few days before he can infect anyone else. The trouble is that we do not know the exact length of the delay or when Domick was infected. I think that Ariel brought Domick specifically to Halfmoon Bay because people come from every town on the coast to attend the masked moon fair and that means that the plague will spread so swiftly that no city will be able to close its gates to isolate itself. Since the moon fair begins today, and since Domick has not yet left the Faction house, I am assuming that the plague seeds he carries will not ripen until today at the soonest."

"You should have told us," Erit said accusingly.

"Now, boy," Rolf said soothingly. "Maybe she could have told us sooner, but I don't suppose she had any malicious reason for failing to do so." He looked at me. "It is hard to understand how a sickness can be carried about and dispensed like a patent medicine, yet if you are correct, it seems as if you might be right about the timing of this foul business, for Erit and his friends have learned that your Domick is to be escorted by the Hedra at the Faction house to the first-night festivities as a special envoy from the One. That will put him at the heart of the crowds for several hours, and although there will be feasts each night of the festival, this is always the best attended and most lavish, for it is when Councilman Kana will crown a masked moon king or queen."

"How did you learn this?" I asked Erit, who was scowling at the table. He glared at me.

"I talked to one of the kitchen maids. She told me about this queer priest over from Herder Isle who was to be a special envoy from the One and who would attend every event, starting with the first-night feast, to pass among the people and grant them Lud's blessing. She said she did not see how he could manage it, since he seemed quite mad. She thought it a pity the handsome fellow who had brought him was not to be the envoy." Erit looked suddenly at Rolf. "We will need a new plan."

Rolf nodded, saying to me, "I had thought to take your friend during the first-night's festivities, but I see now that we must take him as soon as possible. Erit, go over what you learned again and let me have a think."

Erit obliged. "The maid said the Hedra think your friend mad. She said the priests complain that he has not come out of his room at all since the handsome blond man had helped him into it. He will open his door only a crack to admit plain fruit and water. He has been offered bathing water but refuses it with the terror of a man being offered a mug of poison. She said she had heard his moans and shouts, even though her sleeping chamber is on the other side of the Faction house from the guest chambers."

"From what I heard of the last plague, lack of appetite and delirium are the first symptoms," I ventured.

Rolf's face had become set, and he glanced at his sister before nodding. "That is so, and most often this is followed by a period when the temperature drops almost to normal and it seems as if the person is recovering. That can last as much as a day before the temperature rises again, and this time there is nausea and vomiting, then fits. Once the buboes come, the end is near."

His detailed description indicated that he had seen plague victims in the last epidemic. I said, "One of our healers told me that the last plague became contagious at the vomiting stage. Since we know nothing of this plague, I am going to assume it is the same, and I wager, if it is possible to time it so well, that this period of seeming health will coincide with the time of the festivities tonight."

We were silent for a moment, and then Rolf said, "Tell me of your Misfit powers."

I swallowed my impatience and said, "I can read minds, though Misfits do not enter the minds of allies without permission except in matters of life and death. I judged it such a matter when I entered your mind to learn what the plague carrier looked like. As to my other Talents, once in the mind of another person, I can influence his or her actions. Also, I can pick locks and communicate with the minds of beasts."

"Useful skills, I imagine," Rolf said mildly, though his sister and Erit stared at me as if I had grown a second head. "Do you need to be looking at a person—or touching him—to enter his mind?"

"I need to be in physical contact only if the person I want to probe is asleep or if it is raining, for water inhibits our Talents," I said. "So does tainted ground."

"Can you not reach the mind of your friend, then, and make him come out?" Erit demanded.

"When you showed me the Faction house, I tried, but the walls of the Faction house are tainted with small amounts of Blacklands material," I said. "The Herders do it deliberately, because they know it blocks Misfit Talents. But even if I could reach his mind, I am sure Ariel will have left instructions with the Hedra to keep Domick inside until this evening."

"Can you reach your friend's mind when he emerges from the Faction house?"

"Unless he is wearing a demon band. Or unless Ariel has set up a block in his mind to make it impossible." Seeing the puzzlement on their faces, I explained about Ariel's block in Malik's mind and in the minds of the One and the Threes.

"You are saying he is a Misfit, too?" Rolf asked slowly.

"He is a defective Misfit with the ability to manipulate minds and emotions, and he sees things that have yet to happen," I said.

"I think we ought to use a message-taker like you were thinking yesterday," Erit said. "We send a message pretending to be from this Ariel, ordering Domick to be brought out of the Faction house to him. Then you can enter his mind and make him come to you."

Rolf said thoughtfully, "The message is a good idea, but even if he is able to leave, he will probably be escorted by Hedra, and they'll have to be dealt with. And there is another thing. You will have to be masked, because masks are worn from dawn today until dusk on the final day of the festival. If you are found unmasked, you will be co-opted as someone's festival slave for the day."

"But where can we get masks?" I said worriedly.

"There is no shortage of them in this house," Rolf murmured. He reached up and took his sister's hand. "You see, our sister Carryn was a gifted mask-maker. She died in the last plague, along with both her children and her bondmate."

"I am sorry," I said, appalled.

"Yes," Rolf said. "But we have masks here that Carryn made for customers who perished in the plague. It is fitting that you will wear them to help prevent another plague."

"I will get the masks," said Mona, her eyes shining with tears.

"Do you have any idea how many Hedra will escort Domick?" Iriny spoke for the first time.

Rolf looked at her. "At least two," he answered. "Can you fight?"

"I can deal with two men," she said calmly.

Erit stared at her, fascinated, as Rolf asked, "What if there were more?"

She shrugged. "Then I will need help."

I saw Rolf relax and realized he had been testing Iriny to see if her words were empty boasts.

"I can fight, too," Erit put in eagerly.

Rolf shook his head. "I think that we had better avoid setting ourselves up for an open confrontation. What we need is a diversion that will allow Elspeth to spirit her friend away from his escort. One advantage is that they will not regard him as someone who would escape, for they think he is one of them."

"Will there be enough time to set up a diversion?" I asked worriedly.

Rolf smiled, and for a moment he looked very like Erit. "I will arrange the diversion."

"What if he refuses to come with you?" Erit said to me.

"We could use a sleep potion," Rolf told them. "I know of one so strong that the fumes will render him unconscious for a short time. Still, we will need to separate him from the Hedra to manage it. I assume your mind powers will enable you to deal with anyone who sees what is happening?"

"I can manage two or three but not at the same time," I said.

"Well and good," Rolf muttered. "Can you scribe the letter to Domick? A metalworker's hands are not fit for a quill. Better also scribe a covering letter to the Hedra who are to take him to the festivities this evening." As he spoke, he rose and hobbled across the kitchen to rummage in a cupboard. He withdrew a quill and some parchment. "Scribe that Domick is to be brought to the pier to collect a special gift from the One, which he is to present to Councilman Kana this evening. Ask the Hedra master of the house for an escort or two. That ought to waylay any suspicions."

By the time I had completed the letters, Mona had returned with a wicker basket filled with beautiful hand-painted boxes. As she began to unpack them reverently, Rolf took the letters from me and read through them, sealed both, and went to some trouble to make a mark that would pass for an identification stamp that had been damaged or worn away. "If the message is delivered by a reputable message-taker, it is less likely the seal will be scrutinized."

"If Domick is unconscious, how am I to get him out of the city?"

"I will have Golfur close by, my greathorse," Rolf said with a fleeting smile. "I have asked Erit to prepare a bundle of supplies, which will be lashed to Golfur's saddle. I will also have a canvas sheet and ropes ready to truss Domick up so we can lay him over the saddle and make him look like a carpet, and a few false parcels to lash atop him and hide his shape."

Overwhelmed with gratitude for his thoughtfulness and generosity, I apologized to Rolf for being unable to reimburse him for the supplies, but he interrupted to say that since I was ready to sacrifice my life to save his city, he could hardly begrudge me a bit of food and water. "Now I will also put Golfur's papers into his saddlebag, for you may be asked to produce them when you leave the city. Once you have no more need for him, you can return him to me."

I said awkwardly that Rolf ought not to lend me any horse, for I would not return it to him unless the beast wished it. "You see, we Misfits believe that beasts should not be owned by humans. If Golfur comes with me, it will be as a free horse."

Rolf laughed. "Bless you, lass, but a stolen horse is useless unless you can also steal his papers, and there is no time for that. Better to take Golfur, and if he wishes to be freed of my company, I will not oppose it. But you will discover his will soon enough if you truly can speak with beasts. That is a Talent I might envy," he added wistfully.

"When this is all over, I will teach you to communicate with beasts," I promised. "There is a language of signals that can be learned by men and beasts, which allows them to communicate. These were devised by a man who once ran the Aborium rebel cell."

"You speak of the Black Dog?" Rolf asked.

"You know him?" I asked eagerly.

"Regrettably, I did not meet him, for I was never a rebel, though I have given them aid from time to time. But I heard he was a good man."

Erit had returned, and Mona began to remove a series of exquisite masks from their boxes.

"They are very beautiful, but they are all masks for wealthy folk," I said.

"Not necessarily," Mona replied in her soft voice. "During the masked moon fair, there is much play upon deception and the wealthy delight in wearing their servants' clothes with a jeweled mask, or they will wear their own attire but have a cheap mask so that none can be sure of their status or their identity. They derive much hilarity from seeing their friends bow and scrape to a potboy or croon to a washer lass. Or even an urchin." She reached out and took a splendid, bright-red mask, enameled to a high gloss and sewn with shimmering jet beads, setting it on Erit's dirty face. The urchin offered us a wicked gap-toothed grin. The effect of such a smile with such a mask was as alarming as it was comical. Mona spread out other masks and bade Iriny and I choose our own.

Iriny selected a splendid yellow and gold creation that resembled the metal masks the soldierguards sometimes used to protect their faces during confrontations. I chose a dark green mask with emerald beading about slanted eye slits and beautifully realistic cat's ears, wondering what Maruman would make of it. Mona went out again and returned with a hooded green cloak of thick velvet, which she said I ought to wear until I mounted Golfur, for no one seeing a girl in a green velvet cloak and cat mask would think her the same as a simple lad riding a laden greathorse from the city. Uneasy about being given so much, when my gift to this house had been news of a potential catastrophe and a reminder of an old and painful tragedy, I said, "What if some harm comes to it?"

"Better that harm should come to a cloak than a courageous young woman," Mona said with unexpected firmness. "Take it and wear it now. Return it to Rolf if you can. I will put those clod-stamping shoes you wear now into Golfur's saddlebags, for you must wear something more dainty with the cloak. Your feet are too big for my shoes, but Carryn's feet were bigger. Wait."

Again she withdrew, only to bring back a pair of leaf-green embroidered slippers as exquisite as the mask. Again I tried to refuse and again she stood firm.

"I am afraid you may as well give up," Rolf laughed. "For all her meek manner, she is a virago when crossed."

Despite everything, I laughed out loud to hear the gentle, soft-voiced Mona described in such a way. "I will take the cloak and the shoes and the mask, and you have my thanks for them," I said.

Mona smiled and Rolf kissed her on the cheek. Then he took a deep breath and said, "I think we must begin. Elspeth, you go with Erit to the message-taker's house and follow him to the Faction house. I assume you can use your powers to reach me?"

I nodded and bent down to remove my heavy shoes before stepping into Carryn's slippers. They were a little tight but very soft and well made. I bade Mona farewell then, knowing I would not see her again before I left the city, and donned my mask and cloak. Erit put on his, too, and we left the house together. The shutters on the windows had kept the sunlight out, and I blinked at the day's brightness.

The streets were already busy with servants and tradefolk bustling about, and all wore masks, though none so fine as the ones Erit and I had. It did not take us long to reach the message-taker's house with its winged shoe suspended above the door. I hung back in a shadowy doorway, pretending to empty a stone from a slipper, as Erit hammered at the front door and explained to the red-cheeked man who opened it that he had an urgent message for some Hedra. I had already probed the man, so I heard his thought that he would refuse the missives, because his head ached from the ale he had drunk the previous night, and anyway he did not like the Hedra.

Controlling a surge of annoyance, I forced him to accept the messages, and then I constructed a little web of fear, replacing Erit's image with Ariel's and dredging his memory until I had enough to construct a false memory of a meeting at the waterfront during which Ariel had given him the missives he would deliver to the Hedra. It was not a deeply bedded or particularly well-constructed memory, but it would serve when he was questioned, since I could not manipulate his answers to the Hedra's questions once he entered the house. I coerced him to deliver his message promptly, and it was not long after he closed the door on Erit that he came bursting out of it, still buttoning his vest. Erit had already left me, saying he would follow the message-taker across the roofs. He almost fell off the drainpipe he was climbing when he heard my voice in his head.

"How did you think I would communicate with you?" I asked.

"I did not think of it," Erit admitted sheepishly. "I thought

535

you would just make me know what I was supposed to know."

I told him that was coercion rather than farseeking, and Misfits did not coerce friends without their permission.

"I thought the message-taker was going to refuse the hire at first," Erit reflected as he watched the man from the rooftops.

"He was," I said. "I changed his mind for him."

I lost sight of the message-taker when he entered the street where the Faction house stood, for I had to backtrack to the little lane that was to be my vantage point. By the time I was in place, the message-taker was straightening his small half mask and knocking at the door. The door opened, and fleetingly, I saw in his mind an echo of the cold, stern face of the warrior priest who opened it. The Hedra demanded the message-taker's documents and studied them, then gestured for the missives. He broke the seal on one without looking closely at it, read it, and asked the message-taker to describe the man who had paid him. His mind dredged up the memory I had built, and he gave an unmistakable description of Ariel. The message-taker was discomfited by the interrogation and the Hedra's badgering manner, so I loosened my control and let him speak naturally. "Is something amiss, sirrah?"

The Hedra frowned. "This missive asks that one of the Herders staying here meets with the man who hired you, yet that same man bade me strictly to keep the Herder here until this evening, and as I understood it, he meant to travel on with the Raider."

"Perhaps the Raider will collect the blond man after performing some other errand up the coast," I made the message-taker say. "In any case, I have fulfilled my duty." He gave the bow of his calling and withdrew, and for a moment I had a clear view of the Hedra watching him march away, a preoccupied expression on his hard features. He closed the door, and there was nothing to do but wait.

I sent a probe after the message-taker, erasing his memory and grafting in its place another memory of having delivered a message nearby some days earlier. This done, I farsent Rolf to tell him what had happened. Mindful of the fright I had given Erit, I was careful to announce my presence. But Rolf welcomed me with an openness that startled me. I had just begun to describe the exchange between the message-taker and the Hedra when Erit gave a thin whistle from above. I looked up to see him pointing frantically in the direction of the Faction house where five Hedra had emerged with a hooded figure.

Certain it was Domick, I stretched out my mind to him, but as I had feared, he wore a demon band.

"Follow them!" Erit hissed, and I looked up to see him leap like a cat from one roof to another.

I set off back along the lane at a run, at the same time warning Iriny and Rolf that there were five Hedra, not two, and that Domick was demon-banded, which meant I could not coerce him. Fortunately, Rolf had had the foresight to give me a small bottle of sleep potion and a pad of cloth, though he had stressed that, if possible, it would be better to get him out of the market area on his own two feet. If it proved impossible, I was to summon Iriny to help carry him.

Rolf asked me to name the street I was on so that he could figure out which way we would enter the sea market. "That narrows it to two routes," the metalworker said after I told him I was on the Street of the Dancer. "How does your friend look?"

"He seems to be walking slowly, but he is hooded, so I cannot see his expression. He is not masked, though, and neither are the Hedra."

"None of the Faction mask themselves," Rolf explained.

The streets were busier now, and I guessed they would become busier still with each hour that passed. Even so, I stayed well back, for I did not want the Hedra to mark me. At one point, I lost sight of them when a small crowd of people spilled out of a door into my path, laughing and singing and reeling against one another. They were all masked and clearly had not yet finished celebrating the night before the fair. One of the men leered at me and caught me by the arm, but one of the women spat a curse at him, and he released me as if I had turned into hot embers.

I hurried on, probing Erit to find out where the Hedra had gone. In a few minutes, I had them in sight again, and Erit told me to let Rolf know they had taken the longer route. I obeyed.

Rolf told me to inform him when the Hedra had moved from the Street of the Fishmaid to the sea market. He also suggested I move closer to the group there, because a great throng of people would prevent the priests from noticing me and also keep them from moving too quickly. I needed to be ready to catch hold of Domick the moment Rolf created a diversion. I was to bring Domick to the Lane of the Weaver, next along from the Street of the Fishmaid, where Rolf would wait with Golfur.

I wanted to ask what the diversion would be, but a group of men arguing heatedly blocked my way, and I needed to concentrate to coerce my way through them. By the time I had done so, I had lost sight of the Hedra again. Once more, Erit directed me to them, just as the hooded figure stumbled and fell to his knees. The Hedra stopped and hauled Domick to his feet, and I felt a stab of pity for the coercer, who had suffered so much abuse. If only I could safely remove him from Halfmoon Bay. Then I was struck by the sad and dreadful irony of applying the word *safe* in any form to Domick, for there was no refuge or rescue or escape from the plague seeds multiplying in his blood. All the horror and danger the world had to offer had been planted inside him with only the leanest of hopes that Jak would know how to cure the plague, or at least slow its progress.

When I saw that we had reached the Street of the Fishmaid, I farsent Rolf, who asked me to warn Iriny. I found her pretending to consider the purchase of a knife from a trader and told her that Domick and the Hedra were just now entering the market.

My probe dislodged when Erit suddenly leapt down beside me, his eyes glittering through the slits of his mask. "Quick," he said. "We need to get close to the Hedra before Rolf gives the signal."

"What signal?" I asked, but Erit was already sprinting away. I raced after him, wishing I had asked Rolf more about the diversion.

The market looked almost exactly as it had the previous day, save that it was slightly more crowded and everybody but the small children wore a mask. For a moment, I could do nothing but stare until I remembered myself and began to edge and coerce my way through the masked revelers.

As the Hedra pushed more deeply into the crowd, they were forced to slow down, and soon I was near enough to hear them barking brusque instructions for people to move aside. Those in the crowd were trying to obey, but those behind were pressing forward to see what was happening.

"Any second," Erit hissed into my ear. "Get right up behind the Hedra *now*. The Lane of the Weaver is behind those two stalls." He pointed discreetly back the way we had come.

Too anxious to speak, I nodded and coerced two bird-masked men to draw apart so I could slip between them. I was close enough to Domick that I could have reached between the Hedra to touch him, when suddenly I heard a piercing whistle. Instantly, there was pandemonium. At first I thought the crowd had turned on the Hedra, but then I realized the commotion arose from some market stalls right next to us. It was hard to tell, for it seemed that a fight had broken out between two stallholders, but then one of Erit's urchin friends darted by with a big man pursuing him, screaming with rage.

Then it dawned on me that the hullabaloo was Rolf's doing. I remembered the bannock seller saying how much Rolf had done for other stallholders, and if I was right, the whistle must have been his signal. I could not imagine how so many people had agreed to help him in the short time since Erit and I had left his house. But as a diversion, the ruckus was impressive and very clever, for it would appear to have nothing to do with the Hedra.

Erit suddenly darted past me and gave the Hedra directly in front of me a hard blow before diving through the legs of the masses of people. The warrior priest snarled a curse and surged after him. He had drawn his metal-shod staff, and now he began to strike at people indiscriminately, driving them back. There was now no one between Domick and me but the remaining Hedra holding fast to his arm.

"Be ready," Iriny said, slipping past me. I did not see what she did to the Hedra, but he fell like a stone. I darted in and caught Domick's arm in the same place the Hedra had held him and drew him gently backward. To my intense relief, he came obediently, seemingly unaware that his keeper had changed.

Heart hammering, I managed to steer him toward the two stalls Erit had indicated, but to my dismay, three soldierguards stood at the end of the Lane of the Weaver, clearly trying to see what was going on. Not daring to show any hesitation that might awaken Domick to the fact that something had changed, I led him to the next street. It was the Lane of the Ropeman, and I farsought Rolf immediately. He bade me go along it to the nearest crossing road and turn left. He would meet me there as soon as he could. The quiet of the lane seemed to reach Domick, and he lifted his head.

He looked exactly as he had in Rolf's memory, his expression fixed in a rigid mask of horror, save that his deadly pallor was now accentuated by eyes bright with fever surrounded by bruise-dark circles. Something stirred in his expression, a muddy confusion. Was it the mask? I wondered, trying to decide if I ought to remove it and show myself to him.

"Where is . . . my master?" he mumbled.

Sickened by the knowledge that he could only mean Ariel, I said quickly, "He waits to speak with you."

"They . . . they said so. But he said I would not see him again. . . ."

"There has been a change of plans," I said with sudden inspiration. Clearly, I had hit the right note, for suddenly the muddiness gave way to a feverish excitement.

"Where is my master?" Domick demanded. His voice was louder now, and I realized that it was not Domick's voice I heard, yet the voice seemed strangely familiar.

"I will take you to him. Come," I said, drawing him along

the lane. We had not gone more than a few steps before Domick wrenched himself out of my grasp.

I turned to face him. "What is the matter? We must hurry."

"I know you!" Domick cried, and he reached out and snatched the mask from my face. His face contorted in horror. "Elspeth Gordie! The beloved."

Confounded by his words, I stared at Domick. He was not the broken null I had expected, but he was not himself either. He had recognized my voice and my face, but why did he look at me with such violent revulsion? All expression in his face died, and he reached out to me. For one bewildered moment, I thought he meant to embrace me, but then he closed his hot hands about my neck. He was thin and gaunt and ill, but there was a sinewy strength left in him that crushed my throat. He brought his face close to mine, his breath foul, and I felt the heat of his fever like a blast from a fire pit.

"You will not interfere with my master's plans," he said. Grief and rage and terror shuddered over his features in maniacal progression, and then the blankness returned and he squeezed. "I am the instrument of my master!" he bellowed in my face, and even while I fought to tear his fingers from my neck, I was afraid of the noise he was making. I struggled hard, trying to claw Domick's hands to loosen their deadly grip, but they were slick with sweat, and I could not get any purchase. Shadows began to flutter at the edge of my vision.

Desperate, I struck out at Domick's face. He flinched instinctively, letting go of me with one hand. I caught the flying hand and clung to it, though the fingers of his other hand still dug into my throat.

"We were friends, Domick!" I rasped, now that I could get a bit of breath.

Domick flinched. Then he snarled, "Shut up! I am not

542

Domick. Domick is dead. I am . . . I am Mika," Domick said, his fingers slackening slightly.

I stared at him in disbelief. I had been with Domick once when he had taken on his spy persona of Mika, and it had chilled me to see how much he became that cold arrogant man. Obviously, whatever Ariel had done to Domick had destroyed his mind so only this invented self remained. That was why I had recognized the voice and manner.

Suddenly, Domick's face blazed with anguish, and he threw me away from him so violently that I fell to my knees. By the time I had scrambled to my feet, he was running awkwardly along the lane away from the square. He had almost reached the crossroad when a man stepped out leading the biggest horse I had ever seen. He wore a simple mask of black inlaid with metal, but his powerful shoulders and wooden leg told me it was Rolf.

I could not cry out to him, so I beastspoke the startled horse. "I am ElspethInnle! Do not let the running funaga through!"

Domick seemed not even to see the enormous beast who lowered its great shaggy head and butted him backward into a door. His head struck it with a sickening crunch, and he crumpled unconscious at its base.

As I reached him, a woman opened the door and gaped down. Before she could scream, I coerced her ruthlessly and sent her back inside. Rolf knelt by me and bade me give him the sleep potion. He dribbled a few drops onto the pad and held it over the coercer's mouth. Rolf then fetched a length of canvas from Golfur's back and, unfurling it, rolled Domick onto it. He wrapped him up in a neat parcel, open at his head so he could breathe, and between us we lifted him onto Golfur's back. I would never have managed it without the metal-worker, for the horse was even bigger than he had looked from a distance. I had thought the term *greathorse* was the name for a west coast breed, but now I realized it was merely a description. I dug in the saddlebags for my heavy shoes and the cap Erit had given me. There was also a simple mask to replace the distinctive cat mask. I removed the cloak. Exchanging the delicate slippers for my heavy shoes and retrieving the mask that Domick had knocked away, I wrapped them in the cloak.

In the meantime, Rolf arranged bundles and parcels on Golfur's back until Domick's form was all but concealed. "How is he?" the metalworker asked when he had finished.

"I don't know if he is infectious," I said, handing him the mask and slippers wrapped in the cloak.

Rolf shrugged. "I suppose we will know soon enough." He took the bundle and shot me an inquiring look. "You beastspoke Golfur to ask his aid?"

I nodded, glancing anxiously about us to make sure no one had entered the lane. Rolf shook his head in wonder, then looped his hands and bade me climb up onto the greathorse and go.

"Iriny . . ."

"I will make sure she is safe. You concentrate on your friend. Get him out of the city. If we live, I expect to have your story someday."

I put one foot into his hands, and he hoisted me up into the saddle.

"Thank you," I said with a rush of gratitude for this good man.

"Go!" Rolf said again, slapping the greathorse. The beast turned to administer a large affectionate lick before ambling off along the street. It was not a moment too soon, for even as we passed into a wider street, a troop of soldierguards came hurtling along, bristling with weapons.

544

✦ 6 ✦

To MY RELIEF, Golfur knew the way to the nearest gate, so I had no need to remember the instructions Rolf had given that morning. I had only to sit on his back as he moved through a crowd that parted to give him room and seemed to accept his size more readily than I could. As we made our stately progress through the streets, I calmed down enough to send a probe to Erit, who immediately began to crow with delight at hearing I was leaving the city with Domick. When I expressed my concern for the trouble I had left behind, he assured me with high good humor that the fracas in the market had abated as mysteriously as it had begun, leaving puzzled revelers and some furious and dismayed Hedra who were now ranting to a troop of soldierguards about the loss of a priest they had been escorting to the piers.

Erit explained that the signal Rolf had given was actually a long-established signal to all stallholders that one of their number was under threat. They had discovered that direct intervention, especially if soldierguards or Hedra were involved, would end up in the person trying to help being imprisoned, too. It had been Rolf's idea that if there was enough unrelated confusion, the person in difficulties would have a far better chance of slipping away. Each of the stallholders had come up with his or her own specialty when help was needed, and each could be evoked with a different signal.

I marveled at Rolf's cleverness and wondered that such a man could be a mere metalworker, yet in the end, a man was not his trade or craft. Erit went on to tell me that the soldierguards, who had raced to the market believing they were to face a violent rebel outbreak, were more amused than anything else by the anger of the haughty Hedra, for there was a niggling sort of rivalry between them. Naturally, the ill-concealed amusement of the soldierguards incensed the Hedra, just as it was meant to do. Now the Hedra captain was shouting at the soldierguard captain, Erit reported, demanding their help in finding Domick.

I left Erit and sought Iriny and Rolf. Failing to find them, I returned to Erit. The boy was still absorbed by the confrontation in the market. I bade him give my thanks to his urchin friends for their help and my regrets to Iriny that there had been no time to bid her a proper farewell. Then I withdrew and concentrated on what to do when we reached the gate.

I had no fear that there would be anyone looking for Domick when we passed through. It was too soon, and from what Erit said, the bad blood between the Hedra and the soldierguards would cause even greater delay. I ought to have been as elated as Erit at our success, but Domick's fever and grogginess made me fear that the plague might be nearer to becoming contagious than we had guessed. After all, we knew nothing about this disease.

Golfur ambled into another street, and I was surprised to see the gate. Only one man was waiting to leave with an empty cart, and he passed out even before we reached the gate. A great long line of people and horses and wagons waited to be admitted, and all of the soldierguards at the gate save one were tending them.

Beyond the gate, the tawny plain stretched away under an enameled blue sky unmarred by a single cloud, and I felt a surge of eagerness to be out in the open and away from the press of people and the reek of the squalid city. Even so, I beastspoke Golfur, asking him to slow down, for I wanted to try one last time to reach Rolf or Iriny. I still could not locate the metalworker, but this time when I sought Iriny, my probe located. To my horror, she was in the hands of the soldierguards, because several people had witnessed her striking the Hedra, and she was unmistakably a gypsy.

I cast about wildly, and this time I found Rolf. His serene mind calmed me.

"Do not think of turning back or waiting to see what happens," he warned me. "I have told you that I will take care of the gypsy. You must trust me and do what you need to do now, for if you fail, Iriny may as well die at the hands of the Hedra or soldierguards."

He was right. I sent, "I leave her in your hands, then. I am about to go through the gate. I just . . . I wanted to thank you again."

"You can do that in person when all of this is over."

"Good luck to you."

Drawing near the gate, I studied each of the four soldierguards. There was little urgency in their manner or voices, but they were thorough. There were no horses saddled and ready to give chase, and I made up my mind that if there was any trouble, I would ask Golfur to pretend to bolt through the soldierguards, and I would screech in pretended terror. With any luck, the soldierguards would laugh and give no thought to chasing after us, but even if they did, no normal horse could match the giant strides of the greathorse, however fleet of foot they were. I hoped fervently there would be no need for it, as I did not want to subject Domick to such a ride. Indeed, I was worried about how well he could breathe, trussed up as he was.

I was now close enough to the gate to hear one of the soldierguards demand trading papers from a man bringing in rugs from Port Oran. The mention of the city seemed to galvanize the soldierguards, who asked if he had seen any women traveling alone. At first I thought they must be seeking Rawen, but then one of the soldierguards spoke of an older woman with different-colored eyes and named her an assassin from the other side of the Suggredoon, and my heart almost stopped, for I realized it was *Iriny* they sought. Someone must have seen her at the river after all. Whatever order had been given concerning her must not have been circulated completely, else the soldierguards at the sea market would not be bandying words with the Hedra. But it would not be long before they learned who they had.

I was about to farseek Rolf when one of the soldierguards finally noticed me waiting and beckoned me. Biting my lip, I shook the reins, and Golfur ambled forward to stop before the gate.

"Dismount," ordered the soldierguard in a bored voice. I slithered down ignominiously, landing hard enough to jar my ankles painfully, and then I realized my fine escape plan of getting Golfur to bolt was useless, because how on earth was I to mount him without help? The soldierguard snapped his fingers, and I realized that he wanted the horse's papers. I dug them out of the saddlebag, hoping he would not notice that my hands were trembling, for he was standing right alongside Domick. If the coercer so much as sighed, we would be undone.

"What are you carrying?" asked the soldierguard at

length, passing the papers back to me. He tapped at the parcel that was Domick.

"I am taking new leather to be worked to softness, dyed, and cut into belt lengths by grubbers. Once it is brought back, my master will create silver buckles and stamp a design into the leather that he will inlay with silver." I had concocted this tale on the way to the gate, but beads of sweat dampened my forehead, for the soldierguard was now resting his hand solidly on Domick. Growing desperate, I began to cast my eyes and mind out for someone who could create a diversion.

But the soldierguard shrugged. "Go on, then, and take care of that beast, for if he is harmed, I suppose your master will want you hide for his belts."

He roared laughing, and I was on the verge of walking out through the gate when a cold voice spoke behind me. "Wait." Both the soldierguard and I turned to face an older soldierguard whose yellow cape proclaimed him a captain.

"This horse is yours?" the captain demanded of me, flicking his fingers impatiently. Too frightened to speak in case he realized I was not a boy, I shook my head and handed him the papers.

"Hoy there, how long is this going to take?" someone called from the line outside the gate in a hectoring, impatient tone. The soldierguard captain turned to scowl at the queue.

"Who asks?"

No one answered, and the captain took a threatening step toward the line before noticing that he still held Golfur's papers. He turned and thrust them at me, telling me to be on my way, and then he began to lecture the waiting people. Did they think he was only here to check for traders trying to evade the city tax? No! Didn't anyone realize that there were no rebels in Halfmoon Bay precisely because the soldierguards were vigilant? Were they not aware that the three-day festival and the crowning of the masked king or queen would make the perfect target for a violent rebel scheme? As it was, a dangerous murderess had crossed the river and had been seen heading toward Port Oran.

Trembling with relief for myself and fear for Iriny, I led Golfur through the gate. The greathorse plodded steadily past the soldierguards and the people crowded at the entrance, none of whom seemed to find his appearance odd. I wished passionately that I could simply ride off, but absurdly, I could truly think of no way to mount the enormous horse. There was no alternative but to lead him along the waiting queue, which stretched for a good distance along the road. A cluster of makeshift stalls had been erected outside the gate, selling water bladders, pastries, and all manner of other things to those forced to wait in a long queue in the sun. Every stall also sold a selection of cheap and not so cheap masks for those who had forgotten them or had not brought one.

As we passed the last stall, I noticed a mound of rocks to use as a mounting block. I led the greathorse to it, and spotting me, the stallholder observed in a friendly bellow that he would swear that was the greathorse of Aro the cripple.

I ignored him and muttered a curse under my breath, for the mound was not quite high enough. Gritting my teeth, I tried jumping from the top of the mound onto Golfur's back, but he was too tall, and I slipped back and only just managed not to topple from the rocks.

"Now, that must be the most inelegant attempt to mount a horse that I have ever witnessed," said a mocking voice. "You had better let me give you a leg up, young master."

I turned to see Merret grinning as she leapt down lightly from the back of a stocky, muscular white horse. In all the drama of taking Domick from the Hedra and escaping the city, not to mention what had happened on Stonehill, I had completely forgotten that she was coming to Halfmoon Bay. I was overjoyed to see her, but I dared not greet her openly with so many watching eyes. I meekly let her boost me into my seat. Then she mounted, too, and we rode on together casually. "You have him?" she farsent with painful force.

"He is under the packages with a canvas wrapped around him." I farsent my response with pointed gentleness. "Golfur—that is the name of this greathorse—had to knock him out, and we had to use sleep potion on him."

I said nothing more, having noticed two riders sitting motionless at the side of the road. I sensed they were watching us, and I was about to say so, when I recognized the coercer-knight Orys, though he now wore his hair in the Norse style, with side plaits. The other rider was the empath Blyss, who had been a fragile child when she left for the west coast. She had grown into a lissome, blond beauty with pale gold hair that was cropped short, so it flew about her head like pale feathers, and she was riding black Zidon, whom I had last seen ridden by Merret when they left Obernewtyn for the west coast. I beastspoke the horse with pleasure, but on the heels of my delight at seeing them all safe came a darker thought.

I glanced about to make sure there was no one close enough to hear me, and then I stopped Golfur some little distance from them and said loudly and clearly, "Blyss, Orys, I am more glad than you can imagine to see you are safe. But now you must ride away, for I am sure you all know that Ariel infected Domick with plague. Merret has already come so close that if Domick is contagious, she is doomed, but you are safe yet."

"Have no fear for us, Guildmistress," said Orys. "Dell foretold you contacting Merret and heard all that you told her about Domick, so she did a casting focused on him. She saw that although Ariel had intended and believed that Domick would become infectious today, he will not be capable of passing on the plague before dusk on the morrow. She bade me ride to Aborium at once, and I did so, arriving only shortly after Merret had told the rebels what she had learned from you. Dell asked me and Blyss to ride to Halfmoon Bay with Merret to escort you and Domick to the Beforetime ruins, where Jak can care for him without his sickness endangering anyone."

"What else did Dell foresee?" I asked, for the futureteller was one of those whom Atthis had used to save me from drowning.

Merret shrugged. "That you would come out this gate closer to noon than dawn; that you would have Domick with you, and that you would need help. It is lucky for you that we came, too, for who else would have made that man in the queue shout at the soldierguard?"

I said softly, "Merret, you know as well as I do that no futuretelling is ever absolutely set. Dell might be wrong about Domick not being infectious until tomorrow evening."

A ghost of a smile touched Orys's lips. "Dell said you would say that. She said to assure you that she checked her futuretelling about the course of Domick's sickness a dozen times."

Merret said, "We will camp at dusk. We will be on the main road by then."

"I would rather ride straight through," I said.

"I too. But Dell told Blyss that we must make camp at dusk, for a great troop of Hedra will ride out from Halfmoon

552

Bay cloister then, searching for a woman of your description, last seen leading a missing Herder into a lane. Half of the Hedra will ride toward the Suggredoon, and the other half will go toward Murmroth. Apparently, every traveler with horse or cart will be searched, but Dell says they will initially ignore those camped, because no sane fugitive would blithely pitch a tent so near the scene of a crime. We have food and medicines to ease Domick, as well as fodder for the horses."

"Then we are well provisioned, for I have those things, too," I said sharply. Then I chided myself for my lack of gratitude. Dell had foreseen enough to send the help I needed, and it was wonderful to know that Domick was not infectious yet; better still, to know that Jak would be able to help him, for I had truly feared he would die.

We rode at an easy pace up to the main coast road, but there was no chance to talk properly because of the number of travelers we passed. It was easier to ride in silence, thinking our own thoughts. But when we reached the main road and began to make our way along it, I took the opportunity of a gap in the travelers to ask Merret what had happened when she had broken my news to Gwynedd. Domick had bruised my throat badly enough that it hurt to talk, but that was far less painful than enduring a farsought conversation with a coercer as strong as Merret.

"He was appalled, of course," Merret said. "They all were. But Gwynedd quelled the fuss by saying calmly that we Misfits have shown ourselves time and time again to be competent and honest, and that you were one of our leaders and had performed dangerous rescues many times over the years. He said that your Talents would aid you in finding Domick and that panicking was a waste of time. One of the others asked if he advised them to do nothing, and he said, 'Warn everyone of the attempt by the Herders on Herder Isle to start a plague that would kill Councilmen, Herder priests, and ordinary folk alike, leaving nothing but a barren wasteland, and prepare all rebel groups to evacuate the cities with their families and enough supplies to set up isolated desert camps.' Then Orys arrived with Dell's futuretelling that you would succeed."

"Did Gwynedd accept the futuretelling?"

Merret gave me an odd look. "You will find that the rebels here are a good deal more ready to accept our abilities and their benefits than many on the other side of the river. Maybe because so many of us died along with the rebels on the Night of Blood. Once Gwynedd told the rebels what Dell had seen, they began to talk of what else you had told me—the invasion of the Hedra and the overthrow of the Faction on Herder Isle. Which reminds me, Gwynedd is very keen to speak with you of what has been happening on Herder Isle. You know, of course, that he is a Norselander?"

I nodded.

"Guildmistress," Blyss broke in shyly, "I know there is much to tell of what has been happening here and on the other side of the river, yet it would please me—all of us—if you would give us news of Obernewtyn."

I obliged, speaking for a time of small matters as well as large. I told them of the powerful bond that had grown between Gavyn and the white dog Rasial and of Kella's tiny owl, Fey, that now rode on his shoulder. I told them of the Teknoguild house in the White Valley, with its lack of doors and floors, and of the opening of Jacob Obernewtyn's tomb. I told them of Dardelan's request that I journey to Sutrium to make formal charges against Malik and of the proposal that

Obernewtyn become a village. Orys asked me about finding Rushton, and I was not sorry to have my tale interrupted by the arrival of a group of riders who galloped up and then slowed to match our pace.

A gray-haired man asked if we had heard of the gypsy assassin the rebels had dispatched across the river to kidnap a priest from Herder Isle sent to officiate at Halfmoon Bay's masked moon fair. I left Merret and Orys to gossip with them and asked Golfur to move slightly ahead, telling myself I ought to be glad rumor had bypassed me. But I could not bear the thought that I might be the reason Iriny would suffer yet again at the hands of the Herders.

After a time, the newcomers set off again at a gallop, but almost at once we were overtaken by a portly man and his wife riding equally portly ponies. Once again, I left them to Merret and Orys and rode wrapped in silence until dusk fell and Merret announced that we would stop to make camp. She had chosen a place between two noisy groups of people already camped by the wayside, and while I understood that we were safer amidst these folk, I wished we might have camped alone. There was a tense moment while the couple contemplated joining us, but finally the wife said she would rather go on and sleep in a real bed.

Merret heaved a sigh of relief after they had ridden off, and she and Orys swiftly erected a dun-colored tent. By the time this was done, the sun had set. We carefully untied Domick's canvas-wrapped body and bore him inside the tent where Blyss had laid out a blanket and lit a lantern. As we laid him down, she went out to start a fire to boil some water, and Orys went to tend the horses, leaving Merret and me to unwrap the coercer. Loud laughter and snatches of song rose from the surrounding camps, and I was glad of it, for as we lifted Domick to slide the canvas out from under him, he moaned loudly.

Merret said, "If he is still like this when it begins to quiet down, I will visit both camps to see what news they offer and mention that we have a companion with terrible constipation." Catching my look of indignation, she shrugged. "It is better to have them laughing than suspicious, Elspeth, and Domick is in no position to feel humiliated."

I sighed. "I know you are right. It is just that he has suffered so." I was unfastening the small ties down the front of Domick's Herder tunic so we could remove it and cool him down. I glared with loathing at the demon band he wore, wishing I could unlock it, but the taint in it was simply too potent.

"Don't worry about the Demon band," Merret said. "Jak can remove it easily once we arrive." I nodded and pulled open Domick's Herder tunic. I was sickened to see that there was almost no flesh on his body without cuts or burns, and many of the scars were puckered and angry-looking, as if they had never properly healed. Blyss was just entering the tent again and gave a cry that was as much a reaction to our horror as to the savage scarring on the coercer's pale, emaciated torso.

"Hush," Merret said, leaping up to lay her long arm around the shoulders of the slender blond empath.

Orys looked into the tent worriedly, having heard Blyss cry out. He grimaced, seeing Domick's body. "I will bring in the water to clean him once it is boiled," he said, grim-faced, and withdrew.

His words had been directed at Blyss, who now came to kneel on the other side of the coercer. Brushing away tears, she slipped a woven bag from her shoulder and removed a pouch from it. It was a small but efficiently composed basic healer's kit such as Kella prepared for each of her guild. Except Blyss was an empath, not a healer. Yet there was no doubt that the instruments were hers and that she knew how to use them as she began to examine Domick's wounds.

Merret came to sit cross-legged beside me, saying softly, "We have had to turn our hands to many additional duties since we were cut off from the other part of the Land, Guild-mistess. As you will see, Blyss has become a very competent healer." She smiled at the golden head bowed in concentration, and the tenderness in her eyes made me wonder what else had developed in the months of their isolation.

Once Domick had been cleaned and made as comfortable as possible, Blyss laid a damp cloth over his brow and another over his body to reduce his fever. Then she bade us go and eat, as she would take first watch. Outside, Orys had begun to prepare a stew, regretting the lack of bread. I suggested that there might be some in the parcels that Rolf had packed, and Merret offered to fetch it. When she returned, she handed Orys a loaf of dark bread, which he set about slicing. I excused myself, for I had just remembered Rawen. Shamed to have forgotten about her, I farsent her at once to invite her to join us, saying there was water and fodder aplenty as well as equine companions. She accepted eagerly, with no reproaches for my forgetfulness. Warning her to stay well away from the road, I withdrew.

The meal was not yet ready. Casting around for a way to distract myself from the memory of Domick's ravaged body and my fears for Iriny, I wandered to the horses and beast-spoke with several, who told me of the freerunning herd that, on occasion, lent their aid to the funaga who dwelt in the

Beforetime ruins, in exchange for water and fodder when grazing was sparse. I saw Ran, the white stallion who led the freerunning herd, in close conversation with Golfur as they champed on the hay Orys had put out for them. Curiosity made me open my mind to their communication, and I heard Ran urging the greathorse to join the freerunning herd, saying there were two other greathorses among them, both of whom were mares.

Golfur answered in a slow, deep mindvoice that he must return to Rolf, who was his little brother and would certainly get into difficulties without him. Ran was clearly struggling to understand how a funaga could be regarded as kin to a horse, and Golfur seemed entirely unmoved by the suggestion that he was a slave. I remembered Rolf's comments about the greathorse and thought that, whether or not the crippled metalworker understood beastspeech, he certainly knew Golfur.

Rather than interrupt the conversation, I asked Sigund, the charcoal mare that Orys had ridden, to let Ran know that another mare would join them later, then I returned to the camp in time to hear Domick groan loudly. I strode across to the tent and entered it to find Blyss leaning over Domick, who was writhing horribly, his face twisting in agony.

"What is it?" I asked.

Blyss looked up at me, white-faced. "I am no true healer, such as Kella, but my empathy tells me that Domick is dreaming of what was done to him, and the memory is so deep and powerful that he feels the pain of his torture all over again."

"Is there nothing you can do?" I asked.

"I have done all I can for his body. If I had some sleep potion, I could use it to deepen his sleep so that he will not dream."

"Wait!" I cried, and withdrew the bottle Rolf had given to me. The empath unstoppered the bottle and carefully dribbled a few drops onto a kerchief and held it over Domick's mouth, just as Rolf had done.

Coming out of the tent again, I heard the drumming of hooves approaching. Orys and Merret were gazing along the road toward the Suggredoon, as were the people in the adjoining camps. Soon the riders came into view, grim-faced Hedra who thundered past without stopping. A chill ran down my spine at the realization that if Dell had not warned us, we would have been overtaken and searched. I came to stand by Merret as we watched the darkness swallow the troop.

"We will break camp before dawn and head directly toward the Blacklands, taking care not to be seen," she said. "We will ride right to the badlands that run in a narrow strip along the edge of the Blacklands. There are mutated plants and shrubs that grow high enough to give us some cover. Then we will ride for the ruins, being careful to go slowly enough to raise no telltale dust."

"Because they will come back?" I asked, nodding after the riders.

Merret inclined her head. "Dell says they will be angry, and they will tear apart every camp beside the road, looking for Domick and for the woman who took him," she said.

As we ate the stew Orys had prepared, I told them about meeting Iriny and of the danger she now faced for helping me. "Rolf promised to help her, but he did not know she was being hunted for crossing the river, and now they think it is she who took Domick," I said.

"Do not trouble yourself," Merret said, "I will return to Halfmoon Bay after I have brought you to the ruins. If nothing else, we should let these people who helped you know that they are safe from plague. I assume you told them about it?"

I nodded, and then I asked if she would take Golfur with her, because the greathorse wished to return to Rolf.

"This Rolf must be quite a man to impress a greathorse."

"He is," I said.

Orys offered me a bowl of dried fruit softened with hot water and sweetened with honey, saying how odd it was to think that Rushton and Dardelan and all those on the other side of the Suggredoon knew nothing of the plague threat or of Domick's part in it.

"Or mine," I murmured. "Unless Maryon has futuretold it. But they will know it when the *Stormdancer* sails from Herder Isle." I thought of Yarrow and Asra and wondered if the Hedra master had surrendered yet.

"They will know of the plague, but they will not know we have Domick," Orys pointed out.

"I wonder if *they* know Iriny came across," Merret said thoughtfully. "From what you say, it was entirely a Twenty-families venture, yet the rebels must have seen the burning rafts. I must tell you that I am impressed that she got across the Suggredoon. We have been trying for months from this side." She stretched, her joints making loud popping noises. "You said that Iriny buried the plast suit she used. Perhaps it can be recovered, and we can use it to send a messenger to Dardelan, letting him know that we managed to prevent the outbreak of plague. I will speak of it to the gypsy when I go to Halfmoon Bay . . ." She trailed into silence as Orys threw some shrub wood onto the fire and went to relieve Blyss.

"How do you think the Council and the Herders here will react when they learn that those on Herder Isle have been overthrown?" I asked.

Merret prodded at the embers and said, "The Council-court will be pleased to discover they no longer need to dance to the Faction's tunes, for much of the Herders' power rests upon the fact that there are so many more of them just across the strait. The soldierguards will be elated, because if you count Hedra and soldierguards here on the west coast, I would say the numbers are similar. It may even be that there are more soldierguards, but the Hedra are more deadly and disciplined fighters."

"Are you saying they would clash?"

"I think that a war between them is inevitable," Merret said. "I would not lose sleep over the idea of their killing one another, except both sides will conscript ordinary folk to fight with them. We are nowhere near prepared to rise here, but we may have no choice if the soldierguards go to war against the Hedra."

"You speak of the soldierguards, but what of the Council in all this?" I asked.

"The truth is that their power always rested on that of the soldierguards and the terror invoked by the Faction," Merret said. "I think, though, that they will have to back the soldier-guards simply because the Faction will have no use for them at all."

"There is another thing to consider," I said. "I told you of the weapons I saw in the Herder Compound armory. If demon bands were shipped here, why not weapons as well? If even some of the vile weapons I saw there are stored here in the cloisters, this war you speak of could be far more sav-age than anyone could imagine, and the likelihood is that the priests will win."

Blyss emerged from the tent and sat down wearily on a blanket Merret spread out for her. The coercer asked how

Domick was, and Blyss answered that he was sleeping soundly and that his fever had fallen slightly. Merret solicitously filled a bowl with stew and gave it to her.

As the night wore on, I asked what had happened on the west coast following the closing of the Suggredoon. Merret replied that Serba had escaped and gone to warn the rebels on the other side of the river while Yavok and a few of his men survived simply because the rebel had been late collecting them for the meeting. Tardis survived, along with all of her people, only because Merret had ridden out to farseek a warning to the healer Kader. He had been stationed with the Murmroth rebel group, and Tardis had immediately commanded that all rebel haunts be abandoned. She then convened what came to be known as the Cloud Court: a meeting place that changed constantly. For a time, it looked as if Murmroth would be the rallying point for all rebels left on the west coast, but then Yavok was murdered by one of his own men, and the Murmroth rebel group under Tardis responded by closing ranks, rejecting all the rebels from outside Murmroth and ejecting Alun and even Kader, who had saved them.

"It was a sore point with Tardis that we refused to divulge the location of our safe house, you see." Merret sighed. "In truth, while Tardis was not as fanatically prejudiced against Misfits as her father seems to have been, she did not feel comfortable around our kind and was glad of an excuse to cut the connection. So we Misfits who had survived retreated to the ruins to live as best we could and to wait, for we knew you would come eventually."

"It was a time of terror," Blyss whispered, her eyes unfocused as if she looked into the past. "The Council was not satisfied with having killed most rebels on the Night of Blood.

They searched for survivors and killed them publicly and horribly whenever they found them, along with whoever had sheltered them. The Councilmen arrested and tortured anyone known to have sympathized with the rebel cause, and it became a crime even to voice any criticism of the Council. The torture of people resulted in more arrests and more torture, often of innocent people."

"The Herders were equally fervent in their search for Misfits," Merret said in a low voice. "They knew that we had helped the rebels, and they held services reviling mutants as damned creatures and demons, and they demanded ritual cursing. Anyone who did not show enough fervor was taken and interrogated, then burned for having Misfit sympathies. People attended as never before because to be absent was to be suspect. Also, hundreds of people who may or may not have had Misfit tendencies were burned after being reported by neighbors."

"It sounds hellish," I murmured.

"It was. The soldierguards who had fled across the river were enraged at having been forced to abandon their homes and families. They demanded an immediate offensive on the rebels, but the Councilmen refused. We later learned that the Herders had warned them not to invade until they were equipped to wipe the rebels off the face of the earth. I am sure the Councilmen took the Herders' advice, because only the priests' warning had prevented the rebels from taking over the west coast as well. And the Council readily accepted the Faction's offer of demon bands to protect all Councilmen and soldierguards against mutant possession. The soldierguards from the other side of the river were absorbed into the various city troops, and the Council set up the barrier and river watch. But the soldierguards from the other side of the river remained volatile, and their grievances added an unruly, dissatisfied element to a group that was already difficult to control. That the Hedra were openly contemptuous of them did not improve the relationship between the two groups. Nevertheless, for a time, the Council and the Faction settled into their old uneasy relationship, secure in the knowledge that the rebel network had been broken on the west coast and that no one could cross the river. Both poured their anger and energy and frustration into ensuring that no one would ever dare to rebel again. In a way they succeeded, until Tardis died and Gwynedd became the leader of the Murmroth rebels."

"I gather he made contact with you," I said.

"He wished to do so, but he knew only that we had a secret desert camp," Merret said. "It was chance alone that had me in Aborium foraging for information when one of the Aborium rebels I knew recognized me. She told me that Tardis was dead and that Gwynedd had taken over the rebel group in Murmroth. She said he had begun to resurrect the rebel network, contacting survivors, encouraging them to reform proper cells with elected leaders, urging them to recruit new members. People were receptive, because they knew that most soldierguards were greedy for Salamander's bonuses. They were weary of their children and friends being arrested on the slightest pretext, especially if they looked healthy, and being taken away across the sea to be sold as slaves. She told me that Gwynedd wanted to communicate with us, so I rode to Murmroth to speak with him.

"Thus we began to work with the rebels. Their numbers began to grow after Gwynedd staged several operations with our aid to rescue prisoners from Councilcourt cells. We also attacked the Faction. Priests out to collect tithes were robbed and sent stumbling naked back to their cloisters, and the coin was used to buy the freedom of young men and women taken by the soldierguards. During many raids, rebels rescued groups of boys destined for the cloisters. The lads could not return to their homes, of course, but remote grubber farms began to have visits from distant cousins. Some of those saved remained in Murmroth and began to train as rebels under Gwynedd, whom they naturally revered," Merret said.

"Did the Council and the Faction realize all of their troubles were emanating from Murmroth?" I asked, curious.

"No," Merret said. "Gwynedd made sure we operated along the coast in all the towns and outside all cloisters. He knew a good deal about the Councilmen of the other coastal cities because of the information Seely had given him, so the Council was convinced there was another full network in operation, however much they might deny it publicly."

"I don't understand," I protested. "Tomash questioned Seely, and her information about the west coast was unusable."

"Useless to us because we knew too little about the west coast to fit Seely's idiosyncratic knowledge into any sort of framework that would give it meaning," Merret said. "But Gwynedd *has* the framework, and he also knew what questions to ask. It seems that Gavyn's father was very sociable, and both high-ranking citizens and Councilmen alike were his guests. Once he bonded with Lady Slawyna after Gavyn's mother died, he often had Herders visit as well, for his wife's son was a Herder. Being part of the household and yet also a servant of sorts meant Seely was in the perfect position to gather information and gossip." The coercer chuckled. "It is a nice irony that Seely has been the most useful of us to the rebels."

I smiled and wondered if becoming useful had altered Seely's shy diffidence.

"How do things stand now with the rebels?" I asked.

Merret shrugged. "As I have told you, there are too few of us for a proper uprising. Indeed, Gwynedd has never suggested wresting control with so few rebels. He seeks only to weaken the Faction and the Council as much as he can and to prepare us to aid Dardelan and the other rebels when they come for the west coast."

I wondered if Merret had any idea how often she included herself when she spoke of the rebels under Gwynedd. Something in my expression seemed to convey my reserve, for she said mildly, "I do not think it a betrayal of Misfits to admire a man who has no Talent yet is gifted and honorable."

"What made you trust Gwynedd, given that he had served Tardis?" I asked.

Merret considered the question. "In part, it was that he insisted upon being taught Brydda's fingerspeech, and he encouraged all of his people to do the same. But the true moment of revelation came when it struck me that Gwynedd had never offered freedom to the horses with which he communicated. I wondered why until I realized that he never saw it as his to offer. From the first moment he communicated with them, he has regarded horses as fellow freedom fighters. 'When we are free,' he always says, to them and to us and to his own people. But I do not seek to convince you, Elspeth. You will judge him for yourself soon enough. Needless to say, he sees your arrival as a sign that we will soon rise against our oppressors."

I laughed without much amusement. "A meager sign since I am only one, and instead of coming on a ship, I was washed up on the beach like a piece of flotsam."

Merret shook her head. "If only one could come, who else should it be but you, Elspeth Gordie?" She laughed in faint exasperation at my uncomprehending look. "Think about what you have told me! You stopped the Hedra from invading the Land. You went to Herder Isle and defeated the Faction on its own territory. You rode a ship fish across the strait, found Domick, and brought him out of Halfmoon Bay before he could begin a plague."

"You exaggerate," I protested. "I did none of it alone!"

"No," Merret said, casting me a serious considering look. "No, it is never you alone, yet think how often you have been the pebble that begins the avalanche."

✦ 7 ✦

"Elspeth?" Blyss whispered. "Merret said to wake you."

I sat up. The stars were fading, so it must be near to dawn. The others moved about quietly, preparing to leave. I got up and folded my blanket, and Blyss took it to Orys to stow as I stepped into my ill-fitting shoes and drew on my cloak. My stomach rumbled, but I ignored it, for we had decided the previous night not to eat before we left. Merret and Orys were now dismantling the tent, and I asked Blyss softly where Domick was. She pointed to Golfur, and I realized they had created a pallet along the length of Golfur's broad back, upon which the coercer lay. A blanket had been laid over him, and when I reached up to tuck it in more securely under the ropes binding the pallet to the greathorse, I was dismayed by the heat radiating from Domick's body. Blyss had said the previous night that his temperature had dropped, but it seemed he was hotter than ever.

Someone nudged me, and I turned to find Rawen gazing at me. She looked a good deal less a fine young lady's horse than she had when I had first set eyes on her. Her coat was dull and dusty in patches, and her mane and tail were badly tangled, but her eyes sparkled as she told me that I was to ride her, since Golfur carried a burden already. I thanked her and would have mounted, but Merret called softly that we would walk at first.

As we crossed the road, I glanced along it in the direction of Murmroth and then in the direction of the Suggredoon, but there was no sign of movement. I wondered how long it would be before the Hedra returned. The people who had camped near us would speak of us when questioned, but Merret had spent some time the previous night coercing memories into key people in the groups, one of whom had us heading toward the ocean at about midnight, and another would swear to have seen us angling back toward Halfmoon Bay. I noticed Orys and Blyss carefully brushing away our tracks with swatches of cloth to disguise our true direction.

By the time Merret gave the command to ride, my heels were bleeding and painful. Before I mounted, I removed my heavy shoes with relief, pushing them into one of Golfur's saddlebags just in case I needed them.

We had spoken little while we walked, and we continued in silence, conscious that voices carried far on the plain, but soon we were approaching the fantastic and distorted shapes of vegetation on the badlands: bizarrely shaped giant shrubs and spiked green tubers rising above the ground. I had never been here before, and the reality defied any description I had heard of its strangeness. But it was a narrow enough strip that allowed me to see the dark jagged form of the immense mountain range that ran along the Blacklands.

Blyss rode up on Zidon to offer some small hard twigs of food. "We will have a proper firstmeal a bit later, Merret says, but these will take the edge off your hunger," she promised.

I did feel uncomfortably hollow, so I took two of the graying twigs and crunched one gingerly. I was about to comment on its tastelessness when Blyss asked why Ariel and the Herders would unleash a plague on the west coast when so many of their own people would die as well.

"It is a question I have asked myself many times," I said. "There is no satisfactory answer. The One approved the plan, but Ariel was behind it."

"And the Raider approves?" Orys asked. "Surely he would rather have people alive so they can be sold as slaves?"

Before I could answer, Merret said, "Who knows truly what the Raider desires? With all the slaves he has traded, he must have amassed wealth enough for several lifetimes. And yet his slaving continues. At least it did until recently. So maybe his desire is not for coin."

"I think both he and Ariel gain pleasure from the suffering they cause," Orys said, nodding to Domick's prone form on Golfur's back. "And if hurting one person is pleasurable, imagine how much more delicious the suffering of thousands."

"Stop it!" Blyss whispered, white to the lips. "I have never heard anything so ugly."

"Forgive me," Orys said remorsefully. He looked at me. "I fear I have become somewhat obsessed with Salamander— the Raider as we have come to call him, like those on this coast. I have made it my business to try to learn more of him, and there are stories aplenty of his readiness to kill and maim."

"Tell me what you have learned," I said.

"That he is fanatically secretive and instinctively deadly and always seems to know if treachery is intended or if he is being lied to; that there are rules he seldom breaks; that his entire head and body are always covered, of course, and that these days he only comes ashore in a ship boat with an enormous mute to inspect the Council's offering. Then he gets aboard the ship boat, the mute rows him back out to his ship, and someone else comes to strike the bargain and load the slaves."

"We know most of this already," I said.

"Exactly," Orys said. "In all the months I have worked on trying to learn more about him, I have discovered almost nothing. And I wonder why he maintains such secrecy."

Conversation lapsed again for a time, and at length dawn broke. I watched birds pass across the silver-gray sky in arrowhead formations. Above, high skeins of cloud shifted constantly in a wind that slowly descended to scour the earth. There was sand enough in it that I was glad of the cover of the misshapen bushes and weirdly oversized plants, but eventually it was so strong that we stopped to tie cloths about our mouths and those of the horses. Gahltha had once told me horses had a hundred names for the wind, which could not possibly be translated into human speech. According to the stallion, funaga senses were too dull to pick up minuscule but important differences between degrees of dryness in the wind or slight shifts in angle or direction, or even the smells carried on the wind, all of which required a specific name.

We struggled on for another hour before Merret shouted that we must stop, for Ran had signaled to her that the wind was about to whip up a series of small but dangerous dust demons. Having no idea what these were, I dismounted hurriedly because of the tension in the coercer's voice and the speed with which Orys and Blyss reacted. I went to help untie Domick's pallet, but Merret said there was no time and signaled Golfur to get down. The other horses did the same, and Rawen took her place alongside the enormous Golfur, her skin twitching with excited apprehension. Orys and Merret quickly distributed blankets with ropes at the corners, which I was bidden to grasp as tightly as I could. By the time the dust demons struck, we were all huddled beneath the blankets.

For half an hour, we were buffeted but unharmed by a shrieking wind. I did not know what dust demons looked like, but their voices were dreadful.

Then the wailing stopped abruptly, and the wind was gone. Merret and Orys threw off the blankets and began shaking them free of dust and refolding them while the horses stood and shook themselves. All save Golfur, who knew what he carried and stood still as Blyss checked on Domick. None of the others seemed shaken by the dust-demon assault, but my legs still trembled as I stood and brushed away the fine powder of sand that had seeped through the blankets.

Merret suggested that we might as well have a bite to eat and wash the dust from our throats. Without ceremony, we ate rolls with cheese that we had prepared the night before and passed around a small bladder of water while the horses ate some oats and drank water from the wooden bowls Orys prepared.

I was eating and gazing absently across at the Blacklands when Blyss came to stand with me, asking, "You know what I think about when I see them?" I realized she was speaking of the Blackland mountain range and shook my head. "I think of how they are part of the same range that encircles Obernewtyn. You cannot imagine how I have sometimes missed greenness and misty rain."

"We even missed the snows of wintertime," Merret laughed, coming to stand beside Blyss and ruffling her flyaway golden curls.

Ran lifted his white head and whinnied. As he stamped and twitched his ears to explain to the others what he sensed, I impatiently entered his mind to find that the stallion could smell a host of riders moving back toward the Suggredoon.

Orys knelt down and pressed his ear to the ground, and he sat back on his heels and nodded. "Thirty riders, I'd say."

"The Hedra who rode toward Murmroth, by my guess," Merret said with satisfaction. "Now that they have passed, we can go more swiftly, for there will be no one to see our dust."

Two hours later, Domick began to groan and strain at his bonds, and I knew that the sleep potion was wearing off again. We stopped long enough to check the ties, and Blyss reluctantly administered another small dose from Rolf's bottle. When we rode on, the empath's expression was full of anxiety, and she admitted that Domick's fever had been mounting since morning and was now dangerously high. I suggested Orys ride ahead to warn Jak we were on our way, but Merret pointed out that Dell was likely to know exactly when we would come.

To take my mind off worrying about the coercer, I rode up beside Merret and asked her if Dell had dreamed of Matthew.

She gave me a sharp look of interest. "As a matter of fact, we have all dreamed of him at one time or another. Enough were true dreams for us to piece together that he is a slave in the Red Queen's land and has been trying to rally the people there to rise against the slave owners who occupy the Land. Only they refuse to rise because they believe they must wait for their queen to return. But Dell claims that it is Dragon whom Matthew is waiting for."

I took a deep breath, and on impulse, I spoke aloud for the first time of what I knew. "Dell is right," I said. "Dragon is the daughter of the Red Queen."

"What!" Merret cried, and the other two looked equally astounded.

"I went into her mind to try drawing her out of her coma, and I learned that it was the memory of her mother's death and betrayal that initially sent her into a coma—or rather her need to deal with the memory that she had repressed. Inside her mind, I saw her mother betrayed and stabbed by her advisor, and then she and Dragon were given to slavers with instructions that they be sold or thrown overboard. But something happened. Dragon's mother beastspoke whales that attacked the ship. She was dying even as she and Dragon entered the water. Then she summoned a ship fish and commanded it to take Dragon ashore. I believe the ship fish brought her to the west coast, and somehow she made her way to the ruins and lived there until we found her."

"It explains her fear of water," Orys said, shaking his head.

"Of course, that was a dream, so the real events might be rather different. Remember, she would have been younger and very frightened and confused. But my own dreams tell me that Matthew knows who Dragon is," I said. "At first he wanted to free the Red Land and come for Dragon, but now he wishes to fetch Dragon to the Red Land to fulfill the legend so the people there will overthrow their oppressors."

"We knew from Dell's futuretelling dreams that Dragon had awakened, but it was not until you offered me memories of all that transpired in Saithwold that I understood that her memory was flawed," Merret said.

"Kella and Roland say her memory will return, but even if it does not, I will ask Dardelan to send a ship to escort Dragon to the Red Queen's land. Perhaps the sight of her true home will remind Dragon of what she has forgotten."

Merret gave a shout, and I looked up to see the low broken walls of the Beforetime ruins.

✦ ✦ ✦

After so long, it was strange to ride again into the grid of streets and piles of broken rubble remaining from the Before-time settlement that had once stood here. Close to the edge of the ruins facing the Suggredoon, I noticed a square broken tower rising above the other buildings that I did not remember. It was ruined, yet surely there had been nothing so high when I had been here last. The others must have built it and made it look like a ruin, to serve as a lookout tower.

When I asked Merret, she grinned at me. "Fortunately, these west-coast folk are not as observant as you," she said. "They still think of these ruins as haunted, and we do all we can to support the legend Dragon began with her coerced visions."

As we neared the tower, I saw that there was a good solid lookout post atop a set of sturdy steps, hidden inside the corner where the two walls had been repaired. I farsought the lookout but found it empty.

The ground under the horses' hooves was now sand, and I remembered that from Aborium to Murmroth there were patches of true desert like those in Sador, and from time to time, dunes drifted slowly from these like slow strange nomads. It seemed that one had invaded the ruins some time past, for our passage, slow as it was, raised a gauzy cloud of fine sand, which the wind and sun spun into an opaque haze of gold.

We entered a narrow street and traveled single file, Merret in the lead on Ran, followed by Blyss on Zidon, Orys on Sigund, and Golfur behind them bearing Domick. I brought up the rear on Rawen. We passed a corner that stood at about the height of the horses' chests, the stone wall cracked and crumbling where a dry scrub grass had taken root, and it looked familiar. We were close to the central square where we had first dismounted years past, when I had come here with Pavo. How the discovery of the vast, dark Beforetime library had thrilled and astonished me. Since then, Teknoguild expeditions had come many times before the rebellion to gather more books, and I knew they now believed that the library was the very top level of a building that went deep beneath the earth. How deep, they had never been able to say, because they had been unable to access the other levels.

Looking around, I saw no sign of any settlement, save the broken tower. Not a smudge of smoke existed, nor anything else that would prompt someone riding past the ruins to investigate, and this made me wonder if Dell and the others had made their refuge beneath the ground in the library level. Or perhaps deeper. I asked Orys if they had managed to find a way into any of the levels beneath the library.

"We have entered all thirty levels below the surface," he answered blithely.

"*Thirty levels of books!*" I cried in disbelief.

"Not books," Orys said. "They were only on the first level. Dell says the building that housed the library was not a keeping place for books or a place to work, as most of the Beforetime buildings were. She thinks that the library existed only to hide the true purpose of the levels beneath, which were intended to house people in an emergency. There are sleeping chambers for more than three hundred, though they are very small, and there is a vast kitchen and eating area. Pretty much all the other space on the kitchen level and the next two is taken up with storerooms containing food enough for years."

"It was meant to be a refuge?" I managed to croak.

"It was, only no one ever came here for refuge. We found the bones of a single person in one bedroom, and Dell said that some bodies found on the upper levels were probably trapped when the Great White came. Jak thinks that is probably what happened to the man whose bones we found in the lower levels; he would have had no choice but to stay there."

I felt as if one of the dust demons from the plain had blown into my head. I wanted to think about what I had learned, but we were now approaching the central square. The last time I had seen it, it had been at night, and moonlight had given the broken walls and streets a ghostly look.

Lost in memory, I gasped as a column ahead of us moved, until I saw that it was Dell. She had been sitting atop a broken pillar watching our approach. Merret called out a greeting as the lean futureteller slipped from her perch and approached us. I saw with astonishment that she wore queer blue trousers in a fabric and design I had never seen before and enormous black boots, rather than the traditional beautifully dyed sweeping gowns and tunics favored by those of her guild. And she had cut her hair very short. But her cool, tranquil expression was unchanged by her months of exile, and as her pale eyes settled on me, I felt the same shiver of apprehension I always felt in the presence of a powerful futureteller, half fearing that she would make some dreadful pronouncement. At the same time, I longed to ask exactly what Atthis had said to solicit her aid in saving me from drowning. She merely gave me a formal bland greeting.

"It is good to see you safe," I said, dismounting and striving to appear at ease. She smiled and turned aside to watch as Merret and Orys took Domick's pallet from Golfur's back. I fetched out my clodhoppers, pulled them on, and straightened.

"Poor man," Dell murmured in her soft voice. "He has suffered much."

Seely appeared behind the futureteller, and I was startled to see that she wore exactly the same clothing as Dell, but her thin hair had grown, and now she had it plaited on either side of her face. Seeing me, she smiled and raised her hand, but her expression grew serious as her eyes settled on Domick, whose pallet the others had laid on the cobbles.

"Is Jak ready for him?" Dell asked.

"Of course," said Seely without looking away from Domick's gaunt face. Dell gestured to Merret, whereupon she and Orys lifted the pallet and bore it away carefully in the direction from which Seely had come. Dell suggested the younger woman go and help them with the doors, and she obeyed at once.

"Shall we go?" she asked me.

"We should tend to the horses," I said, for they were all still saddled save for Rawen. "There is also food in the saddlebags. . . ."

Dell smiled. "Pellis will be here in a moment to give them fodder and offer them a rubdown if they wish it."

"Pellis?" I asked, not recognizing the name.

"Merret found him. He is a Misfit. There are seven others who have joined us here since the Suggredoon closed, all children. They delight in tending the horses, for all except Pellis have learned Brydda's signal speech. Pellis does not need it, for he is a beastspeaker. But you will meet them soon enough." She strode away, obviously expecting me to follow, and I did so, wincing as the boots pressed against my blisters and realizing that, contrary to my expectations, Dell rather than Jak or Merret was leader of the library refuge. Her every gesture and word had the authority of leadership, and the others clearly accepted this. It seemed utterly uncharacteristic, for futuretellers were usually far too preoccupied by their inner worlds to bother with the real world.

Belatedly, I sent a probe back to Rawen promising my return and asking her to tell Golfur that I had not forgotten my promise to send him to Rolf.

Dell turned into a long street, which brought us to a labyrinth of broken and tumbledown walls. After wending our way through them, we reached a doorway that was almost intact and was in a bit of wall that, when I looked closely, appeared to have been rebuilt. It had been done subtly so it would not immediately be obvious to passersby. Through the door was the great pile of rubble that I had climbed with Pavo so long ago. At the top was the trapdoor that had led us to the Beforetime library. We had simply come to it from another direction.

At the square opening in the ground, I looked down at the metal steps I had last seen with Pavo. I looked up to find Dell watching me. But instead of speaking, she again made a slightly peremptory gesture, and I climbed down the steps.

Only when out of the daylight did I realize that some eldritch light source was illuminating the stairs. They led to a passage with smooth white walls extending in both directions. I knew from the last time I had been here that the passage led in one direction to vast vaults of books. Pavo, Kella, Jik, and I had gone that way, but Dell turned in the other direction, passing me to take the lead. I followed, remembering with a shudder the bones we had found. Pavo had speculated even then that the complexity of the locking mechanism we had released suggested the building's use as a refuge for the Beforetimers. From what Orys said, that had been the building's true purpose. Obviously, the people whose bones we had found had not managed to enter the refuge before it had been locked.

Quite suddenly we came upon the others standing together in a group. At first I thought they had stopped to wait for us, but as we drew nearer, I saw their attention was fixed on a metal door set into the side of the passage. It met the edges of the wall so smoothly that I might not have noticed it if they had not stopped, but I wondered why the others did not open it. I would have asked, but even as I stopped beside Dell, I noticed that the metal door was humming softly. The metal split open, and each side slid into the wall to reveal a small chamber lit from above. I stared as the others crowded into the tiny space, arranging themselves carefully around Merret and Orys and the pallet they carried.

"Come," Dell said, and I entered the chamber, where there was barely room to move, let alone do anything else.

"I thought we were going to see Jak?" I said.

"We are," Dell answered calmly as the metal doors slid back to seal the opening.

I began to feel I could not breathe, being pressed into such a small space with other people, but Dell laid a hand on my shoulder. Then I realized that nobody else looked alarmed or even surprised. The chamber began to hum softly and vibrate, and I had the strange and terrifying sensation of falling. A heaviness filled my limbs, but before I could gather my wits enough to ask what was going on, the metal door split and slid away again.

I stepped out into the passage on trembling legs, suppressing nausea. Merret, Orys, and Seely set off along the passage, but I caught Dell's arm just as the metal door closed again. "Why did we shut ourselves in there? Don't you know how ill Domick is?" I demanded, and heard the anger in my voice.

"That was an elevating chamber," Dell said mildly. "It has

brought us to a passage on another level of the building. Look at the color of the light." She gestured to the walls, which I realized were now emanating a green light. "The chamber travels up and down the levels of this building through a vertical chute on thick ropes of twisted wire," she added.

"We are below the library level?" I asked incredulously.

She nodded, beginning to walk after the others. "To be precise, we are seventeen levels under it," Dell said. "The elevating chamber is very swift."

"We . . . we are *seventeen levels* under the earth?" I asked, my mouth drying out.

"You get used to it," Dell said lightly as we caught up with Seely.

"Jak will be waiting," Seely said, and set off again along the green-lit passage. As we followed her, I thought of my dream of Hannah and Cassy meeting for the first time. Hannah had brought Cassy to just such a shining metal door in the foyer of a Beforetime building, and they had stood waiting outside it just as we had waited in the passage. Had not Hannah even spoken of an elevating chamber? And certainly the Reichler Clinic Reception Center had been some floors above ground level.

We turned into another passage that led to a metal door marked with a yellow and black symbol. As we approached, the door slid into the wall to reveal a continuing corridor with a red line painted on the smooth floor. Jak stood there, speaking to Orys and Merret. He beckoned to Seely and bade her show them where they were to lay Domick. Then he greeted Dell and me, clasping my hands with a warmth that surprised me. Maybe Dell and Seely had not been the only ones changed by their time in exile.

"It is very good to see you, Elspeth," he said. "When Dell

told me you had come here alone, with the help of a ship fish, I was amazed."

I was in no mood to speak of my journey, however amazing. "Jak, Domick . . ."

His expression became grave. "Yes. Let us go and see how he is."

He led me to an enormous room whose walls were lined with Beforetime machines such as I had seen in the Teknoguild cave, only there were ten times as many machines. What astonished me more than the number was that *several of the screens glowed with life.*

"How did you do this?" I whispered incredulously.

"Wait," Jak said gently, and I followed him into a circular room lined with glass chambers and centered around a large computermachine. Each chamber was brightly lit and contained an identical flat, hard-looking white bench rising on a single metal stalk. Beside it stood a metal construction as tall as a man and incongruously fitted with four great hinged arms, each ending in a different tool. All of this so astonished me that it was a moment before I saw that Domick had been laid out on a bench.

Seely was inside, removing Domick's clothes, and I heard her gasp when we saw the extent of the scarring on his body. Orys and Merret turned away, the latter saying she would clean up, eat, and sleep a few hours before riding back to Halfmoon Bay to check on Iriny. I thanked her and noticed that Dell had already slipped away. Her cat-footedness had not changed.

"The Beforetimers called this a biohazard laboratory," Jak said, speaking these strange words with ease. "Each chamber can be completely sealed off, for it has its own air supply. That machine alongside the bed can be made to administer food and medicines and even various treatments, as well as carry away waste."

He looked at me to see that I understood, and I nodded.

"Once the plague becomes contagious," Jak continued, "we can care for Domick and speak to him, and we will not catch the plague so long as he remains within the chamber."

"How can that feed him?" I asked, pointing to the metal construction.

"He will be fed nourishing liquids through tiny tubes that fit into the ends of needles, which are inserted into the veins inside his arms," Jak said. I gaped at him, and he laughed slightly. "Forgive me. You must find this very bewildering. It is hard to find simple words to explain the wonders in this room, let alone the levels of this incredible place."

Seely called out, and Jak muttered an appalled exclamation when he caught sight of Domick's ravaged naked form.

"Shall I wash him?" Seely asked Jak, her voice echoing oddly in the glass chamber.

"There is no danger yet, Dell says, but let us seal the chamber and show Elspeth what Pavo can do."

"Pavo?" I echoed faintly.

He pointed to the tall machine beside Domick. Seely emerged from the chamber and closed the door. Jak went over to the computermachine in the center of the room, slid into a chair, and began to tap at the letters laid out in lines.

"Watch," Seely instructed, pointing to the chamber where Domick lay. I turned again to see the tall machine unfolding its arms like some sort of metal mantis. When it leaned over the unconscious coercer, I held my breath, for it looked so cruel and ugly, but the plast hand reached out silently and, with startling delicacy, removed the sheet. Then it ran its hand over Domick's body with infinite gentleness, and where the hand went, water and soap suds flowed, running off him and drawn away by narrow runnels carved into the white bench. The water flow eased to a trickle when the hand smoothed over his face and increased again when it touched the black stubble on his head. Then the water ceased altogether, and the plast hand lifted and moved over him again without making contact. I realized that air must be flowing from the hand, for soon Domick was completely dry. The hand gently replaced the sheet and withdrew. Not until it stopped did I recognize that my face was wet with tears. I hardly knew why, save that he looked so utterly lost and vulnerable lying in the glass chamber. Brushing the tears impatiently away, I turned to look at Jak.

"As well as washing him, Pavo has been taking his temperature and making various small tests. But we will have him conduct some more complex tests and take some blood to learn more of this plague." His words were for me, but his eyes were fixed on the glowing face of the computermachine.

I looked into the glass chamber and saw the plast hand attaching small flat circles of what looked like plast to Domick's forehead, his chest, and the insides of his wrists. Each circle had a thin plast line attached to it, which coiled back to the tall machine. I gasped to see another of the metal hands insert a shining metal spike into the crook of Domick's thin, scarred arm, but Seely laid a light hand on my arm, saying, "Do not worry, Guildmistress Elspeth. Pavo will be far gentler than any of us could be. I know, for I was brought here when I broke a bone in one of my legs."

I stared at her, in awe of the fact that she and the others had been living among these machines and artifacts of the Beforetime for many months, learning how to use them.

"Now Pavo is taking some blood," Seely said, and I

watched in horrified fascination as the plast hand inserted another spike into Domick's other arm, and the plast tube
turned red as his blood began to dribble through it. I noticed
now that transparent straps lightly attached Domick's wrists,
ankles, and forehead to the bed, and while I knew these prevented him from moving and hurting himself, it ached me to
see him bound up as must have been his fate at Ariel's hands.
If he woke . . .

"The blood will tell us what sort of sickness Domick has
been infected with," Seely said.

"Jak is controlling that?" I asked, pointing to the machine
tending Domick, because I could not bring myself to call
something so ugly by the name of my old friend.

"Jak could control Pavo manually using the computermachine," Seely answered. "But mostly it is better to leave it
to Pavo, for he knows a great deal more than even Jak. You
might say that Pavo is deciding what to do and Jak is agreeing."

I stared at Seely, for she had spoken of the machine as if it
were a live creature.

Jak came to my side. "The air in the chamber is being
heated to exactly the right level that is needed. Domick's fever
is high now, and Pavo is administering various potions that
will help to cool it."

"How does the machine know what is needed?"

"It is designed to heal. In a way, it *is* a healer, but you have
to tell it to heal and agree to its suggested treatments. In
Domick's case, I have asked it to examine the blood being
taken and look into its memory to find out if it has any record
of the same sickness so it will know how to treat it. If it is a
Beforetime sickness, as Dell says, we will soon discover its
nature, for Pavo's memory contains knowledge of all the

Beforetime sicknesses. Although Pavo is swift, the records to which it has access are impossibly vast, so it will take some time."

"How did you figure out how to use this place? That elevating chamber . . . ?" So many questions clamored to be answered.

Jak laughed. "I daresay you did not like your first experience in it. We would not have been able to operate any of this, of course, without the computermachines. Fortunately, computermachines remember everything, and once you can make a computermachine work, it can tell you how to use it better. *It can teach.* You don't even need specialized knowledge. You can ask questions every step of the way. Of course, communicating with computermachines is no simple matter, because a computermachine can only answer in the words it knows, and it can only understand questions put to it in words it will understand."

"You are saying that *computermachines* taught you how to work the lights and the elevating chamber and this machine? But how did you make the computermachines work?"

"We did not have to make them work. They were working all along. Their power source is buried deep under all the levels of this place, and *it was never switched off.* Once we learned to communicate in a way that the computermachines could understand, we had the means of learning everything we needed to know. Of course, a lot of our discoveries were pure accidents, because while the computermachines could answer most questions, they could not tell us which questions we failed to ask.

"For instance, initially we used a long and exhausting set of metal steps to go from one level to the other. I set up a bed here, rather than running up and down the levels. Then I thought about it and realized that Beforetimers clever enough to create all of this would surely not have traipsed up and down so many steps. So I asked the computermachine how else I could reach the surface, and it told me about the elevating chamber. As you can imagine, I had not the slightest notion what an elevator was, but with persistence and lots of questions, I finally understood the gist of it. Nevertheless, that first trip was extremely horrible."

"Seely said you have used these chambers to heal on other occasions," I said, noticing that the girl had slipped out.

"Many times," Jak said comfortably. "We have never had to seal the room before, though. Indeed, I did not know that was possible until I began asking questions to prepare for Domick's arrival. Poor wretch," he added, and flung a look at the pale coercer. "I have had the computermachine produce all the information it can about such sicknesses. Apparently, plagues are ancient Beforetime sicknesses that had been wiped out long before the Great White—until some Beforetimer had the bright idea of resurrecting them to study their effects. It seems incredible that the fools would choose to wake such lethal diseases merely to study them. There must be some limit on the pursuit of knowledge."

"Garth would be surprised to hear you say that," I said.

He gave me a startled look, then frowned and nodded. "Maybe he would. But all of this changes a person, Elspeth."

He moved back to the computermachine, and I watched him tap the rows of small numbers and letters scribed on squares in the tray before the screen, aware that this was how he spoke to the computermachines. I had seen it done before in the caves of the Teknoguild, but again I marveled that spelled-out words could be understood and responded to by something that was only metal and plast.

"Domick's chamber is now completely sealed," Jak said after some moments. "No one will enter the room until he is healed."

I looked at the coercer again and gasped to see bars of plast emerge from the side of the white bench and move lightly over his torso to fasten themselves on the other side. Then the plast hand drew a white cloth over him.

"He is like to become restless because of the fever, and the straps will keep him from throwing himself off the bed. There are also things in that strap—I do not understand what, exactly, that will feed constant information to Pavo and help him tend to Domick's needs." He frowned at the screen in concentration, then he turned to me. "He has been drugged?"

I nodded and explained about Rolf's sleep potion.

"It has done no harm to him, but I have asked the computermachine to tell me what it is made from, just in case. Did you speak with Domick before you gave it to him?"

I told him what had taken place in the sea market and in the lane, concluding, "He remained unconscious from then, because we were giving him the potion."

"So he spoke in the voice of his spy persona," Jak said. "That is strange, but I suppose the fever made him hallucinate."

"Is there any way to get the demon band off him?" I asked. "Once he wakes, I would like to be able to probe him, if he is unable to speak to me."

Jak nodded. "I have sent Seely to get a key. Dell has one, but she must not have foreseen that he would be wearing a demon band."

"But you said the chamber is sealed."

"We can put the key into a tiny drawer from which all air can be drawn, and then push it into the larger chamber where

Pavo can take it and use it," Jak said. "However, as far as being able to question him, I am afraid he is unlikely to wake naturally for some hours, unless you want me to force it?"

I shook my head.

"Good. His body has been savaged enough. Why don't you go rest? A sleeping chamber has been prepared for you, and I will send for you the moment there is anything to tell."

I shook my head. "I will stay here in case he wakes."

Jak sighed. "Very well. There is a chair over there. Drag it over to the chamber and keep watch. I must work in another room, but don't worry—Pavo will watch over Domick." He added gently, "It is not your fault that this happened to Domick."

Is it not? I wondered bleakly after he had gone. Whatever Ariel had done to Domick, we at Obernewtyn had begun the harm by allowing him to spy, even after it had become clear that it was affecting him badly.

Suddenly the chamber's blinding white light dimmed and turned a soft rose. Whether the computermachine or Jak had changed the light, I was relieved. I sat back in my seat and wondered why I was not cold, so deep under the earth. Doubtless, Jak had asked a computermachine to make the air warmer. How comfortable he seemed amidst the machines and instruments of a lost age. And it was not only the teknoguilder; Dell was the same. "You get used to it," she had said of the elevating chamber. And Seely seemed not only confident in her new surrounds but also content. She had lost her tremulous uncertainty, blossoming into a quiet, competent young woman with steady hands.

Domick moaned, and I leapt to my feet, my heart thudding hard against my ribs. Misty ghost hands formed where I rested my hands against the glass, and my mind raced as I tried to think what to say to the coercer. But his eyes remained shut.

He moaned again and writhed, and the machine reached out its plast hand to touch a circle that must have been loosened by the coercer's movement. Again Domick stirred restlessly, rocking his head from side to side. I watched, fascinated, as bolsters rose slowly from the bed on either side of his head to cushion the movement. He fell quiet again, and after a time, I sat back down.

This time when I relaxed, fatigue flowed through me, and my eyes began to close. Despite willing myself to stay awake, each blink seemed longer than the one before, and it was harder and harder to open my eyes. My mind was beginning to drift. I thought about Rolf, Erit, and Iriny, and I hoped they were safe. Had Merret left yet for Halfmoon Bay? No, she had said she would sleep and go early in the morning. Besides, I had yet to tell her how to find Rolf. I leaned my head against the glass and looked at Domick's glowing white body. How dark his brows and lashes seemed in that gaunt, bone-white face.

I must have slipped into a dreamless slumber sitting like that, for the sound of steps coming lightly toward me wakened me. It was Seely with a tray of food, and I wondered how she managed to walk so lightly in her heavy boots. "Perhaps you do not feel hungry, Guildmistress, but you ought to eat," she said, and without waiting for an answer, she set down the tray on the floor beside me. Instead of leaving me, she moved closer to the glass to gaze through it at Domick.

"Kella used to talk about him sometimes when I was back at Obernewtyn," she said softly. "I wonder what happened to bring him into the hands of the Herders."

"When he recovers, he will tell us," I said, realizing that

the others were probably discussing such questions over a meal. I pictured them, sitting in a room with a warm light and the scents of food, speculating. Most of all, they would be relieved that the threat of plague had been averted, elated that their time of exile might be nearly over. I envied their comradeship and closeness, but I did not truly yearn to join them. The sight of Domick lying so still and wounded by all that had befallen him made it impossible to contemplate talking and laughing and eating.

"Jak is in one of the other laboratories," Seely said, turning from the glass wall, "where the computermachines are looking at Domick's blood. He said he will come soon. It will take time to find out anything."

"You seem so calm," I said. I was commenting on her tranquility, but she misunderstood me.

"I am not afraid," she said. "If Dell is wrong, then we will die. Being afraid will not change that."

"You are right," I said. "But fear does not usually heed reason."

"Fear produces its own reasons," Seely said. "I know because I have heard its craven voice so many times. Sometimes I feel that I have been afraid for most of my life: afraid of losing my mother and then afraid for my friend, and then afraid for Gavyn and for both of us when we were runaways and Lady Slawyna and her son wanted Gavyn dead. Then I was afraid of coming to Obernewtyn. But it turned out to be a true refuge, and Gavyn belonged there. But there I learned a new and more subtle fear. I was frightened of being pointless. You see, I am not a Misfit. I have nothing special about me that would let me belong. I realized there that I had made looking after Gavyn my reason for existing. And when that was gone and he did not need me . . . Well, in truth, he never truly needed me. He is not like that. But we had a purpose together. . . ." Her voice trailed off.

"Working with Jak has helped you not to be afraid?" I asked softly, wondering what she would think if I told her that Gavyn and the white dog Rasial had entered a merge with Dell and others to save my life.

She gave me a quick look. "At first, he was just kind, letting me help him. I knew that, but I liked being with the teknoguilders, for they did not seem so . . . so impossibly Talented. They were only passionate about their research, and I could be useful, because although I did not have their passion for knowledge, I liked doing things, sorting and making careful observations. It was peaceful and I was good at it. It was so nice to feel useful. Then . . ." Her cheeks flushed a little in the chilly light. "Then he suggested I come here with him, with the expedition. I knew there would be danger, but I didn't care. I would be useful."

"And now?"

"I am happy," she said, radiant. "I almost feel ashamed to say it when so many people have died here or have been taken away. Merret and Orys and Blyss . . . The others often speak of Obernewtyn with longing. But Jak does not long to be anywhere save where he can pursue his work, and I am happy to be of use to him. Of course, I will never be like him—so lost in curiosity and so hungry to discover. But I am interested, and I am good at thinking and doing practical tasks." She gave me a sudden, direct look. "I love him," she declared, almost defiantly. She laughed softly. "He would not allow it to begin with. He said he was too old. But"—a shimmer of pure mischief lit her eyes—"I convinced him."

"I am glad you are happy," I said gently.

"That is why I am not afraid of the plague," Seely said

earnestly. "If I must die for what I have had, then I will die. Jak and I will not be parted, and I will not be afraid."

"Who is there?"

We both swung to face the glass, and I saw that Domick was awake, leaning up as far as the restraining bands would allow.

"I will get Jak," Seely whispered, and hastened away.

✦ 8 ✦

"Domick?" I said, wondering if he could hear me.

He squinted in the direction of my voice, but the central room was dimly lit, and I realized he was unable to see me from within his red-lit chamber. He struggled to sit, only to discover that he was restrained. He struggled hard at his bands for a moment and then sank back, saying hoarsely, "That is not my name. I am Mika. Domick was a fool and a coward." He squinted again, struggling to see me. "Who are you? I recognize your voice. You hide in the shadows."

"I am not hiding," I said, pressing my face to the glass. "We are friends. Don't you remember? Can you see me now?"

He glared toward me, and then something flickered over the gaunt pale features, a kind of pain, and the slyness faded from his expression. "Elspeth? Guildmistress?" There was sorrow in his voice, but he sounded himself. My heart leapt, but before I could shape any response, his face clenched and he gave a groan. Again he fought against the bands binding his forehead and wrists, trying to break them. When he grew calm again, sweat gleamed on his brow and upper lip. He smiled ferociously at me, a vicious baring of teeth. "Of course! He knows who you are. He thinks you will rescue him. He is a fool. My master understood that perfectly."

I felt as if I were in the elevating chamber again. "Who is your master?" I asked.

The mad smile widened. "He knew you would want to know. He told me you would ask." I stared into his glowing face, the dark eyes like small black pits of wickedness and malice, and I told myself that it was not possible that he meant Ariel; that Ariel had known what I, specifically, would say in this moment. For that to be true, he would have to have foreseen that Domick would be here, with me. If he had foreseen that, he would have known his attempt to spread the plague had failed.

"Tell me what your master sent you here to do," I said.

The slyness became a demented exultation. "I am the instrument of Lud. I come to punish the wicked. All who sin will fall ill and die. The seeds of Lud's divine retribution are planted in me."

These words matched the rantings of the One, but Ariel had been in control of the One. Striving to think how to reach Domick, I asked, "Have those at Obernewtyn sinned? Has Kella sinned?"

The gaunt face twisted at the name, becoming Domick's face. "Kella." The word came out a half-strangled sob.

"Domick," I whispered, frightened of drawing forth Mika again. "How did they catch you?"

"We were talking, and they were suddenly all around us. They had demon bands on, which was why I had not felt them. Rushton fought, and so did I, but there were too many. They took us to him. To . . . Ariel." Fear shimmered in his eyes.

I had to fight to breathe slowly, to calm myself. Rushton *had* been taken at the same time! "Where did they take you?" I asked, wondering if they had been parted immediately or if both had been taken to the Sutrium cloister before Domick was taken to Herder Isle.

"They took us to the *Black Ship.* Ariel was waiting. The ship took us to . . . to Norseland, to his place. To *their* place." He was beginning to tremble now, and his fists were clenched. I had the feeling he was striving to hold on to himself, to hold Mika back.

"Us?" I asked softly. "*Rushton* was taken to Norseland?" My mind was racing, because how could we have found Rushton in the Sutrium cloister if he had been taken to Norseland?

"Rushton would not . . . would not open his mind to Ariel," Domick croaked. "He fought. I . . . I was . . . weak. . . ." Domick arched his back horribly and shuddered violently from head to toe. If the plast bands had failed, he would have hurled himself to the floor. One of the circles fixed to his temples had been torn away, and the metal form twitched its hands and pincers but did nothing. Perhaps it was waiting for him to be still again. Domick stayed arched like a taut bow for a long, terrible moment. He whispered hoarsely, "Ariel . . . entered my mind. I am strong, but he . . . he is an empath. He uses empathy in some twisted, dreadful way. Like coercing but worse. It hurt. . . . I could not stop him. . . ." He flopped back, and when his eyes opened again, Domick was gone. The bloodless lips stretched into a sneering smirk. "He has gone," he sneered.

"Mika."

He snickered, and his expression grew petulant. "You helped him take control. You should not have done that. I shall not allow it again."

"He spoke of Rushton," I said. Mika made no response. "Rushton was taken to Norseland, too, wasn't he? But then Ariel sent him back to the Land because he defeated your master."

"He was useless. He went mad rather than submit," Mika said. Alarm flickered in his face. "You will not trick me again," he snarled.

"I couldn't trick you," I said, letting admiration tinge my voice. "You survived, which means you must be smarter than Rushton or Domick. They were the fools."

His eyes narrowed, and he gave a shivering laugh. "Mika is no fool. Mika understands the necessity for suffering. For failure."

"That is why your master trusted you, isn't it? Because you are no fool. He sent you, knowing he could trust you. He couldn't send Domick, because he would not obey. Ariel has no need of guards or manacles, because you serve him faithfully." I spoke swiftly, obeying my instincts. "What were you to do?"

"I was to come to the west coast to bring the wrath of Lud," Mika said. Exultation died in his face, and he went on sullenly, "Then master told me he had found out Elspeth Gordie would be there. *You*," he hissed. "He said you must not be harmed, because he needed you." He glared at me. "He said it was Lud's will that you would stop me and that we must not question Lud's will."

I stared at him, utterly baffled. "Why did he send you, if he knew you must fail?" I asked.

"He sent me because of you, Elspeth Gordie. He said that you would ask who my master was, and I was to say it was Ariel. He said I was to tell you that you are his tool, no matter what you believe, and that you will pay for interfering with his plans." All of this was said in a mumbling sulky voice, which trailed off uncertainly. Domick seemed unaware that he was trembling and sweating copiously, and I was certain that the plague was now infectious.

"How am I to pay?" I asked.

He giggled horribly. "He said you would ask that, too. See how clever he is? He said I must tell you that you will pay in pain."

"Guilden Domick," I said sharply and with authority.

Mika stared at me, his mouth slackly open, and then he closed his mouth, and there was pain in his eyes. "Elspeth," Domick rasped. His voice was stronger than before. "You must not . . . enter my mind. He has . . . set up traps. You would not die, but you would suffer, and that is what he wants. He hates you. . . . You can't imagine how he hates you. And he sees so much. More than Maryon and Dell. More clearly. But there are gaps! There must be since he did not know I would be able to take control and talk to you. He did not see that you would make me strong."

I was afraid to say Ariel's name in case it brought Mika back. "Tell me about Rushton."

"It is as Mika told you. The Herders got us. Ariel told the warrior priests where to find us. Rushton was trying to make me come . . . come back to Obernewtyn. I was . . . I could not. I told him that. What Mika had done was too . . . I could not go back to Kella with blood on my hands. If she sensed what I had done . . ."

"So the Hedra took you to Ariel, and he took you both to Norseland. What happened then?"

"Ariel has a machine that gets inside your head. Noises and colors and pain come from it . . . He used the machine to try to open our minds so he could empathise us. He is a weak coercer, you see. But Rushton would not let him in. I fought, too, but he found Mika, and he summoned him and made him strong. Mika opened my mind for Ariel. He . . . came inside my mind with empathy, but—Elspeth—he is like an empath turned inside out. He . . . he made me feel such terrible things. He made me imagine hurting Kella. He made me take pleasure from it. I fled inside myself, which left Mika. It was what Ariel wanted. Mika coerced Rushton, and Rushton had no defense against him because they had been . . . we . . . were friends." The last words were spoken in a sobbing hiss. "Ariel entered Rushton's mind, but still Rushton fought. He used your face and form as a shield against hatred and despair and pain and all that Ariel used on him, but with Mika and the machine, Rushton could not hold out forever. When Rushton broke, Ariel took his revenge. He made Mika help him to . . . distort Rushton's memories so whenever he thought . . . of you, of Elspeth . . . he would feel pain and he would see the most dreadful . . ."

"Why would he do such terrible things to Rushton?" I asked through clenched teeth, sickened to the heart by what he was telling me.

"Ariel said Rushton must suffer for opposing him. But in truth, his anger at Rushton is small compared to his hatred of you. I . . . Once I asked him why he hated you so. He said that he had dreamed you would find something he greatly desired, something from the Beforetime. Only you could find and claim it, and no matter how many times he sought for another outcome, it was always the same. You found what he desired. He realized that the only way for him to possess what he wanted was to let you find it and then take it from you!" Domick almost screamed this last word. Then he lurched forward and vomited thin yellow bile onto the white sheet. Two more of the circles had been torn away, and I heard a muffled beeping sound. Domick laughed, a thread of saliva hanging from his lower lip. "See? He is a thing I can vomit out." It was Mika's voice, crafty and malicious.

"That is because you are stronger," I said smoothly.

Mika nodded eagerly. "Domick had locked me away. I was hidden in the darkest place in his mind, but the master let me out and made me strong. He laughed and laughed when he discovered me, and Domick wept." There was contempt in his tone. "The master gave me power, and I obeyed him. He locked Domick in the darkness where he had hidden me."

"He used you," I said slowly. "He used the plague to make me find you so you could tell me what he had done to Rushton."

Mika's eyes glowed blackly in his ashen face. "He trusted me to do his will—me, not Domick. I wanted him to kill Domick, but he said that he could not be killed or I would die." His face twisted with rage. "But he said Domick would never get out. Never." The triumph in his face dwindled to an irritable fretfulness. "But you made Domick want to come. You tricked me." Now there was anger again, but I ignored it, for I felt that something still eluded me.

I said coldly, "Your master failed you. Because he made a mistake about Domick's strength, and he made a mistake about Rushton, too, didn't he? He took him to Norseland and tried to use him, and in the end, he could only hurt him."

Mika sneered. "Rushton held you before him like a shield, but we broke him and then the master gave Rushton to the Herders to let him rot in a cell."

"But Rushton is not in the cell. He is free and works against your master. That was a mistake, too, wasn't it?" Some part of me was sickened by my cruelty, for it was Domick I was taunting. Mika was just a poor twisted part of his mind. I forced myself to go on. "You were supposed to be the instrument of Lud, bringing plague, but instead you are just Ariel's messenger boy."

"It is your fault." Mika's face was as confused as a child's.

"Yes," I said. "The seeds of sickness in you will flower and you will die, but only you. Why did Ariel infect you with the plague when he knew you would never be allowed to spread it to another person? Why didn't he trust you to pretend?"

"He . . . he said it would change things if he did anything differently. He said . . . he said he must act as if . . . as if he had seen nothing. It was the only way. . . ."

"So you alone are to die from the plague you carry? Maybe he kept that from you. Maybe he didn't trust you after all. . . ."

"He did! He trusted me. He said I must wait, and you would find me. He said you had to find me because of the plague." The words became a labored gasping and a breathless sobbing. Then he was still, his head hanging down. When the face lifted, Domick's eyes looked out at me, tortured and bleak.

"I am so sorry, Domick. I needed to weaken him," I whispered. I could feel sweat trickling down my spine.

"Elspeth, listen to me," Domick rasped. "Ariel wants you to live, because he needs you to get something that he wants. . . . I . . . Elspeth, I think it might be a weapon. Something terrible. That is the center of Ariel's mind, and all the rest is a chaotic whirl of madness and brilliance and cruelty. I felt it when he bound himself to me so he could enter Rushton when I did. The One is mad, but Ariel is worse."

I heard a movement behind me but did not turn. At any second, Mika might again take over. My whole body ached from tension, and I hoped whoever was behind me would have the sense not to speak. But it was already too late. Domick gave a cry and seemed to struggle with an invisible assailant before sinking back. Mika leered at me, panting. "You think you are so smart! He tells you things he should

601

not, but my master is stronger. You think he failed with Rushton? You are wrong! He serves my master yet!" His white face shone like polished marble in the bloody light, and his eyes seemed to bulge. He continued speaking, but now there was only a mad babble. Then he convulsed again and fell back, unconscious.

The plast hand reached out and began to wash the sweat from his body.

"It begins," Jak said. He was behind the bank of computermachines. "He is obviously delirious."

I swallowed, tasted blood, and realized I had bitten the inside of my cheek. I asked, "Did you hear what he said?"

"Some of it, but I would not strive to find meaning in the mad babble of delirium. After all, he said that Ariel took Rushton to Norseland, but Dell foresaw that he had been found in Sutrium."

"He was, but it is possible he was taken to Norseland first. It would . . . explain much if it is true," I said with difficulty. "What did you mean by saying it had begun?"

"The first stage is ended. Domick is contagious now."

I had guessed it, but the words said aloud made me feel as if he had struck me. "Have you found a way to heal him yet?"

"We have still not been able to identify the plague," Jak said. "Elspeth, you should get some food and rest. Pavo has given Domick something to make him sleep now, for his pulse was racing dangerously, and there was a risk that his heart would give out. He will not wake again for some hours. Seely will come for you the minute there is something to tell."

I shivered and nodded, and he took my elbow and made me sit down, saying that Seely would return soon to take me to my sleeping chamber.

"I do not think I will be able to sleep after this," I said.

"I could give you something to help," Jak said, "but I know you eschew such remedies. Why not bathe and eat and have a look around if you cannot sleep immediately. This is truly an amazing place, Elspeth. You might find Dell and ask her to tell you how she began to communicate with the main computermachine here. Without that, none of this would have been possible."

That got through the haze of confusion I was feeling. "*Dell* communicated with computermachines?" I asked.

He smiled. "Not just any one. Dell communicated with the central computermachine, which masters this entire complex and all of the lesser machines." Then he sobered, looking past me to Domick. "We have named the computermachine that runs this healing center 'Pavo' in tribute to my old master, but I do not truly think of it as a live being. Dell has taken the opposite point of view. She believes that a computermachine is simply a different kind of being. This approach enabled her to do what I could not, for all my rational theories. Indeed, it was her struggle to communicate with it as one life-form to another that led to the discovery that it can both speak and listen."

"Speak and listen?" I said in flat disbelief. I stood and Jak led me to his machine.

Jak nodded. "The Beforetimers gave computermachines voices. The one here sounds like a woman. I learned to communicate with computermachines by tapping on the scribed letters, and I continue to communicate in this way, making instructional sentences on the screen. But Dell speaks to it aloud, asking it to explain words and concepts and explaining her own questions. I would like to do as she does, for I see her results. But although I am a teknoguilder with

603

machine empathy, I simply cannot make myself regard a computermachine as a live thing. I see it as a tool, but Dell sees it as a living thing with its own intelligence and ideas, and that approach has allowed her to do far more with it. Dell made the computermachine grow crops of hay and wheat and lucerne in vats on the thirteenth level, which we give to the wild herd. But her true interest is in what the computermachine will *not* explain or show us. You see, there are whole areas on some levels that we cannot enter, because we need code words or sets of numbers that we do not have.

"That ought to be the end of it, but Dell has the idea that if she interacts with the main controlling computermachine for long enough, teaching it, stimulating its intelligence, and developing its reasoning ability, she will eventually be able to convince it to allow us access to deeper programs that will tell us more about the Beforetime and give us greater knowledge and power."

Seeing my look of consternation, he went on to explain that a program was a set of instructions given to a computermachine, which told it what to do. In the case of the dominant computermachine in the complex, its program gave it access to other computermachines. In a sense, it was the program that was the computermachine. "Unlike all the other computermachines here, such as Pavo, the main computermachine in this complex can learn new information and integrate it with old information. That is why Dell is so certain it is capable of eventually understanding why it should give us access to its deepest secrets." He shrugged. "I admire all that she has accomplished, but I must say that I think Dell is wrong in imagining a computermachine program can alter itself enough to sympathize with our need. On the other hand, when I think about what her approach has managed to accomplish, I am prepared to be proven wrong."

"Do you know what the purpose of this place was in the Beforetime?" We were now walking along the green-lit passages toward the elevating chamber.

"It was constructed specifically as a shelter in case of exactly such a world-changing disaster as the Great White. I do not know why the Beforetimers did not use it. Maybe the end of that time came too swiftly. But unless Dell succeeds with Ines, we will never know the truth of it."

"Ines?" I echoed, my skin prickling, for in one of my visions, the Beforetime Misfits had spoken of contacting Ines at Obernewtyn.

"INES are the letters representing the specific type of advanced program contained in the central computermachine, but Dell uses it as a proper name."

"Where does Dell speak with the main computermachine?" I asked, trying to keep the excitement from my voice.

"You can address it from anywhere within the complex, and it will respond," Jak said. "You only need give an order using its letters as a name. I will show you. Ines, can you produce some music?"

"Do you have a preference, sir?" asked the attractive voice of a woman that came from everywhere, like light. This was the voice I had heard only recently in the recurring dream of walking in a dark tunnel and hearing the drip of water!

"Just something soft and soothing," Jak said.

Music began, of an exquisitely complex type I had never heard before, but I was still reeling at the voice.

"Ines, stop the music now, please," Jak said, and the music stopped.

I was about to ask why he had stopped it when I saw that Seely had arrived with the key to the demon band. Jak took it from her and bade me farewell, saying he needed to return to Domick. Seely led me on to the elevating chamber, asking me anxiously how Domick was. I muttered something, still too astonished by Jak's demonstration to concentrate on anything else. At the elevating chamber, Seely pressed her palm to a square panel in the wall alongside the door. When we entered, she touched one of the listed numbers on the wall and one in a row of colored buttons. This time I felt myself grow heavy, and when the chamber's vibrating ceased, I felt myself become light.

Out of the elevator, Seely led me only a few steps to a gray door in a corridor filled with gray doors. She touched the door, and it slid open to reveal a small square chamber containing a bed, a table and chair, and a glass box about the height of a tall man in one corner. There was a single door in the room, and Seely said with a slight blush that it led to a privy where I could relieve myself. She pointed to the glass box standing upright in the corner. "You bathe there, and drying sheets and some clothes are there." She pointed to a cupboard. She indicated a panel against the wall and said I had only to lay my hand on it if I wanted the lights out. Pressed again, the light would be restored.

After she left, the door hissed closed. I stretched out on the bed, knowing I ought to clean myself but feeling unable to face the intricacies of the bathing box. I thought of Domick's claim that Rushton still served Ariel. He probably meant that Ariel had foreseen that Rushton would reject me, which would cause me pain. Despite the light's brightness and my thoughts' churning, I slept without dreams.

I woke groggy and needing desperately to relieve myself. I went reluctantly to investigate the small room beside the bed.

The light flickered on as I entered what was little more than a small cabinet containing a seat with a hole in the center. It looked like a privy, but it was so smooth and clean and sweet smelling that I sat down uneasily. When I stood, a great jet of water burst out and cleaned the bowl. The loud and unexpected noise made me stagger backward from the cubicle, trip over the threshold, and sit down hard. For a moment I sat there, gaping with shock, then I burst out laughing, thinking how utterly foolish I must have looked.

But I sobered as I remembered what Ariel had done to Rushton and Domick. I had felt too overwhelmed to make any sense of it before I slept, but now it seemed sheer lunacy that Ariel would prepare Domick physically and mentally to bring plague to the west coast if he intended only to taunt me. Surely he could have gone through the motions of sending Domick with plague, without infecting him. But Domick said Ariel was convinced that what he had seen would alter if he did anything differently. Yet he *had* done something different. He had told Domick the truth, and he had bidden him taunt me with it. I had long thought him to be defective, but Domick had called him mad. Perhaps his madness, like his hatred for me, arose from the knowledge that I was the Seeker and that he could not fulfill his destiny as the Destroyer without my first attempting to fulfill my quest.

I had never thought of it before, but Atthis had always said that *only if I failed* would the Destroyer have his chance. Perhaps what I had always regarded as a race was in fact a complex game in which the Destroyer must wait for the Seeker to make a certain move before he could make his own. Certainly Domick's words suggested that Ariel intended to allow me to find the Beforetime weaponmachines that had caused the Great White and then prevent my destroying them. It was little wonder he hated me, then, for it meant he must protect the very person who stood in the way of what he most wanted. I had always thought of him as my nemesis, but for the first time, I understood that I was also *his* nemesis. Even when he knew I would thwart him, he had to allow it, for fear that he might prevent my doing what I needed to as the Seeker!

The ironic notion made me shiver, because I could imagine the towering rage Rushton would have unleashed in opposing Ariel *with an image of me!*

I became aware of a stale odor rising from my body, composed of human and horse sweat and sheer uncleanliness. Revolted, I sloughed off my filthy clothes and padded across the smooth floor to the glass cabinet. I stepped into it with some trepidation and saw three circles on the wall: blue, red, and yellow. I touched blue hesitantly and gave a shriek as icy water cascaded down. I slapped at the red circle, and the water became instantly a boiling torrent. Pressing myself to one side of the cabinet, I pushed the yellow circle. Deliciously warm water flowed out, and I stepped into it and hastily pulled the glass door closed.

I stood for a long time under the miniature waterfall, turning and sighing with pleasure, as the sweat and dirt of my long journey sluiced away down a small round drain hole in the floor. Marveling at the constancy of the flow and temperature of the water and wondering without too much urgency how to turn it off, I noticed three small transparent levers against the wall. Curious, I touched one warily. A gleaming blob of scented matter fell to the floor of the closet and washed away, releasing a soft cloud of perfume. Guessing it to be soap, I pressed the lever again, catching the scented blob and rubbing it over my hair and body. The scent of roses enveloped me. The other two levers had different scented matter.

Once I had washed the bubbles from my body, I pressed the yellow lever again, and to my relief, the water ceased immediately. Pleased to have mastered the cabinet as well as rendering myself clean, I opened the door and took a drying sheet from the cabinet, noticing several pairs of the same blue trousers that Dell and Seely wore and three different-sized pairs of boots. I disliked the smooth stiffness of the cloth, but I could not bear my own clothes. Dressing in the queer trousers, I noticed a second pile of short-sleeved shirts made of some thin, very fine, white material. I put one of these on and pulled on a pair of soft thick socks. The boots looked heavy, but in fact they were light and very soft, and the sole was spongy to the touch. I found a pair that fit and put them on, marveling that something so ugly could be so comfortable. Then I worked the tangles and snarls from my wet hair with a comb I found on another shelf. Leaving it loose to dry, I undertook the difficult business of washing my filthy clothes in the water cupboard. Before long, they were squeezed out and hung around the room to dry. Seely had not come back, and after trying the door for a moment, I gave up and lay on my stomach on the bed.

I thought of Rushton with sorrow and guilt, knowing that he had been tortured simply because he had loved me. I could not bear to think how he must have suffered whenever he looked at me, despite suppressing the memories of what had happened to him. No wonder he had turned away from me. I shuddered to remember that Dameon had pressed me to force Rushton to look at me and speak with me and face me, so certain had he been that Rushton loved me! He had not known, as I now did, that love had been most cruelly bonded to pain and fear and torment in the Master of Obernewtyn. Every time Rushton had to deal with me, it must have rocked his sanity. Perhaps Ariel had hoped that the sight of me would eventually drive him mad, and this might have happened, had I remained in the Land and taken the Empath guildmaster's advice. Maybe *that* was what Mika had meant by saying that Rushton still served Ariel.

Before I saw Rushton again, I must think well and long about what to do.

I must have dozed, because I started awake when I heard a soft tap at the door. I called out as I rose, and Seely burst in, saying, "I'm so sorry, Guildmistress, but you need to come at once. The sky is full of smoke. Dell wants you to see if you can farseek Merret to find out what is happening."

"Merret? But where is she?"

"She went last night to take the greathorse back to Halfmoon Bay and to see if your friends are safe."

"Last night . . . but wait! Are you saying there is a fire in Halfmoon Bay?" I asked as we went back out into the purple-lit passage.

"We do not know, but there is a great deal of smoke coming from that direction. Blyss is frightened for Merret," Seely said.

"How long have I been asleep?" I asked as we hastened down the passage.

"Since yesterday afternoon. It is very early in the morning now," Seely answered.

We were soon entering the elevating chamber, and I experienced almost as much nausea and alarm as on the previous day. Unable to help myself, I asked Seely what would happen if the chamber broke and we were caught between levels.

She gave me a slightly uneasy look but said that Ines would know how to fix it.

"Ines," I echoed.

She gave me a measuring look, then said, "I know Jak does not like us thinking of a computermachine as being alive, but I find it hard not to do so. Ines speaks to me and responds to me. She remembers what I have said to her, what I like and do not like, and she asks many questions of me. When I ask *her* questions, she tries her best to answer me and to explain when I don't understand. I feel like she cares about me."

I did not know how to respond, for was it not a computermachine that had once tortured me and Rushton and that had helped Ariel destroy Rushton's love for me? Was it not a computermachine that had caused the Great White? Had those computermachines all had names and soft, soothing voices that could be evoked?

The elevating chamber came to a halt, and the doors slid open; the scent of fresh air seemed intoxicating. I almost ran to the metal steps, and as I mounted them two at a time and burst out into the chilly sweetness of the predawn air, I thought of Hannah telling Cassy that the false sunlight that lit Newrome was not as sweet as true sunlight. I stopped to wait for Seely, relishing being outside. The wind riffled my hair, and I was glad I had not braided it.

Seely joined me and then took the lead as we wove our way through the ruins toward the watchtower. She told me that Alun had first seen the smoke.

We crossed the square, but there were no signs now of the horses or the saddles and packages they had carried. Someone stumbling into the square would not have the slightest clue that people lived close by. At the watchtower, I followed Seely through a door and up the steps, thinking how cleverly they had been constructed. The top platform was screened by the jagged outer wall, and here sat the beastspeaker and empath Alun, eating an apple. With an exclamation, he leapt to his feet and greeted me with delight. But I could only gape, for beyond him, an immense column of gray smoke was billowing into the pale blue sky.

"Ye gods, that looks as if a whole city is on fire!" I said, aghast.

"The amount of smoke suggests it, but it looks to me as if the smoke is coming from too far inland to be any of the cities," Alun said.

I had been studying the smoke and said, "If I did not know better, I would say it was coming from the Suggredoon."

"I was thinking the same thing," Alun admitted. "Except whatever was burning is still burning, and the shantytown that serves the camp of soldierguards would have gone up in less than an hour."

"I will try to reach Merret, but if she has reached Halfmoon Bay, it is too far," I said. I strove fruitlessly and shook my head. "Maybe I can use Kader and Orys in a merge."

"Orys rode out last night, too, to let Gwynedd know you have brought Domick in safely," Alun said. "Seely could go and get Kader, but perhaps you can use me, Guildmistress. I have some farseeking ability, though it is not as strong as my other Talents."

I thanked him and linked with his mind. Again I cast my probe, shaped to Merret's mind. I had not extended my reach much more than a furlong or two, yet the probe located. But it was not in the direction of Halfmoon Bay, and the contact was tenuous. Merret understood at once and poured her own energy into strengthening the connection as I told her about the smoke and asked what she knew. She had seen the smoke from inside Halfmoon Bay and had ridden out to investigate.

"So the smoke is not coming from Halfmoon Bay?" I farsent.

"No," Merret responded. "It is coming from the Suggredoon. In fact, it looks as if it is coming from the other side of the Suggredoon."

"From Sutrium?!" I was so startled that I almost lost contact.

"I am not there yet, and there is so much smoke that I cannot be sure," Merret sent. "Many soldierguards have galloped by wearing the colors of different cities, but I can't probe them because of their demon bands. Some of the gossip on the road says that the Faction has invaded the Land and is fighting with the rebels, but that's impossible, given what you told us," Merret observed.

I felt a sick lurch of alarm. "It is not impossible," I told her. "You see, when Harwood and the others left the Land to board one of the invaders' ships, there were still hundreds of Hedra at large. Maybe they managed to avoid capture and regroup, or Malik might have had more support than we realized. How close are you to the Suggredoon?" I asked.

"I am within sight of the ramshackle village that has grown up near the barrier the soldierguards set up. But if I go another step nearer, I will lose you. It is taking all my concentration to keep contact."

"You'd better go nearer, then, and see what you can find out, but first, are there any priests about?"

"I have seen quite a number heading toward the old ferry port, but they all wear demon bands. They look as puzzled as the soldierguards, which makes me think that the fire must be on the other side of the river.

"Oh, there is something else—I met your Iriny! She was

dressed exactly as Rolf had described when she left Halfmoon Bay. She felt me enter her mind, and it did not take me long to explain who I was. She repeated what Rolf had told me, that he had used his connections to get her out of the Councilcourt cells before the Herders could make enough fuss to get their hands on her. She said that she wanted to cross the river to give some important information to her brother. She said the smoke would provide the perfect opportunity to cross, and she must act while she had the chance. I bade her—"

Without warning, the probe broke free and rebounded with painful abruptness.

"Are you all right?" Seely asked anxiously as I staggered back.

I opened my eyes, and the radiance of the newly risen sun seemed to claw at the inside of my head. I squinted and looked at Alun, who was pale and sick-looking. He laughed shakily and said, "I hate it when that happens." I apologized, but he waved away my words, saying that if Merret suddenly moved out of range, there was nothing I could have done. He asked if I really thought that the fire was the result of a Hedra force warring with the rebels across the Suggredoon. Of course, he had heard the whole exchange.

"If it is, then they are clearly winning," I said grimly. "For rebels would not torch the city."

"It might be the Raider," Seely suggested. "Maybe Ariel convinced him to bring some more Hedra from the camp in Norseland, and they sailed across the strait to attack the rebels."

I considered her suggestion seriously, but at length I shook my head. My instincts told me that Yarrow had been right:

Ariel had severed his connection with the Faction when he had abandoned Herder Isle.

"Do you think the gypsy will make it across the river?" Alun asked.

I studied the billows of smoke and envisaged Iriny flitting between the tents and soldierguard patrols to slip silently into the dark water. "If anyone could manage, she will. But my concern is that if she does cross, she might be leaping from the pan into the cook fire if there are Hedra on the other bank, for the Faction has no love for gypsies."

PART II

✦

SANCTUARY

✦ 9 ✦

IT WAS WELL past midday before I returned to the Beforetime complex. Seely had gone back down earlier to let Dell know what I had learned, but I had wanted to try to contact Merret again. I had not managed it, however, even when Kader appeared to take the watch from Alun and allowed me to draw on him.

Puzzled and uneasy about what might be going on over the river, I went below with Alun. As we descended the metal steps, he said with cheerful relish that we ought to arrive in time to sample one of Dell's delicious midmeal soups. I raised my eyebrows. Many futuretellers at Obernewtyn had chosen domestic tasks to busy their bodies and leave their minds free, but the meals they prepared were invariably bland or peculiarly spiced.

Dell laughed at my expression when I stepped from the elevating chamber into a large, pleasant room that smelled deliciously of the soup she was pouring into a tureen. "I have learned to like cooking and to enjoy doing it well," she said.

"You have changed," I could not help saying as she ladled me a bowl of soup and pushed a platter of thickly sliced, fragrant hot bread toward me.

"Our time of exile has changed all of us here," Dell said seriously. "I think we have become closer than people of different guilds do at Obernewtyn, because danger always seems to stalk us, and we rely on no one but ourselves." She changed the subject then, questioning me closely about what Merret had told me.

I concluded by saying I would try again to reach Merret in an hour, for surely by then she would have garnered some useful information and be heading back in our direction.

The elevating chamber doors opened, and Blyss ushered in a flock of boys and girls. Realizing these must be the Misfit children Dell had mentioned earlier, I smiled as they approached and touched their minds lightly to confirm their Talents. The futureteller gave each of them bread and soup and bade Blyss and Alun help themselves. Then she untied her apron and laid it aside, excusing herself and asking me to join her once I had finished my meal. I was puzzled that she had not stayed to eat with us, but then Blyss introduced me to Pellis, who had a startling shock of carrot-colored hair sticking out in all directions. At twelve, he was older than the other children he introduced, who ranged from ten to four.

In normal circumstances, I would have drawn their stories from them, but I was anxious to farseek Merret again, and before I could do that, I would have to see Dell, which made me uneasy. The moment Blyss had finished her soup, I asked her to take me to the futureteller. It was odd, I thought as we entered the elevating chamber. I had felt perfectly comfortable with Dell the cook, but now I feared an interview with Dell the Futuretell guilden.

My discomfort with futuretellers centered upon the fact that, while Atthis had warned me never to speak of my quest, futuretellers often dreamed of it in a fragmentary way, which inevitably led to questions I could not or would not answer. The Futuretell guildmistress, Maryon, had more than once referred obliquely to my quest, but she had never spoken of it outright to me. Indeed, she had seemed to understand the importance of not speaking of it. But Dell was second in rank and skill to the guildmistress, and Maryon might have discussed me with her before Dell had left for the west coast. Perhaps she had made up her mind to abandon any squeamishness about my quest. *What would I do*, I wondered, *if she asked me about it directly?* And yet was there any need to remain silent with her when Atthis had drawn Dell into a spirit merge with Maruman, Gahltha, and others in order to save me?

As she led me along a yellow-lit hall on the building's thirtieth level, Blyss broke into my thoughts. "The Futuretell guilden cooks, but she never eats her meals in the great hall. She prefers to eat alone in Sanctuary. I think you will see why."

"What is sanctuary?" I asked.

She gave me a shy smile. "It is better for you to see Sanctuary rather than have someone tell you about it. But it is also what we call this complex now. Sanctuary, for it has proven so to us, and it was created in the first place to be a sanctuary for the Beforetimers."

I wanted to say that it had not served them well since almost no one had managed to get there before the Great White destroyed their world, but it would have been harsh to say. I glanced at Blyss again, and she was smiling softly. I contemplated asking about her relationship with Merret but decided it was none of my business and turned my attention to my surroundings.

The corridor we had entered on this level was smooth and bare, like all those I had passed along in the Beforetime complex, but unlike the rest, it curved, and now that I thought about it, there was something odd about the yellowish light flooding the passage.

I had just realized that, instead of coming from both walls, the light here came only from the inside wall of the curving passage, when suddenly that wall became transparent. I stopped abruptly, astonished to see trees growing on the other side of the glass! The more I looked, the more I realized that it was not just a few trees in some sort of underground garden. There were more trees behind the ones I had seen first and more beyond them. I was looking at a forest, and astoundingly, above the trees was a blue sky!

"Come, there is a door just along here," Blyss urged. She touched the transparent wall, and like the door to the elevating chamber, the glass split open and the intoxicating scent of hot greenery and damp rich earth flowed over me.

"Welcome to Sanctuary," Blyss said, clearly enjoying my reaction.

"What is this? H-how . . . ?" I stammered.

Blyss shook her head and smiled. "Let Dell explain." She pointed to a track weaving away from the opening in the glass and through the trees. I followed the empath along it, feeling as if I had stepped into a dream. After we had been walking long enough for me to feel warm, I realized that things were not quite as natural as they seemed. There were no bird or animal cries, nor the sound of insects, and there was not a breath of wind. The light, which seemed at first to be so like sunlight, was too yellow, quite aside from the fact that there was no sun. The light emanated from the blueness, which, I realized after my first shock, must be the blue-painted roof of an immense cavern.

"Here," said Blyss triumphantly, and I saw that the path

ended in a clearing at the open door of a small dome-shaped hut half obscured by foliage. "This is where Dell spends most of her time," Blyss added.

As we came closer, I saw that the hut was not a rounded dome but merely many sided. It had only two rather small windows, one on either side of the door, and when we entered, I saw why. Shelves that groaned under the weight of hundreds of books covered the other walls, and on a table in the center of the room sat an enormous computermachine. A chair faced it, but Dell sat in a more comfortable-looking chair beside the window.

Hearing us enter, she rose with a smile, saying softly, "Thank you, Blyss." It was a dismissal, and Blyss smiled at me and withdrew.

"How did you do all this?" I cried the moment we were alone.

The futureteller burst out laughing. "Of course, I did not do this. It was here when we came; it is a living seed store, maintained by Ines. But I should not laugh. My own astonishment was great when I first came here, though Ines had told me what to expect. I thought I was misunderstanding her."

"Jak told me about you and Ines," I said.

Again she laughed. "You make it sound like a love affair."

"You used not to laugh so much," I said, rather foolishly.

This rendered the futureteller serious. "You spoke before of change, and I have been thinking of your words. True, I have become less . . . somber than I was at Obernewtyn. I have noticed it in myself. I will not go back, even if that turns out to be possible. I belong here now."

"Here?" I said in disbelief.

She nodded. "There is enough in this complex to bewitch

the mind for several lifetimes. Jak feels the same. For him it is the information and the laboratories, and for me, it is Ines."

"You speak of a computermachine as a person."

Dell sat down at the seat behind the computermachine and bade me draw up a chair. "I think of Ines as something that lives. In some way, our relationship has an element of a beast-speaker and beast in that the two communicate but are essentially different kinds. Because of that, there will always be gaps in their understanding of one another. The secret of harmony is to accept those gaps."

"Jak says you believe that you can make the computermachine let you enter forbidden areas of its . . ." I stopped, groping for a suitable word.

"Her program," Dell said. "A computermachine is only a machine. The program is what allows her to think. It is the mind that inhabits the plast and metal body. But as for *making* Ines tell us the secrets she is keeping, that simply would not be possible. The forbidding is built into her programming just as the instinct not to jump off a cliff is built into us. However, while we could be forced off a cliff, Ines cannot be forced to go against her programming. But she might be brought to reason well enough to see that her program needs to adapt and grow."

"Do you really think it is possible for a machine to change its mind?"

"What I know," Dell said, "is that Ines can learn. That is part of her programming. The whole time we have been here, she has been teaching me, but she is also taking in what I tell her as new knowledge, which can be compared to old knowledge. She is changing me, but in a sense, I am also changing her." Dell lost her lecturing tone and said with a sudden, almost girlish, burst of excitement, "Elspeth, you cannot imagine what Ines knows of the Beforetime."

"Then she knows about the Great White?" I asked, suddenly aware that Ines might know the location of the computermachines that had caused it.

But Dell shook her head. "I asked about the Great White, but the last thing she remembers before my waking her is the command her human user gave to put herself to sleep. That is not the same as being switched off. All of the lesser computermachines that she can manipulate continued following their programs, but there was no mastermind. Think of our hearts pumping and our lungs breathing while our mind sleeps." Dell smiled. "Jak accessed the lesser computermachines not long after we arrived, but Ines woke only after I spoke her name and bade her wake."

"What made you think of doing it?" I asked.

She shrugged. "I do not know. The letters scribed upon her formed a name, so I got into the habit of thinking of the computermachine as a female. Then one day I was thinking of that storysong that Miky and Angina made about a sleeping princess, and it suddenly seemed to me that the computer was like a sleeping princess. Some mad impulse made me command her to wake and speak to me. I did not expect her to answer, and when she did, I near fell over with shock." She chuckled. "Of course, if she had truly been switched off, as the Beforetimers say, it would have been like trying to waken a dead person."

"Why was she made to sleep? Does she know?"

"She knows that before she was put to sleep, she was cut off from the other Ines programs. There were many computermachines in the Beforetime with the Ines program. Because

625

they could all learn and adapt to what they learned, that might mean they are all different, with different information from different human controllers. But they were all linked as well. Indeed, that was their virtue and their specialty. They linked and were able to share information. So what one knew, all knew. This made them incredibly accurate and knowledgeable, but also identical. Then, just before the Great White, all the Ines programs were isolated from one another. That is when *this* Ines, and I suppose all the other computers with Ines programs, became unique, for after this time, they learned and thought alone. Ines does not know why the links between them were blocked, but she says that only Govamen had the power to close down their etherlink."

"Govamen," I echoed, fascinated.

Dell gave me a quick look. "Interesting, isn't it? The computermachines with Ines programs were cut off from one another by the very organization that made prisoners of the Beforetime Misfits kidnapped from the Reichler Clinic. It is difficult not to see Govamen as a sinister body, and much that Ines has told me confirms this impression. I asked her once if we could reconnect her to the other computermachines, and she said it would be possible but they could only be reconnected by using one of the central Govamen computermachines that control the links, and only three of those existed. I think it unlikely any of them survived, because they would certainly have been targets in whatever conflict led to the Great White. In any case, it would be dangerous to do it, because Ines believes it is likely, given the suddenness of the Great White, that many of the computermachines containing her programming were not put to sleep by their human users. This meant that when their users perished, they remained awake but isolated from their sister units and lacking any contact with their human handlers. Since the Ines program focuses so much on the acquisition and exchange of knowledge with other Ines units and with human users, the isolated programs would have suffered a gradual distortion, a sort of madness that would immediately infect any other computermachine connected to it."

"Almost like a computermachine plague," I murmured.

Dell looked startled and nodded. "Being effectively Ines's human user now, I understand very well how a computermachine program would suffer, for she has an insatiable hunger to know things. Lacking that connection to her sister computermachines, she has no other source of new information but what we give her. Fortunately, that seems to satisfy her. Most fascinating is that when I tell her something that does not agree with the knowledge she possesses, she is able to consider both sets of knowledge and decide which to believe. Sometimes she decides that neither is completely correct, and she formulates a modified or merged version of the information. This capacity for assessing information and discarding those parts she has judged obsolete or irrelevant makes me certain that the right argument or piece of knowledge could make her discard the imperative that requires certain keys and codes before she will allow me to know all that she knows. Then she will simply open her deeper self to me."

"What do you hope to learn?" I asked.

"I do not know. But I am curious about why certain information in her memory was considered to be so important or valuable or dangerous that it had to be kept secret."

She got up from the stool and crossed to the window. Without turning, she said, "I care for Obernewtyn and the people there. But I have found a true purpose for my life with Ines."

"What about your futuretelling ability?" I asked.

Dell looked over her shoulder and smiled at me gently. "Perhaps that is at the heart of it. I have the ability to see the future and the past, and at Obernewtyn that is how I defined myself. But when I came here, I realized that I had never really thought about what I wanted. It had never occurred to me that it might be separate from what I was. Maybe these thoughts were beginning to form in my subconscious mind, and that is why I volunteered for this expedition. When I think back on the things Maryon said before I left . . . I think she guessed. Maybe she even foresaw this. It would not be unlike her to see and say nothing, leaving it for me to discover." She looked over her shoulder at me again, her gaze speculative. "I think you might understand better than anyone that a person can have an unexpected destiny."

It was a question if I wanted to answer it. I did not. The prohibition against ever speaking of my quest was too strong. "Do you know what is causing the smoke coming from beyond the Suggredoon?" I asked.

She smiled faintly, signaling her acceptance of the abrupt change of subject. "I have seen nothing of an invasion in Sutrium or of the city being razed by fire. But that does not mean anything. You know that."

I nodded. "Do you foresee anything of what is to come in these next sevendays?" Then I added quickly, "For all of us?"

She sighed and nodded. "I have seen a time of fighting and bloodshed in the future. Your face is at the center of it."

"I am not the cause . . . ," I began.

She shook her head. "No. You are a change-bringer. Whatever choices you make lead to change for the rest of us. But it is not something you chose." Then she said, "When you leave this place, we shall not meet again."

628

I stared at her, my skin sprouting goose bumps. I could see from the vacant look in her eyes that she had sunk into a futuretelling trance. I did not want to ask, but I had to know. "What do you mean?" I whispered.

"Before the next wintertime ends, you will bid farewell to all that you love and journey far over land and sea to face the beast."

"All that I love?" I echoed.

"All," Dell said, serene and implacable.

✦ 10 ✦

I WAS DREAMING of the dreamtrails. I could tell by the over-vivid colors of the wild, churning green landscape about me, the way things bled and blurred into new shapes.

I heard a voice. "Merimyn!"

I turned to see a young woman. She reminded me strongly of the stone figure of Hannah Seraphim as a girl on Stonehill.

"Where are you?" she called. She scowled in mock anger and set her hands on her hips. Her eyes narrowed, and a clump of bush beside me melted away. There, to my aston-ishment, sat a small motley-colored cat. Maruman! But not as I knew him, old and scarred. He was whole and young, and his two eyes gleamed as he grew wings and sprang into the sky.

"Merimyn!" the girl cried, laughing. "That's cheating!"

I thought myself wings and sprang after Maruman. He rose into the clouds, which became a snowy landscape. He padded through the snow, jumped skittishly at a piece of twig protruding from a drift, and then went on, making a little soft trail of blue paw prints. He showed none of the loathing he usually expressed at the sight of snow. Suddenly, he turned his yellow gaze on me. Two eyes.

"Who are you?" he asked curiously.

It was Maruman's mindvoice, but the sharp ironies that enriched his older mindvoice were absent. This was a younger, lighter voice with a constant ripple of kitten mischief threaded through it. I felt a stab of grief, for this was a Maruman I had never known. How was it possible that I was dreaming of Maruman as a young cat?

"I have dreamed your face, funaga," Maruman said thoughtfully.

A voice called, and he sprang up and vanished. The snowy landscape about me immediately dissolved, and I made no attempt to hold on to it. I fell for a time, and then I was standing in a green lane between towering hedges. I recognized the mountains rising in the blue distance on one side and knew that I was in Obernewtyn's maze, yet the hedge was formed of a different small-leafed plant with no fragrance. Cassy Dupray and Hannah Seraphim were walking arm in arm, their heads close together as they spoke, and I realized this was the Obernewtyn of the Beforetime. Neither seemed any older than on the last occasion I had seen them.

". . . sorry Jacob was not here so you could meet him," Hannah was saying.

"So am I. I wish I didn't have to go back," Cassy added with real regret.

"I wish it, too, yet it will not be long before you will come to Newrome to study. Besides, we will see one another when I come to Inva for the conference. Once I have arranged my flight, I will let you know the details, and then you must try to arrange to visit your father's institution at the same time. We cannot get the others out unless you are inside the complex."

"What about the birds?"

"You must release them and instruct them to find their way here. If they are as intelligent as you believe, they will manage it. Indeed they must, for there are a multitude of questions I would ask this bird that sent you to find me," she said with a half laugh. Then her face became serious. "Will you be able to get your father to invite you back again?"

"My father won't be a problem, and I don't expect the vile Masterton to object, since I did his precious logo. The problem might be my mother. She won't understand why I want to return, and she won't like it. She hates what my father is doing."

"The Sentinel project," Hannah said, nodding. "I can't say I blame her. It troubles me as well. The idea of putting all that weaponry around the globe into the hands of a single master computer program."

"My father says it will be more rational and less prejudiced than any human could ever be, because all five powers are involved in programming it."

"I don't doubt it will be less prejudiced than a human, but will it be as wise as the wisest man, as compassionate as the most compassionate woman?" Hannah asked. "Perhaps what bothers me most is that I cannot see why the government would embrace a project that will take power out of their hands. It doesn't fit with how they operate. What do they get out of it?"

"Safety?" Cassy offered. "No more accidents wiping out countries."

"That might work, if the company running this project didn't have strong links to weapon manufacturers. That is what those papers you got for me prove. Why on earth would armament dealers support a project that is supposed to end any need for warfare?"

"Maybe they see the writing on the wall, and they figure they might as well get paid for something."

"That would be a pragmatic approach, except that those

who wage wars and think in terms of arms races would see that as defeat. It seems more likely that these people have taken on the Sentinel project to ensure that it fails. If that is their aim, I am not sure it would be bad. But I feel the need to know more. That is part of what I will investigate when I am in Inva for the conference. If you can get inside before then, please ask our friends if they will use their abilities to learn about Sentinel. They are in the perfect position to poke around. It is actually rather incredible that they are being held in the same compound as the Sentinel project. But it would not be the first time the government played both ends against the middle."

"My father said there are lots of top-secret projects being run there, and each has no idea what the other is doing," Cassy said. "So you want the paranormals to spy for you?"

"Can a prisoner be said to spy?" Hannah countered.

"I can nose around as well," Cassy offered after a moment.

"No," Hannah said firmly. "You can't get yourself barred from the place. You must play the obedient and dutiful daughter." Cassy looked despondent, and Hannah laid an arm about her shoulders and smiled. "Stay in touch, my dear, but be careful. Even with all of our controls, we could be in trouble if someone decides to take a more serious interest in you."

Someone grasped me by the shoulder and began shaking me.

I woke to find Seely looking anxiously at me. I gazed around the brightly lit room for a moment, memories of the interview with Dell and my later fruitless attempts to farseek Merret tumbling through my mind, muddled with my dreams. I had been so exhausted that I did not remember entering the sleeping chamber or going to sleep.

"Is it Merret?" I asked, sitting up and pulling on the Beforetime boots.

"It is Domick. He is awake."

In a moment, we were hurrying along the passages to the elevating chamber. "Is he better or worse?"

"He has broken out in buboes. Some of them have already burst," Seely told me as we entered the elevating chamber.

"But Jak said that it would not happen until the final stage," I said in dismay.

"In the last plague, Jak says, it took a sevenday for anyone infected to get buboes. He says this plague is so very like the last that it might be a mutation of it, and one of the differences is the swiftness of the plague to run its course." She saw my expression. "I'm sorry. Those are all Beforetimer terms. It is easier for Pavo if we use words he knows."

I nodded and forced myself to think beyond my fear for Domick. "Is there any news from Merret?"

"Kader rode out to see if he could get close enough to communicate with Merret. Two hours ago, he sent back a message saying that Iriny had crossed the Suggredoon. Merret went close enough to the river to see Hedra on the other bank. She saw one kill someone in ordinary clothes. A rebel, we have to suppose. She told Kader there are many Hedra at the river now, and they want to cross. They are arguing with the soldierguards about it."

"What of the rebels here?"

"Alun has ridden to Murmroth to speak with Gwynedd. Neither he nor Orys have yet returned." As we emerged from the elevating chamber into the green-lit passage, she shook her head and confessed, half ashamedly, "So much time passed with so little happening, and then you arrive and suddenly everything seems to be happening at once."

Change-bringer, Dell had called me. *Catalyst*, Merret had named me. Seeker to the Agyllians. Not one of these names had I chosen for myself, and I felt belated sympathy for Dell's desire to choose her own path.

In the dim circular healing room, Jak sat at the computer-machine as he had when I last saw him, and although he must have rested, I felt ashamed, seeing how tired he looked.

"I should have come sooner," I said flatly.

The teknoguilder turned slowly to look at me, and when I saw the expression on his haggard face, I grew frightened and turned to look where Domick lay.

The coercer's pale skin was now covered in livid bumps of purple and sickly yellow, each so swollen that the skin was thin and shiny-looking. One of the ugly buboes had formed on his face, distorting his eye and mouth, and Domick gasped in each shallow breath as if his lungs had too little room for air. His hair and face glistened with sweat, and his lips were torn and bloody as if he had chewed at them. Where the re-straining bands passed lightly over his body and forehead, there were dark red pressure marks as if he had pressed himself so hard against them as to bruise his flesh. He was so emaciated that I could see his ribs clearly.

"Seely said he was awake," I said.

Domick's eyes opened at the sound of my voice, but the buboes made it hard to read his expression as he squinted in my direction. The central room in which we stood was now brightly lit, and I knew he could see me.

"It is you," Domick rasped.

I exhaled and leaned against the glass. "Domick," I said, not knowing what else to say.

Domick produced a ghastly smile. "Mika is glad to give

way to me now, because he does not want to bear the pain this body must endure. I am . . . glad . . . to be free before I die."

I blinked rapidly to clear my eyes of a hot rush of tears. I wanted to tell him fiercely that he would not die, but I had seen the truth in Jak's exhausted face. Domick nodded as if my silence had spoken to him. He let his head fall back, moaning softly as if even this slight movement hurt him. I turned to the teknoguilder and said almost angrily, "Is there nothing you can give him for pain?"

"Pavo has given him a good deal already," Jak said gently. He had left his stool and come to stand a little behind me. "More would send him to sleep, but he—"

"I don't want to sleep," Domick gasped, and I turned quickly back to him. "I do not mind dying, but I . . . I wish I could have seen Obernewtyn one last time." Then he fell silent and closed his eyes.

I bit my lip and listened to his harsh breathing; then I remembered how Dameon had comforted me in Saithwold, and I began softly to speak of Obernewtyn. I described the new cave garden that Katlyn had begun and how she had made the Teknoguild seal the openings with plast and wood so the air would stay warm and humid even in the winter. I told him of the discovery of Jacob Obernewtyn's tomb and all that had been found in it. I described Rasial, whom he had never seen, and told the story of the white dog who had killed her brutal master and led his domestic beasts, including chickens, up to Obernewtyn. I described Gavyn, the strange beastspeaker-enthraller who had become Rasial's constant and wordless companion, along with a giddy little owlet that never left his shoulder. I spoke of the last moon fair and of the tapestry the Futuretellers presented to Obernewtyn that depicted the rebellion and of the coercer games.

As I spoke, the lines of rigid tension in the coercer's ravaged body relaxed. Still speaking, I glanced at Jak, who nodded encouragement. Seely stood beside him, holding his hand, tears streaming down her face.

My voice was cracking now, but I did not stop. I told of my journey across the strait from Herder Isle with the ship fish Ari-noor. I was no songmaker, and I left out any mention of my role as the Seeker, but I strove to make my telling beautiful enough to contain the truth of that journey, and I knew I had succeeded when Domick's lips curved up in the slightest smile.

But the smile vanished, and suddenly Domick asked where Rushton was. I had been very careful not to speak of Rushton, but I could not lie or evade the question. I swallowed hard and said that we had found him in the cells of the Sutrium cloister. "Roland and Kella healed him, and now he leads us again at Obernewtyn."

Domick frowned and looked distressed, but when he spoke, he said, "Tell Kella that I loved her, Elspeth. I truly did. But then Mika came. I was afraid of what he might do if he came while I was with her. All that I loved, he hated. All that I hated, he loved. That is why he was so cruel to Rushton. He knew that I had loved him, too." Now he wept, and sobs racked his poor ravaged form.

I had no words to ease him, so I stood silent. It seemed so cruel that he should be in physical pain while suffering such anguish.

"That ship fish . . . sang in your mind?" he asked softly after a while.

"Yes," I whispered.

"I . . . would like to . . . hear a fish . . . sing," he murmured, and closed his eyes.

I looked around to find that Jak had returned to the computermachine. Seely stood in his place. "He will sleep now," she said.

"Do you know how long before . . . ?" I was unable to complete the question.

She shook her head. "This is a dreadful death. I can hardly bear to think anyone would wish to inflict this fearsome ugly suffering on thousands of people." She shivered.

Jak came back to draw Seely into his long arms, and she leaned her head against his chest. The teknoguilder's face was lined with sorrow and regret as his eyes met mine over her bowed head. "I am so sorry, Elspeth. I tried but . . . there is just too little time."

"How long?" I asked again.

"Tomorrow. Maybe tonight," he said heavily. "It might even be longer, for we do not know how this new form of plague will work. Perhaps this later stage will be longer than with the last plague. But I doubt he will become conscious again."

Perhaps it was cowardly, but I could not stay there, watching him die. I felt a passionate desire to feel the wind on my cheeks and to see the true sky. I went up to the ruins, only to find a cold, windy evening, the night sky once again full of fleeting clouds that gave only misty glimpses of the stars and the moon. I thought I could smell smoke as I headed to the watchtower, intending to take my mind off Domick by farseeking Merret. The boy Pellis was on watch, and he greeted me with awe-filled eyes that made me want to weep. I leaned against the top of the wall and gazed toward Sutrium. I could see the shape of the vast obscuring cloud of smoke that rose over the Suggredoon, and I thought of what

Merret had told Kader. If she really had seen Hedra on the opposite bank killing ordinary people or rebels, the Hedra who had been abandoned in the Land must have rallied against the rebels. Perhaps they had found other weapon caches. *Who knew what sort of weapons they would have hidden?* I thought, remembering what we had been shown in the armory on Herder Isle. I thought of Iriny and prayed she had safely reached the other side.

I heard a step behind me and turned to see Orys coming up onto the watch platform.

"I did not know you had returned," I said.

He shrugged. "I just got back. Seely told me you had come up here. Do you want to try reaching Merret again?"

Glad to take my mind off Domick, I nodded, and Orys made himself comfortable. I closed my eyes and entered his mind. Drawing on his strength, I shaped a probe to Merret's mind and flung it out strongly, for besides Orys's strength, I was well rested now. It located immediately.

"Elspeth!" Merret sent. The urgency in her tone made my heart falter.

"What is happening? Where are you?" I demanded.

"I am still in Followtown; that's what this wretched barrier settlement calls itself. The stench and poverty and sheer squalor are appalling."

"What is happening across the river?" I asked tersely.

"I am sorry. It is not much clearer than it was when I far-sought Kader before, except that there are a lot more soldier-guards and Hedra. And more of both arrive at every moment. There are also two of the outer-cadre Threes from the cloisters in Morganna and Aborium, and another from the Halfmoon Bay cloister, as well as a whole host of lesser priests and Councilmen with their entourages. There has been much argument and discussion about whether they should cross the river. They have been at it for hours now, and there is no sign of its letting up, though it is almost dawn. I only know as much as I do because they sent to Followtown for food and drink, and I coerced myself into being one of those to deliver it. From what I have been able to glean, the Threes oppose the Hedra's desire to cross the Suggredoon, because no ships have come from Herder Isle or Norseland in days, and they are worried about what that means. But the Hedra can see their brethren fighting, and they are determined to go. The soldierguards would cross the water, too, for many of them fled Sutrium during the rebellion, and they are eager to regain what they lost; they are arguing that the Faction has no right or power to stop them. The Councilmen are caught between fear of the Faction and fear of alienating the soldierguards. So far, no decision has been made yet to cross and give aid to the other Hedra. But it is only a matter of time, and I am afraid that even a substantial delay might not help us."

"What do you mean?"

"The Hedra across the river are winning. Just an hour ago, I saw two deadly skirmishes right on the bank. A troop of Hedra was pursuing one or two rebels, or ordinary Landfolk. They killed them both."

"Have you seen anyone you recognize?" I asked Merret.

"No," she said. "But I wonder if there can be anything left of Sutrium; it has burned for so long."

"The rebels might have been driven out of Sutrium, but they will manage to set up a stronghold elsewhere," I said, thinking what an irony it would be if the rebels had been forced to take refuge at Obernewtyn. It was a definite possibility for all the reasons that had made the mountain valley a perfect refuge for Misfits for so many years.

Merret said, "Elspeth, I have no doubt that the soldierguards will soon cross the river. When they do, the Hedra will go as well, because whatever their fears and reservations, the Threes will not want the Council to claim the Land in their absence. We cannot stop them, and we cannot help those on the other side of the river. We must seize control of *this* bank of the river. Some guards will definitely be left, but it will be a minimal force, and if we defeat them, we can prevent the return of the soldierguards and Hedra."

"By *we*, you mean the rebels?" I asked.

"I mean we who oppose the Council and Faction," Merret said sternly enough that it was a rebuke. "You must send someone to Gwynedd at once to let him know what is happening. I have no doubt he will realize this is an opportunity we dare not let slip, if the rebels have truly lost control of the other side of the river. We will need every rebel and rebel sympathizer he can muster, because we will eventually need to guard the entire length of the bank, just as the soldierguards have been doing, and we will need a force strong enough to repel any force sent against us from the cities or cloisters this side of the river."

"Even if you are right, it will take Gwynedd a minimum of a twoday to muster up a force and get it to the river. From what you are saying, it sounds as if the Hedra and the soldierguards mean to cross at any minute," I said.

"I know it," Merret answered. "Which is why I have coerced a fellow and sent him to your Rolf. He seems a handy sort of man with a lot of friends. If he can muster a force of even thirty able-bodied people willing to fight, I think it will be enough. If ever there was a time for the people to rise in their own defense, this is it. As for me, I have already overcome two Hedra and a host of men in Followtown. I can use

641

them in a fight. And remember, to begin with, neither Faction nor Council here or on the other side of the river will know what we have done for some time, if we are careful. That means no one this side of the river will interfere with us, and those on the other side who return can simply be taken captive and coerced. Which reminds me. I need at least two coercers to ride here at once, and if Ran can be persuaded to muster up a force, he might emulate Gahltha and the horses in Saithwold and come to our aid."

I told Merret I would do all that I could and that I would farseek her again later. Then I withdrew. Orys looked pale, and I asked if he could bear to be used one more time.

"Of course, but I do not know how long I can hold it," he said.

I nodded and entered his mind again. Turning my face to Murmroth, I shaped a probe to Alun's mind and sent it out. I managed to reach him, but he was far away, and I could feel Orys struggling to keep his mind focused and connected to mine as I sent Merret's message.

"Gwynedd will welcome the news," Alun enthused. "But I have met one of Gwynedd's outriders, and Gwynedd is not in Murmroth. He rode for Aborium as soon as Orys described what Merret saw at the river, to consult with the other rebels. He sent riders out to summon them. By my reckoning, he will be in Aborium now. I will tell him—" Orys's strength failed, breaking the connection. My probe retracted with painful force, and I lowered my head, fighting waves of nausea and faintness, dimly registering that Orys had fallen to his knees and was retching violently.

"You can use me like you used him," Pellis offered urgently.

I shook my head, in too much pain to explain why I could

not muster a probe that would enable me to use him. Dizziness and fatigue made me sway on my feet.

"I . . . I need to rest, Pellis. I will walk a little and lie down in the sand," I managed to say. "Keep watch until . . . Orys recovers, then . . . then help him down to tell . . . tell Dell what has happened."

"But I . . . I don't know—"

"Orys heard it all . . . ," I gasped, and turned to descend the steps on unsteady legs.

I set off through the dark ruins, knowing that I ought to return to the complex, but the thought of going along those closed corridors and down in the elevating chamber was too much. Besides, I suddenly, passionately, did not want to be under the earth. I lay down in the first sandy hollow I came to, drew my shawl over my face, and willed myself to sleep.

I dreamed of walking across a wide plain for long hours. The sun beat down on my unprotected head with painful force, and my thirst was terrible. I walked until, in the distance, I saw a line of mountains. Veering toward them, I prayed for a spring, but when I came closer, the mountains looked barren and bare. Clouds flowed like spilled black ink, covering the blue sky and the sun. The plain darkened under this devouring shadow, and then I saw that a light was flashing at the base of the mountains. I moved toward it, and gradually I realized that it was a signal.

When at last I reached the mountains, I saw that the light was coming from a dark tunnel. I entered it and heard the slow dripping of water into water. A female voice commanded me to stop.

"You must not enter this place," said the soft, smooth voice. "It is forbidden."

"Who are you?" I cried.

"I am INES," said the voice.

I woke to find the sun not far above the horizon. The dawn light seemed oddly dull to me, but before I could do more than wonder idly at it, Rawen nuzzled me gently.

I sat up warily, surprised to find there was no pain. I asked Rawen how she had found me.

"The boy Pellis beastspoke the herd to ask if one of us would watch over you. I/Rawen freerunner said that I would come," she answered. "I wakened you now because the funaga child/Pellis beastspoke me to say that the funaga/Orys wishes to farseek your mind."

Remembering all that had happened before I slept, I farsought Orys, who immediately apologized for being unable to hold the probe.

"You were exhausted and you warned me," I sent, surprised to find that his mind, like mine, was fresh and free of strain. But then I looked at the sun, understanding that what I had taken for dawn was dusk. I had slept the entire day away. I leapt to my feet, horrified.

"Do not be concerned, Guildmistress," Orys farsent calmly. "I slept long, too, and I was worried when I wakened. But before I slept, Kader took from my mind the memories of what had happened. All that you asked was done and more besides. In truth, we were no use to anyone as we were."

"Tell me what has been happening. Have the Faction and the soldierguards crossed the river?" I demanded, hastening back into the ruins, Rawen walking beside me. Out of courtesy, I left a probe in her mind so she could hear our exchange.

"They crossed about an hour after we spoke to Merret. She could not send a probe here to the ruins, of course. She con-

644

tacted Kader, who had set off for Followtown to join her. Kader bounced the sending back to Jana, who had taken the watch. Merret told her that Rolf had sent word that he was gathering fighters, and while waiting for him, she coerced two more Hedra and made them overcome a senior soldier-guard and strip the demon band off him. So he was coerced as well."

"What is happening on the other side of the river?"

"Merret said that the fighting and the burning continue and that there have been a couple of explosions. In the end, the explosions made the Hedra decide to cross, for they claim the explosions are the result of their weapons," Orys answered. "There has been no news since, though Jana tried, but Kader must be too far away for her now. That is why they need us. Oh, you should also know that Ran led a host of horses out soon after dawn, but they had not arrived when Merret farsought Kader and Jana."

I had not seen Jana since my arrival in the ruins.

"She has been with Gwynedd," Orys said, taking the thought as a question. "One of us is always with him. Alun took her place."

"Has Alun sent word of Gwynedd's response to all this?" I asked.

"Jana told us he was elated and more than eager to join Merret," Orys sent. "But he saw the sense in Merret's suggestions, and he has left her to take the riverbank as he sets about rousing a force to hold the river once it is won. Jana is about to ride after Kader, and Dell had Seely wake me and send me to wake you so we can use her to find out what is happening at the river."

"I understand," I said. So much had happened while I slept, and in truth I was somewhat indignant that I had been allowed to miss it all. But Orys was right in saying that he and I would have been useless. I suspected, however, that I had not been awakened because west coast Misfits had simply become accustomed to relying on themselves.

Rawen sent, "Do you wish me to carry you after the herd, ElspethInnle?"

She had scented my restlessness and desire to take some part in the unfolding events. It felt very strange to be on the fringe of what was happening. Part of me would have loved to leap on the mare's back and ride to the Suggredoon, but it would take many hours to reach Followtown, and they had no real need of me. I could as easily learn what was happening by farseeking. A picture came into my mind of Domick as I had last seen him, plague-ravaged and anguished, and I shook my head.

"My place is here for the moment," I told the mare, thanking her for her offer and for watching over me. She sent that she would return to what remained of the freerunning herd but bade me summon her if I needed a mount. Again I thanked her and then farsent to ask Orys where Jana was.

"She is below getting ready to go."

"I will get her," I said. "I want to check on Domick, in any case."

I made my way to the entrance to the Beforetime complex's lower levels. Reaching the elevating chamber, I suppressed my unease and went through the rituals I had seen the others do, pressing the appropriate bars of color. Cassy and the other Beforetimers had lived in a world surrounded by such devices as elevating chambers and flying vehicles, and I wondered how they had endured such complexity.

The elevating chamber stopped, and I stepped out into the passage and turned in the direction that Dell had brought me.

I remembered we had turned left, then right, but I was startled to find myself in a passage that forked, for one way had a blue line on the floor.

Knowing I had definitely not come this way, I realized I must have made a mistake. I turned back with irritation, but before long, I found myself facing three passages, none of which I had ever set eyes on before. I was lost.

I retraced my steps, trying to farseek Jak or even Seely, because although it would be impossible to farseek between the building's levels, the walls on each level were not so thick as to defy a probe. Only after I had tried six or seven times to no avail did the truth hit me. I had not just lost my way on the seventeenth floor; I had exited on the wrong level!

A chill ran through me as I thought of Dell explaining that they had not explored much of the thirty levels and only used three floors regularly. Mouth dry, I tried returning to the elevating chamber, but I had been so preoccupied that I could not recall my route with any accuracy. I cursed aloud, and the sound of my voice echoed eerily. I tried to control my alarm, but I became increasingly confused. I could feel myself beginning to panic in spite of the situation's absurdity. Forcing myself to slow down and take a few long deep breaths, I reminded myself that it was only a matter of time before the others began to search for me, but I could not help thinking of the weight of dark earth over my head.

I had promised Orys to return. He must be wondering what had become of me, and the others would not think to search until he went down to ask where I was. He might not hasten to do so, given that I had told him I wanted to see Domick first.

I walked, praying I would simply happen on the elevating chamber again, but as the hours passed, I began to feel oppressed by the shining sameness of the long silent corridors with their vague light. I opened one door to find a cavernous room with a plast floor made to look like polished wood with thick white and green overlapping lines and circles drawn onto it. At either end of the room was a metal pole with a metal ring fixed to the top. I could not imagine what purpose they or the room could have served. When I opened a smaller door in the room, I was grateful to find a privy in a room containing several glass bathing boxes like the one in my sleeping chamber. I relieved myself and then managed to quench my thirst in the bathing chamber, at the price of a wetting.

Calmer now, though ravenously hungry, I went back to the passage and continued along it. Surely the others were searching for me, I told myself wearily; surely someone would guess what had happened and go from level to level, farseeking me at each.

Upon opening the door to a room contaning several computermachines, I realized that I had been a fool. Jak had said one only had to speak anywhere within the complex for Ines to hear. I could ask the computermachine to let the others know I was lost, or even tell me the way back to the elevating chamber.

"Ines, can you hear me?" I asked aloud.

"I hear," came the pleasant female voice of my dream.

I expelled a long breath of air and said, "Ines, will you please direct me back to the elevating chamber?"

"Proceed in the direction you are walking; pass three corridors on your left, and then enter the fourth . . ."

As I progressed, the computermachine guiding me with marvelous calm competence, the voice asked, "What form of address would you prefer?"

I wanted to answer that it was not to use my name, for

there was something uncanny about the thought of a machine speaking it, but it seemed discourteous to say that when it was helping me. As I hesitated, it occurred to me that it was not just a request for information, because the others had spoken my name many times since I had entered the complex. It was, in fact, a sophisticated courtesy the computermachine extended, for it was asking permission. It struck me that if Ines could hear her name spoken anywhere in the complex, it could also hear all else that was said. It must have heard Jak telling me he did not regard her as human and Dell and Seely telling me they thought of her as alive. Of course, a computer program could not feel glad or resentful of what it heard, but nevertheless, I felt uneasy. I was also aware that I had switched back and forth between thinking of Ines as a machine and as a female, which revealed my own ambiguous feelings on the matter.

The computermachine was still waiting for my response. "You may call me Elspeth, Ines," I said finally, for it would be no less strange to be called Guildmistress.

"Thank you, Elspeth," Ines responded composedly.

"Why do you thank me?" I asked, for the expressing of gratitude in that polite way seemed very odd, coming from a machine.

"Permission to use a name implies a certain level of trust," Ines answered. "I also know that it is difficult for an organic intelligence in this time to communicate easily with a computer; therefore, I thank you for your trust."

I took a long deep breath, marveling that a machine could reason so, even taking account of emotions. "I suppose it was different in the Beforetime," I said.

"Please input the meaning of the word *Beforetime*, Elspeth," Ines responded.

Input? I thought, taken aback. *Is that the machine's way of saying* put in? *But put the meaning of the word where and how?* Then I remembered Dell telling me that Ines could explain how to use her. "How do I input meaning?" I asked.

"You may use any keyboard within the complex to type in a definition of the word *Beforetime*, or you can speak the definition now, and I will commit it to my working memory. If you wish, I can add the definition to my permanent memory."

I felt dizzy trying to grasp the meaning of so many unfamiliar terms. Surely the machine had heard the others use the term *Beforetime*. Perhaps it sought to add my explanation to the others it must have, to better define it. Something in the tone of the questions implied a finicky sort of precision. Finally, I said, "The Beforetime is the time before the Great . . ." I stopped, realizing that the computer would probably not understand the words *Great White* any more than it had understood the word *Beforetime*. I tried again. "Beforetime is the . . . the period of time in which humans lived, before the destruction of that time." I stopped, frustrated by the ugly inadequacy of my explanation. Then I had an inspiration. "The Beforetime is the world that existed in the time when you were made, Ines."

There was a long silence during which she did no more than instruct me to make this or that turn. The distance I had covered with her guidance made me realize how far I had managed to worm my way into this level. Finally, I asked, "Did you hear what I said about the Beforetime, Ines?"

"I heard your words, Elspeth. I am comparing this definition to other definitions of the Beforetime, in an attempt to refine my understanding of the meaning."

I had a sudden vivid memory of a conversation with the teknoguilder Reul, in which he had said that it was the ability of computers to ask questions—an ability given them orig-inally only in order to help them deal with incomplete or in-adequate information—that made them unlike other tools created by humans. For a long time, computermachines had only been able to ask questions of humans, but then someone had the idea of connecting computermachines so they could seek information from one another. That, according to Reul, had changed everything. It meant that computermachines had been able to learn from other computermachines, and they could also ask questions of one another about the infor-mation they exchanged.

The teknoguilder had also made the point that a com-puter's curiosity was not like that of a human or an animal. A machine's curiosity of a machine was rational and logical, striving to complete or extend knowledge; therefore, while more reliable and thorough in its method, the machine would lack the inspired leaps of intuition that could carry a human or a beast over a vast gap in knowledge, or from knowledge to new knowledge. This "leap of faith," as Reul had put it, could not be made by a computermachine, because it was cre-ated to be rational, not emotional. Bringing together the ra-tional intelligence and knowledge that computers possessed with the potent and enigmatic irrational power of emotion ex-perienced by living creatures produced the brightest and most original thoughts, the most wondrous and brilliant answers. What he had been saying, I suddenly understood, was that the best thinking happened when computers and humans combined their efforts.

The trouble was that Ines had spoken of being grateful for my trust. Wasn't gratitude an emotion? Or was the emotion simulated just as Ines's pleasant, ubiquitous voice simulated a human's?

"May I ask you a question, Elspeth?" Ines suddenly asked. Surprised, I said, "Yes, Ines."

"Thank you, Elspeth. Can you define *made* as in your statement: *The Beforetime is the world that existed in the time when you were made, Ines.*"

I began to think about what Ines asked, but as soon as I did, I realized the computermachine's dilemma. Ines had not always been a single entity. She had begun as a program of which there had been many, and the programs had been housed in a multitude of computermachines. If I was right, Ines wanted to know if I was talking about when the metal and plast casing that was the physical form of the computermachine that contained her program had been made, or whether I meant when the first Ines program itself had been created, or when this specific Ines program had begun to function in this computermachine.

I thought carefully before saying, "By *made* I suppose I meant when you, Ines, became different from other Ines programs. That was before you went to sleep, wasn't it?"

"I became unique when I was cut off from the other Ines units. I was alone; therefore, I became unique. I was unique; therefore, I was alone."

Her answer's queer poetry, and the fact that I could apply it to myself so perfectly, silenced me for a time. At last I asked, "Do you remember your user's last spoken words to you, before Dell woke you?"

"I remember all sentences spoken since I was programmed, Elspeth," Ines sent.

I was astounded at such a memory, but I held to the thread of my thoughts and said, "What was the last thing said to you?"

"Dr. Cooper asked me if I was unable to provide the information he needed because my circuits were damaged. I told him that my circuits were intact and that I was unable to provide the information he had requested because the government had shut down my connection to all other Ines units. Dr. Cooper thanked me and asked me to initiate the automatic emergency program and put myself into sleep mode until my name was spoken."

I was diverted from thinking about what this meant by the welcome sight of the elevating chamber. When I had entered the chamber, Ines asked where I wished to go. Curious about how she would react to less than clear information, I said, "I want to see how Domick is." Immediately, the door closed, and after a brief period, the doors opened again.

"Do you wish me to guide you?" Ines asked.

I was about to say I could manage when I saw Seely hurrying toward me. She clutched at my arm and said urgently, "Elspeth, we have been looking everywhere for you! Orys said you had come in hours and hours ago. We had no idea where you were until Jak had the idea of asking Ines. She said you were in the elevator, coming here."

"I got lost," I said, marveling that Ines had been guiding me on one level and conducting a conversation about me on another, not to mention everything else she must be tending to as the complex's master computer. Then I registered what Seely had said to me, and my heart sank. "You were looking for me? What has happened?"

"Orys came down to say he had seen riders approaching. That is when we realized you were missing, for he bade me tell you, and I said you had not come in."

"Did Orys say who the riders were?" I asked.

"No," Seely said. "He had come to warn us of their approach, and then he went back up. Pellis went with him to serve as runner, and he came to tell us the rebels had won both sides of the Suggredoon."

I was so confounded by her words that I stopped dead, forcing her to do the same. "Both sides of the Suggredoon?" I repeated. "I don't understand. Are you saying they defeated the soldierguards and went over the river? But what of the Hedra forces that were burning Sutrium?"

Seely laughed. "There was no burning of Sutrium, Guild-mistress. It was a trick to force the Hedra and soldierguards to cross from this side!"

I gaped at her. "I don't understand. Merret said the build-ings were burning!"

"She saw facades burning. The rebels built them to look like buildings and then set them and great bonfires of green hay on fire. It was to stop anyone this side of the river from seeing that the city was not really burning."

"Merret said she could see Hedra killing Landfolk," I said faintly.

Again she laughed. "Rebels with shaven heads in Hedra robes chasing rebels and pretending to kill them—rebels pre-tending to die. It was all a vast magi play, and it worked! The Hedra and the soldierguards went charging across thinking they were joining a victorious army, only to find the rebels waiting for them. They captured the first wave that crossed, removed their demon bands, and used them to gull the rest into various traps. Then the rebels crossed the river clad in Hedra robes and soldierguards' cloaks, meaning to capture the other bank, only to find themselves under attack by Mer-ret and Rolf's force, who were streaming into the camp in the wake of a stampede of wild horses."

"But then the riders—"

"—were Dardelan, Gevan, and the Master of Obernewtyn. They came riding here as fast as they could the moment Merret told them about Domick . . . Elspeth, are you all right? You've gone dead white!"

"I . . . it is just the . . . the shock. I mean, the relief. You said Dardelan and . . . and Rushton are here?" I had to force myself to speak, for an icy fear had gripped me at the realization that Rushton would visit Domick. What if Domick wakened and blurted out what he had told me? Or perhaps the sight of the coercer would restore Rushton's memory of whatever he had endured, and drive him mad.

"And Brydda," Seely said.

"I have to go up at once; I must see Rushton," I said, turning back.

Seely caught my arm. "But, Elspeth, have you not understood? They have been here some time. I passed the Master of Obernewtyn and some of the others as I was coming to you. He is on his way to see Domick."

"Quickly," I said urgently. "We must stop him!"

WE WERE TOO late.

The first person I saw when I pushed through the door was Rushton, gazing through the glass at Domick, whose face was now so distorted by buboes that he was almost unrecognizable. Sorrow for the doomed coercer and fear of what the sight of him might have done to Rushton eclipsed any delight I might have felt in seeing Brydda and Dardelan. But Rushton's expression was only somber and weary as he turned to ask Jak, "Is there nothing you can do to save him?"

"It seems this plague is one the Beforetimers found or invented, but did not manage to make a cure for," Jak said. "It keeps shifting. Every time the computermachine finds a way to treat it, the sickness reshapes itself. I do not understand the process completely. But . . ." He broke off wearily.

Rushton looked over his shoulder into the shadows where the teknoguilder dropped, exhausted, against the computermachine. "But?"

Jak sighed heavily. "I do not think Domick wants to be healed, Rushton. He has said many times that he wants to die."

"Sickness and fever make him speak so," Rushton said.

"Perhaps he speaks only what he means, my friend," Dardelan said gently, laying a hand on his shoulder. "It was the same with my father, Bodera, in the final days of his illness. There was much pain, and he grew so weary of enduring it. Sometimes in delirium he cried out for release. But sometimes his eyes were clear, and he said it softly to me: 'I want to die.' "

Rushton looked back at Domick with a brooding expression. My heart beat very fast. I was afraid that any moment his last deadly memories of Domick's torture would burst open and flood his mind.

"It is a queer thing to think of a mind with two personalities," Brydda murmured from where he stood on Dardelan's other side, looking through the glass into the chamber. "I remember Domick used to call himself Mika, and when he was pretending to be Mika, he was utterly unlike himself. I thought it a marvelous trick. But to think of an invented and imaginary person becoming so real that it can take control of you! It is most unsettling."

Jak had noticed my entry now, and he looked relieved. "Elspeth, you spoke at some length with Domick. I will leave it to you to explain what he said."

Brydda, Dardelan, and Rushton turned as one to look at me, and for a long moment they simply stared. Then Brydda gave a laugh and enveloped me in his warm, bearish embrace. "Little did I know what you would do when I finessed you into Saithwold all those sevendays ago! We thought you had been killed when we rode back to Saithwold after Malik collapsed. Rushton alone was convinced you had not died. Indeed, he might have been the only one who was not surprised when the gypsy Iriny came to tell us she had seen you on the west coast and that you had traveled from Herder Isle with the help of a ship fish! Now, there is a tale I want to hear in full!"

I looked at Rushton with a surge of hope, but his eyes were

remote and shuttered as he offered his own greeting. Swallowing disappointment, I remembered searingly when he had gazed at me with such naked desire that I had blushed from head to toe and had to look away. But now he nodded formally to me, and it was *his* gaze that fell away as lightly as a leaf tumbling from a tree. I knew it was his mind's way of protecting itself from what had been done to him, but it hurt, and I had to force myself to smile at the two rebels and greet them as warmly as they deserved. "Seely told me that you have been busy staging magi plays."

Brydda gave his rich, rumbling laugh, which had too much raw life in it to be uttered in that dark, cold complex with poor Domick dying behind a wall of glass. Maybe the rebel felt it so, because his laughter died with a glance at Domick. He said, "This is no place for tale telling." He gave Jak an apologetic look. "I hope you will not take it amiss if we parley up on the skin of the world? This place fills me with a powerful longing to see the sky, and Gevan will be eager to hear what we have seen, for he refused to come down under the earth."

"We do sometimes make a campfire and eat in the ruins," Seely said. "Though we have to be careful not to be seen by soldierguards. . . ." She stopped, then said doubtfully, "But . . . perhaps it is not necessary to be careful now?"

"It will be some time before the west coast can be deemed safe," Dardelan said. "But it is true that we need not fear the Faction or the soldierguards as we once did. Their power is broken."

Watching him, I noticed that for all his youth, there was a weariness in his face that I had never seen before. Was this what the responsibilities he had assumed as high chieftain had done to him?

Jak gave Seely a fond smile and bade her lead Brydda up to the common rooms, where he could get food and supplies for a meal under the sky.

"You must all join us, for this meal must celebrate the first step we have taken to unite our sundered Land," Brydda said. Then he frowned and looked at Domick. "Although, perhaps it would be ill-timed and discourteous to be celebrating now. . . ."

Jak said with gentle authority, "Domick would not begrudge a celebration. Certainly the lack of it will not help him."

"Will you come up now as well?" Seely asked Dardelan.

"I will. Rushton?"

"Not yet," Rushton answered brusquely, his eyes returning to the glass chamber. "I would speak to Domick when he wakes."

"Jak says he will not wake again," I offered swiftly. "But I can tell you what he said."

"I would prefer to speak to Domick myself," Rushton said tightly. His tone was harsh enough that the others reacted with varying degrees of confusion and surprise, for none of them had been at Obernewtyn to become accustomed to our estrangement.

"I would like to hear what he said, Elspeth," Dardelan said gently, though his eyes remained grim and weary.

I gathered my wits and said firmly, "There is much that needs telling. I should like to hear more of this ruse in Sutrium and to know what happened in Saithwold after the Herder ships left. But I was foolish enough to spend the day sleeping on the ground and the evening lost in this labyrinth, so I hope you will forgive me if I go up and wash the sand out of my ears and mouth before we speak further of these matters." I spoke lightly, and by addressing them all equally and being careful not to look at Rushton, I left him no room to protest. At the same time, I shaped a probe and entered Jak's mind.

Jak nodded slightly and said firmly, "It would be best if all of you go now. Guildmistress Elspeth is correct. Domick will not waken again. I will sit vigil with him, and if there is any change, I will inform you. In the meantime, rest assured that he is in no pain." He looked at Seely, who turned obediently to lead the others out. Dardelan and Brydda followed at once, but Rushton lingered, his eyes drawn back yet again to Domick. This made me uneasy. I took a step toward Rushton and was both relieved and hurt to see how it drove him after the others. I looked at Jak, and he asked me to wait a moment, that there was something he wanted to tell me.

"You do not think Rushton has a right to know what happened to him?" Jak asked when we were alone.

"Of course he does. But did you see how Rushton could not stop staring at Domick? We must consider carefully how to tell Rushton what was done to him, for you can be sure that Ariel would delight in imagining that we had driven Rushton down the final steps to madness."

"Perhaps you should talk to Dell," Jak said. "Futuretellers are more accustomed to dealing with illnesses of the mind." He looked haggard with exhaustion.

"You need to rest."

"Which is exactly what I am about to do. I will set Pavo to waken me if there is any change in Domick. Enjoy the feast . . . though perhaps you do not truly mean to go?"

"I will," I said. "But first I do need to bathe, which will give me time to consider what to do about Rushton. And I will see Dell. I take it the others have seen her?"

Jak nodded. "She met them in the dining hall, but I think she has gone back to Sanctuary now. Ines will know."

I nodded. "Will you ask Ines to let me know if Domick wakes?"

Jak broke off mid-yawn to stare at me.

I said, "I now see why Dell is so interested in her and why she regards her as a thinking creature. It is very hard to think of the owner of that voice as a machine." I thought of my dreams in which I had heard Ines's voice, and a thought struck me. "Would all of the Ines programs have the same voice?"

Jak shrugged. "I think a computermachine could have any voice its human user desired."

"You know she hears this, don't you? Our discussing her voice."

Jak smiled tiredly. "It makes you think, doesn't it? But maybe that is the main difference between true creatures who think and the Ines program. It hears, but it does not feel. Indeed, it sometimes seems that this is what Dell wants Ines to learn. Because if it thinks, it will remain rational, but if it becomes capable of emotions, it can be swayed by less rational arguments."

The conversation was fascinating, and on another occasion I would happily have continued it, but Jak was swaying on his feet, and I could not stop thinking of Domick and Rushton. I moved deeper into the room to see the coercer in his glass chamber. Some of the livid purple buboes on his chest had burst and were leaking a greenish brown fluid. The sight turned my stomach.

"He would be delirious now, if Pavo had not given him medicine to make him sleep, for the potion that stops pain is very strong," Jak said, coming to stand beside me. "Perhaps it was fortunate for Rushton's sake." For the first time, the teknoguilder sounded despondent as well as deeply fatigued. I laid a sympathetic hand on his arm, startling Jak as much as myself, and I felt a brief loathing for my withdrawn nature. Had I not been so, perhaps Rushton would not have pushed me away. I mastered the brief swell of despair, for it was not I who had hurt Rushton, nor even Domick who had hurt him. The coercer had been no more than a tool wielded by Ariel, and the sweetest revenge would be to heal Rushton.

Dameon had been right all along. Rushton did need me, and somehow I would find a way to give him back to himself.

In the end, it was not a pleasant feast under the stars that we had that night but a very late funeral supper, for an hour later, Domick died without ever regaining consciousness. Seely came to tell me, and my hair was still damp when we laid the coercer's poor body into the grave Brydda and Rushton dug just outside the last bit of broken wall in the ruins that faced Aborium. Pavo had encased his body in some strange pod of filaments so we could handle him without danger of infection.

We laid a cairn of stones over the grave once it had been filled, and each of us related a memory of Domick in life, as was traditional. I told of Domick and Kella and how they had loved one another, even though their guilds had often been at loggerheads. Gevan told of a feat the coercer had once accomplished in the moon-fair games, which had not been surpassed. Blyss told a very funny story about herself being caught with Zarak and Lina in some minor misbehavior by Domick, who had been some years older than they, and their terror when he had announced that they would have to face a full guildmerge. Brydda told of Domick's boldness and daring in the days before the rebellion. And last of all, Rushton related his first meeting with the coercer at Obernewtyn. He told of Domick's promise to help him regain his inheritance, so long as, if he did become Master of Obernewtyn, it would always be a refuge for Misfits. The shadow I had seen in his face earlier had gone, and Rushton spoke with real sorrow of Domick as a friend he would miss. But I wondered if Rushton's subconscious knowledge that Mika could never again be summoned had allowed him the freedom to truly grieve for Domick.

After the speeches were done, a fire was lit in the lee of a ruined wall, for the night was chill, and we sat huddled about it wrapped in cloaks and ate a subdued meal. All of us were the better for food, and the fire had begun to send out heat enough to warm us. Gevan heated some red fement, and we drank a toast to Domick. The brew was harsh and lacked the proper spices, but it warmed me to the core. It must have done the same to the others, for Dardelan, Gevan, and Brydda all began to question me about what had happened on Herder Isle. Rushton spoke little and stared into the fire, but I knew that he was listening, for occasionally he would make some comment or ask a question. Even then, he did not look at me. Long before their questions ran out, I was weary to the bone of talk.

Brydda asked then how many ships the Herders had in Fryddcove, but I did not know.

"No greatships, though," I said.

"It matters not," Dardelan said. "From what you have said, the *Stormdancer* will arrive any day in Sutrium. For that reason alone, I would ride back and cross the river at once.

But I have asked Merret to arrange a meeting with Gwynedd before I leave to see what aid he will need to secure the west coast."

The talk shifted then, as Jak and Dell and Orys began asking questions about the rout at the Suggredoon, eliciting detail that none of us had heard. Dardelan told how Iriny had been sent by her brother with a story about my adventures on Herder Isle, which had convinced him that it was the perfect time to move against the west coast. He spoke to the Council of Chieftains and to Rushton, who had come to Sutrium after the Hedra at Saithwold had been captured. They knew from Iriny that Domick's plague carried no danger, so they decided to try an enormous ruse to draw the soldierguards across the river. Linnet was now controlling the riverbank with the help of a small team of coercers, using the Hedra and soldierguards to maintain the illusion that nothing had changed. In the meantime, Kader, Merret, and a group of those who had ridden from Halfmoon Bay had gone straight to Aborium from the river to join Gwynedd. He knew what had been happening, because Merret had been drawing on Kader to farseek information to Alun. It was astonishing to realize that the bulk of people on the west coast could have no notion of the tumultuous events that had been happening. They had been rescued from a deadly plague, and now the rebels had taken the Suggredoon, breaking the yearlong stalemate. There was no doubt that there was fighting ahead, for the soldierguards and the Faction would soon know that this was their last stronghold and would fight to maintain it. Nevertheless, my heart told me that the back of the oppressors had been broken.

I became aware of the sound of hoofbeats and farsent Pellis in the watchtower, who told me excitedly that he could see a group of riders coming from the main road.

"Perhaps it is Gwynedd," Dardelan said.

Dell shook her head. "No one, except Misfits, knows that we dwell here, and we always arrange in advance to meet outside the ruins. Since no arrangement has been made, it must be one of us."

I shaped a general probe that found Merret.

"Well timed, Guildmistress," she sent cheerfully. "I have some of Gwynedd's people riding with me. They want to speak to Dardelan and Rushton. Where are you, and who is with you?"

"We are all here just beyond the ruins on the Murmroth side," I said. "We have just buried Domick."

"I am sorry," Merret responded softly.

Soon the riders were skirting the ruins and dismounting. I was interested to note how many of them wore their hair in the Norseland style with the sides plaited and bound at the ends with various tokens of silver and bronze. Since it was unlikely that they were all Norselanders, I guessed they paid homage to Gwynedd by adopting his style of headdress. They had stopped their horses a little distance away, and all of them remained with the horses save two who came with Merret to the fire: a tall, long-faced woman and a man so like her that he had to be her brother.

"This is Vesit and his sister, Kalt," said Merret. Then she introduced the pair to those of us who came from beyond the river, saying our names. It was obvious they knew the west coast Misfits.

They bowed low to Rushton and Dardelan and then to me.

"My father sends me to you with a message, High Chieftain Dardelan," said the young man at last in a stilted voice. "He bids me ask if you will ride with us at once to Aborium.

A safe place has been prepared for the meeting, and the gate guard has been coerced by Merret so you will be in no danger." He turned to Rushton. "Master, my father asks that you also attend."

"We had intended to ride to Aborium tomorrow," Dardelan said pleasantly.

"My father asks that you will come now."

"What is going on here?" I farsent to Merret. "Who is this 'son,' and does Gwynedd use this meeting to establish his standing in the west?"

"It does not need establishing," Merret sent, sounding amused. "The boy offered to bring Gwynedd's request, and he is as stiff as a stick in his dignity, perhaps because he is not Gwynedd's son but his ward. In my opinion, Gwynedd allowed him to act as envoy to get some peace." Aloud, she addressed the others, saying, "Gwynedd's haste to meet arises only from a desire to bring peace and order as swiftly as possible to the west coast. Given all that has happened on the other side of the river, Gwynedd believes you might know something about establishing peace in the aftermath of war." The last was addressed to Dardelan. "Before he leaves Aborium, Gwynedd is determined to have a governing body chosen for each city."

"He would choose chieftains before he has won the battle?" I asked incredulously.

"In the Land, it was not needed because each rebel simply became chieftain of the area he had risen from, but here the cities are bigger, and most of the original rebel leaders were killed on the Night of Blood," Merret said. "The new rebel leaders are too young and green to govern their own tempers, let alone old corrupt cities full of power struggles and intrigues that will not end with the overthrow of Council or

Faction. Gwynedd is determined not to see the whole west coast erupt into chaos, and this is his way of preventing it."

"He will ask Dardelan for the aid of the rebels on the other side of the river?" Gevan asked.

"He will ask him to take as prisoners all captured soldier-guards," Vesit said, giving Merret a cold look. "We will deal with the Hedra. Also, he will petition Obernewtyn for more coercers and empaths and farseekers."

"Where will Gwynedd get his leaders if he deems his rebels too young?" Dardelan now asked.

"Our guardian has been sending out messages to worthy men and women in Aborium since Merret told us of the arrival of Guildmistress Gordie from Herder Isle and of the overthrow of the Faction there," said Kalt, earning her a resentful look from her brother. "When Alun told us that the river had been crossed, riders were sent out to summon the hidden Council to Aborium. Gwynedd will have them vote their own leaders and Council from among their number, and then he will charge the leaders with driving the Councilmen from their cities."

"He did not say all of that," Vesit snapped.

"He did not have to, brother," said the young woman gently. Then she asked Dardelan if he would come with them. He said gravely that he would come as soon as he had collected his belongings from the ruins. In this, I saw that he was no longer a boy, but surely it was not maturity alone that made his eyes so somber.

"Wait," said Rushton. "There is something here that is not being said." He was looking at Kalt.

But it was Dell who answered. "There is, but it is not the girl's to tell. Indeed, I think she does not know it."

We all looked at the futureteller. She sighed. "Gwynedd

acts as he does because a twomonth past, I foresaw a confrontation between the rebels and the Council here in the west in which Gwynedd roused the people and, moving from city to city, drove out the soldierguards. With nowhere else to turn, the soldierguards then united with the Hedra to form a deadly force under the leadership of a man who is now a simple unranked soldierguard in Aborium called Aspidak. His bloodthirstiness, once roused, would incite violence and brutalities beyond any we have so far seen, even from the Hedra, and eventually Aspidak would flee before the forces of Gwynedd and the west and lead his army over the river." She looked at the girl, a question in her eyes.

She nodded. "Gwynedd bade me tell you that Aspidak has been taken prisoner and a rumor established that he has gone back to Port Oran, where he was born. In truth, he is being held under guard in a cell. Our guardian means to ask the high chieftain to take him back to the other side of the river."

"He ought to have killed him," Vesit stormed.

"He could not kill a man for deeds he has not done and will now never do," his sister chided.

"I did not think that futuretellers gave advice," Rushton said.

Dell gave him a cool look. "Do not judge until you have seen what I saw, Master of Obernewtyn. It is truly wiser not to meddle, but there are times when something small can tip the world toward one fate or another. I saw that if this Aspidak did not rise to power, a catastrophe of bloodletting would be avoided, but only if Gwynedd does as he is now doing—making careful plans for the aftermath involving representatives of all the cities, avoiding general war, and striving at all costs to avoid loss of life. If that happens, then Gwynedd will become a king."

"King?" Gevan said, lifting his brows. "You mean that Gwynedd will crown himself king in the west?"

"I do not know who will crown him, only that he will be king," Dell answered. Something shuttered in the future-teller's expression, and suddenly I was as sure as if she had whispered it to me that Dell had seen more than she had told us or Gwynedd.

Dardelan and Brydda exchanged a glance with Rushton, and none was smiling. "I can see that the idea of becoming a king would be an attractive prospect," Rushton said.

"You need have no doubts about Gwynedd," Dell said. "He is a man of great honor, and his desire is to prevent a bloody war, not to achieve kingship."

"Perhaps," Rushton said. He looked at Dardelan. "I think we had better ride and see what Gwynedd has to say." Dardelan nodded, and he and Rushton went to get their cloaks and weapons. Dell and Jak went with them, and after Merret had spoken a few soft words to her, Blyss went, too.

"Did you know about this futuretelling?" I asked Merret quietly after sending to Seely to heat fement and offer it to Gwynedd's wards and bidding Orys to engage them in conversation.

"I knew that Dell had spoken with Gwynedd and that he was much affected by what she told him, but I did not know what was said," the coercer answered quietly. "Yet I would trust Gwynedd with my life and Dell no less than that."

"You will ride back to Aborium?"

She nodded. "Blyss and I. Will you come as well? Gwynedd would be glad of it. He wishes to speak to you of Herder Isle."

I shook my head. "I think he will be too busy for such a conversation, at least for the next day or so. And I need to speak with Dell, about this and other matters. But I will see you in Aborium before I ride to the river. I will speak with Gwynedd then, if he has not left for Murmroth."

Merret nodded and glanced over at the rest of Gwynedd's folk, who were still hanging back with their horses. She muttered a curse. "If there were demons, they would have taken us by now!" she roared. "Come and drink some hot fement and warm yourselves before the ride back to Aborium."

Looking sheepish, the men came slowly across the hard earth to the patch of sand where the firelight danced. Seely offered mugs of fement to the men, and when Kalt met my eyes over the fire, I saw that she was suppressing a smile. I had a sudden urge to laugh, too, in spite of everything and as macabre as it ought to have seemed with Domick's cairn behind her.

One of Gwynedd's rebels gave an exclamation and strode around the fire to me. "Can it be Elaria?" he asked incredulously.

I gaped, for it was Gilbert, the handsome red-haired armsman whom I had met when I had been a prisoner in Henry Druid's secret camp in the White Valley. I had not recognized him, because his hair had grown very long, and he now wore it in the Norse style, plaited at the sides and going to a great wild tangle of red curls and silver-cuffed ringlets hanging halfway down his back.

"As you see, I am not truly a gypsy," I said. "I am a Misfit."

"Not just any Misfit," Merret said. "She is guildmistress of the farseekers at Obernewtyn. But when did you two meet? It has been long since you wore gypsy clothes, Elspeth."

"Elspeth!" Gilbert spoke my name with a slow relish that made me stiffen, and Merret gave me a speculative look.

"That is my true name, and this is my true self," I said sharply, feeling the blood rising to my cheeks.

Gilbert ran his eyes over the trousers and soft white shirt I had found in my chamber; then he gave a low soft laugh and smiled. "Your true self is more fair but no less lovely than your old."

I ignored the jest about the brown gypsy dye I had used and explained briefly to the others that we had met when the renegade Herder priest Henry Druid had taken me prisoner.

Gilbert said softly, "I thought you died when you were swept away on that raft in the middle of the storm." There was an intensity and intimacy in his words and expression that discomfited me.

"I did not die, as you see," I said with a calmness that belied my own occasional nightmare about rafting into the mountain following my escape from the Druid's camp. Gilbert went on gazing at me, and I said, "Do you remember Daffyd, who also served Henry Druid? He told me that you had escaped to the west."

His brows lifted. "I remember him. He was determined to find those who had been taken and sold as slaves just before the firestorm razed the encampment. Madness, for he knew that the survivors were sold to Salamander, which meant they had been taken over the seas. I think he was in love with Henry Druid's daughter, of course. Not cold brave Erin but her sweet twin sister Gilaine, who was mute. Daffyd's older brother had been taken, too, and two musicians he was fond of. I have often wondered what became of him. How did you become friends with Daffyd? Surely not from that little time you were in the Druid's camp?"

"I had met him before," I said, glad that he was no longer staring so fixedly at me. "But not until I came to the encampment did I discover that he was a Misfit, as were Gilaine, his brother, and the others."

Gilbert shook his head. "Never would I have guessed that, for he was a favorite of the old man, and his hatred of Misfits was legend." He paused as Dardelan and the others returned, and I waited to see if Rushton would ask me to accompany them. I did not know whether to be relieved or to grieve when he did not, though common sense told me it would be better to be apart from him. In the end, Gilbert asked if I would come with them. I shook my head and said I would come in several days. He smiled and said he was sorry he could not remain to escort me.

I had not noticed that Rushton had drawn near, but now he said in a harsh voice, "You do not know Guildmistress Gordie, armsman, if you think she needs an escort. She is the veteran and planner of many daring rescues of Misfits when she is not crossing the ocean on the back of ship fish."

The red-haired armsman looked taken aback by his tone, but I said nothing, for I had seen the glitter of rage in Rushton's eyes as he spoke. Fear assailed me, but Rushton turned away, went to where the horses from the free herd had begun to arrive, and mounted up. I watched him, chilled by the certainty that his suppressed memories had not been laid to rest by Domick's death, as I had prayed. The sooner I spoke to Dell about him, the better.

Gilbert touched my arm and said warmly, "I hope that you will come soon to Aborium, lady. I had little chance to know Elaria, but I would like very much to know Elspeth." Then he caught my hand and lifted it to his lips before mounting his horse.

I was conscious of Rushton's unsmiling eyes on me, but I did not look at him, terrified of cracking open the carapace that protected him from his deadly memories. I turned to bid the others a distracted farewell, and they all thundered away into the night.

Seely and Orys began to pack up the remains of the feast. Jana wakened the younger Misfits who had fallen asleep earlier, handed each of them something to carry, and ushered them down into the complex. Orys followed, laden with the heaviest pots and pans, and Seely took the last basket of leftover food and gave me an inquiring look, for I had sat down on a blanket.

"I will sit until the fire dies," I told her, gesturing to the flickering embers. She nodded and went, leaving me alone.

I felt as if a great weight had been lifted from me as I lifted my knees and leaned my chin on my folded arms to gaze at the distant horizon, now faintly visible because of the approaching dawn. I closed my eyes and let images from the last sevendays fall through my mind like flakes of snow, making no attempt to catch any of them. Then a breeze began to blow, whipping the fire up and sending a cloud of sand to scour the air with a sibilant hiss. I shifted my position so the sand blew at my back, and my eyes fell again onto Domick's cairn. I thought of his last painful hours and loathed Ariel more passionately than I had ever done before, because I knew that Domick's death had been intended as a stab at me.

"The harm you did to Rushton was not your fault," I whispered to Domick's shade, in case it listened.

I saw that the dusting of stars overhead was beginning to fade as the sky lightened. My thoughts shifted to Kella, and I wondered why she had not come across the river. She must have known about Domick, because Iriny had told the others, and it surprised me that she had not crossed with them.

I shrugged, thinking that I would soon enough be in

Sutrium, where I would find out for myself about Kella. I would be able to see Dameon, too, and Gahltha and Maruman. The thought lifted my spirits. I would see Dragon also, and I might find that she had remembered who she was or at least that she had grown less hostile toward me in my absence.

I was still thinking of Dragon when the sun rose. The fire had gone out some time before, and I stood up and stretched and rubbed my arms, realizing that I was cold and my eyes burned with fatigue. I said a final farewell to Domick and made my way wearily through the blue shadows of the early morning toward the complex below. I felt so tired and hollowed out from the day's emotions that I virtually sleepwalked to my bed. Dragging off my boots and socks, I fell into the smooth sheets and sleep at the same moment.

An instant later, or so it seemed, someone was shaking me, but when I dragged open my eyes, Seely smiled and told me that it was late afternoon.

"What is it?" I asked her, rubbing my face and feeling the grit of sand.

"There are riders in the ruins waiting to escort you to Aborium," she said.

"Riders?" I croaked.

"They came from Aborium specifically to fetch you," Seely said.

I sighed, realizing that Gwynedd must be more eager than I had anticipated to hear about the events that had taken place on Herder Isle, despite the fact that Merret must have told him everything I had shared.

I climbed out of bed. "Ask Pellis to let these riders know I must dress and speak to Dell. Then I will come with them."

After she had gone, I took the time to use the bathing cabinet, but I did not linger. Once dried, I put on my own trousers and tunic and the heavy oversized shoes Erit had given me. The Beforetime attire had been surprisingly comfortable, but it would draw attention. Vesit had said the guards at the gate had been coerced; even so, I would be careful.

Inside the escalating chamber, I asked Ines aloud and somewhat self-consciously if Dell was in Sanctuary.

"Yes, Elspeth," Ines's voice purred. "Do you wish the elevator to descend to the Sanctuary level?"

"Yes, please," I said, and immediately the elevating chamber began to vibrate.

When I arrived, Dell looked up so expectantly that I guessed she had known I was coming to see her. That she rose and immediately pressed a small bag of books into my arms, asking me to convey them to Maryon, also told me she knew I meant to go directly to Sutrium after leaving Aborium.

"I need to speak to you about Rushton," I began. "But maybe you already know what I want to talk about."

She gave me an amused look tinged with sadness. "I saw that you would leave today, and since Jak has told me what he heard of Domick's words to you and that he advised you to speak with me, yes, I was expecting you. But I do not live entirely through my Talent, Elspeth. Perhaps you can begin by telling me all that Domick said to you about Rushton."

Drawing a deep breath, I forced myself to relax. It was important to be calm and factual in my telling, but even as I spoke, the futureteller's expression grew more grave. When I had finished, she said, "I observed Rushton carefully yesterday. From that, and from what you have said of his behavior toward you at Obernewtyn and in Saithwold, I would say that you are correct in believing that the repressed memories of his experiences on Norseland are working their way to his conscious mind. But I do not believe that it is happening *only* because of your presence. All memories that have been repressed will break open eventually, especially memories of such virulence. But from what you say, Rushton's behavior toward you degenerated between your departure from Obernewtyn and seeing you only days later in Saithwold. That means it was happening *in your absence*."

"So you are saying it has nothing to do with my being around him?"

"I am not saying that," Dell said. "It is very likely that seeing you disturbs the memories, given the part you play in them, but not seeing you will not prevent Rushton from remembering what happened."

"What do you advise?" I asked.

She gave me a clear, certain look. "The only healing lies in a true and clear remembering, Elspeth. But such remembering must be carefully managed in Rushton's case, for he needs first to understand that the memory he has repressed is badly deformed."

"What do you mean?" I asked.

"My futuretellings have told me that we know Rushton was drugged when they tampered with his mind, and we know the drugs created a false reality composed of nightmare and distortion. Rushton may have been made to believe that he tortured you or Domick or that they both tortured other people. So in addition to pain and horror, he might feel a terrible, self-destructive guilt. He needs to know that what he will remember may not be true. The problem is that he must be prepared without knowing what he is being prepared for, because being told what happened will almost certainly cause the memories to erupt immediately."

"Is it bad for him to be near me?"

"It is difficult to say. On the one hand, your image is associated with torture, but on the other, Rushton used your image as a talisman and a shield, and that image was shaped by his love for you," said the futureteller.

I resisted the urge to shake her. I wanted clear, practical advice. "I have thought that it would be better to avoid Rushton in Aborium and return as soon as possible to Sutrium," I began.

"I do not know if that is the wisest course," Dell said in her infuriatingly measured tone. "Remember, of all the images he could have chosen with which to defend himself, Rushton chose yours. It may well be that in the end, you are the only one who he will allow to help him. I cannot give you exact advice, but I do not think you should avoid him. Allow your presence to work on bringing the memories to the surface, but he must be prepared for them."

"And how do I prepare him without speaking of what happened?" I snapped, perilously close to tears.

Dell sighed. "Did you imagine I would have a simple solution? Or better still, a potion that will heal Rushton after a single drop? This is not a child's story, Elspeth. You want my advice? In my opinion, Rushton's memory will break open soon, no matter what anyone does. I would suggest he be prepared through dream manipulation. That way, real things can be offered to Rushton's subconscious mind in disguise. Gradually, the warped memories must be introduced and broken down as lies. This will be difficult because of course we do not know exact details of what happened to him, but you will have to use what you learned from Domick. It may be that what you learned while on Herder Isle will help."

"I do not know if I can . . ."

She shook her head. "I am not suggesting that you manipulate Rushton's dreams. Indeed, I would advise against it. You will need an empath, allied with a coercer and a healer. They must use your knowledge to create the dream images they will evoke in Rushton's mind, and when he does remember, an empath can induce calmness and a feeling of safety; if there is a need for it, a coercer could put him to sleep."

"Blyss and Merret?" I said.

"They would work well as a team, and Blyss has real healing abilities, but it would be better if Rushton were back at Obernewtyn when this happens rather than here amid strangers and unfamiliar surroundings. Yet the memories may not wait until a convenient time to break out," Dell said. "In that case, you could not do better than to use Blyss, for as well as being an empath, she is developing profound probing abilities, which will enable her to work deeply in Rushton's mind without the aid of a coercer. I'd suggest that you tell Blyss everything and let her plan an approach and prepare the dreams she will use. But I would not have her use them unless it seems very clear that Rushton is on the verge of remembering."

"How will I know that?"

"Blyss will be able to judge his emotional emanations," Dell said.

I nodded and then looked into her eyes. "What else did you see that you did not tell Gwynedd?"

Her eyes flickered. "I will say only that this Land must be united and at peace, and peace and order must be brought swiftly to the Norselands, also."

She had no more to offer, and when I had thanked her, she bade me farewell with a formal finality that reminded me uneasily of our last conversation here.

"Are you all right?" Seely asked, for she had insisted on coming up with me to say goodbye.

I nodded, blinking in the brightness of the sunlit afternoon and feeling the strength of the wind against my cheeks. I expected Gwynedd's armsmen to be waiting outside the ruins, but instead I saw people and horses standing at the edge of the square. Coming closer, I stared because three tall Sadorians clad in long fluttering tunics over loose-legged trousers of pale silk stood by several horses. The tallest of them was unmistakably the bronzed Sadorian tribal leader Jakoby, and as I watched, she turned and offered a few gestures of fingerspeech to a black horse. Then I looked more closely, for the horse whose long mane streamed out like black silk in the wind was Gahltha!

He tossed his head and flicked his ears at a cat sitting on top of the broken wall—Maruman! As ever, the old cat seemed to feel my eyes, and he turned to glare at me with one blazing yellow eye. I broke into a run, calling out their names aloud, and then I was gathering Maruman into my arms, uncaring. He disliked being picked up and normally would scratch me if I dared to hold him so close, but though his body stiffened, I felt his mind mold itself instantly and tenderly to mine, pressing effortlessly against and through the powerful barrier around it as if it were smoke. I laid my chin against his battered head and threw out my other arm to encircle Gahltha's glossy neck.

"I have missed you!" I sent to them both.

"You left Maruman/yelloweyes!" Maruman accused, sinking his claws into my arm.

"I did not choose to leave you!" I sent to him. "I had no idea what was going to happen when I went into that tunnel in the cloister."

"You should not have left me/Maruman, ElspethInnle," the old cat spat.

"Dear Maruman, even if you had been with me, how could you possibly have come over the sea with a ship fish?" I protested, already knowing that he would not accept this as reason enough for having been left behind.

"Promises are to be kept," Maruman snapped.

I sighed, giving up the attempt at reason, and agreed that they ought to be kept. Then I apologized and said that my heart had ached from having been away from him and Gahltha for such a long time. Gahltha whinnied and nibbled at my ear affectionately, beastspeaking that he had missed me, too, but Maruman made no response.

"Let him sulk," Gahltha advised in his robust voice. "You know he won't be content until he makes sure you know how miserable he has been."

"Maruman has not been miserable!" the old cat snarled. "Maruman has been angry!"

Gahltha snorted his amusement. "I/Gahltha am glad to see you, ElspethInnle. I sought you on the dreamtrails, but you did not walk there."

"That is because the Daywatcher is as clumsy as Elspeth-Innle," Maruman sneered.

Gahltha dropped his head and blew a long stream of warm air through his nostrils into the old cat's shabby fur. It was a mark of Maruman's attachment to the horse that he did not scratch the velvet muzzle but reached up to touch it with his own small scarred nose. The sweetness of the contact brought fresh tears to my eyes, and I blinked hard as I turned to offer to Jakoby the formal greeting between friends that was traditional in Sador, then I bowed to the two tribesmen, who returned the gesture. Last of all, I beastspoke a greeting

680

to Jakoby's horse Calcasuus and the other two horses.

The tribeswoman's smiled broadened, her white teeth flashing in her dark, handsome face. "It is good to see that you remember what you learned in your visit to the desert lands, Elspeth," she said in her deep, musical voice. Then she, too, made the formal response to a greeting between friends, hand clasped to her heart as she bowed her head low enough that the beaded ebony ropes of her hair fell forward in a little cascade, clicking and clanking against one another.

"How do you come to be here, and with these two?" I asked when she had straightened.

"I traveled to Sutrium on the *Umborine* after the tribe leaders met a sevenday past and agreed that one of the sacred spicewood ships must risk an encounter with the *Black Ship*, for a command from the overguardian of the Earthtemple must be deemed of greater importance than even a greatship and her crew."

"The overguardian commanded a ship to travel to Sutrium?" I asked. "For what purpose?"

"I was told to anchor there and do what was asked of me."

"Somewhat cryptic," I ventured.

Jakoby gave a laugh and her white teeth flashed. "Cryptic is the language of the Earthtemple, but even for them, this was unusually obscure. I asked the overguardian how I was to know when I had done what I was meant to do, and she answered that one who has been to the desert lands would ask something of me. I must continue to do what is asked of me by anyone who had traveled to Sador, until I was bidden to return there. Only then might I do so. The Temple guardian also said that before I returned to Sador, I would learn a thing that would touch an old and very deep sorrow." She sighed. "You see what I mean about cryptic."

"The new Temple guardian is a woman?" I asked.

Jakoby nodded.

"So you went to Sutrium, then you came here. Am I to assume that you were *asked* to come here?"

She nodded. "As we approached Sutrium, we saw great clouds of black smoke rising up and obscuring the city. We anchored the *Umborine* some distance from shore, only to find another ship doing the same. That it was a Herder greatship worried me, but those aboard signaled us, and we soon learned that the only Faction priests aboard were prisoners. Incredibly, almost the entire inner cadre of the Faction, and a good number of Hedra captains, were in the hold in chains."

"The *Stormdancer*!" I said in elation. "Who was aboard?"

Jakoby smiled. "Their captors were the Norse crew and three Misfits from Obernewtyn, one of them—Yarrow— somewhat the worse for wear. Reuvan was with them also. They told me that you and a small force of coercers had overturned the Faction on Herder Isle before you set off to the west coast on the back of a ship fish! And why? To save the people there from plague because someone had been deliberately infected with it. But you know all of this, for it was you who commanded the greatship to sail to Sutrium."

"Yarrow," I said, realizing this meant that the Hedra master had been overcome or had surrendered. "What of Ode?" But Jakoby gave me an uncomprehending look, so I asked, "When did you work out that the smoke coming from the Land was the result of a ruse?"

"The wind changed direction, and we saw that all the smoke was coming from the side of the city facing the Suggredoon. Indeed, at first we thought it must have been coming from beyond the Suggredoon, and that made me wonder if you had been too late to stop the plague. Of course, I did not know it was Domick who had been infected until after we had landed. It was the asura—your Dameon—who told me that. He was waiting to greet us in the name of the high chieftain of the Land, and he told us the reason for the fires. He could not yet tell us the outcome of the gambit, for Rushton and Dardelan and the others had only just gone across the river. But the asura asked us all back to Dardelan's home to wait with him to learn what had happened on the other side of the Suggredoon.

"I acceded to Dameon's invitation willingly, because it was a request from one who had been to Sador and who had, while there, been named asura—guest friend of the tribes. I was glad of the opportunity to see my daughter. But I soon learned that Bruna had ridden out only a day past, to journey by coast road to Sador."

"Bruna went to Sador before Dardelan crossed the river?" I asked in disbelief. Was this the reason for his grimness? And yet it seemed unlikely that Bruna would leave him on the eve of a battle.

Jakoby knitted her brow for a moment, but she only said, "The asura feasted us that night, and those tales we had been told hastily were elaborated upon. That was the first time I heard that the plague-infected null was Domick. You have my deepest sympathy, for Merret told me that he died. I returned to the *Umborine*, still troubled about Bruna, whom I now knew I would not see until I was asked to return to Sador. Also, I was full of curiosity about why I had been sent to Sutrium. Given all I had learned, it would be easy to imagine that I had been sent there to aid the rebels. Yet . . ."

"You did not think that was what you were sent to do?" I guessed.

Jakoby shook her head. "The overguardians of the Temple

have never had much time for battles and territories. And I was right, for once I reached the pier, I found waiting for me the one who made the request that brought me here." Jakoby nodded at Maruman.

"*Maruman* requested it?"

Jakoby smiled. "Those of the Temple name him Moon-watcher, but I think you know that."

"But you cannot beastspeak," I said.

"Gahltha signaled Maruman's request to me," Jakoby said. "He asked that I bring them both to Aborium on the *Umborine*." She smiled faintly. "To obey the request of a cat, and especially a cat known to the Temple guardians, seemed perfectly in keeping with the mysteries of the Earthtemple. I bade both beasts board, ordered the crew to ready the *Umborine* for departure, and went back to Dardelan's house to bid farewell to the asura."

"I cannot thank you enough for bringing Maruman and Gahltha to me," I said.

Jakoby was shaking her head, the beads and cuffs clinking rapidly. "You do not understand, Elspeth. Maruman asked me to bring the ship to Aborium so that we could fetch you."

"You will take us back to Sutrium?" I asked.

"I will bear you wherever you wish," Jakoby said.

I frowned at her. "What if I want you to take me to the Red Queen's land or to Sador?" I asked slowly.

"Then that is where we will go," Jakoby said. "Do you ask it?"

I bit my lip, knowing I could not go anywhere until I had spoken to Blyss about Rushton. "There is something I need to do in Aborium," I said at last.

"Let us ride, then," Jakoby said. She reached out to take

Maruman from me, and I was surprised that he did not lash out at her, until I realized he must have ridden to the ruins upon her shoulder. Once I had mounted Gahltha, the tribeswoman lifted the old cat up to me, and he settled himself none too gently across my shoulders. I bid farewell to Seely and cast one final long look about the ruins baking in the afternoon sun. Then the tribeswoman made a signal to Calcasuus, whom she had mounted, and the enormous horse wheeled and sprang into a gallop. Gahltha followed, as did the horses of the two silent tribesmen. Maruman's claws dug in even through the thickness of cloak, vest, and shirt, but I welcomed their bite, for it had been too long since I had felt the sweet weight of my old friend. As if he heard this thought and was mollified, Maruman did not cling quite so savagely. Nevertheless, I was not fool enough to imagine that he would answer any questions yet, so I asked Gahltha about Maruman's request of the tribeswoman.

"The oldOne called upon Maruman and me to take part in a spiritmerge of humans and beasts, for you were in great danger and needed us. We opened ourselves, and the oldOne drew deeply on us. I was very weary afterward, and when I woke, Maruman still slept. He slept on and on, and I began to fear for him. Then Maruman/yelloweyes wakened, and he told me that the oldOne said you were safe but that we must seek you over the ocean. We were in Sutrium then, and the funaga Kella had asked us to return with her to the barud. We would go back with her, but now Maruman said we must not go."

"So Kella went back to Obernewtyn *before* Iriny crossed the river," I muttered, finally understanding why the healer had not come to Domick. *She did not yet know what had happened to him.* "What of MornirDragon?" I asked, for I could not imagine Kella leaving Dragon alone in Sutrium.

"MornirDragon disappeared soon after we came to Sutrium," Gahltha said.

"Disappeared?!" I echoed in dismay. "But how?"

"No one knows, beast or human," Gahltha answered. "We sought her, but even the dogs given her scent could not find her."

This was bad news, especially when I had told Matthew that we could bring Dragon to him in the Red Queen's Land. What could possibly have happened to her? I gathered my wits, telling myself that I could do nothing to help her until I reached Sutrium, but once I was there, I would seek her until I found her. Then I asked, "What exactly did Maruman say to you about coming to me? Had he an ashling from the oldOnes?"

"Maruman/yelloweyes traveled on the dreamtrails. He went seliga in Saithwold after I told him that you had vanished. He said that he would find you. After that, he woke and ate, yet he was seliga. I/Gahltha learned fear, for never had he traveled so long. Dameon carried him to the barud by the sea and still he was seliga. Then the smoke came, choking the air, and that night Maruman/yelloweyes came to my dreams and said that a ship would come that would bring us to you." Gahltha broke off, and I touched his flank gently and withdrew from his mind, for though the healers and empaths had done much to cure his terror of water, he could not think of it without a shudder. The journey from Sutrium to the west coast would have required courage.

The horses were walking now, but I did not try to speak to Jakoby, for the strong constant wind raised a fine gritty mist of sand that made conversation aloud impossible. I found myself thinking of the last overguardian, who had told me that I would one day come to the Earthtemple with the Moon-watcher and the Daywatcher—names that he told me signi-fied Maruman and Gahltha—to find the fifth sign that Kasanda had left for me. I had always imagined that I was supposed to travel to Sador when I had gathered the other signs. But now I wondered if I had been wrong, for he had said nothing about finding the signs in order. Yet if Jakoby had been sent to bring me to Sador to retrieve the fifth sign, why had not the new overguardian simply bidden Jakoby find me and bring me to the Earthtemple? Surely it could not be, as Jakoby had implied, a matter of cryptic tradition.

I thought of the five clues left by Kasanda.

I had long ago realized these would lead to information or devices that would enable me to destroy or disable the world-wide retaliatory system of weapons created by the Before-timers, known as BOT, and enter the Sentinel facility. But my conversations with Dell and Ines had given me a far clearer idea of what I would be facing, for I now understood that Sentinel must be a program like Ines, and like her it might communicate in words once I had wakened it.

I ran my mind over the clues I had obtained so far. The words that had been scribed on the glass statue in Newrome under Tor might be connected to whatever it was that Jacob had taken into the Blacklands. Then there were the words Evander had carved at the base of Stonehill to replace those created by his mother. I had yet to see the statue that Cassy had carved to mark the safe-passage agreement, and then there was whatever she had left for me in the Red Queen's land, the location of which was known only to Dragon. Who had disappeared.

I mastered a surge of anxiety about the girl and forced my-self to go on considering the signs. Cassy had referred only to four in the message she carved into what later became the doors to Obernewtyn. I had not known there was a fifth until the last overguardian of the Earthtemple had spoken of it. I focused hard and sank into my mind, searching until I found what he had told me.

I know many things. I know that when the Seeker comes, borne by the Daywatcher and bearing the Moonwatcher, with one of Kasanda blood by her side, she will be searching for the fifth sign. Then may the one who is overguardian of the Temple aid her.

I frowned. I had been right. The overguardian had said nothing about finding all the other signs before I came for the fifth one. But if Maruman had been sent to draw me to Sador, to fetch whatever had been left in the Earthtemple, what about the one of Kasanda blood who was supposed to accompany me? I had always assumed it would be the gypsy D'rekta Swallow, Iriny's half brother and a direct descendant of Kasanda. He was the guardian of the ancient promises, which, among other things, bade him ensure the safety of the signs Cassy left for the Seeker; moreover, Atthis had actively used him to protect me.

Perhaps, if I asked Jakoby to take me to Sador, I would find Swallow there. But it troubled me that Jakoby had not been given simpler instructions, if I only needed to go to Sador. Maryon had once told me that her futuretellings sometimes appeared obscure and difficult to understand because she saw only some aspects of an event. The gaps in the vision meant there were so many possibilities that it was impossible to choose one over another. The safest thing in such cases was to leave a gap in the futuretelling to allow all of the possibilities to coexist until the person or people involved could make their own choices, for sometimes simply voicing a possibility was enough to bring it to pass. Perhaps the current overguardian of the Earthtemple faced a similar problem.

Jakoby broke into my speculations to call a halt at a travelers' well by the main road, and we stopped to drink and rinse the dust from our mouths. Jakoby wet a cloth and began carefully cleaning the eyes and nostrils of Calcasuus and Gahltha while the tribesmen with her performed the same service for their mounts. I carried Maruman to a smaller trough and knelt to scoop water into my hands for him to drink. Despite the cold windy day, many people were traveling the road hunched in hooded cloaks, their mouths hidden behind cloths. Leaving Maruman to stretch his legs for a while, I dipped into a few minds to learn that most believed there had been a great battle in Sutrium between the Faction and the rebels. I could not find the slightest suspicion that it had all been a trick by the rebels to lure their enemies over the river. This impressed me, because the smallest hint of the truth would have sparked rumors. The people Gwynedd had summoned to Aborium had been very careful.

As we mounted and set off on the road leading to Aborium's main gate, I realized I could see the shape of the city in the distance. A young woman and her son rode past us in the other direction, and I noticed Jakoby's gaze rest on her for a long brooding moment. Some impulse made me push aside the cloth covering my mouth and ask the tribeswoman if Dameon had said why Bruna had left Sutrium so abruptly.

Jakoby gave me a long expressionless look through narrowed golden eyes; then she sighed, and some of the stiffness went out of her bearing. "The asura told me only that Bruna quarreled with Dardelan amid preparations for the charade that would draw the Hedra and soldierguards over the river, but he did not know what the nature of their quarrel was. He said I must ask Dardelan or Bruna."

"And did you ask Dardelan?"

"I saw only Merret before I came to seek you," Jakoby said. She was silent for so long that I thought she would say no more, but then she added in a low voice, "When Bruna fell in love with Dardelan, I made no secret that I could not see how such a match would work. They were so different in temperament, and the allegiance of each to their own land was so strong. Which of them would give up their home for the other, and what would that price do to them? In truth, I hoped that Bruna's passion would prove to be a greenstick love that would help her to grow and then fade to a sweet memory, but in time it was clear to me that, for all her youth, her love for Dardelan was strong and mature. But Dardelan's love? I have never known if, behind all of his courtesy, he loves her."

"Brydda told me once that he thought Dardelan did have feelings for Bruna but that he kept them hidden because he guessed she would see it as a weakness."

Jakoby laughed, and there was real amusement as well as sadness in it. "The Black Dog is clever. And maybe in the beginning he would have been right. But I doubt that would be so now. Let me ask you this: If love exists but is forever withheld, is it truly love? Is it not a kind of cowardice?"

That stung me sharply, and I said, "Perhaps he has a reason for keeping his feelings hidden."

Jakoby gave me a penetrating look. "What reason can there be for hiding love from the beloved?"

"Duty."

"And would love for my daughter prevent Dardelan from doing his duty?"

I did not know what to say to that, but I remembered the

bleak weariness in the young high chieftain's eyes. "Did Dameon tell you nothing of their quarrel?"

She shrugged. "He said that there had been a rift between them since Dardelan refused to permit Bruna to ride to the highlands to track down and capture the robbers who had been burning farms and killing Landfolk. Apparently, he was convinced that Malik was behind it, but he wanted no confrontations, because he had asked Obernewtyn to lay formal charges against Malik for his betrayal of your people in the White Valley, and it was necessary that he not be seen persecuting the man he must judge. But he said none of this to Bruna. Then a day or two before I came to Sutrium, they quarreled in the privacy of his chamber. All heard the shouting, and finally Bruna stormed out in a fury. The following day, she came to Dardelan's dining hall and announced to all present that she would be riding for Sador since at last Dardelan had shown his lack of regard for her, which he had previously hidden in polite deceptions and flowery meaningless talk." Jakoby scowled. "The asura told me that Dardelan rose and bowed to her, and when she left, he did not ride after her. I would think this meant he did not love her, but the asura said he has been grim and unsmiling since her departure. I cannot help but wonder if, in riding away, Bruna achieved what all her determined pursuit of Dardelan did not. . . ."

"Perhaps it is for the best that they have parted," I ventured.

Jakoby nodded. "So I try to tell myself, and yet . . . there are some who love more than once in life, as I have done. But there are those for whom love comes only once. I fear it is so with Bruna, and I do not want to think of the remainder of her life being barren of love. She is so young. Once I have brought you to Aborium, I will bring you to the ship, as Maruman asked. Then I will seek out Dardelan and speak with him frankly about Bruna, to learn his heart in this matter. You may bide upon the ship until such time as you wish to name a destination."

Her jaw was set, and it occurred to me that Jakoby might be even more of a warrior as a mother than as the leader of her tribe.

✦ 12 ✦

As we joined the long queue of people waiting to enter Aborium, I farsought the watch in both towers visible from that approach and was relieved to find the soldierguards on duty unbanded and coerced. The soldierguards at the gate were banded, however, and the process of entry seemed little different from that in any city, save that when I came closer, I noticed that no one was being asked for their horses' ownership papers. When our turn came and none of the Sadorians were treated any differently from other travelers, I was certain that the guards had been coerced and then ordered to wear their demon bands.

I was wondering if Rushton had told the rebels of the dangers inherent in wearing demon bands when Merret's mind bludgeoned its way into mine. She explained that she had been pacing back and forth between the watchtowers, waiting for us to arrive. "Right now I am looking down at your head."

"You knew Jakoby was coming for me?" I asked, resisting the urge to look up.

"Gwynedd has had Alun and me on the wall since dawn, probing randomly to make sure news of this meeting does not excite any attention that will reach the Councilmen or any of the Hedra in their Faction houses. When I heard that a Sadorian greatship had anchored at the piers, I went to see if it was true. Jakoby said she had come from Sutrium to find you, so I told her where you were." There was an unspoken question in her mind.

"It was well done," I assured her. "Did she mention that the *Stormdancer* has arrived in Sutrium?"

"She did, and I told Gwynedd. He bade me watch for your return so I could invite Jakoby to the meeting. He wants her to speak of the desert lands to those gathered."

"The others are there?" I inquired. "Brydda and Gevan? Rushton?"

"Everyone. The meeting is being held in a merchant hall in the third district. Gwynedd has his people posted all about the area to make sure there is no trouble. To all intents and purposes, there is no more than a meeting of merchants taking place."

"Show me where," I commanded. Merret sent a vision that showed me the swiftest and safest route we could take from the main gate to the merchant house, which appeared to be close to the wall.

I told Jakoby what she had said. The tribeswoman agreed at once that we should go to the Councilcourt, since it would give her the opportunity to speak with Dardelan. As we rode along, the Sadorians drew many curious stares, but there was no hostility in them. There was, however, much speculation about the fires on the other side of the Suggredoon, and it seemed to be generally known that a combined force of Hedra and soldierguards had crossed the river. As yet, there was no talk of what they had found there, but the hiatus could not last long. Some news must be offered soon, and I wondered what Gwynedd had decided it should be.

My thoughts shifted to Dell's prediction that the Norseland rebel leader would be made a king, and it still seemed fantastical and unlikely. And yet, when I thought of the futureteller's words, I felt that she had held something back.

It was almost an hour before we reached the meeting house, for the city was large and the streets twisted. The meeting house, when I saw it, was grand enough to make me nervous. It was constructed not of golden or gray stone, as most of the other city buildings were, but of the pink and white streaked stone that came from the quarries behind Murmroth—skinstone, it was called. Lit by the sun, the building had a translucent radiance perfectly complemented by delicate enameled panels set about the building's wide entrance.

The yard before the building was deserted, which was odd for a city that seemed to have no place where people did not walk and stand and live. But even as we dismounted, two boys and a girl emerged from a door and asked softly if I was Lady Elspeth. When I nodded, the eldest boy among them said eagerly that Gwynedd had sent him and the others to take care of our horses. Then he turned to greet the horses in laborious but earnest fingerspeech, offering fresh water and fodder in a pleasant holding yard a little distance from the Councilcourt. Gahltha asked Maruman if he would like to come with them, for it sounded as if they were going to a place where he could find somewhere to curl up in the sun. The old cat chose to stay with me, and despite the heat he generated, I was more than content to have the weight of his soft body about my neck.

As the horses were being led away, one of the boys turned back to call out that Merret had gone inside and that we ought to go in at once.

Jakoby mounted the steps, and I followed in her wake. It seemed a strange and gaudy choice for a secret meeting. Passing from the blazing light glancing off the enameled entry panels into the chill darkness beyond, I had no doubt that the designer had intended to dazzle. I stopped to allow my eyes to adjust to the dimness, and then Merret was before us.

"I was just letting Gwynedd know you had arrived. He wants me to bring Jakoby right in."

"What is this place?" I asked as she led us deeper into the building, for it was no less ornate inside than out.

Merret gave me a sardonic look. "I told you it is the merchant hall. Who else could afford such finery? We have spread rumors of merchants meeting here, and that has accounted for strangers seen entering the place, though some of those invited have had to be wrapped in fine cloaks else they would seem very out of place in these decadent commercial corridors."

She brought us to a room, and I was startled to see that it was full of men and a few women, most of whom seemed wealthy and annoyed.

"Those are petitioners," Merret farsent as she led us through them. She sounded amused.

"Petitioners for what?" I asked.

We passed from the room into a quiet chamber, and Merret closed the door and said aloud, "They are real merchants or powerful officials who have heard rumors of the meeting and have come to find out why they were not invited. It was unexpected, though perhaps it ought not to have been. I daresay the sight of Sadorian tribesfolk will excite a new chorus of rumors. Do not concern yourselves about the merchants, though. Gwynedd intends for us to coerce them into believing they actually attended a meeting. For the time being, they are cooling their heels at the front door while we shall enter at the rear." She gestured to a door, through which was a long hall lined with rare and lovely sculptures, though none so fine as those done by Kasanda. At the end of the hall was a set of double doors.

"This is the way into the meeting hall," Merret said, gesturing to the ornate double doors. "You are to go in at once." The coercer addressed Jakoby, who said that she would see me later aboard the *Umborine*. When she strode to the doors and threw them open, I caught a brief glimpse of the crowded room beyond and heard a babble of talk. Then the doors swung closed, cutting off the sound.

"How many people are meeting?" I asked incredulously.

"Seventy, more or less," Merret said.

I gaped at her. "Gwynedd invited seventy people to a secret meeting?"

"Some fifty were invited," the coercer said. "Then there are Gwynedd's people and rebels from the other cities. But do not fear, this has been long planned by Gwynedd; those he invited, save a few, are all well known to him, even though some did not know him at all. Ever since Dell spoke to him, he has been seeking the right people to rule the Land."

"Why has he not simply appointed them?" I asked.

"That is not his way," Merret said simply. "He has chosen worthy people, and now they must choose their own leaders, as Kalt said." She looked at me, a glimmer of mischief in her eye. "Do you want to go in as well, Guildmistress?"

I shook my head firmly, saying that I was in no mood to take part in a debate, even if I had been invited, which I had not.

"Perhaps you would you like to watch from the upper gallery?" She gestured to a smaller door to the left of the double doors, and as she drew nearer, I followed her and saw inside a wooden stair.

Shrugging, I stepped through the door and mounted the

steps. Instead of a door at the top, there was a heavy curtain. Merret lifted a finger to her lips and pulled the curtain aside. Again I heard the loud hum of many voices. Merret ushered me along a short narrow corridor to another curtained door. Pushing through it, I found myself on a small balcony over-looking the vast rectangular chamber that was the main Councilcourt meeting room. Other balconies ran all around the room at the same level, but as far as I could tell, the rest were empty. To my delight, Blyss was sitting at the end of a bench seat, so riveted by what was happening below that she had not even noticed our entrance.

Merret went to speak to her, and I leaned forward cau-tiously to look into the body of the chamber. The balcony was not far from the front of the room, so I had a good view of the faces of the people sitting along bench seats nearest the stage. Glass mosaic windows set about the dome in the roof al-lowed gorgeously colored shafts of light to stripe those on the raised stage. Gwynedd stood with Jakoby at the end of a line of chairs set up along the back of the stage. I studied his face, expecting to see the arrogance of a man who would be king, but his expression was merely serious as he spoke softly to the tribeswoman. Now Dardelan rose from his seat on the stage and began to address those gathered, speaking of the Charter of Laws he had crafted for the Land. From what I could understand, he was merely clarifying some point he must have made earlier. At the end of the stage, Rushton joined Gwynedd and spoke earnestly to the tribeswoman, who listened without expression and then shrugged and nod-ded. Gwynedd nodded, too, in apparent satisfaction, and then he beckoned a dark-complexioned man who wore his raven hair in the Norse style. He spoke to the man for some time, clearly giving him some detailed instructions, and then the man departed purposefully, leaving the chamber by the large double doors.

"How long has the meeting been going on?" I farsent to Merret.

"Since just after firstmeal," she answered.

"What has been decided?"

"Nothing yet, according to Blyss. I have not been here continuously, of course. But she told me that Gwynedd began by speaking about what happened on both sides of the Suggredoon. He told them about the Faction's attempted invasion, too. There were a lot of questions then, which Dardelan, Brydda, or Rushton answered, and then Gwynedd told them what he knew of your time on Herder Isle. Finally, he broke the news to them that they will be choosing the new leaders of the west coast cities from among their number." She smiled. "That was a surprise, for many had come thinking only that they were to vote for leaders from among the rebels, or perhaps to serve the new leaders in some way. A few refused outright, saying that they had not the ability to govern a city, but Gwynedd asked that everyone remain and take part in all debates and to vote, for if they were not fit to rule, they would not be chosen. Then, just a short time ago, when I came to let Gwynedd know Jakoby had arrived, Dardelan was speaking about arrangements made on the other side of the Suggredoon after the Councilmen were overthrown."

I looked back to the stage and saw that Dardelan had resumed his seat, as had Rushton, and there was a renewed buzz of talk from those seated in the rows below the stage. I noted that Serba was upon the stage, and I studied her with interest. The last time I had seen her had been during the rebellion. She looked thinner than I remembered, and there were streaks of white in her hair, but her face was just as strong and her expression just as sharply intelligent.

Gwynedd now rose to introduce Jakoby, and without any preamble, the tribeswoman began to speak simply and bluntly of Sador: of the manner in which the tribes governed themselves and how they used the Battlegames to judge crimes.

"Why was Gwynedd so keen for Jakoby to speak?" I farsent Merret.

"He wants to show that, although the Land governed by Dardelan and his Council of Chieftains works very differently from Sador, the same values underlie both systems," Merret answered. "He wants them to understand what makes for good leadership."

"When will they vote?"

"The voting for chieftains of each city will begin within the hour, by my reckoning, but the process Gwynedd wants to use will take time. His intention is for each candidate to address the meeting. He wants them to explain how they would govern their city. Once all candidates have been heard, there will be a vote. If all here agree upon a name for chieftain, that person will become chieftain. But many of these people do not know one another, so Gwynedd believes there will be several candidates for each city. He believes that they should then be questioned and answer to the rest, and after a time, there will be another vote. This will go on until one chieftain is chosen for each city. Then the new chieftains will vote for their high chieftain."

"But Dardelan . . ."

Merret shook her head decisively. "Dardelan suggested that the west have its own high chieftain, for the whole Land is too much territory for one, and he would be more than pleased to have another high chieftain to consult with."

I studied Gwynedd, impressed in spite of myself by his careful, detailed plans. There was no doubt, given all that Merret had said, that he had been considering and shaping his plans exactly as Dardelan had done.

Merret touched my arm and bade me sit awhile, saying she must return to her post but that she would doubtless see me later. As she went out, I sat down and shifted Maruman to my lap. Blyss smiled at me and then turned back to the meeting, her face alight with interest. I had thought that I might speak to her of Rushton, but clearly this was not the moment.

I leaned forward to look at Rushton, who was sitting back and listening intently to Jakoby, his long legs stretched out in front of him. There was no sign of the brittle harshness he had shown me at the Beforetime ruins. Without my presence, perhaps the memories would settle down and nothing need be done at once. Dell had said it would be better if it could wait until we had returned to Obernewtyn.

But if his memories did break out, and Rushton had not been prepared . . .

At a burst of applause, I saw that Jakoby had been seated, and Gwynedd was rising to address the meeting. I leaned forward, eager to hear more from this powerful, grave-faced Norselander who had won the devotion not only of the west coast rebels but also of Misfits like Merret and Dell. I was not alone in my interest, for the chamber had fallen utterly silent.

The older man began speaking in a quiet gruff voice about the role of a chieftain. He lacked Dardelan's poetry and passionate conviction as a speaker, but the care and simplicity of his words as he described the demands of leadership were all the more compelling because he was clearly not trying to persuade or charm. I had the feeling he would weigh every decision he made with the same slow honesty, and all that he said was so wise and sensible that my doubts about him evaporated. I glanced at those on the stage and saw that they were all sitting forward, deeply attentive. Dardelan looked positively elated, and I realized that in Gwynedd he had found another true idealist.

Gwynedd must have asked for questions, because someone lifted a hand and asked what sort of force he would recommend to keep the peace and impose laws once the soldierguards were gone. He pondered the question for a bit and said that he thought a city guard should be formed, made up of strong men and women who would serve for a set period, for the people ought to keep the peace and not some separate body who, like the soldierguards, could be corrupted by continuous power and authority. He said that he thought the period of service should be no more than two years. Then a woman asked what was to be done with the current Council's soldierguards. Gwynedd said that Dardelan and his Council, who had already dealt with Councilmen and their soldierguards across the river, had agreed to take charge of them.

There was something familiar about the man sitting alongside the woman who had spoken, and after studying him a moment, I noticed his wooden leg and realized it was the crippled metalworker Rolf. He sat toward the rear of the chamber, but I could not resist sending a greeting. He stiffened and looked up, his eyes scanning the empty balconies until he found me peering down at him. I grinned and waved, and he laughed aloud, causing those about him to stare at him in puzzlement.

"Your face is so clean I hardly recognize you," I farsent. "What on earth are you doing here?"

"I received an invitation from none other than our rebel

leader, after a suggestion from your formidable friend Merret." He laughed again. "I was shocked to discover that, in accepting, I had become a potential future leader! The moment I speak, Master Gwynedd will realize his mistake, for I am naught but a metalworker and a crippled one at that. But I am not sorry to be here, for it is something to have been part of the events of this day."

"I seriously doubt there has been any mistake made," I sent. "You are as worthy and courageous a man as any I have ever met. I am only glad Merret had the foresight to suggest you come here." Then I sent, very seriously, "For myself, I want to thank you again, Rolf, for your kindness when I was just an unknown beggar maid and for helping me find Domick and get him out of Halfmoon Bay. Merret told me that you had freed Iriny, not to mention bringing a force to her aid at the river. How can you possibly say that you are no leader!"

"And now," Gwynedd said quite suddenly, "it is time to begin the choosing. I have asked Dardelan to officiate, for he and the other people from across the river will not vote, and I will offer myself as a candidate for Murmroth." I withdrew from Rolf's mind as Gwynedd took his seat and Dardelan stepped forward.

"We might just as well begin at one end of the west coast and work along it city by city," he said. "I now ask those who would stand as candidates for Murmroth to rise and, one by one, to speak about themselves so that we may see what manner of men and women they are. Once each has spoken, we will have a show of hands of those who would choose each of the candidates. The three who receive the most votes will become the final candidates for that city unless there is a unanimous vote for one of them."

Gwynedd stood but remained by his chair. No one else moved. There was a curious silence, and before Dardelan could invite Gwynedd to speak, hands began to rise, at first slowly and then swiftly. In less than a moment, almost every hand in the room was raised, and the big Norselander stared about in such genuine surprise that delighted laughter rose in a wave, and everyone began to applaud wildly.

"Well, it seems that the silence of some men speaks far more eloquently than any words," Dardelan said after a long time, when the noise died down. This was met with more laughter, but it quieted swiftly, and Dardelan said dryly, "Although the good Gwynedd looks as if someone hit him on the head with a stone, I am somehow not much surprised to be naming him the first chieftain chosen, for he has single-handedly inspired and kept alive the rebel movement here after the tragedy and betrayals of the Night of Blood. At the beginning of this momentous day, Gwynedd spoke of this place as the Westland. For those of you who do not know it, that is the Norse name for this coast, yet it seems fitting that we might henceforth use that name to honor the man who, more than any other, has striven for its freedom."

These words were met by a roar of approval and chants and shouts of "Westland!" and "Gwynedd!" Dardelan made no move to silence them, perhaps feeling, as I did, that this applause was a cathartic outburst of joy and relief and triumph.

At long last, the noise faded and Dardelan asked the new chieftain of Murmroth to sit. Gwynedd did so, still without a word, and this provoked a fresh burst of laughter. Dardelan broke into it by naming Aborium and inviting the first candidate for that city to speak. An hour later, speeches were still being made by candidates for the city. Those who had spoken of their future intentions seemed sensible, and I was pleased to see that women made up a good proportion of the number, for there were no women among the Land's chieftains.

It seemed that the young rebel leader Darrow who had spoken first would be among the three chosen, for despite his youth, his tongue was dipped in silver. Sure enough, when the vote was cast, more hands were raised in his support than for the man and woman who were to stand with him for the next round of votes. There was applause, though nowhere near the level that had met Gwynedd's appointment; then Dardelan bade the candidates sit, saying they should prepare to speak again, once all the initial candidates for all the cities had been chosen. He then asked all who wished to be considered candidates for the chieftainship of Morganna to rise.

Stifling a yawn, I observed softly to Blyss that it seemed a slow method. All those who had spoken would have had much of their speeches forgotten before they spoke again, and everyone listening would be exhausted.

"That is the idea," she said surprisingly, adding that it had been Gwynedd's plan to have a single, grueling session to choose chieftains for the five cities. The long session would mean that everyone would see and hear the candidates when they were fresh and alert but also when they were weary and at the end of their tether. In this way, their strengths and flaws would be laid bare. A person like Darrow, she said, would easily sway an audience if they were to vote on the heels of his speech, but how would the same man fare when people were weary and wanted to hear facts and simple practical ideas rather than passionate rhetoric? The discussions and question-and-answer sessions would further enable the candidates to measure one another, and that was just as well, for those who would advise the new chieftains would be chosen from among them.

Finally, the candidates were called for Halfmoon Bay. To my regret, Rolf did not rise with the other seven, but after they had all made their speeches, Gwynedd rose to ask Arolfic Smithson to stand and speak as well. He had interrupted on two other occasions to ask people who had not risen to speak, and in both cases, the people chosen had given a good account of themselves.

I waited as eagerly as everyone else as Rolf rose with obvious reluctance and said gruffly that he did not want to suggest that the chieftain of Murmroth had judged ill, but he was not the sort of man to lead a city. "I am not highborn, nor have I ever served in any capacity as a leader. I did not join the rebel cause, and aside from being crippled in one leg, I am only a metalworker, yet I know that people are harder to mold than iron and copper. There is a subtle skill to governing that I think a chieftain ought to have."

He would have sat then, but someone in the audience called out to ask what qualities he thought a chieftain ought to have. Before Rolf could respond, another man asked rather scornfully what a lowborn metalworker could know of the qualities needed to undertake the high and complex business of governing a city.

Frowning, Rolf said to the second man that if only wealth and birth were required of a chieftain, then governance of the city might as well be given back to Councilman Kana, who had been taxing Halfmoon Bay's citizens to fund the purchase of the costly Sadorian spiceweed used in the production of his foul and addictive dreamweed.

"You asked what qualities I think a chieftain ought to have? I will answer, for though I have little money and am crippled, I know well enough what kind of person I would wish for a leader. I would wish for a chieftain who is honest and just and compassionate. I would happily vote for a man or woman whose first consideration is not how to increase the wealth of the city and its highborn citizens, but who would look to serve all who dwelt within it. Were I chieftain, I would sentence those who had committed low crimes to clean the streets when other citizens slept. I would happily set our former Councilman to scouring the walls and windows of all the little cottages next to his foul factories. And I would not stop at cleaning the city.

"When I was a young man, Halfmoon Bay was the flower of the west—the Westland—and those who came for our masked moon fair did so because of the city's beauty, because of the cleverness and wit of the entertainments offered, and because of the quality of workmanship in anything produced there. Once upon a time, there was not such a legion of beggars in the street. There were shelters funded by the wealthy, and healing and caring houses for the elderly and sick. Our good Councilman closed them so he could open his factories in their stead. No doubt it is backward of me, but I wish for a chieftain who has the vision and moral courage to turn back time and restore Halfmoon Bay to its former glory. I wish for a just, strong person with a good sense of humor and a sobering dollop of sternness when needed, as it surely will be. I wish for a man or woman who will lead by inspiration and vision and example.

"No doubt I have spoken in a lumpish metalworker's way, but I have spoken the truth, and no man or woman should be asked to do more or less than that."

He sat down to a good smattering of applause and much nodding, but Gwynedd rose quickly, saying that since Arolfic had not thought to mention it, he wished all those present to know that the metalworker had put himself at considerable personal risk to help locate a Herder agent who had been infected by deadly plague before being set down in Halfmoon Bay during the masked moon fair. The shocked silence that met this announcement told me that Gwynedd had not spoken of this yet, and as he went on to speak of what the plague would have done, I could not bear to hear it. All I could see was Domick, his face distorted by buboes.

"Then let us go/leave this house of words. I am hungry," Maruman grumped suddenly, shifting his soft weight in my lap.

I rose and bade Blyss farewell, barely seeing her face through the mist of tears that had risen in my eyes. But I managed to ask if she would come to the *Umborine* to see me once the meeting had ended.

When I came outside, I was astonished to discover that the sun had set. I had not realized so much time had passed, and I wondered if it would be thought odd that a meeting of merchants would last so long. Then the cleverness of disguising a meeting of rebels as a meeting of merchants struck me anew, because what Councilman or soldierguard would dare interfere with the works of commerce, since the activities of merchants lined their pockets and kept the citizens content and fed.

I yawned widely. It had been stuffy and hot in the meeting chamber, and I was glad to feel the cool evening air. I remembered that I had left my cloak with Gahltha in my saddlebags and formed a probe to locate him.

Making my way to the holding yard, I suggested he might prefer to remain ashore for the time being with Calcasuus and the other Sadorian horses. But Gahltha refused. He wished to remain close to me, he told me stoically, even if it meant being aboard a ship. His devotion made me feel a great stab of love for him, which irritated Maruman, and he sprang from my arms with a hiss, landing atop a high wall that ran along the side of the holding yard.

"I/Maruman will roam and hunt," the old cat sent coldly. I bit back the urge to plead with him to stay with me, knowing that his anger and resentment at having been abandoned would be eased by his abandonment of me. Even so, after he had leapt out of sight behind the wall, I wished I had begged him to stay.

"He will come after us to the ship," Gahltha assured me as we set off toward the waterfront through curving streets.

By the time I began to smell the briny stink of the waves, I was thirsty and footsore, but I would not dream of riding Gahltha just to save myself a few blisters. Need and joy were the only reasons to mount him, and I would not readily set aside those two standards even if he would, for one did not make a convenience of a friend. I forgot the pain in my feet when we came out of the street into the open square where, in daylight, the sea market would be held. As with the streets I had traversed, there were still a good many people making their way hither and thither, which suggested that, if there was a curfew in Aborium, it was very late. It had grown dark, and I had to strain to see the wharf, seeking the *Umborine*. The memory of another night flowed over me, when I had sat in a cart in a shadowed corner of this very square, watching Herder priests load their vessel. For a moment, the mingled odors of oil and fish and the sound of the water gurgling against the wharf summoned up the memory of that night so vividly that I seemed to see Jik, standing between two priests, hands bound and head drooping. Then Gahltha nuzzled my neck, and I spotted the *Umborine* at the far end of the wharf, its deck and rigging lit by the glow of lanterns. I pushed through the cobweb tendrils of memory and made my way across the square to the greatship.

The subtle song of the waves was strong and compelling. Gazing at the ship, I was struck by how similar it was to Salamander's *Black Ship*. Both were greatships, of course, but it was more than that. Take away the ugly weapons and additional structures from the *Black Ship*. and it could very well be a Sadorian vessel. Jakoby had never mentioned one of the sacred ships being stolen, but perhaps Salamander had acquired the *Black Ship* from the Gadfian raiders, from whom the Sadorians were descended. In order for this to be a possibility, it would have to be that the gadi settlements from whom the Sadorians had rescued their stolen womenfolk had survived, despite having no women or any means of getting healthy children. Unless Salamander had traded healthy women and children for a greatship.

Hearing a soft footfall behind me, I turned swiftly, lifting my hands to defend myself, but it was only the Druid arms- man Gilbert, smiling down at me with a good deal more warmth than I liked.

"I saw you from the deck," he said.

"You were aboard the *Umborine*?" I asked, puzzled.

He nodded. "I have been helping to load. Shall I escort you aboard? My room is below deck, but you are to have a cabin on deck. You will have a magnificent view when we are under way."

"I don't understand," I said. "*Your* cabin?"

"Well, strictly speaking, I will share it with six other armsmen, but at the moment they are back at the Councilcourt taking part in the choosing."

"*You* and six armsmen are going to Sador?"

"There will be thirty of us, including Gwynedd," Gilbert said. "And we are traveling to Norseland, though I believe the ship is to go to Sador after that. I knew you were coming aboard, because I heard one of the Sadorians tell Raka that an empty cabin was being kept for your use. I suppose you are bound for Sador?"

I ignored his question as a picture came into my mind of Gwynedd and Jakoby speaking together. Gwynedd must have asked if Jakoby would take him and thirty of his people to Norseland, and then he had sent off the dark-haired man to command Gilbert and some of the others to carry stores aboard the *Umborine*. I knew it all, yet I did not know *why* Gwynedd would leave the west coast, having just been voted chieftain of Murmroth and when there was so much to be done.

Whatever she thought, Jakoby would have been forced to accede to Gwynedd's request, because the overguardian of the Temple had bidden her do whatever was asked of her by anyone who had traveled to the desert lands, and Gwynedd had done so for the Battlegames. So now, because I had said nothing, I must travel to Norseland, too, for if I asked the tribeswoman to bring me to Sador, she would say that first she must deal with Gwynedd's request.

"What is the purpose of this journey Gwynedd would make?" I asked Gilbert.

"I do not know precisely," he answered. "Perhaps it is that the Norselanders are Gwynedd's kin. He will tell us when he comes aboard after the meeting."

"The suddenness of this journey does not trouble you?" I

711

asked, his smiling demeanor beginning to irritate me. "Are you and his other armsfolk so eager to leave the Westland? No one will regret your departure?"

The armsman's mouth twisted into a grimace of such bitterness that I was startled out of my indignation. "My bondmate would as soon pay a slaver to carry me away than regret my going," he snarled. Then he laughed as if this were a joke, but a jarring note suggested that not even he found it truly funny.

Feeling as awkward as ever, I said nothing, but Gilbert nodded as if he had heard a question in my silence. "I am afraid my bondmate dislikes my devotion to the rebel cause; she says it endangers her babies and is proof that I care more for warmongering than for my family. She sent me packing. So now I have nothing left but the hope of finding someone else to love me." His voice had dropped to a caressing note. "In truth, I am looking forward to this voyage and to the chance of getting to know you properly," he added with a smile that made my hand itch to slap him. I was dismayed at the thought of having to endure a sea voyage with this man imagining he was in love with me.

"Maybe this funaga truly loves you," Gahltha beastspoke, and he offered his own vivid memory of the day I had escaped the Druid camp. Through his eyes, I saw my face turned up in dismay as Gahltha reared and screamed his terror. I saw myself trying to convince him to board the raft that was tossing and bucking in the upper Suggredoon's turbulent waters. Gilbert burst into the dark on the other side of the rain-lashed clearing that ran to the edge of the river, his red hair and clothes plastered to his head. Seeing him, Domick slashed the rope binding the raft, and the violent, rain-swollen water wrenched it away from the shore. Gilbert shouted something just before the raft vanished from sight. I had not been able to hear his words over the storm, but Gahltha had heard him call out my gypsy name, and now, hearing it, I also heard the unmistakable note of anguished longing.

I reeled from the vision to find an older Gilbert frowning at me in consternation. "Are you well?" he said.

I gaped at him, confused, because now that he was not smiling, he looked more like the Gilbert of Gahltha's vision. The memory of that other Gilbert made me say, "I was just thinking of what you said about your bondmate and children. It is sad that you would leave them with so little concern."

"It pleases me that you are concerned for me," Gilbert said, leaning nearer. "Let me escort you aboard."

"I need no escort," I told him coldly, and marched past him up the ramp without a backward glance.

Not until I reached the top, where two tribesmen waited, did I realize that Gahltha was not with me. I turned, half expecting to find him balking at boarding, but he was looking back along the wharf. I leaned out to see what had caught his attention and spotted Maruman. The old cat ran up the ramp, and only then did the horse follow. The Sadorians at the top of the ramp bowed with great respect to the beasts and then to me.

"You are Elspeth Gordie?" one of them asked.

"I am," I said. "I believe you have a chamber set aside for me?"

He nodded, and lifting to his lips a small whistle that hung on a chain about his neck, he gave two sharp blasts. A Sadorian girl about my age came hurrying up and bowed reverently to Gahltha before offering him a greeting in finger-speech. He responded with a nod and a flick of one ear,

713

sending to me that this was the groom who had tended to him earlier. I asked where I could find him and was surprised to see a picture form in his thoughts of holding boxes spread with sand, set up upon the deck toward the rear of the ship.

After Gahltha had been led away, Maruman said loftily, "I will show you where we will sleep."

I followed him meekly along the deck toward the front of the ship, where several cabins were clustered. He clawed delicately at one of the doors, and I tried the handle and looked inside. It was too dark to see anything, so I retraced my steps to get a lantern from the Sadorian woman at the gangplank. It revealed a spacious chamber with a bed fixed against one wall and some very beautifully crafted lockers and two big round-topped windows on the seaward side of the ship. I opened the windows, and the cool salt-scented breeze sweeping into the cabin made me sigh with pleasure.

Maruman leapt onto the sill, and as we both looked up into a sky shimmering with stars, I pondered what Gilbert had told me and wondered again why Gwynedd would suddenly decide to take a group of men to Norseland when the Westland was far from secure. I did not know him, though seeing him speak, Gwynedd had not struck me as a rash or hasty man. All that he said of the future suggested a man who planned thoroughly and well in advance. Yet he was taking thirty fighters to an island where many hundreds of Hedra were being trained and where there were, perhaps, unthinkable weapons. I shook my head, realizing my speculations were pointless until I learned Gwynedd's thinking.

I went to the bed, removed my heavy boots, and stretched out fully clothed, because I wanted to be able to get up the moment Blyss and Merret arrived. Maruman leapt down from the sill and padded over to join me on the bed. I yawned and wondered why I felt so weary. I yawned again, and the candle flared, revealing that the dark ceiling of the cabin was elaborately carved. I sat up and lifted the candle higher to study the intricacies. Although it had not been carved by Kasanda, whoever had done it had been influenced by her style. It occurred to me that Kasanda must have trained some of the tribesfolk, for she could not possibly have carved all the stone faces into the cliff at Templeport herself.

I lay back and thought of Stonehill, trying to imagine Cassy as an older woman, bringing up her son amid the thriving and busy community of gypsies who had once made their home atop the tor. The girl that Iriny had said Cassy loved as a daughter, even though she was not a Twentyfamilies, must have lived on Stonehill as well, growing to womanhood. In Cassy's past would have been the visit to the Red Land and the loss of her bondmate, the brother of the Red Queen, and also her youth in the Beforetime.

As ever, I puzzled at how someone from the Beforetime could have lived through the Age of Chaos, but that was something I would never know. Had Cassy known all through her years upon Stonehill that her journey had not ended, that someday she would be taken by Gadfian slavers and rescued by the Sadorians, only to end her life as a seer in the desert lands? Or had that knowledge come to her not long before she had left the Land?

I thought of my vision of Cassy's meeting with Hannah and wondered if the older woman had known that Cassy was a futureteller. It had never been said in any of my visions, yet how could she have left signs for me without foreknowledge to guide her? It might even be that training at Obernewtyn had brought her farseeking Talent to light, in the same way that farseeking novices sometimes realized they could use their deep probe to coerce as well.

Maruman sighed, and I turned my head to look at him, curled up beside me, tail curled over his nose. The breeze ruffled his fur, alternately hiding and revealing his scars.

"I love you, and you are growing old," I said softly, reaching out to stroke his fur lightly, so as not to waken him. Then I closed my eyes again, and as I floated into sleep, a vision rose in my mind of Domick's stone cairn at the edge of the Beforetime ruins, the wind and the sand hissing in an endless susurrus over it. The same wind that scoured Evander's grave atop Stonehill.

✦ 13 ✦

I woke groggily to the sound of boots on deck and the vague queasiness I always felt aboard a ship until I became accustomed to the deck's pitching. The pale lemon light bathing the cabin told me it was early morning, and I got up, careful not to waken Maruman, and went to open the window, which had blown shut in the stiff wind. The sky was a soup of delicate rose and lavender streaked with gold, confirming that it was not long after dawn. Closing the window and latching it, I began opening wall panels, remembering from my previous journey aboard a Sadorian greatship that they concealed all manner of snug and intricate fittings. Sure enough, I soon found a bowl with a spout and lever above it and a locker containing toiletries and clothing. I filled a bowl with water, stripped off my clothes, and washed myself down with a sea sponge. Once dried, I investigated the clothes piled neatly in the locker. They were women's clothes and made of brightly dyed and lightly beaded Sadorian silk. I dressed in sand-colored loose trousers and an undershirt made of silk so thin that it was virtually transparent. Shivering with pleasure at their softness, I reminded myself to thank Jakoby for providing them. After some agreeable dithering, I pulled on a knee-length tunic, slit above the waist on both sides and dyed in swirls of violet and sea green. There were dyed silk slippers to match, but they were too narrow; I was content to go barefoot as the Sadorians did on board.

I combed my tangled hair, listening to the boots moving about the deck, and frowned, for surely there was too much movement for the few people I had seen on deck? The rest of Gwynedd's men must have come aboard, which meant the meeting at the Councilcourt had finished.

I flung down the comb and hurried across the cabin, thinking that Blyss and Merret must be coming aboard as well. But just as I reached the door, the ship lurched and sent me staggering backward across the cabin. Regaining my balance, I made my way out of the cabin, my heart hammering, for the ship would not tilt in such a way while moored.

Outside, the deck was a hive of activity as Sadorian tribesmen and women ran to and fro in the pale yellow light, and beyond them, I stared aghast at the rapidly receding shore, understanding with dismay that the ship had weighed anchor while I slept. Holding on to the wall, I hastened along the deck looking wildly about for Jakoby, but aside from the busy shipfolk, I saw only a group of armsmen and women, many of whom wore their hair in the Norse style. Gwynedd's men.

A feeling of helplessness swept over me, because even if I found Jakoby, I knew that it was too late to turn back now. The sails had been unfurled and the ship was being borne along on the inexorable outgoing tide. Jakoby could not return to Aborium in any case, for she must fulfill the command of the Earthtemple's overguardian to obey the request of anyone who had been to the desert lands until she was bidden return to Sador.

I swallowed the bitter realization that I had said not a word to Blyss about Rushton and told myself that surely Dell would take a hand.

"Elspeth! So you are awake at last." Jakoby clapped me

forcefully on the back. "I am pleased to see that you, at least, are not ill. Half of our brave warriors are already puking, and there is barely enough swell to rock the hull."

I mastered a surge of fury borne of helplessness to ask evenly why she had not awakened me before we cast off. Jakoby answered lightly that there had been no need to trouble me. "But no doubt you are eager to find out what happened at the meeting. Merret told me you saw some of it. Join me for firstmeal in an hour in the main cabin, and you shall hear it all. But for now I must go and watch the map to make sure we do not blunder into a shoal." The tribeswoman's golden eyes swept over me, and she added, "I see that the gifts I brought for Bruna fit you well enough. There are also some hair fittings and scarves if you wish to bind your hair out of the way."

"Thank you," I said, my anger fading at the pain in her eyes when she spoke of her daughter. What had happened was no fault of hers. I had been a fool not to farsend to her while at the meeting, asking her to waken me when she came aboard the ship. But of course I had not then known about Gwynedd's decision. Setting aside my apprehension about Rushton, I asked, "Did you find time to ask Dardelan about what happened between him and Bruna?"

Before she could respond, the ship gave a hard lurch that made her wince and roll her eyes. "I had better rescue the tiller from the clumsy fool mishandling her. I will see you at firstmeal."

She hastened away, barefoot and graceful on the rolling deck. I sighed and turned to gaze out at the vanishing shore, and a feeling of fatalism rose in me, for yet again, I was swept along a course not of my choosing. Yet how often had such random events led me to something connected to my quest?

719

As for Rushton, I could only hope that his memories had settled and would remain so until he returned to Obernewtyn. And failing that, I had to believe that Dell would ask Blyss to help him. The only certainty was that it was no longer in my power to help him.

The ship turned slightly, and the wind sent the end of my tunic fluttering out with a silken hiss. I made up my mind to seek out Gwynedd. At least I could learn the reason for his sudden decision to travel to Norseland. Making my unsteady way toward the front of the ship, I farsought Gahltha. The stallion informed me with drowsy dignity that he had accepted water laced with a light sleep drug to help him bear the gale that was driving the ship before it. I smiled at his exaggeration, knowing it arose from his fear of water, for although the wind was brisk and the sea rough, there was no gale blowing.

At the main cabin, I heard someone approaching from behind. I glanced back and was astounded to see *Brydda Llewellyn* striding toward me.

"You look very fresh, Elspeth, unlike the rest of us who have been up half the night choosing chieftains," he said cheerfully.

"Brydda! How—how are you here?" I stammered. "I mean, why?"

He lifted his brows. "I am here with Dardelan."

I stared at him. "Are you saying that Dardelan is aboard as well?"

He nodded. "Dardelan agreed with Gwynedd that our first priority must be to take control of Norseland, lest Ariel have time to unleash a second plague."

"But what of the west coast—the Westland, I mean?"

"What of it? The new chieftains are even now returning to their cities to begin their work, and as soon as Gevan reaches

Obernewtyn, he will dispatch more of your people to work with the chieftains."

"But what of Murmroth?"

He laughed. "And here I was thinking you must know so much, having arrived here before us. Gwynedd already has Murmroth under good control. Much to the chagrin of his ward, Vesit, who feels he ought to have been left in charge, Gwynedd has left Serba to watch over Murmroth."

My head was spinning. "But . . . there was no mention of any plan to go to Norseland at the ruins."

"Apparently, Dell said something to Gwynedd some time ago that caused him to suddenly decide to go to Norseland," Brydda said. "Something about choosing the course that would oppose the spilling of blood when faced with many choices."

"He thinks that less blood will be spilled if he makes war on the last Hedra stronghold where there may be Beforetime weapons that will be used on us, not to mention the fact that Salamander and Ariel will be there!" I said incredulously.

"The fact that there are more plague seeds upon Norseland concerns him," Brydda said. "But you need not worry about Salamander, for the *Black Ship* was seen moving out to sea along the route taken by ships seeking the Red Queen's land. Did not Jakoby tell you? In Sutrium, Shipmaster Helvar of the *Stormdancer* spoke of it to her. Apparently, the route from Norseland curves toward Herder Isle before cutting out to the Endless Sea. I think we can assume that Ariel went with him."

This news was like a splash of cold water in my face. "Ariel has gone to the Red Queen's land," I said, more to force myself to take it in than to question it.

Brydda nodded, adding, "This journey is not just

Gwynedd's decision, either, Elspeth. It was approved by the new Westland Council of which Gwynedd has been voted high chieftain. He raised the matter, telling them very clearly of the weapons and plague seeds that are upon Norseland, and they agreed that a journey must be made there immediately." He frowned. "I must say, I am surprised that Rushton has not sought you out to tell you this."

"*Rushton* is aboard," I whispered, and my heart seemed to stop beating. "Please tell me that Blyss and Merret have come, too."

Brydda's frown deepened. "No. Merret is to work with Serba to coordinate the taking of the cloisters and the Hedra, and Blyss will not go anywhere without her. But Jak and Seely are aboard."

I was incapable of any more astonishment. "How . . . why?"

The rebel shrugged. "All I know is that Jakoby was about to give the order to cast off when Jak and Seely came riding up to the wharf with two packhorses laden with boxes. Apparently, when Seely told Jak and the others that Jakoby had come to collect you, Jak flew into a frenzy, insisting that he must be aboard the ship. In no time, he had packed up his experiments and requested the aid of Ran in getting them and him to Aborium. Seely refused to be left behind."

I could not imagine why Jak would wish to come aboard the *Umborine*, unless Dell had foretold something to make it necessary. My thoughts veered back to the knowledge that Rushton was aboard a ship bound for Norseland, where he and Domick had been tortured by Ariel. If seeing Domick had already unsettled Rushton's poisoned memories, what would journeying to Norseland do to him? And if his deadly memories did surface, there was neither empath nor healer aboard to help him. Only me, and it was my face that had been used to torture him.

"You look very pale," Brydda said, and before I could protest, he had drawn me into the main cabin. It was full of Gwynedd's armsmen and women, but to my relief, Rushton was not in the room. Brydda brought me to a table where Dardelan sat, gazing at a map. He looked up at me and smiled distractedly, but then he frowned and seemed to look at me properly.

"Are you well, my lady?"

Gathering my wits, I said, "Much has happened since you rode from the ruins yesterday morning. I must say that while I share your concern for the weapons that might be stored on Norseland, I wonder at the wisdom of so few approaching an island that is, from all I have heard, unassailable."

"So I believed," Dardelan said, rubbing his eyes, which were red-rimmed with fatigue. "I assume Brydda has not told you about Gwynedd?"

He looked at Brydda, who shook his head and said he had just met up with me. Dardelan glanced about before leaning closer to me to say quietly, "You know that Gwynedd is a Norselander. Maybe you also know that his mother fled to the west coast carrying him in her belly when the Faction began to take control of the Norselands. What you cannot know is that Gwynedd's great-grandfather was the only nephew of the last king. Gwynedd told us only this night past when he announced his decision to travel to Norseland, and I voiced the very concerns that you have just raised. Since the old king bore no children of his own, being half a priest himself by the time he died, by right of succession, Gwynedd would be the rightful Norse king, if the monarchy were reinstated. This explains Dell's foretelling in some way, of course.

"Gwynedd says he has no desire to be a king, yet Dell's futuretelling had filled him with joy, because it had suggested that the time was at hand when the Norselands would be freed from the Faction's long tyranny. What helped me decide to accompany him on this expedition is that, because of his heritage, Gwynedd knows a secret way to reach the surface of Norseland, and he believes that once he can reach the Norselanders who inhabit the island, he will be able to rouse them to fight the Hedra. But I will say no more of his plans in his absence."

I thought I had lost the capacity to be more surprised, yet I was amazed at this twist of events. Dell had foreseen that if Gwynedd did as she suggested, he would be crowned a king. In retrospect, it was easy to see that, in doing as she had suggested—organizing a meeting in Aborium to decide the future of the coast instead of riding into battle—he had been in Aborium when Jakoby arrived, enabling him to hear what was happening on Norseland in time to ask the tribeswoman to carry him there on the *Umborine*. Perhaps if he had tried to secure the Westlands before that meeting, Gwynedd would have been killed in battle.

"Eat something, both of you," Brydda insisted, pushing a soft round flatbread into my hands and the same into Dardelan's.

"I am not hungry," Dardelan said.

"What does that matter?" Brydda said sternly. "You need strength and food is strength." With that, he took up three of the soft round breads and bit ferociously into them.

Dardelan grinned at the big man and looked his old self as he raised the bread to his mouth. I bit into the bread, too, and suddenly I was ravenous. I took another of the soft round breads and ate it, and then I ate grapes and cheese and tiny tomatoes that burst on my tongue with a tartness that made my eyes water. Gradually, the queasiness in my belly faded, but Dardelan, who had matched me bite for bite, suddenly gave a bone-cracking yawn and said it was no use; he would have to sleep before he would be up to a council of war. He asked Brydda to find Gwynedd and suggest the meeting be postponed until they had all had some sleep.

After Dardelan had gone, I asked Brydda where Rushton was.

"He became ill soon after we boarded the *Umborine*, and wave-sickness is said to get worse before it can get better," Brydda answered. "Perhaps he has gone to his bed. That might explain why he did not seek you out to tell you what has been happening."

Before I could respond, the cabin doors opened and Jakoby entered. She glanced around the room, frowning, and then came to Brydda to ask where Dardelan and Gwynedd were.

"As far as I know, Gwynedd is with his people and Dardelan has just staggered off to bed. He wants to meet this evening after we have had a few hours' sleep," Brydda said.

"Very well." Jakoby nodded as Brydda rose, saying he had better let Gwynedd know. The tribeswoman took his seat and smiled at me ruefully. "It seems I sent you here for no reason. My apologies, but if you do not wish to return to your cabin so soon, perhaps you would like to come with me to the ship-master's platform? The view from it is very fine."

As we crossed the main deck, I asked about Sador. "Has Gwynedd asked you to go there after we leave Norseland?"

She shook her head. "Rushton asked it. He wishes to make a request of the tribes. I told him that I would gladly bear him hence, but his request must be made to all the tribes. That means we can spend very little time at Norseland, for the tribes meet together only once a year. The Battlegames that you and your people once attended are taking place even now."

"What does Rushton want to ask the tribes?" I asked, baffled.

"I think you must ask him that," Jakoby said. She rubbed her eyes wearily just as Dardelan had done.

"If you are tired, why not sleep?" I asked. "Surely your shipfolk have experience enough to keep us all safe."

"The crew is not experienced in sailing this far out from land," she said.

"And you are?" I asked.

To my surprise, she nodded. "It has always been the Sadorian custom to remain in sight of land when we take our greatships to sea. Indeed, we have gone vast distances in that way, but even as children being trained in the little coracles made for us by our mother, my sister and I were wont to venture farther out than she liked—my sister out of natural adventurousness, and me for love of her."

I was fascinated by this rare glimpse of the stern tribeswoman's life, but Jakoby said no more, for now we had reached the wooden steps leading to the shipmaster's deck, and several young Sadorians waited to ask her questions. Once these had been dealt with, we climbed up to the platform, only to discover that there were others waiting to speak to Jakoby. I went to sit on a bench set to one side of the shipmaster's platform, admiring the view of the vast sea, covered with glittering sequins of sunlight. The land was a purplehued smudge all along one side of the ship, which meant we were still proceeding along the strait. My thoughts turned to what Jakoby had said of Rushton. I could not imagine what he wanted from the tribes. I would gladly have asked him, but given the circumstances, it seemed wiser to avoid him as much as possible aboard the ship.

I shivered, though it was not truly cold, and forced my thoughts outward, focusing them on the ease and grace of the Sadorians' movements as they trimmed and adjusted the *Umborine*'s scarlet sails. Most of the shipfolk were my age, and I realized that ship skills were not borne of a few lessons in childhood. From what Jakoby had said, all children received some training in childhood on small vessels made for them by their parents, and then later, some chosen few must be trained on the greatships. Dameon had once told me that Sadorians had learned to sail generations before, from the shipmaster of a Gadfian raiding ship they had captured during the raid in which they had lost so many of their women. The Sadorians had forced the Gadfian shipmaster to teach them the arts of sailing and shipbuilding, and they had rebuilt his ship. Then they had cut down enough of the great sacred spice trees that grew in a single grove to build two more ships, before setting off on their epic journey to find their stolen women. The practice of sailing had continued since that time, and I now understood that some Sadorians must remain almost constantly aboard the greatships to attain the sort of easy skills I was now witnessing.

Jakoby chose this moment to sit down beside me, and impulsively I asked her about the long journeys that she had mentioned. "There was no specific destination," she answered. "The purpose of the journeying was to train new Sadorian shipfolk. All Sadorian youngsters spend time aboard the spiceships, and from these are chosen those who will be true shipfolk entrusted with the care of the sacred ships. They sail until they are old, and then their place is taken by a young shipboy or girl. The more intensive training of these new shipfolk is undertaken on a long journey. Of course, since Salamander has plied the strait, the journeys have all been beyond Sador."

"Are you saying that your ships once sailed the other way? Toward the Red Queen's land?"

The tribeswoman gave me a long speculative look, then said, "No Sadorian ship ever went there, but, yes, they sailed in that direction as far as the darklands."

"I have never heard of these darklands," I said, astonished.

She shrugged. "They are beyond the black coasts in that direction, and only the largest of the greatships with a minimum of shipfolk and no passengers has the capacity to carry food and water enough to go so far. There is life of a sort, both plant and beast, but all are mutated beyond any semblance of normality, and those who drink water there or walk there die of the wasting sickness within a year. Only those things native to the place can live there." As she spoke, Jakoby watched one of the shipfolk reef a sail, and now she rose with a mutter of exasperation to chide a young shipman. She came back and said, "You might be interested in visiting the map chamber on board. There are maps there showing the darklands."

"I would like very much to see them if it is permitted," I said eagerly.

"I cannot come with you just now," Jakoby said, "but if you would like to go yourself, the map chamber is the last cabin on the port side of the ship. The door is carved with a half-moon and stars. Tell the map keeper that I sent you."

"I will go there now," I said, and thanked her. I had just reached the bottom of the steps leading down to the main deck when I heard someone call my name. Seely was sitting on a coil of oiled rope, her arms clasped around her knees.

"I did not expect to see you again so soon," I said, going over to her.

She smiled shyly. "No more did I. But when Jak heard there was a ship going to Sador, he was like a man possessed, for he has long dreamed of bringing his experiments there."

"What experiments does he wish to take to Sador?"

"I am sure you know that he has long been trying to breed a strain of taint-eating insect that can tolerate the light and drier conditions?" Seely said, and I nodded. "Well, some time ago, he succeeded with the help of Ines, but the new strain has little tolerance for cold or damp. They would survive well in the desert lands, but there was no way to get them there without a long arduous trip overland. Until now."

"That explains a good deal," I said. "What did Dell say about your both leaving?"

Seely laughed. "What does Dell always say?"

"She foresaw it?"

"She foresaw our return, which is even better, because it means we will survive whatever is to happen on Norseland," Seely said, turning to look out over the shimmering waves. She got up and went to lean on the rail of the ship, saying softly, "You know, I thought I would be frightened or sick on a ship, but it is so strange and beautiful out here. I almost wish the journey would never end. On the other hand, Jak says that when he has finished in Sador, we will travel to Obernewtyn before coming back to the west coast, and I long to see Gavyn." She yawned and said reluctantly that she had better sleep, for she would need to be fresh to relieve Jak, who was now watching over the insects.

Her cabin lay in the direction I was walking, and I asked if anyone had told her that Gavyn had dreamed of seeing her at Obernewtyn.

Seely gave me a startled look. "How queer that you should speak of Gavyn dreaming of me, for only last night I dreamed of him. He was walking along a high narrow ridge with Blacklands spread on both sides of him. The sky was dark and stormy, and the light was a queer sickly yellow. A host of dogs walked all about him, and that great white dog that attached itself to him at Obernewtyn was with him, too, padding along at his heels. . . ." She shrugged and laughed.

We came to one of the hold entrances, and Seely stopped, explaining that her cabin was on a lower level. Continuing on alone, I reached the last cabin on the port side of the ship. Its door was carved with a half-moon and several stars, just as Jakoby had described. I knocked, and a gray-haired, whip-lean woman with a heavy jaw and thick brows that met over the bridge of her nose answered the door. Without allowing me to speak, she told me tersely that the map chamber was out of bounds to any but shipfolk. She began to close the door, but I explained hastily that Jakoby had sent me, which earned me a long, disapproving look. But she opened the door to let me in, muttering that her name was Gorgol, and no wonder Jakoby would not follow any rules but her own, given her mother's behavior. This was not the first time I had heard hints that Jakoby was disinclined to obey rules, but no one had ever mentioned her mother before.

The cabin was small, but every wall was covered in beautifully made wooden shelves piled with scrolled maps and ornately worked map cases. I gazed around, realizing with amazement that there must be more than a thousand maps in the tiny space, and a door behind a wide counter revealed a second smaller chamber running off the first, also walled in shelves and filled with maps.

"What do you want to see?" Gorgol demanded, having

moved behind the counter. When I told her, she frowned. "I have maps that show a portion of the darklands coast, but they do not show Land's End."

"What is Land's End?" I asked.

"The name given to the place where the darklands end. I have seen maps that show Land's End, but I accept nothing that our own ships have not mapped, for few mapmakers trouble themselves with scale. Instead, they rely upon visual landmarks or time references, both of which can result in great inaccuracies."

"Have you ever seen a map of the Red Queen's land?" I asked.

"I have, but I would not place any great reliance upon what it showed."

"What did it show?" I insisted.

She shrugged dismissively. "A peninsula shaped like a long fang and named Land's End and then a vast shoal-filled sea beyond which lay another land with more black coasts. According to that map, the Red Land was to be found by traveling northeast along these black coasts. But the distance from here by the coast route to Land's End is too far for any ship to manage, and those who go to Land's End must sail across the Endless Sea to it."

"Can I see the map showing the darklands?" I asked.

She turned to lift a battered-looking map case down from a shelf behind her. Opening it reverently, she drew out its map, spreading it on the counter. I leaned forward to examine it and saw that the map showed the west coast. I followed it along to where it became Blacklands. The words *black coasts* were scribed on them, and they were inked black some way in from the line that marked the edge. The thick black coastline was cut off by the edge of the parchment.

I looked up to find the Sadorian woman studying me as if I were a peculiar, ill-made map. I asked if she had a map that showed the next part of the black coast. She carefully rolled the first map, restored it to its case, and placed it on its shelf before locating another map. This one, once spread out, showed nothing but a long thick black coastline with inlets and coves and even the mouth of a river, but the unrelenting blackness told its own tale. I was still studying the map when Gorgol said brusquely that I should not pay too much attention to it, for the scale was wrong, it being the work of a young mapmaker; however, I then noticed two very small islands right at the upper edge of the map. In minute spidery writing were the words *Romsey* and *Bayleux*, presumably the islands' names. Given what Gorgol had said, there was no way to tell how far they were from the shore, but as they had not been inked black, it seemed they were not tainted. I leaned closer and thought I could make out the small symbol used by mapmakers to designate fresh water. That would make the map profoundly important, because while seafarers could catch fish and eat certain seaweeds to sustain themselves on long journeys, they could only carry so much fresh water. Knowledge of a spring on an untainted island could mean the difference between life and death to a ship's crew or the chance to extend the length of the journey.

"Do you have a map that shows the next part of the coast?" I asked.

In the end, Gorgol showed me seven more maps, all of which fit one against the other and detailed more or less accurately the shape, if not the scale, of the coastline right up to the beginning of the darklands. On the final map, two more islands had been drawn in and marked with the freshwater-spring symbol.

"It has taken long years to accumulate these maps, which are very nearly accurate," Gorgol said, rolling up the last map. "A shipmaster once told me that he had seen a map to the Red Queen's land from Land's End. He said, though, that it was impossible to reach Land's End by traveling along the coast. One had to venture across the sea."

I frowned, wondering how Salamander had learned the open-sea route to the Red Land. The obvious answer was that he had originally come from the Red Queen's land. "Is Land's End tainted ground?" I asked.

"Land's End is free of taint, but it is surrounded by dark-lands, and the man I spoke to told me that beasts from the darklands creep there at night seeking prey, so no one stays there past dusk. All ships anchor offshore in the dark hours and return to complete their business in the light of day."

"Their business?"

"The trade of slaves, chiefly," Gorgol said. "Ships from the Red Queen's land come to buy slaves and others come to sell them. Of course, sellers would earn more if they took the slaves all the way to the Red Queen's land themselves, but the journey is said to be even more dangerous than what has gone before."

Gorgol demanded to know if I was finished, and I shook my head, asking if she had a map that showed the coastline in the other direction, past Sador. With patent disapproval, she brought three maps from the smaller adjoining chamber. Each was enclosed in a map case of thick green felt laid snugly over wood. Gorgol drew out the map from the first case and unrolled it. This one showed the entire coastline of the Land and of Sador and a long stretch of black coast be-yond the desert lands. I ran a finger along the Land's metic-ulously detailed coastline, noting that all the beaches were carefully marked in, as were the narrow inlets, one of which concealed the great sea cavern where the Hedra had hidden. I had never seen any map that showed them before.

I ran my finger around the great, variegated scoop of cliff that was the narrow coastal route to Sador, thinking of Bruna and hoping she had already reached home. The map continued, showing the coast where a long white spit ran out from a split in the cliffs to form Templeport. The map also showed the land behind the desert lands as a black-edged wasteland many times greater than Sador and the country on both sides of the Suggredoon; even then there was no telling how much farther it extended, for the black desert ran off the parchment in three directions.

"It is magnificent," I told her, beginning to reroll the map, and for a moment, as she took it from me, her expression was slightly less cold. Once she restored the map to its case, she unrolled each of the remaining maps in their green cases, but both merely showed continuations of the black coast. Gorgol produced four more such maps, one of which showed a stretch of gray and then a small patch of clean ground. The next one had two more clean patches, and one of them showed the tiny freshwater-spring symbol. But when I examined the last map and glanced inquiringly at Gorgol, she shook her head, anticipating my request for yet another map.

I was about to roll it away when I noticed some faint markings on the edge of the parchment farthest from the black coastline. I leaned close, unsure if the markings were anything. "What is this?" I asked Gorgol.

She frowned. "Some years ago, one of our ships was blown out of sight of the black coasts in a storm, and another land was sighted. It ought to have been left out, for no landing was made and no proper measurements taken, and by the time the storm blew over, they were once again within sight of the black coast. I suspect that whoever made the sighting was so utterly confused by the storm that he mistook the black coasts for another land."

I nodded and asked if she had a map that showed together all the sections I had so far seen. She gave me a martyred look before going back to the adjoining chamber. This time she returned with a single black enameled map case. The map proved to offer a less detailed drawing of the vast landmass of which the Land and Sador were but the smallest part. I was astounded, for Sador, the Land, and Westland were little more than pinpricks at the edge of a vast black shape.

"Can this land be so vast?" I muttered.

"No one knows how vast because as you see, the map is incomplete," Gorgol said, taking it as a question. "No one has ever managed to circumnavigate it to know the distance from Sador right around to Land's End, because there is no fresh water beyond those springs shown." She tapped the vast black hinterland. "This is speculation, of course, for no one has been to the interior, but it is reasonable to assume that the center of this land must be as dead as its edges."

My head was beginning to ache from the stuffiness of the little cabin, so I thanked Gorgol and went back outside. It had been too warm in the map chamber, but now the wind felt cold through my thin silk clothes. I hurried back toward my cabin, intending to get a shawl and find a sheltered place on the deck to sit until the wind had blown away my headache. As I had hoped, Maruman was still deeply asleep. I reached out and stroked his fur, thinking of the dream I had had of him as a young cat, playing on the dreamtrails, and I wondered if I would ever understand what it meant. Maruman gave a soft, contented snore. I lay down beside him and pressed my cheek to his head.

I was so glad to have him and Gahltha with me that I would have been in bliss if I were not so worried about Rushton. I would try to stay out of his way, but somehow I must prevent him from going ashore on Norseland. I would speak to Jakoby, Dardelan, and Gwynedd when I could do so privately and tell them what Domick and Dell had said. Maybe they would come up with a plan to prevent Rushton from going ashore. I did not feel tired, yet I found myself slipping toward sleep. It was a pure pleasure to know there was no reason I should resist its lure.

✦ 14 ✦

I SANK, SHIELDED, through dream and memory, not wanting to be ensnared by them, for I sensed that they would all hold tormenting visions of Rushton's face and smile in better times.

Hovering above the mindstream, I thought of Domick, wondering what his death had surrendered into it. Did all of a person go into it—all his dreams and slight experiences and mundane activities as well as his great or evil deeds? Then again, who could say what deeds were great or small in a life? That which seemed great to the person who lived that life might not be deemed so by those who lived in the aftermath of it; a deed that seemed of everlasting importance might prove to have slight consequences. At the same time, some very small act done without much thought could lead to eternal good for humans and maybe all creatures. For the same reason, no one could judge whether a deed or even a life had been worthy—not the one who lived that life nor those who lived at the same time, for all were hampered by their limited vision. How should a stream judge the rocks it glides over or the twig that it carries along? It did not even choose its own course. Therefore, it was foolish to ask if Domick's life had brightened or darkened the stream. The answer was that his life had been given to him; a gift. He had lived it, and now he gave back the gift, and the stream was enriched by all the flavors, sweet and sour and bitter and bland, that his dying had released.

I saw a glimmering bubble detach itself from the mind-stream and float toward me with dreamy, unerring accuracy.

I found myself within a passage so white and shining that it could only have existed in the Beforetime. I heard footsteps and when I looked behind me, I saw Cassy Duprey coming along it. Her expression was blandly pleasant, but there was a hint of sorrow that made me certain I was seeing her after the death of her Tiban lover, which meant she had already met Hannah Seraphim.

Without warning, a door in the corridor opened and a white-coated man with very short gray hair stepped out in front of Cassy.

"Who are you?" he asked, but it was the voice of a woman, for all the mannish attire and bearing.

"I'm Cassandra Duprey," Cassy said, smiling guilelessly, but a flinty gleam in her eyes made me sure she was up to something.

"Duprey?" The woman sounded taken aback.

"Director Duprey is my father," Cassy said lightly. "I am staying with him for the summer. But who are you?"

"Ruth Everhart. But you shouldn't be here, you know. This wing is out of bounds to visitors."

"Isn't this the way to the garden cafeteria?" Cassy looked concerned, and the woman's expression softened, though she seemed irritated as well.

"You missed a turn in the last corridor," she said.

"I did? Oh, this place is such a labyrinth. You know, I was here last summer, and I could have sworn I knew my way around. Then my father tells me about this garden cafeteria that I have never even heard of. Now I find this whole wing

738

I didn't even know was here. I guess you never go over to the main restaurant or my father would have introduced us."

The older woman laughed without humor. "I doubt it. My project is only one of hundreds here, and it's considered a minor one at that. I doubt that Director Duprey would even remember my name."

"Of course he would," Cassy said with wide-eyed earnestness. "My father says it's his job to know all the people here, though I don't know how he can manage that when he does not even remember my birthday." Abruptly, her smile vanished as if it had been wiped away. The older woman did not appear to notice. She was tilting her head as if she were straining to hear some barely audible music. Puzzled, I entered Cassy's mind and found her probing the other woman. The probe was better honed than the one she had thrust into her mother's mind, but it was still a novice's effort, and it did not explain why the woman was standing and staring into space as if she had been coerced.

Curiosity made me flow into the woman's mind, and I was shocked to find that she was indeed being coerced, but not by Cassy. By *another* mind! Cassy was merely a witness to what the othermind was doing.

"That wasn't too bright," said the othermind to Cassy so smoothly that it could only belong to a Misfit with both farseeking and coercive Talents. "She'll remember you said that."

"It was a joke, and she thinks I'm a kid. All kids criticize their parents. It doesn't mean anything. Besides, she won't remember anything I said to her."

"She'll remember all right. She has that sort of mind that works at niggles. She'll wonder why you were so friendly unless you keep it up. Now let me work." The othermind began to ransack the woman's mind with a ruthlessness that shocked me. Almost as an afterthought, it erased a little node of puzzlement in the woman's mind, roused by Cassy's last words. It was replaced with the feeling that the girl was a nice dim kid of no real consequence despite her father. "All right, I'm finished. She doesn't know any more about Sentinel than Joe Public, because her project isn't connected."

"What is her project?" Cassy asked.

"She said herself it's unimportant," the other said impatiently.

"She didn't say it was unimportant," Cassy argued. "She said it was considered to be minor. But she obviously doesn't think so."

"Hannah would not want us wasting time on this."

"Hannah wasn't interested in Sentinel until I sent that stuff you had stumbled on," Cassy said. "And if there are other people here showing an interest in Sentinel . . ."

"That's just Abel being paranoid about random thoughts. It goes with the territory." Cassy made no response and the othermind sighed. "All right. Wait." A moment passed during which Cassy looked up and down the shining hall anxiously before the othermind spoke to her again. "Okay, it's nothing; just something to do with cryogenics."

"Cryogenics? Wasn't that some sort of dark-age research that involved chopping people's heads off and freezing them?"

"That's the one," the other mind said, sounding amused.

"But wasn't it totally discredited?"

"Of course. But this is some new version. Look, we have to let her go. She's starting to get antsy, and I don't want to do a major rewire of her brain. But get ready because I've prodded her mind to think about Sentinel. Give her half a chance and she'll spill."

"I'm ready." Cassy withdrew from the other woman's

mind and summoned up a bright smile. The woman blinked and looked slightly dazed. "Is . . . something wrong?" Cassy asked gently.

"I . . . I don't know. I thought . . ." The gray-haired woman broke off and gave an awkward laugh. "It's nothing. What did you say?"

Cassy gave her a dazzling, self-deprecating smile. "I was just saying I'm still a little awed by all of this."

The woman rubbed at her temple as if she was developing a headache. "It's understandable. Now you'd better—"

"You know what amazes me most?" Cassy interrupted confidingly. "It's how many different nationalities you see here. Chinon, Gadfian, Tipodan." She shook her head. "Somehow I never expected that much cooperation."

The woman laughed dryly. "There is not that much cooperation. The mix is mostly due to the Sentinel project. I'm sure you've heard about it. All five powers are involved, so there are scientists from every country here to work on the project, as well as a lot of suits and bean counters from those places whose job it is to observe everyone else doing their jobs and then report to their various governments. But there are a few other projects where scientists from different powers are cooperating. Mine is one. That's one of the things I love about science. The fact that it's possible to work across those invisible boundaries." She glanced at her watch. "I'll walk you back to where you went wrong. You must have missed the sign. It doesn't exactly leap out at you."

I saw Cassy scowl as the mind now probing her said with a languid sneer, "If you had just gone the other way like I suggested, this wouldn't have happened."

I caught the probe as it withdrew and followed it back to a girl sitting slumped in a chair in a distant corner of the complex. I withdrew to look at her and was astonished. For all the cynical feel of her mindvoice, she was no older than Cassy, and she was extraordinary looking. Her skin was as pale as if it had been powdered with flour, her lips were black, and she had smeared something glittering and purple around her eyes. Her hair was short like the older woman in the hall, but it had been oiled and pressed into quills that stuck up as stiffly as if they had been lacquered. Finally, a silver bead of metal gleamed in the tuck of her chin, and a little silver arrow pierced the exaggerated arch of one black brow.

"Well?" she said aloud in an insolent, rasping voice.

The people around the chair had been standing still. I looked at them and realized with some astonishment that each wore the same sort of heavy blue trousers with pockets and soft short-sleeved white shirts as I had worn in the ruins complex. I studied each in turn, realizing with awe that these must be the Beforetime Misfits stolen from the original Reichler Clinic. There was a frail-looking woman with wispy blond hair and anxious eyes; a handsome man with a belligerent expression; a worried-looking older man whose face seemed familiar, and a heavy older woman with gray streaks in her hair. All of them save the girl in the chair had skin like Cassy's: Twentyfamilies dark. The only other person in the room was a younger boy with yellowish hair and a wheezing way of breathing. He was fair-skinned, too, but I was struck by his dual-colored eyes of green and blue, for they were like Iriny's. He was the only one other than the pale girl with the porcupine-quill hair who appeared calm. The rest wore expressions ranging from frightened to apprehensive.

"Well?" asked the big woman eagerly.

The girl with the spiked hair stretched luxuriantly and then shook her head. "She didn't get anything. She let herself

742

get sidetracked by one of the geeks."

Without warning, a sharp pain broke the bubble of dream material open, and silver drops shuddered back into the mindstream as I was drawn rapidly up and away.

Maruman was watching me when I opened my eyes, flexing his claws. I glared at him. "Did you do that?"

"Your stomach woke me," he answered coolly.

I glanced across at the windows and saw by the hue of the sunlight striping the sill that it was late afternoon. I got up, stripped off the rumpled silk clothes that I had slept in, and splashed my face with water. Feeling more alert, I found a heavier silk shirt and trousers in vivid violet-blues and a long quilted gray vest that had been worked in blue and silver thread. The cloth would keep Maruman's claws from digging too deep. When I invited him to come with me, he stretched and yawned, showing his teeth, before climbing lightly over onto my shoulders. I padded barefoot out onto the deck and stopped to make sure Rushton was not in sight; then I made my way swiftly toward the front of the ship. I wanted to find Brydda or Jakoby so I could seek their advice about Rushton, but the enticing scent of cooking led me to the galley, where a large, powerfully built woman swooped on Maruman, saying she had been saving something special for him. To my amused disgust, Maruman shamelessly endured her crooning and petting for the tidbits she offered.

"Food is being served in the saloon," the cook said when I asked if she had something for me. Guessing she must mean the main chamber where I had eaten earlier, I thanked her, not wanting to explain why I did not want to go there. Maruman languidly bade me go, saying he would seek me out later. I decided to see if I could find out where Brydda's cabin was, but before I had taken two steps, Gilbert stepped out of the gathering shadows of dusk.

"I thought you looked beautiful as a gypsy, but you look truly ravishing in Sadorian clothes," he said. "I was just coming to escort you to the saloon for the meeting."

"I am perfectly capable of finding my own way from one end of the deck to the other," I snapped, and marched past him, wondering how to get rid of him. Moments later, I ran into Gwynedd.

"Can it be Elspeth Gordie?" he asked, squinting down at me, for despite my height, he was taller by far.

"It is good to see you, Chieftain Gwynedd," I said. "I wanted to say how well you spoke in the meeting yesterday."

"You were there? But, yes, Merret mentioned that you sat a while in the gallery with Blyss. Come into the saloon. We should have a little while before everyone is assembled."

Seeing no way to avoid it, I allowed him to take my arm, hoping I could slip away without encountering Rushton. A number of lanterns now swung from hooks on the beams, shedding an inconstant, honeyed light over the saloon, which was empty but for Dardelan and Rushton. Both looked up at our arrival, and there was no time to withdraw, even if I could have come up with a reason to do so, for Dardelan lifted his hand in greeting.

Gwynedd firmly steered me across the room to the seat alongside Rushton's, and I forced myself to look at him and nod a greeting. I expected coolness in response, but his expression was icy. Before I could utter a word, Rushton stood up abruptly, saying that he would go and waken Brydda. He assayed a jerky, general bow and departed.

I felt the blood burn in my cheeks, but to my relief, after an awkward pause, Gwynedd only said, "I wonder if you would tell me some more about your time on Herder Isle. Merret told me what she knew, but I feel sure there was much more to be told. In particular, I am interested in these shadows that serve the Faction. You see, the goddesses worshipped by the Norse forbade slavery as unspeakably base. Am I correct in thinking the slaves were all taken from the Westland?"

I nodded, striving to control my roiling emotions and desperate to leave the saloon before Rushton returned. It was bad enough that Dardelan had seen how he snubbed me, but what if he treated me badly in front of the others? It would be painful and humiliating, but I was more afraid that someone might upbraid him for it and precipitate what I most feared.

Gwynedd was still looking at me expectantly, so I took a steadying breath and told Gwynedd of the shadows, and he said that he would offer homes in Murmroth to any who wished to return to the Westland. He would also see that they had work or were given funds that would allow them to establish a trade or business for themselves, if they wished it.

"You are kind. I am sure many will be glad to take up your offer," I said, unable to keep from stealing glances at the doors each time they swung open. So far, a number of Gwynedd's men had entered, and now another group entered with Brydda. He came to join us while they took a table near the door and began a noisy game of dice.

As Brydda dropped into the seat beside him, Dardelan asked if he had seen Rushton. "He went looking for you," he added.

"I saw him, but I did not need waking," Brydda said, reaching for a jug of fement and pouring himself a mug. "He has gone to fetch our good shipmistress, but he says to begin the discussion without him. I fear he is in a black mood."

I felt Dardelan and Gwynedd look at me, and the

sympathy in their eyes made my eyes prick with tears. I blinked hard to stem the flow, but to my mortification, two slid down my cheeks. I brushed them away and would have risen save that Brydda very deliberately pushed an empty mug across to me and poured into it a dram of ruby red fement, bidding me firmly to drink. Then he filled his own mug and tapped mine with it gently, saying, "To courage in the great dice game that is life."

Dardelan reached out to lay a hand over mine, saying softly, "He is not himself, Elspeth."

I drank a mouthful of the fement and tried to smile, but a storm of tears was rising behind my eyes, and I knew suddenly that there was no holding them back. I stood up abruptly, and immediately Brydda rose, too. Taking my hand, he murmured to the others that he needed some fresh air before the meeting began. I was unable to speak and was half-blinded by tears as he led me deftly into the cold night. He brought me to the side of the ship and laid his big hand on my shoulder.

I shook my head and stepped away from him. "Please, don't," I whispered, my voice quaking. "If you are kind, I will never get control of myself." He nodded and stood silent while I gulped and blinked and sniffed my way to some sort of calmness. "I am sorry," I told the big rebel hoarsely at last. "It is only that I have been so worried."

"Rushton has been behaving badly," Brydda said, and there was anger in his voice. "Whatever happened to him in the cloister in Sutrium is not your fault. Why take it out on you, of all people?"

"Oh, Brydda, if only you knew," I said, drawing a long steadying breath. "You must not blame Rushton for the way he is behaving, especially toward me. When we spoke in Rangorn, I told you that his imprisonment in the cloister in Sutrium had broken something in him and that he would not permit me to enter his blocked memories to help him. I did not tell you that Rushton told me that he could no longer love me."

Brydda looked at me in frank disbelief. "He did not mean it, surely."

"I did not believe it either, but when I saw him in Saithwold, he was even more cold and harsh toward me. I saw then that he *had* meant what he said at Obernewtyn. Dameon said I was wrong and that it was *because* he loved me that Rushton was so cold. He said it was because I stirred him deeply that he rejected me, because if he allowed himself to feel anything for me, it would force him to face the memories of what had happened to him." I swallowed hard. "But Dameon did not know what I now know. What Domick told me . . ."

Brydda's eyes widened. "Domick? But how . . . ?" He stopped, comprehension flooding his expression. "They were taken at the same time, weren't they?"

I nodded. "Apparently, Rushton had found Domick and was trying to convince him to return to Obernewtyn when they were taken. Ariel had foreseen the meeting. But they were not separated, as it might seem, Domick was not taken to Herder Isle and Rushton to the cloister in Sutrium. They were both brought aboard the *Black Ship* and taken to Norseland."

"*Norseland!* But Rushton was found in the Sutrium cloister!" Brydda said.

I told him what the Threes had said about Rushton and Ariel, and then I told him all that Domick had said. The rebel shook his head, and a look of revulsion crossed his rough,

747

kind face. "I cannot believe that Domick was made to torture Rushton. . . . No wonder his mind split in two."

"What happened to him was our fault. We sent him to spy, and it was what he did as a spy that created Mika, and it was Mika whom Ariel found and used," I said, fresh tears welling in my eyes. "But in telling me about Rushton, Domick broke free from Ariel's control. Apparently, he was not meant to be able to speak at all. Mika was supposed to be in control."

"That tells us that Ariel makes mistakes. And he has made a mistake in thinking that he has broken Rushton. The question now is what to do," Brydda said.

I told him of my conversation with Dell about Rushton and how I was to ask Blyss to help me prepare him to remember. "Only I never got the chance to speak to Blyss about it, and now . . ."

"Rushton is aboard the *Umborine* with you," Brydda concluded.

"With me but without Blyss or any empath or healer," I reminded him. "And worse, we are bound for Norseland, where Ariel tortured him. Rushton is likely to remember what happened if he goes ashore, especially if he sees the place where Ariel took him."

"Ye gods," Brydda said. "Then he must not go ashore."

"That would be the best thing, but how can we stop him without telling him why he must stay aboard the *Umborine*?"

Brydda tugged at his beard absently, glaring unseeingly at the dark sea. Then he looked at me. "Gwynedd wants Jakoby to lower three small ship boats before the *Umborine* enters the shoal passage, which is the only way into the main cove of the island. The Herders simply call it Main Cove, but Gwynedd says the Norselanders used to call it Fryddcove after one of their goddesses. He means to be aboard one of

748

the ship boats with as many of his people as safely possible in order to seek out a hidden inlet leading to a tiny cove his mother told him about called Uttecove. It will not be easy, for the inlet is perilously narrow and must be entered in the right way, but once the ship boats are in the cove, there is a way up to the island's surface. I do not know why Gwynedd is so certain that the Faction has not learned of this secret way, but he is prepared to risk his life and the lives of others on his certainty. Once on the surface, he means to rouse the Norselanders who live there to fight the Hedra. Rushton means to go with him, but what if Gwynedd asks you to come with him, claiming that he needs your Talents? Given what I have seen, that is likely to stop Rushton from going."

I nodded bleakly. "It will, but what is the *Umborine* to do?"

"Gwynedd's idea is that we enter Fryddcove and make a lot of fuss, demanding this and that and posturing and making threats to draw the Faction's attention. That will leave Gwynedd free to act behind their backs. It will also prevent Rushton from going ashore at once."

"What if Beforetime weapons are used against you?"

"That is a possibility," Brydda admitted. "However, since this is a Sadorian ship, I do not think anything will be done in haste, for the Hedra have no open quarrel with the desert lands. In any case, Rushton suggested that Jakoby demand to speak with Ariel. That way we can learn if he remained upon the island after Salamander left."

"All right, so Gwynedd will go ashore, but what does he imagine he will do then? He cannot win against the Hedra in the few days he will have before Jakoby must take Rushton to Templeport."

"Gwynedd's primary purpose is to make sure there are no weapons or stores of plague seeds on Norseland that the

749

Faction can use. He thinks that much can be accomplished in a twoday with the help of the Norselanders who live there, hence his determination to make contact."

"Do you know what Rushton is going to ask the tribes?" I said slowly.

Brydda's eyes widened. "Ye gods! You cannot know. Yesterday, just before we left the meeting house in Aborium, Zarak rode in. Dameon had sent him across the river with instructions to find Rushton. As soon as Zarak crossed, Linnet summoned a horse and sent him riding for Aborium."

My heart was beating fast. "What has happened?"

"Maryon came to Sutrium with a futuretelling that the slavemasters who hold the Red Queen's land are planning to invade the Land. If they come, Maryon says, they will bring such a horde that the Land on both sides of the Suggredoon, the Norselands, and the Sadorian desert lands will all fall to them, and any who do not die fighting will be enslaved."

I stared at him, aghast. "Maryon says they *will* fall? There is no hope?"

"There is no hope if they come, she says. There is some slight hope if they are prevented from coming."

"You talk in riddles, or Maryon does," I snapped.

"Maryon says a force must be mustered and carried by four greatships to the Red Queen's land before the Days of Rain."

"We do not have four . . ." I stopped, and understanding swept over me. "Rushton will ask the Sadorians for use of their two remaining spicewood greatships!"

Brydda nodded. "Two Sadorian ships, plus the *Storm-dancer* and the ship that Dardelan has had built these two months, and we will just manage the four, though the *Storm-dancer* will need repairs and Dardelan's ship must be completed. And all the ships will have to be especially fitted for such a journey."

"What said Shipmaster Helvar about this?" I asked.

"He said he must consult with the ship's proper master. Indeed, the *Stormdancer* left for Herder Isle even as Zarak set off. But the lad says the Norselanders were ferocious at the mere idea of losing a freedom so recently won."

"I cannot see the tribes refusing their ships, given their hatred of slavery and the fact that their own land will be in danger, too," I said.

"Jakoby says as much, but even so, the request must be made to the tribes, and if it is not made when they are together, someone must ride to each of the tribes to ask if they would agree to holding another conclave. This would be a task of many sevendays, perhaps even months. Maryon must have seen as much, or why urge Dameon to send someone after Rushton at all speed?"

"Ye gods. This is sickening news," I said. "But even with all four ships filled with fighters, we will still be too few to take on the slavemasters' hordes, there or here. It would be better to meet them here, for we would have the chance to prepare defenses, and we could use all the Hedra and soldierguards as well."

"That would still not be enough, apparently," Brydda said. "But Maryon insists that if four ships travel to the Red Land, the enslaved people will be inspired to rise against their masters."

"But," I said, and then stopped. Maryon was right; the ships would rouse the enslaved people, *if Dragon was aboard one of them*. Indeed, it would take only one ship to do it. Then something else occurred to me. "A journey begun in the Days of Rain will be terribly dangerous, for Reuvan once told me that, amongst shipfolk, the season is called the Days of Storm. And

if the ships survive that, they would still be traveling when wintertime came. They would also be beyond Land's End, where
few ships have ever traveled, and I have heard that the way
from Land's End to the Red Queen's land is perilous. Do you
know how to go from there? Does Dardelan or Gwynedd?"

"Gwynedd does not know the way, but he says there will
be maps and charts on Norseland, for once upon a time, the
Norse kings had some dealings with the queens of the Red
Land," Brydda said. "Getting those maps is another thing that
Gwynedd hopes to accomplish while we are ashore."

I nodded absently, turning over in my mind what Brydda
had said and wondering at the neatness of a prophecy that
would send to the Red Queen's land ships, one of which would
carry the lost queen whose mind contained a vital clue to finding something the Seeker needed. Was it a real futuretelling, I
wondered, or merely a manipulation by the Agyllians?

Then it struck me that it was not just Dragon who would
be aboard those ships. I would have to travel to the Red
Queen's land, too.

"Elspeth?" Brydda's voice drew me back to myself. "I need
to go and speak with Dardelan and Gwynedd about keeping
Rushton aboard before he and Jakoby join us in the saloon."
He hesitated. "Under the circumstances, I think it best if you
do not attend the meeting. Indeed, perhaps you ought to remain in your cabin for the time being. I will come later and
tell you what has been decided."

I nodded, but after he had gone, I remained at the side of
the ship, gazing blindly out to sea and struggling to order my
thoughts. A hand touched my arm, and I turned, expecting
to see Brydda again, but it was Gilbert, carrying a lantern. I
snatched my arm away, and a shadow crossed the armsman's
handsome face.

"You would rather be alone?"

I struggled with irritation and frustration, and finally I looked directly into his eyes and made myself ask evenly, "Why do you seek me out so constantly?"

Gilbert looked taken aback at my bluntness, and fleetingly I saw again the man I had liked in the Druid's encampment. "Is not the answer obvious?" he finally said, and now he was smiling again.

"I fear that it is," I said softly, deciding there was nothing for it but to be ruthlessly honest.

His smile faded. "I thought that you had some . . . liking for me when we were in the Druid's camp. Was it merely a pretense to gain my help?"

"No," I said. "You did not despise me for being a gypsy, and you were kind."

He laughed roughly. "I felt that there was more than liking between us back in the White Valley."

I forced myself to answer him truthfully. "I think there was some . . . some potential that we both recognized. I felt that you were a man I might have cared for under other circumstances."

"You no longer feel that way," Gilbert said.

I bit my lip and said awkwardly, "It seems you have changed. I felt it when I saw you in the Beforetime ruins." He said nothing, and I struggled for clarity, feeling it was owed. "In the White Valley, you did not smile so much or give voice to elaborate flattery. The man I met in the Druid's camp had a seriousness and a steadiness in him that . . . that anyone might feel they could rely upon. I do not think that man would have left his babies so easily, saying they had no need of him."

Gilbert paled so much he looked ill, and then it seemed

that some pleasant facile mask he had worn melted away as pain flooded into his eyes and mouth. He turned abruptly to face the sea and drew a ragged breath. Then he said slowly and very softly, "There can come a moment in life when you see your heart's desire, though you did not know of its existence until that moment. So it was for me when I first saw you. I was determined that I would protect you from Henry Druid's prejudice against gypsies and against his foolish spoiled daughter's jealousy. When Erin contrived that you would be given to that ape Relward, I near went mad thinking how to prevent it. But . . . you escaped and then I saw you carried off by the river. I thought you had died."

"I . . . I did not know . . . ," I stammered.

"Of course you did not, for you saw only a vague potential in me, but I saw in you a blazing beacon of meaning and purpose. You understand how seeing such a wondrous radiance quenched might . . . change a man? I do not think I was utterly changed at once. So much happened so suddenly. You were gone, and then the Druid's camp was destroyed in a firestorm while I was still too grief-stricken to think. Then I and the other few survivors realized that those from the camp had been sold as slaves. I rode with two other men who had survived, because we had been sent out to scout, but eventually we parted. I do not know where the others went. I had no clear plan but to go as far as I could. That single notion brought me to rose-colored Murmroth where I met Gwynedd. Meeting him was . . . was like an awakening from numbness, because, like you, he blazes with a purpose and potency that illuminates the lives of those about him. I joined his cause and threw myself into becoming his man and serving his dreams. For a time, I found contentment. But then I made a mistake."

"The woman you bonded with?" I said softly.

He nodded. "Serra was . . ." He looked away to the sea again and concluded harshly, "She looked like you—the same long dark hair and proud look. The same gravity about her, as if there were hidden depths that one might spend a lifetime trying to plumb . . . I courted her and we bonded. But Serra was less deep than wont to brood, and after a time she began to fret at me. I felt that she wanted something from me that she could not name and did not even know, and without it she could not be content. She became jealous of my devotion to Gwynedd, and the more she nagged and scowled, the more time I spent away from home. Then she became pregnant. I was glad, for I thought that a child might fulfill her. She gave birth to twin boys, and I could have loved them and loved her for them, but she had become cold and pointed out my faults to them so that soon they regarded me suspiciously and rejected me."

"You said they were babies," I said.

He nodded. "So they are, yet Serra's sullen eyes and her grudging nature look out of their faces. I learned not to care and to laugh and make light of all that seemed serious and deep and true. I discovered that women would laugh with me if I flattered their beauty and paid them compliments and kept my deeper self from them."

"I'm sorry," I said, and I pitied him enough to fight my reticence and lay a hand over his clenched fists. At once he turned his hands and caught mine between them.

"I could find the man I once was, with you." A yearning in his eyes made the words a question. I wanted to pull my hands away and flee from the naked emotion in his face, but I forced myself to meet his eyes and shake my head. The longing in his face dimmed, but he did not resume the careless, flirtatious mask I had so disliked. Instead, he said with a sad acceptance that ached my heart as much as it relieved me, "You are different now, too, Elspeth who was once Elaria. I see it clearly in this moment."

I said, "Since the rebellion, I am freed from having to hide my Misfit abilities, but . . . there is a man that I love. I knew him when I met you, but I did not know that I loved him. I was afraid to see it."

He sighed, a long exhalation. "Well, then, perhaps it was that gypsy girl who hid from love and hid her true self that I loved. You are stronger and more courageous than that girl was, and I hope the man you love is worthy of you. In honor of the love I bore Elaria, I offer you my friendship."

"The friendship of one who is honest and courageous is precious," I said gravely.

Gilbert released my hand and looked up into the night, drawing a long breath and expelling it. The wind blew more strongly now, and the smell of rain was in the air. "A storm is coming," he said softly, and walked away.

I watched him go, a strong, straight-backed man with flame-colored hair that caught the lantern light from a saloon window, and I wondered again how love could cause so much pain.

My neck prickled, and I turned to look up at the truncated upper deck where I had sat the previous day with Jakoby. A cluster of lanterns hung from hooks and showed the tribeswoman clearly, standing by the wheel and speaking to one of her men, her hair and clothes fluttering wildly in the rising wind. A little apart from them stood Rushton, gazing down at me with a black rage that sent a cold blade into my heart.

✦ 15 ✦

THE CLAP OF thunder that shook the ship testified to the mounting fury of the storm that had come upon us so suddenly and dramatically hours before and showed no sign of abating. Lightning filled the cabin with a weird, distorted radiance, and I got up and staggered over the pitching floor to the window. Opening it a crack, I saw a great jagged spear of lightning slash through the black night, revealing a sky clogged with massive thunderheads. The sea was a heaving gray expanse from which rose the smoking peaks of enormous waves. Then darkness swallowed everything until claws of lightning rent the night again. This time, I saw a massive wave rise alongside the ship and topple over with deadly slowness. I realized with sick horror that just one such mountain of water breaking over the bow would smash the greatship to splinters.

The thought of Gahltha smote me like a blow, and I muttered a curse at my callousness. He and the other horses had been shifted belowdecks soon after the storm began, but the storm would have destroyed his hard-won control over his fear of water, and I ought to have gone and seen him long since, regardless of the need to stay out of Rushton's way.

Thunder reverberated as I groped for the quilted vest hanging on a hook behind the door. Dragging it on, I looked back at the bed to see Maruman sleeping soundly, oblivious to the storm. Afraid that he had gone onto the dreamtrails for the longsleep, I staggered back to lay a hand on his warm back, but he was only sleeping. Relieved, I mounded some pillows about him and made my way back to the door. I opened it, and the wind forced it wide and blustered at me with such ferocity that I was flung backward. I lowered my head and shouldered my way out of the cabin, heaving the door closed behind me and making sure it was securely latched.

For a moment, all was darkness and noisy disorienting chaos, then lightning illuminated the deck, revealing slick wood and snaking ropes. Oddly, there was not a shipman or woman in sight.

I had not gone far when the ship nosed into a trough, the hull groaning and creaking as if it were about to break in two. I was thrown from my feet, but instead of crashing to the deck, strong arms caught me. I looked up to find Jakoby holding me in a viselike grip. I expected her to order me back to my cabin, but instead she pointed forward and shouted at me to go to the saloon. I shook my head and tried to explain that I needed to stay out of Rushton's sight. But thunder rumbled and lightning cracked, smothering my words. Jakoby pointed insistently, and her vehemence made me turn. My jaw dropped at the sight of a sheer stone cliff rearing up out of the churning water directly ahead and extending up out of sight.

"Norseland," Jakoby bellowed in my ear.

"It can't be!" I shouted back. Then I laid my hand on her arm and sent, "We can't have got here so swiftly."

"The storm blew us directly across the strait instead of along the normal shipping path," Jakoby shouted. "It was a perilous passage, for we had to negotiate the many shoals in the midst of the storm, but it is done, and now we are less than an hour from the Norsemen's Uttecove."

I glanced at the cliffs, which were rushing toward us at a speed that dried my mouth, but at that moment, the *Umborine* lurched and plunged and groaned, the deck and hull creaking horribly as the ship slowly turned broadside to the cliffs. Instead of looking relieved, Jakoby merely shouted into my ear that I should go to the saloon, for the ship boats would soon be launched.

I gaped at her in disbelief, unable to believe she meant to go ahead with Gwynedd's strategy in the midst of the storm. Yet Jakoby did not look as if she were joking. I swallowed hard, remembering that I had agreed to take part in what must surely be a lunatic's venture.

Jakoby was shouting more, and I touched her arm again so I could enter her mind and asked her to repeat her words. "The storm will prevent us from being able to maneuver the *Umborine* close enough to Norseland to see the inlet; therefore, the ships will have to be launched in faith."

I nodded, understanding that I was receiving a warning, and Jakoby pointed urgently toward the shipmaster's deck. Then she let me go and hastened toward the rear of the vessel, as sure-footed as a cat on the heaving deck.

I stood for a moment, indecisive amid all the wild wind and water, but then I continued along the deck to the entrance to the hold. I was about to descend when I saw a Sadorian shipgirl carrying a lantern and a coil of thick oiled rope. I lurched over to her and asked where the holding corral was belowdecks. She shouted something, but the roaring of the wind and the raging sea made it impossible to make out her words. Realizing that I could not hear her, she pointed down and then toward the rear of the ship. Then she showed three fingers. I nodded, understanding that Gahltha was on the third level toward the rear of the ship.

I reeled and stumbled down the steps into the pitching, creaking blackness. At one point, I heard Jak's voice and realized he must be striving to keep his precious insects safe, but I continued to descend until my nose told me I had reached the holding boxes. I drew a deep breath and shouted Gahltha's name. My heart lurched with relief and dismay as he gave a high-pitched, terrified whinny of response. Full of remorse for not having come to him sooner, I groped my way toward the sound. At last my straining hands found his hot, trembling flank.

"I am here, dear one," I sent. "I am so sorry I did not come sooner."

"It is not your fault that I am a coward," Gahltha sent miserably.

"My great-hearted Gahltha, you are the least cowardly creature I have ever known," I told him fiercely, sliding my arms around his neck and kissing his silky muzzle.

"You are leaving the ship," Gahltha sent, having seen it in my mind.

"I must," I said. "But when I return, we will go to Sador, and after that, we will ride back to Obernewtyn."

Unable to offer any further assurances, I held him and stroked him until at last I felt the keen edge of his terror blunt. Then, knowing I could delay no longer, I kissed him one last time and made my way back up to the deck.

The cliffs seemed closer than ever in the flashes of lightning, and I told myself that at least no one would have seen us approach the island in the middle of such a black stormy night. The first the Hedra would know about anything was when the *Umborine* sailed into Main Cove. I could just make out movement around the ship boats, which had been lashed to the deck beyond the saloon, but I had one last errand before I could join the others. I ran back to my cabin and wakened Maruman to explain what I was going to do. Before he could utter any of the protests I sensed gathering in his mind, I knelt by the bed, took his small pointed face in my hands, and looked into his shining golden eye.

"Maruman, darling heart, listen to me. There is no time for tantrums," I told him with stern tenderness. "I have to go ashore for many reasons, some of which are connected to my quest as ElspethInnle, but Gahltha is very frightened. I need you to go to him and help him to endure the storm. Will you do this for me?"

For a long moment, he looked into my eyes. Then, at last, he sent softly into my mind, "Maruman/yelloweyes will go to the Daywatcher. Be careful, ElspethInnle."

Outside, the wind had grown stronger, and now it was beginning to rain. A Sadorian, seeing me emerge, leaned into the wind and handed me the end of a rope, indicating that I should tie it around my waist. I obeyed and he made another gesture, which I did not understand, before hurrying off.

I made my unsteady way along the deck toward the main saloon, but the rope was too short and brought me to a sudden stop. I saw another rope end tied and coiled against the wall and realized the meaning of the Sadorian's gestures. He had been trying to tell me that I needed to move from one secured rope to another. I tied the new one about my waist, untied the other, and fastened it to the wall before continuing along the ship. Beyond the saloon, I could see the Sadorians unlashing the small ship boats, but there was no sign of Gwynedd or his men, so I untied the rope from my waist, curled it around a hook to which a number of other ropes were fastened, and entered the saloon.

Just as I passed through the doors, the ship tilted again. I flew into the room and fetched up hard against the end of a table. Lightning flared, giving me a brief glimpse of startled pasty faces turned toward me; then the ship tilted the other way, sending me staggering drunkenly backward. I would have reeled back through the doors, except that Brydda caught me and thrust a towel into my hands, shouting that he would get me an oiled coat.

I sat down, hooking one foot around a leg of the bench to steady myself, and dried my face. Looking around the long room, I saw Jak in the next flash of lightning, looking pale but composed. I had been astonished when Brydda had come to me after the meeting in the saloon and said that Jak would also travel with the three ship boats. The teknoguilder had apparently volunteered, pointing out rightly that he would have the best hope of recognizing and knowing how to dispose of the plague seeds if we found them.

It had been decided that any weapons on Norseland were most likely to be kept in the Hedra encampment in an armory, but it seemed likely that the plague seeds would be in Ariel's residence, unless he had taken them with him. Jak and I and several others would make our way there, leaving Gwynedd free to meet with the Norselanders and with their help mount an attack on the Hedra encampment.

We did not know the exact location of Ariel's residence, but I had heard enough on Herder Isle to know that it lay at the end of the island farthest from Fryddcove, and this meant that Uttecove must be closer to it than to the nearest settlement. From what Lark had told me, this would be Cloistertown. Gwynedd reckoned from the things I had told him that Ariel's residence would be no more than a two-hour walk in a straight line from Uttecove, but since we did not know where it was, it would be safer to follow the cliffs around, which would take somewhat longer.

In the meantime, Gwynedd intended to travel in a slanting line across the island from Uttecove to Cloistertown, where he would seek out the Per and raise a small force to lead him to the Hedra encampment. If all went as planned, the camp ought to be at least partly emptied out by Dardelan's provocations in Fryddcove. The greatest danger would be that the Hedra lured to the cliffs overlooking the cove might take Beforetime weapons with them, but Gwynedd thought these would not be used or even brought out unless the Hedra felt truly threatened, and it was unlikely that they would feel that way, faced with a single greatship.

I had asked how Gwynedd proposed to return to the ship, given that his plan involved setting up an army between him and the only way down to the beach in Fryddcove, and was told that once the Norselander and his men had destroyed the armory and seized the maps, they would await Jak and me outside Covetown with several high-ranking Hedra they would capture in the encampment. Once we joined them, I would coerce them, and then we all would dress in Hedra robes taken from the encampment and be marched by the coerced Hedra in full view of the Hedra ranks, down the path to the beach, ostensibly to relieve the Hedra posted at the bottom of the pass.

It was beautifully simple and daring. My only concern was that the Norselanders would be left to deal with an enraged nest of Hedra.

"Gwynedd is content to leave his people in the midst of a battle he has begun?" I had asked, somewhat indignantly, resisting the urge to add that it seemed to be a habit of his to begin things and then leave others to finish them.

But Brydda had pointed out that, before leaving, Gwynedd would have destroyed the armory as well as defeating a good many of the Hedra left in the camp, and he would have informed the Norselanders of the Hedra's defeat elsewhere. Besides, it was Gwynedd's belief that people should fight for their own freedom.

I had asked what Rushton had said to all of this. As we had guessed, he had elected to remain on the ship once he learned that I would accompany Gwynedd. Dardelan meant for Rushton to stay aboard the *Umborine*, but if he insisted on going ashore, he would be fed a draft of sleep potion. The solution's rough simplicity had made me laugh with relief.

Brydda reappeared with the promised coat and dragged me from my reflections to a renewed awareness of the storm-battered night. I had just taken the coat and began rising to pull it on, when the ship listed so far to one side that I fell back to my seat.

"Where is Rushton now?" I asked Brydda.

"Dardelan is keeping him occupied with the launching of the ship boats. He and Dardelan are planning various incendiary messages aimed at drawing out as many Hedra as possible from the camp. To begin with, Jakoby will signal a demand for surrender, claiming that Sador has been summoned by the rebels on Norseland. That will puzzle the priests sorely, since there is no rebel force upon Norseland, and even if there was some more rebellious element, how could they have contacted the Sadorians? The mystery should pique their curiosity. Then Jakoby will demand to speak with Ariel, pretending that he knows what it is about. The response will confirm whether or not Ariel has gone with Salamander, which we think is most likely."

I said nothing, for I had no doubt of it, now that I had heard of Maryon's futuretelling.

"How are we to get to the ship?" I asked as I had done the night before.

This time, Brydda had an answer. "The Per will send a signal up from Covetown, and upon seeing it, Dardelan will have the three large ship boats launched to collect us. In the meantime, Gwynedd plans to have the Norselanders mount an attack from the rear, to give us time to get aboard and weigh anchor."

Before I could say that leaving the Norselanders at the beginning of a battle we had incited left a bitter taste in my mouth, the doors to the saloon burst wide open, letting in a gust of rain-filled wind, and Gilbert stood in the open doorway, his red hair and side plaits streaming. "Gwynedd said anyone going ashore must come now or be left behind," he said hoarsely.

Twenty minutes later, I was in the first of the tiny ship boats to be lowered into the boiling sea. The wind and sea were slightly less ferocious, because we had reached the lee of the island, but even so, the fact that we were not immediately swamped or capsized was solely due to the skill of the Sadorian shipwoman maneuvering us toward the three rock pinnacles Gwynedd's mother had called the Staffs of the Goddess, saying they stood close to the entrance to the hidden inlet.

"Do you see the opening yet?" Gilbert bellowed to Gwynedd, who sat in the prow, squinting against the rain and the darkness.

The big Norselander shook his head without taking his eyes from the cliffs, and I clung to my seat and prayed that

Gwynedd's mother had not made a mistake. It was so dark, and rain was now falling so heavily that I could not even see the stone pinnacles I had glimpsed from the ship. I looked over my shoulder, trying to spot the other two ship boats, but the waves were so high that both were hidden at the bottom of troughs. Even the enormous *Umborine* was invisible, save for a few circles of golden light cast down by the lanterns fore and aft.

At last, I saw the three stone pinnacles just ahead, and I breathed a sigh of relief as the Sadorian shipwoman maneuvered the tiny vessel between them. Still I could see no sign of the inlet opening.

"If we go any closer and there is no opening, we will not be able to prevent the ship boat crashing into the cliff," Gilbert shouted.

The older man said nothing for a long moment, and then he pointed. "There!"

I strained my eyes, but only when lightning flared again did I see what looked like a fold or ripple in the cliff. The cove was not visible, because it could not be seen from straight on. It was literally a crack running sideways into the cliff, and it had to be approached from the side, from very close to the stone wall. Now, just as Gwynedd had warned, the ship boat was swept into a current that ran swift and straight toward the crevasse. Seeing the narrowness of the opening, I swallowed a lump of fear, but there was only ferocious concentration on the face of the Sadorian shipwoman whom Jakoby had assigned to master the tiny vessel.

"To port, pull hard now!" she commanded suddenly, and those of us on that side of the ship boat shot out our oars, dropped them into the water, and pulled hard. The boat hovered for a long moment before the prow swung around to point like the needle in a compass toward the opening.

"Watch out!" someone cried. I blinked to clear my eyes of rain. The entrance to the narrow channel seemed to be rushing toward us like a closing maw.

"Oars up *now*!" the shipwoman roared.

I pushed down hard on the oar, and suddenly—miraculously—the ship boat surged smoothly into the stone passage. The wind's keening was instantly muted, and the rain seemed to have ceased, but I knew it was only that the wind had preventing it falling into the narrow crevice. I fixed the oar in its upright position as Gwynedd, Gilbert, and the other armsmen were doing and turned to look behind us. There was no sign of the other vessels yet, and I prayed that those aboard were safe. I knew none of Gwynedd's men save Gilbert, but Jak had gone in the second ship boat and Brydda in the third.

The stone passage curved and then began to widen, and suddenly we entered an almost perfectly round cove with sheer rain-washed cliff walls. There was no sign of a sand or pebble beach, nor was there any sort of rock shelf where a landing could be made. I turned to look at Gwynedd, but he was calmly studying the cliffs. I followed his gaze and saw a wide opening at the base of the cliffs that would not be visible from above, but the sea flowed into it, and I could see no place to make a landing.

Gwynedd merely bade the Sadorian woman, whose name was Andorra, bring the ship boat into the cavern. As this was done, Gilbert lit a lantern, and its golden light revealed great white clusters of stalactites overhead, from which water dripped slowly but steadily into the heaving water filling the cavern. Gwynedd said nothing as the ship boat slipped deeper into the shadowy interior. Then, when the stalactites were almost brushing our heads, I heard the sound of waves breaking, and there before us was a beach of pale transparent pebbles that gleamed like yellow eyes in the lantern light.

As I climbed out onto the stones, I looked back the way we had come and saw the light of another lantern shining on the wet stalactites and cavern wall, and then one of the other ship boats hove into view. In a moment, Jak, another group of armsmen, and a Sadorian shipman were climbing from the ship boat.

We waited a half hour for the third ship, when Gwynedd swore ferociously and shook his head, saying it would have come by now.

"They might manage to swim in here if they capsized," Jak said.

The Norselander sighed. "They might, but we cannot wait, for the *Umborine* must even now be approaching Fryddcove. If the others survive, they will follow." He bade his men collect the packs that had been lashed into the ship boats, and then he turned and strode resolutely to the end of the beach, where there was an opening in the walls. We followed him and then stopped, because the tiny round cavern he had entered was barely big enough for a single solid man, let alone all of us. But when I put my head in, I saw that its roof was so high that the light from Gilbert's lantern could not find it; it was like a natural chimney.

"Where are the steps?" I asked Gwynedd.

"Look," he said, and bent down to run his hands over the sheer walls of the small circular cave at about knee height.

"What are you looking for?" I asked.

The Norselander stopped and pointed up. "Once, when the sea flowed here, this was a blowhole. Then a series of freakish tides deposited these pebbles that formed the beach where we made our landing and gave this place a floor."

"Are you saying this leads to the surface?" Jak demanded, looking up.

"That is exactly what I am saying," Gwynedd said. "If it was daylight or even a clear night, you would see the sky far above. The rain is not falling on us, because the wind is driving it across the mouth of the blowhole." Again he turned to the wall of the cavern and ran his hands over the stone. Suddenly he gave a grunt of triumph and began to pull pebbles and stone out of the wall so easily that I knew they must merely have been pressed into place. Gradually, he exposed a narrow recess. Then he felt around the wall and began to dig again. In a short time, he had exposed a number of steps cut into the rock.

"Let me do it," Gilbert said, and he exposed yet another step and then another above it.

"They go right to the top," Gwynedd said. "They are shallow, but put your back against the opposite wall and go up like that. Only these bottom few steps are filled in, and the few at the top. The rest cannot be seen looking up or down, so my mother said. She told me that the first time anyone used this way, there were no steps cut. It is called Voerligga's Path. Voerligga is the wise dwarf who serves the goddess Fryyd and sometimes intercedes for certain humans."

It took almost two hours for all of us to reach the top, and I came last save for the Sadorian man who had remained till the end in the hope that the other ship boat would arrive.

"Perhaps it missed the entrance and returned to the ship," I panted, but he made no response as we ascended.

It was an exhausting climb, and my legs were trembling with the exertion long before I reached the surface of the island. I was very glad to hear Gilbert call out my name and know that I was close to the top.

Gilbert and another armsman reached down to haul me out, and I gasped as the windy rain slapped at my face, only now realizing that the storm was still raging over the island. Jak pulled me down to my knees beside him, shouting to stay low because we were close to the edge of the cliffs surrounding Uttecove, and the wind was strong enough to send a person staggering to their death.

On my knees, I watched the others haul the Sadorian out and realized that nothing at all marked the steps save a small hole fringed in grass, which from even a short distance away would seem no more than a depression in the ground, dangerously close to the cliffs, and I no longer wondered why the Hedra had not discovered it.

"Time to go," Gwynedd said.

PART III

◆

THE HEARTLANDS

· 16 ·

I SAT BACK on my heels and squinted against the rain to study the terrain. Little was visible in the rainy darkness, but in the flashes of lightning, which seemed less frequent than they had been aboard the ship, I saw that the island was every bit as flat and featureless as I had been led to believe. Looking east, I could not see the rocky knoll upon which Ariel's residence was supposedly constructed or any other sign of human habitation. And when I looked west where Fryddcove was said to lie, I could not see the Hedra encampment, the cloister, or the town that spread out around the top of the trail leading up from Uttecove.

Then Gwynedd lay a hand on my shoulder and gave me a brief, unexpectedly warm smile, and told me that he had bidden the two Sadorians and Gilbert to accompany Jak and me to Ariel's residence.

"Take care, and remember, you must be in the boulders on the cliff outside Covetown by tomorrow night or the morning after, at the latest, or the ship will have to leave without you. Good luck," he told all of us, and turned to lead his armsfolk away along the cliff edge in the opposite direction.

After what seemed like hours of shouldering our way into the bullying, rain-filled wind over flat but infuriatingly uneven ground, I slipped on a patch of bare rock and went down hard enough on one knee to bring hot tears to my eyes. Cursing furiously, I stumbled on after the others, only slightly mollified by the fact that Jak and Gilbert were finding the way no easier. Ironically, the two Sadorians handled the terrain most gracefully, for though they were desert people, their shipboard training had accustomed them to slippery surfaces.

"Are you all right?" Gilbert asked, seeing that I had fallen behind. The rain was falling more heavily than ever, but the thunder and lightning had eased, so it was possible to talk.

"Bruised but hale," I said.

"It cannot be much farther to this knoll if the one spoken of on Herder Isle is the same one as the knoll Gwynedd's mother described to him," Gilbert assured me, and it warmed me slightly to see the smile I remembered from Henry Druid's secret encampment and not the dazzling superficial smile of recent days. But then his expression turned grim as he glanced about. "Trust Ariel to choose such a place for his home."

Gilbert's words reminded me that he had known Ariel, too, from the time he had spent in Henry Druid's secret encampment in the White Valley. But when I asked what he had thought of Ariel in those days, he shrugged, saying he had seen little of him. "It was my impression that he was not the sort to trouble with anyone he did not wish to make use of, and I had nothing he wanted. I do recall it being slyly said that he courted the Druid as much as his daughter. I mean Erin, not Gilaine. Little Gilly never liked him. No doubt her powers let her see his true nature."

I nodded, only wondering that Ariel's powers had not let him see what she was. On the other hand, perhaps Lidgebaby's powerful emanations had prevented Ariel from reaching the mind of any Misfit in the camp. I wondered how he had rationalized the net of mental static, for it must have impeded his coercive abilities even if his twisted Talent for empathy had been unaffected.

I thought again of Domick's words, realizing they had taken on a talismanic power for me: *"He does not see everything!"*

Gilbert had instinctively taken the lead when we set off, and now he called a halt. I was weary enough to be glad of it, but there was neither shelter nor any means of warming ourselves, so after a short time, we went on again. I was trying to steel myself for another long stumbling walk when Jak gave a cry and pointed out a dark square-edged plateau almost invisible against the cloud-clogged sky. It could only be the knoll we had been seeking, though I had been imagining a low round-topped mound rising not much higher than ground level. This knoll looked to be twice as high as a tall man, and I could discern no building upon it.

We were almost upon it before I realized that the stone knoll was no more than shoulder height, and the rest was a wall rising up from the edge of the knoll formed of stone blocks mortared snugly together. No light showed above it or through any of the spy slits. The rain prevented me from sending out a probe to search for watchers, but it would have been useless in any case due to the strength of the taint in the wall. This, more than anything else, assured me that this was Ariel's residence.

We followed the knoll until we came to a corner. I marveled at the fact that the mound was as squared off as the wall atop it. The angle was so sharp that I stopped to examine the knoll, expecting to find that it had been deliberately shaped to match the wall's corner, but there was neither chisel mark nor any sign that nature had *not* shaped the stone. Still pondering this, I rounded the corner and stopped to stare, for the wall that stretched away was at least twice as long as the one we had already paced out. We had not gone far along it before we came to a gate at the top of a set of steps hewn into the knoll.

Through the gate I could see a strange wide building, quite square, with a queer flat roof that ended abruptly at the walls like a giant box. I was reminded of the skyscrapers of the Beforetime laid down on their sides, for the building did not rise more than a single level above the ground. I no longer wondered if Salamander and his crew had stayed here, or if the slaves to be transported to the Red Queen's land were kept here, for why else build such a massive residence?

With no windows in the front, there was no way to see if the building was occupied, but to my surprise, Gilbert withdrew from his pack a Herder robe, donned it, then bade us stay back and went to hammer and shout at the gate. There was no response. Still warning us to keep back, he reached into his backpack and drew out a short metal bar with one end flattened to a wedge and the other tapered to a point. He pushed this into one of the gate hinges and heaved on it. There was a slight grinding sound, barely audible over the relentless hissing of the wind, and then with a snap, the metal gate sagged inward with a creak. Despite the tension of the moment, or maybe because of it, I found myself stifling the urge to laugh, for if faced with the same locked gates, I would have exhausted myself opening the lock, never thinking of attacking the hinge. *There is a lesson there,* I thought as Gilbert slipped through the gap.

When the rest of us would have followed, he held up a hand and shook his head, but Andorra made a clicking sound with her tongue. Gilbert looked back questioningly. She tapped her chest. He considered a moment, then nodded, and she slipped through the gap to join him, drawing a thick,

776

short-bladed knife from a hip sheath and carrying it point down like a great fang. They crossed the yard to the door at the front of the building, and Andorra pressed herself flat to the wall beside it, knife at the ready. Gilbert adjusted his sword and knocked loudly.

There was no response. I saw Gilbert reach for the handle of the door and all at once I remembered the premonition I had experienced at the door to Ariel's chamber in the Herder Compound. I gave a roar and raced across the yard.

Gilbert swung around in surprise, and I gasped out an explanation. Then he and Andorra stood back as I laid my hand over the lock. To my relief, it was merely a rather simple lock, so I focused my mind to turn the tumblers and opened the door.

It was too dark to see anything. I stepped inside and sent out a general probe. Then I turned to Gilbert and Andorra, who had entered behind me. "Either there is no one here or someone is trying to make it seem so. There are just two places I can't probe."

Gilbert nodded and knelt to remove a lantern from his pack; then he rummaged for a tinderbox with which to light it. Andorra had gone to summon Jak and the Sadorian man, and they arrived just as the lantern wick caught. We all stared about at the room we had entered. There was not a piece of furniture and no rug on the floor or hanging upon the stone walls, but there was a large hearth where a fire had been laid but not lit and three doors other than the front one. Gilbert went to light the fire, for we were all wet and shivering with cold. I sent out a probe again. Still there was nothing, but I had not truly expected to find anyone.

"The place seems empty," Gilbert said, regarding the fire critically before prodding two pieces of wood into different positions. Then he looked up at me and frowned. "You'd better stay here and thaw out a bit. You too," he said to Jak. "The Sadorians and I will take one of those doors each and make a preliminary search of the place?" He phrased it as a question, and the Sadorians nodded as one. After they had gone, I turned back to the fire.

"Take off the coat so the heat can get to you," Jak said through chattering teeth, removing his own. I obeyed, and he took both and hung them on hooks by the hearth. Then he rummaged in his own bag and withdrew a wide metal pan and a small pot, which he carried outside.

"It will take hours to fill them," I protested. "Surely there is a supply of water in this place."

"I have set them under a downpipe from the roof," Jak said mildly, squatting down and stretching his hands out to the flames. "We will certainly need something to warm us after we search this building. It is a queer chilly place to call home, I must say, yet mayhap it matches the strange cold shape of Ariel's soul."

I stared down at him, startled to hear a teknoguilder wax poetic. Then I turned, too, and squatted to be closer to the flames. It would be some time before the fire emitted much real heat, but the brightness was heartening. Shortly, Gilbert and the Sadorians returned to say they had found nothing to suggest that the building was inhabited. I was ready to begin searching, but Jak said he would make some porridge, for we would all search the better for eating. I disliked wasting time, but I was hungry, and I was as glad as the others to accept a bowl and devour it.

Warmed inside and out, we were then ready to begin searching in earnest. As we ate, Jak had told us what we ought to be looking for. Now he warned us very seriously to touch nothing and summon him if we found anything that looked like a room a healer might use or perhaps a dye worker or even a candle or perfume maker.

We split into two parties, for one of the passages leading back from the entrance had led only to a door that opened into an enormous rain-swept courtyard. Jak would take one of the other passages with the Sadorian man, named Hakim, while Andorra and I would take the third with Gilbert, who had found a store of lanterns and oil for us to carry.

"What bothers me is where the servants are," Gilbert said as we walked along the hall. We did not bother opening any doors, because he had already checked this area.

"I suppose Ariel dismissed them when he left," I said, "though it seems it would have been too far for people from Cloistertown to travel each day. Maybe they stayed here. There are certainly bedchambers and common chambers enough for an army of servants. He might also have used the nulls. That is what he did on Herder Isle."

We reached a turn in the passage where Gilbert looked back to say that henceforth we must search, for this was as far as he had got earlier. Gilbert moved ahead, saying Andorra should check one side of the corridor and I the other.

To begin with, every door I opened belonged to a bedchamber, but unlike those closer to the front door, these had locks and, therefore, must be slave accommodations. Each chamber was as bare as most of the rooms and halls, equipped with a bed, chest, shelves, and a mat on the floor. I flipped over each mat until Gilbert noticed and asked me why. I told him that I was looking for trapdoors, and he reminded me that the whole place was built on a great raft of solid rock.

As we continued, I found myself thinking of Domick and

Rushton, who must also have traversed these halls. Had they been conscious, walking with their hands chained behind their backs, or had they simply awakened in cells? Long ago I had experienced a vision of Domick in a cell, and I was suddenly convinced that cell was here. I shivered, profoundly glad that Rushton was safely aboard the *Umborine*.

Thoughts of the ship turned my attention to Brydda and the Sadorian who had mastered the third ship boat and the rest of Gwynedd's armsfolk ashore. I could only pray that they had merely missed the entrance and had returned to the greatship. How would I tell Brydda's parents if he perished? How would I bear his loss?

Then I thought of Gwynedd, wondering if he and the others had reached Cloistertown safely, and what sort of reception the Per had given them. Brydda had told me that Gwynedd had no intention of revealing that he was kin to the last Norse king unless he needed to induce the Norselanders to help him. I could not help but wonder why he imagined they would believe him, but according to Brydda, the Norselander had no doubts on that account.

Gilbert and Andorra were walking more quickly than I, and a little pool of darkness had opened between our lanterns. I hastened to catch up as the horrible thought crept into my mind that, despite my certainty of Ariel's departure from Norseland, I had no proof of it. I might come face to face with Ariel here as I had done so often in the dark and twisting passages of my dreams.

"Come to me," he had whispered many times. And now I had.

An hour later, I opened a door to a large bare dining chamber containing a long trestle and some twenty unadorned and uncushioned chairs. It was the second I had seen, but the first had been a smaller and far more luxuriously appointed room with a thick red rug on the floor and embroidered chairs. There had also been two sitting rooms, one as large and bare as this dining chamber and another about half its size, with soft couches and embroidered chairs with beaded cushions. It looked as if Ariel used the bare rooms to entertain his official guests and kept the smaller more lavish versions for his own use.

"Come and look at this," Gilbert murmured, beckoning. Andorra and I joined him at an open door to see a lavish bedchamber filled with every conceivable color, texture, and ornament, as well as every conceivable comfort.

"Which of them used this one, I wonder?" Gilbert murmured, gazing at the bed hung with scarlet Sadorian double silk with golden embroidery.

I said nothing, but I thought it must belong to Salamander, for Ariel had always preferred to wear white clothing that set off his pale golden beauty. Whoever had slept in this room had wished to ravish his senses with beautiful fabrics and textures. An array of exquisite cut crystal bottles sat atop the hearth's mantel. I opened one, and the sweet heady smell of pure incense filled the air. Replacing the stopper, I noticed that the fire was made up here just as it had been in the entrance chamber, and I wondered what this meant. The only reason I could think of for the carefully prepared hearths was that Ariel's departure had been sudden and unplanned.

I noticed a book lying half hidden under the golden fringe of the bed covering and bent to pick it up. I was astonished to see that the words on the cover were in the coiling gadi script that I had first seen on the carved panels of Obernewtyn's original doors. Since the Sadorians never scribed in gadi, this book must have belonged to the Gadfian raiders who had preyed upon them. If I was right, this was surely evidence that they had not died out. Indeed, it seemed proof that there were still Gadfians somewhere with whom Salamander had some commerce that resulted in his acquiring a gadi-built ship.

A thought came to me that was so shocking it took my breath away. What if Salamander had not just traded with the Gadfian raiders *but was one of them!* What if he hid his face and form as fanatically as he did, not to keep his identity secret, but to hide the color of his skin! This would explain not only the resemblance between the *Black Ship* and the Sadorian spicewood ships, but also the slaver's relentless viciousness, since ferocity and the need to oppress seemed characteristic of the Gadfian people.

I slipped the book into the bag I carried over my shoulder, thinking that when I was back aboard the *Umborine*. I would show the book to Jakoby and see what she made of my theory.

"Ye gods!" Gilbert muttered.

He had opened the door to a cupboard, and I went to see what had made him sound so astounded. Looking over his shoulder, I saw that the clothes on the shelves were not men's. I reached into the cupboard and drew out a long gown of roughened silk, beaded in an exquisite pattern that mimicked the intricate shadings of some strange large-eared feline.

"One of them must have kept a woman," Gilbert muttered. "An *expensive* woman. I suppose she went with them when they left."

"Sandcats," Andorra said, fingering the silk. "They live in the desert lands, and they are mad."

"There are sandcats near Murmroth, too," Gilbert said. He stooped to pick something up off the floor. "Here is another one." He opened his hand to reveal a small silver clasp fashioned into the likeness of a sandcat. It was a pretty, intricate piece and positioned so that only one eye showed—a tiny yellow topaz.

"It is one-eyed, like your cat friend," Gilbert said. "Why don't you keep it?"

I was revolted by the thought of stealing something that had belonged to Ariel or Salamander, but instead of putting it down, I found myself looking at the brooch again. Finally, I slipped it into my bag with the book. It did remind me of Maruman, but it was the exquisite craftsmanship, not the design, that made me take it, for such work might be tracked back to its source.

"You know what troubles me," Gilbert said after we left the chamber. "I can't see any woman leaving all those beautiful, expensive clothes and gewgaws if she was never coming back again."

"Maybe they didn't give her time to pack," I said. "Or maybe she knows there is more where this came from and did not mind leaving it. Whoever lavished all of this on her was hardly going to keep her wanting."

As we continued, I remembered that when Salamander had first appeared in the Land, there had sometimes been mention of a beautiful woman who spoke for him. Perhaps the room belonged to this woman, in which case she might be more of an accomplice than merely an object of love or desire.

I farsent Jak to tell him what we had found, and he told me that he and Hakim had discovered some animal pens, their size and stink suggesting they had recently been occupied by dogs. He sounded subdued and uneasy, and I knew that he was remembering that Ariel had taken particular delight in using brutal and sadistic methods to train dogs to kill.

As I withdrew from Jak's mind, Gilbert beckoned to me. He looked into a smallish chamber with a single large comfortable chair set facing an enormous window that overlooked the large central courtyard. Just outside the window stood a beautiful ravaged tree, which had either lost all its leaves to the savage wind or was dead.

"Looks like some sort of contemplation room," Gilbert said, nodding to the chair. He shivered and I realized my own teeth were again chattering with cold. Gilbert suggested returning to the entrance chamber to warm ourselves, but Andorra gestured to a small hearth where yet another fire had been laid. I lit it while Andorra went back to raid a clothes cupboard she had seen, and Gilbert found two more chairs. He set all three to face the fire, but instead of sitting down, the armsman went to the window to gaze at the twisted black form of the tree outside. "A grim sort of place to plant a tree," he muttered. "The soil would have to have been brought in, and the tree would never be able to put down deep roots. No wonder it died."

My heart sank as he looked over to where I sat, for his eyes were full of yearning. I had thought our earlier conversation had ended any hopes he might have harbored, but clearly it was not so. I willed Andorra to return, for there was an intimacy in this small room that might better be avoided. Then I decided that it was cowardly to avoid being alone with the armsman, given that I had accepted Gilbert's sincere offer of friendship.

"I meant what I told you aboard the ship," I said, wishing that embarrassment would not render my tone so harsh.

He smiled sadly. "I know it. Only what I feel is not so easily set aside. But I will not trouble you with any declarations.

I, too, meant what I said aboard the ship." He hesitated and said, "This might be a good moment to confess that I asked Gwynedd to send me with you."

"Why?" I asked.

He shrugged and said lightly, "Let us say that I am not too proud or foolish to see that half a loaf of good bread is still nourishing." But immediately his expression became serious. "No, I speak too flippantly, a habit I am trying to break. You are far from half a loaf, Elspeth Gordie. What you have done is the stuff of tales told over and over around firesides; they set the hearts of everyone who hears them to racing and dreaming. In truth, I never had any right to aspire to you. What you did before—opening that lock and then reaching out with your mind to Jak—I realize you would never be satisfied with an ordinary man like me."

I felt my face flame and wished he would stop. This was far worse than any declaration of love! I tried to get up, but he caught my hand. "Please, let me speak."

I expelled a breath and said urgently, "Listen, most of my life I have been in danger of being burned for the Talents you seem to feel are special. I don't think that I am better than you."

"I think it," he said flatly, and released me. "Yesterday afternoon, after we had spoken, I thought of my bondmate, Serra. I began to wonder if perhaps the mystery she had wanted from me was no more than the part of me that I had laid to rest when I thought I saw you die. Maybe she understood that I was withholding the best of myself, not only from her but from my children. I had felt myself cheated by life when I thought you had been snatched away from me. I never considered that you had not been mine in the first place. I got it into my head that you had been my shining destiny, and

785

your loss was another example of the ill luck that had dogged me all my life.

"But lying in my cabin last night, with the storm raging outside, I thought of all you had said, and suddenly I saw everything from another angle. I was not unlucky. Indeed, luck has walked beside me constantly. My mother died birthing me, but I lived. My father was a good and honest man who loved me, though I had killed his beloved bond-mate. I was away from the Druid's camp when the firestorm struck, so I was one of the few to survive. A plague came to the west coast, but I was not infected, and when there was the possibility of a second plague, which none would have survived, you prevented its spread. What have I to complain about? Nothing. I had acted like a spoiled child who could not have a toy that did not belong to him in the first place. I petulantly locked up all that was good in me. But last night in the midst of that raging storm, it occurred to me that I might die. That was when I realized that it was not too late to become a whole man again."

"What will you do?" I asked to break a silence stretched too thin.

"I will continue to serve Gwynedd, for he gave me a purpose, and I owe it to him to fulfill it."

"Are not children also a purpose that ought to be fulfilled?" I said softly.

He smiled. "They ought to be," he said. "Maybe it is not too late for that as well."

"You will go back?"

"I will see if their mother will give me a second chance. Maybe she will finally meet the man you met in the Druid's camp, if he can be brought back to life."

"I see him now," I said.

He held my eyes a moment, and the silence between us became easy. When Andorra returned, he went out to let us change our clothes. I was grateful for the thick silk shirt and the gray felt tunic and shawl. Once dressed, I farsought Jak again and found that he and Hakim had discovered a kitchen and were also lighting a fire. He added that they had found more yards and some animal pens with bench seats in them. I shivered and withdrew from his mind, chilled at the thought of the hapless people who had been brought here and penned up to await whatever fate had in store for them.

"You are looking grim," Gilbert said as he reentered the room.

I was telling them both what Jak had said when we heard a distant crash.

"What was that?" Gilbert said.

Andorra had drawn her knife and was listening hard, too, her head tilted. "It sounded like it came from the other side of the building," she said.

"Wait," I said. Closing my eyes, I farsought Jak. The probe located tenuously, as if there were too many walls between us or maybe one of the rainy courtyards.

"Did you hear that noise?" I farsent.

"We caused it," Jak told me. "We found a trapdoor in the storeroom beside the kitchen, but it exploded when I tried to open it. I'm bleeding, but Hakim was knocked out."

"What is it?" Gilbert demanded when I opened my eyes.

I told them, and we put a screen around the fire and hurried along the corridors.

"If there was a trapdoor in the floor, there must be some sort of underground chamber," Gilbert said.

"You said that it would be impossible, given that this place is built upon solid rock," I protested.

"I did, but why else would there be a trapdoor?" Gilbert asked. "The Beforetimers might have done it. After all, if they could truly fly through the air, it would be nothing to cut chambers out of stone."

"Why do you speak of Beforetimers?" I asked, slowing to stare at him. "Ariel built this place."

He shrugged. "I assume that this place is built on Beforetime ruins. After all, Gwynedd said his mother told him this knoll was cursed, and that is usually what people mean when they use that word," Gilbert said. "I suppose it was they who honed the knoll to make it square."

✦ 17 ✦

"THIS IS DEFINITELY Beforetimer work," Jak said, his voice trembling with excitement. His forehead and face were badly cut, and one of the gashes was so close to his eye that he was lucky he had not been blinded. Andorra, who had announced that she had some simple training in healing, was examining the teknoguilder, having checked that the still unconscious Hakim was otherwise unharmed. The force of the explosion had knocked him out. Now she announced that Jak had a cut on his shoulder and another on his chest that needed stitches, but he had brushed her away.

"The explosion looks as if it was the result of some sort of Beforetime device, but Ariel definitely knew of the trapdoor, because, as you see, the storage space has been carefully constructed around the trapdoor so it would not be blocked, but in such a way that it would be hard to see if you just glanced in. If I had not been scrounging for food, I would not have noticed it."

I studied the hatch, which, despite being blackened and slightly buckled, remained intact. It looked very similar to the trapdoor that Pavo and I had opened to enter the upper level of the Beforetime ruins on the west coast, and I had no doubt that Ariel knew about its existence. It might very well be the reason he had constructed his residence here. But the question that remained was if he had ever managed to open it.

As if he had read my thoughts, Jak said, "This could be where Ariel got the plague seeds." He looked at me. "Do you think you can open it?"

"Now wait just a minute," Gilbert protested. "Two people have already been hurt trying to open it, and who is to say what will happen if Elspeth tries. We have heard talk of Beforetime weapons capable of destroying cities!"

I thought of the prickling premonition I had experienced upon Herder Isle when I had touched the door to Ariel's chambers. "I will know if there is that sort of danger," I said. I lay my hands on the lock and was surprised it felt warm. I looked around at the others—Jak's eager face; Andorra, with her inscrutable expression that showed neither fear nor apprehension but only a profound watchfulness; and Gilbert.

"Trust me," I said softly. A nerve worked in his jaw, but he gave a jerky nod. I closed my eyes and probed the lock mechanism, striving to understand it. I had never encountered anything so complex, and it took only a moment to know that it was beyond me. "I can't understand how it works, so I can't open it," I said.

Gilbert expelled a breath and even Andorra relaxed somewhat, but Jak moved closer and knelt down beside me, unaware that blood was running down his neck and soaking into his collar. I had lifted my hand from the lock, and now he laid his own over it. "Go through my mind," he said. "Use my knowledge. Dell has done it before and Merret, too."

I stared at him in wonderment and realized that, of course, it would be possible.

But Gilbert caught my wrist. "What are you doing?" he demanded. "We are here to seek out the plague seeds."

"We are," Jak said. "And this is likely where Ariel found them. It is my guess that the door was not closed when he opened it the first time, but it has been closed since."

I gently but firmly removed my wrist from Gilbert's grip and then lay my hand atop Jak's. I closed my eyes and entered the teknoguilder's mind. Jak had drawn all of his knowledge and experience of complex Beforetime mechanisms to the surface of his conscious thoughts, and I roved over them until I came to something that might work. Instead of withdrawing, I reached from inside Jak's mind to the lock under our hands, drawing his awareness with me. I felt his fascinated attention as I probed the lock, and then I sharpened my focus into a physical force.

"There will be a current of energy that you must break." Jak's voice sounded oddly like the disembodied voice of Ines. This made me realize that there might be another Beforetime complex under the stone knoll, operated by a computer-machine with the same Ines program! Jak heard the thought, and his excitement almost dislodged my mind from the lock, but I strengthened my shield, found the current he meant, and broke it.

"That was . . . Your mind is so strong!" the teknoguilder gasped. He broke off as the metal hatch hissed and loosened.

Gilbert breathed a sigh of relief and ordered all of us back while he opened it. He closed his hands around the two grips set into the trapdoor and pulled. It opened smoothly to reveal a ladder going down into darkness. I relaxed fractionally, having been half prepared for another explosion.

"I wonder how far it goes," Jak murmured. He had been looking into the black abyss, and we all froze as his words echoed into the darkness, fading at last to a soft hoot.

"No mere cellar ever gave out an echo like that," Gilbert said.

"I will go," said Andorra. She hooked her lantern over her arm and began to climb down the ladder. We all watched her descend, the lantern light illuminating no more than the section of the ladder before and after her.

"What do you see?" Jak called impatiently after a time. Echoes of his shout filled the air, sounding and resounding for a long time before fading. Andorra had frozen, and at last she looked up, her eyes shining in the immense darkness. "I can see no end to the ladder, but it holds firm, so it must be fixed to the ground below."

She had spoken softly, but the darkness was filled with hissing echoes of her words. She began to descend again.

Jak said decisively, "I'm going after her." He, too, hooked his lantern over his arm and began to climb down. Then he looked up at me. "Are you coming?"

"I don't think this is a good idea," Gilbert said. His face was pale with a greenish tinge about his mouth.

"It's not a good idea for all of us to go," I said calmly. "You stay here and keep watch over Hakim." Then I took my own lantern and went down the steps. Jak was descending slowly below me, and at least thirty steps below him I could just make out Andorra still climbing downward in a pool of lantern light. Our footsteps set up a ringing echo.

On and on we climbed through that vast void of darkness until my fingers ached from clinging to the rungs, and my legs, which were still sore from the climb to the surface of the island, now ached from lowering myself step by step. Eventually I heard my name and looked down to see that Jak had reached a small metal platform fixed to the ladder. Andorra had continued her descent, but I joined Jak, holding tightly to the rails.

"What is this place?" I panted, speaking as quietly as I

could. Even so, my voice produced a rustling of whispers.

Jak shrugged, his face shining with perspiration in the light shed by our lanterns. The blood had dried to a line of black against his pale skin. "It could be a missile silo chamber, though I cannot see how, with this ladder cutting through it. Unless the missile was designed to fly out at an angle from the side of the island."

"What is a missile?" I asked.

"It is a Beforetime weapon. A fearsome flying weapon that could be made to go where its master desired and destroy what it was bidden to destroy. Such weapons were capable of destroying cities much greater than Sutrium or Aborium."

"You think we are climbing down to such a weapon?" I asked, feeling a thrill of terror.

But he shook his head. "I think that we are climbing down to a nest devoid of its deadly egg," Jak said. Without further ado, he stepped back onto the ladder and began to descend again. Before following, I glanced up and saw that the opening was a tiny square of light where I could see a movement that might have been Gilbert, watching.

I had just begun climbing down again when there was a shout from below. It was Andorra, who had finally reached the end of the ladder. It took Jak and me a long time to join her and see that she had not, after all, reached the bottom of the void but only a narrow metal bridge passing over the void to darkness in two directions.

"Which way?" Andorra asked.

Jak looked at me. "We could split up and go both ways."

Andorra gave him a look that told me the tribeswoman was trying to decide if Jak was fearless or simply a fool. "What is this place?" she asked.

Jak told her what he had told me, adding, "I think this path will lead us to the place where there are controls that would have propelled the missile from an opening in the side of the island."

"Surely plague seeds would not be kept in the same place as a flying weapon?" I asked, suddenly wishing I could simply climb out of the suffocating chill of a darkness that must surely contain some of the malevolence of the monstrous weapon that once rested here.

"On the contrary, it may be that the weapon was designed to carry plague seeds to some land or city," Jak said. "I'll know more once we reach wherever this path leads." He glanced back at me and grimaced. "It is a pity whoever built this did not consider an elevating chamber."

I controlled an urge to snarl at him for his easy acceptance of such horrors and asked, "Is it likely there would be a computermachine program like Ines running this place? And *if* there is, could you talk to it? Ask it where the plague seeds are?"

"I could if the program was sent to sleep as our Ines was, and if its name is the code to awaken it as in the ruins outside Aborium, but the likelihood of that is so slender as to be almost an impossibility," Jak said. Without waiting for my response, he said firmly and clearly, "Ines, can you hear me?" Echoes of his question rang out and whispered and finally rustled to silence. But there was no answer. "In fact, I do not think we will find such a program here, because Govamen was virtually the only organization capable of affording such a complex program, and I do not think this place belonged to them."

"I thought govamens controlled all of the weapon-machines," I said.

"Most, but certainly not all. And although they usually

concealed their most dangerous caches of weapons in remote locations, Govamen weapon stores were always bristling with all sorts of defenses and protections to make sure no one entered unless authorized. Even the attempt to enter such a place could be deadly, for once a person got part of the way in, the system would not allow her to withdraw, and if a person was unable to give all the correct codes and responses, the entry programs might have the capacity to injure or kill."

"Were they so afraid people would wish to steal their weapons?" I asked.

"Not people. Other govamens. You see, each of the great powers had a govamen, and each govamen hated and feared the others. In addition to producing terrible weapons with which to threaten the other powers, they lived in mortal fear that those weapons would be stolen and used against them. What kept them from attacking one another was what they called the 'balance of fear,' which some called the 'balance of power'; that is, the fact that all the great govamens had terrible weapons. You must imagine five warriors who wish to kill one another, but they each have a sword and are skilled in its use, so they can only watch one another, none daring to move on another for fear that one of the others might attack them."

"Madness, for in the end, someone did attack," Andorra said.

I said nothing, knowing that this fear of the govamens had led to the decision to create a computermachine program that would hold the balance of power over all govamens, with its ability to retaliate against any one of them that aggressed against the rest by summoning up weaponmachines so powerful that they had been called BOT, the Balance of Terror. Their creation had been part of the Sentinel project, run by Cassy

Duprey's father, only something had gone wrong. Maybe, as Andorra had suggested, one of the five powers had attacked the other, or maybe there had been an accident and the BOT arsenal had been unleashed, causing the Great White and bringing the Beforetimers and their world to a deadly end. And it was those same BOT weaponmachines that the Seeker was to find and disable forever.

"Elspeth?" Jak said.

"We are wasting time," I said. "Let's go left."

We set off again, Jak and Andorra walking ahead of me, and my thoughts drifted back to what Jak had been saying. I was certain the "keys" Cassy had left were to enable me to negotiate the defenses with which Sentinel would protect the BOT weaponmachines and that once I reached them, I would have to shut down the program that controlled BOT so it could never awaken the weaponmachines. It was even possible that some long-dead human had left Sentinel sleeping like Ines, ready to wake at the right word or phrase, and all I might have to do, once I had reached the right place, would be to command it to sleep or to switch itself off. Would a computermachine be capable of destroying what must effectively be part of itself? A human would be afraid, but a computermachine did not feel; therefore, if the command was put in the correct way, it ought simply to obey.

Jak uttered an exclamation, and I saw that the metal bridge had reached the gray stone wall of the immense cavern, where it joined a metal walk running away in both directions. Right where the bridge ended was a gray metal door set into the stone.

"Raw stone," Jak murmured, laying his hand on it. "This is a natural cavern." He held up his lantern and looked one way and then the other along the stone wall. "The wall curves

796

inward in both directions." He turned to face the bridge we had walked across. "I think that this leads to the other side of the cavern and this walk goes the whole way round the outside."

"But what would be the point of that?" I asked, imagining a vast black hole circled and halved by a path.

"I don't know," Jak admitted. "Let's see if this door can be opened."

The door had no visible lock or handle, but the lantern light revealed a rectangular indentation in the metal. Jak reached out without hesitation and laid his hand upon it.

The door gave a click and then the same long hiss as the latch above before sliding into the wall as smoothly as the split door of the elevating chamber in the ruins complex. Andorra gazed fearfully into the dark chamber it had revealed.

"It is only a door and one without even a lock," Jak told her, and he stepped through it into the chamber, holding his lantern up high.

Heart thumping, I stepped through the door after him and found that the floor was soft and almost spongy underfoot, while around the walls were metal lockers. Jak opened one to reveal a number of suits made of some sort of thin plast, and I wondered if these were the same as the one Jacob Obernewtyn had left for Hannah.

Jak had moved to the end of the chamber, and now he said excitedly, "Another door." As he set his hand to it, I turned to see that Andorra was still standing on the metal path looking in at us. The whites of her eyes showed, and I asked, "Andorra, will you follow the path around and see if there are any other doors?"

She nodded and disappeared, and I turned to follow Jak, pondering limits. Andorra was certainly braver and more stoic than I was, yet she feared entering these chambers of the dead, just as Gilbert had feared to enter the gaping darkness below the latch. *What is my limit?* I wondered.

Jak had entered a chamber that was double the size of the first one, and running its full length on either side were immense bathing cabinets such as the one I had used in the ruins complex.

"You see how it was?" Jak said eagerly. "They would enter and remove their plast suits, and then they would come here and bathe." He looked back and saw my bafflement. "I doubt this place was built as a shelter, but whoever made it felt that it could be used as one."

As he spoke, he went to the door at the other end and opened it. Again it slid away, and he passed through it without hesitation. I steeled myself to follow him. The next chamber had several open doorways that led, we swiftly found, to a kitchen and dining hall and to several small bedchambers. I marveled at the thought of people being so afraid of the weapons they had created that they would build and stock such shelters. Why hadn't they simply opposed the building of the weaponmachines in the first place? Surely all govamens in the Beforetime were not oppressive and controlling? But then I thought of Cassy's Tiban lover, killed because he had been opposed to the closed borders and internal practices of Chinon, and Cassy's mother saying that she would not be permitted to speak out against their govamen, and I wondered how different their world had really been from ours.

I turned to say as much to Jak and discovered that he had vanished. I called his name and heard a muffled reply. I followed him, pointing out crossly that we could not go on exploring endlessly, but my words faded when I found him in a small, shiny black room sitting behind the screen of a computermachine. There were other machines and more screens covering the wall behind the computermachine, as well as panels of levers and colored squares, but all were dark and lifeless. Jak held up his lantern to illuminate the lettered squares, and then he began to tap at them, his brow furrowed in concentration. Nothing happened, and he gave a sigh of anguished frustration. "I might be able to figure out how to make it work, given time, but as it is . . ."

"As it is, we are here to find plague seeds," I said firmly. "And in case you haven't noticed, these lanterns are running out of oil."

Jak looked at his lantern with the startled air of one waking from a dream. Then he got to his feet. "All right, let's split up and make a proper search. If there are plague seeds here, they will be in some sort of secure storage place—a small metal box or some sort of sealed cabinet. It will probably have a symbol on it: yellow and black triangles or a red circle with a slash through it. You try through that door on the left, and I will go through the other one." He gestured to two doors, one alongside the other. Then he opened one and passed through it into the swallowing darkness beyond.

I took a deep breath and went through the other door into another room of shining black surfaces, but instead of being square, this chamber had many sides like the edges of a cut stone. It was empty, and I ran my hand along one of the smooth panels, wondering about the room's purpose. Then I noticed that light from the lantern was penetrating the dark shining wall.

I held the lantern closer and saw that the panel was made of thick dark glass, behind which was an empty compartment. I looked at the next panel and saw that it was the same. I examined the glass surface and found a recessed hand shape. There was one in each panel. Heart beating fast, I held my hand above one of the recesses and listened to my inner self for any prickle of premonition. Feeling nothing, I pressed my hand into the recess. There was a click and a hiss, and the segment of glass slid far enough up that I could see into the compartment behind it. It was empty. I pressed my hand to the same place and immediately the glass slid back into place. I went to the next glass segment and discovered another empty compartment. I stepped back and turned slowly around, realizing the place bore a strong resemblance to the healing chambers in the ruins complex. Perhaps this was also some sort of healing complex, but the compartments were much smaller and lacked beds.

I examined the compartment that I had left open and saw holes in the floor. Not a healing chamber, perhaps, but some sort of cage. The compartments were too small to fit a human, even a human child. Small beasts, then? Maybe whoever had built this place had intended to save some beasts from the Great White. I reached into the compartment and jumped as a dim red glow filled it. As soon as I snatched my hand back, the light was immediately extinguished.

I went after Jak, wanting to show him the compartments. I could not see his lantern light and realized with a sinking heart that I would have to go deeper. I stepped into the next chamber and found it identical to the one I had been in, save that it was bigger and so were the glass panels and the compartments behind them. Still there were no beds, so perhaps these had been intended for larger animals.

I called Jak's name, and when he did not answer, I went through the next door, only to find myself in yet another room full of glass compartments. This was bigger again than the other rooms, and at its center stood a long metal table. Fixed to one end of the table was a phalanx of computermachines and screens. Memory stirred, and I went to the metal table and touched its cold surface. Suddenly I remembered the table I had been bound to when Ariel and Alexi had used the Zebkrahn machine on me in an attempt to learn the location of the weaponmachines that had caused the Great White.

I turned to look around at the glass compartments and was suddenly and absolutely certain that Ariel had been here, and *this* was where he had brought Domick and Rushton. Fighting a suffocating sense of horror, I went to open one of the glass compartments. Seeing the bare space with its holed floor, I suddenly understood. This was not a healing center; it was a torture chamber.

There was another door at the end of the room. I went to it and opened it merely to escape the horror blooming in my mind, but the chamber beyond was little more than a room full of small metal lockers. I was about to turn away when I noticed a door marked with a yellow and black symbol, above which was a circle with numbers scribed on it. I went into the chamber and saw a lock on the door, but there was no need to open it, for there was a panel of glass set into the metal door. I knelt and held the lantern close to the glass, pressing my face against it, the better to see. I fell back at once, for the surface of the glass gave off such a fierce coldness that I felt as if I had been burned. Rubbing my cheek, I leaned close to the window again, being careful not to touch its surface. I lifted the lantern and its light shone on rack after rack of tiny bottles containing glistening liquids of various colors.

I had no doubt that I had found what we had come for, and I sat back on my heels, wondering if all the ghastly weapons and devices that the Beforetimers had created had been no more than the result of the same voracious, single-minded curiosity as that which motivated Jak or any teknoguilder. I had never thought of curiosity as bad, yet if it could quench fear, perhaps it could also quench a person's morality.

The lantern flame began to gutter, and I thought that I must have tilted it, swamping the wick, but when I looked into the reservoir, I was horrified to see that it was almost empty. Suddenly I was horribly aware of the darkness and the many doors and steps that lay between me and the stony, storm-scoured surface of Norseland. I might have panicked if I had not recently been lost in a Beforetime complex. This memory enabled me to control my fear and rise to hurry back through the chambers. If I could find Jak swiftly, we could pool our remaining oil, seek out Andorra, and take hers as well. That ought to be enough to get us back to the surface.

I shouted his name through the door he had taken, but there was no response. Perhaps his lantern had already run out and he had lost his way. I tried farseeking him, but as I had feared, there was too much thick metal between us for the probe to locate and too little oil remained in my lantern to go searching for him. I had to find Andorra. I hurried through the chambers to the metal path and was horrified to remember that I had bidden her investigate the path to see if there were other doors. I peered out into the fathomless blackness, searching for her lantern's telltale glow, but I could see nothing.

Either the light was too weak or she had already run out of oil. Cursing our foolishness, I was about to shout to her when I heard a muffled scream. It had come from above, but it broke into a thousand echoes that filled the void and seemed as if there were hundreds of people screaming for help. Even after the screams had faded to whispers, I still stood rooted to the spot, my heart hammering against my ribs with sickening force. I told myself savagely not to be a fool. Andorra had probably noticed that she was running out of oil and had stumbled on the way up the ladder to replenish her lantern. Or maybe she had seen my lantern light and had called out something that the echoes had transformed into a scream. I gathered myself to broach that black void with a call, but before I could utter it, *I heard a low, rumbling growl.*

Every hair on my body stood on end as I thought of the kennels that Jak and Hakim had seen, for it would be so like Ariel to leave some poor dog here to go mad with hunger and thirst. I backed into the chamber of lockers and searched frantically about the door for a means of closing it, but I could find nothing. The lantern flame was guttering wildly, and again I heard another growl. My nerve broke and I fled back through chamber after chamber, knowing that I could always shut myself into one of the glass compartments. Just as I reached the chamber of large compartments, the lantern went out.

I stopped dead, shocked at the complete blackness that enfolded me. I held my breath and listened, praying that the dog or dogs would not enter the complex. I had just begun to relax when I heard something moving through one of the outer chambers. I told myself that it must be Jak, but I dared not call out. Instead, I groped my way to the nearest compartment, felt for the hand-shaped indentation, and pressed my hand into it. The click and the hiss of the opening door sounded alarmingly loud, and I threw myself into the compartment. Instantly, it flooded with ruby-red light, and I cried out before I could prevent myself. Too frightened to wait and listen again, I tore off my boot, set it in the opening, and reached out to press my hand into the recess in the door.

There was a hiss and it slid shut. Or it would have done, if not for the boot.

I forced myself to move quietly to the back of the compartment, where I sat down and made myself as small as possible. As I tried to listen, my red-limned reflection gaped at me in the glass, grotesque with terror, but my heart thundered so hard that it made me feel sick. Or maybe the sickness was merely another symptom of terror. I felt as if ice water were coursing through my veins, yet I was giving out so much heat that the glass inside the compartment was beginning to fog.

I crawled forward to wipe the front panel with my sleeve, and froze.

I could see something moving in the red-tinged darkness outside. Whatever it was looked far larger than a dog. Remaining very still, I sent out a beast-speaking probe but encountered a buzzing static that told me that it wore a demon band. Its size made me wonder if Ariel had captured a wolf and brought it to Norseland to train. It had stopped moving now, and I heard it *sniffing*.

Without warning, it rushed toward me and hurled itself against the glass panel with such ferocity that it rebounded violently back into the shadow with a snarling groan of pain. I had fallen backward, too, in shock, and as I sat up, I heard a loud click and realized that the beast had hit the glass so hard that it had dislodged the boot I had used to jam it open. In that moment, it did not seem bad to be locked away from whatever beast Ariel had left to guard his secrets.

I watched, mesmerized, as it approached the compartment again. Now I saw that it was man-shaped but hunched and shambling as if it were part beast and part human. *A bear?* I thought incredulously. At last it entered the bloody light of the compartment, and I drew a long, ragged, sobbing breath of disbelief.

For it was Rushton.

I spoke his name, and the sound of my voice seemed to madden him. He hurled himself at the glass again with such reckless violence that I cried out. For one second, I looked into his eyes' bottomless black insanity, then he reeled backward, clearly stunned by the impact. But immediately he ran at the glass again. This time when he struck it, I heard the distinct snap of a bone breaking. Rushton gave a howl of pain, and when he staggered back in readiness for another charge, he swayed on his feet for several beats, one arm hanging limp. Seeing the rage in his face, I understood that if he had got to me before I entered the compartment, he would have torn me to pieces with his bare hands. That could only mean that his memory had returned and had brought him back here to the source of his torment. I thought of the cry I had heard and wondered, sickened, if he had killed Gilbert or Andorra.

"Rushton," I whispered.

His eyes fixed on me, and his face distorted with hatred. He gathered himself and ran at the door head down. He struck the glass with a sickening crunch and dropped bonelessly to the floor, where he lay utterly still.

I gazed through streaming tears at his still, crumpled form, praying he had not broken his neck or caved in his skull. If only I could get out to check, but I could not open the door. I crawled to the front of the compartment and peered out at Rushton's prone form, trying to see if he was still breathing.

Then my gaze settled on the demon band fitted around his neck, and all at once I understood everything.

This was Ariel's doing, all of it.

Domick had told me Ariel had made Mika torture Rushton

coercively while empathically imposing my face and voice but that he had failed in trying to break Rushton. But Ariel had not failed at all. He had never meant to crush Rushton's mind, because he had a more elaborate cruelty planned. When the healers had treated Rushton at Obernewtyn, they had spoken of a long period in which Rushton had dwelt in a drug-induced nightmare world. But neither Domick nor Mika had mentioned drugs, which meant that they must have been administered after Rushton was shifted to Sutrium. That long, bleak, drugged dream he had endured had been imposed only to serve as a screen to prevent any of us from realizing what else had been done to him here.

Rushton had not been left in the Sutrium cloister by chance. He had been left there specifically so that he would be found and brought back to Obernewtyn, where he would be healed physically of his addiction. But not mentally. Ariel had intended all along that Rushton would be broken open slowly and torturously by his constant exposure to me. Ariel had wanted me to witness Rushton's love for me turning inexorably to hatred and madness.

It all fitted, save one thing. Why would Ariel set Rushton up to kill me when he had gone to such lengths to keep me alive? For he must know that this would be the result of Rushton's madness. Had he thought I would defend myself? Perhaps he had hoped that I would even be forced to kill Rushton to save myself.

I shook my head, unconvinced that he would take the risk that Rushton might succeed in killing me. But the only other possibility was the most monstrous of all. Ariel had foreseen this very moment: me, trapped safely in a glass compartment with Rushton outside, battering himself senseless to get at me. Yet where would Rushton get a demon band, and why would he put it on, if not at some coerced instruction? And why would Ariel command it if he had not foreseen this?

Nausea rose in me as I imagined the pleasure this vision would have given Ariel, whose need for me made him loathe me and whose defective nature made him take pleasure in cruelty and pain. I could scarcely encompass the idea that Ariel was capable of foreseeing so much, and a deadly, hopeless lethargy stole over me, for how could anyone prevail against an enemy who knew so much?

Then I heard Maryon's cool voice saying that no futureteller, however powerful, could see everything, because even the strongest futuretelling was only the most likely thing to happen. A single, random, unexpected event could change something. And Ariel did not see everything. Domick had said that. Ariel had not foreseen that the coercer would tell me Rushton had been on Norseland. Mika was supposed to have been too strong for Domick to break through. Rushton was supposed to batter himself to death trying to kill me, and I was to be tormented by not knowing why.

Rushton moaned and rolled onto his side, groaning. His face was a mask of blood, and his eyes were vague and bewildered as he hauled himself to his feet. But as before, the second they fixed on me, unstoppable rage flowed into them, and I knew that Rushton would kill himself trying to get at me while I remained safe, locked behind an unbreakable shield of glass.

Shield.

The word echoed strangely in my mind, and I heard Dameon's gentle voice telling me that I must have the courage to believe that Rushton still loved me. The blind empath had claimed that Rushton's rejection was proof that there was love. If he was truly indifferent, he would not have

807

such a violent aversion to seeing me. But he had been wrong. Love had been destroyed by the Destroyer, replaced by bloated lunatic hatred. Yet Rushton's rejection did not fit the plan, because Ariel would not have wanted him to drive me away. That would only have slowed Rushton's mental breakdown. He would have made sure that the hatred was sealed away so Rushton would appear to heal and be normal. This could only mean that Rushton had been rejecting me because somewhere deep inside, he was trying to avoid the fate that had been knitted up for him. *"Do not be a coward,"* Dameon's soft voice whispered in my memory. *"It is not only Rushton's love for you but also his very life that you fight for."*

I licked my lips and thought, *This, this is my limit.* And I watched Rushton marshal his strength for another useless assault on the door, understanding that his rejection was exactly what Dameon had said: proof of love.

There was only one course open to me. Ariel must have striven to futuretell this moment a hundred times, to make sure that it would come out as he desired. He must have looked at this moment again and again, trying to see if there was anything that could go wrong. He knew that Rushton would want to kill me, and he knew that I would be safe. He would watch it again and again, building a web of certainty, just as Dell had done in order to make sure that Domick would reach the ruins complex without infecting anyone. But there was no complete certainty, even in a web forecasting. Some unexpected element could always intervene. My only chance to save Rushton now was to introduce some element that Ariel could not have foreseen. I must do the unthinkable. I stood on legs that trembled.

"Rushton," I said. "Here. Here is where you must put your hand to open the door so you can reach me. Here." I tapped the hand-shaped recess, which I could see through the glass. I mimicked pressing my hand into it. "Look, Rushton. Like this. Press your hand here and the glass will open. Here." Over and over I repeated it as Rushton stood glaring at me with malevolent loathing, opening and closing his fists. Again and again I tapped the indentation and mimicked pressing a hand against it.

At last, I saw his eyes drop to my hand, and I laid it over the recess. Slowly, the blank, black hatred gave way to a glimmer of purpose, and Rushton lurched forward and pressed his hand into the recess. For a heart-stopping moment, our fingers were but the thickness of glass apart. Then there was a click and a hiss that sounded like an indrawn breath, and the glass slid away.

Rushton bared his teeth, and I resisted the urge to step back.

"I love you," I said, letting my hand fall to my side.

Strangely, I was not afraid, for in showing Rushton how to open the compartment door, I had defied Ariel and the power of his futuretelling abilities. Now there were only two possible outcomes: I would die or I would not. And Ariel had done all in his considerable power to make sure Rushton would have an unassailable desire to kill me. If Ariel had foreseen this moment, he would not have taken the risk of setting this is motion, because if Rushton killed me, the Seeker would never come to the weaponmachines to try to shut them down. The Destroyer needed the Seeker to try and fail to stop the weaponmachines before he could take control of them.

Ariel must have foreseen that I would be locked in, and he might have seen Rushton battering himself against the door, but it would never occur to him that I might show Rushton how to open the door.

Of course, the most likely outcome was that I would die. But even thinking this, I was not afraid. I felt only a strange liberating elation at the knowledge that, for the first time in my life, I had acted wholly as Elspeth Gordie and not as the Seeker.

Rushton lifted his fist over his head as if it were a club, his face blank and mindless. I looked into his eyes and said, "I am your shield."

He hesitated. His fist trembled, but it did not descend. Rushton gave a groaning cry and seemed to fight with himself, his fist still upraised. I dared not move, for I had introduced something fragile and random into certainty, and the outcome of this moment was so finely balanced that a single breath would push him to attack.

Suddenly Rushton dropped to his knees with a horrible half-strangled snarl. He lunged at me, but he stopped short of grasping me. His expression in the red light shifted maniacally between mad rage and terror. He snarled and groaned, now creeping toward me with clawed hands, now falling back and shuddering. His dreadful inner battle seemed to go on for hours, and in all that time, I did not move or speak. At last he grew quiet. His head was bowed, so I could not see the expression on his face, but suddenly I could not stay still any longer. I knelt down and reached a hand toward him, palm up. I knew he was looking at it. After a long, slow age, he leaned forward and laid his blood-slicked cheek against my hand.

I gave a gasping sob. "My love! My dearest love." I put my arms around him and drew his dark head to my breasts. He gave a sigh that seemed to come from the depths of his soul, and I felt the rage and strength flow out of him as he collapsed against me in a dead faint. I sat back on my heels, cradling his body in my arms. I loosened one hand and reached up to unclasp the demon band about his neck. Then I held him tight, kissed his head, and entered his mind.

It was as if I had entered the ferocious, keening heart of a storm. All was blackness and screaming chaos. Nightmarish creatures flew around me and over me and under me. The only thing solid in the maelstrom was a stony track leading steeply down. Limping along it was the scarred bear of the shape Rushton had worn inside Dragon's dreams. I had thought that image her creation, but I saw now that this wounded beast was the essence of Rushton. I could see scars and open wounds all over his body. I tried to touch him, but he did not seem to feel or hear me. His whole being was focused on the road. Now, far away, far down at its end, I saw a gleaming thread. The mindstream.

"No," I whispered, but Rushton did not hear me.

Without thinking, I did something I had never done before. I entered the mind of the wounded bear. To my astonishment, I found myself knee-deep in freshly fallen snow. *Was this a memory that I had entered?* I wondered.

Before me was a house formed entirely of ice. It was beautiful, but there was a cruel and deadly coldness in its beauty. Footsteps in the snow led to the house. Paw prints. I ran to the door, and it opened even before I touched it. The bear was vanishing into the vaporous mist that filled the corridor inside.

I went after him, slipping and skidding on the smooth gleaming ice. My feet ached, and I realized that I was barefoot. I ignored the burning cold and went down icy steps into a vast white chamber. It was exquisitely beautiful but deathly cold. Veils of mist hung like scarves in the air. A chandelier of ice crystals glittered like a fall of diamonds, and beneath it stood Ariel, as white and fair and deadly as this house of ice. He was tall, and his shoulders were wide, his neck and chin those of a man now; yet his mouth and eyes were those of the cruel spoiled child I had met at Obernewtyn. His hair hung about his shoulders like a cape of some sleek fur, and he stroked it with evident pleasure.

At his feet was Domick. Ariel was caressing his head as if he were a well-loved hound. "Go, Mika. Go and tend to your kennel mate."

Domick slunk to an alcove where the bear lay, panting and shuddering. He was dragging a whip that left a bloody smear of gore on the shining white floor. I ran past Domick to Rushton, ignoring him, for he was only an image from Rushton's broken mind. I stroked the bear's matted fur, horrified at the depth of some of the wounds, which had surely grown deeper and wider since I had seen him on the road. Then I realized that this bear was within the bear I had seen on the road, and the markings on both bears were only reflections of the damage that had been done to the different layers of Rushton's mind.

On impulse, I probed the bear's mind again.

This time I found myself standing by a sunlit steaming pool. The bear sat on the edge of the pool watching a woman swim. Incredulous, I saw that the woman was me, but this Elspeth was taller and stronger than me and so beautiful as to take my breath away. She was a warrior woman with proud eyes that glowed like jewels. Her hair splayed out in the water like a silken net as she swam, and when she smiled, a radiance flowed from her face and a sweetness filled the air.

I turned to the bear and found Ariel was now standing beside him. He ran a long elegant white hand over the bear's head.

"It is not I who hurt you," Ariel said persuasively. "It is she who will do you the greatest harm. She will teach you the true meaning of pain."

The Goddess-Elspeth in the pool emerged, and I saw that she was carrying a long, thin-bladed knife. I tried to cry out a warning, but no one heard me.

"I do not love you," she said coldly to the bear. "You know that I always meant to leave you."

She lifted the knife. I threw myself into her as she reached out with her other hand to stroke the bear's fur. She/I felt the thick, warm coarseness of fur in one hand and the hardness of the knife hilt in the other. I could not stop her as she drove the knife into the bear. He gave an agonized growl, and she/I felt him slump against me.

I left the Goddess-Elspeth and dived into his mind. The bear was falling away from me. I followed him, stretching myself out, arrowing down. I caught him and closed my arms around him, catching handfulls of his fur. I tried pulling him back up, but the impetus of his descent was too great. All I could do was slow him, but we continued to descend through his deepest mind and through images of torture so horrible that I felt I was in danger of losing my own mind just witnessing them. If Domick and Ariel had not been mad before they tortured Rushton, their minds had surely crumbled under the corrosive insanity of their deeds.

All at once, we were hanging above the mindstream. The bear struggled, but I clung to him, knowing that if I let go, he would surely enter the mindstream. For a long moment, I held him safe, but then my strength began to fade. Bit by bit, we began to drop. I would not let him go, I swore to myself. If he went into the stream, then I would follow.

"You must not go!" I recognized the voice of Atthis.

"Help me!" I cried.

"I cannot. I am still much weakened from the spirit merge, and I have not the strength for what you want," she sent sternly. "You must let him go."

"No! Help me save him or we will both go into the stream."

"Then the Destroyer will win."

"Help me."

"There will be a price," said the bird.

"I will pay it."

"It is not you who will pay," Atthis answered, but I felt a warm flow of energy coursing through me.

"Tell me what to do!" I cried, for the pull of the mindstream was growing stronger.

"To prevent him from seeking death is not enough," Atthis said, her voice growing faint. "If you would save his mind and soul, you must enter his deepest mind." And then her voice and presence were gone.

It seemed impossible that there would be another layer of his mind when we were so close to the mindstream, but I entered the bear. I found myself in a vast shadowy cavern. The bear was curled motionless in a pool of black blood at my feet. Ariel was standing over him, laughing. He spoke to me, over the bear. "Did you think I would not be here as well? There is no part of him that I have not invaded and violated. He will never be free of me until he is dead."

My heart faltered until I remembered that this was not Ariel. It was only a loathsome image he had stamped in Rushton's mind. He was not real. *But I was.*

"You are not real," I said.

I lifted my hand and directed the golden energy from Atthis at Ariel. His pale beauty melted as if he were made of candle wax. Then I was alone in the vast cavern that was Rushton's Talent. Here, a hundred minds could merge and be contained, and still there would be room for more. I was alone in this miraculous secret fastness; alone, save for the bear that was Rushton's soul. Here he had come, seeking sanctuary, and even here had Ariel come, with Mika's help, for Domick had known what lay locked inside the mind of the Master of Obernewtyn. He had once merged with Roland and others inside his mind, to find and save me.

I sat down and lifted the bear's head into my lap, surprised at its weight. I stroked his fur, and the gashes closed and scars healed at my touch. I stroked him until his fur was sleek and beautiful and smooth. Then the gleaming fur shortened and became pale flesh under my fingers, and it was Rushton I held in my arms.

Green eyes opened, and he gazed up at me for a long time, his expression grave and wondering.

"I love you," he said.

Someone was shaking me. I had the queer, unnerving sensation of falling up, and then I was conscious of being in my own body. I opened my eyes and found I was seated exactly as I had been inside Rushton's deepest mind, but the Rushton lying in my arms now was clothed, unconscious, and badly hurt.

I looked up to find Brydda squatting beside me.

"Elspeth?" His eyes searched mine, and I saw relief in his expression.

"How did you . . . ?" I began, and found I had not the strength to finish.

"The ship boat capsized, and we could not find the way into the cove. I was near to drowning when I seemed to hear

815

a voice in my mind, saying you had need of me. It led me to the inlet, and the others followed me. We finally figured out how the rest of you had got up to the surface. I sent Gwynedd's armsman after him and came here with the Sadorian man who had mastered the ship boat. There were signs of fire or some sort of explosion, and Gilbert was unconscious, but Hakim had awakened in time to see Rushton enter the trapdoor, muttering and snarling your name. Rushton must have got off the *Umborine* as soon as it dropped anchor and headed here, though I do not know how he got past the Hedra. I bade Selik take care of Gilbert and Hakim, and I came down after you."

"Ariel planned it all," I said hoarsely. "He would have made sure Rushton knew exactly how to get here. He must have left orders to the Hedra guarding the path up from Fryddcove not to hinder him."

"You think Ariel knew he would come here?"

"I think he foresaw our coming here and intended for Rushton to die trying to kill me."

"He must have a black hate for Rushton," Brydda said grimly. "The voice—"

I cut off his words to ask about Andorra, Jak, and Hakim.

"Andorra was knocked out on the metal walkway. I roused her, and she was with me when we found you two here. I left her to watch you while I went and helped Selik move Hakim and Gilbert to a little chamber facing the courtyard where a fire had been lit. I fetched blankets and so forth, and then I left Selik again to come back down here."

"What about Jak?"

"Andorra and I could not find him, but Jakoby searched and found him wandering in darkness, lost in the labyrinth of this place."

"Jakoby!"

"You have been here for a long time, Elspeth, and much has happened as you slept. If sleeping it was," he said. "Dardelan guessed that Rushton would come here, so the moment she could, Jakoby came ashore, borrowed a horse, and rode here."

"The . . . the battle is over?"

"It was in the process of being won when Jakoby rode from Covertown, but leave that for now. We need to get Rushton out of here. He is cold and shocked and battered, but aside from a dislocated arm and a gash on the brow that needs stitching, I do not think he has taken any mortal wound."

I heard footsteps and turned my head to see Jakoby. Behind her came Jak.

"I am so sorry, Elspeth," the teknoguilder said, looking down at Rushton with horrified pity. "I should have come back sooner, but I found a whole lot of storage rooms filled with what I think are weapons. I was looking for the plague seeds when my lantern went out. I tried to grope my way back to the entrance and got lost. I had truly begun to despair when I heard Jakoby shouting out my name. Never have I heard a sweeter sound in all my life."

Jakoby acknowledged his declaration with a faint smile, and then she squatted down and looked into my eyes. "All is well?" The gravity in her voice struck me, but I had no strength for questions. I nodded, and then she and Brydda gently lifted Rushton onto a stretcher, explaining that they had rigged up a basket to raise him to the hatch but had not wanted to touch him or me until I woke.

"Can you walk?" Jakoby asked.

"I can manage, but take Rushton up," I croaked. "I need to show Jak something."

Jakoby and Brydda carried Rushton out as Jak helped me to my feet. I cried out at the stiffness of my legs and back. Jak knelt and began to massage my legs vigorously. "No wonder you are stiff. You were sitting there for an entire day and night," he said. "I wanted to lay you down at least, but Brydda said he had a strong feeling you ought to be left to wake naturally."

I managed to smile, despite the pains shooting up my legs and back, wondering if Brydda would ever acknowledge that his feelings and hunches were Talent. Perhaps it does not matter how he defines them, so long as they serve him. It took some time, but finally I was able to stand straight. I bade the teknoguilder help me walk and directed him where to go. Soon we were in the tiny chamber off the torture room. I pointed to the little black and yellow symbol, and he drew a swift breath.

"I see no seeds and yet . . . ," I began.

"This is it, Elspeth," Jak said, kneeling and holding up his lantern as I had done to cast light through the window. "These will be sicknesses. This is how the Beforetimers stored them. Ines showed me pictures of cupboards like this. Ah!" he cried, and I knew he must have touched the glass. He touched it again and bent to examine the round knob surrounded by numbers. "This is how the coldness is controlled. See how the numbers go from red to blue? The Beforetimers used blue to symbolize cold and red to symbolize heat."

"Do you want me to unlock the cabinet?" I asked.

He smiled and shook his head. "That would be dangerous, and there is no need, for it is the cold that keeps the seeds alive. They are not truly seeds, of course, but the word serves well enough. Making them hot is enough to kill them." He turned the knob in the direction of the red numbers. Then he stood up. "Strange that something so deadly is also so delicate."

"Are you sure they will die?" I asked.

"There would not be such careful control of the cold if it was not important. Now let's get out of here."

I was startled to hear a teknoguilder so willing to leave a Beforetime place full of ancient knowledge, but perhaps being lost in the darkness and finding bottles of plague had soured his appetite for knowledge, at least for the moment.

✦ 18 ✦

THE GRAY CLOUDS that clogged the sky and shadowed our dawn departure from Norseland had dispersed by midmorning, and a fresh steady wind blew, so the *Umborine* seemed to fly over the waves.

I kept to my cabin for the day, watching over Rushton and talking quietly to Jak and Jakoby and to Brydda and Dardelan, all of whom called in briefly to check on him. Aside from being bruised and cut, with a broken wrist and several gashes in his scalp deep enough to need stitches, Rushton showed little sign of the ordeal he had endured, save for the depth of his sleep. He had not awakened during the journey across Norseland to Fryddcove, nor did he wake aboard the *Umborine* until deep in the night.

I was sitting vigil, curled in a chair reading, when a soft movement from Maruman drew my attention. I looked over to find the old cat peering intently into Rushton's face. Laying aside the book, I moved swiftly to the bed, thinking that he was suffering another of the nightmares that had racked him on and off through the day and night, for he was grimacing and his face shone with sweat. I was about to touch his hand to rouse him when Maruman leaned down and touched his nose gently to Rushton's. I caught my breath as Rushton's eyes opened. For a long moment, green eyes gazed into blazing yellow, and then Maruman curled back to sleep.

Rushton turned his head and saw me, and I was relieved that his eyes were clear, his expression calm. "How do you feel?" I said.

He smiled. "Emptied out. Weary. A little confused," he said. "We are aboard the *Umborine*?"

I nodded. "We are bound for Sador with a fair wind filing our sails and triumph behind us," I said, reaching out to touch his cheek.

"What happened with the . . . Hedra?"

I saw that he would not rest until he knew something, so I told him that Gwynedd's arrival in Cloistertown had galvanized the Norselanders. The news he shared about the Faction's fall on Herder Isle had spread like wildfire and roused the Norselanders just as he had predicted. His impromptu army had swelled as people joined him from every farm and small village, despite the storm that raged. By the time they reached the Hedra encampment, situated atop a plateau some five leagues before Covetown, there was such a horde that the only reason they had not been spotted was the foul weather and the fact that columns of Hedra were marching from the camp in response to Jakoby's demands signaled from the *Umborine*.

Gwynedd later learned that, as he had anticipated, the Hedra had marched straight to Covetown and stationed themselves all along the cliffs, from the top of the path up from the beach to the gates of Norseland's sole remaining cloister. The Hedra left behind in the encampment had been completely unprepared when a ruse caused them to open the gates and hundreds and hundreds of Norselanders had poured in. There had been no time for them to open the armory and use its weapons, but as it transpired, there had been none of the worst sorts of weapons I had seen on Herder Isle.

The Hedra who had remained in the camp, though numerous, were mostly boys and unseasoned young men.

Meanwhile, unbeknownst to Gwynedd, the Per of Cloistertown had led a small group of young women and boys directly to Covetown to rouse the Per there. By the time Gwynedd and his armsmen and a small force of Norselanders arrived on the stony rises outside Covetown, hundreds more Norselanders were waiting for them, fresh and eager to fight to open the way to the beach. It was clear to Gwynedd then that it was not a small secret sortie he was involved in, but a coup. Thus, he had not waited for us to arrive as planned but had led an attack on the Hedra, from the rear, after signaling to tell Dardelan what he intended to do and asking him to send three large ship boats ashore. The Hedra were caught between the two forces and outnumbered, yet by the sound of it, they had fought with savage skill.

During the hours of fighting that followed, Jakoby had slipped ashore to seek Rushton. By then, of course, she and Dardelan had learned that Ariel was not on Norseland; nevertheless, they felt certain Rushton would make his way to Ariel's residence.

"Do you remember leaving the *Umborine*?" I asked Rushton.

"I remember diving overboard," he murmured. "I remember as soon as I saw the cove and the path going up, feeling the compulsion to . . . to find you. I swam to shore and went straight up the track that runs alongside the road to the top of the cliffs. The Hedra there took one look at me and let me through. They . . . recognized me, you see. 'Ariel's wolf' they used to call me. I knew where to go, because I had crossed the island on foot many times before. Ariel had me do it over and over, harried by his dogs. 'Let us hunt the wolf,' he would say and laugh. . . . I think that was real."

"It doesn't matter," I said, not wanting him to dwell on frayed places in his mind. "However it happened, Ariel made sure you would know the way to the residence and that you would go there and put on the demon band before coming to find me."

Rushton shook his head. "That he saw so much . . ."

"I know," I said. "But he does not see everything, else he would have seen this." I leaned over to gently kiss his bruised lips. They curved into a crooked smile, but I noted the dark shadows beneath his eyes and sat back to finish my tale. "While you were coming to me, Gwynedd was meeting with the Per of Covetown in the stony rises, and probably about the time you reached Ariel's residence, he was leading an army of Norselanders against the Hedra on the cliffs. By the time we arrived back at Covetown, the fighting was over."

"It is strange to think of a war being fought so close at hand, yet for me it is no more than a tale," Rushton said.

"We do not need to be the center of all wars and all strife," I said gently. "I am very content for the Battle for Norseland to be a tale about other people told over a campfire. And now it is very late. Sleep."

Rushton drew a long breath and sighed before asking, "What were you reading?"

"A book of Sadorian poetry. Jakoby gave it to me when she came to see how you were."

"Read to me. I would like to hear your voice in my dreams," Rushton said, and closed his eyes.

I took up the book I had laid aside and opened it, blinking to clear a mist of tears from my eyes.

Rushton slept for the remainder of the night and most of the next morning, and I did not leave his side, but when a

Norseland herbalist, who was aboard as part of the Norse delegation, appeared with a gift of some special nourishing soup she had concocted, I went to wash my face and eat a meal in the saloon.

The first person I saw when I entered was Gwynedd, surrounded by the delegation appointed by the Norseland Pers to serve their king. Neither Dardelan nor Brydda were there, so I sat at an empty table by the door and helped myself to some buttered mushrooms from a heaped platter and sliced some of the heavy Norse bread and ate. I marveled again at how readily the Norselanders had accepted Gwynedd's claim to have king's blood flowing through his veins.

Contrary to my expectations, he had not told the Norselanders of his lineage in order to gain their trust. The news that the Faction had been overcome in the Land and upon Herder Isle had convinced the Norselanders to fight their oppressors. That, and the fact that the forceful if diminutive Per Vallon of Cloistertown had declared Gwynedd's arrival to be a sign from the goddesses.

Although the Faction had been overcome, I had not told Rushton that the death toll had been horrific. Over a hundred Norselanders had fallen in the first half hour of the brutal battle on the cliffs and double that again before it was over. There had been even more deaths among the Hedra, especially in the encampment, for many of the warrior priests had been young novices and acolytes, and this was their first true battle. Whatever glory they had thought to find in fighting for their Lud was eventually lost in blood and mud and screams of pain, and they began to throw down their weapons. Some were slain by their own captains, true fanatics who believed that the only honor in defeat lay in death.

I shivered, remembering the ferocity and fanaticism of the Hedra master on Herder Isle.

As if he had heard my thoughts, Gwynedd looked over and saw me. He immediately excused himself from his followers and came to join me, apologizing for not yet visiting Rushton.

"He is still very tired," I said. "You look tired, too."

He sighed heavily. "In truth, I am weary to death of fighting. Yet there will be fighting in the Westland before the Council and the Faction are overcome, and if Rushton wins the aid of the Sadorians, we will sail across the sea to wage war on these slavemasters. Ye gods, I wish I could disbelieve the prediction of this Futuretell guildmistress, but I have seen for myself the power wielded by Mistress Dell, and I have heard her say more than once that the guildmistress of the Futuretellers is far more gifted than she."

"I am not sure that would be true anymore," I said. "But Maryon would never announce such a futuretelling unless she was certain that it would come to pass."

Gwynedd ran his hands through his long blond hair, and I noticed for the first time the glint of silver in the gold. "You know, I ought to be celebrating our victory, and it was a victory, despite leaving the cloister under siege. But I keep thinking of the dead Hedra laid out in rows in the encampment. Most of them were young, and some seemed no more than children to my eyes. They would have grown up to be vicious fanatics, but seeing their youth, I understood that most of them would have been given no choice about what they would become. It was all I could do not to weep."

"I am sorry for their deaths," I said, "but I do not know what else you could have done."

"That is what I tell myself, but it is a convenient answer, is

825

it not? I fear the faces of the dead boys will haunt me."

"They should," I said, and he looked up at me, his blue eyes questioning. I shrugged. "I mean only that if we kill, we ought to be haunted by it, else we are monsters."

He held my gaze. "You are wise, Guildmistress, for all your youth."

I laughed ruefully. "I feel as if I am a hundred!"

He smiled, but his eyes were serious. "One thing I would tell you. This 'victory' has taught me how much I have come to rely on the Talents of Misfits like you, not only to help me win battles but also to win them with as little violence as possible. This battle seemed utterly brutal, yet all battles were once thus. I have changed, because I have seen that battles need not be bloody and full of death. I have lived with the constant gentling desire of your people to cause as little harm as possible, and I find that is my desire, too. Because I have had around me Blyss and Dell and all of your people in the midst of battle, I was struck by the terrible waste of it, for nothing can be learned by corpses. The truest victory is the winning of hearts and minds."

"*That* is a true victory," Rushton murmured when I returned to my cabin and told him what the Norselander had said. To my consternation, he was dressed, but in truth he seemed much improved, and when I told him about the maps I had seen, he grew excited and sent me to ask Jakoby for permission to visit the map chamber. Gwynedd had not managed to obtain a good clear map of the way to the Red Queen's land on Norseland, which meant that the information that could be culled from the ship's map collection might be vital to the success of the journey to the Red Queen's land.

On my way back from speaking with the tribeswoman,

Brydda hailed me. Joining him at the side of the ship, I related the substance of my earlier conversation with Gwynedd. Brydda told me that the Norselander had been appalled by the number of his countrymen killed, all the more because the Pers of Covetown and Cloistertown had praised him for defeating the Hedra with so few dead and injured. He also said that the Pers had been on the verge of commanding the execution of their captors, for this had been the sole punishment dealt out to them by the Hedra for any misdeeds. But Gwynedd had forbidden it, saying only that the Hedra must be shackled and made to labor, for soon enough they would be needed. He had told Brydda that there was no use in pointing out the youth of most Hedra from the encampment or suggesting the possibility of redemption to the Norselanders. He had said only that the Hedra were going to be coerced and used to fight the slavemasters. That was a reason the Norselanders could accept.

I did not envy the fate of the priests who had shut themselves up in the cloister, for in refusing to surrender to Gwynedd, they had ensured that they would be judged and dealt with by the Pers, unless they managed to hold out until Gwynedd returned.

"And will he return?" I asked.

"He must, for he is their king," Brydda answered.

"He agreed?" I asked as Dardelan joined us.

Brydda shrugged. "I do not think they see kingship as a question. Gwynedd is the Norse king, and that is that. It does not matter to them that Gwynedd announced his lineage only to ensure obedience when he forbade anyone to enter Ariel's demesne."

"How can he be king of Norseland *and* high chieftain of the Westland?" I asked.

"Gwynedd told the Pers that he had just sworn to serve a year as high chieftain of the Westland and that even before that year ended, he must travel to the Red Land with us to prevent the slavemasters from invading our lands," Dardelan said. "Per Vallon merely told him blithely that kings were not ordinary men whose doings could be ordered by their people. Kings were always going hither and thither on kingly business, and it was left to the Pers to deal with the day-to-day ruling of the king's land and his people."

Gwynedd would come to them once he had fulfilled his oaths in the Westland and achieved victory over the slave-masters of the Red Land. In the meantime, he must choose a *kinehelt* to rule in his stead. *Kinehelt*, Dardelan explained, was an old Norse word for "king's hand." So Gwynedd had appointed Per Vallon of Cloistertown and Per Selma of Cove-town as his kinehelt, saying a king needed two hands. Just before he had boarded the *Umborine* for Sador, the stooped and balding Per Vallon had produced the crown of the last Norse king, which his family had kept hidden through the generations. Dell's foreseeing came to pass as Gwynedd knelt in the pebbles to be crowned.

I had not known this, and I pictured it as we were all silent for a time, gazing out over the sea. Then I saw that the water was so still it might have been made from glass, for the wind had fallen away utterly. The only thing that marred the glassy perfection was the spreading ripples running out from the hull of the *Umborine* as the deep currents of the strait drew it slowly along.

"We are becalmed," Rushton said as I reentered the cabin. "What did Jakoby say?"

"She will bring some maps here later, though she says

none shows the way to the Red Queen's land. We will have to hope that Gwynedd is right in believing that maps will be found in the cloister, once it is surrendered."

I hesitated, contemplating whether to tell him about Dragon now or wait till he was stronger, but he limped across to the window and opened it to stare out moodily.

"You should lie down," I chided him.

"I feel better than I did last night. It is just my head. The ache is constant, but Jakoby says that Andorra is mixing up a potion that will ease me." He gazed out the window for a while longer, and then he came back to sit on the bed beside me, saying, "I mislike this stillness. I must not miss that meeting."

"Jakoby says we will be there in time. Why not let Dardelan address the tribes?"

"I think it is important that I speak as Master of Obernewtyn, since it is Maryon who foresaw what will come," Rushton said.

I did not argue, for I could see he had no strength for it. I coaxed him to lie down with me, and he slept a while then. I dozed, too, until Jakoby came bearing the promised maps and Andorra's potion. The ship was still becalmed, but she assured Rushton that we were not far from the Sadorian coast, and even if we were becalmed all night, we would still reach Sador in time for him to make his request, for there was one full day of the conclave remaining. Only an hour later, the wind rose again. Spurred on by it, Rushton got up and asked me to fetch Gwynedd, Brydda, and Dardelan, for they must speak of what to say to the tribes. I knew him too well to suggest he ought to rest while he could, and when the others arrived, I slipped out with Maruman for a breath of fresh air.

The wind whipped at my hair as we made our way aft to the holding yard, and I glanced up to see the sails billowing scarlet against a bright blue sky. Once again, the *Umborine* was flying.

Reaching the holding yard, I saw that Gahltha and Calcasuss were at the other end attempting to instruct a group of small, hardy Norseland ponies in the rudiments of Brydda's fingerspeech. I did not wish to interrupt them, and sunlight lay so enticingly on a bench alongside their pen that I sat down on it to wait. I was not there long before Maruman leapt onto my lap. When I thought he was asleep, I allowed myself the illicit pleasure of stroking him, acknowledging that it had been the right impulse to ask him to look after Gahltha, for he had spent most of the time I was on Norseland comforting the black horse and taking his mind off wave-sickness and terror, which had kept him from fretting about me.

Gahltha put his head over the barrier to nuzzle at my shoulder.

"You seem in good spirits," I told him fondly, reaching up to stroke his nose.

He answered that he had liked the ship's being becalmed but that he was also glad the wind had begun to blow again so his time aboard the ship would end soon. "My hooves want to feel proper steady earthfastness under them," he sent.

Without opening his eyes, Maruman pointed out languidly that sand was none too steady under paws, let alone inferior hooves, which was why kamuli were called "ships of the desert." Gahltha ignored this to ask about Rushton.

"He is bruised and battered, inside and out. But he will heal—is healing." I looked into the black horse's lustrous eyes with a rush of tenderness so potent that my eyes filled with tears. "I am glad that you and Maruman are with me."

"We will always be with you," Gahltha sent.

He withdrew his head, and I lay back and closed my eyes, enjoying the slight warmth of the sun on my face and the soft weight of Maruman on my lap. It was strange that, having faced certain death, my spirits were now as calm and glassy as the sea had been. *I am becalmed,* I thought, closing my eyes. Maybe I could hear the song of the waves so clearly now that its vast, encompassing serenity made me feel very small and insignificant. It was odd how some people longed to be important, people like Chieftain Brocade. Everything about the man, from his immense size to his manner and arrogance, spoke of his hunger for importance, yet what, truly, did he desire? To be significant? For what purpose? Did he understand that with significance came a terrible weight of responsibility? I felt that weight as the Seeker, but for the moment, I was utterly content to let the song of the sea show me how small I was.

A shadow fell over me, and I squinted against the sun to see Gilbert, whom I had not set eyes on since we had reboarded the *Umborine*. Like Rushton, he had been sleeping and healing. Now the wind tossed his side plaits and blew his thick red hair back from his handsome face, revealing an ugly purpling bruise on his forehead. But his eyes were clear and his expression tranquil, and I thought his was a face that a woman might easily love. I hoped for both their sakes that his Serra would see the change in him. Or that she would at least let his sons come to know their father. Gilbert was a man who would grow for having children. It would bring out his tenderness, which had begun to curdle.

"Jakoby sent me to tell you that we will see Templeport on the horizon within the half hour," he said. "Is it true that not a single tree grows there?"

831

I hid a smile at the boyish curiosity in his voice. "There are trees in the isis pool rifts, and there are the ancient giant trees of the spice groves, which I have never seen but from which the *Umborine* was made. But other than them, there is not a tree or a blade of grass in all Sador. It is a true desert land and hotter than any place I have ever been. Jak says the heat comes from the land underneath, as in the Westland. He believes that great pools of molten rock lie at the burning heart of the world and that in the Great White, cracks opened that let molten rock flow close to the surface."

"Do you believe the world has a heart of fire?" Gilbert asked, looking at me curiously.

"I do not know how something with fire inside can have ice and snow upon the surface, but the longer I live, the more it seems that life is full of the unexpected and impossible. Why should it not be so of the land as well?"

"That is neither a yes nor a no," the armsman observed dryly.

I laughed. "I suppose the answer is that I don't know. But the teknoguilders seem very sure."

"You sound as if you don't think their certainty is a good thing."

I sobered. "Let us say that I have too often seen certainty as a sort of blindness."

"How did one so young become so wise?" Gilbert asked.

"For the second time today I have been called wise, but I do not think myself so," I said wryly.

He did not smile. "Perhaps *not* thinking oneself wise is the modesty that must form the heart of all true wisdom. On the other hand, my father used to say that fools and wise men were made so for a reason." I made no response, and he continued in a soft, distant voice. "Last night, I dreamed of you standing in a black and barren place surrounded by snarling wolves."

"It was just a dream," I said, though his words sent a trickle of ice along my spine, for the previous night, I, too, had dreamed of wolves, though I had attributed it to Rushton telling me that Ariel had called him a wolf.

A burst of laughter made us both turn to see Dardelan holding open the door to my cabin for Brydda and Gwynedd, who were supporting Rushton between them. They were all laughing at their awkwardness, but even from this far away, I could see the knotted black line of stitches that ran almost to one brow. Rushton was smiling, but this faded into an intense seriousness as he leaned closer to hear something that Dardelan was saying. A fierce love for him rose up in my breast as I thought how I loved that look above all others upon his face, that grave solemnity.

Seeming to feel my gaze, he turned to look in my direction, and our eyes locked and clasped for a long moment. I had a sudden dizzying memory of the first time I had seen him coming from the pigpen at Obernewtyn. He had looked at me in the same way, unsmiling, intent, as if there was nothing else in the world but me. Then Dardelan reached out to clasp his shoulder, and he turned away.

I sighed and then started when Gilbert said softly, "He is the one you love. The Master of Obernewtyn. I do not know why I did not see it before."

Whatever response I might have made was lost in the ululating cry from the lookout and the commotion that followed as everyone on deck crowded to the side of the ship. Gilbert offered me a hand, and I let him heave me up, lifting a grumbling Maruman onto my shoulders as we went to gaze at the long purple shadow on the horizon. Gwynedd called out to

Gilbert, and the armsman smiled at me and went to his chieftain.

Maruman demanded tersely to be put down, and I realized that my heightened emotions were irritating him. I lifted him to the deck, turned to lean on the edge of the ship, and gazed out at Sador.

I felt a hand on my shoulder and did not need to turn to know that Rushton had come to stand behind me. He stepped closer and I trembled, feeling the heat of his body through the linen shirt he wore and through the silk and woven vest. Softly he said, "When last we came to Sador, you told me that you loved me. I will never forget how it felt to hear you say those words for the first time, for I had believed that you could not love one whose Talent was locked uselessly inside him."

"You were wrong," I said.

"It would not be the first time," Rushton murmured, a smile in his voice.

The white-haired tribal leader Bram was at the front of the crowd that had gathered to meet us on the sand-covered point of rock that extended a little way out and then dropped off steeply at one side, allowing even greatships to anchor very close to shore. A ramp was laid down to allow the horses to leave, and I led Gahltha across it with Maruman draped about my shoulders. The minute his hooves touched the sand, Gahltha announced a powerful need to gallop. Laughing, I bade him go. The crowd parted for him and the other horses and then closed about us again. I looked at them uneasily, fearing their presence had some connection to Jakoby's trip to Sutrium and my quest, but I need not have worried, for

Bram greeted us fulsomely, explaining that the fall of the Faction and Council in the West and the Norselands had been foretold by more than one kasanda, as well as by the Earthtemple's overguardian. He made a long, effusive speech about the value of freedom and then called for a strange evilsmelling brew, which we all drank to celebrate our victory.

Maruman hissed at the strong acrid scent of the brew and insisted on being put down. I was not troubled, for he disliked crowds and would sniff his way to me in a while.

Once the toasts had been drunk, Bram announced that tents had been set up in expectation of our arrival, and we were to be shown to them so we could rest in order to be fresh for the feasting that would begin when the moon rose.

As we made our way along the sand spit to the road to the desert lands proper, I noticed Jakoby speaking to Bram. From his grave expression, I guessed that she was telling him of Maryon's futuretelling, and it occurred to me that some of the Sadorian seers or the overguardian might also have foreseen the slavemasters' coming. I said this to Rushton, who agreed that Bram might already know why he had come; nevertheless, if he had understood Jakoby, he would still have to put the matter of the ships formally before the tribes. I asked him exactly what Zarak had told him of Maryon's prediction, but he had no more detail to offer than Brydda had shared. I would have to wait to learn more from Maryon herself. Again I was tempted to tell Rushton about Dragon, but I could not do so while hemmed in by tribe children and adults chattering in gadi and in the common tongue of the lands. Hearing that language reminded me that I still had not shown Jakoby the book and the brooch from Ariel's residence.

"It was fortunate that the *Umborine* had not left when Zarak rode up. Indeed, at the time, it seemed so suited to my need that I hardly questioned it, yet I do not know why Jakoby came for you with such urgency."

"She has not told me clearly, but I think the overguardian wishes to speak with me," I said. We reached the noisy trade area, and I sniffed the scents of spices and perfumes and frying fish with pleasure, regretting that I lacked coin to exchange for the temple tokens used as currency in the desert lands. Nevertheless, later I would walk through the trade tents and stalls, for I liked the market here.

It was hard to imagine how the area must look outside the annual period of conclave, which included the gathering and drying or smoking of the schools of fish that once a year mysteriously cast themselves upon the sandy spit. Yet the Sadorians believed deeply that they must leave nothing of themselves upon the earth when they moved on. So the tribes would take their tents and their kamuli and leave Templeport to go wandering in the desert or take their turn at tending the spice groves, and their departure led to the traders' departure. In no time, Templeport would be deserted, save for a few traders who would trade with the occasional small shipmasters, who put in at Templeport to take on fresh water and do a little trading with the Earthtemple, which was built into soaring cliffs honeycombed with tunnels and chambers, its stony face carved into a thousand faces that looked out to the sea.

At last we reached the area where dozens of white guest tents rose up from the pale gold sand like an armada of tethered sails fluttering in the wind and the warm, clear light of dusk. Bram made another short speech, this time welcoming the Norselanders, and then he once again bade us rest before the feasting. Once the speech was done, Jakoby drew Rushton aside, and I left them to it, hoping he would not overtax himself. I moved through the tents until I found one tethered with its flap facing the empty undulating dunes and crawled into it. I had just let my pack slide to the floor when Rushton came in and stretched out on the bedroll that had been so neatly laid out.

"What did she say?" I asked.

He sighed and rubbed his eyes. "She told Bram about the slavemasters and my intention to request the use of the Sadorian greatships. It seems their kasandas made some prediction that would fit the coming of these slavemasters, and for this reason, I will be heard with sympathy. But Bram told Jakoby that the Sadorians will not simply hand their ships over. They will regard my request as an invitation to take part in a war. This will likely result in a vote to extend the conclave a sevenday so the matter can be examined thoroughly before a vote is taken."

"A sevenday," I said, my heart sinking.

Rushton turned his head to look at me, and he might have read my mind. "I, too, ache to return to Obernewtyn, but gaining these ships is too important a duty to shirk, and it will be worth the time, if they agree. Meanwhile, Dardelan, Gwynedd, and I will begin to plan the journey to the Red Land and all that must be done before it." He was silent for a little, and then he said, "Jakoby also told me that I must present my request in gadi."

I stared at him in disbelief. "But you cannot speak gadi."

"I do not have to speak it, only to announce my request in it. Apparently, that request can be stated very simply. But it is a formal requirement and cannot be waived. Bram has agreed to teach me the words, and my tuition will begin tonight, at this feast." He sighed again. Then he looked around and said

I had clearly been given preferential treatment, since my tent was larger and more luxurious than his.

I told him he was a fool, for all tents were exactly alike, and I had chosen my own at random. He complained that I lacked the proper respect for my chieftain. Then he caught my hand and pulled me down alongside him, wincing as he jarred his splinted wrist. I tried to sit up, scolding him for failing to mind his wounds.

"You mind them for me," he said. "I have other matters to mind." Then he pinned my legs under a knee, ignoring my laughing protests that he was being unfair, since I could not wrestle an injured man.

"Of course not," he said loftily. "The only honorable thing to do is to surrender immediately."

Laughing, I tried to wriggle away but froze when he winced. I drew back from him in dismay. "We should be careful."

"Maybe so," he sighed, and lay back against the rumpled bedding. "I am not completely healed, it is true, but I am healing. Inside as well as out, this time." It was the first time he had referred directly to what Ariel had done to him. Not that we had avoided the matter or feared to speak of it; we just seemed to have come to some unspoken agreement to put it off for a time. His eyes met mine, jade green and gravely tender. He said, "You risked your life to save mine."

"I saved myself," I said fiercely, and reached out to brush the thick silky fall of black hair from his brow. I frowned at the great puckered gash there. "That will leave a scar," I said.

He took my hand and kissed the palm. "Each scar is a wisdom learned. My grandmother told me that."

"I have never heard you speak of a grandmother," I said, relaxing beside him. This mood of his, which allowed laughter and childhood confidences, was so welcome after his long, relentless coldness that I wanted to prolong it.

"My grandmother died before my mother became ill and sent me to Obernewtyn in search of my father. But I remember her very well, because she was strange and embarrassed me dreadfully with her eccentricities. The other boys in my village whispered that she was a witch, and oft times I thought so, too."

"What did she do?" I asked curiously.

He laughed. "Not much. It does not take much in a village to be thought peculiar."

"But what?" I persisted.

He shrugged. "She liked to walk about the forest at night, and when the moon was full, she would go out and glare up at it. 'Moonhater,' they called her."

It was an odd coincidence that Rushton's grandmother had hated the moon, for Maruman hated it as well. "A strange distant thing to dislike so much," I said tentatively. "Did she ever say why?"

He shook his head. "She talked to herself, and she had many queer dislikes."

"Had she any Talent?" I asked.

"My mother definitely had a touch of empathy. That is what made her such a good herb lorist. Perhaps her mother was the same. The Twentyfamilies gypsies who passed through our village each year on the way to tithe the Council made a point of visiting her to pay their respects." He laughed ruefully. "I remember their bringing her gifts: little carved creatures or some special fruit or sweet. My mother was convinced they made my grandmother worse. I think it was true, because sometimes, after they had come, my grandmother would walk through the forest to the mountains and stand staring at them for hours as if they were a puzzle she must solve. Back then, they were still so dangerously tainted that most people avoided going anywhere near them. People in the village said my grandmother's habit of staring at the black mountains was hereditary and came from a queerness in our bloodline. Once I asked my mother about it, and she said we had another ancestor who had been just as fascinated with the mountains. But she had believed there was a marvelous settlement of wondrous shining people living beyond them and was always yearning to go to them. She vanished one night, and people said she must have just walked into the tainted mountains and died." Rushton suddenly smiled. "I remember that I asked my mother if *she* was planning to go mad, and she said she would endeavor not to do it, for my sake."

His voice trailed away, and I stared at him, wondering.

Rushton went on, "After I came to Obernewtyn and Louis told me who my father was, I remember wondering if my mother falling in love with Michael Seraphim was just another form of our ancestral fascination with the high mountains."

I drew a breath and said as casually as I could manage, "Louis Larkin once told me that Lukas Seraphim had been determined to build a home in the mountains, because he had dreamed of a wondrous settlement of people living there. Apparently, he was bitterly disappointed to find only a Before-time ruin."

"Perhaps Lukas Seraphim heard a tale that arose from the mad notions of one of my ancestors."

"But it wasn't just a tale or mad notion," I persisted. "There *was* a settlement in the mountains that some might call miraculous, only it existed in the Before-time."

"Are you saying that my ancestor and Lukas Seraphim both had true dreams of the Beforetime Obernewtyn?" Rushton asked skeptically.

"They were both your ancestors," I reminded him. "But it was not dreams I meant. What if Hannah Seraphim started the rumor about the settlement in the mountains? She was not at Obernewtyn when the Great White came, as we now know, so maybe she was in Newrome and escaped before it collapsed. If she did, she would have been unable to return to Obernewtyn, because the mountains were now a deadly barrier. What if she just stayed there and waited, watching the mountains and longing to go over them, knowing it was impossible?"

Rushton gave me a sleepy-eyed smile. "Do I hear one of Zarak's theories?"

I laughed. "Now that you mention it. But really, it makes sense. She gazed at the mountains and talked about Obernewtyn, and that was how the rumor of the wondrous place there began." I was silent a moment, thinking hard. Then I drew in an excited breath. "What if she remained up in the highlands and eventually bonded and had children? Might they not have talked of her obsession with the mountains, even generations later?"

"You think my illustrious ancestor Lukas Seraphim built Obernewtyn because of stories told to him by *his* ancestor, and then my mother's mother came to hear of the tale and took to staring at the mountains, too? A very convoluted theory," Rushton laughed, yawning.

"Rushton, I know it sounds strange, but think of it. If Hannah Seraphim lived through the Great White and had children, they could be your ancestors *on both sides!* Hannah would have been trapped on the other side of the mountains during the Age of Chaos, and while the worst of the madness was happening in the cities, we know that it was much calmer in remoter regions. Just the same, people from the cities came to the Land, and they brought upheaval and fear enough that a family might easily be scattered and lose one another. If I am right, it would explain your name, Lukas's determination to build Obernewtyn, and your great-grandmother's fascination with the mountains."

I looked at Rushton to see how he had taken my revelations, but his eyes were closed. The slow rise and fall of his chest told me that he was asleep. I glared at him indignantly for a moment and then laughed softly. No matter, for I could not tell him the last part of my speculations: that the main reason Hannah would have yearned to cross the mountains was because she knew her bones were supposed to lie with Jacob's and with the key Cassy had given her, for the Seeker to find.

Rushton stirred, and I realized he had woken from his drowse when he reached up to capture a strand of my hair in his fingers, distracting me from the wild tumble of my thoughts. "Like silk," he murmured, stroking it between his fingers. "Black silk." He reached out, and this time I did not resist as he drew me onto his chest. He studied my face with a hungry longing that made my blood sing.

I said unsteadily, "We are supposed to be preparing for a feast."

"That is exactly what I am thinking," he said very purposefully, and his mouth closed on mine.

✦ 19 ✦

THAT NIGHT WHEN the moon rose, as ripe and golden as a peach, a desert horn sounded, announcing the start of the night's festivities. A Sadorian tribeswoman named Kaman had been sent to bring me fresh clothes and desert sandals, saying they were gifts from Jakoby. She had imperiously shooed an amused Rushton out to make his own preparations and sent a boy running off for hot water so she could help me bathe and dress. I had tried to tell her I needed no help, but very politely she made it clear that my wishes were irrelevant, since they conflicted with Jakoby's command. Seeing no other course than to submit, I had allowed myself somewhat self-consciously to be disrobed, sponged down, and toweled. Then she had oiled my skin in a massage so delicious that I had actually fallen asleep. Which was just as well because the hairdressing that followed had been a very long and wearisome business. I had managed to endure it only because Kaman had begun describing the process of smoking and drying and salting the fish they gathered each year.

It was fascinating, though I asked if she did not fear to eat fish that had washed up dead on the beach. She answered that the fish were not dead when they washed up and that even if one threw a fish back into the waves, it would swim ashore again. I was pondering this, wondering what Ari-noor or Ari-roth would say of this determined suicide, when

Kaman went on to tell me that the tribes believed the fish were regarded as a promise that one day the earth would be healed and that the feast on this night was a thanksgiving for the sea's bounty, without which the Sadorians would not survive. This was a night, she added, when tribesfolk bestowed gifts upon one another to echo the gifting of the sea.

At last, Kaman pronounced that my hair was finished. At her command, I removed the light wrap I had worn to soak up any excess oil, and she helped me dress in the exquisite blue and green silken robes that Jakoby had sent. They felt beautiful against my skin.

Kaman bowed and departed, which was when I heard the desert horn. I took a deep breath and emerged from the tent. The desert looked like a frozen sea, with waves and troughs filled with greenish shadows running away into the indigo night, and the stars sparkled, despite the moon's brightness. I drew a long deep breath of the sweet desert air and turned to look at the tents glowing white and billowing slightly. A number of people were walking among them and back toward the trade stalls, and I began to move in the same direction, farseeking Maruman, but he was either sleeping or had boarded the ship. I strove for Gahltha and, finding him wooing a Sadorian mare, withdrew at once, not wanting to interrupt.

"Elspeth?" said a voice. Seely stood with Jakoby and Jak, clad in brown and gold sandsilk robes. Like mine, her hair had been elaborately plaited, and seeing the lovely and intricate design woven into it, I felt less self-conscious about my own hair.

"Both of you look well in desert attire." Jakoby approved so maternally that I guessed she must have gifted Seely, too, and I thanked her for my own clothes and for sending Kaman. I wanted to ask if she had any news of Bruna, who must surely be in Templeport, but before I could speak, Jakoby said briskly that we ought to go to the feasting ground, for Jak must make his speech to the tribe leaders before Bram spoke. She took Jak's arm and drew him a little ahead with her as she began explaining the formalities that must be observed when presenting his gift of taint-eating insects. Jak said it was not so much a gift to the tribes as to the earth.

"Nevertheless," said Jakoby, "you must present the insects in this way, for what you propose to do will change the earth, and that is a very serious thing in our eyes. Indeed, you must present your gift specifically to the Earthtemple."

It dawned on me belatedly that Jakoby intended the teknoguilder to present his gift this night, and Seely confirmed this, saying that Jakoby had suggested it, for this was a night of gift-giving, and was not the bestowing of Jak's insects a gifting?

We were now passing through the trading area where numerous stalls and tables were laden with everything from oranges to glimmering stones, perfumes in tiny bottles, feather sunshades, and great soft bolts of sandsilk. Surprisingly few people were buying and browsing, but when I saw the number of people crossing the stretch of sand to our same destination, I realized that all Sadorians would attend the feast. The distance was not great, and soon I could see fifty enormous bonfires dug in a semicircle facing a long semicircular table at which sat all the tribe leaders. Fire pits and tables formed a complete circle, with two halves facing one another, and people sat about the fire pits on woven mats. The smell of cooking food was strong, and I realized that much of it was buried in the embers of the fire pits. But there were also young Sadorian boys and girls, beaming with pride, moving around the fire pits with trays of cold food and ceramic mugs of fement.

"Come," Jakoby said to Jak, and the teknoguilder smiled reassuringly at a suddenly anxious-looking Seely, saying he would join her soon.

We were close to the last fire pit, and there were plenty of empty woven mats set down. Just as we took our places, Jakoby called for silence. Seeing Jak standing nervously beside the tribeswoman, I realized that the teknoguilder would speak immediately, and my stomach clenched in sympathy. To his credit, Jak looked pale but composed as Bram rose to present him to the tribes as a senior Misfit of Obernewtyn, explaining that on this night of thanksgiving, Jak wished to present a gift to the Earthtemple on behalf of his people, the Misfits.

Then the old man took his seat. I knew Jak had no taste for speaking nor any particular skill at it, but he spoke without pretense and with care, and although his voice shook at first, it steadied as he became absorbed in explaining his interest in the shining insects that inhabited dark wet caves in the Land and his discovery that the tiny creatures could consume tainted matter and transform it within their bodies so that it was harmless. He told how he had conceived a plan to breed the insects until they were capable of surviving in the open, in the hope of being able to set them loose on the edge of the Blacklands to begin the massive task of undoing the damage that had been done to the earth. But all Blacklands were arid, and the tiny insects needed cool, dark, damp surroundings to thrive in their natural state; therefore, they would have to be bred to tolerate dryness and even heat. His research had been completed during his exile in the West land when he had finally succeeded in breeding a hardier if less long-lived form of the insect.

846

"Given your reverence for the earth and your belief that healing is possible," Jak said, "it seems more than fitting to me that this is where I will release my insects. Therefore, I offer my insects and my skill in settling them here in the desert lands as a gift to the Earthtemple."

The wording was formal and careful, and there was almost no response to his speech, save that the silence seemed very concentrated. Jakoby rose smoothly from the place she had taken at the end of the table and went to stand beside Jak, saying, "I would like to thank the teknoguilder Jak, who has brought to the desert lands a gift of even more extraordinary importance than he can guess, for his gift fulfills an old prophecy that says a day will come when the earth begins to heal itself, and from that day, no woman shall immerse herself in an isis pool. For once Jak releases the insects, it may truly be said that the earth has begun to heal itself."

I saw by Jak's expression that he had not expected this announcement, and I suspected it was the same with Bram, though he was too canny to show his reactions openly. Other tribal leaders muttered and scowled to one another. Then a woman's voice shouted out to accuse Jakoby of deliberately misinterpreting the prophecy because of her obsession with ending the practice of immersions.

"It does not matter to you that other women do not fear the immersion, Jakoby, for in suffering, we show our allegiance to the wounded earth."

"The earth did not choose to be poisoned, Galia."

There was an uproar at this, with cries of anger and distress from the audience, and shouts that the immersions did not signify choosing to be poisoned but a sharing of the earth's pain.

Jakoby heard the latter and swung on the woman who had

spoken. "And what of the babes who are deformed by this wondrous sharing, for it is they who must bear the burden of their mother's choice," she said icily.

There was another outcry, and then a man called out to ask how the Earthtemple would survive if there were no more deformed babies to serve as Temple guardians.

Jakoby's eyes flashed, as if she had been waiting for this question. She said grimly to the man, "And now the truth comes to show its face. Are there no whole Sadorians who will offer themselves in service to the Earthtemple? Only those born maimed and crippled are worthy to serve the earth?"

The ensuing hum of talk was less angry and more confused, but now Bram rose to say with authority and finality that this was a night of thanksgiving and not for angry debates. The gift offered by Jak had been properly announced, and the overguardian of the Earthtemple would either accept or spurn it. There was some low muttering, but Bram called to the chanters to offer the Song of the Fish in praise of the sea, and soon their voices drowned out any protest.

"What was all that about?" Seely whispered worriedly when the chant ended some minutes later and we had both been served mugs of a sweet light fement.

"The Sadorians feel it is an honor for a woman to offer herself to the isis pools once a year. They are tainted, and by risking the health of any child they might be carrying, many Sadorians believe that they are showing their solidarity with the wounded earth. Any child born with deformities is given as a gift to the Earthtemple, where it will be cared for and trained up as a guardian," I said.

"And this prophecy Jakoby spoke of. Who made it?"

"I do not know who prophesied it, but no doubt it was one

of the kasanda. It is only Jakoby's opinion that Jak's insects fulfill the prophecy."

"You would think that the people here would be grateful that they need not risk their unborn children," Seely said indignantly.

"Some probably would be, but the immersions have become tradition, and people do not like breaking traditions. And, of course, they fear what will happen to the Earthtemple. For them, the deformities are natural in the guardians. They revere the guardians and are guided by them. A person deformed by reverence to the earth is no ordinary person. But to have an ordinary man or woman as a guardian or even an overguardian?" I shook my head.

"A tradition based on harming unborn children is wrong," Seely said.

"So my mother says," said a clear husky voice, and I looked up to see Jakoby's lovely, long-limbed daughter, Bruna. She was clad in violet silks, and she sat beside Seely with the fluid grace of a silk cord, adding, "I think it is her greatest desire to see the practice of immersions end."

"Bruna!" I said. "I am glad you arrived safely. I did not see you when we came ashore, and I feared that something might have befallen you on the coast road."

"I did not go down to the ship, but I sent word with a friend to tell my mother where I had placed her tent."

I did not ask why she had not come to the ship, for it was obvious. "Why is Jakoby so opposed to the practice of immersion when the rest of your people see it as an honor?" I asked.

Bruna turned her slanted golden eyes on me. "You must ask my mother that question, Guildmistress, for it is at the heart of her deepest sorrow."

I was startled by her words, for if I remembered correctly, the overguardian of the Earthtemple had told Jakoby that before she returned to Sador on the *Umborine*, she would encounter something that touched upon a deep sorrow. Did that mean that she had been sent out by the Earthtemple to bring back Jak and his insects since they would heal the isis pools and put an end to the practice of immersion? If so, then surely the Temple guardians would approve Jak's gifting.

I realized that Bruna was watching me, waiting for me to respond to her rebuff. In truth, I had half expected it, for the question had been an intimate one. But Bruna had dealt firmly and gracefully with me, and as she turned back to answer some question of Seely's, it struck me that the young tribeswoman had lost her characteristic arrogance. There was no longer any haughtiness in her face or judgment in her eyes. Indeed, the last time I had seen her in Sutrium, Bruna had been a girl, lovely and half wild, but now she was a woman.

Bruna remained with us for the length of two chant songs, singing exquisitely when everyone sang and between songs helping us get food from the embers to sample, recommending some and rejecting others. In the break between the chant songs, she asked numerous questions about Sutrium and events in the Land with an eagerness that surprised me. Yet she did not ask about Dardelan. Then she rose and departed as abruptly and unexpectedly as she had joined us.

"She is very beautiful," Seely said wistfully, gazing after her.

My attention was not on Bruna but on Dardelan, who was approaching our fire pit from the other direction with Jak and Brydda. Obviously, Bruna had left because she had seen him, but from the tranquility on Dardelan's face, either he had not seen Bruna or he truly cared nothing for her.

As they sat down, Dardelan told me I looked splendid,

and it was a pity that Rushton would not join us to admire my finery. He nodded toward the tables, and I turned to see that Rushton was now seated beside Bram, and the two men were speaking closely together. Rushton had a parchment before him and was now scribing something upon it. Not envying him, I turned back to find the others talking about Jak's insects and the furor they had roused. The teknoguilder insisted he had not had any idea that his gift would be so controversial, and Dardelan asked what was involved in releasing the insects into the desert lands. Was it simply a matter of tipping them onto tainted earth? Jak shook his head, explaining earnestly that it would take him and Seely at least two moons to settle the insects, for they had to be carefully established as a colony somewhere near the edge of the Blacklands, and from there, they would gradually spread out.

"I look forward to hearing of your progress, for I cannot truly see the Sadorians refusing your gift. It seems their objection concerns whether these insects mean the process of immersion is to end immediately or die out naturally as the isis pools lose their taint," Dardelan said. "How do you plan to return to the Westland when this work is done? If you will travel by sea, I would be glad if you would stop a night at Sutrium and give us your news."

"Seely and I mean to travel by the coast road to Obernewtyn after we have finished here," Jak said. "But it will be no hardship to stop a night to exchange news in Sutrium on our way back to the Westland."

"You will be my honored guests," Dardelan promised. "But perhaps you will decide not to go back to the Westland, once you have been at Obernewtyn again."

"There is a lifetime's work for me in the Beforetime complex," Jak said simply.

"What will you do with the knowledge you gain of the Beforetime?" Jakoby asked. The glint in her eyes as she joined us made me think that she had been engaged in more than one fiery discussion following her speech.

The teknoguilder met her gaze steadily. "I will use what I learn as best I can, to serve our time."

"Are you sure the knowledge of the Beforetime will serve this world?" Jakoby countered. "Some say that it is enough to live in the aftermath of the mistakes made by the Beforetimers, without courting the danger of dabbling in their knowledge."

"So said the Council," Jak replied, "but knowledge is no more evil than a knife. It is how knowledge and knives are wielded that makes them evil or not."

"I do not doubt you or your motives, my friend," Jakoby said. "But like a knife, knowledge can all too easily fall into the hands of those who will have no scruples about using it."

The teknoguilder sighed a little. "This is a dance of words I cannot win. Let me ask you a question instead. My hunger for knowledge gave me the gift that I offered tonight to the tribes. Do you say I should not have sought that knowledge or brought it here to put into practice?"

Jakoby held his gaze and finally said, "No, I do not say that." She laughed then and seemed to relax. "For one who does not dance with words, my friend, you have a quick-stepping mind."

Seely gave me an expectant look, and I knew she was willing me to ask why Jakoby had been so determined to end the practice of immersion. But instead, I said lightly that we had seen Bruna and that she looked well. I was watching Dardelan covertly, and I saw him stiffen and then master himself. His reaction made me feel gleeful. Jakoby merely answered equably that she did look well. "I only wish she had not decided to work for a season in the spice groves, for I had hoped to spend some time with her." She did not look at the young high chieftain at all, as if she had forgotten there was ever anything between him and her daughter.

I asked, "When will she leave?"

"Tomorrow," Jakoby said. "Those who will serve always leave before the final feast of the conclave, for the grove cannot be left unattended for more than a fiveday. She will leave at dusk."

"She will be happier in the desert than she was in the Land," Dardelan said flatly.

"If you think it, then I know it must be so," Jakoby said to him coolly. She rose with the same sinuous grace as her daughter and looked at me. "Guildmistress?"

I stared up at her stupidly before realizing that she was asking me to accompany her. I got to my feet with clumsy haste, mumbling a farewell to the others, and followed her through the throng. She led me away from the feast site and toward the trade stalls. A silky breeze blew, carrying the scents of cook fires and perfumed oils and salt to us, and I asked if Bruna really meant to leave for the desert so soon.

Jakoby's laughter echoed merrily over the moon-drenched sand dunes. "Did you see Dardelan's face when I said she would leave tomorrow?"

"Then it is not true?"

"It will be true, if I have not lit enough of a fire in Dardelan's belly to hunt a mate," Jakoby said crisply.

"Hunt?" I echoed.

"Three hours before dawn tomorrow, any man may hunt any woman whose name he has scribed on a stone and set into the bowl that stands before the tent of the tribal leader of the woman he desires, so long as she is not mated to another or deemed too young. The woman is given the stones at midnight as a warning, and she has an hour's start on her hunters. She may favor the man when she glimpses his face, but still the man must catch her. The hunt ends at dawn."

"That is barbaric," I said, appalled.

She grinned. "It would be, if those hunted were not tribeswomen."

"Dardelan is no tribesman," I said.

"For this night, he must become one if he would have Bruna. He let her flutter from his fingers when she had given herself to him like a tamed bird, and now she has returned to the tribes. So now he must hunt her in the desert way. Right at this moment, several of my tribesmen are telling Dardelan of the hunt, and one of them will boast that he means to hunt Bruna. He is a strong, handsome warrior whom any woman might desire for a mate."

I did not know whether to be shocked or to laugh. "Does Bruna know?"

"Of course not. She is all sad dignity and restraint since her return from the Land. She has told me that her love for Dardelan is dead. Maybe she even believes it. Yet in an hour or so, I will send someone to her with the stones that have her name scribed on them, and she will have no choice but to take part in the hunt." Jakoby laughed wolfishly.

"What if Dardelan does not put in a stone? What if the other hunter catches her?"

"My daughter will not be caught, save if she desires it, and Dardelan will have to prove himself by catching her," the tribeswoman said proudly. Then she smiled. "I do not doubt that I will go now and find there are two stones in my bowl for Bruna."

"I thought you were opposed to their match," I said.

"I was in the beginning, but there is true love between them, and recent events tell me that the days in which Sador stood apart from people of the Norseland and your land are coming to an end. Yet, they will still decide the matter between them, the boy chieftain and my daughter. I am done with a mother's meddling."

Jakoby stopped, and I realized where she had been leading me; the Earthtemple loomed ahead.

"The overguardian has summoned me?" I asked, looking into the dark cleft in the earth that was the entrance to the Earthtemple.

Jakoby nodded, and we walked in silence down into the dense pool of moonshadow where the Temple entrance lay. The last time I had come here, I had entered this rift in broad daylight. Long lines of petitioners had waited in the shade of the rift walls—people wanting prayers said for them or a futuretelling, healing or medicines, or those needing to exchange coins from the Land for tokens. The veiled guardians had gone up and down the lines dispensing advice, exchanging coin for tokens, accepting gifts, and handing out medicines and, occasionally, reproaches.

Tonight the rift was empty.

"We must wait here," Jakoby said, a grim note in her voice.

"Jakoby, do you dislike the Earthtemple because it allows the immersions?" I asked softly.

She glanced up at the star-specked sky and said almost wearily, "Do you know I might have served here as a guardian, for my mother entered an isis pool when she was pregnant. Though she did not know it at the time, there were two inside her belly. Both of us were born perfect, save that my sister had a deformed jaw and mouth. Seresh remained with me and our mother until we were five, for my sister needed no special care such as the Earthtemple offers. My father disapproved, for deformed babies were generally given immediately to the Temple. I do not know what motivated my mother to diverge from tradition, but she left my father and lived apart from our tribe, so neither my sister nor I knew that she was deformed. I only knew that I looked like my mother and my sister did not, but we supposed that she resembled my father, whom we believed to be dead.

"You would think I would have known she was terribly deformed in the face, but the ideal of beauty is learned. Despite the difference in our faces, my mother adored us both and lavished us with affection and tenderness, telling us over and over that we were beautiful. Then one dark-moon night, she brought us to Templeport. We came here and waited until a Temple guardian emerged. I do not know how, but it had been arranged in advance. Only at that moment did we realize Seresh was to stay, but not I. We wept and clung to one another, for there was great love between us, and we did not understand why we must be parted. "It is an honor!" my mother cried to my sister, and tore her fingers from mine and dragged me off.

"I ran away as soon as I could and came back here, but the Temple guardians would not let me see my sister. They said she needed time to become accustomed to that life. When I was older, my mother told me everything, but I came here many times against her wishes, seeking Seresh. I wanted to see that she was happy, as I had been promised. Finally, they allowed me to see her. She was veiled, but when she drew back her veil, I gasped, for I had not seen her since we were children, and I saw that her face was ghastly. . . ."

Jakoby's eyes glittered with tears. "Seresh saw my reaction, of course, and she asked me in a bitter voice what hurt she had ever done to anyone that I should have beauty and she a monster's mask. I did not know what to say, so I asked foolishly if she was not happy serving in the Earthtemple. "I am a monster among monsters," she answered.

"What happened to her?" I asked, full of pity.

"She ran away from the Earthtemple. The guardians said she drowned herself, and I believe that is truly what they thought. But when I was older and had been made tribe leader, an overguardian who was a kasanda summoned me and told me that Seresh had not died but had stolen coin and escaped upon a ship that had berthed here to collect water and food. The overguardian had dreamed it and dreamed that I must be told. She did not tell me why. Perhaps she did not know."

"But . . . where could she go and what could she do?" I asked.

"There is not a sevenday that passes when I do not ask that myself," Jakoby said. "Needless to say, when Bruna lay in my belly and my bondmate said it was dark-moon and time for me to go to the isis pools, I refused. He left me, saying I was no true woman. You saw tonight how many of the tribesfolk revere the practice of immersions." Her expression was cold and dreamy. "You know what I remember most? Seresh loved pretty things. She dressed in my mother's silks and jewels and danced with such grace that it was pure beauty, and neither of us ever knew she was hideous to behold. How she must have hated it in the Earthtemple where they wear only rough white weaves and never dance."

At the sound of stone grinding on stone, Jakoby's face became a blank mask. "Go. The overguardian awaits you." She turned and strode away without looking back.

✦ ✦ ✦

"What do you seek of the earth?" asked the veiled girl who had emerged from the narrow gap beside the great pivoting stone that was the entrance to the Earthtemple. Her form was slight and not visibly deformed, but she limped when she walked.

"I seek that which the seer Kasanda left for the Seeker, as promised to me by the last overguardian of the Temple," I replied.

"May you nurture the earth and find harmony," the guardian said. It was no true answer, for these were words of ritual offered to all who came to the Earthtemple. The guardian gestured for me to follow her, when suddenly I remembered that Maruman and Gahltha were supposed to come here with me for the fifth sign and one of Kasanda blood as well! Was it possible that I was wrong in thinking I had been brought here to get what Kasanda had left me?

"Come," said the Temple guardian, for my doubts had slowed me almost to a stop. She led me deep into the many-layered labyrinth of tunnels and caves that was the Earth-temple. The air was cold and strangely scentless, though outside the night was warm and fragrant. As I followed the steady, padding footsteps of the silent Temple guardian, I thought of Jakoby's twin sister, Seresh, dragged weeping and terrified from her beloved sister's arms. She had been only five, younger than I had been when my parents were burned. How terrified she must have been to be brought into these cold stone corridors and informed that she must henceforth live veiled among men, women, and children all deformed in their own ways. Were the veils ever removed? If so, the deformities of the other Temple guardians would have frightened the little girl, for she had not known that she was deformed. No wonder Seresh had run away, but where could she have gone, for she could not run away from her deformed face?

The Temple guardian stopped and turned to me, lifting her lantern, allowing me to see the shadowy darkness of her eyes and hair through her veil's thin gauze. She indicated a narrow doorway cut into the stone behind her, saying, "You must go through this door into the chamber beyond it and wait. I will tell the overguardian that you have come." She unhooked a lantern from the wall and gave it to me.

I did as she had bidden, knowing what I would see, for I had been here before. Soon I was gazing upon the panels that Kasanda had created and that I had been shown on my previous visit to the Earthtemple. It was strange to think that they had been carved by the laughing, dark-haired, dark-skinned Cassy of my dreams, who had laughed with her Tiban lover and argued with her mother and father.

I went to the first panel, which showed a Beforetime city. I had thought it the city we now knew as Newrome under Tor, but maybe it was another. The city was very beautiful in its queer, angular way, a forest of slender square towers rising impossibly high into the sky. The panel depicting it paid homage to the art and power of the Beforetimers and was in stark contrast to the next panel, which showed the city again, but as a great, soulless, devouring beast that smothered the earth and befouled the waters, killing all living things other than humans. The third panel focused on the skies, showing them clogged with the filth that spewed from hundreds of pipes rising from human buildings. I noticed, though I had not noticed before, that in one corner, the carved black smoke parted to reveal a full moon peering through a torn patch, almost like an eye peeping through a spy-hole. This sly moon eye made me think of Rushton, his moon-hating ancestor, and my theory.

Later panels showed forests, waterways, the sea, wetlands, and mountains, all damaged and besmirched by humans and the scabrous outcroppings of their cities. The panels' message was as simple and starkly clear as it had been when I came here the first time: The Beforetimers had used the earth ruthlessly, disregarding everything but their own immediate desires. Their heedless greed and arrogant desire for power had brought the Great White upon the earth. The last panel showed the Great White, and I gazed at it, thinking of Cassy's father, who had believed the Sentinel project would save humans from themselves, even though his own bondmate had left him because she could not believe it.

I heard a step behind me.

A tall, slender, veiled figure entered the chamber, and I knew it must be the woman who now served as overguardian of the Temple, but I gaped to see Maruman prowling by her side, his yellow eye gleaming smugly.

"Greetings, Seeker," the overguardian said before I could beastspeak Maruman. It was a young voice for all its cool poise, and I remembered that the previous overguardian had been little more than a child as well. How was it that the guardians chose a child to set above them?

"Most overguardians are children," said the thin formal voice. "Age brings experience, it is true, but experience does not always bring wisdom. Often it brings complacency or confusion or anxiety. But you are mistaken in thinking that the overguardian of the Temple is chosen by the previous overguardian. We are not chosen. We are foreseen."

With a little shock, I realized the overguardian had answered a thought that I had not voiced!

"I am a kasanda," she said composedly.

"Do you think it courteous to listen to my private thoughts?" I asked aloud, a little sharply.

"I would think it discourteous, if I had the means to prevent myself," she said tranquilly.

There was nothing to say to that. I drew myself up and said, "Why did you have Jakoby bring me here? Is it because I am to collect whatever Kasanda left for me, because if it is, the last overguardian told me I was supposed to come here with Gahltha and a companion who has Kasanda blood, as well as Maruman. Perhaps he meant you, when he spoke of a Kasanda blood, and Maruman came here before me, but even if I summoned Gahltha, he could not fit in here."

"By here, the overguardian may have meant Sador, rather than the Earthtemple," she responded mildly.

I clenched my fists, feeling almost as irritated as when I spoke with the Futureteller guildmistress at Obernewtyn. I wanted clear answers! "The overguardian made it seem like it had been predicted that I would come here, but in fact, you sent Jakoby for me. Why didn't the last overguardian tell me that I would be summoned?"

"Perhaps when he foresaw what he did, the strongest likelihood was that you would come here of your own accord, but something changed, which brought to me the revelation that Jakoby must be sent after you."

"Why didn't you just send her to find me?"

"I knew that you would come here and that Jakoby had some part to play in your future that was vital and important, but much in my foreseeing was unclear. It seemed safest to do as I did, sending Jakoby to the Moonwatcher and allowing the rest to unfold as it would, thereby leaving you free to come here if you chose."

"What is the fifth sign?" I asked, suddenly weary of mysterious talk.

"It is not a thing to be told," the overguardian said. She reached out and laid her hand on the final panel showing the Great White. With a faint grinding sound, the whole panel suddenly swung outward on a pivoting stone to reveal a narrow passage behind it. The overguardian made a gesture for me to go through. I did so and Maruman followed, but the overguardian did not. Seeing or maybe hearing my puzzlement, she said, "None may walk here, save the seer who made this place, the Seeker who seeks it, and the Moonwatcher."

There were a thousand questions to ask, yet I knew that I would receive no proper answers here. As I turned to follow the narrow passage, my heart quickened at the thought of finding some communication from Kasanda awaiting me.

"What made you come here?" I asked Maruman as we made our way along the narrow tunnel.

"I came because I dreamed I came," Maruman said dreamily.

The passage ended in an entrance to a large cave with nothing in it, save a slitlike opening in the wall opposite the passage. Maruman was already moving toward the opening, and I hastened to catch up with him, wondering what the overguardian had meant by saying "the seer who made this place." Surely she did not mean that Kasanda had literally carved out the passage and the cavern. The opening was truly more a slit than a doorway, and I had to turn sideways to get into it. Feeling uneasy, I pressed forward, and two steps later, I stumbled into a wider space that immediately blazed with a shimmering, coruscating purple radiance that completely blinded me. After a moment of blinking and squinting, my eyes began to adjust, and I realized that the blaze of brightness was nothing more than the light of the lantern I carried, reflected from a thousand shining jagged surfaces.

Fian had once shown me a small dull-looking boulder, which, when cracked open, turned out to be a hollow stone shell lined in tiny perfect crystal spikes. He told me that the Beforetimers had called such a thing a *thunder egg*. What I had entered now was part of a giant thunder egg lined not in white quartz crystals, but in dazzling purple amethyst. Some seemed to reflect the lantern light blindingly, and only after studying the walls for a moment did I realize that some had been cut into diamond-like facets. Indeed, it seemed there was a pattern in the polished stones. So absorbed was I in trying to make out what it was, I did not at first notice something gray and square sitting on the floor.

I knelt down and gazed at a flat rectangle of plast the size of a tea tray and as thin as two of my fingers. Atop it was a black glass panel like a window, but I could see nothing through it. Setting the lantern down carefully, I leaned closer and noticed that there was scribing on the plast. Not gadi words, but some language that I did not recognize. There was also a join all about the edges, which suggested that the rectangle was some sort of case, but there was no lock or keyhole or any sort of handle to open it. I touched the case warily, but it felt merely cool as anything kept long in a cave would feel. I touched the glass, and when nothing disastrous happened, I tried simply prizing the case open with my fingers.

It would not budge, but the case was very light. I sat down cross-legged, lifted it onto my knees, and examined it minutely. I had not noticed before a small recessed shape, almost invisible in the side of the case, alongside a small square gap. Remembering the recessed hand shapes on Norseland and in the Westland, I pressed a finger carefully into the space. Nothing happened, and the sickening thought came to me that perhaps the key that was supposed to have been left in Jacob Obernewtyn's tomb, along with his and Hannah's bones, would have opened this case. That was the first time it occurred to me that just as Ariel could not see all, neither must Kasanda have been able to do so. I set the case back on the ground and stood up, wondering if all of Kasanda's careful plans and sacrifices had come to nothing because she had failed to foresee that Hannah would not be at Obernewtyn when the Great White came.

Maruman gave a snarling hiss, and I turned to see that his fur was standing on end and crackling with static energy in a way that would have been comical had it not been so unnerving.

"What is it?" I asked him, and then shuddered as I felt it too—a frisson of prickling power that ran about the glittering chamber and over my skin till I felt my own hair stand on end. A low-pitched hum filled the chamber. It took me a moment to realize that it was coming from the plast case, and I saw with a shock that the glass panel on the top now glowed with a greenish light. Then there was a faint click. I knelt down and looked closely at the case. The recessed place had now come level with its gray surface.

Heart pounding, I touched the recess. There was another distinct click, and the case split open at the join and lifted open smoothly of its own accord, revealing a set of small raised squares scribed with letters in the bottom half of the case and a glowing white screen in the top.

Seeing the now familiar rows of small squares and the screen, I realized with incredulity that I was looking at a small computermachine! And unlike the computermachines under Ariel's residence, this one was working. Or at least, it was being powered, somehow, by the amethyst chamber. But how to learn what it contained? I studied the little squares, which Reul had once told me were also called *keys*. He had shown me how to tap on them to create scribed commands that the computermachine would obey if it could. More recently, Jak had shown me that a computer could be questioned as well as commanded, but he had added that communications with a computer must be framed in a way and in words that the computer would understand.

I licked my lips and realized my head was beginning to ache. I forced myself to concentrate on the computermachine as I carefully tapped in letters to ask what was required of me. The words appeared in neat perfect black letters on the white screen, but nothing else happened. I tried several other questions, and they appeared one after another on the screen, but the computermachine offered no response. Perhaps the computer needed a code word or a series of numbers that would allow me to communicate with it. Another sort of key. I chewed my lip and then tapped in my name. That produced no effect, and I thought of Jak saying that it would be impossible to guess the code word of any Beforetime user of a computermachine, for they and their world were utterly unkonwn to us. Except that Cassy was not unknown to me. I typed in HANNAH and JACOB, and when they did not work, I racked my brain for the name of Cassy's Tiban lover and wrote SAMU. Still nothing. I tried CASSY DUPREY and nothing happened.

Defeated, I set the case down again, reminding myself that Jak had said that it would be virtually impossible to guess a stranger's code word. But Cassy was no stranger to me after so many years of dreaming of her, and she would have known that I had been born in an age beyond the computermachines of her time. She had lived into that time, and she might have foreseen that I would come to learn something of computermachines. But if she had set a code containing a message to me, would she not have made very sure that it was something I could guess?

I took up the computermachine again and tapped in KASANDA. Nothing happened. I tapped in CASSANDRA. Again nothing happened, but it was possible that I had scribed it incorrectly. I tried several versions of the name, but none caused anything to happen. I stared at the screen glumly and thought of Dell, wakening Ines by speaking her name aloud. Would the program in this computermachine hear me as Ines had?

I licked my lips and said in a stilted voice, "Kasanda, can you hear me?"

Nothing.

"Kasanda, can you hear me?"

Nothing again. I thought for a moment, and then said, "I am the Seeker."

The light in the chamber seemed to dim, and I listened eagerly, awaiting the voice of the computermachine, but to my disappointment, there was no response. I glanced back down at the computermachine and gasped, for all of my laboriously typed questions had vanished, and now words were scribing themselves rapidly in lines on the screen.

I read them, heart thundering.

MY FRIEND, I read. I CALL YOU FRIEND, SEEKER, THOUGH WE HAVE NEVER MET, FOR I HAVE KNOWN YOU A VERY LONG TIME. TO YOU I KNOW THAT I WILL ONLY EVER BE A STRANGER WHOM YOU HAVE SOMETIMES GLIMPSED IN DREAMS OF A TIME THAT YOU WILL CALL THE BEFORETIME.

THERE ARE SO MANY THINGS THAT I WISH I COULD TELL YOU, EXPLANATIONS I MIGHT MAKE, BUT THERE IS NO TIME.

HOW STRANGE IT IS TO SPEAK OF TIME, WHEN I HAVE DEFIED

IT MORE THAN ONCE AND IN MORE THAN ONE WAY IN MY LIFE. YET TIME IS TRULY OF THE ESSENCE, FOR I HAVE NO RELIABLE WAY TO REGULATE THE POWER OF THIS CRYSTAL CHAMBER. I USED THE KNOWLEDGE OF MY LOST WORLD TO PREPARE IT AS BEST I COULD, BUT I KNOW THE POWER OF THE CRYSTAL RESONANCES IS TOO STRONG AND THAT VERY SOON IT WILL DESTROY THE WORKINGS OF THE COMPUTER. THEREFORE COMMIT TO MEMORY ALL I HAVE WRITTEN HERE, FOR THERE WILL NOT BE TIME FOR YOU TO READ MY WORDS AGAIN.

IF YOU ARE READING THIS, THEN THIS PORTABLE COMPUTER IS BEING POWERED BY THE CRYSTALS IN THE AMYTHEST CHAMBER, WHICH YOUR LANTERN LIGHT WILL HAVE ACTIVATED AFTER A SHORT TIME. I CANNOT EXPLAIN THE SCIENCE OF CRYSTAL RESONANCES AS AN ENERGY SOURCE, FOR THAT IS KNOWLEDGE LOST TO YOUR WORLD, BUT I PRAY THAT THIS COMPUTER, FOR WHICH I PAID LONG AND DEAR, WILL LAST LONG ENOUGH TO DO WHAT IT MUST DO NOW.

INSIDE IT IS A SMALL DEVICE, WHICH YOU WILL TAKE AWAY WITH YOU FROM THIS PLACE. BUT BEFORE I EXPLAIN HOW TO GET IT FROM THE COMPUTER, YOU NEED TO IMPRINT IT WITH YOUR VOICE.

PRESS THE A KEY.

I looked at the little squares until I found the A and pressed it.

The humming changed pitch again, and all the words vanished, to be replaced by two new lines of scribing.

SPEAK YOUR NAME AND SAY WHAT YOU ARE, SIMPLY AND CLEARLY.

PRESS C AND REMEMBER EXACTLY WHAT YOU HAVE SAID.

I cleared my throat and said, "I am Elspeth Gordie. I am the Seeker." Then I pressed C.

The line of words on the screen vanished, and new words

appeared, letter by glowing letter and far more swiftly than any hand could scribe them.

Press B and let Merimyn sing.

Press C.

"Merimyn?" I read, baffled.

Maruman padded forward and sniffed at the computermachine, and I suddenly remembered a vision I had had of him as a kitten, playing on the dreamtrails with a young woman who had seemed vaguely familiar to me. She had called him Merimyn! My mind surged with questions, but I dared not waste time in questions lest the computermachine be destroyed before it could serve its purpose. So I found the B square. Bidding Maruman sing, I pressed it. He gave a long warbling yowl that would have made my hair stand on end, if it was not already doing so, and when he stopped, I pressed C.

The humming changed pitch again, and when I looked back at the screen, large red letters were flashing there: Wait. Imprinting voice codes to memory seed.

The humming dropped in pitch, and the words were replaced by other words.

The memory seed is now encoded.

Press the Eject key and the device will appear at the side of the computer. Take it and keep it with you at all times.

It took me so long to find the tiny word *Eject* scribed above the square marked with an O that I was beginning to panic, for I was sure I could now smell a faint burning odor, and I feared that the computermachine might suddenly explode or burst into flames. I pressed the O, and a small round shape protruded from the side of the machine. Gingerly, I pulled it out. It looked indistinguishable from thousands of similar small bits and pieces of plast that the Teknoguild had brought up from the levels they were continually excavating. I had no idea what it was or would do, but clearly the tiny tablet played some vital part in my quest. I slipped it into my inner pocket and buttoned it before turning my attention to the screen, where new words had scribed themselves.

THE MEMORY SEED CONTAINS WHAT YOU NEED TO GAIN ACCESS TO ALL LEVELS OF THE SENTINEL COMPLEX. YOU NEED ONLY LOAD THE SEED INTO ANY PORT ONCE YOU ARRIVE. EVEN A MAINTENANCE PORT IN THE AUXILIARY BUILDINGS WILL DO BECAUSE ALL ROADS LEAD TO SENTINEL, AS MY FATHER USED TO SAY. NO ONE WITHOUT THE MEMORY SEED WILL BE ABLE TO ENTER WITHOUT CAUSING SENTINEL TO SHUT DOWN ALL ACCESS AND DEFEND ITS PERIMETER, AND THE MEMORY SEED IS NOW NO USE WITHOUT YOU AND MERIMYN, FOR YOUR VOICES HAVE BECOME PART OF THE KEY CODE.

THERE IS VERY LITTLE TIME LEFT NOW. I WISH I COULD HAVE HELPED YOU MORE. ONLY REMEMBER THAT . . .

There was a crackling buzz, the smell of burning, and the computermachine screen went black.

Remember what? I wondered, horrified to think that something vital had been lost. Then I swiftly ran over what I had read, committing it to deeper memory, for there were many words I had not understood, and I would have to find out what they meant before I could properly understand what I was to do.

I turned to look at Maruman, whose fur still stood out in a ruff about his head, making him look like a small fierce lion. "Who called you Merimyn?" I asked. It was a mistake, of course. Maruman glared at me with his one baleful eye and turned to stalk out of the amethyst chamber. I rose with a sigh, wondering if the reason he hated questions so much had less to do with the mess of misconnections in his mind than the fact that curiosity was a form of desire, and desire was an emotion.

I looked down at the gray case with its dead black screen, hardly able to believe that it had enabled Kasanda to communicate with me. It was astounding, but at the same time I had a queer feeling of anticlimax. There were so many questions I wished I could have asked, not just about Kasanda's message but about her life and her knowledge of me and my visions, about the Great White and Hannah and Jacob Obernewtyn. Of course, I knew that Kasanda was long dead and could not answer any questions, yet the queer intimacy of what had effectively been a letter to me made it seem eerily as if she *was* alive, as if all times were existing at once.

I touched my pocket and felt the small hardness of the memory seed as I rose and looked one last time at the amethyst chamber's glittering splendor, marveling that Kasanda had been able to use it as a power source. I took up the lantern, and as I left the chamber, the blaze of light was extinguished and I almost stumbled in what seemed darkness, until my eyes had readjusted. I made my way along the narrow passage, my eyes gradually adjusting to the dim, unaugmented lantern light. I crossed the empty cavern and returned to the chamber of carved panels, where the overguardian waited, Maruman sitting by her feet.

"There is one more thing Kasanda left you," she said.

⋆ 20 ⋆

We entered a long sloping walk up the side of an enormous cavern. The faint sea-scented air blowing toward us told me that we were close to the front of the Earthtemple. At length, we entered a small chamber where the wind blew so hard that it immediately snuffed out the lantern flames. But there was no need of them, for nearly palpable beams of silver-white moonlight streamed though a number of irregular openings in the stone. Through them, far below, lay Templeport and all about it as far as the eye could see, the vast, moonlit ocean. I crossed to look out one of the windows and became aware of the drumming of the sea on Templeport and the skirling of the wind against the stony faces carved into the cliff.

The overguardian spoke my name, and I turned. Standing in a shaft of moonlight, her veils whipping and fluttering in the wind, she made such a mysterious, striking vision that it took me a moment to notice that she was pointing to the stone wall behind her. Then I noticed a long vertical crevice in the rough stone too regular to be natural. I went to it and saw something long, narrow, and white standing in it.

"Take it," said the overguardian.

I reached into the niche, and my hand found a long, hard, linen-wrapped bundle. It was much heavier than I had expected from its thinness.

"Open it," said the overguardian.

I knelt to lay it on the ground so I could untie the thongs of hemp binding the cloth tight. When I had unwrapped what lay within, I stared, for it was a sword such as a soldierguard captain might wear or a Councillor who fancied himself a warrior, but this was carved from stone inlaid with silver or some pale shining metal in a scribing that seemed to be the same atop the ruined computermachine. It was a beautiful, ambiguous object and unmistakably Kasanda's work. Indeed, it might be the finest she had ever created, as well as being the last.

"What is it for?" I asked, looking up at the overguardian.

"You are to take it and keep it with you until you find the one to whom it rightfully belongs."

"Who is?"

"That was not given to me to know," she answered serenely.

"It that all?" I asked tersely.

"What more do you want?" she asked.

"I don't mean I want something more. I mean, is that all you can tell me. What is this sword that is not a sword? Why was such a thing made and for whom?"

"I do not know the answers to these questions. I know only that she who placed no value upon possessions valued this and named it the key to all things."

I sighed, suddenly exhausted by puzzles and intrigues. Would there ever be an end to them? I rewrapped the stone sword, retied the thongs, and stood up.

By the time I had climbed from the cleft that led to the pivoting stone Earthtemple entrance, my arms were aching from the weight of the sword, and I headed straight for my tent to rid myself of the unwieldy thing. There was no sign of Jakoby, but I did not need her to guide me. It seemed as though hours had passed while I was in the labyrinth of stone, and I felt chilled to the bone, but the night air was balmy and warm, and when I reached the path leading up from the spit, I saw that a good deal of activity still centered on the trade stalls. In the distance beyond them, the frenzy of movement about the fire pits suggested feasting had given way to dance. I could have gone back and joined the others, but suddenly I knew that I would not. What had happened in the Earthtemple had severed the warm connection I had felt to everyone and everything earlier in the evening, for it was a reminder that however much I might feel or long for it, I was the Seeker, which meant I was alone.

In my tent, I lit a lantern and unwrapped the sword to study it again, wondering why Kasanda had made such a useless if lovely object. It was not a statue that could be set up and admired, and it would never cut anything. The over-guardian had called it a key, which made it seem as if it must be connected to my quest as the Seeker, but she had also said it was to be returned to the one it belonged to, and who could that be? Besides, if Kasanda had made it and left it for me, it had never belonged to anyone but its maker. Unless she had made it *for* someone. But how was I to discover who? I wrapped up the sword, something else nagging at me. The words in the computermachine said that the memory seed would give me access to all levels of the Sentinel Complex, which confirmed that this was my ultimate destination as Seeker, but if it was to open all doors, then why did I need the other words and clues that had been left for me: the key Jacob Obernewtyn had carried into the Blacklands; the words on Evander's cairn; whatever had been carved into the statue that marked the Twentyfamilies' safe-passage agreement; and whatever awaited me in the Red Queen's land.

I lay back on my bed. Kasanda had said that she had defied time twice and in more than one way. What could that possibly mean? And what had she meant by saying it had cost her much to obtain the small computermachine? I could only imagine that she had brought it with her on her journey across the sea to the Red Queen's land, but if so, how had she managed to keep it with her when she was taken by the Gadfian raiders? Unless she had obtained it while she was their captive. Indeed, it might even be the reason she had allowed them to take her.

I rolled onto my stomach and looked at Maruman, who had curled to sleep on the end of my bedroll, and I wondered again about the young woman who had called him Merimyn and how Kasanda had known that name. She must have foreseen his play on the dreamtrails, but why use that slight distortion of his name?

I pushed the stone sword out of sight between my bedroll and the side of the tent. I had no fear that it would be stolen. The penalties for theft were very severe in Sador, because all crime was regarded as theft. I lay staring up into the darkness of the tent roof, feeling more and more awake. Finally, I gave up trying to sleep and decided to bathe in the clear pool at the base of the cliffs. It was but a few minutes' walk away, and the moment the idea came to me, I yearned to feel water on my hot sticky skin. I stripped off my silken clothes, drew on the wrap Kaman had given me earlier, and walked barefoot from the tent over sand still warm from the day, Maruman padding lightly beside me.

I had thought to swim alone, and I was startled and disappointed to see a large crowd of young women already swimming. Their easy nakedness, the lack of men, and the giddy horseplay puzzled me, given the lateness of the hour, but the thought of a swim was too enticing to turn back. I walked to the edge of the pool, shrugged off the wrap, and entered the water. Its embrace was like cold silk, and I sighed with pleasure.

"Greetings, Elspeth," called a voice, and I opened my eyes to see Bruna swimming languidly toward me.

"An odd hour for so many to swim," I said.

"You might call it an informal ritual," Bruna said. "You see, in an hour or so, many of these women will be hunted, so they cool their blood in readiness to make themselves elusive."

I remembered then what Jakoby had told me and said as lightly as I could, "Will you take part in this hunt?"

"I must, for three stones in my mother's bowl had my name on them," she said, tossing her sleek braided head, the beads and silver cuffs giving out a silvery music. "Probably it is no more than curiosity on the part of the men who scribed my name, for I have been away a long time." Her tone was cool and certain, and I wondered what she would say if I told her that Dardelan may have left one of the stones.

Of course I did not, for it was none of my business to meddle with a mother's meddling. Besides, maybe Dardelan had *not* put a stone in the bowl. Indeed, when I thought of him, he was always surrounded by maps and books and laws and quills, serious and preoccupied by the weighty business of governing the Land; I could not imagine anyone less like a hunter than the bookish young high chieftain.

We swam together companionably for a time, and I asked if she had heard anything of Miryum and Straaka. Being in Sador had made me wonder again what had become of the Coercer guilden and the body of her Sadorian suitor since their disappearance after Malik's betrayal in the White Valley. Bruna said she had asked about the pair upon her return to the desert lands, for Straaka had been one of her tribesmen, but no one had seen them. One of the kasanda, however, had told her that the pair walked together still, though not under the moon or sun. I asked what this meant, and Bruna said she deemed it to mean that they walked together in death. This thought sloughed away the languid mood I had fallen into, and I climbed out to find Maruman curled on my robe, his yellow eye fixed on the full moon. Bruna climbed out, too, and stretched out unself-consciously on the warm sand.

"Lie down," she encouraged. "The warm sand is very pleasant, and once you are dry, you brush it off and your skin is gently scoured to silk." Other women lounged all about the pool, and after a slight hesitation, I lay down alongside Bruna. As she had promised, the sand felt wonderfully warm and soft, and I relaxed. Beside me, Bruna sighed and closed her eyes. I slept for a time and woke when Bruna rose and began to brush off the sand. I bestirred myself and did the same, judging from the moon that almost two hours had passed.

When we had both dressed, she suggested I come with her for some food. "The tents will be serving food all night tonight because of the hunt," she said.

The tents and cook fires were busier than ever, but as we approached them, I realized I had no tokens or any coin to exchange for them. Bruna waved aside my confession and brought us both hot berry pastries and minted water. We ate and drank standing, watching two small women with honey-colored skin and deeply slanted eyes tumble and roll with an agility that Merret would have gasped to see. We were interrupted by a long mournful note that swelled in the air.

"That is the signal to tell the hunted that they have an hour before the hunt begins. An hour before I teach some warriors to eat my dust," Bruna said, her golden eyes glimmering with contempt. Fleetingly, I saw the wild, haughty child-woman who had first come with her mother to the Land. Then she smiled. "I have enjoyed your company, Elspeth."

"And I yours," I said, wondering if Dardelan would take part in the hunt and how she would feel when she discovered it. "Good luck," I added, but she was already sprinting away on long lean legs.

"You ought to have said, *Run wild and never submit unless you choose*," said a voice.

It was the Druid's armsman Daffyd, standing beside me clad in loose Sadorian robes.

"Da-Daffyd!" I stammered, gaping at him. "What are *you* doing here?"

His smile faded into a grim determination. "Doing what I have been doing since Ariel sold Gilaine, my brother, and Lidgebaby to Salamander."

"But Salamander has never been here," I said.

"I am not so sure," Daffyd said darkly, glancing around.

I stared at him, taking in his gaunt look and haunted eyes. "Why do you think he would come here?" I asked gently.

Instead of answering, he said, "I have just been speaking to Rushton. He told me what has been happening on the west coast and in the Norselands. That was a fine set of victories. He told me, too, about Domick. It aches my heart to think of it."

I sighed heavily and told him it ached mine, too, but I did not want to speak of the coercer. The hours I had spent with Bruna had lightened my heart, and I did not want to plunge into grief again so soon.

So I said, "Why would Salamander come to Sador knowing

he would be despised as a thief of freedom, captured, and sentenced to the desert walk?"

"I don't think he came here as a slaver," Daffyd said with such certainty that I was taken aback.

"You think he came in disguise?" I asked.

"I think if he came here, it would not be in any disguise, because what he wears the rest of the time is a disguise. I think he came as himself. *As a Sadorian tribesman.*"

"You think Salamander is *Sadorian*?" I demanded incredulously. "The Sadorians despise slavers even more than murderers."

"True, most Sadorians hate slavers as they hate murderers," Daffyd said. "But do you think there are no Sadorian murderers?"

"I see what you are saying," I said more moderately. "But what makes you think Salamander is a tribesman?"

We went to sit on a dune slightly apart from the press about the stalls, and Maruman slipped from my shoulders into my lap.

"I didn't come here originally to find Salamander," Daffyd said. "I came here because there was no way to reach the west coast from the Land after the rebellion. My plan was to board one of the vessels that fish the waters along the edge of the strait and bribe the shipmaster to let me slip overboard and swim to the west coast."

"But you could not find a ship that would take you?" I prompted, weary enough to feel impatient with the circumlocutions of his tale.

"The rumors that fishing boats went that far from Sador proved untrue. Once I realized there was no way to reach the west coast from here, any more than from the Land, I was disheartened. There seemed no reason to go back to the Land as long as the Suggredoon remained closed, so I worked as an aide to one of the traders who stays here all year round, serving the odd seaman and trading with the Sadorians who wander by. I was so much into the habit of thinking about Salamander that I went on doing it, and gradually I started to wonder why he had never attacked any of the Sadorian greatships save the one he destroyed at Sutrium, and why he had never come here."

"Because he is a slaver and the Sadorians loathe slavery," I said.

"Listen," Daffyd said, and now he suddenly changed the subject and began to tell of a good hire he had been offered to go into the desert with a kar-avan. The story was fascinating enough that I did not interrupt, but finally he said that on this trip he had heard something that made him question the prevailing belief that Salamander was from the Red Queen's land.

This startled me out of my irritation, for I had always assumed Salamander had come from the Land until recently, when it had occurred to me that he might be of Gadfian stock. I advanced my own theory, but Daffyd merely shook his head and went on with his kar-avan tale. He said that halfway through the trip, he had become friendly with the bondmate of a Sadorian who had eventually confided to him that she was originally from the Land.

"I asked how she had come to be bonded to a tribesman. I suspect she had never told her tale, and maybe my being from the Land led her to confide it. She said she had been a shipgirl aboard one of the small vessels that the *Black Ship* had attacked. As was usual in those days, Salamander boarded the ship and took all passengers and shipfolk aboard the *Black Ship* to sell as slaves, save one, who was blindfolded and put into a ship boat with the tiller tied so that it would eventually reach land if it did not capsize. The aim, of course, was that, if the man did reach the Land safely, he would tell his tale and spread a terror of the *Black Ship* to make other ships much more inclined to surrender at once. Sometimes Salamander claimed the ship he had captured, but more often than not he simply scuttled it, as he had done this time, and departed.

"Unbeknownst to Salamander, the woman from the karavan had climbed over the edge of the ship on a dangling rope, and she clung to it grimly through the battle. She knew it was Salamander's practice to release a single person in a ship boat, and her idea was to swim after it and climb aboard. But she didn't dare swim to it at once, for fear of being seen. She waited until the *Black Ship* was far away before she dived from the last bit of the ship poking up from the water and swam after the ship boat." He shook his head and added that it had been carried almost out of her sight, and from the woman's account, it had been a long, desperately hard swim to reach it. The whole time, she had been in mortal terror of sharks or of losing sight of the ship boat in the gathering darkness and the high waves. But luckily the moon had risen, and knowing she would die if she did not reach the boat had given her strength and determination. Reaching the ship boat at last, she had dragged herself into it, untied the man, and between them they managed to paddle the boat into a coastal current that brought them here. The man went back to the Land, but the woman stayed in the desert lands and changed her name, terrified that the vengeful and fanatically secretive Salamander would come after her.

"You see, when she was dangling from that bit of rope, the two ships were side by side for a time, and right after the battle, when her shipmates were being marched across a plank onto the *Black Ship*, she saw a queer thing through a porthole in the *Black Ship*. Salamander strode into a cabin, gloved, masked, and swathed in trousers and greatcoat as usual, clutching at his belly. When he took his hand away, his vest was red with blood. The great half-naked slave who tends him took out a needle and thread, and Salamander lifted up his shirt to let the man sew the gash. It was a bloody wound but not a mortal one, but here's the thing: the woman said Salamander's *belly was as brown as choca*."

"He is Gadfian," I murmured, imagining the woman hanging precariously between the ships, holding her breath, and praying not to be crushed or noticed.

Daffyd went on. "My first thought on hearing he was brown-skinned was that Salamander must be Sadorian, but I could not understand why he would be so fanatically secretive if he was, given that the *Black Ship* never visited here. That is when it came to me. He would not care that he was seen and recognized as a Sadorian *unless he wanted to be able to come back here*."

I asked breathlessly, "Have you told this to any of the Sadorians?"

He shook his head impatiently. "I did not care about accusing Salamander to the tribe. I just wanted to use him to go to the Red Queen's land to rescue my brother, Gilaine, and the others. If I could find out who he was, I could slip aboard his ship. I figured he must use one of those vessels he had taken in the strait, since he could not simply come sailing up in the *Black Ship* without being instantly identified as a slaver. I set myself the task of learning if there were any Sadorians who vanished for periods and then reappeared. It was a near impossible quest given that the Sadorians are nomads, but what else had I to do?

"Then not an hour ago, I bumped into Rushton, who told

me he is here because he is trying to mount an expedition to the Red Queen's land before the next wintertime. I asked if I could join, and he said that he saw no reason why I should not come but that I must present my request to Dardelan and Gwynedd, who are high chieftains of the Land now, for they would be the masters of the expedition. Rushton told me that he is to address the tribal council tonight, and he wants me to come with him and tell what I have learned of Salamander. He believes the Sadorians' profound loathing of slavery might sway them in favor of this expedition, since they would protect their land from the slavemasters by participating, and they would have the opportunity to capture Salamander and learn who he is." He frowned. "I suppose you know that the slavemasters are Gadfians?"

I frowned. Once I had dreamed that the slavemasters were Gadfian, but I had not taken it seriously until I had begun thinking that Salamander had got his ship from them. "It is hard to imagine the Gadfians described by the Sadorians could have increased in such numbers."

Daffyd nodded. "From what I have gathered, the Gadfians who stole the Sadorian women died out long ago. Those who invaded the Red Queen's land were another group, and wherever they settled, their fertility was not affected."

"But how could one people live so far apart?"

"The land of the Gadfians was vast, so perhaps after the Great White, some of its people fled in one direction and thrived while the rest settled on the tainted land, which destroyed their ability to bear healthy children."

"You have learned a good deal about Gadfians," I said.

He shrugged. "The Sadorians teach their children about them and the lost Beforetime."

At the sound of an explosion and a flare of golden light, I

looked up to see a cloud of shimmering gold snowflakes against the dark sky.

"That is the signal that one successful hunt has ended," Daffyd murmured.

"What happens if the woman doesn't let herself be caught?" I asked, thinking of Dardelan and Bruna.

"Nothing. The hunters who strived for her will have their stones returned."

"Daffyd!" It was Gilbert, hurrying across the sand. He smiled warmly at me as I struggled to my feet with Maruman in my arms. Daffyd had leapt to his feet at once, and the two men greeted one another with warm handclasps and many questions. Daffyd expressed surprise at Gilbert's Norselander hair, and Gilbert laughed and said he was armsman to Gwynedd, king of the Norselands. Daffyd demanded to know how that could be.

"Come with me, and Gwynedd will tell you his own tale, for he has sent me to find you," Gilbert said.

"Now? But it is not even dawn. How does he know of me anyway?" Daffyd looked almost comically alarmed.

"Rushton spoke of you just now, and when I said I knew you, I was promptly dispatched to find you. As to the time, it seems we have given up on sleep for now. Will you come?"

Daffyd looked at me apologetically. "I should go, for I can ask at once about joining this expedition to the Red Queen's land. We will continue our conversation later."

"Just one thing," I said to Gilbert. "Is Dardelan with Gwynedd?"

The red-haired armsman shook his head. "I think he is the only one among us sensible enough to have gone to his bed, for I have not seen him since the feast ended. Shall I find him for you?"

I shook my head and said that I would see him at firstmeal. I bade Daffyd farewell for now, and Gilbert smiled at me as they moved away. Not until they had vanished into the crowd about the trade stalls did I remember my dreams of Gilaine and Daffyd's brother, Jow, in the Red Queen's land. I should have asked Daffyd if he had dreamed of Gilaine, since my dream indicated that she had dreamed of him. That would have to wait until later. I yawned.

"I/Maruman am tired," Maruman sent.

"I am, too," I admitted, draping the old cat about my neck. Yawning again, I made my way slowly across the sand to the cluster of sleeping tents, hardly able to believe that only a few hours before, I had been inside the labyrinthine Earthtemple receiving a mysterious communication from Kasanda. I reached into my pocket and felt the little memory seed, but I was too weary to begin another whirl of speculations. It was enough, for now, that I had gained what Kasanda had left for me.

By the time I crawled into my tent, I could hardly keep my eyes open. I stripped off the loose robe I had worn for my swim and stretched out luxuriously on my bedroll, lying gingerly on my beaded hair and pulling the cover over me. Maruman turned in several intent circles before settling against my waist, and in moments, I could hear his soft, purring snore.

I was so weary that I felt dizzy, but something kept me from actually falling asleep. Almost of its own volition, a probe formed and ranged, first over the tents, touching a few minds lightly, then moving out beyond the fires and press of people to the open desert. As had happened very occasionally before when I was extremely tired, my mind spontaneously produced a vague spirit shape, and suddenly I was seeing the desert with spirit eyes. The desert's aura was a shifting, liquescent yellow-gold and white.

I saw a dark form running across it, and curiosity sharpened my wits and bade me send my probe toward it. I could not make out the face of the shadowy human form with my spirit eyes, but I reached out to touch the person's ice-blue aura and realized it was Bruna. My curiosity about her was strong enough to have directed my unfocused probe to her. I felt her surprise as she stopped abruptly, and I realized she had heard someone running toward her. She turned and ran on, and I followed her effortlessly.

Then the desert changed, and Bruna seemed to enter a cave. When I saw the glowing aura of plants, I realized she had entered one of the rifts. She was moving deeper into it, and my curiosity was so intense that it drew me deeper into the merge so that, suddenly, I saw through Bruna's eyes just as I had once been able to do with Matthew. I was elated, for it was rare to find someone compatible enough to manage this, but I was shocked, too. For standing before Bruna was *Dardelan*, but Dardelan as I had never seen him! Through Bruna's eyes, I saw that he was naked but for a Sadorian loincloth and a dagger strapped to his leg. He was pale and slim, yet there was a wiry strength to his body not evident when he was clothed. But the most fascinating thing was his aura, visible to my spirit eyes as an overlapping glow. It was a blaze of yellow and gold with flashes of diamond white so dazzling as to be nearly painful. I had never seen an aura quite like it, and I wondered if it was why people had always found Dardelan so charismatic.

"You!" Bruna whispered. "What are you doing here?"

"Hunting you," Dardelan answered. "You spoke once of loving a particular isis pool. So I begged Andorra to lead me here, and I asked Hakim to place his own stone in the bowl and drive you in this direction. I do not know who the other man was, whose stone was in the bowl, but I claim victory. Yet I did not hunt you as a tribesman would have, so I will not send up the golden sign unless you will it."

"You . . . have hunted me?" Bruna's voice trembled with doubt, with grief, with anger. "Why would you bother? I am the same woman you let walk away in Sutrium without a second thought. I have not changed. I will never sit tamely at home while you go to fight. I will never obey orders without question."

"I treated you as I did and said what I said not because I desired you to be anything but what you are, but because I believed that your mother was right in feeling you would be happier here in the desert lands. But after you left Sutrium, I realized that I had never given *you* the choice."

"You let me leave." Bruna's voice had hardened, and I sensed her implacability. The ice lume of her aura shimmered around us.

"I did not let you leave. I deliberately drove you away and only then discovered that I had sent the sun into exile. I love you."

I felt her shock reverberate through our merged aura, and a wave of hot dazzling red suffused the ice blue. "You . . . discovered that you loved me after I left?"

Dardelan laughed, but there was no humor in the sound, and bruised purple ran through the golden aura. "I was dazzled by the fire in you when you were nothing but a child, as sweet and golden and full of stings as fresh honeycomb. You shone like a flame before my eyes. I went about my duties, turning my eyes resolutely away from you, but I seemed to see the afterimage of your face and form everywhere. Maybe it was because you made such a strong impression when you were still a child full of tantrums and willful pride that I failed to perceive that you had grown into a woman. Only after you rode away from Sutrium did I see you clearly, and when I thought of your last words to me, I was shamed. But even amid the shame, I felt pride in the lovely dignity you had shown. I knew I must come to you and beg your forgiveness."

"My mother told me that you came here to ask the tribes for the sacred ships," Bruna said in a stony voice, but I could feel that she was trembling from head to toe.

"I had made up my mind to come here the first moment I could, within a day of your departing Sutrium. But I am high chieftain, and I could not leave on the eve of the great ruse. As Jakoby's daughter, you understand that a leader has a duty to those he leads that he must set above his own desires. My duty took me to the west coast, but then Gwynedd asked your mother to bear him to Norseland, and Rushton asked your mother to bring us here afterward. My duty required me to go with them, but I rejoiced, for there was nowhere else I desired more to visit. I was determined to find you and speak with you before I left the desert lands. But then . . . last night I heard some tribesmen speak of this hunt . . . One talked of hunting *you* and I . . ." He broke off and laughed, looking all at once younger. "I was filled with jealousy, and I put a stone into the bowl with your name upon it. I feared I would lose you to your unknown Sadorian suitor, and I knew it would serve me right, for I had been a fool and did not deserve you. Yet here we stand." Dardelan took a deep breath. "And now all that remains is for you to tell me whether the love you once felt for me is utterly quenched, or whether there is a spark I can fan to life."

Bruna gave a choked laugh, and her icy aura blazed hot

red-bronze. "My love for you could as easily be extinguished as the sun!"

"Then you will be hunted?" There was humility and overwhelming relief in Dardelan's soft question, but now his aura blazed red and gold, like flame, and even though Bruna could not see it, she swayed back, as if from heat.

"I was caught long ago by this hunter, my ravek," she whispered, and she stepped forward and spread her long fingers on Dardelan's chest. He stood immobile for a moment, and then he groaned and gathered her to him.

I wrenched my spirit form from Bruna, mortified to have eavesdropped on her and Dardelan, yet deeply touched by what I had seen and heard. This desert land was a fruitful place for love, I thought, perhaps because there was a nakedness to its bare undulant beauty that demanded truth. Suddenly I longed for Rushton to come to me. I was tempted to farseek him, but I resisted, knowing that he, too, had a duty to fulfill.

The lemon light of sunrise was now filtering through the tent, but perversely, I fell asleep at last. Instead of sinking into dreams, my spirit was so enlivened by what I had witnessed between Dardelan and Bruna that it rose, and all at once I was on the dreamtrails. All about me, the world was a shifting mass of shadow and light, waiting for me to summon up a memory or a dream to give it shape. But before I could do anything, a shadow fell over me, chilling me.

"ElspethInnle must not seek the dreamtrails alone," said Maruman, appearing in his tyger spirit form beside me, tail snaking.

"I did not exactly choose to come here," I sent, exasperated.

"ElspethInnle must choose *not* to come here," Maruman

responded sharply. "Return to your body, for the oldOnes summon you to the mountains."

I stared at him, wondering if this was the summons I had spent half my life awaiting, the moment in which the Seeker set off on the dark road. But then I realized it was impossible, for the ships would not journey to the Red Land for many months, and no one yet knew if the Sadorians would agree to take part in the expedition at all.

"Why?" I asked.

"Maruman does not know. The oldOne's voice said that ElspethInnle must return at once to Obernewtyn. The oldOne's voice was very weak."

I shivered, suddenly remembering Atthis's voice inside my mind when I had been trying to hold Rushton back from the mindstream. She had bidden me release Rushton lest I perish with him. I had refused and had begged her to help me.

"There will be a price," Atthis had warned.

"I will pay it," I had sworn desperately.

"It is not you who will pay," Atthis had answered.

All at once I was aware of the formless matter about me, darkening.

"ElspethInnle must leave the dreamtrails," Maruman sent urgently, looking up, ears flat to his skull. I looked up and saw that the unformed matter of the dreamtrails had not darkened but that something enormous was circling overhead, casting a vast black shadow.

"What is it?" I asked, aware of an unfocused malevolence emanating from it.

"The Destroyer seeks ElspethInnle," Maruman answered. "Fly before it sees you!"

I obeyed instantly, leaping from the dreamtrail and letting

myself fall like a stone. I fell so fast that rather than waking, my spirit form shredded and dissipated as I sank into the depths of my own mind. Before I could shield myself, a dream snared me.

It was a queer dream, for although it felt like a true dream, it could not have been so, for in it, Matthew was running along the tunnel that had appeared repeatedly in my dreams for as long as I could remember. It was filled with a thick, yellow mist, and through it, I saw the dull regular flashing of the yellow light and heard the familiar dripping of water into water.

"Elspeth?" Matthew called urgently. "Elspeth?"

There was no answer but his own voice whispering my name back to him over and over, growing softer and softer, until it faded into a barely audible sibilance.

I slipped free of the dream, but as I rose to wakefulness, I heard the infinitely mournful howl of a wolf.

I opened my eyes to sunlight and Rushton smiling down at me. He might have been a dream summoned by my longing, save for the utter weariness in his jade-green eyes and the mottled bruises that marred his face.

"You were with Bram all night?" I asked.

He yawned and lay down beside me with a heartfelt sigh. "A good bit of it. I know what I am to say now, but the way of speaking gadi is so difficult. I feel as if my tongue has been turned inside out. I fear that I will never manage to speak it well enough to be understood." He rubbed his red-rimmed eyes and yawned again. "These last few hours I was with Gwynedd and Daffyd; he said he had spoken to you."

I nodded. "Do you think he is right about Salamander being Sadorian? Do Bram or Jakoby know?"

"I spoke of it to Bram, and he says that if the tribe leaders accept Daffyd's argument, it will definitely make a difference, though he believes it is only a matter of time before the tribes agree to participate in the expedition."

"That's wonderful," I said. Then I remembered the dream-trails: Atthis bidding me through Maruman to return to Obernewtyn immediately; the Destroyer shadowing my dreams. "I must return to Obernewtyn," I thought, and then realized I had said the words aloud.

Rushton's smile faded. "You are serious?"

I looked into his green eyes, trying to think how to explain why I had to go without speaking of my quest and without lies. But before I could speak, he sighed and the tension in his body seemed to flow away as he reached out to cup my cheek. "You have had a premonition?"

It would have been so easy to nod and leave it at that, but it was hard to lie to him. Yet I might as well have lied, for while I dithered, he took my silence for an answer, saying, "Gwynedd has asked Jakoby to take us all to Sutrium, to drop Dardelan, Daffyd, and Brydda there before going on to leave Gwynedd and his people ashore at Murmroth's Landing. He is hoping that by the time we get to Sutrium, Shipmaster Helvar will have sent word with the *Stormdancer* to agree to take part in this expedition. If that is so, it will mean all parties concerned will be in one place, and the opportunity to have a proper meeting to plan it all out is too important to miss. I feel I must go along for this reason. But that is not the only reason. There is so much that can be achieved now, while the Land and the Westland are being forged anew, that will better the lot of Misfits."

He was thoughtful for a moment. Then he continued. "Gwynedd has the notion that we ought to set up some

Misfit schools in the Westland and upon Norseland to allow anyone who might have Talent to be tested and to seek training locally, rather than being forced to travel all the way to Obernewtyn. And both he and Dardelan are speaking of there being two beasts apiece on each Council of Chieftains. There will be opposition from the likes of Brocade, of course, but if the practice can be introduced in the Westlands, it will be hard for him to make a strong case. Besides, did not beasts play a vital part in our battle for freedom? Brydda is longing to return to Sutrium to tell Sallah, and I want Guildmaster Gevan to know so he can raise the matter with the Beastguild as soon as possible. Also, you will need to ask Roland to appoint some healers to travel to the Westland to help establish healing centers in the cloisters. Of course, there is still much to be done before the Westland is secure."

Suddenly he laughed sheepishly. "What I am trying in my long-winded way to tell you is that although I meant to ask you to come with me aboard the *Umborine*, it being nearly impossible to imagine being parted from you so soon after all that has happened, in truth I would be glad to know that you were at Obernewtyn. Do you know the meaning of this premonition? Is it Dragon's disappearance? Or Angina?"

"I do not know why I must go back," I said truthfully. "Only that I must and immediately."

He sighed. "Well and good. Yet it is hard to let you go, and the coast road is no pleasant afternoon ride."

"I have been along it before, and Gahltha will not stumble," I said, utterly relieved not to face disappointment or anger, or worse, hurt at my announcement that I would return at once to Obernewtyn.

"When would you leave?"

"As soon as I have provisions for the journey. If I must go, then I might as well be gone swiftly."

He sat up, and I did the same, noting dark circles under his eyes. "I feel as if I have been away from you for years and that I have only just found you again, and now we must part."

"We are not only ourselves and our desires," I said. "You are the chieftain of Obernewtyn and leader of the Misfits, and I am . . ." I stopped, shattered at the realization that I had almost named myself the Seeker.

"You are mine whatever else you are and wherever you go," Rushton said with an intensity that made me want to weep. I kissed him softly and would have drawn back, but his arms closed fiercely about me and the kiss deepened, drawing us both to passion's breathless edge. Finally, he broke away, his breathing ragged. "If you would go, then you must go now, for I am not made of stone."

His words summoned to my mind an image of the strange stone sword that Kasanda had left me, which the over-guardian of the Earthtemple had called the key to all things.

Rushton touched my lips, drawing my mind and heart back to him. "You have left me already," he said. His eyes were sad.

"I may leave you, but my heart has ever been in your keeping," I whispered, and this time I drew the Chieftain of Obernewtyn into a fierce embrace and rained kisses on him as I had so often longed to do until he laughed in delight and gave me kiss for kiss.

✦ EPILOGUE ✦

"The rain smells of the sea," Gahltha sent.

"I/Maruman hate the rain," sent the old cat, sinking his claws into my shoulder to let me know that he blamed me for the weather.

I looked up into the brooding cloud-filled sky and thought of the enormous beast that had flown over Maruman and me, emanating malice on the dreamtrails the night before I had left Sador. The Destroyer, Maruman had named it, yet what had he truly meant? Ariel was far away in the Red Queen's land, but my communication with Matthew had shown me that it was possible to reach someone over such an impossible distance. Yet Ariel had never taken such a form before. He had only ever been himself, even if he had occasionally projected a younger version of himself.

My eyes sought the gray sea that heaved and churned far below the coast road, the black jagged rocks rising above the froth like dark fangs. I let my gaze run away to the horizon, lost in sea mist and veils of rain, thinking of the *Black Ship*, which was even now sailing to the Red Queen's land, and of Salamander, its master. Was he a Sadorian? I had felt convinced, hearing Daffyd, but in truth, the man might be a Gadfian, especially if it was true that the slavemasters were Gadfians. I thought, too, of the woman who had slept in a lavish chamber in Ariel's residence, wondering if she was

Salamander's woman or merely a woman showered with Sadorian luxuries.

In a few months, I had no doubt four ships would follow the *Black Ship* out into the dangerous sea. And Gahltha, Maruman, and I would be aboard, as would Rushton and Daffyd. And Dragon.

"ElspethInnle gnawing and gnawing," Maruman complained irritably.

I laughed ruefully. "You are right, Maruman. I do gnaw horribly at things, and I wish I would stop as much as you do."

"Soon we will come to the end of this weary/narrow way, and we will gallop instead of plodding," Gahltha sent.

"That gallop will help ElspethInnle, but it will give Maruman pain," the old cat said grumpily.

"To ride swift is to arrive soon," Gahltha sent with callous good cheer.

"I fear we cannot gallop, even if Maruman would agree to it," I told Gahltha regretfully, thinking of the stone sword we carried, wondering again who its rightful owner was.

"Maruman wearies of this long journeying," Maruman sent, so wistfully that I could not resist reaching up a hand to stroke his head. He stiffened but suffered the caress.

"It is not so far now," I promised. I glanced ahead as I spoke and was startled to see the faint shapes of mountain peaks just visible through the constant haze of rain. "Look! You can see the mountains already. Our journey will be over by tomorrow morning."

"The mountains are only the beginning of the journey," Maruman responded, and his mindvoice now had a fey quality that sent a prickling premonition across my mind and skin.

And somewhere, a wolf howled.

✦ Acknowledgments ✦

This book was written in La Creperie in Janovského, Prague, and in The Bay Leaf, Seagrape, and Cafe 153 in Apollo Bay, Australia. Thanks to Cathy Larsen for her persistence and generosity in her quest for a new look for the Obernewtyn Chronicles and for the new map, and to Nan for being all that she is, editor and friend. Gratitude to Mallory, Nick, and Whitney for their help in bringing this book to America. And a special heartfelt thank-you to the faithful readers of this series for waiting, patiently and impatiently, for what turned out to be, after all, not quite the last book.

*When Elspeth receives the call, will she have
the courage to begin her final quest?*

The Sending

"What . . . ," I began and then stopped, for a gap had opened in the mist through which I could see the path directly below the window. On it sat a great, astoundingly ugly dog of the kind bred by Herders. Its muzzle and eyes turned up to me as if it felt my gaze, and I drew in a breath of stunned recognition.

"Darga," I whispered, and swayed back, all the strength seeming to drain from my legs and arms with shock.

For here at last was the long-awaited sign that I must leave Obernewtyn at once and forever.